Murder
Most
Irish

Murder Most Irish

Edited by

Ed Gorman, Larry Segriff,
& Martin H. Greenberg

BARNES
&NOBLE
BOOKS
NEW YORK

Contents

Introduction

If you grew up in the America of the 1940s, there was a good chance that you came to associate Irish matters with Bing Crosby–Barry Fitzgerald movie musicals; St. Patrick's Day parades; and jigs danced by grade school kids with pomaded hair, emerald green costumes, and eager immigrant smiles.

When I was ten or so, I saw Sir Carol Reed's brilliant movie *Odd Man Out,* and realized that the homeland of my grandparents was a far darker place than all the sentimental songs indicated.

You can follow the strife in Ireland all the way back to 795, when the Vikings invaded; or to 1160, when the Normans appeared, all bloody blades and territorial ambition; to 1534, when the British king, Henry VIII, began to fix his eyes on conquering the island; to 1603, when James I seized Catholic land in Ulster and gave it to the Protestants; and to 1916, the year of the Easter Rebellion, when the British executed fifteen rebel leaders and sparked the troubles that continue to this day.

So there you have the two sides of Ireland: light and dark. The sentimental poems and ballads are no less true and honorable and necessary than the bloodier ones. Life is a matter of contrasts and mixtures, and nowhere are these contrasts and mixtures better found than in the soul of the Irish people.

In this anthology, you'll see all the moods of Ireland on display. James Joyce, Sean O'Faolain, and Peter Tremayne show us the changing face of Ireland across different eras; classic detective writers Edmund Crispin and Freeman Wills Crofts show us how the land and its legends can be integrated into fair-clue puzzles; Mary Ryan, Michael Jahn, and Morris Hershman use Irish traditions to illuminate the psychological aspects of their stories; and such contemporary masters as Edgar award–winner Clark Howard, Robert J. Randisi, Bill Crider, and Wendi Lee give us snapshots of modern-day Ireland.

You'll also find first-rate stories from Mary O'Reilly and Jon Breen, plus a delightful Nicholas Blake tale that proves that the Irish spirit can easily be transplanted to England. As authors as disparate as William Trevor and Brian Moore have proven, a lot of great Irish stories are set in Britain.

The two novels, by John Brady and Ann C. Fallon, are especially notable. John Brady has been called "The Simenon of Ireland," while Ann C. Fallon has been called "The Agatha Christie of Ireland." Their novels complement each other perfectly–John Brady's moody procedural, which exposes the darkness of contemporary urban Ireland, contrasted with Ann C. Fallon's tale of small-town suspense.

These stories will teach you a lot about the history of Ireland. But most of all they'll entertain you. Because that is Ireland's greatest product, if you will–centuries of fine storytellers. From the ballad writers of the misty years of prehistory; to the literary icons James Joyce, William Butler Yeats, and Oscar Wilde; to the long list of thriller writers who came along in the thirties and forties and fifties ... storytelling has long been Ireland's forte.

We hope you enjoy reading this book as much as we've enjoyed editing it.

–Ed Gorman
1996

ḣemlock at Vespers

A Sister Fidelma Mystery

PETER TREMAYNE

S ister Fidelma was late. The vesper-bell had already ceased pro-
claiming the arrival of the sixth canonical hour, the times set aside
for prayers, long before she reached the dusk-shrouded gates of the
grey stone abbey building. The services were over and the community
had already filed into the refectory for the evening meal as she, having
cursorily brushed the dust of travel from her, entered and hurried
towards her place with arms folded into her habit, her head bent in
submissive attitude.

While her head was lowered, the keen observer might have noticed
that there was little else that was submissive about Sister Fidelma's
bearing. Her tall, well-proportioned figure, scarcely disguised by her
flowing robe, carried the attitude of a joy in living, a worship of
activity, rather than being cowed by the sombre dignity associated with
a religieuse. As if to add to this impression, rebellious strands of red
hair broke from beneath her head-dress, adding to the youthful col-
ouring of her pale, fresh face and piercing green eyes which hardly
concealed a bubbling vitality and sense of humour.

The refectory hall was lit by numerous spluttering oil lamps whose
pungent smell mingled with the heavy aroma of the smoky turf fire
which smouldered in the great hearth set at the head of the chamber.
Lamps and fire combined to generate a poor heat against the cold early
spring evening.

The Abbess had already started the *Gratias* as Sister Fidelma, ignoring the scandalised or amused glances from the lines of Sisters—each expression fitting their individual characters—slipped into her place at the end of one of the long tables and genuflected, slightly breathlessly, and with more than seemly haste.

'*Benedic nobis, Domine Deus, et omnibus donis Tuis quae ex lorgia liberalitate Tua summus per . . .*'

The sudden cry of agony was followed by several seconds of shocked silence. Then the cry, a harsh male howl, came again followed by a crash of someone falling and the sound of breaking pottery. Sister Fidelma, eyes wide at the unexpectedness of the interruption, raised her head. Indeed, all those in the great refectory hall of the abbey had done so, peering around with excited whispers.

All eyes came to stare towards the end of the hall, to the table which was usually occupied by the visitors to the House of the Blessed Brigid in Kildare. There was a commotion near the table and then Sister Fidelma saw one of the community hurry forward to where the Abbess, and the other leading members of the House of Brigid, stood behind their table which was placed on a slightly raised platform to dominate the hall.

She saw Sister Poitigéir, whom she recognised as the sister-apothecary, lean forward and whisper excitedly into the Abbess's ear. The Abbess's placidity of features did not alter. She simply inclined her head in dismissal of her informant.

By this time a babble of sound had erupted from the hundred or so members of the community gathered to partake of their evening meal following the celebration of vespers.

The Abbess banged her earthenware mug on the table for silence, determined to finish the formula of the *Gratias*.

'. . . *summus per Jesum Christum Dominum nostrum. Amen.*'

Across the hall, Sister Fidelma could see two members of the community labouring to carry what appeared to be a man's body from the refectory. She saw Follaman, a large, ruddy-faced man, who looked after the male guests at the community's hostel, enter the refectory and help the sisters with their burden.

'*Amen.*' The word echoed raggedly but there was scarcely another sound as the hundred members of the community slid into their seats. This was the moment when the meal usually began with the handing round of bread, but the Abbess held her hand to prevent the monitors from commencing to dispense the meal.

There was an expectant silence. She cleared her throat.

'My children, we must delay our repast a moment. Our guest has been taken ill and we must await the report of our sister-apothecary, who believes that our guest may have eaten something which has disagreed with him.'

She stilled another eruption of excited murmuring with a sharp gesture of her thin white hand.

'While we wait, Sister Mugain shall lead you in the devotion ...'

Without further explanation, the Abbess swept from the platform while Sister Mugain began intoning a mixture of Latin and Irish in her shrill voice:

> Regem regum rogamus
> In nostris sermonibus
> anacht Nóe a luchtlach
> diluui temporibus

> King of Kings
> We pray to you
> Who protected Noah
> In the day of the Flood

Sister Fidelma leant close to Sister Luan, a gawky girl, beside whom she sat.

'Who was the person who was carried out?' she asked softly.

Sister Fidelma had only just rejoined her community after a two-week journey to Tara, the royal capital of the five kingdoms of Ireland, seat of the High King.

Sister Luan paused until the strident tones of Sister Mugain paused in her chant:

> Regis regum rectissimi
> prope est dies Domini ...

'It was a guest lodging in the tech-óired. A man named Sillán from Kilmantan.'

Each religious house throughout the country had a quarter named the tech-óired, a hostel where travellers lodged, or where important guests were given hospitality.

'Who was this man, Sillán?' demanded Sister Fidelma.

An imperious hand fell on her shoulder. She started nervously and glanced up, firmly expecting a rebuke for talking during the devotions. The hawk-like features of Sister Ethne gazed disapprovingly down at her, her thin lips compressed. Sister Ethne, elderly and pinched-faced, was feared by the younger members of the community. Her pale, dead eyes seemed to gaze through anyone she looked upon. It was whispered that she was so old that she had been in the service of Christ when the Blessed Brigid had come to this spot a century before to establish the first religious house for women in the country under the great oak tree from which her church took the name Kildare, the Church of the Oak. Sister Ethne was the *bean-tigh*, the house steward of the community, whose job it was to oversee the internal affairs and running of the community.

'The Abbess requires your presence in her chamber immediately,' Sister Ethne sniffed. It was a habit with her. She could speak in no other way except to punctuate her sentences with disapproving sniffs.

Wondering, Sister Fidelma rose and followed the elderly religieuse from the hall, knowing that the eyes of all the sisters were following her in curiosity, in spite of their bent heads as they continued their pious chanting.

The Abbess Ita of Kildare sat before a long oak table in the chamber which she used as her study. Her face was set and determined. In her fifties, Ita was still a handsome, commanding woman, whose amber eyes usually shone with a quiet jocularity. Now it was hard to see their expression for they sparkled unnaturally in the flickering reflective light of the two tall beeswax candles which lit the shadowy room. The sweet scent of wild hyacinth and narcissus blended to give a pleasant aroma to the chamber.

'Come in, Sister Fidelma. Was your trip to Tara successful?'

'It was, Mother Abbess,' replied the girl as she moved into the chamber, aware that Sister Ethne had followed her in and closed the door, standing in front of it with arms folded into her habit.

Sister Fidelma waited quietly while the Abbess seemed to gather her thoughts. The Abbess's gaze suddenly seemed to become preoccupied with a pile of half a dozen small rocks which lay on the table. She rose, with an apologetic gesture, and gathered them up, dropping them into a receptacle. She turned, reseating herself with a contrite smile.

'Some stones I was gathering to create a small rock garden.' She felt urged to explain. 'I dislike clutter.' Abbess Ita bit her lip, hesitated and then shrugged, coming abruptly to the point.

'Were you in the refectory?'

'I was. I had just arrived at Kildare.'

'A problem has arisen which is of great concern to our community. Our guest, Sillán of Kilmantan, is dead. Our sister-apothecary says he was poisoned.'

Sister Fidelma tried to conceal her astonishment.

'Poisoned? By accident?'

'That we do not know. The sister-apothecary is now examining the food in the refectory hall. That was why I forbade our community to eat.'

Sister Fidelma frowned.

'Do I take it that this Sillán began to eat before you had finished the *Gratias*, Mother Abbess?' she asked. 'You will recall that he cried in agony and collapsed while you were not yet finished.'

The Abbess's eyes widened a little and then she nodded, agreeing with the point.

'Your perception justifies your reputation as a solver of mysteries, Fidelma. It is good that our community is served by one skilled in such matters and in the laws of the Brehons. Indeed, this is why I asked Sister Ethne to bring you here. I know you have just returned from your journey and that you are fatigued. But this is a matter of importance. I would like you to undertake the immediate inquiry into Sillán's death. It is imperative that the matter be cleared up as quickly as possible.'

'Why so quickly, Mother Abbess?'

'Sillán was an important man. He was in this territory at the request of the Uí Failgi of Ráith Imgain.'

Sister Fidelma realised what this meant.

Kildare stood in the territory of the petty kingdom of the Uí Failgi. The royal residence of the kings of the Uí Failgi was situated at the fortress of Ráith Imgain, to the north-west of Kildare on the edge of the wasteland known as the Bog of Aillín. Several questions sprung into her mind but she bit her lip. They could be asked later. It was clear that the Abbess had no wish to incur the enmity of Congall, the petty king of the territory, who was known simply as the Uí Failgi, for, under the Brehon law, the petty king and his assembly granted the land to the community of Kildare and they could just as easily drive the community out if displeased. All ecclesiastical lands were granted by the clan assemblies, for there was no such thing as private property within the kingdom of Ireland. Land was apportioned and allotted at the decision of the assemblies which governed the tribes and kingdoms.

'Who was this man Sillán, Mother Abbess?' asked Sister Fidelma. 'Was he a representative of the Uí Failgi?'

It was Sister Ethne who volunteered the information, punctuating the sentences with sniffs.

'He was an *uchadan,* an artificer who worked in the mines of Kilman-tan; so Follaman, who looks after our hostel, told me.'

'But what was he doing here?'

Did the Abbess cast a warning glance at Sister Ethne? Sister Fidelma caught only an involuntary movement of Sister Ethne's eyes towards the Abbess and by the time Fidelma glanced in her direction the Ab-bess's features were calm and without expression. Fidelma exhaled softly.

'Very well, Mother Abbess. I will undertake the inquiry. Do I have your complete authority to question all whom I would wish to?'

'My child, you are a *dálaigh* of the Brehon Court.' The Abbess smiled thinly. 'You are an advocate qualified to the level of *Anruth.* You do not need my authority under law. You have the authority of the Brehons.'

'But I need your permission and blessing as head of my community.'

'Then you have it. You may use the *tech-screpta,* the library chamber, to work in. Let me know when you have something to report. Go with God. *Benedictus sit Deus in Donis Suis.*'

Sister Fidelma genuflected.

'*Et sanctus in omnis operibus Suis,*' she responded automatically.

Sister Ethne had placed two rough, unglazed earthenware lamps, their snouts fashioned to support a wick, to light the dark shadowy vault which was the *tech-screpta,* the great library of the community which housed all the books and treasures of the House of the Blessed Brigid. Sister Fidelma sat at the library table, in the chair usually occupied by the *leabhar-coimdaech,* the librarian who guarded the great works contained in the chamber. The treasure trove of manuscript books hung in rows in the finely worked leather book satchels around the great chamber. The *tech-screpta* of Kildare even boasted many ancient 'rods of the *fili,*' wands of hazel and aspen on which Ogham script was carved from an age long before the scribes of Ireland had decided to adopt the Latin alphabet with which to record their learning.

The *tech-screpta* was chilly in spite of the permanent fire which was maintained there to stop dampness corroding the rows of books.

Sister Ethne, as steward of the community, had volunteered to aid Sister Fidelma, by finding and bringing to her anyone she wished to examine. She sniffed as she endeavoured to adjust the lamps to stop abrasive smoke and reeking tallow odour from permeating the library chamber.

'We still start by confirming the cause of Sillán's death,' Sister Fidelma announced, once she had noticed that Sister Ethne had finished her self-appointed task. After a moment's reflection she went on: 'Ask the sister-apothecary to join me here.'

Sister Poitigéir was nervous and bird-like in her movements, reminding Sister Fidelma of a crane, moving with a waddling apprehensiveness, now and then thrusting her head forward on her long neck in an abrupt jerking motion which seemed to threaten to throw the head forward off the neck altogether. But Sister Fidelma had known the sister-apothecary since she had joined the community at Kildare and knew, too, that her anxious idiosyncrasy disguised a keen and analytical mind when it came to the science of botany and chemistry.

'What killed Sillán of Kilmantan?'

Sister Poitigéir pursed her lips a moment, thrusting her head forward quickly and then drawing it back.

'*Conium maculatum,*' she pronounced breathlessly.

'Poison hemlock?' Sister Fidelma drew her brows together.

'There was no questioning the convulsions and paralysis. He expired even as we carried him from the refectory hall. Also ...' She hesitated.

'Also?' encouraged Sister Fidelma.

Sister Poitigéir bit her lower lip for a moment and then shrugged.

'I had noticed earlier this afternoon that a jar containing powdered leaves of the plant had been removed from my apothecary. They were there this morning but I noticed they were missing two hours before vespers. I meant to report the matter to the Mother Abbess after the service.'

'Why do you keep such a poison in your apothecary?'

'Properly administered, it can have good medicinal use as a sedative and anodyne. It serves all spasmodic affections. We not only have it in our apothecary but we grow it in our gardens which are tended by myself and Follaman. We grow many herbs. Hemlock can heal many ailments.'

'And yet it can kill. In ancient Greece we are told that it was given to criminals as a means of execution and among the Jews it was given to deaden the pain of those being stoned to death. I have heard it argued that when Our Lord hung upon the Cross He was given vinegar, myrrh and hemlock to ease His pain.'

Sister Poitigéir nodded several times in swift, jerky motions.

Sister Fidelma paused a moment or two.

'Was the poison administered in the food served in the refectory?'

'No.'

'You seem positive,' Sister Fidelma observed with some interest.

'I am. The effect of the poison is not instantaneous. Additionally, I have checked all the food taken to the refectory for the evening meal. There is no sign of it having been contaminated.'

'So are you saying that the poison was administered before Sillán entered the refectory?'

'I am.'

'And was it self-administered?'

Sister Poitigéir contrived to shrug.

'Of that, I have no knowledge. Though I would say it is most unlikely.'

'Why?'

'Because taking poison hemlock results in an agonising death. Why drink hemlock and then enter into the refectory for an evening meal if one knows one is about to die in convulsions?'

It was a point that seemed reasonable to Sister Fidelma.

'Have you searched Sillán's chamber and the guest quarters for the missing jar of powdered hemlock leaves?'

Sister Poitigéir gave a quick, nervous shake of her head.

'Then I suggest that is your next and immediate task. Let me know if you find it.'

Sister Fidelma asked to see Follaman next. He was a big burly man, not a religieux but a layman hired by the community to take care of the guest quarters. Each community employed a *timthirig*, or servant, to look after its *tech-óired*. It was Follaman's job to look after the wants of the male guests and to undertake the work that was too heavy for the female members of the community and assist the sisters in the harder chores of the community's gardens.

Follaman was a broad-shouldered, foxy-haired man, with ruddy complexion and watery blue eyes. His face was dashed with freckles as if a passing cart had sprayed mud upon him. He was in his mid-forties, a man without guile rather like a large boy, still with the innocent wonders of youth. In all, a simple man.

'Have you been told what has transpired here, Follaman?'

Follaman opened his mouth, showing blackened teeth. Sister Fidelma noticed, with some distaste, that he obviously did not regard his personal cleanliness as a priority.

He nodded silently.

'Tell me what you know about Sillán.'

Follaman scratched his head in a bemused fashion.

'He was a guest here.'

'Yes?' she encouraged. 'When did he arrive at Kildare?'

Follaman's face lightened with relief. Sister Fidelma realised that she had best put direct questions to the man, for he was not the quickest wit she had encountered. She assessed him as slow in thought, without perceptive subtleness.

'He came here eight nights ago, Cailech.' Follaman addressed all the sisters formally by the title 'Cailech,' the term given by the lay people to all religieuses meaning 'one who had taken the veil,' from the term *caille,* signifying a veil.

'Do you know who he was? What brought him here?'

'Everyone knows that, Cailech.'

'Tell me. For I have been away from Kildare these last two weeks.'

'Ah, yes. That is so,' agreed the big man, having paused a moment to examine what Sister Fidelma said. 'Well, Cailech, Sillán told me that he was a *bruithneóir,* a smelter, from the mines in the Kilmantan mountains.'

'What mines would those be, Follaman?'

'Why, the gold-mines, Cailech. He worked in the gold-mines.'

Sister Fidelma successfully prevented her eyes from widening.

'So why was he in Kildare? Surely, there are no gold-mines here?'

'It is said that the Uí Failgi asked him to come here.'

'Indeed? But do you know why?'

Follaman shook his head of reddy hair.

'No, Cailech, that I do not. He spent but little time in the guest-house, sleeping there and then leaving at daybreak only to return for the evening meal.'

'To your knowledge, where was Sillán during this afternoon?'

The big man scratched his chin thoughtfully.

'It was today that he came back early and stayed in his chamber in the guest-house.'

'Was he there all afternoon?'

Follaman hesitated. 'He went to see the Abbess soon after he returned. He was with her awhile and then he emerged from her chamber with anger on his face. Then he returned to his own chamber.'

'Did he say what had angered him?'

'No, Cailech. I asked him whether he required anything. That being my duty.'

'And did he call for refreshment?'

'Only for water ... no, he asked for mead. Nothing else.'

'Did you take the mead to him?'

'I did. In a stone jar from the kitchens.'

'Where is it now?'

'I have not tidied the guest-house. I think it must still be there.'

'Do you know what poison hemlock is?'

'It is a bad thing. That I know.'

'Do you know what it looks like? The shape and colour of the plant?'

'I am only a poor servant, Cailech. I would not know. Sister Poitigéir would know such things.'

'So Sillán called for mead. And you took it to him. Did he drink straightaway, or did you leave the jar with him?'

'I left it with him.'

'Could anyone have tampered with the jar?'

Follaman's brow creased with a concentration of effort.

'I would not know, Cailech. They could, I suppose.'

Sister Fidelma smiled. 'Never mind, Follaman. Tell me, are you sure that Sillán stayed in the *tech-óired* all afternoon until vespers?'

Follaman frowned and then shook his head slowly.

'That I would not be sure of. It seemed so to me. And he began preparing to leave the abbey at first light. He packed his bags and told me to ensure that I had saddled his chestnut mare in readiness.' Follaman hesitated and continued sheepishly. 'That was when he had to accompany me to the stables, Cailech. So, yes, he did leave the hostel after all.'

'For what purpose did he go to the stables with you?' Sister Fidelma frowned, puzzled.

'Why, to show me his horse. We have several whose shades are the same to me. You see, I lack the ability to tell one colour from another.'

Sister Fidelma compressed her lips. Of course, she had forgotten that Follaman was colour-blind. She nodded and smiled encouragingly at the big man.

'I see. But Sillán made no mention of what had angered him, or why he had decided to depart?'

'No, Cailech. He just said that he was bound for Ráith Imgain, that is all.'

The door opened and Sister Poitigéir returned. Sister Fidelma glanced towards her and the sister-apothecary nodded swiftly in her bird-like manner.

Follaman looked from one to the other, puzzled.

'Is that all, Cailech?'

Sister Fidelma smiled reassuringly.

'For the time being, Follaman.'

The big man left the library room. Sister Fidelma sat back and studied the closed oak door with a frown. There was a discordant bell ringing distantly in her mind. She rubbed the bridge of her nose for a moment, exhaling in annoyance as her thoughts became no clearer. Then she turned to the anxious Sister Poitigéir with an inquiring gaze.

'I found a jug of mead in the chamber occupied by Sillán. While the mead disguises the unpleasant odour of the hemlock, nevertheless I was able to discern its traces. A draught of such a mixture would be enough to kill a strong man. But there was no sign of the bowl of crushed leaves taken from the apothecary.'

'Thank you, Sister Poitigéir.' Fidelma nodded. She waited until the sister-apothecary had left before she stretched back into her chair and sighed deeply.

Sister Ethne regarded her with perplexity.

'What now, Sister? Is your inquiry over?'

Sister Fidelma shook her head.

'No, it is not over yet, Sister Ethne. Far from it. There is, indeed, a mystery here. Sillán was murdered. I am sure of it. But why?'

There came a sudden sound of a commotion from the gates of the abbey, which were usually shut just after vespers and not opened until dawn. Sister Ethne frowned and strode as rapidly as dignity allowed to the window of the *tech-screpta*.

'There are a dozen horsemen arriving.' She sniffed in disapproval. 'But they bear a royal standard. I must go down to receive them.'

Sister Fidelma nodded in preoccupation. It was only when Sister Ethne went hurrying off to fulfil her duties as the steward of the community that a thought crossed her mind, and she went to the window and gazed down at the courtyard below.

In the light of the flickering torches she saw that several riders had dismounted. Follaman had gone forward to help them. There was light enough for Fidelma to see that they were warriors and one carried the royal standard of the Uí Failgi of Ráith Imgain while another held the traditional *ríchaindell,* the royal light which, during the hours of darkness, was always carried to light the way of a great chieftain or his heir-elect. The new arrivals were no ordinary visitors. Sister Fidelma forgot her training, pursing her lips together in a soundless whistle.

It was only after the passing of a few minutes that the door of the *tech-screpta* flew unceremoniously open and a stocky young man entered, followed by another man, with a worried-looking Sister Ethne trailing behind. Sister Fidelma turned from the window and regarded the intruders calmly.

The stocky young man took a pace forward. His richly decorated clothes were still covered in the dust of travel. His eyes were steel-grey, piercing as if they missed nothing. He was handsome, haughty and his demeanour announced his rank.

'This is Sister Fidelma.' Sister Ethne's voice almost quavered, even forgetting to sniff, as she nervously pushed her way through the door to stand to one side of the young man.

Sister Fidelma did not move but stood regarding the young man quizzically.

'I am told that Sillán of Kilmantan is dead. Poisoned. I am told that you are conducting an inquiry into this matter.' The phrases were statements and not questions.

Sister Fidelma felt no urge to reply to the young man's brusque manner.

She let her restless green eyes travel over his features, which gathered into a frown at her lack of response. She paused a moment and then moved her gaze to the muscular warrior at his side, before allowing her eyes to move to the clearly nervous Sister Ethne. Fidelma's raised eyebrows asked a question.

'This is Tírechán, Tanist of the Uí Failgi.' Sister Ethne's voice was breathless.

The Tanist was the heir-elect of the kingship or chieftaincy; an heir was elected during the reign of a king of clan chieftain, which prevented any successional squabbles after his death or abdication.

Sister Fidelma moved back to her chair and sat down, motioning Tírechán to be seated on the opposite side of the table to her.

The young prince's face showed his astonishment at her behaviour. Angry blood tinged his cheeks.

'I am Sister Fidelma,' she announced, quietly, before he spoke, for she saw the words forming to burst from his lips. 'I am a *dálaigh* of the Brehon Court, qualified to the level of *Anruth*.'

Tírechán swallowed the words that had gathered on his lips and a look of understanding, mingled with respect, spread over his features. A *dálaigh*, an advocate of the Brehon Court, especially one qualified to the level of *Anruth*, could meet and be accorded equality with any provincial king or chieftain and could even speak at ease before the High King himself. An *Anruth* was only one degree below the highest professorship of *Ollamh* whose words even a High King would have to obey. He regarded Sister Fidelma with a slightly awed air of surprise at her attractive youthfulness for one who held such authority. Then he moved forward and seated himself before her.

'I apologise, Sister. No one had informed me of your rank, only that you were investigating the death of Sillán.'

Sister Fidelma decided to ignore the apology. The Tanist's bodyguard now drew the door shut and stood before it, arms folded. Sister Ethne, a worried expression still on her features, realising that she had neglected to introduce Sister Fidelma in proper form, still stood where she had halted, her lips compressed.

'I presume that you knew the man Sillán?'

'I knew *of* him,' corrected the Tanist of the Uí Failgi.

'You came here to meet him?'

'I did.'

'For what purpose?'

The Tanist hesitated and dropped his eyes.

'On the business of my chieftain, the Uí Failgi.'

'The man is dead. Poisoned. Perhaps it might help in this inquiry if you were more specific.'

Tírechán exhaled in annoyance.

'Very well. The man Sillán was commissioned to come to this district by the Uí Failgi ...'

Sister Fidelma smiled thinly as the man hesitated again. He obviously had difficulty speaking of the private business of his chieftain.

'Perhaps I can help?' Fidelma encouraged, as the thought suddenly took shape in her mind. Indeed, the logic of the idea was unquestionable. 'Sillán was from Kilmantan, whose hills are full of gold-mines, for do we not speak of that area as Kilmantan of the gold? Sillán was a *bruithneóir*, a qualified artificer. Why would the king of Ráith Imgain ask such a man to come to Kildare?'

The Tanist stirred uncomfortably beneath her amused but penetrating gaze. Then he responded with almost surly defiance.

'I take it that what I say shall be treated in confidence?'

Sister Fidelma showed her annoyance at such a impudent question. 'I am a *dálaigh* of the Brehon Court.' She spoke quietly. The rebuke needed no further embellishment.

The cheeks of the young prince reddened. But he spoke again as though he had need to defend something.

'Since the twenty-sixth High King of Milesian descent, the noble Tigernmas, first had gold dug and smelted in Ireland, gold has been searched for throughout the country. From Derry and Antrim in the north, south to the mountains of Kilmantan and the shores of Carman, gold-mines have been worked. Yet our need for gold to enhance our courts and to increase our trade is not diminished. We look for new mines.'

'So the Uí Failgi asked Sillán to come to Kildare to search for gold?' Fidelma interpreted.

'The production of gold has not kept pace with the demand, Sister Fidelma. We have to import it from Iberia and other far-off places. Our need is keen. Are not the Eóganacht of Glendamnách at war with the Uí Fidgente over possession of the gold-mines of Cuillin in the land of holly trees?'

'But why would the Uí Failgi think that there was gold at Kildare?' demanded Sister Fidelma abruptly.

'Because an aged man recalled that once the lands of Kildare held such a mine, knowledge of which has long passed from the minds of men. Seizing on this old man's recollection, the Uí Failgi sought out Sillán whose fame for seeking the veins of gold was legend among the mountain people of Kilmantan. He asked Sillán to come to Kildare and seek out this lost mine.'

'And did he find it?'

An angry spasm passed the face of the Tanist.

'That is what I came to discover. Now I am told that Sillán is dead. Dead from poison. How came this to be?'

Sister Fidelma wrinkled her nose.

'That is what my investigation shall discover, Tanist of the Uí Failgi.' She sat back in her chair and gazed meditatively at the young chieftain.

'Who knows of Sillán's mission here?'

'It was known only to Sillán; to the Uí Failgi; to myself as Tanist and to our chief Ollamh. No one else knew. A knowledge of the whereabouts of gold does harm to the minds of men and drives them mad. It was better not to tempt them by spreading such knowledge abroad.'

Fidelma nodded absently in agreement.

'So if gold had been discovered, it would have been of benefit to the Uí Failgi?'

'And to his people. It would bring prestige and prosperity to our trade with other kingdoms.'

'Sillán came from the territory of the Uí Máil, might he not have spoken of this enterprise to his own chieftain?'

'He was paid well enough,' frowned the Tanist of the Uí Failgi, his features showing that the thought had already occurred to him.

'But if the Uí Máil, or even the Uí Faeláin to the north-east, knew that there was gold in Kildare, surely this might lead to territorial dispute and warfare for possession of the gold? As you correctly state, there is a war between the Uí Fidgente and Eóganacht of Glendamnách over the mines of Cuillin.'

The Tanist sighed impatiently.

'Kildare is in the territory of the Uí Failgi. If the neighbouring chieftains invaded Kildare, then the wrong would be theirs and our duty to prevent them.'

'But that is not what I asked. Might this discovery not lead to enmity and warfare?'

'That was why the mission was so secret; why none but Sillán was to know the reason for his being in Kildare.'

'Now Sillán is dead,' mused Sister Fidelma. 'Did you know he was leaving here to return to Ráith Imgain tomorrow?'

The Tanist's face showed his surprise. Then a new look replaced the expression, one of scarcely concealed excitement.

'Which means that he must have found the gold-mine!'

Sister Fidelma smiled a little as she sought to follow his reasoning. 'How do you arrive at that conclusion, Tírechán?'"

'Because he had only been here eight days and no other reason would cause Sillán to return to the Uí Failgi other than to report his success.'

'That is a broad assumption. Perhaps he was returning because he realised that this search for a legendary gold-mine in Kildare was a hopeless task.'

The Tanist ignored her observation.

'Are you sure that he was leaving Kildare tomorrow?'

'He told our *timthirig*, Follaman, that he would be leaving,' Fidelma assured him.

The Tanist snapped his fingers, his face agitated.

'No, no. The mine must have been found. Sillán would not have given up the search so soon. But where, where did he find it? Where is the mine?'

Sister Fidelma shook her head slowly.

'The more important question to be resolved is how Sillán came by his death.'

'By the grace of God, Sister Fidelma, that is not my task,' the young man replied in a thankful tone. 'But my chieftain, the Uí Failgi, will need to know the location of the gold-mine which Sillán must have discovered.'

She rose, inviting the Tanist to do so.

'You and your men are doubtless staying the night at our *tech-óired*. I suggest, Tírechán, that you now go and cleanse the dust of travel from yourself. I will keep you informed of anything that you should know.'

Reluctantly, the Tanist rose and motioned to his bodyguard to open the door of the *tech-screpta*. On the threshold he turned hesitantly as if he would press her further.

'*Benedictus benedicat,*' Sister Fidelma dismissed him firmly. He sighed, grimaced and withdrew.

When he had gone, she resumed her seat and spread her hands, palms downward, on the table. For a moment or so she was completely wrapped in her thoughts, forgetting the presence of Sister Ethne. Finally, the *bean-tigh*'s rasping cough, as the steward tried to attract her attention, stirred her from her contemplations.

'Is that all now, Sister?' asked the *bean-tigh* hopefully.

Sister Fidelma rose again with a shake of her head.

'Far from it, Sister Ethne. I should now like to see Sillán's chamber in the *tech-óired*. Bring one of the lamps.'

The chamber in the *tech-óired,* or guest's hostel, was not dissimilar to the cells occupied by the members of the community. It was a small, dark, grey stone room with a tiny slit of a window over which hung a heavy woven cloth to keep out the chill night air. A small cot of pine wood, with a straw palliasse and blankets, stood in one corner. A stool and a table were the only other furnishings. On the table stood a single candle. The hostel was provided with only poor lights. The candle was simply a single rush peeled and soaked in animal grease. It gave scant light and burned down very quickly, which was why Fidelma had the foresight to bring one of the oil lamps with her.

Sister Fidelma paused on the threshold of the room and examined it very carefully as Sister Ethne set down the lamp on the table.

Sillán had apparently already packed for his journey, for a heavy satchel was dumped on the foot of the bed. It was placed next to a smaller work-bag of leather.

Sister Fidelma crossed to the bed and picked up the leather work-bag. It was heavy. She peered inside and saw a collection of tools which, she supposed, were the tools of Sillán's profession. She laid the bag aside and peered into the satchel. These were Sillán's personal effects.

Finally, she turned to Sister Ethne.

'I will not be long here. Would you go to the Mother Abbess and tell her that I would like to see her in her chamber within the hour? And I would like to see her alone.'

Sister Ethne sniffed, opened her mouth to speak, thought better of it, bobbed her head and left the room.

Fidelma turned back to the satchel of personal belongings and took them out one by one, examining them minutely. When she had done so, she explored the interior of the satchel with her fingertips, raising the lamp in one hand and examining the dust on the tips of her fingers with a frown.

She then repeated her careful examination with the tools and implements in Sillán's work-bag. Once again she ran her hand over the dust in the bottom of the bag and examined it carefully in the light.

Only after a careful examination did she replace everything as she had found it.

Then she lowered herself to her knees and began a microscopic examination of the floor, slowly, inch by inch.

It was when she was peering under the wooden cot that what seemed a small lump of rock came in contact with her hand. Her fingers closed around it and she scrambled backwards into the room and held it up to the light of the lamp.

At first sight it seemed, indeed, just a piece of rough-hewn rock. Then she rubbed it on the stone-flagged floor and held it once again to the light.

Part of it, where she had abraded it, gleamed a bright yellow.

A satisfied smile spread over her features.

*   *   *

Abbess Ita sat upright in her chair, her calm, composed features just a little too set to be an entirely natural expression. It was as if she had not stirred from the chair since last Fidelma had seen her. Abbess Ita regarded Sister Fidelma with her amber eyes wary as a pine-marten might watch a circling hawk.

'You may be seated, Sister,' the Abbess said. It was an unusual invitation, one showing deference to Sister Fidelma's legal status rather than her religious one.

'Thank you, Mother Abbess,' Fidelma replied, as she lowered herself into a chair facing Abbess Ita.

'The hour grows late. How does your inquiry progress?'

Sister Fidelma smiled gently.

'It draws towards its conclusion,' she answered. 'But I am in need of further information.'

Abbess Ita gestured with one hand, a motion from the wrist only, as if in invitation.

'When Sillán came to see you this afternoon, what was said which caused him anger?'

Abbess Ita blinked; the only reaction which expressed her surprise at the directness of the question.

'Did he come to see me?' she asked slowly, parrying as if playing for time.

Sister Fidelma nodded firmly.

'He did, as you know.'

Abbess Ita let out a long sigh.

'It would be foolish to attempt to conceal the truth from you. I have known you too long, Fidelma. It always surprised me that you chose the life of a religieuse rather than pursue a more worldly existence. You have a perception and a reasoning that is not given to everyone.'

Sister Fidelma ignored the praise. She waited quietly for the Abbess to reply to her question.

'Sillán came to apprise me of certain things which he had discovered. . . .'

'He had discovered the lost gold-mine of Kildare.'

This time Abbess Ita could not conceal the faint ripple of muscle as she sought to control the astonishment on her face. She struggled to compose herself for some moments and then her lips became thin in an almost bitter smile.

'Yes. I suppose that you learnt this much from the Tanist of the Uí Failgi, whom I am told has just arrived seeking hospitality here. You doubtless know that Sillán was a man skilled in the profession of mining; that he had been sent here by the Uí Failgi to find an ancient gold-mine and explore its potential.'

'I do. But his mission was a secret known only to Sillán, the Uí Failgi and his Tanist, Tírechán. How did you come to learn about it?'

'Sillán himself came to tell me about it this very afternoon.'

'Not before?'

'Not before,' agreed the Abbess with emphasis.

'Then tell me what transpired.'

'It was after noon, well after the noon Angelus, that Sillán came to see me. He told me what he was doing in Kildare. In truth, I had suspected it. He had arrived here eight days ago and carried credentials from the Uí Failgi. What could a man from Kilmantan be doing here with approval of the Uí Failgi? Oh, I had heard the ancient legends of the lost gold-mine of Kildare. So I had suspected.'

She paused for a moment.

'And?' encouraged Sister Fidelma.

'He came to tell me that he had found it, had found the old gold-mine which had been worked centuries ago and had explored some of its passageways. Furthermore, he declared that the gold-seams were still in evidence and were still workable. He was leaving Kildare tomorrow to report his find to the Uí Failgi.'

'Why, then, Mother Abbess, did he break secrecy with the Uí Failgi and tell you this?'

Abbess Ita grimaced.

'Sillán of Kilmantan respected our community and wanted to warn us. It was as simple as that. You see, our abbey lies directly above the mine workings. Once this was known, then there is little doubt that the Uí Failgi would have ordered our eviction from this spot, this blessed spot where the Holy Brigid gathered her disciples and preached under the great oak, founding her community. Even should our community be simply ordered to move a short distance, we would have to give up the holy soil where Brigid and her descendants are buried, their clay mingling with the earth to make it sanctified.'

Sister Fidelma gazed thoughtfully at the troubled face of the Abbess, listening to the suppressed emotion in her voice.

'So the only purpose he had in telling you this, Mother Abbess, was to warn the community?'

'Sillán, in his piety, thought it only fair to warn me what he had discovered. He merely wanted to give our community time to prepare for the inevitable.'

'Then what angered him?'

Abbess Ita compressed her lips a moment. When she spoke, her voice was firm and controlled.

'I tried to reason with him. I asked him to keep the secret of the lost mine. At first I appealed to him by virtue of our common faith, by the memory of the Blessed Brigid, by the faith and future of our community. He refused, politely but firmly, saying he was bound by honour to report his discovery to the Uí Failgi.

'Then I tried to point out the greater implications. Should news of the gold-mine be broadcast, then war might follow as it has done at Cuillin.'

Sister Fidelma nodded slowly as Abbess Ita confirmed her own thoughts.

'I am aware of the conflict over the mines at Cuillin, Mother Abbess.'

'Then you will realise that Kildare, while in the territory of the Uí Failgi, is but a short distance from the territories of the Uí Faeláin to the north-east and the Uí Máil to the south-east, with only the desolate plain of the Bog of Aillín to protect us. The word *gold* will cause a fire to be lit in the hearts of chieftains avaricious for the power it will bring. This dear, green spot, now so peaceful and so pleasant, would be stained red with the blood of warriors, and of the people that once lived here in harmony with the green plains and hills of Kildare. Our community of Kildare will be swept away like chaff from the wheat.'

'Yet why did Sillán become angry?' pressed Sister Fidelma.

The Abbess Ita's expression was painful.

'When I had told him this, and when he still insisted that his duty lay in telling the Uí Failgi, I told him that his would then be the responsibility for what followed. I told him that God's curse would pursue him for destroying the peace of this land. That he would be damned in the next world as well as this one. The name Sillán would become the synonym for the destruction of the holy shrine of Brigid of Kildare.'

'What then?'

'His face reddened in anger and he flung himself from the room, averring that he would depart at first light.'

'When did you see him again?'

'Not until vespers.'

Sister Fidelma gazed thoughtfully into the eyes of the Abbess Ita.

The amber orbs smouldered as they reflected back Sister Fidelma's scrutiny.

'You dare think...?' whispered the Abbess Ita, her face pale, reading the suspicion in the younger face before her.

Sister Fidelma did not drop her gaze.

'I am here as a *dálaigh*, Abbess Ita, not as a member of your community. My concern is truth, not etiquette. A man lies dead in this abbey. He was poisoned. From the circumstances, it was a poison that was not self-administered. Then by whom and for what reason? To keep Sillán from revealing the secret of the lost mine to the Uí Failgi? That seems a logical deduction. And who stands to gain by the suppression of that knowledge? Why, none but the community of this abbey, Mother Abbess.'

'And the people of the surrounding countryside!' snapped Abbess Ita, angrily. 'Do not forget that in your equation, Sister Fidelma. Do not forget all the blood that will be saved during the forthcoming years.'

'Right cannot be served by wrong, it is the law. And I must judge what is lawful. Knowing that it was the law that I must serve as a *dálaigh* of the Brehon Court, separate from my role as a member of this community, why did you ask me to investigate this matter? You yourself could have conducted the inquiry. Why me?'

'In such a matter of importance, a report from a *dálaigh* of the Brehon Court would carry much weight with the Uí Failgi.'

'So you had hoped that I would not discover the existence of the gold-mine?' frowned Sister Fidelma.

Abbess Ita had risen in agitation from her chair. Fidelma rose so that her eyes were on a level with the Abbess's own agitated gaze.

'Tell me directly, Mother Abbess: did you poison, or arrange to have poisoned, Sillán to prevent him speaking with the Uí Failgi?'

For several moments there was an icy silence. The sort of silence which precedes an eruption of the earth. Then the Abbess Ita's anger faded and a sad expression crossed her face. She dropped her gaze before the younger woman.

'Mine was not the hand that administered poison to Sillán though I confess that the heaviness of my heart lifted when I heard of the deed.'

In the quietude of her cell, Sister Fidelma lay on her cot, fully clothed, hands behind her head, staring into the darkness. She had extinguished the light of her candle and lay merely contemplating the shadows without really registering them as she turned over in her mind the facts of the mysterious death of Sillán.

There was something staring her in the face about this matter, a clue which was so obvious that she was missing it. She felt it in her being. It was there, in her mind, if only she could draw it out.

She had no doubt in her mind that Sillán had been killed because of the knowledge he possessed.

And Sister Fidelma found herself in sympathy with the suppression of that knowledge.

Yet that was not the law, the law that she was sworn to uphold as a dálaigh of the Brehon Court. Yet the law was simply a compact between men. Rigid law could be the greater injustice. While the law was blind, in an ideal world justice should be able to remove the bandage from its eyes long enough to distinguish between the unfortunate and the vicious.

Her mind spinning in moral dilemma, Sister Fidelma drifted unknowingly into a sleep.

Sister Fidelma became aware firstly of someone pulling at her arm and then of the dim tolling of the Angelus bell.

Sister Ethne's pale, hawk-like features cleared out of the blurred vision as Fidelma blinked and focused her eyes.

'Quickly, Sister, quickly. There has been another death.'

Fidelma sat up abruptly and stared at Sister Ethne in incredulity. It lacked an hour before dawn but the bean-tigh had already lit the candle in her cell.

'Another death? Who?'

'Follaman.'

'How?' demanded Fidelma, scrambling from her cot.

'In the same manner, Sister. By poison. Come quickly to the tech-óired.'

Follaman, the timthirig of the community, lay on his back, his face contorted in pain. One arm was flung out in a careless gesture and from the still fingers, Sister Fidelma followed the line to the broken pottery below. It had once been an earthenware goblet. There was a dark stain of liquid which had seeped into the flagstone below.

The sister-apothecary was already in the room, having been summoned earlier, and had examined the corpse.

'The goblet contained hemlock, Sister Fidelma,' bobbed Sister Poitigéir quickly as Fidelma turned to her. 'It was drunk in the same manner as Sillán drank his poison. But Follaman drank the liquid in the night and no one heard his final cries.'

Sister Fidelma surveyed the scene grimly, then she turned to Sister Ethne.

'I will be with the Mother Abbess for a while. See that no one disturbs us.'

Abbess Ita stood at the window of her chamber, watching the reds, golds and oranges of the rising dawn.

She half-turned as Sister Fidelma entered, then, ascertaining who it was, she turned back to the open window. The sharp colours of dawn were flooding the room with a pleasant, golden aura.

'No, Fidelma,' she said before Fidelma spoke. 'I did not poison Follaman.'

Fidelma's lips thinned.

'I know that you did not, Mother Abbess.'

With a surprised frown, Abbess Ita turned and stared at Fidelma for a moment. Then she motioned her to be seated and slid herself into her chair. Her face was pale and strained. She seemed to have slept little.

'Then you already know who the culprit is? You know how Sillán and Follaman died?'

Sister Fidelma nodded.

'Last night, Mother Abbess, I was struggling to decide whether I, as a dálaigh, should serve the law or serve justice.'

'Is that not the same thing, Fidelma?'

Sister Fidelma smiled softly.

'Sometimes it is; sometimes not. This matter, for example, is a case where the two things diverge.'

'Yes?'

'It is obvious that Sillán was killed unlawfully. He was killed to prevent him revealing his knowledge that a gold-mine is situated under these venerable buildings. Was the person who slaughtered him right or wrong to kill him? By what standards do we judge? The taking of a life is wrong by our laws. But if Sillán had disclosed his knowledge, and that knowledge had led to the driving forth of this community from its lands, or had led to warfare between those who would then covert these lands, would that have been justice? Perhaps there is a natural justice which rules above all things?'

'I understand what you are saying, Fidelma,' replied the Abbess. 'The death of one innocent may prevent the deaths of countless others.'

'Yet do we have the right to make their choice? Is that not something which we should leave in the hands of God?'

'It can be argued that sometimes God places in our hands the tools by which His will is carried out.'

Sister Fidelma studied the Abbess's face closely.

'Only two people now know of Sillán's discovery.'

Abbess Ita raised an eyebrow.

'Two?'

'I know, Mother Abbess, and you know.'

The Abbess frowned.

'But surely the poisoner of Follaman knows?'

'*Knew,*' corrected Sister Fidelma softly.

'Explain.'

'It was Follaman who administered the hemlock which killed Sillán.'

The Abbess bit her lip.

'But why would Follaman do that?'

'For the very reason that we have discussed, to prevent Sillán telling the Uí Failgi about the gold.'

'Yes, but Follaman...? He was a simple man.'

'Simple and loyal. Had he not worked here at the abbey as the keeper of the hostel since he was a boy? He loved this place as much as any of our community. He was not a religieux but he was as much a member of the community as anyone else.'

'How did Follaman know?'

'He overheard you and Sillán arguing. I suspect that he purposely eavesdropped on you. Follaman knew, or surmised, what profession Sillán practised. He might well have followed Sillán on his explorations. Whether he did or not is beside the point. When Sillán came back yesterday afternoon, Follaman certainly deduced that he had made some find, for Sillán told Follaman that he would be leaving for Ráith Imgain the next morning. He probably followed Sillán to your room and overheard what passed between you.

'Since you could not act against the laws of man and God, he would serve a natural justice in his own way. He took the jar of poison hemlock from the apothecary and when Sillán asked for a drink, he supplied it. Follaman did not know the precise quantity needed and so Sillán did not suffer the full effects until after the bell called the community into the refectory for the evening meal following vespers.'

Abbess Ita was following Sister Fidelma closely.

'And then?'

'Then I began my investigation, and then the Tanist of the Uí Failgi arrived seeking Sillán or an explanation for his death.'

'But who killed Follaman?'

'Follaman knew that sooner or later he would be discovered. But more importantly in his guileless mind there was also the guilt of having taken a man's life to be considered. Follaman was a simple man. He decided that he should accept punishment. The honour-price of a life. What greater honour-price for the life of Sillán could he offer than his own? He also took a draught of the poison hemlock.'

There was a pause.

'It is a plausible story, Sister Fidelma. But how do you substantiate it?'

'Firstly, when I questioned Follaman, he knew all about Sillán's profession. Secondly, he made two slips. He told me that he had seen Sillán coming from your chamber with anger on his face. Your chamber is on the far side of the abbey to the hostel. Therefore Follaman must have been near your chamber door. But, most importantly, when I asked Follaman if he knew what hemlock looked like, he denied any knowledge.'

'Why is that damning?'

'Because one of Follaman's duties is to help in the herb garden of the community, and Sister Poitigéir had just informed me that she grew hemlock in the garden for medicinal purposes; the very plant used in the apothecary came from the garden. And Sister Poitigéir said she was helped in this task by Follaman. He knew what hemlock looked like. So why did he lie to me?"

Abbess Ita sighed deeply.

'I see. What you are saying is that Follaman tried to protect us, protect our community here at Kildare?'

'I am. He was a simple man and saw no other way.'

The Abbess smiled painfully.

'In truth, Sister, with all my knowledge, I saw no other path that would have led to the same result. So what do you propose?'

'There are times when the law brings injustice with it and the triumph of justice is mankind's only peace. So the question is between justice or the stricture of the law.' Fidelma hesitated and grimaced. 'Let it be natural justice. I shall officially report that the result of my inquiry is that Sillán met his death by accident, so did Follaman. A contaminated jug of water, which had been made up by Follaman to destroy the vermin in the abbey vaults, became inadvertently used to mix with the mead in the hostel. The contaminated jug was not discovered until Follaman had also died.'

Abbess Ita gazed speculatively at Sister Fidelma.

'And what do we tell the Tanist of the Uí Failgi about the gold-mine?'

'That Sillán had decided to return to Ráith Imgain because the legend of the gold-mine of Kildare was simply a legend and nothing more.'

'Very well.' The Abbess had a smile of contentment on her face. 'If this is what you are prepared to report, then I endorse your report with my authority as the head of this community. In such a manner may our community be saved for future generations. For the falsehood of the report, I absolve you from all responsibility and sin.'

It was the smile of the Abbess which troubled Fidelma in her decision. She would, for the sake of natural justice, have held her tongue. But the relieved complacency of Abbess Ita suddenly irritated her. And, if she carefully analysed herself, was it not that her pride in her reputation as a solver of mysteries had been pricked?

Sister Fidelma slowly reached into her robe and pulled out the small piece of rock which she had picked up in the chamber that Sillán had occupied. She tossed it on the table. The Abbess gazed down at it.

'It was part of Sillán's proof of his discovery. You'd better keep that safe with the other pieces of gold which Follaman gave you after he had poisoned Sillán ... at your instruction.'

Abbess Ita's face was suddenly ashen and the whites showed around her amber eyes.

'How...?' she stuttered.

Sister Fidelma smiled bitterly.

'Do not fear, Mother Abbess. All will be as I have said it was. Your secret is safe with me. What I do is for the good of our community, for the future of the House of the Blessed Brigid of Kildare, and those people who live within the peace of the shadows of these walls. It is not for me to judge you. For that you will have to answer to God and the shades of Sillán and Follaman.'

Abbess Ita's lips trembled.

'But how...?' she whispered again.

'I have stressed that Follaman was a simple man. Even if he had the wit to understand the implications of Sillán's find for the abbey and the community around it, could he really have taken the poison hemlock and administered it?'

'But you yourself have demonstrated he could. Sister Poitigéir told you that Follaman helped her attend the plants in the herb garden and would know what hemlock looked like.'

'Follaman knew what the plant looked like, yes. But he would have to be told what the crushed leaves of hemlock were. You need to discern colours for that. Follaman could not pick out a bowl of crushed hemlock leaves by their purple spots and white tips once the distinctive shape had been destroyed. You see, what was staring me in the face the whole while was a simple fact. Follaman was colour-blind. He could not discern colours. Someone would have had to have given Follaman the poison to administer.'

Abbess Ita's lips were compressed into a thin, hard line.

'But I did not kill Follaman,' she said fiercely. 'Even if I admit that I suggested to Follaman that our community would best be served by the demise of Sillán, even if I admit I showed Follaman a method to do that deed, who killed Follaman? I did not do it!'

'No,' replied Fidelma. 'It was as I have said. At your suggestion, Follaman administered the poison to Sillán because you told him it was God's will. You used him as a tool. But he, being a simple man, could not live with the guilt he felt in taking a life. He took his own life in self-retribution, as I have said. He had not given all the hemlock to Sillán but kept some aside in his room. Last night he drank it as a penance for the deed. His was the penance, Mother Abbess, but yours is the guilt.'

Abbess Ita stared at her blankly.

'What am I to do?' she demanded, but her voice broke a little.

Sister Fidelma gave a slight smile of cynicism.

'With your permission, Mother Abbess, I shall be leaving Kildare this morning. I will make my report to the Tanist of the Uí Failgi first. Do not worry. The good of the community is uppermost in my mind. That good outweighs the law. But I shall make a pilgrimage to the shrine of the Blessed Patrick at Armagh to pay penance for the falsehood of my report.'

Sister Fidelma paused and gazed into the troubled amber eyes of the Abbess Ita.

'I cannot help relieve your guilt. I suggest, Mother Abbess, that you acquire the services of a sympathetic confessor.'

A Gift for Friendship

MORRIS HERSHMAN

O nly one man has a better reason than I to feel satisfied. Hasn't a painful task been done and success been his? Doesn't the police force itself as much as admit in so many bitter words that the particular case cannot be solved?

Absolutely yes, to all of that. And yet, very slightly but perceptibly, I have a feeling of furtive, hard-to-identify dissatisfaction. It does seem that the perfect accomplishment of a difficult goal is not enough to ensure happiness.

Let me see if I can't identify the reasons for that elusive itch. Can I go back in the mind's eye, trying to remember the feeling, the look-over-your-shoulder tautness, that for a while was so much of everyone's life in the village?

As we join our friends (as they used to say just before the start of the broadcast of a serial episode on Radio Eireann back when I was a lad), Brendan Roche has hurried over from his house up the street in vain hopes of hearing good news. He hasn't heard it and he is upset. Brendan speaks:

"What a shame that you didn't see anything," he says to his host, shaking that big horselike head of his. "Nobody else was so likely to see anything, and you've always had such splendid eyesight."

A downcast Kieran Cavanaugh says, "All I saw was some stranger's car roaring past the far end of the street."

"Do you at least know what make or model it was? Did you get the license number?"

"It happened too quickly," Kieran says, forbearing to add that the knowledge would have changed little because when he saw that car the horrid event itself was taking place elsewhere. Kieran has always been a gentleman to the fingertips.

Brendan turns to the police detective–from the great metropolis of Clonmel itself, to be sure–who has been slogging gamely from house to house and asking whether anyone has noticed anything that might be of help in this damnable situation–though not in those words.

"Mr. Cavanaugh here was on duty as the neighborhood block watcher," Brendan says. "He's the one to have seen some criminal hurrying out of that house where the crime took place."

And he looks at me for agreement, which I reluctantly grant in the form of a half-nod. It happens that I have dropped in unannounced on Kieran, too, as many have, and I hear him admitting he has been useless. It would be clear to a deaf man just how much Kieran absolutely hates having to say so.

Brendan stops rubbing Kieran's face in it, and doesn't leave until he is certain that Kieran won't get into any trouble over the mistake. The detective looks approvingly after Brendan and says that Mr. Brendan Roche seems like a fine upstanding fellow.

And that was the first time I saw Kieran shrug, after a pause, at Brendan Roche's name. He might have been saying clearly that no one could expect much in the way of progress with the likes of Brendan Roche around. But that would be unheard-of from Kieran, who always supported block watch members over anybody else in the village, and was especially a good friend with Brendan. I don't think anybody had ever before seen Kieran, of all people, behaving like what my sainted mother liked to call an itch....

Kieran was, as my elephant memory reminds me, the one who first suggested a block watch to keep crime at bay in our village of Meela. The young had been racketing about in the late-night hours, mopping up enough Guinness to lose all sense of proportion at their age. Someone had pitched a rock into Father O'Hickee's domain, the Church of the Blessed Martyr, during an evening Mass. A wave of thefts had come and gone as quickly as the dog-racing season in a Clonmel February. Worst of all, there had been several night burglaries of homes, all committed by strangers who had been observed through a series of unrepeatable accidents.

Kieran suggested that we eliminate the factor of happenstance by a block watch. Softly he explained that the neighbor on duty two nights a month would walk back and forth during a four-hour stretch, ready to telephone a special number at the police building in Clonmel should the need arise.

He first talked about it to me at the Gasworks, as our local pub was impishly called. It seemed sensible to me, but I only agreed with it as something that ought to be done sometime.

Brendan Roche, to whom Kieran suggested the idea during one of their occasional piss-ups in Kieran's ever-hospitable surroundings, took the notion and ran with it. It was a short time after Brendan's only child, a daughter, had trudged off to college. He himself was ready for almost any distraction. Of course, Brendan gave credit where it belonged, but he was so busy making plans and handing out assignments that a few of the others figured he was being exception-ally modest.

The idea was only accepted, I think, because' we all knew without saying it that soft-voiced Kieran Cavanaugh and loud-but-mostly-amiable Brendan Roche would take responsibility for whatever might go wrong. Kieran once told me, chuckling all the while, that his wife and Brendan's said that the real work would be dropped over the shoulders of the team spark plugs. I wouldn't insist that the two good ladies were entirely wrong.

Think of last night's hellishness, if you need a perfect example. Kieran had taken Teddy O'Callaghan's duty, as he or Brendan often had to, because Teddy had responsibly agreed to help when needed and then backed out uniformly at the last minute. Kieran's own duty that night followed Teddy's, so he had done both jobs without com-plaining. Brendan himself had performed a similar double stint not long back. When bad trouble showed its ugly head after two pretty efficient months of the block watch, it's no wonder Kieran had been too tired to do what was necessary.

He had, though, volunteered to do one thing as soon as possible, minutes after finding out that Owney Maguier, the carpenter, had been fatally hit over the head with one of his own hammers. The detective had put off notifying Owney's widow, who had traveled southeast to visit her sick father. Kieran took it on himself to phone her in Rosslare with the awful news, admitting bluntly that he'd seen nothing useful on his block watch and offering no excuses for having let the killer get away unseen. Just like Kieran, that was, conceding his faults, being the first to tell her that he had accepted responsibility for not living up to his duty.

Kieran's wife, Lillian, said to him over early supper, "Owney is known to have carried on with any number of women in the village."

"I think I've heard something like that, too, dear."

"What Dellie Roche told me," Lillian added, referring to Brendan's wife, "is that his Agnes was very cool to doing it as soon as they'd been married for six months or so. Owney took up his new hobby afterwards and was very successful."

"Did you hear this from Dellie?"

"Oh yes. When the ladies get together, they speak from the heart."

If Kieran wondered what his wife's contribution might have been to such a gabfest, he didn't say.

I can't remember who told me that when Brendan came by the house later on, Kieran told his friend that he and Lillian would be going out to the pictures as soon as the children were asleep. There wasn't a word of truth in that. Kieran went back to watching Southend versus Mansfield on the telly and cheering Paul Holland on to greater triumphs, if that were possible for Southend's star midfielder. He turned down the telly with a feeling of relief, as ever, and welcomed me when I appeared at the door.

My wife and I invited the Cavanaugh elders for a supper during the week, and it surprised me hardly at all when Lillian steered the talk around to the subject of the first murder in the history of Meela.

"It can't be hard to imagine how Owney Maguier got what was coming to him," Lillian said pensively over her portion of a salmon which looked as if it, too, had been hit with a hammer. Only because she was so poor a cook, as I've often said to others at the Gasworks, did my missus insist on having guests at a sit-down supper every two weeks. "It's really as plain as could be."

"I suppose so," my missus said, not excessively happy about it herself.

I asked, "How could either of you know what happened to Owney, or how it happened?"

Lillian took the question seriously. "Dellie Roche was always telling us what she heard about Owney. Fascinated by him, she was—in a detached sort of way, you must understand."

Kieran was smiling. "You've both made up your minds to tell us

what you think or what Dellie Roche does, so why not get it over
and let the men have a quiet glass afterwards?"

"It's very simple," Lillian said only a little coolly. "Owney invited
some new woman over to his place, with Agnes being gone for a few
days. He'd done that sort of thing in the past. The new woman—I
would think it was Jennie Meserve, but Owney always liked his
women more filled out—agreed to come over. She would have been
impressed by Owney's gentlemanly manners and good looks. If he'd
lived to eighty, Owney would still have looked like a thirty-five-year-
old who worried a lot, I do believe."

"And when the woman came over," I said, rushing to the point,
"Owney did his best to take care of her."

"Don't be vulgar, dear," my missus said. "But basically you're right,
and the new woman became testy about it, you might say."

"That's what Dellie Roche might say," Lillian contributed, "only she
wouldn't be so even-tempered about it."

My missus started to talk about how reliable Brendan's Dellie could
be at passing on the spiciest gossip.

There was an argument getting under way between myself and both
women, when Kieran stopped it cold.

"This salmon of yours is just delicious," he said, lying in only one
word. "You must let Lillian have the recipe."

"I'll prepare it for you, dear," Lillian promised between clenched
teeth, "exactly according to the directions."

Let me tell you that Kieran was behaving in a very strange way toward
Dellie Roche's husband. He made several clear complaints about his
best friend in Meela. I can't be the only one who heard.

Kieran must have known that his behavior was unsettling to his
many friends, and tried to justify himself by telling a few of us later
in the week that he'd visited Roche—as he now called him—that Monday night. He'd carried a specially inscribed tee shirt for Brendan Roche
to send his college daughter. The way Kieran told it, he spent hardly
five minutes with Roche and the devoted Dellie. He insisted he hadn't
wanted to stay for another minute.

Just about an hour before the block watch monthly meeting ("like
rehearsing the ñags ahead of the Curragh racing," as Kieran and Brendan had always told the lazier members with one voice), I ran into
Kieran. I suppose he could have been looking for me, as the missus
skeptically suggested long afterward. I didn't care. I had married two

months after he did, and my twin girls were just about the same age as his twin boys, so we've been special friends over the years.

Kieran was taking a warm bag of food out of his car. As manager of the Fish 'n' Chips on Commerce Street, I congratulated him on his and his family's excellent taste in fast food, but wondered why he wasn't coming to a meeting this once.

"I won't be at any of the meetings from now on," Kieran answered with overdone rue. "Roche told me on the phone that he's going to demand I be dropped from the group. He isn't backward about coming forward, I'll say that much."

"You? Dropped? Any mistake you made could happen to each of the others, too," I said aggressively, as if I were ordering one of the helpers to put more salt on the chips before cooking them. "If Brendan Roche won't live with that, he can take the first train to hell, far as I'm concerned."

And half an hour before the meeting, I'll be damned if Kieran didn't phone me to suggest that a new rule be made which would keep any neighbor from doing two consecutive tours of duty, as he was pleased to call it. Wouldn't such a procedure help prevent similar possible foul-ups?

I'll never believe that Kieran was glad to know afterward about the arguments at that meeting, which soon got out of hand. Even what started as a proper analytical discussion of whether Paul Ince would be leaving the Manchester United team to play for Internazionale in Milan turned into a spirited discussion in which tempers were lost and stayed that way.

I had talked to most of the others beforehand, so nearly everybody had come loaded for bear, but it was Brendan who caught most of the pellets. It was made clear that a tin-pot dictator was the member who wouldn't be in the block watch from now on.

Roche swore that he'd never so much as thought of demanding that we drop Kieran, of all people, but couldn't say what made Kieran lie about it. Just before he left, under a hailstorm of jeers, I heard him mutter, "But what made him *lie* like that?"

Kieran said no more against Brendan Roche, but his pointed silences made it clear he wanted nothing whatever to do with his former very good friend. Not, it seemed, since the recent foul murder which the police were now admitting wasn't likely to be solved this side of paradise.

None of us spoke up for Brendan to Kieran or vice versa. Both were liked and respected, and it was impossible to backtrack far enough to find out what misunderstanding had led two good men to this painful rupture.

Soon enough Brendan made it clear he couldn't keep on living near somebody who had betrayed an innocent man. Word got around that the Roche holding was for sale, and at about as much as his great-great-whatever had paid for it at about the time when Saint Patrick's grandfather walked the earth. At this year's deflated prices, buying it was a good piece of business for somebody.

I dropped in on Kieran late one not-too-misty Sunday afternoon in April. He and his sons were warming up on their lawn, and he asked me to join them in cracking a shin or two at soccer. The biggest advantage in having young sons, Kieran liked to say, is that a man his age or mine can always get a game if he wants one.

Shane, Kieran's younger one by three minutes, was handling the ball while describing the game like some commentator on the telly. "Collymore has the ball now and is moving ahead with it ... moving ahead...." Shane turned, losing the ball to his older brother and all the time burbling excitedly if not being consistent in his attitude. "Well played, Collymore, oh, very well played...."

The ball, with which contact was suddenly lost, dribbled toward Kieran, who normally could have seen a living fly, but ignored this as if he didn't know it was there. His suddenly drained face looked almost the color of cream Belleek.

Glancing to where he had moved, I couldn't help noticing the curb from the corner of my eye. All three members of the Roche family were in their six-year-old glass-topped red Corvette and starting off, a truck with furniture and other belongings having got under way minutes before.

Kieran, turning, disregarded plaintive calls for the ball from the troops. He could clearly see Roche and Dellie stolidly ignoring the house across the street, that house where Owney Maguier had met a philanderer's end little more than a month ago.

Although Kieran's face still looked haunted, he suddenly nodded in the direction of the car. Nodded reassuringly, I thought.

Which is when the realization crossed my mind that his sharp vision had picked out someone near the Maguier home on that tragic late night. He had protected one person from possibly being recognized in future as having been on or near the premises at that terrible time. And it mattered so much because that particular person was supposed to have been far away from the village. So Kieran had alienated his greatest friend forever, practically forcing the man and his family out of the area in a powerful example of friendship that could never be known by the recipient. Kieran had seen (how could I doubt it any longer?) Brendan Roche's only daughter.

A Study in White

NICHOLAS BLAKE

'Seasonable weather for the time of year,' remarked the Expansive Man in a voice succulent as the breast of a roast goose.

The Deep Chap, sitting next to him in the railway compartment, glanced out at the snow, swarming and swirling past the windowpane. He replied: 'You really like it? Oh well, it's an ill blizzard that blows nobody no good. Depends what you mean by seasonable, though. Statistics for the last fifty years would show—'

'Name of Joad, sir?' asked the Expansive Man, treating the compartment to a wholesale wink.

'No, Stansfield, Henry Stansfield.' The Deep Chap, a ruddy-faced man who sat with hands firmly planted on the knees of his brown tweed suit, might have been a prosperous farmer but for the long, steady, meditative scrutiny which he now bent upon each of his fellow-travellers in turn.

What he saw was not particularly rewarding. On the opposite seat from left to right, were a Forward Piece, who had taken the Expansive Man's wink wholly to herself and contrived to wriggle her tight skirt farther up from her knee; a desiccated, sandy, lawyerish little man who fumed and fussed like an angry kettle, consulting every five minutes his gold watch, then shaking out his *Times* with the crackle of a legal parchment; and a Flash Card, dressed up to the nines of spivdom, with the bold yet uneasy stare of the young delinquent.

'Mine's Percy Dukes,' said the Expansive Man. 'P.D. to my friends.

General Dealer. At your service. Well, we'll be across the border in an hour and a half, and then hey for the bluebells of bonny Scotland!'

'Bluebells in January? You're hopeful,' remarked the Forward Piece.

'Are you Scots, master?' asked the Comfortable Body sitting on Stansfield's left.

'English outside'–Percy Dukes patted the front of his grey suit, slid a flask from his hip pocket, and took a swig–'and Scotch within.' His loud laugh, or the blizzard, shook the railway carriage. The Forward Piece giggled.

'You'll need that if we run into a drift and get stuck for the night,' said Henry Stansfield.

'Name of Jonah, sir?' The compartment reverberated again.

'I do not apprehend such an eventuality,' said the Fusspot. 'The stationmaster at Lancaster assured me that the train would get through. We are scandalously late already, though.' Once again the gold watch was consulted.

'It's a curious thing,' remarked the Deep Chap meditatively, 'the way we imagine we can make Time amble withal or gallop withal, just by keeping an eye on the hands of a watch. You travel frequently by this train, Mr–?'

'Kilmington. Arthur J. Kilmington. No, I've only used it once before.' The Fusspot spoke in a dry Edinburgh accent.

'Ah, yes, that would have been on the 17th of last month. I remember seeing you on it.'

'No, sir, you are mistaken. It was the 20th.' Mr Kilmington's thin mouth snapped tight again, like a rubber band round a sheaf of legal documents.

'The 20th? Indeed? That was the day of the train robbery. A big haul they got, it seems. Off this very train. It was carrying some of the extra Christmas mail. Bags just disappeared, somewhere between Lancaster and Carlisle.'

'Och, deary me,' sighed the Comfortable Body. 'I don't know what we're coming to, really, nowadays.'

'We're coming to the scene of the crime, ma'am,' said the expansive Mr Dukes. The train, almost deadbeat, was panting up the last pitch towards Shap Summit.

'I didn't see anything in the papers about where the robbery took place,' Henry Stansfield murmured. Dukes fastened a somewhat bleary eye upon him.

'You read all the newspapers?'

'Yes.

The atmosphere in the compartment had grown suddenly tense. Only the Flash Card, idly examining his fingernails, seemed unaffected by it.

'Which paper did you see it in?' pursued Stansfield.

'I didn't.' Dukes tapped Stansfield on the knee. 'But I can use my loaf. Stands to reason. You want to tip a mail-bag out of a train–get me? Train must be moving slowly, or the bag'll burst when it hits the ground. Only one place between Lancaster and Carlisle where you'd *know* the train would be crawling. Shap Bank. And it goes slowest on the last bit of the bank, just about where we are now. Follow?'

Henry Stansfield nodded.

'OK. But you'd be balmy to tip it off just anywhere on this Godforsaken moorland,' went on Mr Dukes. 'Now, if you'd travelled this line as much as I have, you'd have noticed it goes over a bridge about a mile short of the summit. Under the bridge runs a road: a nice, lonely road, see? The only road hereabouts that touches the railway. You tip out the bag there. Your chums collect it, run down the embankment, dump it in the car they've waiting by the bridge, and Bob's your uncle!'

'You oughta been a detective, mister,' exclaimed the Forward Piece languishingly.

Mr Dukes inserted his thumbs in his armpits, looking gratified. 'Maybe I am,' he said with a wheezy laugh. 'And maybe I'm just little old P.D., who knows how to use his loaf.'

'Och, well now, the things people will do?' said the Comfortable Body. 'There's a terrible lot of dishonesty today.'

The Flash Card glanced up contemptuously from his fingernails. Mr Kilmington was heard to mutter that the system of surveillance on railways was disgraceful, and the Guard of the train should have been severely censured.

'The Guard can't be everywhere,' said Stansfield. 'Presumably he has to patrol the train from time to time, and–'

'Let him do so, then, and not lock himself up in his van and go to sleep,' interrupted Mr Kilmington, somewhat unreasonably.

'Are you speaking from personal experience, sir?' asked Stansfield.

The Flash Card lifted up his voice and said, in a Charing-Cross-Road American accent, 'Hey, fellas! If the gang was gonna tip out the mail-bags by the bridge, like this guy says–what I mean is, how could they rely on the Guard being out of his van just at that point?' He hitched up the trousers of his loud check suit.

'You've got something there,' said Percy Dukes. 'What I reckon is, there must have been two accomplices on the train–one to get the Guard out of his van on some pretext, and the other to chuck off the bags.' He turned to Mr Kilmington. 'You were saying something about the Guard locking himself up in his van. Now if I was of a suspicious turn of mind, if I was little old Sherlock H. in person'–he bestowed another prodigious wink upon Kilmington's fellow-travellers–'I'd begin to wonder about you, sir. You were travelling on this train when the robbery took place. You went to the Guard's van. You *say* you found him asleep. You didn't by any chance call the Guard out, so as to–?'

'Your suggestion is outrageous! I advise you to be very careful, sir, very careful indeed,' enunciated Mr Kilmington, his precise voice crackling with indignation, 'or you may find you have said something actionable. I would have you know that, when I–'

But what he would have them know was to remain undivulged. The train, which for some little time had been running cautiously down from Shap Summit, suddenly began to chatter and shudder, like a fever patient in high delirium, as the vacuum brakes were applied; then, with the dull impact of a fist driving into a feather pillow, the engine buried itself in a drift which had gathered just beyond the bend of a deep cutting.

It was just five minutes past seven.

'What's this?' asked the Forward Piece, rather shrilly, as a hysterical outburst of huffing and puffing came from the engine.

'Run into a drift, I reckon.'

'He's trying to back us out. No good. The wheels are slipping every time. What a lark!' Percy Dukes had his head out of the window on the lee side of the train. 'Coom to Coomberland for your winter sports!'

'Guard! Guard, I say!' called Mr Kilmington. But the blue-clad figure, after one glance into the compartment, hurried on his way up the corridor. 'Really! I *shall* report that man.'

Henry Stansfield, going out into the corridor, opened a window. Though the coach was theoretically sheltered by the cutting on this windward side, the blizzard stunned his face like a knuckleduster of ice. He joined the herd of passengers who had climbed down and were stumbling towards the engine. As they reached it, the Guard emerged from the cab: no cause for alarm, he said; if they couldn't get through, there'd be a relief engine sent down to take the train back to Penrith; he was just off to set fog-signals on the line behind them.

The driver renewed his attempts to back the train out. But what with its weight, the up-gradient in its rear, the icy rails, and the clinging grip of the drift on the engine, he could not budge her.

'We'll have to dig out the bogeys, mate,' he said to his fireman. 'Fetch them shovels from the forward van. It'll keep the perishers from freezing, anyhow.' He jerked his finger at the knot of passengers who, lit up by the glare of the furnace, were capering and beating their arms like savages amid the swirling snow-wreaths.

Percy Dukes, who had now joined them, quickly established himself as the life and soul of the party, referring to the grimy-faced fireman as "Snowball," adjuring his companions to "Dig for Victory," affecting to spy the approach of a herd of St Bernards, each with a keg of brandy slung round its neck. But after ten minutes of hard digging, when the leading wheels of the bogey were cleared, it could be seen that they had been derailed by the impact with the drift.

'That's torn it, Charlie. You'll have to walk back to the box and get 'em to telephone through for help,' said the driver.

'If the wires aren't down already,' replied the fireman lugubriously. 'It's above a mile to that box, and uphill. Who d'you think I am, Captain Scott?'

'You'll have the wind behind you, mate, anyhow. So long.'

A buzz of dismay had risen from the passengers at this. One or two, who began to get querulous, were silenced by the driver's offering to take them anywhere they liked if they would just lift his engine back onto the metals first. When the rest had dispersed to their carriages, Henry Stansfield asked the driver's permission to go up into the cab for a few minutes and dry his coat.

'You're welcome.' The driver snorted: 'Would you believe it? "Must get to Glasgow tonight." Damn ridiculous! Now Bert—that's my Guard—it's different for him: he's entitled to fret a bit. Missus been very poorly. Thought she was going to peg out before Christmas; but he got the best surgeon in Glasgow to operate on her, and she's mending now, he says. He reckons to look in every night at the nursing home, when he goes off work.'

Stansfield chatted with the man for five minutes. Then the Guard returned, blowing upon his hands—a smallish, leathery-faced chap, with an anxious look in his eye.

'We'll not get through tonight, Bert. Charlie told you?'

'Aye. I doubt some of the passengers are going to create a rumpus,' said the Guard dolefully.

Henry Stansfield went back to his compartment. It was stuffy, but with a sinister hint of chilliness, too: he wondered how long the steam heating would last: depended upon the amount of water in the engine boiler, he supposed. Among the wide variety of fates he had imagined for himself, freezing to death in an English train was not included.

Arthur J. Kilmington fidgeted more than ever. When the Guard came along the corridor, he asked him where the nearest village was, saying he must get a telephone call through to Edinburgh—most urgent appointment—must let his client know, if he was going to miss it. The Guard said there was a village two miles to the northeast; you could see the lights from the top of the cutting; but he warned Mr Kilmington against trying to get there in the teeth of this blizzard—better wait for the relief engine, which should reach them before 9 P.M.

Silence fell upon the compartment for a while; the incredulous silence of civilised people who find themselves in the predicament of castaways. Then the expansive Mr Dukes proposed that, since they were to be stuck here for an hour of two, they should get acquainted. The Comfortable Body now introduced herself as Mrs Grant, the Forward Piece as Inez Blake; the Flash Card, with the over-negligent air of one handing a dud half-crown over a counter, gave his name as Macdonald—I. Macdonald.

The talk reverted to the train robbery and the criminals who had perpetrated it.

'They must be awfu' clever,' remarked Mrs Grant, in her singsong Lowland accent.

'No criminals are clever, ma'am,' said Stansfield quietly. His ruminative eye passed, without haste, from Macdonald to Dukes. 'Neither the small fry nor the big operators. They're pretty well sub-human, the whole lot of 'em. A dash of cunning, a thick streak of cowardice, and the rest is made up of stupidity and boastfulness. They're too stupid for anything but crime, and so riddled with inferiority that they always give themselves away, sooner or later, by boasting about their crimes. They like to think of themselves as the wide boys, but they're as narrow as starved eels—why, they haven't even the wits to alter their professional methods: that's how the police pick 'em up.'

'I entirely agree, sir,' Mr Kilmington snapped. 'In my profession I see a good deal of the criminal classes. And I flatter myself none of them has ever got the better of me. They're transparent, sir, transparent.'

'No doubt you gentlemen are right,' said Percy Dukes comfortably.

'But the police haven't picked up the chaps who did this train robbery yet.'

'They will. And the Countess of Axminster's emerald bracelet. Bet
the gang didn't reckon to find that in the mail-bag. Worth all of
£25,000.'

Percy Dukes' mouth fell open. The Flash Card whistled. Overcome,
either by the stuffiness of the carriage or the thought of £25,000-
worth of emeralds, Inez Blake gave a little moan and fainted all over
Mr Kilmington's lap.

'Really! Upon my soul! My dear young lady!' exclaimed that worthy.
There was a flutter of solicitude, shared by all except the cold-eyed
young Macdonald who, after stooping over her a moment, his back to
the others, said, 'Here you—stop pawing the young lady and let her
stretch out on the seat. Yes, I'm talking to you, Kilmington.'

'How dare you! This is an outrage!' The little man stood up so
abruptly that the girl was almost rolled onto the floor. 'I was merely
trying to–'

'I know your sort. Nasty old men. Now, keep your hands off her.
I'm telling you.'

In the shocked silence that ensued, Kilmington gobbled speechlessly
at Macdonald for a moment; then, seeing razors in the youth's cold-
steel eye, snatched his black hat and brief-case from the rack and bolted
out of the compartment. Henry Stansfield made as if to stop him, then
changed his mind. Mrs Grant followed the little man out, returning
presently, her handkerchief soaked in water, to dab Miss Blake's forehead. The time was just 8.30.

When things were restored to normal, Mr Dukes turned to Stansfield. 'You were saying this necklace of–who was it?–the Countess of
Axminster, it's worth £25,000? Fancy sending a thing of that value
through the post! Are you sure of it?'

'The value? Oh, yes.' Henry Stansfield spoke out of the corner of
his mouth, in the manner of a stupid man imparting a confidence. 'Don't
let this go any further. But I've a friend who works in the Cosmopolitan–the company where it's insured. That's another thing that didn't
get into the papers. Silly woman. She wanted it for some big family-
do in Scotland at Christmas, forgot to bring it with her, and wrote
home for it to be posted to her in a registered packet.'

'£25,000,' said Percy Dukes thoughtfully. 'Well, stone me down!'

'Yes. Some people don't know when they're lucky, do they?'

Dukes' fat face wobbled on his shoulders like a globe of lard. Young

Macdonald polished his nails. Inez Blake read her magazine. After a while Percy Dukes remarked that the blizzard was slackening; he'd take an airing and see if there was any sign of the relief engine yet. He left the compartment.

At the window the snowflakes danced in their tens now, not their thousands. The time was 8.55. Shortly afterwards Inez Blake went out; and ten minutes later Mrs Grant remarked to Stansfield that it had stopped snowing altogether. Neither Inez nor Dukes had returned when, at 9.30, Henry Stansfield decided to ask what had happened about the relief. The Guard was not in his van, which adjoined Stansfield's coach, towards the rear of the train. So he turned back, walked up the corridor to the front coach, clambered out, and hailed the engine cab.

'She must have been held up,' said the Guard, leaning out. 'Charlie here got through from the box, and they promised her by nine o'clock. But it'll no' be long now, sir.'

'Have you seen anything of a Mr Kilmington–small, sandy chap–black hat and overcoat, blue suit–was in my compartment? I've walked right up the train and he doesn't seem to be in it.'

The Guard pondered a moment. 'Och aye, you wee fellow? Him that asked me about telephoning from the village. Aye, he's awa' then.'

'He did set off to walk there, you mean?'

'Nae doot he did, if he's no' on the train. He spoke to me again–juist on nine, it'd be–and said he was awa' if the relief didna turn up in five minutes.'

'You've not seen him since?'

'No, sir. I've been talking to my mates here this half-hour, ever syne the wee fellow spoke to me.'

Henry Stansfield walked thoughtfully back down the permanent way. When he had passed out of the glare shed by the carriage lights on the snow, he switched on his electric torch. Just beyond the last coach the eastern wall of the cutting sloped sharply down and merged into moorland level with the track. Although the snow had stopped altogether, an icy wind from the northeast still blew, raking and numbing his face. Twenty yards further on his torch lit up a track, already half filled in with snow, made by several pairs of feet, pointing away over the moor, towards the northeast. Several passengers, it seemed, had set off for the village, whose lights twinkled like frost in the far distance. Stansfield was about to follow this track when he heard footsteps scrunching the snow farther up the line. He switched off the torch; at once it was as if a sack had been thrown over his head, so close and blinding was the darkness. The steps came nearer. Stansfield switched on his torch, at the last minute, pinpointing the squat figure of Percy Dukes. The man gave a muffled oath.

'What the devil! Here, what's the idea, keeping me waiting half an hour in that blasted–?'

'Have you seen Kilmington?'

'Oh, it's you. No, how the hell should I have seen him? Isn't he on the train? I've just been walking up the line, to look for the relief. No sign yet. Damn parky, it is–I'm moving on.'

Presently Stansfield moved on, too, but along the track towards the village. The circle of his torchlight wavered and bounced on the deep snow. The wind, right in his teeth, was killing. No wonder, he thought, as after a few hundred yards he approached the end of the trail, those passengers turned back. Then he realised they had not all turned back. What he had supposed to be a hummock of snow bearing a crude resemblance to a recumbent human figure, he now saw to be a human figure covered with snow. He scraped some of the snow off it, turned it gently over on its back.

Arthur J. Kilmington would fuss no more in this world. His brief-case was buried beneath him: his black hat was lying where it had fallen, lightly covered with snow, near the head. There seemed, to Stansfield's cursory examination, no mark of violence on him. But the eyeballs started, the face was suffused with a pinkish-blue colour. So men look who have been strangled, thought Stansfield, or asphyxiated. Quickly he knelt down again, shining his torch in the dead face. A qualm of horror shook him. Mr Kilmington's nostrils were caked thick with snow, which had frozen solid in them, and snow had been rammed tight into his mouth also.

And here he would have stayed, reflected Stansfield, in this desolate spot, for days or weeks, perhaps, if the snow lay or deepened. And when the thaw at last came (as it did that year, in fact, only after two months), the snow would thaw out from his mouth and nostrils, too, and there would be no vestige of murder left–only the corpse of an impatient little lawyer who had tried to walk to the village in a blizzard and died for his pains. It might even be that no one would ask how such a precise, pernickety little chap had ventured the two-mile walk in these shoes and without a torch to light his way through the pitchy blackness; for Stansfield, going through the man's pockets, had found the following articles–and nothing more: pocketbook, fountain pen, handkerchief, cigarette case, gold lighter, two letters, and some loose change.

Stansfield started to return for help. But only twenty yards back he noticed another trail of footprints, leading off the main track to the left. This trail seemed a fresher one–the snow lay less thickly in the indentations–and to have been made by one pair of feet only. He followed it up, walking beside it. Whoever made this track had walked in a slight right-handed curve back to the railway line, joining it about one hundred and fifty yards up the line from where the main trail came out. At this point there was a platelayers' shack. Finding the door unlocked, Stansfield entered. There was nothing inside but a coke-brazier, stone cold, and a smell of cigar smoke....

Half an hour later, Stansfield returned to his compartment. In the meanwhile, he had helped the train crew to carry back the body of Kilmington, which was now locked in the Guard's van. He had also made an interesting discovery as to Kilmington's movements. It was to be presumed that, after the altercation with Macdonald, and the brief conversation already reported by the Guard, the lawyer must have gone to sit in another compartment. The last coach, to the rear of the Guard's van, was a first-class one, almost empty. But in one of its compartments Stansfield found a passenger asleep. He woke him up, gave a description of Kilmington, and asked if he had seen him earlier.

The passenger grumpily informed Stansfield that a smallish man, in a dark overcoat, with the trousers of a blue suit showing beneath it, had come to the door and had a word with him. No, the passenger had not noticed his face particularly, because he'd been very drowsy himself, and besides, the chap had politely taken off his black Homburg hat to address him, and the hat screened as much of the head as was not cut off from his view by the top of the door. No, the chap had not come into his compartment: he had just stood outside, enquired the time (the passenger had looked at his watch and told him it was 8.50); then the chap had said that, if the relief didn't turn up by nine, he intended to walk to the nearest village.

Stansfield had then walked along to the engine cab. The Guard, whom he found there, told him that he'd gone up the track about 8.45 to meet the fireman on his way back from the signal-box. He had gone as far as the place where he'd put down his fog-signals earlier; here, just before nine, he and the fireman met, as the latter corroborated. Returning to the train, the Guard had climbed into the last coach, noticed Kilmington sitting alone in a first-class apartment (it was then that the lawyer announced to the Guard his intention of walking if the relief engine had not arrived within five minutes). The Guard then got out of the train again, and proceeded down the track to talk to his mates in the engine cab.

This evidence would seem to point incontrovertibly at Kilmington's having been murdered shortly after 9 P.M., Stansfield reflected as he went back to his own compartment. His fellow-passengers were all present now.

'Well, did you find him?' asked Percy Dukes.

'Kilmington? Oh, yes, I found him. In the snow over there. He was dead.'

Inez Blake gave a little, affected scream. The permanent sneer was wiped, as if by magic, off young Macdonald's face, which turned a sickly white. Mr Dukes sucked in his fat lips.

'The puir wee man,' said Mrs Grant. 'He tried to walk it then? Died of exposure, was it?'

'No,' announced Stansfield flatly, 'he was murdered.'

This time, Inez Blake screamed in earnest; and, like an echo, a hooting shriek came from far up the line: the relief engine was approaching at last.

'The police will be awaiting us back at Penrith, so we'd better all have our stories ready.' Stansfield turned to Percy Dukes. 'You, for instance, sir. Where were you between 8.55, when you left the carriage, and 9.35 when I met you returning? Are you sure you didn't see Kilmington?'

Dukes, expansive no longer, his piggy eyes sunk deep in the fat of his face, asked Stansfield who the hell he thought he was.

'I am an enquiry agent, employed by the Cosmopolitan Insurance Company. Before that, I was a Detective Inspector in the CID. Here is my card.'

Dukes barely glanced at it. 'That's all right, old man. Only wanted to make sure. Can't trust anyone nowadays.' His voice had taken on the ingratiating, oleaginous heartiness of the small business man trying to clinch a deal with a bigger one. 'Just went for a stroll, y'know—stretch the old legs. Didn't see a soul.'

'Who were you expecting to see? Didn't you wait for someone in the platelayers' shack along there, and smoke a cigar while you were waiting? Who did you mistake me for when you said "What's the idea, keeping me waiting half an hour?" '

'Here, draw it mild, old man.' Percy Dukes sounded injured. 'I certainly looked in at the huts: smoked a cigar for a bit. Then I toddled back to the train, and met up with your good self on the way. I didn't make no appointment to meet–'

'Oo! Well I *must* say,' interrupted Miss Blake virtuously. She could hardly wait to tell Stansfield that, on leaving the compartment shortly after Dukes, she'd overheard voices on the track below the lavatory window. 'I recognised this gentleman's voice,' she went on, tossing her head at Dukes. 'He said something like: "You're going to help us again, chum, so you'd better get used to the idea. You're in it up to the neck–can't back out now." And another voice, sort of mumbling, might have been Mr Kilmington's–I dunno–sounded Scotch anyway–said, "All right. Meet you in five minutes: platelayers' hut a few hundred yards up the line. Talk it over." '

'And what did you do then, young lady?' asked Stansfield.

'I happened to meet a gentleman friend, farther up the train, and sat with him for a bit.'

'Is that so?' remarked Macdonald menacingly. 'Why, you four-flushing little–!'

'Shut up!' commanded Stansfield.

'Honest I did,' the girl said, ignoring Macdonald. 'I'll introduce you to him, if you like. He'll tell you I was with him for, oh, half an hour or more.'

'And what about Mr Macdonald?'

'I'm not talking,' said the youth sullenly.

'Mr Macdonald isn't talking. Mrs Grant?'

'I've been in this compartment ever since, sir.'

'Ever since–?'

'Since I went out to damp my hankie for this young lady, when she'd fainted. Mr Kilmington was just before me, you'll mind. I saw him go through into the Guard's van.'

'Did you hear him say anything about walking to the village?'

'No, sir. He just hurried into the van, and then there was some havers about its no' being lockit this time, and how he was going to report the Guard for it.'

'I see. And you've been sitting here with Mr Macdonald all the time?'

'Yes, sir. Except for ten minutes or so he was out of the compartment, just after you'd left.'

'What did you go out for?' Stansfield asked the young man.

'Just taking the air, brother.'

'You weren't taking Mr Kilmington's gold watch, as well as the air, by any chance?' Stansfield's keen eyes were fastened like a hook into Macdonald's, whose insolent expression visibly crumbled beneath them.

'I don't know what you mean,' he tried to bluster. 'You can't do this to me.'

'I mean that a man has been murdered, and when the police search you, they will find his gold watch in your possession. Won't look too healthy for you, my young friend.'

'Naow! Give us a chance! It was only a joke, see?' The wretched Macdonald was whining now, in his native cockney. 'He got me riled—the stuck-up way he said nobody'd ever got the better of him. So I thought I'd just show him—I'd have given it back, straight I would, only I couldn't find him afterwards. It was just a joke, I tell you. Anyway, it was Inez who lifted the ticker.'

'You dirty little rotter!' screeched the girl.

'Shut up, both of you. You can explain your joke to the Penrith police. Let's hope they don't die of laughing.'

At this moment the train gave a lurch, and started back up the gradient. It halted at the signal-box, for Stansfield to telephone to Penrith, then clattered south again.

On Penrith platform Stansfield was met by an Inspector and a Sergeant of the County Constabulary, with the Police Surgeon. Then, after a brief pause in the Guard's van, where the Police Surgeon drew aside the Guard's black off-duty overcoat that had been laid over the body, and began his preliminary examination, they marched along to Stansfield's compartment. The Guard who, at his request, had locked this as the train was drawing up at the platform and was keeping an eye on its occupants, now unlocked it. The Inspector entered.

His first action was to search Macdonald. Finding the watch concealed on his person, he then charged Macdonald and Inez Blake with the theft. The Inspector next proceeded to make an arrest on the charge of wilful murder....

The Inspector arrested the Guard for the wilful murder of Arthur J. Kilmington.

Kilmington's pocket had been picked by Inez Blake, when she pretended to faint at 8.25, and his gold watch was at once passed by her to her accomplice, Macdonald. Now Kilmington was constantly consulting his watch. It is inconceivable, if he was not killed till after 9 P.M., that he should not have missed the watch and made a scene. This point was clinched by the first-class passenger who had said that a man, answering to the description of Kilmington, had asked him the time at 8.50: if it had really been Kilmington, he would certainly, before enquiring the time of anyone else, have first tried to consult his own watch, found it gone, and reported the theft. The fact that Kilmington neither reported the loss to the Guard, nor returned to his original compartment to look for the watch, proves he must have been murdered before he became aware of the loss—i.e., shortly after he left the compartment at 8.27. But the Guard claimed to have spoken to Kilmington at 9 P.M. Therefore the Guard was lying. And why should he lie, except to create an alibi for himself? This is Clue Number One.

The Guard claimed to have talked with Kilmington at 9 P.M. Now, at 8.55 the blizzard had diminished to a light snowfall, which soon afterwards ceased. When Stansfield discovered the body, it was buried under snow. Therefore Kilmington must have been murdered while the blizzard was still raging—i.e., some time before 9 P.M. Therefore the Guard was lying when he said Kilmington was alive at 9 P.M. This is Clue Number Two.

Henry Stansfield, who was investigating on behalf of the Cosmopolitan Insurance Company the loss of the Countess of Axminster's emeralds, reconstructed the crime as follows:

Motive: The Guard's wife had been gravely ill before Christmas: then, just about the time of the train robbery, he had got her the best surgeon in Glasgow and put her in a nursing home (evidence of engine-driver: Clue Number Three). A Guard's pay does not usually run to such expensive treatment: it seemed likely, therefore, that the man, driven desperately by his wife's need, had agreed to take part in the robbery in return for a substantial bribe. What part did he play? During the investigation the Guard had stated that he had left his van for five minutes, while the train was climbing the last section of Shap Bank, and on his return found the mail-bags missing. But Kilmington, who was travelling on his train, had found the Guard's van locked at this point, and now (evidence of Mrs Grant: Clue Number Four) declared his intention of reporting the Guard. The latter knew that Kilmington's report would contradict his own evidence and thus convict him of complicity in the crime, since he had locked the van for a few minutes to throw out the mail-bags himself, and pretended to Kilmington that he had been asleep (evidence of Kilmington himself) when the latter knocked at the door. So Kilmington had to be silenced.

Stansfield already had Percy Dukes under suspicion as the organiser of the robbery. During the journey Dukes gave himself away three times. First, although it had not been mentioned in the papers, he betrayed knowledge of the point on the line where the bags had been thrown out. Second, though the loss of the emeralds had been also kept out of the Press, Dukes knew it was an emerald necklace which had been stolen: Stansfield had laid a trap for him by calling it a bracelet, but later in conversation Dukes referred to the 'necklace'. Third, his great discomposure at the (false) statement by Stansfield that the emeralds were worth £25,000 was the reaction of a criminal who believes he has been badly gypped by the fence to whom he has sold them. Dukes was now planning a second train robbery, and meant to compel the Guard to act as accomplice again. Inez Blake's evidence (Clue Number Five) of hearing him say, 'You're going to help us again, chum,' etc., clearly pointed to the Guard's complicity in the previous robbery: it was almost certainly the Guard to whom she had heard Dukes say this, for only a railway servant would have known about the existence of a platelayers' hut up the line, and made an appointment to meet Dukes there; moreover, if Dukes had talked about his plans for the next robbery, on the train itself, to anyone but a railway servant, suspicion would have been incurred should they have been seen talking together.

Method: At 8.27 Kilmington goes into the Guard's van. He threatens to report the Guard, though he is quite unaware of the dire consequences this would entail for the latter. The Guard, probably on the pretext of showing him the route to the village, gets Kilmington out of the train, walks him away from the lighted area, stuns him (the bruise was a light one and did not reveal itself in Stansfield's brief examination of the body), carries him to the spot where Stansfield found the body, packs mouth and nostrils tight with snow. Then, instead of leaving well alone, the Guard decides to create an alibi for himself. He takes his victim's hat, returns to the train, puts on his own dark, off-duty overcoat, finds a solitary passenger asleep, masquerades as Kilmington enquiring the time, and strengthens the impression by saying he'd walk to the village if the relief engine did not turn up in five minutes, then returns to the body and throws down the hat beside it (Stansfield found the hat only lightly covered with snow, as compared with the body: Clue Number Six). Moreover, the passenger noticed that the enquirer was wearing blue trousers (Clue Number Seven). The Guard's regulation suit was blue; but Dukes' suit was grey, and Macdonald's a loud check—therefore, the masquerader could not have been either of them.

The time is now 8.55. The Guard decides to reinforce his alibi by going to intercept the returning fireman. He takes a short cut from the body to the platelayers' hut. The track he now makes, compared with the beaten trail towards the village, is much more lightly filled in with snow when Stansfield finds it (Clue Number Eight): therefore, it must have been made some time after the murder, and could not incriminate Percy Dukes. *The Guard meets the fireman just at 8.55.* They walk back to the train. The Guard is taken aside by Dukes, who has gone out for his 'airing', and the conversation overheard by Inez Blake takes place. *The Guard tells Dukes he will meet him presently in the platelayers' hut:* this is aimed to incriminate Dukes, should the murder by any chance be discovered, for Dukes would find it difficult to explain why he should have sat alone in a cold hut for half an hour just around the time when Kilmington was presumably murdered only one hundred and fifty yards away. *The Guard now goes along to the engine and stays there chatting with the crew for some forty minutes.* His alibi is thus established for the period from 8.55 to 9.40 P.M. His plan might well have succeeded, but for three unlucky factors he could not possibly have taken into account— Stansfield's presence on the train, the blizzard stopping soon after 9 P.M., and the theft of Arthur J. Kilmington's watch.

Blood Is Thicker

ANN C. FALLON

Other James Fleming Mysteries: *Where Death Lies,
Dead Ends, Potter's Field,* and *Hour of Our Death*

Chapter One

Mr. Sweeney rubbed the large red knuckles of one hand with the reddened fingers of his other and then held both hands near the steaming electric kettle. The back room of the little shop was cold and dark in the gray Irish dawn.

"Tea, Brendan?"

"Right, Da!" his son called from the front of the shop.

Mr. Sweeney opened the box of Lyons Green Label and shook a palmful of the loose tea leaves into the warmed pot. While the tea sat stewing, he took down a naggin of whiskey from the shelf with the stores of paraffin and poured a capful into his own mug. He filled both mugs and brought them out to the shop.

"Papers late today?" asked his son, who took a split second to look up from the counter where he was sorting the mass of post. Letters and packets and parcels were piled high on either side of him. He carefully held each piece up to his good eye and then placed it in the appropriate pile.

"Sean will be here any moment now," he said to his father as he took his mug of tea and stirred it vigorously. A splash fell on one of the parcels and the ink began to spread.

"Damn!"

Brendan dreaded Tuesdays. Tuesday was Old Age Pension Day in Kilmartin, County Wexford, and the safe was bulging with cash. Brendan, who, with his father, ran the local shop, also ran the small branch post office, which was housed in the front corner. So on Tuesdays not only did he have to sort the mail before Sean arrived on his bicycle to deliver the first round, he also had to pay out the pensions and stamp the pension books and chat ceaselessly to a day-long stream of retired locals. Tuesday was always a day of irritation made more burdensome by his fears of the post office being robbed by IRA terrorists.

"Why are those bloomin' papers late today?" grumbled his father as he peered around the posters that hung faded in the small dusty window. He looked at his pocket watch and then at the clock on the wall.

"The five-thirty is twenty minutes late, and it's not even raining," mumbled Mr. Sweeney into his mug. He stamped his feet to get the circulation going. Suddenly, headlights swept through the shop, announcing the arrival at last of the bus from Dublin. It drew up at the bus stop in front of the shop, and the conductor tossed the roped bundles of papers onto the rough pavement. With a tip of his cap he withdrew and the bus rumbled off.

"Bloody bus company. Hah! Nothing changes."

Brendan smiled. He'd heard his father say the same thing every morning for virtually the last twenty-five years, since he was a small boy. It was true. Nothing changes.

The small old man looked like a sprite in the early morning light, hopping out the door to carry in the load of newspapers. For a man of seventy years, he was remarkably strong. He cut the strings with his kitchen knife and worked at top speed to sort the newspapers into piles, setting the bulk aside for sale to the passing trade, but more important, marking the name of the relevant subscriber at the top of each in the remaining pile. He watched the clock, he watched the window, he watched for the brightening light. At six A.M. by his clock he unlatched the front door and the shop was officially open to the public. As he turned he heard the knob rattle. But he didn't acknowledge it. He beetled around the far side of the counter, smiling to himself as he lifted the flap of wood, lowered it, and then stood at the ready.

"Mr. Sweeney!" said a reedy voice.

"Mr. Sinclair," replied Mr. Sweeney, looking up in mock astonishment at the tall, angular figure that peered down at him like a heron.

"Papers late today, Mr. Sweeney?"

"Indeed they were, Mr. Sinclair."

"I don't suppose ..." said Mr. Sinclair, thinking that he had caught Mr. Sweeney out at last.

"But of course, your papers are ready ..." Mr. Sweeney handed Sinclair his four papers. Three English and one Irish, the latter a token gesture to the country his parents had adopted.

"I see ... well, I thank you. And now if you just let me have a tin of Three Nuns. Ran out, exceedingly tiresome. Must have a morning pipe, you know. Gets the blood running ..." He turned at the sound of a car outside. "I say, would you credit that?"

Brendan and Mr. Sweeney looked up from their tasks and followed the direction of Mr. Sinclair's beaky gaze out the window.

"A hearse, is it?" Mr. Sweeney moved quickly to the door. Brendan, with his appalling sight, saw nothing but a blur beyond the dusty windows. "What's the alarm?" he asked, surprised at the reaction of his father.

"It turned, Brendan, it turned into the lane!"

Sinclair and then Mr. Sweeney hurried outside and watched the hearse as it carefully made its way up the narrow stony lane. Sean the post-man was pedaling furiously up the road. Where the lane met the road, he crossed over to the shop. His pink eyes in his broad white face were popping.

"It overtook me just off the main Dublin road, but I followed it," he told them breathlessly. He was a plump man to undertake such a strenuous pursuit. "... I never imagined it would be turning into Moore's!" The three men stood in silence. Sean produced a question-able handkerchief and dabbed his sweating face, Sinclair filled his pipe automatically, and Sweeney once more rubbed his stiffening hands. They lost sight of the hearse where the lane curved and was shrouded by hedging, but they still stood, waiting.

The black hearse was very new. It was still colored the traditional black, with silver-trim filigree on the roof, but it had opaque windows at the sides and rear. The hearse slowed on the gravel of the circular drive in front of the large granite-fronted manor house that was known as Moore's. With a whirr the rear door opened automatically, and with a louder whirr a flat panel slid out. Two young men jumped from the front of the car and lowered the plain wooden coffin onto the gravel. Seconds later the hearse drove off, even as the panel whirred back and the door clicked shut. The car accelerated, the noise of its tires now rumbling across the quiet fields on either side of the lane. Without stopping, it swerved out of the lane and onto the road.

"Harvey's–of Dublin."

"Not a'tall! Smith's–out of Wexford."

"Neither. They were local. Fred told me only the other night at the Drooping Well that his brother-in-law had just bought in a new car for the company." The other two men looked skeptically at the third.

"Pity Brendan couldn't see it, he might have known," mumbled Mr. Sweeney as he turned into the shop.

"Da?"

"Most strange, Brendan. A hearse it was, seemed to go up to the farm and then came back. Probably made a mistake in the address."

"A pretty alarming mistake," said Sinclair.

"Well, glory be to God, we're standin' here," said Sean excitedly, "and someone could be dead up at Moore's."

But they continued to stand, ruminating like the cows in the fields around them.

Violet Moore strode down the center aisle of the cowshed, her boots splashing in the streaming waters. She pulled her anorak tight around her neck, sheltering against the steam rising from the backs of her beautiful beasts. Brushing aside wisps of steel-gray hair, she watched the young man bent to his work. Queen Maeve swished her tail.

"Liam," Violet said sharply.

"Miss Moore," returned a voice.

"How is Maeve milking now?"

"Much improved, Miss Moore, much improved," the voice drawled.

"Deirdre has mastitis. I want no more of it."

"It happens, it does that," the young man replied diffidently.

"It doesn't happen at Moore's, I tell you."

Liam stood. Despite the cold of the dawning day, he was stripped to the waist, sweat and condensing steam rolling off his body. He detached the milking unit from the teats and moved slowly around the cow and on to the next. His slow, rhythmic movements maddened Violet, and she fleetingly regretted hiring him. But he was good, very good, with her cattle. It was his wry smile that was not so good. She started to speak again but refrained. She recognized a free spirit and knew if she pushed too hard, Liam would drift off into the light of day, as he had drifted in from the port of Wexford one late summer afternoon.

"Today's yield will be up, by the looks of it," Liam commented matter-of-factly. He thumped the switch on the wall and Deirdre's udder wobbled from side to side as the milk was squeezed alternately from each teat.

"I'm glad to hear it," said Violet as she walked on down the shed, patting a beast here and rubbing another's underbelly there. Yes, she loved her beasts.

She crossed the cobbled yard to the dairy barn. Both pasteurizing units were in operation, and the black tubes throbbed with a life of their own. Milk flowed into the large stainless-steel tanks, where it was heated to 161 degrees, then passed through the coolers and on to the clattering packing machine, to be fed into hundreds of cartons. Delicious, cool, pasteurized nonhomogenized milk. She smiled. Kevin, the farm manager, was tearing open a brown box packed with flattened triangular cartons. Randomly he took out a fistful, flicking through them with his thumb.

"These bloody things are still sticking together. Banjaxes the machine. I'll have to phone ... Morning, Violet," he called over his shoulder.

"Good morning, Kevin," she replied.

Two scrawny boys, their school day still ahead of them, packed the milk crates furiously, filling them and stacking them near the door of the modern barn. Violet's pride and joy, the new barn stood in stark contrast to the surrounding house and outbuildings, which looked in the half-light as though they had grown from the rock of the ground—mottled gray and brown, covered with moss, ivy, and lichen—and a fine mist now moving in from the surrounding fields.

"Kevin, tell Liam to put the cattle out to grass in the lower field, but only until noon. I don't want them to get too giddy. It's early days yet, despite the growth."

"Right you are," replied Kevin, smiling at the tenderness in her voice as she spoke of her cattle. She knew how they would lift their heads on this their first spring morning out to pasture. How they would sniff the air and move warily at first, stiff and strange after their winter of confinement in the cowsheds. For nearly three months, they had been housed.

"Moira is about to drop. I've got the calving stall ready. Shall I call you?"

"Call me." Violet looked up as she saw Paddy, her milk deliveryman, hovering inside the door of the dairy. The scrawny boys scrambled to drag the milk crates outside.

Paddy stood aside and then came toward her reluctantly. She liked his subservience. And then again, she didn't. So obsequious, she thought.

"Yes." She spoke sharply, angry even before she heard his request.

"Miss Moore, I think you'd better come 'round the front."

"The front? Is it the truck?" she asked in alarm, visions of undelivered milk flashing before her.

"It's not the truck, but there's something you should take a look at ..."

"Where's Lily then ... or even Rose?"

"Ah, now you won't be wanting to alarm Rose ..."

Violet glared at the man.

"Lily!" She raised her voice, trying to locate her sister amongst the numerous outbuildings.

There was no answering voice. "Probably with the hens—if she's out of bed at all!"

"I think it would be best if it was yourself, Miss Violet."

Violet Moore marched out of the barn and across the second yard, then cut around the rear of the house. She wrenched open the wooden door built in an archway in the wall that surrounded and protected the main house and farm buildings. Her three dogs came yelping at her heels, eager for their morning run. She passed down the side of the house and rounded the corner, Paddy hurrying behind.

At first she didn't see the simple pale wooden box. It seemed to blend in with the gray and tawny gravel. It was some sort of crate, but as she moved closer she slowed and then paused.

The dogs raced up behind and then went forward to sniff at it.

"Sit!"

Lily came up beside her, and then Rose, who gripped her arm.

"Violet ... what does it mean?"

At first Violet didn't answer, the four of them stood, a silent group surrounding the simple coffin. Then, at last, she spoke. "Fetch Kevin," she said to Paddy, "and have him bring a claw hammer and the tire lever."

Kevin worked quickly, hands trembling, his heart thudding in his chest. He wasn't quite sure if he should even be doing this, but then, perhaps it was a bad joke. There was no need for the police to witness a joke in such bad taste. No, a joke it was, and they'd keep it quiet, just amongst themselves. He pried up the nails on one side and then, drawing breath, forced the lid back and quickly turned his head.

"Jesus, Mary, and Joseph!" gasped Paddy. Kevin crossed himself and stared hard at the clouds scudding above them. Lily turned away as Violet moved forward slowly, Rose sheltering behind her. For an instant Violet hesitated, and then bending down, she peered at the composed gray face of the man in the coffin.

"Oh, God," she whispered hoarsely, "Jack."

"No, it cannot be," cried Rose. "Not Jack. Not my Jack."

Lily came to put her long thin arms around Rose and pulled her away. The three sisters stood silently in the rain, now pouring down.

Violet stepped back from the coffin and turned to Kevin.

"Don't let the cattle into the fields today ... And Kevin, get this box into the barn."

Chapter Two

As the burgundy Citroen CX sailed along at cruising speed, James Fleming leaned back and smiled. This was a promising start to the week.

Dun Laoghaire. Bray. Wicklow. Arklow. Gorey. The small towns of southeast Ireland flashed past to his right as his attention was caught on the left by breathtaking views of the coastal waters sparkling in the early morning light. Smugly, he sped for a stretch alongside the Wexford train. He recognized it easily as a GM 141 class, the older type of locomotive. Yes, thought James, it was good to get out of the city. He had been working at Fitzgerald's, the Dublin law office, for quite a while without a break, and he knew he was starting to get the wanderlust again.

James smiled to himself. He would never have credited Gerald Fitzgerald—the senior partner, and a difficult man at the best of times—as being sensitive to the needs of his staff. Perhaps Gerald, who had been the Moores' family solicitor since St. Patrick was in knee breeches, had indeed perceived his restlessness. Obliged to go to London, it was James he had chosen to travel down to Wexford to attend to the Moores.

Well, it would be routine enough, thought James. A dead brother, three spinster sisters on a country estate. An old Protestant family. It would be a simple matter to handle the funeral arrangements for them, muddled and unworldly as they probably were.

The Wexford countryside was looking its best. Fertile fields unrolled on either side of the road, shimmering a soft green gouache—early growth which in summer would feed the county's renowned dairy herds.

The Moores owned a dairy farm, James recalled from the file, but he was not familiar with their village of Kilmartin. Gerald was from the same place. James vaguely remembered him talking about Kilmartin over dinner the night he had been made a partner in Gerald's small Dublin law firm. The Fitzgeralds came from strong Protestant farmer stock. Gerald probably went to dances and church fetes with the Moore sisters, thought James. His portly build, encased in a three-piece suit and bursting his waistcoat at the seams, made picturing him as a raw, bespectacled youth a little difficult.

That dinner at the Gray Door had been splendid. The cold borscht to start, and the tender baby ribs, which melted in his mouth. He recalled asking the Russian chef for the recipe for the marinade. And the man had given it to him too. But the third bottle of Bordeaux had erased it from memory.

James sighed. His breakfast of sausages, eggs, two rashers, and a slice of black pudding at Bewleys seemed a long time ago. Black pudding—an interesting euphemism for coagulated pigs' blood, he thought. He glanced around him, trying to orient himself. A road sign indicated a small village ahead, and he accelerated. And then he slowed. The village consisted of a crossroads with two pubs and a shop.

James parked the Citroen at an angle to the curb, got out, and stretched his long, lean body. He ran his hand through his thick, light brown hair and rubbed his face and neck. He shook one leg and then the other, shaking the creases out of his expensive and well-cut chalk-stripe suit. Dismissing the two plastic-looking pubs at a glance, he entered the shop and purchased a couple of bread rolls, a quarter pound of Irish cheddar, and two slices of Limerick ham with a lovely trimming of pure white fat. The sullen girl who served him placed them in a bag without a word.

He drove on, seeking a more attractive pub, and covered the next twenty miles well over the speed limit. Yet he was still overtaken, the second time by a farmer with a bale of hay in his trunk. The one characteristic that the Irish farmer shared with his counterparts on the continent was the incredible speed at which he drove on the narrowest of roads.

James was surprised when he came quite suddenly upon the village of Kilmartin. After one long S bend in a particularly lush area, the road straightened to reveal a pretty little village clustered around a crossroads. James quickly noted with approval the charming architecture of the little Anglican church. It stood on a small rise, with its churchyard laid in front like a somber apron. He slowed as he passed a row of houses sitting cozily shoulder to shoulder on the broad pavement. The spire of the Catholic church rose up at the far end of the village, but before he reached this landmark, he spotted the local pub with the intriguing name of the Drooping Well.

The bar was cool and dark, with red Formica tables and aluminum-legged stools that scraped and racketed on the Spanish flagging. Cheery wrought-iron lamps dotted the walls and swung over the long bar. James was amused at the pub's striking resemblance to the myriad little bars that dotted the Mediterranean island of Ibiza. Someone here has been on a few sun holidays, he thought wryly.

"When you're ready," James called. In answer he heard movement from behind a striped curtain at the end of the bar. And then silence. James seated himself on a bar stool and stared at himself in the mirror. At last a big, gruff man came out to him.

"A pint of Guinness."

The man took a pint glass and pulled the spigot.

"I haven't had any lunch, but if you could let me have a knife and a plate ..." There was no reaction from the barman, but James knew country bartenders well enough to wait. However, after five minutes he began to wonder if the man had heard him.

The pint stood on the drip tray as its head settled. James debated with himself. If he asked again, he ran the risk of offending the man. If he didn't and the man hadn't heard him, he would be left pulling the bread apart and eating out of the bag. Or worse, being glared at by the man himself. James rattled his bag gently and was just about to open it when the barman reappeared with a fresh trout, cooked to perfection and garnished with a sprig of fresh parsley.

"Caught it this mornin'," he said succinctly, and added, "you won't get the likes of that in Dublin."

James glimpsed the man's own kitchen behind the curtain and his lunch on the table. Silently, the man finished pulling the pint, laid it reverently on the bar, and returned to his meal.

James enjoyed the fish and a second pint while he casually studied the bar's patrons. The young man in the corner, with the bottle-thick glasses, amused him, speaking earnestly to his very upper-crust companion. James wondered idly if Jack Moore, now deceased, had frequented this companionable little pub. Refreshed, James returned to his car and drove slowly until he spotted the lane that should lead to Moore's farm. He pulled the car onto the right shoulder and stopped.

It was a lifelong habit, one that bespoke James's orderly, observant nature. He held his map against the wheel, but really was noting the small shop cum post office, the green mailbox to its right, the bus stops on either side of the road. He watched as the bread van unloaded its delivery of sliced pans and turnovers. He saw the turf, machine-cut and stacked at the door of the garage that adjoined the ancient shop. He saw movement in the window of the shop, and in his mirror observed two or three women stepping from their front doors, not acknowledging each other, intent on sweeping the steps or studying the flowers in the small front gardens that ran the length of the row of houses.

Typical, thought James. Country people were notoriously nosy. Even a strange car stopping briefly could draw their attention. But then, his burgundy Citroen CX even drew attention in Dublin. He folded his map with elaborate movements, put the car in gear, and turned up the lane to Moore's.

"Miss Violet Moore? I am James Fleming, Gerald Fitzgerald asked me to come down to help ..."

Violet Moore opened the door wider and stepped back as James entered the flagstone entrance hall.

"Mr. Fleming." Violet extended her hand, and James was surprised at the strength of her grasp.

As they walked toward the drawing room, James offered his condolences.

"Yes, yes," answered Violet abruptly, "now if you'll please excuse me, I want to see to some things in the kitchen."

James stood with his back to the fireplace and rocked on his heels as the fierce heat toasted his legs. He took a few seconds to revise his expectations. Violet Moore was no simple country spinster, but a woman who impressed with both her physical and personal strength. The large drawing room betrayed these characteristics. Here was no shawl-covered piano with framed photographs of distant cousins and long-dead relations, no flowery curtains and chintz-covered chairs. There were, as he noted, one or two good paintings from members of the Royal Irish Academy hanging on the hessian-covered walls. There was a tasteful three-piece suite of Scandinavian design which toned beautifully with the heavy woven toast-colored fabric that dressed the windows. A nineteenth-century rolltop desk stood in the corner, covered with neat stacks of business correspondence. A bowl of hyacinths sat in early bloom on the low coffee table. No, this was not what James had expected. And now his curiosity was aroused.

He took the heavy silver tray from Violet's hands as she reentered the drawing room. The aroma of fresh coffee filled the large, bright room. Violet poured in silence, asking only if he would take a drop of whiskey in his coffee. She fetched the bottle from the well-stocked sideboard.

Everything to hand, thought James, signs of an orderly, an active life. He waited for Violet to speak. When she did not, he began to ask a few leading questions.

"I understand that Mr. Fitzgerald has been your family solicitor for many years," he said encouragingly.

"Quite."

"I know from him that he was most regretful that he could not come down himself. He had an extremely pressing situation to deal with in London, a situation which he assured me that only he could attend to ..."

"Yes, he mentioned some such issue on the telephone."

"Well, Miss Moore, I will do my best to stand in for him ..."

"I'm sure you'll do as well as another," Violet replied, and refilled their cups.

James paused for a moment, musing. He seemed to be pulling teeth here. He was beginning to sound to himself like a barrister grilling a witness.

For the second time he wondered at her delay in getting to the point. Thinking he might have underestimated her grief and ability to cope, he took the initiative.

He placed his coffee cup down with a gesture of finality. "Miss Moore ... I think Gerald told me that your brother died here at the house. If you'll permit me, I'll begin now to make the necessary arrangements. I took the liberty of locating a few undertakers in the telephone book. Perhaps, if you'll tell me whether you have a preference, I'll make a few calls?"

Violet seemed to hesitate.

"I take it that a doctor has been called ... or perhaps was with him when he ... when he passed away." James realized suddenly that he didn't even know the cause of the man's death, and he paused.

Violet Moore sighed and then abruptly stood up.

"I think that—"

She was interrupted by voices from the doorway.

"Vi? What does he say? Oh, oh dear, oh dear ..." Rose rushed into the room, breathless and plump, her wispy, faded hair askew, her small hands twitching the gray and pink cardigan around her little body. James smiled. She was at that moment more like the White Rabbit than any pantomime figure. He waited to see if she'd pull a watch from her gaping pockets.

"Rose!" Lily's firm but kindly voice followed Rose from the hall. Her tall, thin frame wavered in the doorway and then she came forward, bringing a sense of calm to the group. She was followed in by a young man.

"Mr. Fleming," Violet Moore said, "my sisters, Rose and Lily. Oh, and this is Kevin Manning, my farm manager."

Kevin nodded, smiling broadly, relief in his eyes. Oh, thought James, this man seems awfully glad to see me.

"Well, what does he say?" demanded Rose again, petulantly. "Is it all over with? Can it be done?"

"Rose," whispered Lily, "I really doubt it can be done that way."

"But it must, it must. And in our own plot—"

"No!" said Violet, almost shouting. "Certainly not in our own plot! I forbid it."

Rose started to cry into a crumpled tissue. Kevin stood looking awkwardly out the window. He turned, caught James's eye, and raised his eyebrows significantly.

"Vi ..." Lily spoke in her modulated voice. "Time is passing. It's been hours now ..."

"Of course it's been hours ... we had to wait for Mr. Fleming." She glared at James, seemingly blaming him for the long drive down from Dublin.

"Well," said James cheerfully, "I am here now. If someone would—"

"Of course. I was just about to bring you, Mr. Fleming, when my sisters interrupted. If you'll come this way."

They made an awkward parade as they fell into a loose line behind Violet. She strode ahead, leading the way through small interconnecting halls, through the vast farmhouse kitchen to the cold room, then out the back door. They quickly crossed the courtyard between the house and the barn, dodging wild, bright raindrops which were falling from a blue sky. "March weather!" grumbled James half to himself. The whole journey was accomplished in an uncomfortable silence. As they approached the barn, James's thoughts became wilder, but nothing had prepared him for what he saw as his eyes adjusted to the dim interior.

The plain wooden coffin was laid out in the open space in the center of the barn, supported by bales of hay at the head and foot.

"Lay a jug of whiskey at my head and feet ..." The words of the old Irish waking song flung themselves into his thoughts. He shook his head.

Rose had started to cry again.

"Miss Moore?" James directed his look at Violet, but she remained silent. He wanted some answers now.

"Mr. Fleming, at dawn this morning I was summoned to the front of my house by my deliveryman, Paddy. When I came around to the front from the barn, I saw this coffin lying on the gravel near the doorstep. Kevin opened it. After my sisters and I ascertained that it contained the dead body of my brother, I had the box brought in here. I rang Fitzgerald, as you know, and told him that my brother had died." She stopped, apparently having said all she had to say.

The silence was heavy, but the air was sweet with the smell of the hay, the smell of a summer long since past. "And throw the chaff into the fire ..." James whispered. He glanced at the faces of the people standing with him, all heads bent as if in silent prayer, all but Violet's.

"Well, Miss Moore, I must admit this is not what I was expecting."

"I assure you, Mr. Fleming, neither was I."

"You must help me here," said James more firmly. "I need some more information before I act."

Silence.

"Did you phone the police?"

"I did not."

"When did you last see him? Alive."

"I couldn't say. At least twenty-five years ago."

"Twenty-five years ago?" echoed James.

"Twenty-seven," interrupted Rose. "Twenty-seven years!"

Again there was silence.

"You are certain it is your brother?" James asked.

"At first I was not." Violet glared at Rose as her sobs grew louder. "But on a closer look, I knew it was he."

"He did not live in the vicinity then, I take it?"

Violet shook her head but failed to elaborate. James wondered why the others did not speak. He looked appealingly at Lily, but she glanced quickly away. Rose, head bowed, was sobbing into a handkerchief.

"And you were certain at that time he was dead?" he asked.

"Yes, quite dead. There was no mistaking the look of death on his face."

James was finding this more and more curious, but the presence of the dead body spurred him into action. The body had been here since dawn, it had been lying in the barn for almost eight hours now. Alone. That struck him forcibly. No one with the body. The body itself banished to the barn with the feed, sweet as it was, for the cattle. Ah, there was no tender parting and farewell here.

"Because of the circumstances, I think that I should look at the deceased now." He didn't ask permission. There seemed no reverence here. But he was mistaken. Both Lily and Rose fell back, and Kevin sighed such a sigh as to be heard. But he came forward and, together with James, lifted the lid and stood it upright against a bale of hay.

"Oh, Jack, oh my darlin' Jackeen." Real sorrow filled Rose's voice as she moved forward to stroke the dead man's face and smooth the lapels of his overcoat.

James considered the corpse before him. The gray, thin face was cold and dead, composed in death, a handsome face, that of a man around fifty. The knot in his tie sat well in the white linen collar. The overcoat was of rich Donegal tweed, the hair groomed, the skin smooth.

He whispered a short prayer and then wondered at the death of this prosperous man, at the manner of his coming to this house, at the manner of his coming to his death.

His somber thoughts were pierced by a shriek from Rose as she suddenly moved back from the body.

"There's blood! Blood!" she cried before she collapsed.

When James returned to the drawing room, the three sisters and Kevin were all standing ashen-faced, tumblers of brandy in hand. They seemed to be huddling near the fire for warmth, although James found the room stuffy now.

"From what I could see, there is a wound in Mr. Moore's chest," he said. "There was a great deal of ... blood. The overcoat was not ... bloodied, and seemingly concealed the wound and the bloodstains on the shirt and suit from our view. If Rose ..." He hesitated, looking at her. "If Rose hadn't ... Well, we will deal with what has to be done."

"Which is what?" snapped Violet.

"Which is, we wait for the police," answered James, looking sharply at her.

"You had no right—"

"I had the responsibility, Miss Moore. Your brother is dead. Every aspect of this situation is—to say the least—unusual, if not bizarre. Of course the police have to be informed. As an officer of the court, and," he added more kindly, "as your solicitor per diem, I have to handle this situation accordingly."

"Mr. Fleming," Rose spoke for the first time directly to him. "Do you think, do you think ... oh, it's too terrible to contemplate ..."

"What Rose needs to know, and so do I," said Lily softly, "is this: do you think that Jack might still have been alive this morning when Vi ... when we found him out front? Do you think if we had helped him then, he...?" Lily shuddered.

"As you helped him twenty-seven years ago," hissed Rose to Violet. James saw Violet lift her hand to silence Rose.

"That he might still be alive?" finished James. "I don't know, Miss Moore," he said gently to Lily. "Let us hope not, for his sake."

"For all our sakes," said Kevin.

"The police no doubt will bring the examiner with them," explained James. "It is, as you can see, not merely a question of a death certificate. I admit at first I thought that once a doctor ascertained the cause of death and signed the certificate, we could have gone ahead with the funeral arrangements, but ... well, now I'm afraid there will be questions, and you must be prepared for a delay."

"And scandal," said Violet bitterly, "the scandal." She stood apart from the others, glaring first at them and then at James. "My purpose in calling you was to avoid just such scandal. If Fitzgerald had come himself ..." She nearly spat the words at James.

"I assure you, Miss Moore, once Gerald or any solicitor had noticed the blood, there would be no other course. If it hadn't been Rose and myself, the doctor would have called the police."

"What need did he have for a doctor? We could have buried him in the fields."

"That's enough, Violet!" said Lily.

They all fell silent again. The sound of tires on the gravel only increased the tension in the room.

As James went toward the door to admit the police, he addressed them all. "I advise you to describe simply and accurately what happened today. This situation is very serious. Your brother was murdered. For his sake and yours, this matter must be cleared up."

James stood in the driveway surveying the rolling fields and breathing in deeply the cool air of the waning day. The setting sun lent a piquancy to the scene, a melancholy. The air was still, a few birds calling sleepily to their new mates as darkness fell. After the surprising and terrible events of the day, James welcomed the hush.

He walked down the drive, aimlessly kicking stones out of his path. He had been favorably impressed by the local police. They had been efficient as they silently went about their tasks. The medical examiner had arrived in his own car and checked the body over superficially. He had said that it seemed death was caused by the wound in the chest. A grizzled, cross old man, he had not been more forthcoming. And not in the least consoling. Still, he couldn't be expected to say more until the postmortem was completed. The body was removed by Feeney's Undertakers to Wexford General Hospital. James took his small notebook from his inside jacket pocket and consulted it. He wanted to check that he had made careful note of all the details. He sighed. He was genuinely too tired to return to Dublin. He was even too tired to drive the five miles to the nearest country hotel. He had decided to take advantage of Lily Moore's suggestion that he stay the night.

James opened the gate in toward the field and then latched it behind him. It was pleasant to walk in the quiet fields. The grass was short and the heavy evening dew barely wet his shoes.

He sighed again. He would have to ring Gerald in the morning. He hadn't wanted to bother the old man at the end of what was probably a long, strenuous day in London. What did Gerald make of Violet Moore? he wondered.

Violet. Lily. Rose. James thought of those parents long dead who had named those three baby girls after flowers, no doubt wishing for them each a life of beauty, of grace, of love. No doubt wishing for them one day families of their own, little baby flowers of their own. James mused. Maybe he would have had baby girls or baby boys of his own by now, if things had worked out with Teresa. He smiled at the sentimental picture he had created of himself and Teresa with a babe in arms. A girl. It would have been a girl. He saw the evening star and made a wish on it, as he always did—when he chanced to see it.

He hopped the dry stone wall that divided the field from the road, and continued wandering along the lane, heading toward the main road. Violet. No, she was no shrinking, hidden little thing. Instead—more like the words her name resembled—violent, violate. Such strength, such anger. So very much the head of all she surveyed, her sisters included. Did that include the brother too? He had hoped for more information when the police had questioned the sisters. He recalled their answers.

When their brother Jack had left home some twenty-five odd years ago, he had gone to England. He had corresponded with the sisters from London, and when he moved on to America, they virtually lost touch with him. It was an old story. Were the parents dead then? James was more curious than the police for all the small details. Why had the young man left Kilmartin? Safe to assume there were no prospects on the farm. Or perhaps he had aspirations? He had struck James as looking like a businessman, smooth-skinned and rich. Perhaps he had left Ireland to seek his fortune, first in London and then in Boston. Like the hundreds of thousands of Irish before him.

And then—nothing. No word, for months. Perhaps the odd card, and then silence. They didn't even know if he had married or if there were other family members somewhere, worried and frantic ... Violet didn't seem interested, but Rose did, and Lily too. Rose had clearly missed him the most. She had spoken affectionately of Jack as she remembered him, a young boy close to her own age. She had praised his skills around the farm, his way with the animals, and would not be silenced by Violet when she talked of his love of the land.

Lily had little to add. She had, however, been able to produce a Christmas card sent nearly ten years after he'd left home. She had even saved the envelope, which was postmarked Boston. The police would start there, of course, as well as the Irish ports and airports.

Nothing had been found on the body that would identify the man. No papers of any kind, and no money. Their first thought was robbery, and the absence of the usual things a man carries in his pockets lent weight to that idea. But if robbery had been the motive for the murder, then why did the murderer choose this bizarre method of getting rid of the body? James's mind reeled with questions and he felt the need to unwind. Suddenly he found himself back at the Drooping Well, where he had eaten lunch all those long hours ago, when he had breezed in so confidently from Dublin.

He chose to sit this time in the lounge, in a corner. He knew that he would be quickly identified as the Moores' solicitor from Dublin, and he didn't want to engage in any close questioning by the locals.

James could see the bar from the lounge. It was filled to capacity with a talkative crowd, thick blue smoke encircling the heads of people as they drank their pints. He spotted his trout-cooking barman from lunchtime, ordered a whiskey, and settled back, allowing the fatigue to flow out of his body. He thought again of the call he would have to make to Gerald, and could hear the old man firing questions at him. One of the major characteristics of all lawyers, that. Curiosity masked as professional concern. James smiled. He suffered the same malady.

He loved his job. And he loved the life it had brought him, full of incident, rich in detail. He thought of those early years when he was clerking in Fitzgerald's. He had looked forward to the day when he held power in his own hands. He had moved up to title transfers and searches. In a way, he had loved that. He enjoyed the central idea of property, of ownership, of tracking title deeds and, in the course of that, unearthing so many wonderful, intricate stories. Property was a passionate concern of the people. He had quickly come to realize the enormous truth behind the old truism: Irish people loved the land, their property, in a mystical way. Through conveyancing he had moved on to wills and estates. And now he was in his element. True, much of it could be routine. Quite ordinary people sensibly making their wills and disposing the bits and pieces of their lives amongst their families. But the gems, fewer in number perhaps, made up for the routine nature of his work.

It was the large estates, the family disputes. It was the disposal of property out of the family. It was the dredging up of all the details, of finding long-lost relations who were named beneficiaries in some old bachelor's will. These were the human mysteries that intrigued James. The intricacies and entanglements and priorities of peoples' lives, which were revealed in the making of the wills and in their execution.

And then when he had had his fill, James was in a position to arrange his schedule and take off for three or four weeks at a time. If he hadn't been able to do that, he could never have indulged his passion for train travel. Yes, this was to be the year of Peru. In fact he had forgotten about the shots, and realized he had better see to that soon. And a visa. Peru had no embassy in Ireland. He would have to apply to their consulate in London for that. This was a trip that Teresa would have objected to strongly. No sense of adventure, that was her problem. Another girl would have jumped at the chance.

He ordered his final whiskey. It wouldn't do to return to the house too late. He had become cognizant of the early hours kept by the household, dictated by the needs of the cows and the milking schedule.

He walked back briskly, relaxed and ready for the day ahead. Lily had waited up for him. He was later than he realized.

"Not to worry, Mr. Fleming. I have difficulty getting to sleep, and I don't rise as early as my sisters. I do very little of the manual work on the farm." She briefly touched her chest, as if indicating a weak heart. "No, my part in this business is the paperwork, the accounts and so on." She sighed gently; a disappointed sigh, thought James. "And the hens, of course!" she added, smiling.

She led James into the big kitchen, her gentle voice pointing out the old range-style cooker, the hooks in the ceiling where fresh-killed game used to be hung, the mechanical bellows in the now defunct fireplace, and the warming oven in the wall which they still used to let their yeast bread rise. She wasn't merely polite. Her conversation flowed easily, her ideas interesting and her voice murmuring mellifluously. It was one of the most soothing, well-modulated voices James had had the fortune to hear, and he encouraged her to talk. She made coffee on milk, and the sweet taste brought back strong memories of his college days when he indulged himself similarly after an evening of study. As Lily's voice flowed on like a low sonata playing background to his thoughts, he wondered what in this whole situation had triggered off so many disparate thoughts and memories. Fatigue, he decided, unconvinced. And although Lily seemed inclined to talk, he drew himself gently away.

His room upstairs and down the end of a long, narrow corridor was quite spartan. But it was the size of the room itself that dwarfed what would have been adequate furnishings in a more modern house. There was a single bed with a cozy, old comforter in red and brown stripes, a bedside table, two fireside chairs at the small fireplace, a towel stand, and a marble-topped washstand, of the type now seen only in good antique stores and upscale country inns.

He switched off the bedside lamp and undressed by the light of the small fire that glowed in the grate. Wrapped in the duvet, he sat for a long while at the window, the heavy chintz curtains thrown back to reveal the brightness of a country sky at night. Even with the window closed he could hear the howl of a dog, the sharp yelping of what he took to be a fox, and other, to him unidentifiable, sounds of nature carrying on its life. He had traveled far. To Russia, to India, to vast countries and high plateaux. But he had yet to encounter the quality of loneliness that filled the Irish countryside, by day and by night.

Chapter Three

The news of the events occurring daily at Moore's Farm spread along the route of Paddy's milk truck. And although the outlying village was alive with gossip and rumor, it was the row of houses nearest the farm and Mr. Sweeney's shop that fathered the most piquant analysis.

Paddy had come to the farm only in recent years, and as a consequence, was the most disinterested disseminator of information. There are two types of Irish country people: those abundantly endowed with the gift of imagination, and those who are not. And Paddy fell into the latter category. He enjoyed his current notoriety, however, as the man who had first set eyes on the coffin that early spring morning. But he never embellished the story. Each day he would merely report to his customers the bare facts. And so with their milk and cream he also delivered the latest movements of the Moore family. There was no betrayal in this. And although the Moores mightn't like it, they would not have expected anything else. Paddy told the neighborhood about the body, and about himself and Kevin removing it to the barn. To the barn, mind you! That caused more stir amongst his listeners than the actual discovery of the coffin itself. And then he was able to tell of Mr. Fleming, from Dublin, who had come down and who had stayed the night. Now, that wasn't news. Hadn't the whole of the pub seen him on the night in question? Paddy, being as he was, was not chagrined, and merely continued to report what he saw.

Eileen O'Grady's information was infinitely more satisfactory. Eileen did out for the Moores—that is, she was their daily help who cleaned and cooked and washed. She had been working up at Moore's for donkeys years; in fact, as a young girl she had known Jack. When she first left the convent school at fourteen, she had gone to work in the dairy barn and often used to see Jack when he came in from school. A fine-looking lad he was, she always said, full of life, full of fun. He used then to speak of the farm and what he would do when he came into the property. And now he had come back to his own place, as unexpectedly as he had gone.

Eileen embellished on the current events, although for the most part they needed no embellishment. Few believed that Violet was cast down with grief and that Rose herself was at death's door, but the stories were good and Kilmartin enjoyed them for the romances they were.

"Brendan! God bless the poor souls up at the farm, but you wouldn't know Miss Violet, she's gone so thin." Eileen stood in the crowded shop, well-aware of her audience, but nonetheless addressing her remarks to Brendan alone. Brendan nodded encouragingly, for that moment resembling a friendly, curious St. Bernard dog.

"Ah, I'll need a packet of J-cloths as well, Brendan," Eileen examined her list, "and some Vim, a packet of Sunlight Soap, mmm, and some vinegar for the windows ... God bless them up there, they're in a bad way. A good spring cleaning will bring some needed fresh air into that house, I tell you. Rose took to her bed even before your one—what's his name—Fleming, went back to Dublin."

"But Mrs. O'Grady, we all know that now ..." Brendan let his phrase hang in the quiet air of the shop. He expected more recent information from Eileen and he hadn't got it. In his mild way, Brendan could elicit all kinds of details. And he liked to be accurate. Between taking calls on the official post-office telephone for some of the neighbors whose phones had yet to be connected, and taking telegrams for all and sundry—but mainly the guests at the local hotel—and then again, between sorting the mail and having an interest in who was receiving what, Brendan knew far more about his neighbors than they would have guessed. But to his eternal credit, the things that he knew and the things that he found out rarely went beyond Brendan himself.

As if in answer to Brendan's unspoken criticism, Eileen leaned forward and, in a conspiratorial whisper, announced to the assembled crowd that the police were expected at the farm this very afternoon. She might have told more but for the disgruntled complaining of Mr. O'Dwyer, who had come in to buy a single stamp and had now been standing in the queue of shoppers—who had not come in for stamps—for nearly half an hour. The shoppers let him jump the queue. O'Dwyer was a mystery to his neighbors, as he seemingly took no interest in the current affairs of Kilmartin. And he stood like an incubus silencing the excitement of the small crowd. But despite his lack of curiosity, O'Dwyer knew everything that John, his neighbor on the left, knew. And that was considerable. John and O'Dwyer were to be seen on any fine day confabbing over the hedge that divided their two back gardens. On a hot day they were to be seen confabbing over the low wall that divided their small front gardens. And although the only converse he held with anyone else consisted of "It's a grand day, missus," or "There's no toleratin' this weather," O'Dwyer could build a nest in your ear, if he chose.

"Of course the police are comin' up here again," snapped O'Dwyer. "Isn't it a murder they have on their plate?" He turned on his heel with his stamp in hand and left.

No one till this point had spoken the word *murder,* and it sent a chill through the people in the shop.

"Ah, God rest his soul," said Eileen seriously, and she took her parcels and left the shop.

"It's a bad business," said Mr. Sinclair sententiously, in the shop for the third time that day.

Brendan's trade had increased appreciably since Tuesday, with people coming in for items they could easily have done without. But it was one of the places in the village where a bit of news might be gleaned. For those of the village who did not frequent the pub, it was either that or wait until Sunday after Mass or after Morning Prayer— if you were Protestant, that is—where news could be garnered and satisfyingly analyzed. The morning rush finally ended, and Brendan and Mr. Sweeney drew a mutual sigh of relief.

"Tea, Da?"

"That would be very welcome," answered Mr. Sweeney as Brendan disappeared into the small back room to plug in the electric kettle.

"What bickies are we having today?" he called.

"Whole Wheat, I think, but with the milk chocolate," Mr. Sweeney replied as he took down the two round packets of biscuits from the shop shelf and slit the paper with his knife. It was just past one o'clock, and he took the key from the pocket of his dusty waistcoat and locked the glass cage that sat in the corner of the shop. He sighed as he did so. The cage was an awful curse. All steel and bullet-proof glass. He'd never get used to it. At seventy he was too old for new tricks. On the other hand, he had got used to the time lock on the safe. He shook his head at the memory of how he'd take the receipts for the day's work at the small post office and stash them under the counter—and it had been safe enough for all those years. But not now. Not with the IRA robbing post offices in nearly every county in the country. He glanced up as a sudden gust of rain struck the front window of the shop. Oh, he'd got used to the safe. But the cage now was hopeless. The grill in the window was too low. His customers couldn't adjust to bending down and hollering through it, and now that he was just a little hard of hearing, he couldn't get used to it either. What's more, the little tray was far too small to be practical, especially paying out the pensions and the child allowance. Did they think up at the General Post Office in O'Connell Street in Dublin that all he did was sell the odd stamp? He was humphing to himself when Brendan returned with the steaming mugs.

Trade was relatively slow at lunchtime, and Mr. Sweeney and Brendan took turns eating lunch in the small kitchen at the back of the shop, but they always began their break with a reviving cup of Lyons tea, the Green Label blend.

"I saw the unmarked police car go up the lane," offered Brendan.

"Did you indeed?" Mr. Sweeney was full of interest. "And when?"

"Oh, about an hour ago. It was when I was getting out the two bales of turf at the front, you know, for Mrs. Byrne."

"Mrs. Byrne? How could she manage ... Mr. Byrne usually gets it for her."

"He had to go in to work early today, I saw him on the bike as I was opening this morning. Mrs. Byrne is pretty inventive. She brought up the wheelbarrow, and lifting the turf in and out is no problem for her ... I wonder if they came bearing news or came with more questions?"

"News, I hope. They must be worn out with questions," replied Mr. Sweeney. "And what can the Miss Moores tell the police? Jack is gone this twenty-seven years."

"Did you know him, Da?" asked Brendan.

"Oh, aye, I knew him. Of course he was younger. I knew the whole family. Your grandfather was still alive then, and he used to do a roaring trade with not only the Moores, but all the big farms around here."

Brendan sighed to himself. They could still be doing a roaring trade if his own father had been more enterprising and not merely content to let things roll along. Things would be different when he took over himself some day.

"I remember when Jack went away because it was the spring and they were very busy up at the farm. They were calving, and they still had the sheep then. It was lambing time too. Everyone was surprised he had taken it in his head to leave just then when he was most needed ... but he was young. Youth is heedless of such responsibility." Mr. Sweeney peered at his son of twenty-seven years and then continued.

"Anyway, it was the spring that you were born, and it stayed in my mind ... for some reason or other. Of course, old Moore was dead, long dead, and the mother, well, I think she was dead a year or two. I do know that it was Violet who was running the farm. She used to come down here to do her business. Of course, there was no manager then, just herself with Rose and Lily and Jack all making it work. It wasn't easy. But she did a splendid job. Although I never agreed she should have given up on the sheep. But then, farming is difficult enough."

"Well, perhaps she wanted to concentrate her resources on the dairy end of things," commented Brendan.

"That's true, I imagine, looking back. After that she really made the dairy a going concern. They always did wholesale, but she brought in the retail in a big way. In fact, we were her only retail outlet for her milk. Father encouraged her, I remember, to go into the delivery business. For a single woman she did well, although she sorely missed Jack at the time. He would have been a big help to her in those early days. She was bitter. She would never mention him. Of course, I would know when they'd get a letter. When he first went, there was a letter a week, postmarked from London."

He paused to peel his apple, which he accomplished in a single movement with his pocketknife, leaving a continuous curl of skin on the counter.

"There was a gap. Rose or Lily would always ask me if there were any letters. Violet never did. After a while there were letters from America. Different cities, you know. Then just the occasional letter, always from Boston. I assumed from that that Jack had settled there ..."

"And then they stopped, did they?" Brendan prompted.

"And then they stopped. We all thought that he had no doubt married and settled down. It was common then, Brendan, even more so than now. The men would leave, and then lose touch ..." Mr. Sweeney sighed.

"Well, according to Eileen, Violet Moore said that he never did marry," Brendan said, resuming the conversation.

"Now that's a surprise. But the police couldn't be mistaken about that, it's too easy to check. Paddy's brother-in-law, the policeman, told him yesterday that all Jack's papers and luggage and passport were found in his room at the Shelbourne. The Shelbourne, that's Jack all over. The poshest hotel in Dublin. I'd say he enjoyed coming back and staying in style ... Who would believe it? Dead after only a few days."

"Well, if they had the passport and the return plane ticket, they must have an address," concluded Brendan.

"Aye. And it would be easy enough to check with the Boston police ... at least to see if there was family out there."

"No, Eileen told me, no family, no wife, no one," insisted Brendan.

"Strange, that ..."

"Strange?"

"It's strange to me anyway," said his father. "I remember Jack was a grand one for the girls. In fact he had been very involved just before he left."

"With a local girl?"

"Mmm, what?" Mr. Sweeney plucked a banana from a bunch on the counter. "Oh yes, a local girl, there was some scandal or other." He retired to the kitchen with his banana and apple and a wedge of cheddar cheese, leaving Brendan to cope for half an hour with the few soggy patrons that the March wind blew to their door.

James Fleming picked up the phone in response to his secretary's buzz. His mind was traveling on the narrow-gauge tracks that twisted between the Peruvian Andes. A thousand adventures among ancient civilizations were about to unfold.

"Your mother on the line."

He thought rapidly. He had neglected to mention the Peru trip to his mother. She considered this railway nonsense an aberration brought on by advancing bachelorhood. He would have to tell her. And she would want to see him. Surely he was booked solid night and day for the foreseeable future.

"Mother!"

"James!"

No, he couldn't possibly make the church fete on Saturday. No, nor the Gaiety Theatre on Thursday. No, not even the wine and cheese party at the museum. But yes, all right, he was free on Sunday. Yes, he would ring her on Friday to confirm.

James tapped his hand on the desk diary. He had to get his shots on Saturday. He was fortunate that Dr. McCormak was willing to take him then. With any luck he'd be deathly ill with the reaction to the smallpox vaccination and could legitimately miss this bloody drinks get-together at his mother's. He looked up guiltily when his secretary came in. Maggie flirted briefly with him as she went over his schedule for the day. He had a lunchtime meeting at the Berkeley Court, but grimaced when the wind flung the rain against his window. It couldn't be helped. The contact was important; he might be able to bring in the business of a large estate. Gerald would be pleased if he pulled this one off. And they did serve excellent lamb at the Berkeley Court.

"Any word from Mr. Fitzgerald?"

"Oh yes, I should have told you. He rang this morning from London just after the office opened ..."

"Did he...?"

"No, he didn't comment that you weren't here. Another one of your late nights, I suppose." Maggie flashed a knowing smile that James chose to ignore.

"Well...?"

"Well? Oh, he was in a dead rush. He said to tell you that you were to hold down the fort, that the probate was more complicated than he had expected, that you were to pull in the fish at the Berkeley today ..." James looked up quickly, impressed yet again with Gerald's control of the minutiae of the practice.

"And...?"

Maggie checked her notebook. "And that was all for you ... Of course, I have volumes of the other three partners as well."

"Nothing about the Moores?" James asked, surprised.

"Oh, wait, yes, sorry. When the body is released for burial, you are to attend the funeral in his absence and take care of flowers, et cetera."

"Nothing about the murder?" James had sent Gerald the salient details of Jack Moore's death on the fax machine.

"Nothing."

"Are you sure?"

"Nothing."

"When is he returning?"

"He says he doesn't know. Could be away the whole week, maybe longer," she answered with a grin.

When Maggie left the office, James rapidly scanned *The Irish Times* for the day. If he had missed the funeral, Gerald would be ... but no, there it was. The Anglican Church, Kilmartin, funeral service Friday, three P.M. Burial private, Wexford Town Cemetery.

That means they released the body to the family, thought James. When he left Moore's Farm, he had given Violet the number of the undertaker he'd dealt with. They were an old Wexford firm, very respectable and very discreet. Through the undertaker he had arranged to purchase, at Violet's insistence, a plot in a new cemetery outside

Wexford town. He turned again to the death notice. Yes, it was there
and not in the family plot in the churchyard that Jack Moore was to
be buried. Violet was to have her way after all. James thought of
Rose's tragic face and Lily's sad one. He checked his desk diary and
penciled in the funeral. He wouldn't mind spending some time in the
village. There were still some questions of his own he'd like to find
the answers to.

"Maggie, I'll be going to Wexford on Thursday afternoon, and I'll
be back on Friday evening ..." He paused as she put him on hold.
"And Maggie, arrange for appropriate flowers to be sent from Mr.
Fitzgerald and the partners to the Moores. You'll find the death notice
in today's paper. Jack, Jack Moore of Wexford."

He put down the phone, drew out his private notebook, and made
a few jottings. Yes, he'd like this bizarre situation to be put to rest,
for his own satisfaction, if not for Gerald's, before leaving for Peru.
He had carefully gone over his schedule on his return from Wexford.
Something about that trip had made him both restless and energized.
He wanted to be up and doing. He thought he saw a real possibility
to take four weeks off from the firm in May. His own cases would
either be concluded or could be put on hold for that month. He certainly had the time coming to him. Gerald would surely be finished in
London. Although there were so many probabilities in the situation,
he felt he had assessed things accurately. One of the two juniors could
take care of his ongoing work while he'd be ongoing from Lima to
Huancayo, 120 miles of track twisting through the rarefied air of the
Andes. And then on from Huancayo to Cuzco. He would invest in a
new rucksack at Johnston's of Wicklow Street. He would get his shots
and get deathly ill and miss his mother's cocktail party on Sunday.

A nervous sun peered from behind the bundling clouds of March
as James stepped out the front door. A nice lunch at the Berkeley,
and all's right with the world.

James was surprised to see the number of cars parked outside the
house when he arrived at Moore's Farm to accompany the three sisters
to the church. Violet Moore had given him the impression on the
telephone that it would be quite a small group of mourners.

"Mr. Fleming, I'm happy to see you again!" Kevin strode toward
James, slapping the Citroen on its flanks as if it were one of his cows.
His look of relief was even more evident this time. "That's a grand
car you have. Very swank."

James smiled. Somehow Kevin looked all wrong in his three-piece tweed suit, biceps straining the seams, his bright red face beaming over his tight collar. But by the time James had got out of his car, he realized that Kevin was visibly troubled.

"It's a bad business, this," muttered Kevin. "I don't believe they should be upsetting Miss Moore today of all days ..."

"Who?" asked James, intrigued.

"It's not so much the local men, though God knows they have been in and out of here all week. It's this pair of special police from Dublin I object to."

"The Special Branch! When did they first show up?"

"About an hour ago ... no warning, nothing."

"Did you catch a name?"

"It's one Detective Inspector O'Shea. Pleasant enough. I know his name since he collared me this morning in the new barn. Had a few questions. Introduced himself. Pleasant enough, as I say, but ..."

They entered the hall and James heard the booming voice. He had met O'Shea a few times but was certain the man would not recall their fleeting encounters over the years in Dublin. But he did.

"Fleming! Glad to see you again. How's the train trekking?" O'Shea was a big, hearty man with a sonorous voice. He gave people an instant feeling of security.

"You've a great memory there," answered James affably. "Peru is next on the agenda. I hope to take the train that runs at the highest elevation in the world."

"The devil you are. Great stuff! Great stuff!" The two men strolled into the drawing room, which was empty but for O'Shea's sullen-looking assistant. "Where's Fitzgerald these days? Not retired is he?"

James explained that Gerald was on business in London.

"Pity," remarked O'Shea. "He's from these parts. Might have been able to shed some light on the situation."

"Mmm. Any news on Jack Moore's previous history?" asked James.

"Well, that depends on what you've already heard. We know that he arrived two days before the body was founded here. He came through Dublin Airport on a flight from London. We're a bit puzzled that he didn't take a direct flight from Boston. On the other hand, he only made a connection at Heathrow. He didn't stop over at all ... Tell me now, do you know the family long yourself?"

"Not really." James was deliberately vague. "He didn't have family there ... in Boston." James hazarded this comment knowing that if Jack had, the body would have no doubt been flown back to the States.

"No. Apparently he was a successful businessman but he didn't have family. We're working with the Boston police to check on his friends. It seems he liquidated all his assets in the States—the Internal Revenue Service there is going to forward the details. But we already know now that he sold his contracting firm for a good price. And the way things are out there, he might have had stocks or investments. We're waiting to get the whole picture."

James's ears pricked up. This was something that hadn't occurred to him. If Jack's estate was substantial, Violet Moore might just ask him to manage the situation for her. If indeed there was no family, then Jack's three sisters might well be the beneficiaries. He beamed to himself, already relishing the thought of one or two trips to Boston. He'd never been to Boston, but he knew of a nineteenth-century eccentric who had built fifty miles of track in eastern Massachusetts just to tour his cranberry bogs. Had an 0-4-2 steam locomotive and several open-ended Pullman cars. That was style. And this enthusiast's delight was only a few hours' drive from Boston. He started guiltily when the three sisters entered the drawing room, somber in black mourning dress.

As Violet paused to speak to O'Shea, Lily drifted over to James.

"Mr. Fleming. I'm glad to see you here, but I was wondering ... is Gerald Fitzgerald with you?"

James thought he detected a note of longing, or was it dissatisfaction? He stiffened, slightly offended. "I'm afraid not, he's still detained in London. But I know that he would have wanted to be here with your family."

Lily nodded.

The undertaker's limousine was now at the door, and James was asked to ride with the sisters. He saw other cars leaving the farm, Kevin's amongst them. Violet was bitter during the short ride to the church.

"It's outrageous, I tell you. They could have come yesterday, they could have come tomorrow. But today! O'Shea knew it was the day of the funeral." Rose wept softly, but Lily was conciliatory.

"Violet, I don't think they can pick their moment. He has to come down from Dublin when he's free to do so ..."

"Yes ... yes ... I suppose it's for the best. The sooner this mystery is cleared up, the better. I cannot bear the scandal. If they solve this today, at least the gossip in the village will die down. With luck it will be a nine-days wonder."

James pondered, not for the first time, Violet's reactions. Even taking into account the Irish penchant for saving face, he did think that at least her curiosity at finding the murderer of her only brother would outweigh her sense of scandal.

They all fell silent as the car pulled in through the gateway of the picturesque church and drove slowly up the graveled path to the side door. The hearse was already at the door, and once the family was seated, the men would bring in the coffin.

James attempted to keep his mind on the service, out of respect for the deceased, and for the most part he did so. But he hadn't known the man, and found his mind wandering. Something seemed to be stuck in the back of it, some detail nagging at the edges of his memory. He tried to clarify it, to no avail.

He observed the congregation. The small stone church was full, each of its long wooden pews creaking under the burden. Without warning, the organist switched from the Bach to a hymn James didn't recognize. Everyone got up. Violet, flanked by Rose and Lily, stood erect in the front pew. James, positioned a few rows back, concentrated on Rose, but she was steady on her feet. Several well-heeled types were amongst the general village population. Then James spotted Mr. Sweeney and Brendan from the shop. And Kevin and his wife. And Paddy with his, looking distinctly under the weather.

The nagging thought returned, even as the clergyman addressed the congregation. James listened intently as he spoke of Jack Moore, a man he obviously had not known. He smiled at the irony of the situation and thought of the numerous funerals he had attended. Funerals where glowing words were spoken by one man about another, in most cases by a man who had never really known the other. Form and substance. So much of what was significant in life was governed solely by form and not by substance. Did it trivialize events, perhaps even emotions? he wondered. Violet, now ... she was breaking with form. And in a dramatic way. True, outside the environs of a small Irish village, the question of where a man was to be buried might seem slight. But her decision was of epic proportions in its context. She wasn't keeping up form. Jack, her only brother, was to be buried in a new, and worse, a public cemetery far from his birthplace. And not in the family plot barely a hundred yards from where his sisters now sat.

What, he wondered with increasing intensity, was the bad blood between Jack and Violet Moore? What had such a powerful hold that even in the face of his death, in the face of his murder, she would not bend? She would not bow to her sister's obvious desires to have Jack buried in the family plot in their own parish church. She would not bow in the face of the speculative gossip of the surrounding countryside, even though she seemed to live in dread of that very gossip. Yes, she was an intensely private person who was now leaving herself open to unceasing speculation as to her motives.

James's attention was caught again, and he focused his wandering thoughts on the clergyman's summation. He was naming the bereaved sisters individually, offering to each in turn consoling words appropriate to their personalities. Or so he thought. Oh, yes, he'd be careful to do that, to say the right things to some of the most wealthy and substantial members of his parish, members who without doubt had contributed to every fund-raising event this man and his select vestry could devise. Substantial. Was this the only substance that countered mere form? Shakespeare was mistaken. It wasn't the deeds that lived after men, it was their money—that was the substance the world recognized. And who better than James to know the truth of that; he who spent his working life helping people distribute their wealth from beyond the grave. Writing wills and probating wills and executing wills. And did that apportionment of wealth, that allotment of what the world called substance, parallel the dying's portioning out of affection to the inevitable survivors? Love parceled out in the form of property and belongings, stocks and shares, silverware and jewelry?

The congregation was rising, and James suddenly realized the service was nearly over. The undertaker's men were standing by the coffin, ready to move the trolley, on which it rested, slowly up the aisle, on silent wheels.

That was it! The undertaker's men. Surely they would know—who had contacted them, where had they picked up the body, where indeed had they coffined the body? He stirred restlessly in his seat. He wanted to get back to the house to speak to O'Shea. He stood up as the pews began to empty in an orderly fashion, and as he followed, was surprised to see O'Shea at the back of the church. A very large man trying to look inconspicuous and failing.

When they exited, the people gathered on the steps to offer their condolences to the Moore sisters. But Violet brushed such niceties aside and headed straight for the funeral car. Rose and Lily, however, remained. James stood nearby. He noted that the assembled crowd of friends, neighbors, and business acquaintances were with one accord warm and sincere in their expressions of sympathy to the two sisters. He watched as Lily graciously accepted the handshakes and kind words and then capably invited old friends back to the house for refreshments, after the private burial in Wexford's new town cemetery. Many of the congregation asked either Rose or Lily if they could also speak with Violet; many looked around inquiringly to see if they had missed her somewhere in the crowd and confusion at the door. Some, as they passed the funeral car in which she sat, tipped their hats or waved gloved hands gently, solicitously. James found it hard to reconcile Violet's perceptions of her jackal-like neighbors with these polite and appropriate expressions of respect if not, in this case, grief.

James watched as Rose, a bit addled, a little bit muddled in her grief, was greeted warmly by a number of women; members, he discovered, of the Irish Countrywomens Association, of whose local branch Lily had been a founding member.

Nothing was said the entire journey to the cemetery. The hearse and their car slowed passing through each village, as caps were removed and people crossed themselves out of respect to the unknown dead. James observed each sister in turn, each silent and preoccupied.

The new cemetery was painfully so, with sapling cypresses, mud everywhere, and three yellow excavators parked just yards from where they stood. The graveside service was mercifully brief, with even the clergyman seeming anxious to be done and away from the terrible emptiness of the place. Lily kept her arm around Rose, supporting her as they both stood a little distance from Violet. There were no tears.

It was with a great sense of relief that James alighted from the funeral car into the brisk fresh air and armed both Lily and Rose into the house. Sandwiches and tea were served in the seldom-used dining room, and the people who had come back for the wake spoke quietly amongst themselves. Violet, after a few broken conversations, left; ten minutes later, as James was sipping a welcome cup of tea, he spied her through the window, crossing the yard, dressed in her anorak and boots. Eileen, however, continued to move among the visitors with trays of sweets, while Kevin, looking uneasy, stood at a side table pouring drinks with a heavy hand.

James was surprised yet again to see O'Shea mingling with the guests, and curious when he beckoned him with a sober look.

"Fleming," said O'Shea brusquely, "when this group disperses—which

I hope will be sooner rather than later–I am going to question the Moores."

"But you've been through all that. Surely today of all–"

"Must be done. And done today," O'Shea cut in.

"But it's routine questioning, surely."

"Pardon me, Fleming. I'm telling you this since you are, I take it, their solicitor, acting in place of Gerald Fitzgerald. Personally, I would have thought a murder serious enough to merit the old man's presence."

James bridled. "O'Shea! I am here in a professional capacity. But I assure you that having got to know the Moore sisters, I am also taking a personal interest in this case. I can speak on their behalf, and I assure you that they are anticipating a speedy solution to this tragic murder of their brother."

O'Shea smiled wryly. "In that case, I'm glad I spoke. I think you should be present when I question them."

"Of course. But before we get to that, I've been wanting to ask you about this hearse business. Have you located the undertaker who delivered the body here?"

"We're working on it, we're working on it." O'Shea's tone was dismissive, and James reluctantly let the matter drop.

O'Shea questioned Rose first, and James had the strong feeling he had done it merely to get Rose out of the way. Between her sobs and tears she had little to tell O'Shea about Jack except what a grand lad he had been and what a happy childhood they had shared. Her mind seemed locked in a time warp where the remote happy past was far more vivid to her than the unhappy present.

"If he hadn't gone away then, this wouldn't have happened," she repeated, seemingly illogically connecting the two events. "He could have stayed on here, and in the end he would have married Kathleen and we would have had little babies, fat little babies in the house. Oh, I would have loved his fat wee babes just as my own–" Rose fell into a paroxysm of weeping, and O'Shea and James stood helplessly by. She turned and ran to the door, calling to Lily, who came quickly.

"That's quite enough, Mr. O'Shea." said Lily, her mild demeanor lending even more force to her words. She looked reproachfully at James. "Young man, I think you could look after our interests as well as Gerald would."

She brought Rose to her room, and on her return she took a seat by the fire, composed once more.

"Mr. O'Shea," she said, taking the initiative, "we have all been ques-tioned by the local police. We were all questioned at the inquest. And I, and my sisters also, have given statements to your assistant. I really don't think that we have to undergo this ordeal again!"

"Miss Moore, believe me when I tell you that I sympathize with your situation. And I imagine you are tired after the strain of the funeral. But I think you'll agree that a speedy end to this situation would be a great relief to all concerned." O'Shea glanced at James, who nodded.

"Very well, Inspector."

"I only have one or two very specific questions. Firstly, concerning the murder weapon. We believe that the murder weapon was a carving knife from your own kitchen. Can you tell me when was the last time you saw that knife?"

"No, I cannot," Lily said simply.

O'Shea leaned back in his chair.

"Now, Miss Moore, I'd like you to recall the day and the evening before you all found the body of your brother ... Can you think of any unusual—let me say, any out of the ordinary—occurrences in or around the farm?"

Lily shifted in her seat and then withdrew an untipped cigarette from her pocket. O'Shea leaned forward to light it. She inhaled deeply, looked at James and then at O'Shea.

"There was one odd thing ..."

"Go on," said O'Shea keenly.

"It happened the night before we found ... Jack's coffin. I had meant to ask Violet about it, but the events of that day knocked it out of my head. Not having seen Jack for so many years, and then to see him again dead ..." Lily's voice trembled.

"I was very restless that night, which is not unusual for me. I had been reading, and I must have dozed off, because my book had fallen off the bed. I think now that it was the noise of the book hitting the floor that woke me. Whatever it was, I couldn't go back to sleep. I got up and turned off the light and walked over to my window. I felt some fresh air might help me. I started to open the window on the right-hand side when I glanced down into the yard.

"I thought I had seen some movement. In fact, I thought I had seen Violet. I peered through the glass and indeed it was Violet. I was so relieved. You see, I sleep so badly that I was relieved to think I had slept through the night. When I saw Violet, I assumed she was on her way to the milking and that it must be near dawn. I continued to open the window, but it was quite stiff, and as I stood there, I saw her stop. She seemed to be speaking to someone. It was a man. And again, thinking it was time for the milking, I assumed the man was Kevin." Lily paused and smoothed her skirt. She seemed preoccupied.

"And was it?" asked O'Shea.

"Well, the extraordinary thing was that just at that moment the telephone rang in the hall downstairs. I didn't want it to wake Rose, so I rushed down to answer it ..."

"Yes?" said O'Shea impatiently. James looked at him inquiringly, but O'Shea ignored him.

"Well, you see, it was Kevin on the telephone. He was calling with a message for Violet. He might be late coming in, in the morning, because his car had broken down or something. And he wanted to warn her to expect trouble with the calving of Moira. In case she went into labor during the night."

O'Shea looked blank. "The carving of ..."

"The calving," interjected James. "This is the calving season."

Lily continued. "Kevin was apologizing for ringing so late, and I thought that that was a bit odd, still believing that I'd just seen him with Violet in the yard ... in fact, still believing it was dawn. But as I stood there at the phone, I looked up at the grandmother clock and it was only half-twelve. No doubt Kevin will remember his call. He doesn't keep such late hours as a rule."

"So what you're saying is—be careful now, Miss Moore, this is very important—what you're saying is that you saw your sister Violet in the barn with an unidentified man between midnight and twelve-thirty?"

"I will say it was a man I didn't know."

"Was it your brother, Jack Moore?" asked O'Shea.

Lily lowered her head and sighed. Silence filled the room. Ominous. Disturbing. James jumped as the telephone, as if on cue, rang shrilly in the hall outside the door. He went to answer it. It was for O'Shea. Lily didn't look at them as she passed through the hall and into the kitchen.

O'Shea spoke for some moments and then hung up. He lit a cigarette, then called his assistant from the kitchen and asked him to come inside to take notes. And he asked Eileen to fetch Violet.

When Violet appeared, she was still wearing her boots and anorak, her face perspiring.

"This bloomin' business of the funeral has upset all our routines," she addressed them abruptly, "and I've neglected the cattle. Moira is finally about to drop her calf. Kevin's going to need me. I can only spare you a few minutes." She glared at O'Shea and then at James.

O'Shea spoke. "Miss Moore, I'm afraid this is a very serious matter. I need your full attention. I am going to caution you now. As you see, your solicitor is here and my assistant will take notes."

James was as startled as Violet. What O'Shea was suggesting was ridiculous.

"Two pieces of information have just come to hand, two pieces of information that fit quite neatly together, I'm afraid. Firstly, a witness has placed you in your dairy barn at the approximate time of Jack's death."

"Yes." Violet looked at O'Shea quizzically.

"Secondly ..." O'Shea took a long pull on the stub of his cigarette and threw it behind him into the fire. "Secondly, the knife which my men discovered in the same barn some days ago—"

"What knife?" Violet exclaimed.

"A kitchen knife ... a kitchen knife which your own, er, woman, Eileen O'Grady, identified as belonging to your kitchen."

"Eileen? When did you ... I don't ..."

James cautioned Violet with a wave of his hand not to say any more. O'Shea waited, but Violet remained silent.

"Furthermore, I have just been informed that this knife, found in the barn, is certainly the murder weapon ..."

Violet swayed slightly, and James moved to put a supporting hand beneath her elbow.

"... and that your fingerprints and only yours were found on the knife. I'm afraid, Miss Moore, that I must bring you to the police station to formally charge you with the murder of your brother, Jack Moore."

Chapter Four

Gerald Fitzgerald looked somber as James concluded his report. "But I thought the body was only in the barn after it was discovered at the front of the house. The murderer hardly killed Jack in the barn and then had a hearse drive it around to the front."

"Agreed. But O'Shea didn't deign to explain his thinking to us. It seemed enough that he had the murder weapon with Violet's fingerprints on it, and only hers. That the body was found at her house.

That she was seen at the barn with an unidentified man by her own sister at the approximate time of Jack's death. And that the knife was found hidden in the barn."

"Did Violet offer any explanation?" asked Gerald.

"No," she said nothing. Nothing at the bail hearing and nothing since she's been released."

"You took care of the bail?"

"Yes, there were no problems there," replied James.

Gerald was silent. James glanced around the comfortable sitting room. The furnishings indicated both Gerald's prosperity and his taste. Or perhaps his wife's taste. James remembered Mrs. Fitzgerald as a kindly, maternal woman who had taken a warm interest in his early career. He missed her gentle humor. Gerald had changed after her death. He had become more remote in the past year, and everyone at the law office had noticed it. Since they had had no children, James reflected, Gerald must feel loneliness even more sharply.

"Gerald, old man, let me leave you in peace. We can discuss this—"

"Nonsense, I have too many questions. Firstly, I must say this. I think you very remiss in not attending the inquest in Wexford, mmm?" Gerald glared at James and shifted the big wing chair to a more upright position. He seemed to be coming to life again, as the color flooded his face.

"I've close-questioned myself about that, Gerald," James said seriously. "When I left Moore's Farm that morning, after having telephoned you in London, there seemed no question of the family being involved in Jack's death. The coroner had called the inquest for Wednesday. The body was still to be examined and the postmortem performed. I should add that it did stay in my mind during that week. I rang the coroner and learned from him that they were only calling on Violet, Kevin, and Sean to give testimony. In fact, that evening I rang again and was told that no other person had come forward with information that was new. The jury returned an open verdict—that Jack was murdered by person or persons unknown. Not in my wildest dreams did I think that Violet had anything to do with it. And I might add, I still don't."

"Your loyalty to our client is impressive, James, after so short an acquaintance."

"I'm not sure it's loyalty at all, Gerald. Strangely enough, it's a gut feeling—call it a fancy of my own—but I don't think Violet capable of such an act."

"I'm amazed to hear it. As I remember Violet, she is a tremendously capable woman, a very determined woman, perhaps I might even call her a ruthless woman."

"Are you telling me you believe she did it?"

"Well, actually no. One doesn't like to think of one's longstanding clients suddenly as murderers. However, we must deal with the reality of the situation. Obviously O'Shea considers her to be the murderer. He's shrewd and generally successful, good at his job. If he has charged her, then it is with good reason. She had the means–the knife, of course. And apparently, according to Lily's still dubious statement, Violet had the opportunity. But that's assuming a lot. Lily did not identify the man as Jack, now, did she?"

James's face brightened considerably. Listening to Gerald seemed to get things back into perspective.

"And then there's motive, Gerald. What possible motive could she have had? O'Shea has nothing there, or he would have hinted at it, I'm sure of it!"

"Right! Now listen to me. Firstly, I am putting you in charge of the case. I know, now that I'm back, you probably assumed it would fall in my provenance. But I am not feeling well–with this heart thing of mine. More importantly, you have been, as it happens, Johnny on the spot. Further, you have some empathy with the Moores. And finally, I think we need your active involvement in the case. There are a number of things I want you to do down in Wexford, and you are more able than I to make flying trips in your most suitable car." Gerald smiled at James.

"Now, while you're here I want to call Lincolns Inns and see if we can get hold of Madigan. So pour yourself another brandy and one for me–it has great medicinal properties." He winked at James and turned to the phone at his elbow.

As James poured out two healthy measures of Hennessey into the Waterford Crystal snifters, he considered Gerald's idea. James didn't know Madigan well, since he'd never had occasion to be involved in a criminal suit, and he wondered at the wisdom of calling in the renowned barrister. It was like a signal to the man in the street that the accused was probably guilty. James even felt that way himself. Madigan's fame was based on often successfully defending what seemed to be hopeless causes. There was a suspicion even in the Inns of Court that many of his clients had indeed been guilty and had been set free on mere technicalities and loopholes cleverly manipulated by Madigan. James sighed. He did not want to see Violet tarred with the same brush, tainted in advance by an association with Madigan.

Gerald looked somber when James handed him his brandy, and he drank it down at a gulp.

"Madigan can't do it for us. He claims he has too many briefs as it is, and a number of those are no doubt capital cases. We'll have to call Sheridan. He's sound and experienced, but ... well, Madigan's brilliance and fire just aren't there." James nodded, relieved. Sheridan was indeed solid and middle of the road. Convinced as he was of Violet's innocence, James did not believe she needed the Machiavellian maneuvering of Madigan. Or the public interest his presence would immediately generate. But as he left Gerald's that night, he had a twinge of regret, and hoped that his new client would not suffer adversely for the lack of Madigan's ingenuity.

"But James, it's such a change for you. So exciting! Now just put the smoked salmon sandwiches at the back of the dining room table, that's it."

"A change from what?" James felt his voice rising as he helped his mother set out what she fondly called canapes.

"Oh, you know, James–from all that dull office work you do ... I'm sure there's more to the law than clerking ... now put the cucumber sandwiches at the front, there we are."

"You know, Mother, I've been a partner for some years now, and–"

"Oh, but darling, of course, of course. Gerald is so generous. Of course he would do his best for you. But now this. This case will be in all the papers. We'll finally see your name in print. I'm certain that Gerald will give you a lovely raise and perhaps a lovely little promotion as well. Now, your father at your age ..."

James tried valiantly to block out his mother's voice. It was always the same. He wondered yet again how his mother sailed blithely through life, getting all the essential details wrong and yet getting the larger picture so often right.

He heard her high-pitched voice from a great distance–calling from the African Room, her name for the room in which she housed all the trinkets she had carried back from what to her was still the dark continent. The room was bright and airy, with a bay window letting in the morning sunshine. He wished that this room had been here during his residence in the house. His mother suffered from that peculiarly Irish disease of "adding on." To date she had added on three rooms to the original house, and was now considering converting the garage.

She was arranging glasses on trays and trying to find space on the sideboard amongst the twenty or so carved elephants that reposed there. A lion looked benignly down on their heads from an embroidered cloth.

"Now, James, when you're serving the drinks–"

"The what!" James's voice was definitely an octave higher whenever he visited his mother. "I thought I was a guest?"

"Don't be ridiculous, James, you're my son. Now, in Africa, of course, we'd have a native boy. And since your brother Donald can't get away from his rounds, as he says, you'll have to do."

James thought dark thoughts about his younger brother, now a junior medical resident, but certainly senior to James in sensibly wriggling out of his mother's parties.

His mother was the most popular woman James knew, and this was borne out yet again by the crowd of corpulent, well-dressed friends who were massed on the doorstep. James greeted them as he admitted them into the reception hall.

"James!" most of them exclaimed, as though they hadn't seen him for a generation. With his arms piled high with coats, he could barely shake hands.

"Just popping in ... service was so very long this morning. Absolutely parched. Vivienne ... Vivienne ..." The swarm of thirty churchgoers buzzed into the drawing room from the hall as James sighed and threw the coats on the hall stand. He had spotted a few younger types–in fact, young women. His mother was going to try again.

The babble of voices rose around his ears as he poured large drinks and made small talk. Through the mass of bodies he had spotted a young, attractive woman perched uncomfortably on the arm of one of the fireside chairs. Eventually he carried two stiff G and T's to her side and introduced himself.

She looked up gratefully and then shrugged. She was balancing a plate of cucumber sandwiches in one hand and a cup of tea in the other.

She smiled an engaging smile and told him she was Hilary. And then she shrugged again.

James hastily pulled over one of the many small wooden tables that represented an elongated elephant with a sort of rimmed tray stuck to its back.

"We might as well make use of one of these beasts of burden."

Hilary laughed, and suddenly James was conscious of his mother's eyes upon him. From afar he heard again her high-pitched voice.

"You've met, you've met! How perfectly extraordinary! Now, Hilary, isn't he just all I've told you? Your aunt and I think you two are just perfect together. James, don't slouch your shoulders like that." James watched as an embarrassed blush crept up Hilary's neck.

"Young people need to be taken in hand," James's mother barreled on. "After all, James is getting a bit long in the tooth—oh, heavens, what am I saying? But of course—child bride, child bride. I always said Mr. Fleming just robbed the cradle when he married me. Now, Hilary, we can't say that about you. This business of women having careers. Much too silly. Marriage and babies, that's what I say—"

"What is it that you do, Hilary?" James's cool voice cut through his mother's matchmaking. But without taking any notice of him, she had moved on, urging cucumber sandwiches on her tipsy morning revelers.

Hilary struggled to her feet, placing her refreshments on the mantel. "Well, actually, I'm an executive secretary with the Peat Board ..." As she said it she laughed merrily once again, and James suddenly felt very aware of her cornflower-blue eyes and the mass of auburn hair that fell to her shoulders in wonderful disarray.

"And I know what you do. Why, we all do ..."

"Oh, yes," replied James hesitantly.

"Of course. You're senior partner in that big law firm. In fact, according to your mother, you are head of the firm in all but name. She tells me that Mr. Fitzgerald is practically in his dotage, and but for you, the firm would be dying with him."

James wasn't sure if Hilary spoke tongue-in-cheek. Had she already got the measure of his mother?

"In that event, she'll probably have told you about my black belt in karate ... which happened to be an orange belt in judo," James added wryly, and watched her face.

"But of course." She smiled.

James decided he could do worse than while away the remainder of the party in Hilary's company—and avoid his mother. At least for now. He gestured toward the garden door of the African Room.

"Then let's step outside to the jungle, and I'll show you some of my better holds."

James regretted his decision to drive down to Wexford on St. Patrick's Day. Never before had he realized that every village and town celebrated after Mass with a parade of its own, no matter how ragtag. His jaw clenched yet again as his CX was forced to crawl behind slowly moving marchers and floats.

Eventually he reached Kilmartin and pulled in at the Drooping Well, only to discover that it was closed for the extended holy hour. Irritated and tired, he drove on to Riders Inn, a small country hotel some miles distant which he had heard good things about from Gerald and where Maggie had booked him a room.

Two hours later James sighed and stretched his feet out to rest them on the fender of the large hearth fireplace. St. Patrick's Day had improved rapidly once he had reached Riders. The remains of an enormous afternoon tea lay scattered on the table at his side. He stretched like a fat cat, full of scones and butter and jam, wafer-thin sandwiches, and fat raisin buns. More holiday makers entered the peaceful country parlor. James stirred and regretfully left his seat.

Upstairs in the cool, sparsely furnished room, he gazed out the small window over the basin as he washed. Just a hint of pale green had touched the leafless trees that bordered what would soon be a lush garden. White wrought-iron benches and tables stood lonely, waiting for the summer. Yes, he would definitely return to this place, he mused, when he needed respite from his labors.

The small oak bar he had spotted earlier drew him back downstairs. He was just diving into a large G and T and a 1957 issue of *Country Life* when a voice broke in on his solitary enjoyment. He looked up, slightly annoyed.

"Compliments of the house," said a stout woman with pale gray hair pulled tightly into a bun. "It's Mr. Fleming, isn't it?"

James accepted the second gin and tonic and asked the woman, who was both owner and manager, to join him.

"Many thanks," James said genially. "I've only been here an hour, Mrs. . . . ?"

She smiled. "Rider, believe it or not."

"Mrs. Rider. And I know that I will be returning many times."

"Well, Mr. Fleming, I can tell from your car and your appearance, you're not a commercial traveler. Perhaps you are . . ."

"A solicitor—for my sins, as they say. Actually, I should be in Kilmartin, but I underestimated the holiday traffic. I think I'll have to hold off my visit until tomorrow. And no harm done, since I've been seduced by your teas and am looking forward to your dinner!"

"Kilmartin? . . . That's a mere stone's throw from here. Sure I know it well—" She broke off suddenly. "Well, Mr. Fleming, I suggest that you walk in our gardens before dinner. There's a stretch in the evenings now, each day a cock's step longer than the day before. The air will whet your appetite." She left abruptly, leaving James puzzled.

But his unspoken question was answered that evening after the splendid dinner of grilled lamb chops, new potatoes drenched in butter and parsley, and some impossibly early fresh peas. Mrs. Rider joined her guests in the sitting room for coffee as heavy and grainy as only Irish country people made it.

"It occurred to me that as you are a solicitor, you were somehow involved in the recent unpleasantness they've been having in Kilmartin," said Mrs. Rider as she handed him his coffee.

"To be honest, I am," said James, heaping brown sugar into his coffee from the silver bowl which Mrs. Rider offered him.

"I am an old friend of the Moore sisters," she said guardedly.

"Ah, I understand. Well, I am acting as their solicitor and I've come down to do a bit of work on the case. I'm doing some background work, actually."

"It's a terrible scandal here in the county, Mr. Fleming, as I'm sure I don't have to tell you. But then, I detect a Dublin accent."

"True, true. I don't know this area well, although I'm getting to like it. If there's anything you feel you could tell me about the Moores ..."

"I hardly think ..." Mrs. Rider, as edgy as a thoroughbred horse, began to move away.

"I mean, if you think it would be of help to Violet Moore. You were saying earlier that you were friends." James smiled encouragingly as Mrs. Rider sat down.

"Well, first I can assure you that I do not for an instant think Violet committed this horrible murder. It's ridiculous to even picture her plunging a knife into a man's chest, let alone into her own brother!"

"I agree," said James, "and not just because she is my client."

"Glad to hear it. Obviously you can't know Violet as I do. You see, we were in boarding school together. It was a small Protestant residential school for girls—since closed, I'm afraid. We were there together for six years, and after that we kept in touch for, oh, I'd say ten, with perhaps a twice-yearly visit. She was very bright. I always thought she should have gone on into a profession, but nothing would shake her determination to stay on at the farm.

"I had mixed feelings when her mother died and left the farm to her, and the others, of course. I felt that she would never escape the farm. But that was the foolishness of youth. As time passed I realized she had no desire to leave, it was her one true love–her passion, you might say. We drifted apart after my marriage to Captain Rider. Violet was at my wedding, but later, when my children came along, our interests diverged. In latter years we've met only at the races or the odd auction, the occasional party. But she never changed from that determined young woman I knew."

"Can you tell me, Mrs. Rider, had there ever been anyone special in her life?" James was inwardly thrilled to come upon this chance to find out about Violet Moore's early life.

"No, not to my knowledge. At the time when all of us girls were starting to go out socially, doing a bit of traveling, going up to Dublin in some cases to take up jobs, she remained on the farm. Then there were those few years when there was a flurry of weddings. She always attended, she always seemed in great form. The rest of us girls tried to arrange dates with brothers, escorts at weddings, you know the thing. But she never ... well, she never did click with anyone in our circle. I think she scared the boys off. On the other hand, any number of the girls in our general circle were absolutely mad about Jack. He was younger, but it didn't matter, he was a lovely-looking lad, big, strong, lively. But he had no time for us!"

"Why was that?" James's ears pricked up at the mention of Jack.

"Well, I do recall that he was gone on a girl, as we used to say. She certainly wasn't in our circle. That I do remember. But she was a local girl, from one of the outlying farms around Kilmartin. I can't recall her name; I'm not sure that I ever met her. But wait ... wait ..."

James waited, hopeful.

"Yes ... It was Walsh! In fact, it was the same name as some of my distant cousins in the north. I remember working out at the time if they were related. I have it ... Kathleen Walsh!"

"Do you know if she is still in the area?"

"Oh, I have no idea. It's all so long ago. The things I'm recalling now are from that period of time that seemed so full of high emotion and sudden passions, courtships and engagements and pretty country weddings. But you're closer to that time of one's life than I.

"We were all in the whirlwind days of meeting our partners in life. What I remember is that Kathleen had a huge family of brothers, and that Jack was–unfortunately, in some opinions–mad about Kathleen. Why he or she broke it off, I have no idea. Of course she was Catholic, so her family mightn't have been too keen. I don't suppose

Violet would have been thrilled either. Anyway, one day they were madly in love, and the next day he was gone."

It was midnight when James sat at the small dressing table in his room, quickly jotting down notes of what he had learned from Mrs. Rider. Despite the long day, he felt elated. The cool of the room was stimulating after the warmth of the oak bar. He found his mind racing ... he was enjoying his new role as sleuth.

On reviewing the information he had gleaned, he wondered again at his mental excitement. He was building up a picture of the victim. But what in the end did the doings of Jack Moore at the age of twenty have to do with his death? James sighed. Somewhere in his gut he sensed that the clue lay in the past. He only hoped that it did not lie in Violet's past as well.

Jack, it seemed, had loved Kathleen. And he had gone away. And in all those following years he had never married. Had she been his only love—in all that time? James's thoughts drifted to Hilary.

No! There was no comparison. He could never forget Teresa. He would never forget, either, how she had fallen out of love with him. But had she actually said that? He had bought her ticket. He had waited for her on the platform. And then, at last, she had arrived. Late. And only to tell him she couldn't go, wouldn't go. But he went ahead as planned, on his Siberian Express trip across Russia. Alone. It was only for six weeks, but when he returned she told him she had met another man. God, it was four years now. She was married, she had a family already. And he was here brooding alone, his life on hold. Could it be you only love like that just once? He shook the thought away. He stretched out on the bed and fell asleep dreaming of a big country breakfast.

As James approached the tenth cottage in the row of twelve houses that sat so cozily just a few yards from the lane to Moore's Farm, he smiled. The residents had certainly done a lot with a little. Eileen O'Grady's house, for example, was painted a deep cream and the stone window ledges and door were trimmed in a brick red. James had to bend down to fit his tall frame through the open door.

Eileen gave James a quick tour of her house and extensive garden to the rear. It was a traditional cottage garden, examples of which James had only ever seen at botanical shows. Although it was early spring, much of the garden was a riot of color, provided by daffodils of every shade of yellow, shy primroses, and some early and vivid tulips. The fruit trees were showing blossoms too, especially the cherries. A row of hawthorne trees in white and pink screened the garden from the wind that raced across the open fields at the back. Eileen took great delight in showing James her spuds and onions, already planted in neat rows. Her herb garden, although a bit barren this early in the season, scented the air with its rosemary, chives, and mint.

"I must say these houses are deceptive," said James when they returned to the sitting room. "From the front I thought they would be small indeed!"

Eileen laughed. "Everybody who comes the first time says that, Mr. Fleming; you're not alone. Sit yourself down. These cottages were built in 1820," she said proudly. "The fields at the back hadn't been drained then, and it was marshy, wet land—perfect, it seems, for the growing of flax. There was a mill here, built by a Dutchman, I think. The foundations are still there where it crumbled away. He was an enlightened man and built these cottages for the workers, who grew the flax and prepared it to be made into fine Irish linen."

James noted the signs of nineteenth-century architecture, including the dutch oven beside the fireplace. He noted too the enormous picture of the Sacred Heart with the small red electric light burning in front of it. It was the largest picture in a room full of pictures and photographs. After they were settled, he got to the point of his visit.

"Mr. Fleming, I'd do what I can to help Miss Moore," said Eileen in response, settling her small, chunky print-clad body into the chair. "But all I can tell you is that the knife the police showed to me was the very knife I had used in that kitchen many a day."

"Well, then," said James, "can you say for sure when was the last time you saw it?"

"Indeed and I can. I had bought the family a good-size roast for their Sunday dinner. I put it in the oven myself on Sunday morning when I came in from Mass. It would have been ready with the roast potatoes when Miss Violet and her sisters came in from Morning Prayer."

"And did you serve the dinner?"

"Oh no. On Sundays I only prepare the meal. Lily would do up the vegetables, and Miss Violet always carved the meat, whether it be flesh or fowl."

"And did you see the knife after that, after Sunday?"

"No, I didn't. I clearly remember looking for it when I came back in Sunday evening to do the washing up. I remember knowing there was an empty space in the knife rack on the kitchen counter." She shuddered.

James waited as Eileen pottered out to the kitchen to make tea. His first call in Kilmartin had not been helpful to Violet's case. Eileen, he could see, would make a useful prosecution witness.

"Eileen, I've heard a little about Jack, about Mr. Moore, actually about his early life here in Kilmartin ..."

"Well, now, I didn't know him very well. We were in different social circles in those days–him being a Protestant. O' course I'd see him up and down the lane, maybe goin' for the bus or goin' back and forth with the hay or the silage on the big trucks. Sometimes I'd see him on the tractor crossing over the road to the bottom fields."

"In that event, I suppose you didn't know of his friendship with Kathleen Walsh?"

"Oh, now, we all knew of that around here. My eldest brother, Kieran, hung around with one of the Walsh boys. Oh, it was a big family, sir, five brothers and then a little slip of a girl comin' along at the end of the day. They doted on her, I can tell you. A sweet dark-haired thing. They was fierce jealous when she started going around with Jack. Y'see, the mother was dead. An' the boys, they had got used to her looking after them. They needed a woman on the farm, it's a big working farm, still is, and a crop farm." Eileen refilled his cup and offered him a slice of fruit cake. "And there was another thing. The Walshes, they were Catholic ..."

"And do you think that was the reason that Jack and Kathleen didn't marry?"

"Well, I'll put it this way, neither side was willing to see that wedding take place. Violet certainly did not want the two farms coming together in any way. I do sometimes think that's why she never married herself ..."

"I don't understand."

"Why she never married herself? It's as though she couldn't bear to share the farm, or even expand it by means of marrying into another of the landed families hereabouts."

James cordially continued to listen as Eileen began to talk about her own children, all of them in England now. He could afford to relax a bit, he felt, having found a small piece of the puzzle.

But getting information out of Mr. Sweeney at the post office was another story. James had waited patiently as the old man served his postal customers. He was impressed with the glass-and-steel cage that housed the branch office, and thought to himself at what cost the GPO had installed these up and down the country. Only to be undercut, he smiled wryly, by the likes of Mr. Sweeney, who conducted most of the postal business outside the booth, on the shop counter, scurrying back and forth to get the required stamps and to make change in the separate cash drawer. Sweeney had a huge range of stock, among it items James hadn't seen since he was a child. Boxes of wax firelighters and paraffin sconces. Ten glass bottles filled to the brim with the old-style penny candies and boiled sweets. He had tinned meats, side by side with writing materials, jars of cigars standing on the counter with baskets of fresh eggs from the local farms, slabs of sticky brown gurr cake and unwrapped loaves of bread. The boxes of milk cartons reposed on the neat, even stacks of turf. In a mere twenty square yards Sweeney's shop housed items to meet every possible casual or immediate need. The whole atmosphere gave James a wonderfully strange sense of security.

James couldn't resist buying a chunk of the gurr cake. The sticky taste of molasses, raisins, and currants brought back a happy memory of when he and a boyhood friend with their red lemonade and gurr cake—survival food, they called it—took the train to Killiney one hot summer day and climbed the head where it jutted out into the sea. There they had lain in the grass and counted the Dublin trains as they passed under the tunnel that cut through the granite rock of the tiny finger of land.

The last customer gone, Mr. Sweeney brought James to a small, comfortably furnished back room with two overstuffed chairs and a chintz-covered table, with a set of white-and-blue-striped delft china standing ready for use. The kettle was coming to a boil, and Sweeney proceeded to make a mug of tea strong enough for a mouse to trot across.

James sensed that Mr. Sweeney knew a very great deal about his neighbors past and present. On the one hand, James admired his unwillingness to chat with a total stranger, but on the other, he found his reticence frustrating.

But the sum of what he learned from Mr. Sweeney was directions to the Walsh farm, something James could have discovered for himself. As he was leaving the little room at the back of the shop, Brendan approached in a conspiratorial whisper. While James ostentatiously purchased two local papers and a second slab of gurr cake, Brendan explained his father's attitude.

"Mr. Fleming, I trust that you are only doing your best for Miss Moore. My father's always been a reticent man. It's one way to survive in a country town, as I'm sure you'll appreciate."

"Brendan, anything you can tell me would be a help right now. You must see that as an outsider I am at a loss. Sometimes I might not be asking the right questions, and that's when I need people to offer me information."

Brendan hesitated. "I'm not sure I can tell you any more than my father, except ... well, except the morning they found the body up at the farm, we saw ... I mean ... the hearse was seen."

"What! You actually saw the hearse?" James's enthusiasm was not exactly professional in manner.

Brendan smiled. "Yes. My father and I were here in the shop. Mr. Sinclair and my father saw the hearse turn into the lane and return. At the time, of course, we were curious. But the car was so quick, we thought it had taken a wrong turning. Later we figured that it was the very car that had delivered the coffin we heard about."

"Did you tell the police?"

"No. Unfortunately they didn't question us," Brendan added, disappointed to have been left out of the excitement. "Sean, our postman, had already spoken to them."

"And O'Shea, the detective from Dublin?"

"No, he didn't question us either. We weren't called at the inquest because Sean was, and after all, he had got the better view, I suppose, having followed them on his bike. Mr. Sinclair, now, he felt he'd got a good view, and was only dying to be called at the inquest. But he wasn't. He was quite annoyed."

As James returned to his car, he realized that the police hadn't made much of the hearse. The postman had apparently given his evidence at the inquest, and that was enough for them. James felt discouraged. Perhaps he was beating a dead horse over this issue of the hearse.

He decided then that there was nothing for it but to visit the Walsh farm. The answer was there, he now felt certain. How he would pry out that secret—of that James was less certain.

Brendan smiled as he saw Mr. Sinclair hustling into the shop.

"But why hasn't he called to interview *me*? And where has he disappeared to, that's what I want to know! You are sure, Brendan, that you mentioned I saw the hearse?"

"Well, I said it as clearly as I could," Brendan responded, a little annoyed at Sinclair's inference.

"Whom were you hoping to see?" Mr. O'Dwyer had glided in to the shop and startled both Brendan and Sinclair.

"That Fleming character. I fully expected him to come to question me about the hearse I saw ... we saw."

"Hoping for your moment in the sun, Sinclair?" said O'Dwyer dryly as he waited for Brendan to make up forty-four pence postage out of the odds and ends in his glassine-paged stamp book. Patrons of the branch office rarely got a single stamp in the denomination they required.

"Of course not. I wish only to do my duty."

"Too bad you hadn't thought of that when the inquest was held." O'Dwyer's tone was teasing.

Sinclair's voice rose to a shriek. "I wasn't called to it! How many times do I have to tell you people that?"

"What is it this time?" Three heads swiveled to observe Kevin standing in the open door of the shop. Their curiosity on seeing him was palpable, and Kevin laughed a hearty laugh.

"Recent events have certainly livened up the gossip in this half-barony."

"I don't think that's appropriate, coming from you." Mr. Sinclair drew his thin frame together, distaste in his voice.

"Oh, drop it, Sinclair. You're as nosy as an old cat. And you've a lot of company. Everyone in the row houses is positively demented to know what's going on. Eileen can't walk three feet without being attacked. And Paddy's milk round takes two hours longer to get through, what with one customer after another demanding news."

"Well then, what is the news? You should know, if anybody."

"Ah sure ..." Kevin looked serious for the first time. "Life goes on, as it should. Miss Violet is up to her eyes with the calving. She– We– None of us really talks about it up at the farm. And anyway, she'd hardly discuss it with me." As he talked, Kevin helped Brendan drag out two enormous bags of commercial fertilizer from the corner.

"I'll leave you with this, though it's not news. Miss Violet ... well now, she certainly could kill a fly." Kevin smiled broadly at his own little joke. "And I've seen her put down her dogs over the years, and a horse, without it taking anything out of her. But her brother, now, there's not a snowball's chance in hell of her takin' a knife to her brother."

"You mean you know that for a fact?" Sinclair inquired in his thin voice.

"I know it like my own name. I've worked with her many a year, since I was a lad. I know because I know what family means to her, I know what that farm up there means to her. Do you think she'd jeopardize that farm for anything?" Kevin's face grew florid.

"Then if they're so great on family, why did Lily say what she did?" O'Dwyer's serious voice broke in on Sinclair's mumblings.

"How the hell...?" Kevin dropped the sack on the floor. "Oh, what's the point, everybody knows everything in this place. I suppose Eileen...?"

"Not a'tall. It was Rose herself who told me, after a fashion. I met her at the coop market on Saturday morning. She was full of it, told everyone within earshot. I fear this whole business has pushed her further into that foggy, foggy dew. What does interest me is, how is Violet taking it? Her own sister doing the dirty on her."

"What 'dirty'? Lily merely told the police she thought she saw Violet with a man at the barn."

"A man she said was you!" said Sinclair.

"And which wasn't. For Jaysus sake! That should show how important her statement is. She thought she saw Violet and meself. And I'll tell you it wasn't me. So if the man wasn't me, then maybe the woman wasn't Violet!"

"Interesting, Kevin," remarked Mr. O'Dwyer caustically. "But we know it wasn't you, because there's real evidence. The vet spoke to you. Your wife presumably can vouch for you. And Lily herself said she got your call on the phone."

"Well, I see that the whole village knows all my movements anyway!" said Kevin heatedly. "But that doesn't weaken my argument. My point is, Lily thought it was me until she knew otherwise. She might have done the same over Violet. She might have thought the woman was Violet until she knew otherwise."

"In that event, who was it?"

"How the hell should I know? I'm demented thinkin' about it."

"What does Violet Moore say?"

"I heard she said she was in her room. And of course there's hardly a witness to that."

"I'll tell you what bothers me in this story," Brendan intervened. "It's that Lily didn't wait to speak to Violet whenever she came in from the barn. Wasn't she just dyin' of curiosity? She knew it wasn't Kevin, once she'd got the phone call."

"Well, they don't ..." Kevin hesitated, conscious he was about to say too much about the family that employed him. He tossed the bag of fertilizer over his shoulder, preparing to leave. "I'll tell you this," he added, red in the face, and not from exertion. "I don't know how people live in this blasted village. What goes on behind their own front door is nobody's business ..."

"Naiveté doesn't suit you, Kevin," O'Dwyer cut in.

"All right. I'll just finish this. Things aren't what they seem ..."

"Humph!" exclaimed Brendan, and then coughed to cover it.

"Miss Violet and Miss Lily, they're not as thick as we'd all like to think, if you take my meaning?"

"Are you telling us that Lily wouldn't have asked Violet what she was doing talking to a man in the barn at twelve-thirty at night?" said Sinclair.

"Well, at least not straight away."

Mr. O'Dwyer moved to the door and held it open for Kevin to carry out the sacks. "It's all right, Kevin," he said, defusing the tension. "We believe you, when thousands wouldn't."

"I'll tell you this," said Kevin, still striving to have the last word. "They all carry on exactly as before. Miss Violet, now, she's gone a bit thin and grim-faced. But other than that, I see the three of them at morning coffee. And when I take my dinner in the kitchen, they chat or not, as the case may be, exactly as before. Rose and Violet were loading the truck this morning 'cause Paddy's boy was sick and it was business as usual." And with that, Kevin escaped through the door.

As those neighbors chatted and gossiped, Violet at that moment was seated at the fire, alone in her sitting room. It was true. She had striven very hard to maintain a semblance of normalcy. But inwardly she was tired. Very tired. She glanced across at Lily, seated at the desk, running up the weekly milk bills to be delivered with the milk early the next morning. Neither had yet spoken of the extraordinary information Lily had freely offered O'Shea.

"The Feeneys haven't paid their bill in six weeks," Lily said from the corner.

"I hear there's a new baby in that house," replied Violet.

"Shall I leave it awhile, then ..."

"Mmm, they're old customers. I should think we could carry them a bit, don't you?"

"Have you decided about the fete?" murmured Lily, still busy at her books.

"I think we should leave it ... for this year." Violet's voice held a sigh. Ever since her father's time there had been a summer fete on the grounds of the Moore farm, barring the year her mother died. They had always raised a goodly sum for the church restoration fund.

"I think that's a mistake," said Lily matter-of-factly. "It will only give rise to even more talk."

"But people will merely come to peep and pry ..."

"I think you underestimate your neighbors. It's a month away yet. Talk is dying down already, I suspect. No one coming to the fete will be ignorant of the situation. It's not as though we draw crowds from far and wide ..." Lily's voice held an unspoken question.

"All right, don't cancel it yet. I'll think about it a little longer."

Violet surprised herself. It was seldom that she was so indecisive. Perhaps the situation was exacting its toll on her after all, sapping her energies.

She was almost glad Fleming had called, even if it had only been a lightning visit. Arrogant and impertinent though he was, at least he was trying to help, more robustly than it was likely Gerald Fitzgerald would have done. He probably wouldn't have had the time nor the inclination. Wedded to his law books, she thought bitterly. Always the same. Drawn to the big city, the bright lights, and the theatre of the law. He'd be as much at sea here in Wexford now as the smart-aleck Dubliner. She had been right all those years ago. Fitzgerald's heart never lay with the land. She could remember the resentment in every line of his body when he was put to the haying each summer on his father's farm. Those had been good days. She had loved going to the local farms to help with the haying. Turn and turn about. The young people would come to Moore's to help as well. It was a shame the way all these modern machines had killed off those happy times. Now a tenth of that number could accomplish the haying, and in half the time. The dances had been good too. Fitzgerald was always there, but he seemed then to have eyes only for Lily. Maiden spinster Lily. That would never have worked. And she had been proved right about Fitzgerald when he sold the farm after his father's death, despite the fact that there had been a depression and prices were bad. She remembered that Lily had not been pleased when she had beat him down and bought half his fields for next to nothing. But it had been important to expand the farm at that time.

Typical Fitzgerald. Couldn't be bothered to come back to Kilmartin himself, so he had sent his protégé. Young Mr. Fleming—wet behind the ears. And now he was off to visit the Walshes. She hadn't seen any of them in years. All that nonsense was in the past, buried in the past.

She rested her head in her hands and sighed. Then she felt Lily's eyes on her and straightened her back. It wouldn't do to give way in front of Lily. Not now.

The Walshes. It wasn't to their advantage either—to speak of that ancient business. And what could it have to do with this present mare's nest? Fleming certainly seemed pleased as punch with that theory of his. But it was preposterous. The enthusiasm of an amateur and a fool. She stirred restlessly. Perhaps it would have been better to discourage him. But then she was certain that would whet his curiosity further. She shivered. She seemed to hear the rattling of old bones in the closet.

James had devised a plan of sorts while he drove, but as he approached the long lane to the Walshes' farm, he grew apprehensive.

Now, four short, wiry men the color of acorns, and all remarkably resembling each other, watched him approach. He had had difficulty finding them. There had been no answer to his ring at the bell, and he had had to clamber through the muck in the yard, ruining his black wingtips in the process. They stood silently, staring not too inquisitively as he walked toward them.

James felt a chill up his spine. The sun had sunk behind the outbuildings, and although there was light in the pale blue and orange sky, there was no warmth in the air. He glanced at their faces and realized if his hunch was right, he could be looking at the face of a ruthless murderer. But which face? Which of these four stern faces held a secret from the others? Or were they all involved? His thoughts were fragmented as he introduced himself.

"Fleming. James Fleming. I'm Miss Violet Moore's solicitor. Would you mind if I ask you a few questions?" James offered his hand, but when no one took it, he dropped it to his side.

"Concernin' what?" said one of the four nut-brown men. James had difficulty understanding a much thicker Wexford accent than he had encountered up till now.

"Well, I think you probably heard about the death—rather, the murder—of Jack Moore."

Four heads nodded almost imperceptibly.

"I was wondering if you might have any information to give me," said James simply. He found he could no more be subtle with these men than he could plough a straight furrow.

The one who seemed to be the eldest waved James into the barn. With trepidation James followed them, and like them, took a seat on a bale of straw.

"You'll find no sympathy here, Mistur Fleming. Jack Moore was a dead man to this family for more than twenty-five year'. There's nothin' that any of us can tell ya."

"If you'll just permit me to ask a few questions, then. About the past ..." The four men glanced at each other and then gave the slightest of nods. The eldest, for that was how James perceived him, spoke for them all.

"It depends," he said laconically.

"Depends?" murmured James.

"On the question."

"I need to know a little about Jack's, em ... Jack's friendship with your sister. In fact I'd like to speak with her if I could."

There was a long silence as the eldest Walsh brushed the straw off his striped navy wool jacket. For a few moments James thought that he hadn't been heard.

"Mr. Fleming, Jack Moore came damn near to ruinin' our Kathleen's life. If it hadn't been for him, the darlin' girl would be with us still ..." He smiled slightly at James's look of alarm. "Our sister is in London."

Another brother spoke with some bitterness. "Aye. And she's married to some pommie bastard too. To my mind that Jack Moore did ruin her life. She was so embarrassed when he took off, without a word to her. One day he was here fillin' her head with grand promises of her life with him, how they'd be livin' up at the big house, how she'd never have to dirty her pretty little hands again. As if waitin' on him was a privilege compared to lookin' after us. One day he was here, and the next day he was gone. No girl could put up with that, what with the neighbors whisperin' and all."

"And you've no idea why he just picked up and left, in the middle of things, so to speak?" asked James, puzzled by this bit of new information. Somehow the pieces weren't falling into place as he had hoped. "Surely they kept in touch? He must have come back at some time, or written to her?"

"We had our suspicions all right," offered the eldest brother. "We knew she'd gone up the big house to see the sisters, but Violet Moore told her some story or other. And then one day she too was gone. She left us a letter that she'd gone to London with a girlfriend and not to worry. There was nothin' to do about it. We accepted she was gone."

"Can you tell me, is this the source of the bad blood between yourselves and the Moores?"

"You might say that."

"Do you know if Jack and your sister got together again in London?"

"Not likely. About two years later she wrote to say she was getting married to some medical student and asked if any of us would come over for the weddin'. But there was too much to do here at the farm ..."

"And has she been back?"

"Not a'tall. She's a family of her own. She sends the odd card and photo but ... ah, she's dead to us now."

James felt suddenly, oddly depressed. He was tired of these stories of departure, of partings that weren't really partings but escapes, flight from one type of loneliness to another.

The brothers stood up with one accord, and James followed them lethargically out of the barn.

"You wouldn't by any chance still have her address, would you?"

"It's in the kitchen drawer," said the eldest brother. "Billy will get it for you."

James was surprised. Were they simply trying to get rid of him? He copied the address from the crumpled piece of paper, thanked them with a nod, and returned through the muddy yard to his car.

Human warmth and the sound of animated voices, food for his belly and pints for his soul—that's what was needed now, James decided. He turned his car into the car park of the Drooping Well. He shook off the chill of the day and of his unfruitful conversation with the Walshes and seated himself in a cozy corner. The sausage rolls, heated for a minute in the microwave at the bar, seemed like a full-course meal to his hunger. He was just ordering another when Mr. Sinclair slithered to his side.

"A word, Mr. Fleming?"

"By all means, Mr. Sinclair, I've been meaning to speak to you." He was amused at the beam that lit up Sinclair's face.

James listened attentively and sipped his pint in comfort as Sinclair told him in minute detail of what he had witnessed the morning of the discovery of the body, including a detailed description of the hearse, its silver filigree and its unusual opaque windows.

Satisfied with the information, James turned the conversation to other things. He had recognized in Sinclair the gossip of the most useful sort. Willing to talk but not to embroider.

"Tell me, Mr. Sinclair, if you can, the meaning of the extraordinary name of this pub?"

Sinclair smiled and launched into his story.

"It's a short story, really, but most amusing. The pub used to simply be called Murphy, after the owner and his son after him. But Tom Murphy decided not only to improve the interior—the evidence of that eclectic style you see before you—he also decided to improve the exterior and give it a more memorable name than the name it was known by. He came up with the name of the Dropping Well on account of the well out back, but his wife, who had a sense of humor and was a bit piqued at her husband's recent performance after a few pints, altered the name on the order docket for the sign makers. The sign makers, who, let's face it, must have had a sense of humor also, never questioned Murphy. And the damage was done! But the name caused such an amount of fun here in the pub and in the vicinity that Murphy had the good grace to let it stand. As he said, as a warning to all the other husbands who came in to the pub for a drink!"

James and Sinclair had a good laugh together, and the mood was comfortable. James sipped his pint and stored the tale in his memory. It would bear repeating.

"I'm just amazed that the Walshes talked to you." Sinclair's voice broke in on his thoughts.

"Why is that?"

"Surely you've heard that story?" His voice rose with enthusiasm.

"I know that Jack Moore left Kathleen standing at the altar, so to speak. And that she went to go and live in London, and she married there." James smiled. "The Walsh brothers certainly seemed put out by the fact she abandoned them to look after themselves."

"Is that all you know?"

"Mmmm." James watched silently as the barman put up the shutters and lowered the lights. He checked his watch. Damn, he thought, closing time. And yet he observed that nobody moved. The barman locked the door. After a few minutes the pub's patrons started ordering their pints in earnest. James leaned back and relaxed. It would be a good long night's drinking for the locals now.

Sinclair settled comfortably to his second hot whiskey. He virtually licked his lips as he launched into his story.

"Ah, now we all remember the night Jack left Kilmartin. But the Walshes remember it most of all. There'd been trouble brewing for a long time, as I told you. This night it was very crowded here in the pub. It was old Tom Murphy's place then. It was a very warm night. Virtually everyone here had been at the haying all day, and the rest of us had been at the horse trials. People were tired but in great form. The sun had been splitting the stones for days.

"There had been a bit of singing, a lot of chat, and more than a lot of drinking. Jack was at the bar, full of himself, tellin' one and all who'd listen how he and Kathleen were gettin' married soon, and that Violet and the Walshes would just have to get used to the idea.

"Remembering back, I'm sure now that he knew Mike Walsh was within hearing. Suddenly, like a pot coming to boil, voices were raised. Mike—he was the second brother—went for Jack. He was pretty tipsy, and wild in any case. As I say, he went for Jack. People pulled him off Jack. Old Tom had got the stick ready, but he didn't need it. He and the barboy dragged Mike out, but everyone heard him."

"Heard him?" said James anxiously.

"We, all of us, heard him say he would get Jack. That no snot-nosed Protestant would marry his sister. That he'd kill him first."

"We all knew that it was the drink talking. Jack was shaken a bit at first, but then laughed it off. Or so we thought. I clearly remember that Jack stayed on for a few more pints and then rolled off home, as merry as ever."

"As it turned out, the next day the Walshes came to the pub. They were looking for Mike. They said he hadn't been home all night and they assumed he returned to the pub. You could drink all night in those days—much as we're doing now."

James took the hint and ordered another round, but he drank slowly, concentrating on Sinclair's remarkable story.

"Mike Walsh was missing all that day. In the end, one of the hired help found his body out in a field that had already been cut. It was in a narrow stream that divides two of the Moores' fields. Lying there at the bottom, the body couldn't be seen from the lane. The chap who found him had been cutting across the field to another where they were working. He was a young lad and he got an awful shock. Apparently Mike was lying as he had fallen, face forward, his arms spread out on either side. There were bruises on his head and face, and he had died from a blow to his head. There was some talk that he had really drowned, that lying unconscious in the water, he had swallowed water and drowned there." Sinclair shook his head sadly.

"There was a lot of drinking at the wake and a lot of speculation as to why Mike was in the Moore's field at all. I was there for part of the wake, but it went on all day and night. The Walsh boys got plastered and went looking for Jack Moore. They swore it had to have been him that did it. The police had found a rock covered with blood, near the body. But they still had ruled it an accident: that Mike had been cutting across the field in the dark, intent on carrying out his threat to kill Jack. And with drink taken, he must have lost his footing and fallen into the stream, hitting his head as he fell. Almost everyone except the Walshes seemed to accept that. The Walshes believed that Jack had fought with Mike and pushed him in the stream and left him there to die.

"A few of us followed the Walsh boys up to the Moores'. We knew that Violet and the sisters were alone there.

"There was a powerful scene on the front steps. The Walshes demanded to see Jack, but Violet wasn't having it. A lot of words were said in the heat of the moment, but she finally demanded they leave or she'd get the police. Then Danny, who was a farmhand there at the time, came to the front door with a shotgun. They never did get to see Jack ... I must say Violet looked magnificent that day. She was in her full health and youth, her eyes flashing and her hair blowing in the wind. Facing down those wild Walsh boys, she was a woman to be reckoned with, and there's no mistake."

Sinclair paused, saving his best till last. He ordered another whiskey and James a pint of stout while James fidgeted. At last the drinks came.

"It transpired that ... Jack had left Kilmartin. In fact, he had left Ireland. None of us knew what to think. The Walshes, of course, swore that it was a sure sign that Jack had murdered Mike and fled the country. But the police had questioned Violet, and she had told them that Jack had come directly home that night from the pub. They had been able to check the times Mike left and when Jack had left. Jack had been at home with Violet at the time the doctor said that Mike had died. There were no other signs of a fight and no witnesses.

"Violet brassed it out. She said that Jack had not gone that night, but rather the next day. That he'd heard about Mike's death and he didn't want to cause the Walshes any more grief. She claimed he'd said that if he hadn't been joking about Kathleen in the pub, Mike wouldn't have lost his temper.

"Violet explained that obviously Mike had been on his way to confront Jack, and being drunk, had fallen into the stream. But that Jack felt so bad, he wanted no more to do with the family. She went on about how he was just a young lad, that he'd never really been serious about Kathleen ... which of course served to enrage the Walshes even more. At the time, she seemed to make sense. Jack was young, and wild. We even thought that perhaps he had got in over his head with Kathleen, and that he had seen a way out of the marriage and tying up with a family where there'd always be bad blood."

James sat back, astonished at what he'd just heard. "And was that it?"

"Pretty much. At the time, we all supposed that Jack would come back in six months, or a year at most. That he'd wait until things died down and then return to the farm. And in the way of things, we all gradually forgot about him. Except the Walshes. They continued to claim that Jack Moore had killed their brother. When Kathleen went off, it just cemented their bitterness. They keep to themselves and ... well, you've seen them for yourself."

James was glad of Sinclair's invitation to spend the night. The local bed-and-breakfast was in darkness, and he knew he couldn't drive to Riders, having drunk over the legal limit. He walked with Sinclair the mile to the house, and as he walked, he considered what he had just heard. He realized that the Walshes might indeed have been willing to give him Kathleen's address in London—just to distract him, to get him off their trail.

His heart lifted as he looked out over the somnolent fields. He glanced up the hills and wondered in which field Mike Walsh had died. This was a major breakthrough. Here at last was a tie-in, a motive for someone to have killed Jack Moore on his return to Ireland after twenty-seven years. A believable motive. For James knew that in Ireland there was seldom a more powerful motive for murder than revenge.

Chapter Five

At first I thought that this Walsh story was a bit farfetched," commented Gerald, getting up from his desk and stretching his arms to meet behind his back. "But I'm growing more intrigued as you talk!"

He turned abruptly and faced James. "I suppose you've heard the office gossip?" Gerald indicated his chest with the stem of his pipe. "There is no call for alarm, and I don't want our clients getting wind of it."

"To be honest, Gerald, I've heard two or three versions from the staff already. What did happen when I was in Wexford?"

"A turn, as they say. Even I thought it was the end. But Dr. Barry at St. Vincent's assured me it was a terrific attack of indigestion. The old ticker will be fine. I just have to watch the angina."

James returned Gerald's smile and, with him, shrugged off the news of his attack. But privately he wondered at Gerald's gray color and his lack of animation. He looked older today than his fifty-five years. As if he had read his thoughts, Gerald came around from behind the desk, sat in the easy chair beside James, and rested his head on the chair back.

"I'll tell you this, James. The attack scared me. When I was lying at home in bed—couldn't sleep of course—I had some time for reflection. Scenes from my childhood in Kilmartin came back to me as vividly as this conversation. Rural Ireland is a very different kind of environment in which to grow to manhood. I imagine you've picked up on some of that difference even in your short stay in Wexford? It's not that values are so very different. But aspirations are. The sense of pride is stronger. The land is full of contradictions. The people hold on to their privacy to the point of obsession. Yet at the same time they are always self-conscious in the real sense of the word ... always aware of living their lives out in a public arena, a theatre where all the players are known by name, where the actors and the audience constantly change places with one another. Oh, the scrutiny!" Gerald stared out the window, as the faint noise of traffic in Merrion Square reached them.

James considered Gerald's words. Although he had traveled to apparently exotic places which had served to point up the larger contrasts between Ireland and other countries, he had never looked at Ireland in this way. Chagrined, he realized that he had adhered to the stale generalizations that people applied to his own country. He knew the timetables of trains in Italy. He knew the timetables of trains in Ireland. But what of it? Had he seen the people and had he come to know them?

"I'm not sure what you're driving at, Gerald," he said at last.

"It was your mention of the Walshes. Believe it or not, the name triggered off the strangest memory. But I see that it is just of a piece. Confined to bed as I was, I had time to cast my mind back to those early days in Kilmartin. And the Walshes now are fresh in my mind. I used to play handball with one of the Walsh boys."

"Then can you also remember when Mike Walsh died?" James asked, astonished at this coming together of apparently diverse connections.

"Yes, actually, I do now. There was a tremendous amount of speculation. I was a student at Trinity when the whole incident took place.
But on weekends at home–the odd time I returned–there was still talk."

"Did you believe that Jack Moore had killed Walsh?"

"No, not for a minute. But I do remember that there were a lot of
questions as to what Mike Walsh had been doing in that field."

James was insistent. "Don't you see? The significant feature is what
the Walshes believed and might still believe about Jack Moore. The
location of the body in that field on Moore's Farm may have served
to convince the Walshes that Jack did indeed kill their brother, despite
the fact you say that the police considered his death an accident. It
strengthens my theory that they held a grudge–for years–awaiting an
opportunity to strike back at Jack."

Gerald caught some of James's enthusiasm. "I see your point, and
I'm glad of it. Sheridan may be able to use the implications of what
you're saying to throw some doubt on Violet's motives–by shifting
attention to the motives of the Walsh family. It could be enough to
plant the idea in a jury's mind. I'll put through a call to Sheridan now
and give him what we've got. He was on to me yesterday. It seems
that the Director of Prosecutions has nearly completed the Book of
Evidence. He will be approaching the High Court this week, looking
for the case to be put on the docket for June. You see, my boy, we
only have the months of April and May to gather as much evidence
as we can for Sheridan. I want you to give this case top priority.
Let's have a look at your calendar and see what we can do to clear
the decks."

James let himself in to his own spacious and comfortably decorated
flat. Switching on the gas fire he poured himself a brandy and sat
heavily in his swing leather chair.

He couldn't shake his present mood, nor did he want to. He sat
back letting the myriad images of the past few days rush into his
mind, seeking for the key to his depression. He had grown almost
used to these moods–if not black then certainly dark brown–overtaking him, ever since his breakup with Teresa. But this time the
mood took on a different aspect, and he sensed it was because the
source was different.

Sinclair. Was it Sinclair? James had been surprised at the evidence
of prosperity in his home, although the man's taste was most definitely
austere. Sinclair had inherited money. And by investing it safely and

wisely, he had made money. He could satisfy all his wants, and with each passing year, as James guessed, his eccentricities had intensified.

And Gerald. Gerald depressed him as well. He had seemed so negative about his early years in Kilmartin. And now a widower with no children. Empty houses full of empty rooms.

Silence filled his own sitting room. Was he going down the same road? he wondered as he opened his briefcase. The question remained unanswered as he finally settled down to his work.

James's mood was markedly different when, at eight A.M. exactly, the 737 lifted off the runway in a perfect takeoff. He smiled as he leaned back in his seat and accepted a drink from the Aer Lingus hostess. The last few days at the office had been productive. He had freed up some of his billable time and concurred with Gerald that a personal visit to Kathleen Walsh Banks was certainly in order. And now London, one of his favorite cities, lay ahead, holding the answer, he believed, to the questions surrounding Jack Moore's life and death. Surely it must be Kathleen who could establish for him once and for all the fatal connection between her brothers and Jack Moore.

At Heathrow Airport James indulged himself by renting a Jaguar, and was in the outskirts of London in record time. He checked into the small, comfortable hotel and as he quickly unpacked, wondering yet again at the Walsh brothers' willingness to give him their sister's address. But for all that suspicion, he was grateful. Tracking her down under her married name after more than twenty years would have taken more time than they could afford, now that the trial date had been fixed for June fifteenth.

The day was still young, only eleven A.M. James sat on his bed, took out his notes, and checked Kathleen's address. He knew London well, and her home was a mere half hour's drive in traffic. He had already decided not to phone her. The element of surprise was too important.

And suddenly James knew he could not justify putting off the evil hour any longer. If he was to see Kathleen alone, it made sense to try to visit her during the day.

Driving south, out toward Wimbledon, he tried to organize his thoughts. But his incipient dread of this meeting only increased as he approached the intersection that his map indicated would lead him to Buttonwood Road. His palms were sweating as he parked the car at the corner of the street. Eyes peering from behind curtains did not need to see a stranger emerge from a Jaguar at Mrs. Banks's very door. He walked slowly down the road, glancing surreptitiously at the numbers on the doors of the neat, prosperous brick-fronted terraced houses. As number 89 neared, he tried to compose himself in the manner of an insurance agent. He was sorry he didn't have a case of samples to disguise his approach. Wildly he thought that perhaps she wouldn't be home, perhaps she worked, perhaps he wouldn't have to fulfill what he now realized was a rather unpleasant mission.

Kathleen Banks opened the door at the first ring. James would have known her for a Walsh—she was small and wiry, fit and brown, with a strong look of her brothers. But she was also meticulously dressed and groomed, her dark hair gleaming in the watery London sunshine.

"Mrs. Banks?" James asked after a brief hesitation.

"Yes?" she replied, suspicion in her voice, her eyes swiftly glancing to see if he carried a sample case or a Bible or copies of the *Watchtower*. She closed the door slightly, shielding herself.

"My name is James Fleming. I am a solicitor with the Dublin firm of Fitzgerald's." James spoke quickly as he observed her expression grow guarded. "Please, Mrs. Banks, your brothers in Kilmartin gave me your address. I must speak to you."

Suddenly she became conscious of how long he had been on the step. She glanced up and down the road, and then through clenched teeth said, "I will allow you to step into the hall, but you must show me some identification."

In the small, bare foyer she glanced at James's business card and at his driver's license and even scrutinized his passport.

"This way," she said finally, and walked stiffly into the sitting room. "Please sit down. I can only give you a very few minutes. I have another appointment." With this she glanced through the white curtains that draped the large picture window.

"This is rather awkward, Mrs. Banks, and may well take more than a few minutes." He turned aside from the anger and fear in Kathleen Walsh's face. Taking out his notebook, for want of something to do with his hands, he glanced unnecessarily at a few pages. Still she didn't sit, but stood as if holding herself together with her tightly folded arms.

"I am representing a Miss Violet Moore in a legal matter." James watched her reaction, trying to gauge his next step, but she looked toward the window.

"Go on," she said finally.

"Believe me, Mrs. Banks, I wouldn't have troubled you except for the fact that this truly is a matter of life and death."

"Whose life? Whose death?" Kathleen hissed, gathering herself together as if coiling to spring.

"Violet Moore's life. Jack Moore's death."

He waited, but she didn't speak, didn't question his extraordinary statement.

He tried again. "Mrs. Banks, I understand that your connection with Ireland is long broken. But the events I need to ask you about happened many years ago, before you left Kilmartin. I believe that if you could answer some questions for me, you may well help us build a case that would serve to clear my client's name."

"Violet Moore's name?" Kathleen smirked and stopped herself. "I haven't heard her name in twenty-seven years." Her face reddened. "Yes, I can tell you she was proud of her name. But surely you know that by now."

James was surprised at the vehemence in her voice. She stared down at her fingers, pushing the cuticles back fiercely but absentmindedly.

"You said just now, something about her life and Jack Moore's death?" she asked. James nodded. "I take it then that Jack ... Jack Moore is ... dead?"

"Yes, he is."

"Does this have something to do with his will, then?" Alarm filled her face. "Does it? Is there something in his will that ... relates to me or someone else?"

"I'm not at liberty to discuss the will at this time," James said, trying to keep her interest. But he failed.

"Mr. Fleming, I know that as a solicitor what is said to you in confidence is nearly as sacred as what a doctor might hear ... therefore I tell you I do not want my husband or children to know anything of your visit or our conversation. This issue is closed." She moved abruptly toward the door.

"Mrs. Banks. Believe me"—a certain sympathy filled James's face and voice—"I would never harm you. What I need to know are the details of the night that your brother Michael died."

Kathleen's face was blank, as though she hadn't heard him.

"Mike, your brother. Do you remember that there was talk that Jack Moore was involved?"

"Jack Moore, is it? He was nothing, nothing but a boyo, that's what we called them then. One of the lads ... He left Kilmartin at that time.

Went off to make his fortune in the big wide world. And did he?"
She looked sharply at James. "Did he make his fortune and go back to
the big house and live it up in fine style with his county friends and
his county relatives?"

"Well, he made a great deal of money."

"And Violet? You said she was your client. Trying to break the will,
is she, trying to do his children out of their money?" Bitterness welled
up in her, overpowering her. She closed her eyes then, shaking her
head.

"I can't help you, Mr. Fleming. Mike died. Jack left. Violet stayed.
That's all I know—and you, no doubt, know all that already."

Disappointed, James stood up and walked with her to the doorway.
"Jack Moore is dead. Yes. But he was murdered ..."

"Sacred Heart of Jesus ... leave me, leave me alone." Kathleen covered her face with both hands.

He saw his chance and took it.

"Kathleen. Listen to me." He spoke rapidly, urgently. "There are no
children. Jack Moore never married. Never had family. His corpse was
found in a pauper's coffin dumped on his sister Violet's doorstep.
Listen to me! He'd only been back in Ireland a few days. That is why
I'm here. To discover who wanted Jack Moore dead."

It was some time before she composed herself. At last she sat down
and indicated to James to do likewise.

"Mr. Fleming," she said finally, "first I want you to tell me about
Jack Moore's will. Am I mentioned? Or anyone I might know?" Kathleen's face was hard again, and the line of her jaw tightened, making
her look less the English housefrau and more the Irish harridan.

James was surprised by the question, but he answered it. "I can't
reveal the contents to you, but I think I can tell you that you were
not," he lied smoothly.

"Then I say again, I cannot help you."

"But Mrs. Banks, Violet Moore is my client. She is being charged
with murder. You must see how unlikely that is. A woman such as
she—"

"Hah! A woman such as she indeed. That's my point exactly. I
wouldn't lift a finger to help her, even if it were in my power—which
I assure you it is not."

"But surely ..." James paused at a loss, "you wouldn't want an
innocent woman to be punished. More than that, surely you would
want Jack Moore's murderer to be caught."

"Let me be straight with you. I loved Jack Moore. And I foolishly thought he loved me. But he didn't. He left me, well, virtually at the altar."

"You were to be married?"

"Well, we would have married, I was fairly certain of that at the time, but ... he left Kilmartin and circumstances changed."

"Mrs. Banks, that's precisely what I need you to tell me about. I know there was some talk that Jack had quarreled with your brother ... talk that he had perhaps even caused his death—accidentally or intentionally. Didn't you feel anything then or since? Didn't you wonder that Mike might have been killed by your ... fiancé?"

"No! No, no, no. How could I think that, for Jesus' sake? I never believed Jack had anything to do with poor Mick's death. I just figured that he fell in his drunken state. It wouldn't have been the first time. But I think you're driving at something. I would prefer you to be straight with me." She waited, calmer now. "It seems to me that you have someone on your mind—someone who might have wanted to kill Jack. Tell me—who?"

"It has occurred to me, Kathleen, that your own brothers might have believed that Jack killed Mike that night in the field. They ... indicated to me that they blamed Jack for your leaving Ireland ..."

"For my leaving them, more like," she interposed.

"Well, yes. They feel he ruined your life and possibly killed their brother. Surely there is a reason that Jack Moore was killed in Kilmartin, where he was born and bred—and not in Dublin or America. It stands to reason that it was someone in Kilmartin who hated Jack."

"Mr. Fleming, you're more naive than you look. Are you seriously asking me to clear Violet Moore of this charge of murder by shifting the blame to my own brothers? That is what you're trying to say, isn't it? That my brothers bore a grudge against Jack for twenty-odd years. For Mick's death and my leaving them. And that the moment his feet touched Irish soil, they murdered him? Do you seriously think that even if they were guilty as hell, I would trade their lives for Violet Moore's worthless existence?"

"With or without your help, I will find the person who killed Jack Moore."

"Let it go."

"No, Kathleen, I will find the truth. No matter how much digging, no matter how much raking up of the ancient past."

"Is the past never to be dead and buried?" Kathleen's voice was now almost pleading.

"No!" James wondered at his own obsession. Not until now had he realized how committed he was to this pursuit. And not because he believed in Violet Moore's innocence. Or now even in her worthiness.

"Violet Moore is innocent."

"Innocent, is it? Ah, Mr. Fleming, it's all in how you define that word!"

"If she didn't kill Jack—and I believe that she didn't, although she'll say nothing in her own defense—then she's innocent."

"Oh, she's guilty all right!" Kathleen said, her voice hissing. "And I can tell you that she'll say nothing to defend herself because she knows her own guilt. She lives with it every day, and has for twenty-seven years."

"Kathleen." James turned and faced her. "If you know Violet is guilty, then tell me that at least. This truly is in confidence. It would help me to know if she killed Jack, even though I am committed to her defense. Perhaps ... perhaps there were extenuating circumstances. I don't know. But I will know the truth."

They sat in silence for what seemed hours.

At last Kathleen turned toward him. "Before I speak to you, you must swear, professionally and as an honorable man, that you will not reveal to a soul what I am going to tell you."

Desperate, James swore to her satisfaction. But he was uneasy.

"I am only telling you this now because I realize that in your determination to find the truth, you may come upon a fact that could destroy many lives." She paused and then continued. "Jack Moore and I were very much in love. In love the way seventeen-year-olds can be, passionately and foolishly. I was foolish, and I found that I was expecting our baby. It was early on, and I told Jack straight away. It took the wind out of his sails for a few days, but he came around. We had talked of marrying all along in that idle way, ignoring the differences in our background, and our religion." She stopped and peered at James. "Have things changed at all ... in Ireland I mean?"

James shook his head.

"Not in two decades?"

"No," said James simply.

"No," she said sadly, "I suppose not."

"Go on," James urged.

"What he said was that he would speak to Violet. He knew she'd go mad, but he was the real boyo, and the farm was one quarter his, as he always told me. Ah, he was full of talk, but I was willing to believe in it then, and in him.

"There was terrible trouble that morning when Mick hadn't come home and then when he was found dead. The house was in an awful state. The brothers were crazy with grief. Outsiders wouldn't have seen it, but we were a close family then and it was ... it was a terrible shock."

"It must have been," James murmured.

"There were the police, of course, and then the arrangements for the wake and the funeral. I didn't see Jack at all. I was at home the whole time cooking and cleaning and sitting with the body. And there was no one sympathetic to my knowing Jack. No one brought me news of him in that house. Jack didn't come, but I didn't expect him to. He wasn't welcome in my home at the best of times. I heard the talk that he was involved, but I never believed it. I figured he was keeping out of the way. But then after the funeral, I heard talk that he had left home ... I waited for word of him and got none. Finally I was so desperate for news, I went up to the manor to speak with Violet Moore."

Kathleen stopped and looked away.

"To be brief, Mr. Fleming, she told me that she knew about the baby. And that Jack was gone to London, that he had run away from his responsibilities, as she put it. I was only seventeen, and I panicked. My brothers would never have me if they knew about the baby. My mother was dead, God rest her soul, and Jack was gone to London. Violet said she'd help me. And she did, as I thought at the time. She made all the arrangements, told me what to say. Just before I started to show, she took me to a convent down in the country, where the nuns looked after bad girls like me. And when the time came, the nuns—with her encouragement, no doubt—arranged for a family to adopt my baby ... my baby girl." Tears rolled down Kathleen's face and she didn't brush them away. "I wasn't allowed to meet them. I wasn't allowed to know any details. I wasn't even allowed to say good-bye ..."

"Did you ever...?"

"No, I never saw her again. I never had word of her. I left as soon as it was all over, and I came here, to London, and here I am still. Violet had told me to go to Australia and had even given me the fare. But I didn't have the courage ... it was too far, too far from all I'd ever known."

"It must have been very lonely for you."

"Save your pity. I have a good marriage. And two fine sons. Which is why, Mr. Fleming, I swore you to secrecy. No one except Violet Moore knew this story. And Jack. Not my husband, not my sons. Not even my brothers. And no one must ever know. It would destroy the peace and happiness I've worked so hard for ..." She stared at James. "I was afraid that if you pressed Violet Moore for details, she'd reveal all this to you. But now even if she does, I have your solemn oath that you will never use it."

"Yes, you do," said James reluctantly. "May I ask you this? When you questioned me so closely about the will, were you...?"

"Oh, God, it wasn't for myself, if that's what you mean. I wondered for a few moments if maybe Jack had mentioned our child in his will. I thought perhaps, perhaps ..."

"That he had remembered her, thought of her during all those years?" said James.

She nodded. "One more thing, Mr. Fleming, if ... if in your pursuit of truth you learn anything of my little girl, would you please let me know somehow, someday. And on your oath promise me that if you do, you will never betray me to her? I've been betrayed too often in my life."

"Are you sure, Kathleen? Don't you want to...?"

"No!" Kathleen interrupted emphatically. "Never! I assure you. Let me be dead to her. But she will never be dead to me, please God." She shivered.

"Then I promise."

For the first and only time, she smiled at him. A lovely, warm smile that lit her face from within and showed him what perhaps the real Kathleen was like—with her husband, her sons, her own friends. He wondered at himself as they parted on the steps that he had not had the sense to place Kathleen in his imagination as a woman with a full life, and not merely a factor in a situation that was long dead if not buried. Once again he felt like the specter at the feast.

The afternoon flight back to Dublin had been dreary. As James sought out his car in the long-term car park, a fine, heavy drizzle began to fall, drenching his hair and shoulders even as he stood unlocking the car. There was nothing more dismal than Dublin Airport in the rain, he thought crankily, unless it was Shannon Airport in the rain. Why tourists didn't turn and run at such a climatic greeting he never knew.

The highway was empty and equally dreary. James's thoughts turned to Kathleen as he drove. Had he really learned anything or was he just fooling himself?

He turned down Dorset Street and into the top of O'Connell Street. The mass of wet shoppers bustling at the Henry Street crossing looked dowdy and drawn after the glamor of London. Grim faces bent into the rain and wind. Suddenly he wanted out. Out of Ireland, out of his job, out of the messy situation that he saw brewing ahead like the storm clouds that brooded over the Dublin Mountains.

Chapter Six

Shocking! Absolutely disgraceful!" Sinclair addressed the air, thinking he was alone outside the forlorn-looking shop.

"Talking to yourself again, Sinclair?" A wry voice startled him, and he jumped lightly off the step and onto the gravel.

"Don't you agree then, Kevin?"

"Agree that it's a disgrace you can't get your tobacco whenever you want it, Sinclair?"

"Is that what you think?" squawked Sinclair. "Then what are you doing here yourself?"

"Just checking to see if the shop is open—like yourself," Kevin said amicably. "But I agree, it's a shocker. I don't know anyone who hasn't taken it to heart. I am not sure whether to go up to their house. You know ..." he finished lamely.

"Mmm, I agree. It wouldn't be seemly, but still ..."

"Come on, let's have a word with Eileen, she'll know what's new, if anyone does."

"Are you mad? It's not yet seven, man, we can't go knocking on her door, close as it is."

Kevin glanced down the row of sleeping cottages, all of their front curtains still tightly drawn, the morning sun just slanting across the tops of their gray slate roofs.

Then the door of number 10 opened and Eileen stepped out, complete with head scarf and bag clutched under her elbow. She walked determinedly toward them without seeing them, her head bent into the wind.

"Good morning, Eileen," both men said together. She looked up and smiled.

"My first customers, is it?" She took a key from her pocket.

"I say," said Sinclair, bemused.

"And what do you say? A tin of tobacco, Mr. Sinclair?"

The men followed Eileen into the shop as she unlocked and turned on the lights.

"God, it's damp in here. Three days makes a terrible difference."

"There's an old paraffin heater in the back," said Kevin. "I can light it for you, if you like."

"Ah, none of that smelly paraffin for me, thanks all the same. Mr. Sweeney said I would be able to use the bar heater."

"That's a concession, knowing him."

"Well," said Eileen kindly, "he's in a bad way yet, and I think he's glad of my help."

"Help?" Sinclair quivered with curiosity.

"Mmm, I'm going to help run the shop as best I can. He thought half days to start. As soon as I heard the awful news, I offered to do whatever I could. Mr. Sweeney thought since I lived so close by and knew most of the customers, that it might work out."

"And the post office?" asked Kevin.

"Sacred Heart, are you serious?"

"I guess that was a silly question."

"No, no, dear, it's just the thought of it. I'm not qualified. The post office wouldn't allow it. But I swear it would scare the wits clean out of me, I'm sure, after the terrible things that's gone on here!"

Eileen had started checking a handwritten list.

"There'll be no papers today, of course, nor milk, but I can get them going tomorrow. And then there's, mmm, the bakery's deliveries and the eggs. God, I don't know how those two manage." She sighed and looked around. "I think for today if I can just manage the dry goods ... and the prices. Lord, are the prices marked?" She read over the list again and then located a master price list crumpled and faded, lying under the long counter.

"Definitely half days to start. Actually, Brendan is none too bad. He's still got a terrific headache from the concussion, and that's affecting his eyes. But he said that he thought he'd be in, in a few days, if the doctor says it's all right."

"And poor Mr. Sweeney?" asked Kevin, plugging in the bar heater and positioning it near Eileen's feet, but safely away from the shelves and goods.

"Oh, he's very shaky. Of course he claims he's grand. The doctor says he must rest. He got a terrible blow to the chest, you know."

"No, we didn't know, Eileen, for heaven's sake! Everyone has a different story," Kevin said impatiently. "For God's sake don't keep us in suspense."

"I'm not, I'm sure," Eileen said huffily. "You're like two old cats around a plate of gizzards!"

"Then take pity on us, ma'am," wheedled Sinclair.

Eileen shot him a look.

"He got a blow to his chest when those gurriers shoved him with the end of one of their guns. He made a rush at them, you see!" she said triumphantly.

"So the papers got it right. What a foolish man," said Kevin soberly.

"Foolish, maybe," said Sinclair, "but true to form. He's a tough old bird. And he hates this kind of thing with a passion." Sinclair was strident. "He took his job with the post office very seriously indeed."

"Well, he didn't take this here glass cage seriously enough," Eileen added, annoyed. "If he'd been in it–"

"If he'd been in it, he'd be dead now, and that's the truth!" a fourth voice added.

"Ah, it's yourself, Mr. O'Dwyer," Eileen said smoothly. "Can I help you?"

"I think it's you that's needing the help, but if you will, I'll take a tin of cat food. The old moggie's off her food, and I thought I'd give her a treat."

He counted out the thirty-seven pence, which in turn Eileen counted out into her hand and then threw in the till.

"If you don't keep a running account," imposed Sinclair, "you won't know where you're at, at the end of the day."

"Mr. Sinclair, can I help you?"

"A tin of Three Nuns please, four ounces," he said, and paid, noting with satisfaction that Eileen wrote down the transaction.

"He could be dead ..." said O'Dwyer. "With the door open to the cage the way Sweeney always kept it, they could have shot him in the cage like fish in a barrel. God knows why they didn't anyway."

"I agree," said Kevin, "it was a miracle that they chose to knock them both out, instead of using their guns."

Eileen shivered. "Oh, dear God, it could have been so much worse. Yes, they could have been dead here on the floor." She looked at the floor and crossed herself.

"And was it the IRA, like they suggested on the papers?"

"Well, my sister's son's wife's brother in the police told the family that they were fairly certain. Even though the IRA haven't claimed it. From the description of the way they were dressed ..."

"And the manner in which it was done," added O'Dwyer. "It had all the earmarks. Brutal, brutal."

"Do we know what they got?"

"Oh, they got it all. You know it was Tuesday. They got the old-age pension, they got the children's allowance, they got all the cash. Begod, they even took the stock of stamps."

"You seem to know a lot about it, O'Dwyer," said Sinclair.

"Aye, that's because I read the papers I buy."

"Sure, what would those reporters know, they only talked to the police in the town."

"Enough, enough of this palaver," interrupted Eileen. "Scat, the crowd of you! I've got to think, and I can't with this gossipin'. Have you no homes to go to?"

"Right, then, we're off," Kevin said amiably, and held the door quite pointedly for the other two men to leave. "And good luck to you for taking this on."

"I can't believe this," exclaimed James. "Why didn't you tell me straight away!"

Gerald was startled at James's reaction. "Well, I'm telling you now. What's the matter? It has no bearing on our case."

"Well, I ... well, we don't know that yet."

"Do you mean the IRA?" Gerald snorted.

"We just can't dismiss it!" James tried to cover it, but he failed. He was shaken by the news that Mr. Sweeney and Brendan had been brutally attacked in Kilmartin the day he flew out to London. And by the terrorist Irish Republican Army, from all accounts.

"And you say they're all right, yes?"

"Yes, they're not dead or dying, if that's what you mean. But I think the reports indicated they were badly injured, head wounds or chest wounds ..."

"Christ!"

"You'd think you knew them well." Gerald's tone was annoyed. "I knew Sweeney before you were born ... but on the other hand ..."

"On the other hand, you wouldn't know him if you fell over him."

"No," said Gerald, taken aback. "Nor the son."

"I do know them; I feel as though I know them. If there's nothing doing here, Gerald, I'd like to go down to see them."

"There's nothing on, but I wanted you to take over the Molloy case. The family home is being auctioned, and as their solicitors, one of us should be there. The money from the sale is to be divided four ways, and there's sure to be murder over it." Gerald smirked. "They're a greedy bunch."

"Gerald, can't Bill Carey look after that one? And allow us to concentrate on this situation? We can't leave any avenue unexplored. Who's to say there isn't a tie-in? Nothing happens in Kilmartin for donkeys years, and then within a matter of weeks there are two major crimes." James's voice rose. Even as he talked, he convinced himself of a connection. "Maybe it was the IRA. Maybe it was someone copying their modus operandi."

"Maybe. But there hasn't been any IRA activity in Wexford for some time. However, check it out if you must. You cleared your desk before you went to London. And speaking of London—was it worth the trip?"

"Yes and no. The Walsh sister—Kathleen—absolutely does not believe that her brothers were capable of killing Jack Moore. She believes that Mike fell because he was drunk. She said it wasn't the first time that kind of thing had happened."

"Well, doesn't it disprove your theory of a longstanding grudge?"

"Perhaps. But she struck me as a kindly person, incapable of believing the worst about her brothers. And she did admit, in a roundabout way, that they had been angry at Jack for leaving Kilmartin and for leaving her—they were sweethearts, remember? And they were annoyed that she chose to emigrate after Jack had gone. Naturally they would hold Jack accountable for their sister leaving Ireland." James fudged, trying to avoid mentioning Kathleen's pregnancy, as she had requested. "I still feel there's life in this theory, Gerald," he added weakly.

"Okay, maybe. We just need enough to sow doubt in a jury's mind that Violet was the only one who might have wanted to kill Jack. You've worked hard at this case, and it's paying off. You have found somebody who had a motive—revenge. Our side does not have to prove that the Walshes did it! Listen, I'll set up a meeting with Sheridan and he can talk to you, if that will help?"

"After I get back from Kilmartin?"

Gerald shrugged. "If you insist."

"I do."

James returned to his office. He gathered his briefcase and buzzed Maggie to book him into Riders Inn.

She buzzed back. "Would that be a single or a double?"

The hues of a hearth fire tinted the road and the fields as they fell away on either side. The sun had sunk behind the hills on his right as James drove fast into the village of Kilmartin. He slowed the car outside Sweeney's shop and was heartened to see a light burning inside.

"Mr. Sweeney," he called robustly as he burst in the door.

"Mr. Fleming—you put my heart crossways in my chest, barging in that way!" Eileen primped her hair and straightened the apron she wore over her clothes.

"Is he here, or Brendan?"

"No, I'm sorry. Hadn't you heard?"

"Yes, yes," James cried impatiently, unbuttoning his Crombie over-coat. "But when I saw the light ..."

"I see. No, they're both still laid up I'm afraid, but I was speaking to Brendan only this afternoon over the telephone there, and he says he'll be in to work for a few hours in the morning. Thanks be to God," she muttered under her breath.

"Can they see people, visitors, I mean?"

"Now *that* I can't say, Mr. Fleming."

"No, of course not. Right! I'll be staying at Riders and, well, I'll ring them from there. Blast! It's so late now, I imagine it'll have to wait until morning. Just tell me—are they both all right?"

"As far as anyone can tell. Brendan was concussed, but I think he's okay. Mr. Sweeney, now, it's hard to say. Oh, Mr. Fleming, he's not a young man to be takin' such a beating."

"Beating?" James shook his head. "Those bloody bastards!"

"They were that and more. The mothers who bore them should fall down on their knees."

"Take care of yourself, Eileen. Perhaps I'll drop in on you tomorrow." James waited by the door until she had locked up and started back to her cottage.

He was getting to be a sentimental fool, he thought ruefully as he put the car in gear and headed for Riders. He wondered how he would while away the evening now, pent-up energy cramping his limbs.

He needn't have troubled himself on that score, he realized later, as

Captain Rider's widow forced him around the gardens in virtual dark-ness on a "turn before dinner."

"And have you made any progress on the case?" she asked after their pleasantries were exchanged.

"It's difficult to say if it's progress. I'm down here now to learn more about the attack on Sweeney's shop."

"Dreadful business. I assume you're making a connection between the murder and the attack."

"Well, yes, I hope to."

"You're not alone in that. Many of us have been thinking along those lines. I hear a lot, you know," she said in answer to James's look of surprise. "Tending behind the bar. Local people have been speculat-ing too—like yourself."

"And what have they been coming up with?" said James, knowing that he was grasping at straws.

"The gist of it is this. They're saying that the way in which Jack Moore's body was, well, disposed of—at dawn, on the steps of his ancestral home—had all the signs about it of the IRA. On the other hand, the IRA don't usually use knives. If we can say 'usually' in this distressing circumstance.

"This village and its surrounding lands have been quiet for many years. Suddenly, within a matter of weeks, there are these two atro-cious happenings! And since it seems that it was the IRA who robbed the post office, people are thinking that perhaps it was some sort of revenge against the village itself, as Jack Moore's home. But perhaps you'd like to discuss it with Inspector O'Shea?"

James stopped in his tracks. "O'Shea? Here?"

"Why yes, he's staying overnight, like yourself. Although he arrived early this morning."

"Do you know why?"

"I know he was making inquiries in the neighborhood."

"The usual stock answer, in other words."

"I'm afraid so," said Mrs. Rider as they turned back toward the inn. "I'll seat you at his table if you like. I do that sort of thing very smoothly."

"I have no doubt," said James, laughing, "but I couldn't stomach a meal sitting opposite O'Shea. Let me enjoy your fine cuisine in peace."

And it was indeed an exquisite meal. The salmon cutlet had been perfectly prepared, the chicken consommé equally superb. A generous slab of apple tart swimming in cream made James feel like a boy again.

And what's more, he had enjoyed every morsel despite the knowledge that O'Shea was seated a few tables behind him. It was when coffee was served that he saw the inspector approach, and glanced up with what he hoped was a disinterested expression.

"Fleming!" boomed O'Shea. Certainly all the diners would now know who he was, James thought wryly.

"O'Shea, no less." James laid it on thick.

"How did you find this little bijou?"

"I might ask you the same," and with more justification, thought James, annoyed.

"Oh, knew it for years."

"A likely story ..."

"And you?"

"Oh, the same story." Checkmate, O'Shea, James added silently.

"I see. Well, will you join me in the bar?"

Together they walked in.

"Two pints of stout, there, Mrs. Rider," O'Shea ordered lustily. Mrs. Rider caught James's eye and smiled demurely.

"By all means, Inspector. I'll bring them to your table."

When they were seated, James got to the point. "Let's eliminate the cut and thrust, shall we, O'Shea?"

"I thought I was doing all the parrying."

"Glad to hear you admit it." James smiled. "Seriously, you're down here because of the post office business, aren't you?"

"A related affair, certainly."

"O'Shea?"

"All right, all right. Yes. I am."

"But you're murder squad."

"Last I heard." O'Shea was facetious.

"In other words, O'Shea, you're down here to establish a connection between Moore's death and the hit on the post office. Yes?"

"If there was a connection, yes, I would establish it."

"But ..."

"Who's to say?"

They leaned apart as Mrs. Rider placed two pints on the table before them. Other patrons gradually filled the small room, until smoke and the press of bodies raised a canopy of privacy over their heads.

O'Shea settled back and contributed the smoke of his untipped cigarette to the general fog.

"O'Shea, can you share what you've found out?" James was blunt.

"Well, I don't see why not. You seem to think I take sides in this kind of endeavor. I assure you, I do not. I do my job. I let the barristers do theirs."

"But that's nonsense. You work, in effect, for the Attorney General, who prosecutes. And you can keep me and the likes of me in the dark or not, as you choose."

"But I choose not to keep you in the dark, Fleming, you or anyone else, insofar as it does not interfere with the A.G.'s functioning in a case."

"Can you tell me anything? You see, I believe there's a connection between the two events. The murder and the hit on the post office in Sweeney's shop. Perhaps revenge is the common denominator. In that case, it puts my client well out of it. The two events are 'political,' as they say. Unless you're about to suggest Violet Moore is an agent of the IRA." James laughed mirthlessly.

"Stranger things have happened, believe me, Fleming. But no ... to be fair, I would not think that of Miss Moore."

"Thank you," James said, signaling for another two pints from the bar.

"The trouble with you, Fleming, is that you sit there smugly assured that there's no way Violet Moore nor the likes of Violet Moore would dirty her hands with the IRA. And what do you base that assumption on?" O'Shea jabbed his cigarette offensively in James's direction. "I'll tell you. It's based on nothing more than the fact that you're a Prod." He smiled as James jumped and looked around to see who had heard.

"That's right. Because you're a Prod and grew up with them, because you've been in your secure little nest of prosperous businessmen and successful professional men and charitable ladies who look on the Queen of England as one of their own and who endow the arts and run homes for indigent Masonic spinsters, you think to yourself: 'Ah, no upstanding, prosperous, landed Anglo-Irish gentry or jackeen would dirty their hands with the IRA ...'"

James felt his face redden both at the description of his kind and the fact that O'Shea had read him so well. "And I'd be right," he said defensively.

"And that's where you're wrong. Why man, have you forgotten your own history? If it weren't for the Prod patriots over the centuries, we wouldn't even be having this conversation."

"That was then—"

"And this is now."

"Is this a personal attack or what, O'Shea? Because I don't intend–"
James was rising from his seat as he spoke.

"Hush, man, hush." O'Shea motioned with his hand for James to sit
down. "It's just those self-assured airs of yours that riled me. Look,
have another pint on me and I'll give you a little modern history
lesson." James was slightly mollified.

"Don't fool yourself that these IRA Provos are all a bunch of hot-
headed youths, adopting guerrilla-style tactics and running around with
Russian-made weapons. Man, these bastards are training in the Middle
East, they're on speaking terms with the likes of Gadaffi. They're single-
minded, they're arrogant, most of them are dirt poor, most of them are
Catholic or were ... and what does that mean? That's a discussion for
another day. I tell you, Fleming, this isn't my scene, as you know. I've
never been in the Special Branch, and I don't want to be. But I read
between the lines, as you should. And hear the talk. Man, these people
are politicized. They have education. Some of them are Marxist, some
of them are a new breed. But are you aware of that? And if you don't
bother your arse to know what's going on under your very nose, do
you think those fools that give them money know more than you?"

"Hold on, O'Shea. Hold on. I don't need a lecture from you. You
don't know the first thing about me. There's something more to this,
something more than the drink talking. What the hell is this all about?"

"Sorry. Sorry. It's true. Fleming, I was taking it out on you. I've had
some information from the States. The FBI was tipped by the IRS–
that's the Internal Revenue Service, if you didn't know–and they followed up the lead. In fact it was an obvious route to go. We had
asked them to look into it ourselves."

"Look into what?"

"Moore's politics. Prosperous Irish-American, very low profile, no
family, et cetera. Anyway, they think they've turned up a connection
with NortHelp."

"The Northern Irish aid group?"

"That's it. The American CIA have to take it from there because
the FBI sources only take it as far as that side of the Atlantic."

"Is it true?" James's face showed his astonishment.

"Well, let's say I've seen the faxes of his tax returns. They seem to
show in outline form that he may have been making large–very large–
contributions to the 'movement,' in the shape of NortHelp. The dates,
however, are sporadic, with long periods of time where there was
no activity."

"Major money?"

"Perhaps."

"And recently?"

"Within the last twelve months."

"I can't believe it."

"Why? Because he was a Prod like yourself?"

"Frankly, yes. What a route to go!"

"Listen, neither of us knew the man. Who have we met yet who knew him?"

"True, but we know—I think we know—that he belonged to no typical Irish-American organizations. I've seen Sheridan's research. He didn't even subscribe to an Irish-American paper, for God's sake."

"True but they're on every newsstand in Boston, I can tell you."

"And you're saying that he could have been getting his picture from such sources—about what's been going on here in the last twenty years? It's bizarre. I'm sorry, O'Shea. I don't buy it."

"Don't. It's no skin off my nose. But I don't see why you're holding on to your self-generated picture of the victim. Listen. He goes to London or wherever. And then he lands up in Boston. There's an Irish mafia there, just as in New York. Our version of the old boy's network, I suppose. Your old emigrants' network." O'Shea laughed at his own wit. "So let's say he gets his feet on the ground. Works hard, keeps his nose clean, makes progress in a career and branches out with investments and stockbrokering. Ends up owning his own firm. Meanwhile he's willingly lost all contact with home, but that's not to say that he isn't like millions, man, millions of Irish in Canada and Australia, in London and the States. They get nostalgic for the oul' country. They wear green on Paddy's day. They read in the papers about the struggle of the oppressed. They look in their wallet and they say: I can be part of that great historic struggle. I can make myself a part of history, I can cover myself with the glory that shines on the likes of Emmet and Wolfe Tone and Parnell—all Prods by the way. And all they have to do is lift a pen or a phone."

"So you are describing Jack Moore: no family, few friends, just acquaintances—if we believe the reports—no church affiliation."

"Exactly ... when you have nothing, you search for something. You buy into a dream and become part of it—with money."

"Well!" James sounded relieved. But he was anxious for additional proof of a direct connection between Jack Moore and the IRA. "Then tell me this, then. Did he make large contributions to anything else?"

"Yes. The United Fund, a hospital for children, some local campaign funds. Those contributions were sporadic too."

"In other words, reflecting perhaps what was going on in his life at the time?"

"I hadn't thought of it that way, but yes, your analysis is right on the mark. He reads something, or sees something, an appeal in the papers or on TV, and he breaks out the checkbook."

"So you view the NortHelp contributions in the same light—that is, sporadic and impulsive?"

"Don't cross-examine me, Mr. Solicitor, that's the barrister's job."

"But you obviously take my point?"

"Yes, Fleming, I do ... But I'm not saying that he couldn't have had a serious committment to the IRA."

"Then you do believe there's a connection between his death and the IRA, and between the robbery and the IRA."

"I didn't say that."

"Why else would you be here? O'Shea, how long have you known all this about Jack Moore?"

"Not long."

"But you suspected something of the sort when you came down to take charge of the Moore case."

"Yes, the manner of his death ... well, actually, the manner in which the body was disposed of—at dawn, on the steps—it all pointed to revenge. It pointed for that reason to some political connection. And the ordinary murderer generally does not have those kinds of resources at hand."

"So, you're telling me that even though you suspected something political, as you so nicely put it, you still went ahead and charged my client? Someone with absolutely no political connections and, for God's sake, no motive to kill her own brother, whom she hadn't seen in nearly thirty years!" James's voice rose and his hands tightened around the pint glass.

"Fleming, Fleming. Everything's political." O'Shea's booming voice dropped to almost a whisper and his strong face was somber. "There was obviously the pressure from the Attorney General. You know that."

"But you know that too."

"Yes, of course, but he was under pressure from the American embassy for a quick solution."

"What!"

"Shh, man. I'm being frank with you, but please grow up. If you want to stay in this business, you can't possibly remain this naive."

"I'm not naive. I expect sworn officials of the department, including the Attorney General, to keep their oaths."

"Hold on. Do you think I could ignore the fact that the body was found on Violet Moore's front step? That the weapon was found in her barn? That the weapon was from her own kitchen, with her prints on it? For Chrissakes! Could I finally ignore that her own sister pinpointed her in conversation with an unknown man around the time of the death? The evidence was too strong not to bring a charge. The Attorney General saw that. If it kept the Americans happy, then that was a bonus."

"And why the hell were they involved?"

"Because Jack Moore is, was, an American citizen. He got his papers years ago. As an American citizen he was under the aegis of the embassy as soon as he landed here. Normally they would take no interest in one of their citizens visiting his former homeland, but they could hardly overlook the fact that he was murdered!"

"And no doubt they had some quick tip about the NortHelp connection?"

"Perhaps. We have no way of knowing that."

"I'm not as stupid as you seem to think, O'Shea. They don't want that made public. A prosperous American who has given major money to NortHelp, killed twenty-four hours after his arrival in Ireland."

"I don't think our government would want it either. Wouldn't do the Tourist Board a lot of good when they were planning their ad campaign. Go home to die: visit Ireland! Send money first!"

"Your gallows humor is ... well, gallows humor."

"Sorry. Here. How about another drink?" O'Shea was conciliatory.

"Listen, O'Shea. If Jack was giving major money to the 'cause,' why would the IRA want him dead? Surely they would be killing the golden goose."

"To be honest, I'm not sure yet. That's what we're working on. But there have been one or two precedents over the years. It runs like this.

"The donor decides, perhaps because his contributions are so large, that he wants a more direct involvement in the 'struggle.' He may want to dictate where or how the money is spent. He talks with the organizers and they get anxious. The message is relayed through the grapevine. He comes over to check it out for himself. And hey, presto!

"Alternatively, there's been one or two cases where the happy camper becomes disillusioned with the way the 'cause' is being served. He reads about the killing of an innocent family returning home from their holidays, blown to smithereens because their green van is mistaken at a distance for a British Army vehicle. The happy camper isn't happy anymore. He's got innocent blood on his hands. And because he's been a big contributor and, up till then, stroked by the powers that be in the States or wherever, he complains to them, perhaps attempts 'political' argument and high philosophical discourse. And getting nowhere, he says he'll blow the whistle on the whole thing, that he'll go public—with what little he knows, which is usually damn all. But in their case, unlike Oscar Wilde's aphorism, any publicity of that kind is bad publicity."

"So steps are taken?" James was horrified at the scenario.

"Too much to take in?"

James was silent as he stood up to leave.

"Before you go, just tell me how your trip to London prospered?" O'Shea smiled.

"Is nothing sacred?" James asked wearily.

"Very little, I'm afraid, Fleming. But you're learning."

"Good night ..."

"Right."

James fell into bed exhausted. And it seemed a mere matter of moments when the pale morning sunshine fell across his face through the narrow window whose curtains he had left undrawn in his weariness.

After indulging in a cholesterol-laden and infinitely satisfying Irish breakfast of sausages, rashers, black and white pudding, two eggs, and beautifully grilled tomatoes, followed by white toast, brown bread and marmalade, and an enormous pot of strong tea, he felt fit and anxious to be off to visit the Sweeneys.

He arrived at their house without warning them in advance, hoping that this would strengthen his chances of actually getting in to see and talk to both Brendan and Mr. Sweeney.

It was on a low hill, and the garden and buildings were half hidden from sight by hedges of boxwood and holly. But the view from the house and from the rear of the house was magnificent, commanding the valley in which nestled the tiny village of Kilmartin, its main road meandering like a stream between the hills and fields and farms. The air was beautifully fresh and bracing. James closed his eyes for a few seconds and had the sensation of a cool, fragrant shower washing his skin and his hair. Thoughts of house hunting drifted into his mind. Yes, he wanted a house, one with cozy rooms and poky cupboards, a farmhouse kitchen and a spacious garden with, yes, potatoes growing, and onions. He sighed and opened his eyes.

He lifted the heavy brass knocker and waited for the low linteled door to open.

Brendan peered blindly through the crack that eventually appeared. "Yes?" he said questioningly.

"Brendan. It's James Fleming, Fleming, from Dublin."

"Oh, goodness, wait ... wait ..." Brendan fumbled in the lower pocket of his baggy cardigan and pulled out his glasses, which he placed carefully and gently on what James realized was a very bruised nose.

"James ... James ..." Genuine pleasure filled his voice as he led James into the small oak-beamed hallway. "Please, follow me, this way." Brendan turned first to his left and then to his right. "Here, in here." They entered a small room crowded with massive oak furniture from the twenties. Full as it was, it was still very cold.

"Da, Da! It's James Fleming from Dublin. You remember?"

"Of course I do," Mr. Sweeney said crossly, turning stiffly in his chair.

If Brendan hadn't directed his attention to the wing chair drawn up to the cold hearth, James would not have seen the tiny man who huddled there in a large, crocheted afghan of more colors than Joseph's coat. A low table with the remains of breakfast was to his side.

Brendan fussed and stewed until Mr. Sweeney snapped at him to bring up a chair closer to the hearth. Why, James could not fathom, until he sat and saw a few red embers still glowing beneath a mountain of ash.

Brendan stood rubbing his hands nervously.

"Tea, Mr. Fleming?" asked Sweeney the elder.

"No, thanks, I just had breakfast."

"Not to worry. Bring us in a fresh pot anyway, Brendan."

"Right, right." Brendan left the room, not to return for a very very long time.

James weighed what to do, and took the bull by the horns at risk of offending the old man.

He knelt on one knee easily and swiftly and drew over the cover from the grate. Spotting the shovel and an empty coal hod, he lifted out the mass of ash that had fallen under the grate and which was choking off the fire from what little coal remained. Small flames leaped up, fed with this new breath of air. James shook down the fire a second time and loosened the ash and quickly tonged a few pieces of coal onto the heart of the fire.

"Not too much there, Fleming."

"Oh, no sir, just a few bits and pieces to keep it alive."

"Right, we wouldn't want a blaze on a warm spring day such as this." Mr. Sweeney pulled the afghan round his neck and tentatively stretched his slippered feet toward the warmth.

James smiled inwardly and felt the better for easing the old man's stiff limbs with the help of the fire.

"It's Brendan, you know, he can't see to do it properly. Humph." Sweeney stirred in the chair with irritation at his son.

"It's just the two of you, then?" James said conversationally.

"Yes, sadly, the missus died some years ago. But we manage, usually." Mr. Sweeney glared at the wall which, James assumed, the room shared with the kitchen. He was glad Brendan couldn't see that look. The sooner the two of them were back at work, the better, he realized.

"Mr. Sweeney, I was terribly sorry to hear of your trouble. How are you feeling now?"

Sweeney rubbed his chest. "I'm not a complainer, Fleming, but I can tell you, not even when I played Gaelic football did I experience such a blow nor the pain I've had from it ever since. But it lessens slightly each day. Dr. MacIntyre comes up to see me. There's little he can do. It's bruised muscle, a damned nuisance. You see, I'm fit as a fiddle otherwise, but if I go to lift my arms, it pulls the muscle, and here I am rabbiting on ..."

"No, no, no. I'm interested. Please finish what you were saying."

"Well, as far as I can remember, the burly young gurrier hit me with the butt end of his gun—I'd hardly call it a rifle—a big, mean-looking yoke, it was. I was making a rush at him, and he caught me full in the chest. It knocked the wind completely out of my body and, well, MacIntyre said I fainted."

"And a good thing too, in a way."

"Not a'tall. If I had taken the blow, perhaps I could have tackled him."

James looked at the wizened, determined face and held his tongue.

"What do you think yourself?" he said after a silence.

"About what?"

"About the robbery?"

"No doubt in my mind it was the IRA boys, the Provos. They wore balaclavas. There were two of them, you see. Youngish, from the quick way they moved. Dark jackets, those jeans everyone wears nowadays, and black balaclavas."

"Did they speak?"

"Oh, indeed. They rushed in the door. It was before five-thirty that morning. I was waiting on the papers to arrive, and of course they hadn't. On the other hand, it was the bus driver who found us. Few others would have been about at that time. Unless it was Sinclair." He laughed at his own little joke and winced with the pain the laughter brought.

"Could you tell anything from their voices?"

"Well now, there's a thought. No one has had the sense to ask me that. But now that you do, it reminds me. I would've said the accent was Sligo."

"Sligo?" Brendan's voice squawked from the doorway as he balanced a tray of tea and cookies with one hand and shut the door behind him with the other. He placed the tray on the small round table near the heavily curtained east window.

"Sligo?" he repeated. "Are you saying that their accents were Sligo? Not a bit of it."

"And why not?" Mr. Sweeney bristled.

"I'll tell you. It was Donegal and no mistake, and I'll ring the station today and tell them to put it in my statement."

Mr. Sweeney considered for a moment. "Brendan, I have to agree."

"Of course you do." Brendan beamed. "You see, James, I was little help to the police. When one of the men leaped over the counter, he pushed me out of the way and knocked my glasses off. I couldn't see a thing after that, but I went toward their shapes. I heard them call to each other just before I was struck in the face.

"And that was it. But accents are a bit of a hobby of mine. Because the old eyes aren't so good and I often can't make out people's dress or appearance, I take a little bit of pride in placing their voices and their accents. And I do believe that these two thugs were from Donegal. But, yes, Da, close enough to the Sligo border to put you in mind of Sligo."

"Well, that certainly would seem to lend credence to the Provo theory. Donegal is a county known for spawning and then hiding these political types, being, as it were, next door to Northern Ireland," James said.

"Political types!" Sweeney's voice rose toward a shriek. "Don't grace them with such a word. Politics is *not* their game."

"I apologize, Mr. Sweeney, of course you're right." James sipped his tea and somehow found an appetite for the Ginger Nut biscuits piled on his plate.

"There's no doubt in either of your minds it. was the IRA, then?" James asked as he ate.

"None whatsoever. They were experienced. They moved like lightning. They were familiar with the glass cage. I admit the door of it was open. I had been counting the money to get ready for the various payouts. It was the first Tuesday, you know," Mr. Sweeney added a bit sadly. "I've always done it that way, you see."

"And it's been a very efficient system, Da," Brendan said gently, and caught James's eye.

"He's afraid now that Dublin will take away the post office from us."

"Oh, 'twould be a blessin'. I'd be glad to see the back of the old thing. Bloomin' cage and endless work. You agree, Brendan, don't you? You'd hardly miss sorting the mail every day?" Sweeney peered at his son.

James knew immediately how very much Brendan would miss that, but said nothing. Inadvertently, a sigh escaped his lips.

"It's a dreadful business ..."

"The post office?" squawked Brendan.

"No, no, I mean, this attack on you both. I'm just very glad you're well, that you're here to tell the tale."

"Indeed. But the police will never catch them. They're in Donegal as we speak. Playing at war games amongst the rocks," Sweeney added with some bitterness.

"How's it going with Miss Moore?" Brendan asked, changing the subject.

"Well, Brendan, I'm hoping to tie this attack on the post office in with the murder. It's a bit complicated, but I thank you for being so frank with me about your experiences, both of you. I'll go now, I don't want to tire you."

"Man, we're both tired with the inactivity. Next time I see you, I hope it's across the counter of me shop." Sweeney's grip was surprisingly strong as he shook hands with James. Brendan went ahead and unlatched the old plank door. "It was nice of you to come, James." Brendan beamed at him. "Sure, we'll be all right. I expect to be in the shop tomorrow, if you'll be coming by?"

"You never know, Brendan."

James climbed back into his car, sad, in a way, that he wouldn't be dropping in to the shop on the morrow. His home, such as it was, was elsewhere. He breathed a little good-bye to the village of Kilmartin and turned the fast car on the road to Dublin.

Chapter Seven

In the end James was astonished how easy it all was.

There, for anyone who might be interested, was the information that Kathleen Walsh was so desperately trying to conceal. It had been a simple matter of patient reading at the Central Office for the Registration of Births, Marriages, and Deaths. He knew the birth had taken place at the end of the year in which Jack Moore had left Ireland, twenty-seven years ago. And he also felt that the convent where Kathleen had gone would most likely have been in one of the less populated counties; in other words, far from Dublin and its environs, and also far enough away from Wexford. Consequently, he had started on the western counties first, and by the end of the afternoon had found the listing.

As he folded up the bit of paper on which he had copied the date and place of birth, all kinds of thoughts raced through his mind. It struck him forcibly that Baby Girl Walsh might know—if she were alive—that she was illegitimate, and would know the names of her parents, for Kathleen had named John Stuart Moore as the putative father. Their two names were linked at least in one legal record, if not on a marriage certificate.

Did Baby Girl Walsh ever wonder about that young mother listed on the record as living at home, or about the young father listed as farm manager, both living in the county of Wexford? Did she even know that their names were there for her to see? Did she wonder why she had been born in a convent in Tipperary? If she hadn't applied for a passport or for a driver's license, then she might not.

The nun with whom he had spoken over the telephone had been less than helpful. He had said simply that he wished to locate a child born at the convent. She had stated categorically that it was impossible. But as James well knew, in Ireland nothing is impossible. But no amount of wheedling and persuasion had helped. Just seconds before she rang off in a huff, he requested she inform the Mother Superior that he was coming to the convent anyway.

The drive to Tipperary was extremely pleasant, but finding the con-

vent at the farthest reaches of the town of Thurles was less pleasant. He took three wrong turnings, the third into a winding country
road that crossed and recrossed a river, only to deteriorate to a
boreen and then end in a rutted field. He knew he had scratched
the car. His temper rose. For all he knew, he had followed the River
Suir back to its rise in the Slieve Bloom Mountains. A heavy rain
began to fall, further obscuring his vision. He saw not a soul in the
surrounding mountain fields, and he drove back to the so-called
main road. Then he began all over again, this time ignoring the
signposts that had misled him. Finally, as his exasperation reached
exploding point, he made a turn, and through the dripping wind-
shield and the dripping trees which intensified the torrent of rain,
he spotted a gray stone building, grim and foreboding. Not even the
stone cross that surmounted its perfectly rectangular construction
would distinguish it from a prison or a reformatory or, for that
matter, an orphanage.

The flat windows showed no light, and looked for that reason as
though no glass shielded them. In vain James tried to read the small
brass plaque on the right side of the double entrance doors. Bent
against the rain, he threw his raincoat over his head and ran lightly
up the steps. THE CONVENT OF OUR LADY OF PERPETUAL HELP.

"Oh my!" he mused aloud. Nothing could have looked more austere
or been so misnamed, at least to the outside observer. He started to
turn back in order to lock up his car, but glancing at the bleak and
deserted landscape, he decided not to bother. He pulled the old-
fashioned brass-handled bell and waited. And waited. Undecided
whether to ring again or just stand there like a fool, he was startled
to turn and see that the door had been opened a crack. He bent down
to see a tiny, wizened white face.

"I am here to see Mother Superior," he shouted against the wind,
feeling foolish as he mouthed the words. Mother of what? he was
wondering. And superior to what? A small stream of water suddenly
dribbled into his collar. Then the door closed on him. They were
refusing to let him in! His fist was just on the point of pounding it
when the door opened a second time.

"Your name?"

"Fleming, Fleming!" James shouted, half in anger, half in embarrassment.

"No need to shout. I have perfect hearing despite my age," she
announced, finally admitting him into the lobby. In James's haste to

shed the dripping coat and wipe his damp neck, he failed to notice at first the splendor of this large entrance hall.

The parquet floor gleamed as if newly laid. On one side of the hall stood a long table, its polished mahogany catching the light from the brass hanging lamp that shed a softness and an illusion of warmth. The little nun took James's coat into a tiny room off the lobby where a crackling fire burned in a small grate. She swiftly hung the coat and spread its skirts wide for it to dry. An antique umbrella stand stood at the ready, and James, without an umbrella, suddenly felt that he wasn't quite the well-dressed man in this little nun's eyes.

To the rear of the vestibule facing him was a wide wooden staircase, uncarpeted and gleaming like the mahogany table. He noticed then the small door tucked beneath the stairwell and the larger, more imposing carved wooden doors opening off either side of the lobby. The nun turned the ornate handle on one of them and said briskly, "Walk this way please, Mr. Fleming."

He entered a surprisingly beautiful room, with pleasing proportions, despite the height of its ceiling. Another fire lit the room with its welcome warmth. A rich Persian carpet, slightly worn in places, was laid in the center of the wooden floor. Two overstuffed couches stood facing each other, and a low round table between them held current news magazines. On either side of the fireplace were two half tables, companions, with bowls of daffodils that were sisters to the ones James had seen in the hallway. Their yellow trumpets were so bright, interspersed with others of such a delicate hue as to be almost ivory, that they made him smile. A simple painting of the Madonna and child hung over the fireplace, and James gazed at it. Always wary of the Catholic penchant for overstatement, he was surprised at the beauty of the painting. Not an old master certainly, but striking in its portrayal and its lack of garishness. He glanced around. An equally simple statue of the Virgin stood discreetly on a table in the corner by the window which fronted the drive, and where he could see his car standing in the torrential downpour.

Suddenly the car and the world outside seemed very distant. He was unaccountably warm and peaceful. He shook himself. He could hear ... nothing, nothing but his own breath. He strained and still could hear nothing. "Quieter than a church," he said to himself, smiling. "And more welcoming."

A fire burned on the hearth, and he spread his hands to the warmth. He did not hear the handle of the door turn, nor did he hear the footfalls of the tall woman who approached. He sensed rather than saw her, and turned quickly. She seemed to glide across the floor.

"Mr. Fleming." It wasn't a question. She extended a cool, thin hand and grasped his firmly. "Please, sit down."

James did as he was bid, trying to evaluate what manner of woman was in front of him. "Mother Superior?"

"Yes," she said simply.

He waited, assuming she would ask him to call her something more reasonable. Even "Sister" would be more amenable to him at this point. He waited in vain.

The silence lengthened. She didn't offer to assist the conversation with the usual platitudes such as "How may I help?" James became tongue-tied.

"My card," he said at last.

"Thank you. I shall take it for my records, but I have already ascertained your credentials through a friend in Dublin."

"A friend?"

"A clerical friend."

"I see," said James, taken aback. "And you know why I am here?"

"Yes. I know what you want. That's why your first request was refused. But since you insisted on coming in person, I will certainly talk to you. But I can only refuse you again."

"But you don't know which child's adoption I am concerned with . . ."

"I assure you it makes no difference. The policy applies to every child—without exception."

"Mother . . . Superior, I am involved in a case where my client is accused of murder. She is a Miss Violet Moore, who arranged for a young mother to come here. I believe my client is completely innocent. That means someone else committed this terrible crime and may well go free."

"How can this possibly be connected with an adoption? From the note I have here, it was an adoption that took place many many years ago. You must take my point."

"No, Mother, you must see my point. The murdered man was the father of the baby girl born at this convent twenty-seven years ago!"

The nun's facial muscles twitched ever so slightly. Curiosity widened her pale blue eyes, but only fleetingly. Years of self-discipline reasserted themselves.

"Please, don't tell me any of the details. I shall make an effort now to forget what you have already very ill-advisedly told me. You see, nothing you can say will alter the fact that our adoption records are sealed. Don't you think over the years we haven't had other similar requests from solicitors, from erstwhile family members, from people who have gone abroad? Regardless of the cases these various people could and did make, our policy remained and must still remain sacrosanct and in force. You know that as well as I do, Mr. Fleming."

Her tone and manner were implacable. James wondered why he had bothered to come.

"As you must understand, Mr. Fleming, it is not a case of my changing my mind. The policy is there to govern those of us who have been chosen to govern. I merely abide by that policy. I might add, I believe in that policy. It has served the children, their parents, and their adoptive parents very well for many many years. Our function here is very delicate. We deal with people at their most vulnerable moments. We deal with the young mother at that emotional time of giving birth, we deal with her when she gives up that baby she has borne. And we deal with those anxious, childless couples whose lives are changed forever by an act of physical love between two people months before, people they will never know. A few seconds of, let us say, biology?—and four or five or more lives are changed forever. It is a sacred trust, and I won't be the one to break it."

The Mother Superior stood up gracefully and her austere expression softened for a moment. "I wish you and your client well, Mr. Fleming. Good-bye."

James, chastened and stymied, took her hand briefly and walked ahead of her to open the door.

Mother Superior touched a small silver bell that stood on the hall table. "Sister Benedicta will see you out," she said as she glided soundlessly from the lobby and disappeared in the shadows behind the staircase.

James stood waiting, a picture of discouragement. The sense of peace the convent had brought to him on his arrival was shattered, but he glanced kindly at the little old nun who had admitted him.

"Your coat, Mr. Fleming," she said, bustling as a tiny house martin might have bustled if encumbered by a long black habit and white coif. James followed her into the small "drying room."

"The rain has stopped, Mr. Fleming. Merely an April shower. I was just going out to the garden."

"I'd love to see it," said James.

"By all means," she said, delighted. "The scents after a rain such as this are heady, as though the flowers and herbs are giddy from their long drink." She pulled on a rain cape and led him from the lobby, down the granite steps, past his car to a wide garden James hadn't noticed in his dash through the torrential rain. She was correct, he thought. The intermingled scents rose up and were wafted toward them on a brisk spring breeze. He followed Sister Benedicta down the narrow little paths of paving stones and listened attentively as she explained her goals and aspirations, for this garden was now in her care in her retirement from years of active service in the convent.

"This is my herb garden. The comfrey's doing well, but of course it loves rain. The chives are flourishing too. But the parsley, now, and the rosemary—they're a bit slow. Now see this lemon verbena, delicious." She handed him a tiny leaf to rub between his fingers. The scent of lemon was powerful. "You are an exceptionally good listener," the little nun chirruped up at him. James had been stooping for some time to catch the words of the ancient nun.

"Well, I must tell you, my mother keeps a fine garden, as do many of her friends in Dublin. I've often visited them, and this is one of the nicest I've ever seen."

Sister Benedicta glowed with pride. "Oh, it is a dear occupation of mine. No matter what the irritations or sorrows of the day, they are soon forgotten working in a garden. And they are soon replaced by a sense of tranquility that I find sometimes even more potent than the tranquility of the chapel. But don't tell Mother I said that!" Her birdlike voice sent a peal of tinkling laughter through the quiet garden. In a separate bed were the flowers. She bent to pick a nosegay, among them the daffodils with the pale trumpets he had noticed inside. As she worked, James chatted and she listened, hungry for news of the outside world.

"I am working on a case now," he said, his voice neutral, "most interesting. In fact it might interest you, Sister."

"Indeed?"

"Yes, it involves a lovely girl, a girl who was born here, in fact, about twenty-seven years ago. I work on wills, you see, that's my main job at the solicitors firm I am with." James fudged the truth unmercifully.

"And might this girl stand to inherit?" Sister asked, intrigued now.

"Indeed, she might. A considerable fortune. I ... well ... perhaps I shouldn't ..."

"Oh, but Mr. Fleming, look around you. Who would I be tellin', except the flowers and the fields?" She beamed up at him. As an afterthought she added, almost to encourage his confidence, "I may well know her. I was a midwife in those days, you see. I knew all the girls and their wee ones. And I've followed many of them over the years."

"The mother was from Wexford, and her surname was Walsh." James thought of Kathleen's tragic face, and told her mentally that telling this little nun was no betrayal in the sense she meant it. Especially since this little nun might well have delivered her daughter.

"Oh, indeed and I do remember her, so well. That was one of the most successful adoptions we ever had, but of course you know that yourself?" She looked questioningly at him.

He jumped. "Oh, yes, yes I agree. Her parents are exceptional people ..." he hazarded.

"Oh, yes indeed. They weren't young, of course, but so ... let me say, loving. I knew that morning when they took Baby Walsh away that it was a dream come true for them and that she would have a beautiful life. And to think she is so successful now. I remember her mother, she wasn't more than a child herself, but she never struck me as musical. Strange, isn't it?"

"Indeed, it is. But who knows how these talents arise—musical ability, artistic ability. Sometimes there is no correlation ..." James waffled on.

"Well, then it's a gift in the true sense of the word. And she has the gift of music, that is sure. So young and already making a name for herself. And now you say she may have wealth too?"

"Ahh ... she might indeed."

By now they had walked to the boundary of the garden, and here he made his farewell. He was sorry to leave the peaceful garden and the sweet-voiced old woman with the ageless face. As he started the engine, he cringed to hear it roar and sully the silence, however briefly. Nevertheless, he tooted his horn, waved, and was pleased to see Sister Benedicta give him a return wave.

James's heart soared. He could barely enjoy the drive back to Dublin, anxious as he was to pursue the leads that Sister Benedicta in all her innocence had given him. A girl with a career, music; in the public eye; and parents who lived in Dublin and who would be just that bit older than most parents of a daughter of twenty-seven. "God bless you, Sister Benedicta, your name truly suits you," murmured James as he hit the highway and let his car fly.

*   *   *

"Flanagan!" James stood on the pavement hailing his friend. A short, stout, bearded man threaded his way through the traffic stalled at the long light at the corner of Stephen's Green.

"Fleming," said Matt, slightly out of breath. "It's good to see you, you old bastard!"

"Likewise I'm sure. Come on, we'll be late ..."

"As usual." Laughing, the friends took the steps two at a time and entered the imposing cold hall of the College Club.

"This is a bit extravagant, isn't it, Fleming?" said Matt as they were seated at one of the white linen-covered tables near the impossibly high Georgian windows that fronted the building.

"Not a'tall. I'll put it on my tab."

"And put it down as a business expense for one of your poor, ignorant clients?" Matt laughed.

"Perhaps, perhaps ..."

"I must admit, James, I've always wanted to see the inside of this place. Ever since school, passing by on the pavement looking up at the white heads in the window with cigars or pipes sticking out of their gobs. What are the fees again?"

"You don't want to know."

"Come on?"

"Well, I think they went up, maybe fifteen hundred pounds a year, around there."

"Lord. And for that you get ..."

"Well, we can eat here like this."

"And pay?"

"Of course. And there are private rooms at our disposal–for parties or perhaps business matters, or just for a place to come and read the papers in peace."

"God, you're a snot!" Matt said, smiling.

"So what else is new?"

"You and your type have to get your peace and quiet. Not like the working stiffs like me. I have my staff room for that–but so do the other twenty faculty members. Not much peace and quiet in there, I can tell you."

"Don't give me that. I've been in your staff room. And I clearly remember cozy broken-down armchairs and tea always brewing and fireplaces burning brightly."

"Ah yes, but that was at my old school. You haven't bothered your arse to visit me at the tech. All shiny bright and spanking new. The staff room has walls made of cinder block—you can't hang a bloody thing on them unless you use tape, and then it dries up from the central heating and falls off. I assure you we have color-coordinated red plastic chairs and Formica tables. God, it's awful."

"Flanagan, these things take time. The likes of you will soon introduce civilized living to the staff room."

"Impossible. For that you need drafty windows, creaking wooden floorboards, and a fireplace that doesn't draw. But I'm not discouraged, the staff are suitably crazy. If that changes, then I'll give up and go become a tree farmer."

"That's no sacrifice. You never saw yourself as a vice-principal anyway. You'd probably love tree farming."

"I might, but I doubt Dorothy would."

An ancient stooped waiter approached. James ordered and then resumed their conversation over a glass of sherry each.

"So how is Dorothy? And my godson and his three brothers?"

"Two brothers, don't get ahead of yourself there, Fleming!"

"Sorry. Everyone I know has so many children, I lose track sometimes," James said sheepishly.

"Don't worry, your day will come." Matt attacked his beef and vegetables. Through his cabbage he assured James that he would succumb to marriage sooner or later, but as his oldest friend, he advised him to make it sooner.

"And why is that?" asked James.

"Because, my good man, you are getting bloody set in your ways." He waved his fork to indicate their surroundings, and bits of cabbage flew in a small arc around them.

"Bachelor life—that's what this is. Fast cars, indifferent food, good clothes, and not a good woman in sight. How do you stand it?" Matt laughed.

"I don't really," James said seriously.

"I know that," said Matt, "that's why I can chance saying all this to you ... I saw Teresa last week."

"And?"

"And she looks great. She still has those great knockers, in spite of the two kids."

"Two?"

"Mmm, one within this last year. She's in the same badminton club as Dorothy. You know they're cousins ten times removed, or some female nonsense like that. They went for a vodka and lime, and when I collected Dorothy, we spoke for a few minutes."

"Two?"

"Yes, two. Now, what about it? Any woman on the horizon?"

After this news, James attempted to divert the conversation, but Matt persisted.

"For God's sake, James, you were with me the first time I met Dorothy, that night at the dance ..."

"And you were with me the night I met Teresa ..."

"Jesus! Fleming, let it go. No one else is telling you, so I will. Let it go. Get on with your life. Let me tell you, a few snot-gobblers rubbing mashed banana down your suit will give you a whole new perspective on your life!"

"Are you trying to put me off?" They laughed together and moved on to other subjects. This was the start of Matt's midterm break, which lasted ten days, so they made arrangements to meet again.

"Great dinner, Fleming. I won't thank you, since you can afford it and I can't," said Matt as they crossed to the Green, walking toward James's office.

"Tell me, Matt, have you heard of a young musician who's been making a splash in the papers in the last year or so?"

"Look who you're askin'! Is it your memory's going as well as your mind?"

"Right. Okay. But ask Dorothy, would you? She was civilized when she married you, unless you've rubbed off on her. She might know."

"I will, since I see you're serious. What's it about? A case? Or an affair of the heart?"

"Oh, it's a case. I'll tell you a bit about it on Friday night." They parted and James returned to the unwelcome news that his mother had phoned.

"What did you tell her?" James groaned into the intercom.

"I told her exactly what time I expected you in the office," Maggie's voice crackled with irony through the receiver. A faint buzz reached his ears. "If I'm not mistaken, that should be your mother now." Maggie was laughing as she switched off and then put the call through.

"James." His mother's voice was icy and James shivered.

"Mother, dear, how are you?"

" 'Mother dear' my foot. Do you realize how long it's been since—"

"But of course, it's been ages. You have no idea ..." James listened with half an ear to his mother's complaints as an idea—a brilliant idea, he felt—formed in his mind.

"Mother, I must see you."

"But that's just what I've been saying."

"No, seriously, I must see you ... tonight."

"Tonight, but that's ridiculous. You know perfectly well that to-night's my bridge night. You're just like your father. He always expected me to drop everything and join him. He never did like bridge either—"

"Mother!" James's voice was stern.

"Yes," she said sweetly.

She always did like it when I'm bossy, thought James. "I'll be over around half-eight."

"Yes, dear, and where are we going?"

"No, I said I'd be over at half-eight."

"I heard you, dear."

"I see. Right, Mother." James sighed. His mother never stayed home. "You pick the place, just be ready, please." James said it without hope. His mother was infamous for never being ready.

And this time she wasn't ready either. James lounged in the love seat by the dwindling fire. No need to feed it if we're going out, had been her excuse. He'd heard it all before. He glanced around the room. Every available surface was covered with memorabilia of one sort or another. Photos of Donald and himself in their prep school uniforms, all shiny hair and crooked teeth. Photos marking every step of their mutual careers in medicine and law. There was even a framed press release of when he became a member of Fitzgerald's firm.

He wondered idly why his father had never branched out on his own, always preferring the security of being a partner in a large firm of solicitors. He wondered too how he himself had ever lived in this house. Few memories attached themselves to the items in the downstairs reception rooms. No, his haven had been his own room, but he was reluctant to go up to it now. He knew his mother hadn't touched it since he'd moved out. And not because she kept it as a shrine to her eldest son, but merely because she hadn't got around to it. She had cleared out Dad's things fairly quickly, James recalled, but without a doubt she had loved her husband, and he knew that she cherished his memory deeply and privately. As his mother entered the room he looked at her with more compassion than he had for a long time.

"The Park House," he suggested hopefully as he helped her on with her coat and untangled her scarf from her sleeve.

"No, not the Park House. The bridge club always refresh themselves there, and I did make elaborate excuses why I couldn't play tonight. No, I think O'Byrnes would be better."

James groaned inwardly. The same old place. He would know half the clientele, since half the clientele lived in his mother's immediate neighborhood. And then he realized that that was exactly it. His mother wanted her friends and neighbors to see him with her. In his present mood, it was a small concession.

As he'd anticipated, the O'Neills were there—husband and wife greeting him with enthusiasm. And so too were the Connollys, who grilled him—not only about himself, but about what little information he had on his brother Donald. They were accompanied by Mrs. Greene, a lovely old widow, whom they often brought out for a drink. She patted James's hand as if he were still ten, and smiled benignly as he sat and chatted briefly.

At last James and his mother settled in a quiet corner. As they sipped their tonics and nibbled a few dry-roasted nuts, James listened patiently while his mother caught him up on the various births, marriages, and deaths that had occurred in the last six weeks in her large circle of associates. Having depleted her store of information, she was persuaded to take a small sherry, and James broached the purpose of his visit.

"Mother, I know how very up-to-date you are on the music scene in Dublin ..."

"More than you are, certainly, James, and more's the pity. When I think of the money we threw away on your piano lessons ... And Mrs. Kehoe swore you had promise."

James laughed. "She swore every one of her students had promise."

"Yes, well now that she says it about your mother, I think you had better keep your levity to yourself. You know I've told you I'm taking lessons. I've told you more than once, James!"

"As I was saying–"

"That I know the music scene, yes, dear?"

"Do you know, I mean, have you heard of a young Irish woman who's been doing rather well lately? I'm sorry to admit I don't even know what instrument she plays, but I've heard in a roundabout way that she's, ahh, making a name for herself. Does any of that ring a bell?"

"But James, you can be talking about only one person, Sarah Gallagher!" He looked blank. "Humph, you are impossible, James, I can't bear it when you are so thick. Sarah Gallagher, the violinist. She's been the talk of the town since last season. How can you have escaped hearing about her? Don't you read the paper?"

"Of course, but—"

"But nothing, my dear. And what kind of people do you associate with that they haven't even mentioned her in conversation? Train enthusiasts." She spoke the last two words as though these innocent buffs carried the black plague from one train station to another.

"Allowing for my own thickness and the ignorance of my friends, could you perhaps deign to enlighten me about this person?" James's tone was lightly teasing.

Vivienne Fleming drained her sherry, and was forced to add that at least James's father had shared her interest in classical music! She sighed heavily, and James quickly signaled for another small sherry.

"All right, James, I just felt I had to clear the air."

Obviously, thought James to himself.

"Sarah Gallagher is from Monkstown. Really, no one knew of her until last season when she made her Dublin debut. Serious musicians, of course, had heard of her through reviews of her Italian debut two years ago. She's about twenty-three, perhaps twenty-five. Perfectly lovely, if you can judge from her photographs in the paper. I unfortunately did not get to hear her play last year. She performed twice with the RTE symphony at the National Concert Hall. In no time all the tickets had been sold out, and that was the first year I let my season ticket lapse since your father died. Very stupid of me."

"And she plays the violin?"

"Yes, and apparently she is extremely gifted. They speak of her as being one in a line with the likes of John O'Connor or James Galway."

"In other words?"

"In other words, you with the tin ear, an artist of international repute, an artist of serious potential, someone who will be recognized outside this wretched little island of ours!"

"Is that it?"

"Of course that's it, what more do you want?" His mother's voice grew suspicious. "Why are you pumping me, anyway?"

"I can't tell you that, at least not yet." James smiled his most charming smile to deflect his mother's intense curiosity.

"James, you are insufferable. You are, at least in this, exactly like your father. I can still hear him saying those exact words ..."

"Yes, Mother, and so can I ... and you know why?"

"Yes, I suppose so. This must be one of your so-called 'cases'—you've inherited your father's secretive ways." Mrs. Fleming was rankled, and the sherry had made her cheeks glow.

"Secretive ways! I think, if anything, I inherited his disposition to be not only discreet, but to keep professional confidences confidential!" James stressed the last word. "I mean it, Mother, this is strictly between you and me. You have been a big help to me, but I can't tell you about it all yet." His voice held the promise he would tell her at some future date, which seemed to satisfy her.

"I can help you further, perhaps, James. I have a ticket for one of the two concerts Sarah Gallagher will be giving this month. They're as scarce as hen's teeth. I was lucky to get the one I got."

"But surely we could attend together."

"Gladly, but I truly was able to purchase only one ticket. You take it, James. Apart from all your subterfuge, you might actually enjoy the splendid music."

"Thank you. I'll make it up to you. By the way, do you know the family?" His mother's circle of acquaintances was so large that James felt anything was possible.

"No, I don't. But Mrs. O'Hara's cousin has relations in Carlow on her husband's side who are second cousins to the family. That's how I know they're in Monkstown. An old Catholic family, I believe." James's mother said this with a tinge of disbelief that a Catholic family could produce an artist of such stature, and she bore it with a personal sense of long-suffering tolerance for such aberrations. "Though of course Mr. Joyce was a Catholic," she added, apropos of nothing.

James smiled and held his tongue. He had learned long ago that it was impossible to make a dent in his mother's fixed beliefs. Though immensely popular, and with friends of every persuasion, the experience had done nothing to alter certain of her inherited ideas. She "drew lines," as she was fond of telling him in his youth. These invisible lines were indeed invisible, except to those who knew her best. And James, after battling his way through five years at Trinity and a liberal education, finally gave up. He had realized that if important real-life experiences had failed to change her ways, then nothing theoretical or even merely logical would shake them.

He drove his mother home and collected the ticket. She exacted her price, however—he wasn't to get off lightly—for he found himself committed to escort her to a wine-and-cheese affair for the Dog and Cats

Home on Grand Canal Street. Nonetheless he felt mean-spirited when he refused her offer of coffee and biscuits which he knew from long experience would be stale. As it was, she happily shut the door on him before he had reached his car. He could just see her through the hall window haphazardly piling her badminton racket into yet another capacious tote bag, looking forward to her match and morning coffee—on the morrow, as she had said.

The feeling of excitement in the concert hall was almost palpable. And James caught the anticipatory buzz as he moved from the lobby, where champagne was flowing freely, and toward his seat. He mentally thanked his mother again for the superb third-row-center seat—despite the price she would extract. He was virtually in line with the low dais on which Sarah Gallagher would stand, just to the left of the conductor.

In the intervening days, James had read articles and reviews on Sarah Gallagher in past issues of various papers. He was embarrassed after the fact to realize just how much coverage had been afforded this violinist, and that he had blithely missed all of it. Dorothy Flanagan had phoned him one night, confirming all his mother had told him but adding little else. And she hadn't mentioned Teresa. James didn't know whether he was glad or not, but he didn't inquire.

A few very discreet calls around town to various solicitors he knew and trusted had yielded more information. The Gallaghers were extremely comfortable. It was old money and very low profile. The father was now in semiretirement, and as a family, they had led extremely quiet lives with their only child, Sarah. He had learned too that there was a strong connection with the Church. Mr. Gallagher was an all-but-anonymous and very large contributor to the archbishop's personal favorite charities. Although James hadn't established a connection with the Convent of Perpetual Help he'd so recently visited, he felt at this point he didn't need to make one. Ireland was, after all, Ireland.

James read the program and learned that Sarah Gallagher had studied with private teachers in Ireland as a young girl and at the National Academy of Music. At an early age she had won a scholarship for a summer to Florence and, while studying in a classroom environment, was spotted by a maestro who had since taken control and direction of her studies and her public career. Excerpts of reviews from various continental papers were all in agreement. Sarah was a violinist of exceptional precocity, brilliance, and potential. Maturity could only bring more.

A whisper over the front rows like a breeze over a field of barley.
Head leaned to head, and mouth was placed to ear, up and down the
rows to James's left and right. And James followed with his eyes as
programs were discreetly pointed in the direction of an elderly man
and his younger wife, who moved slowly and shyly down the right-
hand aisle to two end seats in the first row.

James was bemused. These two surely were Sarah's parents. Why,
then, didn't they sit to the left, where they would have had an unobstructed view? But as James observed their quiet demeanor—the lowered eyes, the slight discomfiture, their awareness that too many eyes
were on them—he realized they hadn't wanted to be even in a minimally
more exposed spot than they were already. The audience shifted and
cleared its collective throat as the orchestra and then the conductor
took their places. A hush fell as Sarah Gallagher came to the front of
the stage and the first notes of the Paganini and Fritz Kreisler set
pieces were struck. The music was magnificent and, to James's ears,
turbulent, emotional, stirring. He was no judge of her technical brilliance, but the music and Sarah's persona quickly melded into the one
experience. He was thunderstruck. Thunderstruck simultaneously by
the power of the music and the beauty of the violinist. It was only
during the intermission that James regained his presence of mind in
time enough to glance over at the Gallaghers and see them beaming
with pride, shaking hands discreetly with people who seemed to be
close friends, and shaking their heads in unison at what James took to
be invitations to withdraw to the lobby or one of the various bars.
They resumed their seats as the well-wishers moved away to refresh
themselves, and James followed suit.

He indulged in a Gauloise in the lobby, one of the few occasions
when he permitted himself to smoke, and he listened attentively to the
fragments of conversations that flowed around him in the crush of the
crowd. The mood was ebullient, not a murmur contradicted it. James
returned to his seat at the first bell, anxious for the remainder of
the concert.

The second half rivaled the first. The music held fewer fireworks,
yet somehow carried one a step further. Her violin sang and wept,
lifting his heart along with it. Haunting melodies hung in his ears, filled
his head just as the applause filled the hall. For an Irish audience, it
was unusually demonstrative. James's eyes held the figure of the slender
young woman in the simple blue scoop-necked dress. Her mahogany
hair swept up at the back, her throat and the line of her chin were

indelibly printed on his memory. The sway of her body, the lift of her elbow, the movement of her wrist, these too were etched on his mind. James stood on the steps of the Hall as the crowd broke up and people hurried to their cars. He could hardly distinguish between the impression Sarah Gallagher had made on him and the impression the music had left behind. The only thing certain was that thoughts of murder and illegitimacy were very far from his mind this night.

Chapter Eight

WW hat is it?" Mrs. Fleming's cross and groggy voice whispered faintly into the receiver.

"Mother, it's James!"

"James?"

"Your son!" James fairly shouted.

"How could you possibly disturb your mother at this hour? What time is it?"

"It's eight o'clock in the morning, for God's sake!"

"Are you ill, James? You seem so overexcited. Perhaps you have a fever."

"Mother, wake up, for God's sake! I need to ask you a few questions."

"All right. I'm sitting up now. Hold on while I plug in the Teasmaid."

James listened impatiently at his end to the sounds of his mother fiddling ineffectually with the silliest gadget yet conceived by modern man: a device that heated water and brewed horrendous tea at one's bedside. They were a favorite of the older generation, and James had duly given one to his mother one Christmas past. After a few muttered but mild curses, his mother returned to the phone, her voice a bit stronger.

"Such a nuisance ..."

"The tea maker or me?"

"Both, if you must know. Your brother Donald never wakes me up at this hour. All right now, what on earth's the matter?"

"Mother, I went to Sarah Gallagher's concert last night. It was everything you said it would be. I need to meet her, and I wanted to know what you could do for me."

"Most extraordinary, James. However, since, as you know, I'll do anything for my eldest son, I'll see what I can manage. I'll ring Mrs.

Smythe after breakfast, she's with the Dublin Musical Society. I think
I heard her talking the other night at the Mothers' Union—something
about young Sarah Gallagher. But please, James, let me get back to
you ... now, good-bye!"

His mother rang off firmly, but her words set James's mind racing.
He had to meet Sarah, and as soon as possible. He hoped it could
further his case, but underneath he knew that he was smitten, capti-
vated, at least from afar.

True to her word, Mrs. Fleming phoned back by noon, having ma-
neuvered an invitation for James to accompany her to a small reception
which the Musical Society was giving in Sarah's honor following her
second and final concert at the National Concert Hall.

The venue at the Baptist Hall on Leeson Park seemed a most unlikely place to hold such an event, but James kept his criticism to
himself as he entered the modern but rather bleak building. A long
table was set with urns of tea and coffee and trays and plates of fairy
cakes, Madeira cake, and currant buns. James cringed. It had all the
trappings of a church fete. Surely this was not the arena in which
Sarah should be shining. However, he quickly noticed that although
the crowd was not as glittering as that at the concert, it seemed to be
a crowd of true enthusiasts. Soberly dressed for the most part, the
guests, he soon learned from his mother's adept introductions, were
the heart and soul of the classical music community. Many teachers of
music were there, members of the Academy, the music critics from all
the papers and magazines—all mingling and speaking knowledgeably
about music in general and Sarah Gallagher's talent in particular. He
spotted her immediately, dressed in a simple two-piece sea-green knit
dress, the soft cowl neck falling gracefully around her throat. She
moved easily from one cluster of attentive listeners to another, laughing
gaily or listening intently. Confident, self-assured. And not in the least
as James had fantasized. At last she approached the small circle where
he and his mother stood. James was embarrassed to find himself moving
slightly behind his mother as introductions were made, like a small boy
at a wedding finally meeting the glowing bride. But his mother, as
usual, was superb.

"Miss Gallagher," she said, her voice rising with enthusiasm and
forcefulness. "This is my son James. He has, I am afraid to admit, a
tin ear. But after hearing you play last night—after I so nobly sacrificed
my own ticket to him—he has become an admirer. In fact he threatened
me with loss of sleep if I didn't arrange for him to attend this evening

and have the pleasure of meeting you. James!" His mother tugged at his sleeve, and James's face grew crimson.

"I assure you that there is a kernel of truth in what my mother says, Miss Gallagher. I did indeed enjoy your performance very much. And yes indeed"–James nodded at his impossible mother–"Mrs. Fleming here did indeed give me her ticket, much to her own loss, I'm sorry to admit."

"Well, perhaps you shall both hear me play when I perform in Dublin next season." Sarah was distant but polite. James sensed her slipping away, and tried desperately to hold her attention.

"Miss Gallagher, have you ever ridden on a steam train?"

"Pardon me?" she said, and smiled at last.

"James!" Mrs. Fleming interrupted, and James stepped on her toe. No matter. "Miss Gallagher, please excuse my son. He is a solicitor, but he insists on taking an absurd interest in trains. Trains of any kind. I hardly think that Miss Gallagher travels by public transportation, James."

"Indeed. But you might enjoy this, Miss Gallagher–an annual event organized by the Irish Steam Train Society. The ride is worth the price of a ticket, believe me. You see the coastline of the whole city–from Bray to Howth–in a most pleasurable way, going back to a more gracious era."

"It sounds delightful." Sarah nodded.

"The line runs along the sea. It's a rare treat now. A steam train, I mean."

"And do you travel often by train?"

"Ah, no, not here in Dublin at least, not often, but I've traveled abroad on trains. I am a true buff, as my mother mentioned." James smiled at his mother's back as she moved discreetly away.

"And where exactly have you traveled?"

"Most recently in Russia, but really all over the world. My next trip will be Peru, I hope, if I ever finish this–" The words froze in his mouth and a look of horror flickered over his face. Sarah was startled.

"Is there anything...?"

"No, not. I just wondered ... I mean ... I have yet to travel the trains in Italy. In fact all I know at present is that Mussolini's single greatest achievement was making them run on time ..." James blundered.

Sarah looked at him quizzically. "That's an unfortunate memory. I assure you Italy has more to offer than worn-out stereotypes."

"As does Ireland. Ireland has improved in the years you've been away."

"Quite." Sarah moved off ever so subtly, ever so firmly. "Good night, Mister ... er?"

"Fleming. James. James Fleming." James Fleming inadvertently followed her for a few steps, fairy cake in hand, looking as gormless as he felt.

He was subdued as he drove his mother home, but she read his thoughts.

"Not a success, I take it, James."

"Unmitigated disaster."

"I agree. I've rarely seen you so charmless."

"Thanks." His tone was bitter.

"Honestly, there you were. The best-looking, certainly the best-dressed. Smooth as silk under all kinds of circumstances, and there you were, behaving like a schoolboy, wet behind the ears."

"Don't you want to add that I had egg on my face?"

"And currant buns in your hands ... honestly, James. I did my best."

"Well, you'll have to do more. I ... I wasn't myself tonight. I have a great deal on my mind ..."

"I realize that, James. It's this case you're working on. I've never seen you quite so preoccupied with work before." She paused. "She was interested, you know."

"Pardon?"

"Miss Gallagher. She was interested in whatever that was you were saying about the excursion."

"Are you trying to make me feel better?" said James desperately.

"Not in the least. You know that. No, I could tell that for one brief shining moment you had caught her attention. Pursue it," said his mother.

"Honestly?"

"Yes."

"Will you help me?"

"If I must," Mrs. Fleming laughed gaily. "Tell me what you want."

"You tell me. What would be appropriate? Do you think ... do you think you could have some get-together at the house?"

"That's a possibility."

"Catered?"

"Catered, of course not."

"Catered." James repeated, brooking no argument.

"If you pay," said Mrs. Fleming sweetly.

"Certainly. But get somebody good. Not one of your dowdy ..."

"Dowdy friends, James dear?"

"Sorry. Don't tease me, Mother. This is important."

"So I see, dear. Will you come in and discuss it, then?"

"Sorry, Mother, must dash."

James sped away from his mother's house and slowed down at the intersection. He wished, excited as he was, that he had someplace to dash to. But, as usual, there was not.

The next morning, when he entered his office, a message from his mother lay on his desk. He returned her call.

"It's all set," she announced triumphantly.

"I can't believe it!" exclaimed James. "You are a wonder!"

"I'd love to take all the credit, darling, but actually it was a stroke of luck. Mrs. Smythe–you remember her from last night–rang quite early. She knew that Miss Gallagher had been hoping to meet Chris Reardon, the young Irish composer. He couldn't make the party last night, but Mrs. Smythe has got hold of him–he's free on Saturday night–and Miss Gallagher has agreed to come along after a dinner with some family friends. It will be quite an honor to have two people of such renown to the house, James!"

"You really are terrific, Mother," said James appreciatively. "Now, what's the plan?"

The party on Saturday night was a success, in everyone's judgment. The caterer had chosen well, and the platters of hors d'oeuvres kept coming, conversation flowed like wine, and the mood was not merely jovial, but ebullient. James as the male, as his mother so delicately put it, played host to his mother's hostess, and the early years of boredom and adolescent resentment paid off. James was witty. James was entertaining. Best of all, thought James, James was intriguing.

Sarah arrived fashionably late and was swept into the mood. James nodded and served her but kept his distance for some considerable time. She was not there, after all, to meet him, but to be introduced to Reardon, who had yet to show up. Timing was all, as his mother noted, and since looks and youth were definitely on his side in this company, only his ineptness could bungle it. He felt Sarah's eyes following him occasionally, and he let his wit and charm shine most evidently whenever she was near. Choosing his moment, he approached bearing champagne in fluted Waterford glasses.

"Share a loving cup with me," he whispered, and felt a sense of achievement when she took the glass from his hand and smiled at him.

"You are James, the James I met the other evening?"

"The very one," returned James, laughing, "but in my true colors this time."

"Were you flying false colors then?" said Sarah.

"Hardly false, only the motley of a complete idiot!"

"Hardly an idiot, sir, since you were praising me," returned Sarah lightly.

"Seriously, Sarah–may I call you Sarah?" James went on without waiting for an answer. "I wasn't myself and I apologize. I'm seldom intimidated, but you see, it's true what my mother told you. I know so very little about music, I was truly tongue-tied ..."

"But you know a great deal about trains?"

"Oh, please, spare me my blushes!"

"And a great deal about the law, I take it?" said Sarah more seriously.

"That I leave for business hours," James said hurriedly. "Trains, and other things, occupy my off hours."

"What you said about them did actually interest me. I was even considering ..."

"Being my traveling companion?"

"Perhaps ..." Sarah laughed.

"I am at your service. If you're free tomorrow, I'll get tickets for the excursion and prepare a picnic, Madam, or is it Ms.?"

"Perhaps it's Mrs. ..." Sarah said coyly, and laughed at the expression on his face.

"You jest?"

"Yes, all the time." She smiled. "But I'm free tomorrow afternoon. I'll attend Mass with my parents at the Pro-Cathedral, and after that I'll be free until tea time."

"That's good, because the train leaves at noon. I'll collect you."

"No need. I'll meet you on the platform at Bray–say a quarter to twelve?"

"That's music to my ears ..."

"Oh, dear, James, please ..." Sarah turned lightly and walked off to meet the composer, who had arrived at last.

"I have a tin ear," called James to her retreating back, "not a tin heart!"

"That remains to be seen," she answered without turning.

James hummed off-key as he helped his mother clear away the debris of a roaring success.

"She's nothing what I expected," said his mother as from a great distance.

"Mmm?"

"She's not what I thought. James, are you listening to me?"

"No, Mother, I'm not. Did you say you were expecting?"

"James!"

"Sorry. No, she's not what I expected either. Although I'm not sure how I'd explain it."

"I'll tell you, you dim-witted male. She's as independent as hell."

"Mother!"

"It's true. She's—how would you say it? Yes, you think she 'goes against type.' "

"Not that exactly, Mother. It's just that I had expected that she would be terribly airy-fairy, head in the clouds. She appeared to be so ethereal on stage, so transmuted in time and place. You know yourself her features are so ... so ..." James ended awkwardly.

"How appearances can deceive, then, James," said his mother. "She's spunky and feisty and independent. For heaven's sake, child, she's lived abroad for years, she's traveled extensively. She's not a little convent girl from Monkstown."

"I know that! And I wasn't picturing her that way. It was more that I thought she was, well, more like her music, if you grasp my meaning."

"Yes. Yet again you have projected a personality on to a girl that has nothing to do with the reality. And so yet again you have to go back to square one and try to find out what she's really like."

"I know you'll laugh at this, Mother, but we, Sarah and I, are taking the steam train excursion tomorrow afternoon—from Bray to Howth ..."

"And back again, I assume? Well, at least for once your enthusiasm for trains and for young women have not been mutually exclusive."

"I don't get it, Fleming," Matt snorted, and wiped his mouth with a coffee-stained handkerchief. He and James were eating kabobs in pita bread in the front seat of James's car.

"What don't you get?" James mumbled through bits of lettuce and dripping sauce. He groaned as a mayonnaise-covered lump of lamb landed on his knee.

"You sound to me like a man in love."

"Do I?"

"Suspiciously so. What I want to know is exactly how many times you've gone out with her?"

James beamed. "The train ride and the picnic–of course it rained– and then the theatre, and every day since then. And last night I had her over to dinner."

"So ... what's going on here?"

James put down his food, his appetite gone. "Did you invite me to lunch to give me a spot quiz ... if you call this lunch?"

"Sure, this is lunch. I wanted to give you a change of pace from your club and your fancy restaurants. You need to get down with the real people!" Matt grunted through his lettuce.

"Please, Matt, next time I'll pick the place ... and I won't let so much time pass either."

"Good, but don't change the subject. Now, what has this musical dream machine got that all the others haven't, up till now?"

"I've given that a lot of thought, believe it or not," said James to his old friend. "I think it's what you were getting at just now when you asked what she's got. She's got a life, and it has nothing to do with me. She's beautiful, of course. And sexy in a highstrung kind of way. But she's verbal and witty and bright. She doesn't seem to mind that I know next to nothing about music. Because that's her life. And it's full. Do you get my drift? I don't smell marriage a mile away when I'm with her. I don't suddenly see myself as a potential marriage part-ner! No, Sarah is as free as her music ..."

James sighed like an adolescent as Matt roared. "I'll tell you, Fleming. You're attracted because she's safe. She's not looking to get married. And perhaps she is unattainable. You know what I think?"

"Do I have a choice?"

"No. I think this is just another in a long line. Sarah the unattainable. No commitment on either side. Am I right?"

"I don't know." James was glum.

"Then think about it. And rev up this car because I'm going to be late–I've got to collect two geese at the Connolly Station left-luggage counter. My daft cousin sent them down from Sligo. Good layers, she claims. P'rhaps one will lay me a golden egg!"

"There's more to it than I've told you," James said quietly as they drove.

"Oh God!"

"I think I might be falling in love with Sarah. Not with the idea of her. But with *her*. And I think she may well have some feelings for me. Serious feelings. But she's tied into a case I'm involved with and I ... I don't think ethically I should be seeing her."

"Well, this is more complicated than analyzing your love-life. What are you doing? Using her to get information?"

"For God's sake! Will you listen to me for a minute. I've got myself in a terrible jam."

Matt said nothing.

James's thoughts were grim and muddled as he longed to discuss the issue with Matt. But now he felt he had said too much. He had been very discreet with Sarah, and still they had seen a great deal of each other. After their picnic at Howth he had seen her for a part of each day or evening for over two weeks. And he had found that the more time he spent with her, the more what he knew about her background increased in importance. He had already been looking for physical resemblances between her and Kathleen in London. He had begged off meeting her adoptive parents in Monkstown because of his growing obsession with her past. Was Jack musical? The thought was ludicrous. There were times when he saw Jack's chiseled, dead gray face superimposed on Sarah's vital one. God, that way madness lies.

"Matt. Sarah's adopted."

"So? Is that a problem for you or for her?"

"No, she's very good about it. She's known since she was a child and she has no problem with it."

"She's not one of these people who want to seek out their biological parents?"

"No, not in the least. She loves her parents deeply, and her own life is so full I don't think she's felt that need, the need to find out ..." James's voice faltered.

"Is there more to this, James?"

"Yes. You see, because of another situation, let's say, I happen to know who her real parents were. Who her mother is, I mean. Her father died recently. I know the whole background. But this is so silly. She was two or three days old when the Gallaghers adopted her. It's just, I can't get what I know about her background out of my mind." *And how can I tell her?* he thought. *How can I tell her her father was murdered and her mother is married in London? How can I tell her that her uncles are four thick, bitter farmers? Or that her three aunts are shriveled spinsters with no life of their own? That her aunt is accused of murdering her natural father? God, if only I could dissociate all this from that brilliant girl.*

"Look, Fleming," Matt said at last, "you've got your emotional lines and your ethical lines crossed. You'd better uncross them."

"I know, but it's tough. I never intended to get involved. I was acting the part of sleuth, enjoying myself. How could I know that she ... Oh God!"

"There's another thing?" Matt's voice was neutral. "Is it because what you know about Sarah's natural parents doesn't live up to your, let us say, social expectations?"

"Yes! Yes! Is that so wrong? Sarah's incredible. She's everything that's gifted and lovely ... Yes, you're right there. I am a snob, and I don't want her to know about her background ... And I don't ever want to be the one who has to tell her either! You see, there's nothing in her that stems from her past! And she knows nothing at all about that past. All she knows is that she was adopted at birth."

"Then leave it at that. Accept it, as Sarah has."

If only I could, thought James, and a shiver ran down his spine. As soon as the case came to trial, there was a real possibility that Sarah's connection to the principals involved might become known. How would she take it? And as important, what would she think of his duplicitous role in the situation? He had to act. He had to prevent this case from seeing the light and glare of publicity, a publicity that would possibly destroy Sarah's career, in Ireland at least, and destroy the relationship he believed was developing between them.

Matt paused as he got out of the car at the station. "Dorothy's giving me a lift home. She'll be so thrilled with the geese!" He grinned, and then more seriously added, "Ring me!"

"In another lifetime," said James grimly, "when it's over."

James's voice was curt as he greeted Violet Moore when she opened the heavy front door.

"I'm surprised to see you again," Violet said conversationally, but her look was guarded.

"Really?" James commented, slightly sarcastic.

"Please, this way."

James followed her into the sitting room. "Lily and Rose? Are they joining us?" he asked.

"No."

"Good, because I have a number of things to say to you, Violet ... that are, I think you will agree, of a very personal nature."

Violet sat down, and for the first time James saw a look of strain and fear pass across her face.

"Firstly. I have been puzzled from the beginning as to the reason why Lily claims she saw you the night of the murder. You have refused to discuss this with me, but I'm afraid I have to insist. I think I should tell you that our case for the defense is going rather badly." James hoped to shock Violet, and he was pleased to see he had succeeded.

Violet was silent however.

"I need to know now, today, if you were in the barn on the night in question."

"No, I was not." Violet's voice was firm.

"Then it follows that Lily is lying?"

"Yes, it follows."

"Violet, how can you be so calm? Have you questioned her about this? Don't you see how damaging her statement is, how incredibly damaging her testimony will be—if it comes to that in court?"

Violet nodded almost imperceptibly.

"Have you discussed it with her?" James felt like shrieking, trying to shake this woman's calm demeanor.

"I can't." Violet's voice was strained and she twisted her fingers in her lap.

"You can't or you won't?" pressed James.

"Both. Don't you see there'd be no point? I know she's lying. And I know why she's lying."

"Then for God's sake, tell me! It will help your case. We must break her testimony. You live every day in this house with her. It's beyond me. It's truly beyond me. How can you live every day with this knowledge and still not confront her, challenge her? My God, I don't know how you can stay in the same room with her. You still tell me that she's lying?"

"Yes."

"And that you know why?"

"Yes."

James waited. He began to pace the room, allowing her silence and his own anger to build.

"Why isn't Fitzgerald handling this case?" she said at last.

"He is. He's in charge of the case. He has been from the beginning."

"Then why isn't he here?"

For a moment James wondered the same thing, but he carried on. "Because, Miss Moore, as you well know, it is I who have been doing all the legwork in this case. That's my job. I report to Gerald. Believe me, he is intimately involved in all that I do."

"He knows you're here, then."

"Yes. Call him if you don't believe me." James took a chance.

"I do believe you."

"Then trust me too," James's voice was softer.

"This will do neither you nor me nor the case any good."

"Tell me anyway."

She looked him straight in the eye and spoke without flinching.

"Lily lied because she hates me. It's as simple as that."

He waited for her to elaborate, but she didn't. "Simple! Do you seriously expect me to believe this? That she is simply lying, that her lies could support a case that could send you to prison, that could destroy your life, Miss Moore!" His voice was scoffing and his disappointment great.

"It is the truth!" Violet's voice was ice cold.

"Miss Moore. I've done a lot of investigation into the background of this case. At no time have you told me the truth, or offered to tell me, or helped me in any way. What I now know to be the truth I have had to seek out for myself."

Violet stood up suddenly, angry and defiant. She pushed past James and walked to the door. "That's enough!"

"It won't work with me, Miss Moore. I'm not leaving until you help me help yourself."

"You are leaving now, Mr. Fleming. No one, no one speaks to me in that way."

"No, Miss Moore. You can't bully me. I'm not some frightened, pregnant seventeen-year-old girl." The words had the effect he had hoped for. Violet staggered as though he had struck her.

"Yes. I know. I know a lot. And I think you'd like to know what I know."

"How dare you pressure me."

"Because I want to save your life."

"Why?"

"Because I don't believe you killed your brother."

"Not good enough ..." Violet smirked.

"Because I don't want a young woman's life destroyed. Because I don't want the sins of the father visited on the daughter. Because I don't want your dirty laundry, Miss Moore, your very dirty laundry, washed in public."

Still Violet refused to react.

"Speak, woman, do you hear me! Speak."

"You've found her!" Violet whispered. "You've found that baby girl?" Her voice rose. "You fool, you meddling, bloody fool! Don't you see what this will do to me, to the farm? How dare you interfere in my affairs like this!"

"Because, Violet, I am trying to save your life. What is the farm to you, woman, if you are incarcerated for the rest of your life–and for a crime you claim you did not commit?"

"How dare you! I did not kill my brother!"

"Then let me help you. Help me to help you. For God's sake, for your own sake, tell me the truth once and for all! Tell me why Lily hates you, tell me why you denied burial of Jack's corpse in your family plot, tell me about Kathleen ..."

"And about their baby?"

"Yes. And about their baby."

ChapteR Nine

"I suppose it all started with my own grandmother," Violet Moore said wearily as she glanced at the now roaring fire.

"My grandmother, now that's going back a bit. My grandmother was an only child, and she inherited this land from her father before her. I never knew her, but my own mother used occasionally to speak of her. I'd say she was probably a hard woman, but then she needed to be. A woman on her own, a young woman, and all this land." Violet waved her arms expansively.

"Her holdings were even more extensive than what we–what I– have now. There were fields scattered all through these parishes, some even stretching up to the Wicklow border. Good land for the most part. She was young. She sold some and she lost others, but in the end she consolidated and held fast to her property. The deeds and Land Registry documents fill a steamer trunk, I assure you. When I was a girl I used to go up to the attic and pore over them and try to make sense of it all. You see, I loved the land even then, and the buying and getting–it was all so ancient and intriguing to a young child like myself. It was romancing really ..." She sighed.

"In any event, Grandmother married Grandfather. I never knew him either. After fathering three girls, he died. It sounds, when I put it like that, that the effort wore him out." Violet laughed mirthlessly at her own coarseness.

"From what little I know, he was a weak man. He brought only one small field into the family. He was the last in a long line of a Clare family that had lost its land over the years, for various reasons. But poor management must have been one of them, because he nearly ruined this farm. After his death it was as though my grandmother had never been married, except for the fact of the three daughters. My mother was one of those three daughters.

"A harder life you'd never meet, Mr. Fleming. You see, there was the land but no money. Land rich, cash poor. Grandmother kept a small dairy herd. They had chickens and a kitchen garden. Mother often repeated how she walked to school, three miles, barefoot. But she wasn't alone. It was like that in those days. She was the eldest and must have got the best of what was on offer because in time her two sisters died. One of TB and the other–oh, it must have been dreadful–the other of brucellosis.

"And there she was, left alone with Grandmother. It seemed as though there were nothing but women in this family as far back as time itself. Women somehow perpetuating themselves. It was as though the men were there merely to extend the line, and when their role was played, when their bolt was shot, they faded and died.

"This is how I grew up, Mr. Fleming. With stories of the women of my family going back generations. Women who had held on to this farm and this land despite the fact that they were alone almost all of their lives.

"Matriarchy, I suppose that springs to your mind? But what else is Ireland but a matriarchy? And hasn't it always been so? Hasn't it always been Mother Ireland? And the *sean bean bocht?* And in all of her guises. Hasn't it been the Fine Old Woman with the four green fields? And haven't our images been the likes of Queen Maeve, Deirdre of the Sorrows? And hasn't she always–since before Yeats and after–been the proud, the mystical, the powerful woman, the mother and the fatal lover?

"And I ask you, Mr. Fleming–if this isn't all Greek to you–isn't that image of Ireland the right and true one? Woman as life-giver, woman as sustainer. Women have always loved the land, but they loved it with sense, good common sense. It didn't take hold of their imaginations and cause them to go mad. They loved it as they loved their children. They didn't let it get into their hearts, but into their minds. And they didn't see land as power—they saw it as life. There's a difference, Mr. Fleming, believe me.

"What monuments do you see in this country to women, to the image of woman, to the great Celtic women? One. And it's a grave. A great cairn on Cnoc na Ri in Sligo, but it's a grave nonetheless.

"What are the monuments and statues you see in Dublin—men and images of men, Celtic heroes and fallen heroes, men one and all. Oh yes, don't interrupt. I know the poor little head of the Countess in Stephen's Green. Pleasant bits of greenery grow around that sculpture and ignoramuses walk by it and idly wonder who that woman might have been.

"Oh, wait, and haven't I forgotten? Indeed and I have. There is now a great statue, isn't there, Mr. Fleming? Right in O'Connell Street for all to see. Anna Livia. Oh such a monument to womanhood. A river. A river famous for what? Named by Joyce and made famous by Joyce. Its entire meaning endowed by him. A bony Medusa-headed corpse in my opinion. Aptly named by Dublin's wit."

"Anna Rexia?" James smiled.

"The floozy in the jacuzzi ... more like. Oh, will that keep us quiet? Yet another sculpture by yet another man!"

James shrugged, at a loss for something to say against this tirade.

"I'll tell you where the images are. In churches. That's what Rome did for us. What pagan sculpture could be allowed to stand, what Celtic and pre-Christian image would stand before the all-consuming ocean that was Rome? Rome! That what it couldn't wash away it subsumed into its very self. And so what images of woman did we inherit from Rome? We got what they chose to give us. Maiden madonnas. Meek and mild. In every village and town, statues and shrines to the Virgin, an even less fecund image than that of the Madonna. And then what does Catholicism give us? Hey presto! A miracle at Knock. And why wasn't it in the heart of Dublin instead of Knock? Because it was the most depressed area of the country at the time. Mayo. Who was in Mayo but ignorant, poor, suffering farmers—who would question such a wondrous thing? It gave them hope and the strength to go on in the blackest of the black times.

"And ever since, hasn't our little island had its fair share of reported sightings? And what does Rome say now, in the modern world? Well, it says neither one thing nor another. And now what do we have, in the middle of this Kerry babies scandal, with unwed mothers murdering their babies or throwing them into the sea—we have the moving statue at Ballinaspittle."

"And hundreds saw it move!" James added.

"And in the dark and in the night two men come and smash the poor plaster statue and smash its head and break off its folded hands. Ah, that was an act that spoke louder than words, Mr. Fleming."

Violet stood up suddenly and walked to the sideboard, where she poured two brandies. James watched as she stood there, quieting herself.

"I seem to have digressed. But in this long and perhaps tiresome digression, I think you will finally follow the thread of my thoughts. You must understand. I haven't talked about these events for a very long time.

"My mother was a very strong woman. Physically as well as emotionally. She ran the farm and increased the herd successfully. She had learned much already from growing up on the land, but she had no formal schooling in agriculture. So she read and she studied and she gleaned all she could from the farmers hereabouts and from the auctioneers, from the financial pages of The Irish Times. She had an acute mind. People used to say she had a head on her shoulders like a man's. It drove her mad. She raised three of us girls and my brother Jack with no help. Because there was none. No relatives. No friendly uncles to take us on outings. I tell you we worked hard and we saw her work hard. She instilled in me—perhaps because I was the eldest, perhaps because I was most like her—such a love for this land that whenever I had to leave it I became physically sick. Homesickness, you see, is a real and not an imagined ill.

"Mind you, she wasn't affectionate herself. I think perhaps Rose minded that, of the four of us. Perhaps Jack too. When we were mere gossoons, she'd take each of us in turn and tell us that the time for kissing and holding was at an end. And so it was. But Rose, Rose never accepted it. She'd hang on mother's skirts until even she wearied of it, and then she hung on to Lily's skirts. It suited them both. It still does."

Violet glanced up at the door almost as if seeing those two young children, clinging to each other, come tumbling into the room. Suddenly James had a sense of the history of this house in which he sat. It was, for a brief moment, as though all the many personalities that Violet had sketched out for him were crowding into the room. Stern-faced women and sickly men, dying children and children dying for affection. He saw a long line of a family that had seemingly passed on its strengths in the only form it recognized as strength—a hardness of heart and an obsession with the land.

"History repeated itself in my family, Mr. Fleming, in a bizarre pattern. Mother married Father and they had three daughters and a son. Father was the only child of an old Kildare family who'd gone into trade, seed and grain I think. He had a bit of family money and took an interest in this farm, I was told. But he died a year or two after Jack was born. I didn't know him. Or should I say, I cannot remember him.

"I was coming up to my majority when Mother fell ill. She never told me or any one of us. The girls and Jack were still in short skirts and short pants, for God's sakes ... 'teenagers,' as they say now—foolish term. I had done well at school. Mother had insisted I get an education. And despite my homesickness at the boarding school, I did very well. But I lived for the day I could return home, and home I came. It was as Mother intended—but how could I know that then? She had cancer. She had seen a doctor, and he told her out straight, as was the way. And she told no one, as was the way. She sickened before our ignorant eyes.

"The morning of the day she died, she milked half the herd by hand. I ask you ..." Violet looked away for some few seconds, but her face was impassive. The burden of her story weighed down on James like a heavy blanket. He didn't speak, for he knew to some extent that Violet was talking to herself.

"That afternoon, after taking a very small midday meal, she said to us all that she wanted to lie down for a rest. This was so unusual that we were speechless, but we never questioned Mother ... I know"—she glanced at James—"it's almost impossible to make outsiders understand. But she went upstairs ..."

A chill of recognition ran through James as he heard in Violet's words a faint echo of the lines of an old ballad he'd sung as a child: "She went upstairs to go to bed/And calling to her family said/Bring me a chair till I sit down/And pen and ink till I write down ..."

"She went upstairs and took up her pen and wrote down that she'd left her will all properly drawn and told where it was kept, what solicitor to contact, that sort of thing. All very efficient. She laid it on her desk with her watch beside it. Oh, I forgot the main item she left—a short letter.

"However it was, I noticed she hadn't come down from her rest, but I didn't want to disturb her. She was a cantankerous woman at the best of times. But Rose was mooning around. She had wanted to make dumplings for tea—a dreadful cook she was—and she just had to know if Mother would like a bit of dumpling with her beef. She trotted up to Mother's room—of course it had to be Rose. It would be Rose.

"She opened the door, and it was dark, the curtains were drawn." James felt the recognition again, and the melancholy ballad ran through his mind: "They found her hanging from a rope ..."

James shook his head and thought of Rose, poor poor Rose. He felt sorrow for Rose the living person that he knew, and not for the unknown woman who took her life in the face of a debilitating illness.

"The letter—the letter told us—told us about the cancer. She didn't offer an explanation. It wasn't lack of courage ... I think it was pride, perhaps, and now that I'm closer to her age at the time of her death, I think also it was the awful thought of weakening and losing, of being dependent on anyone else but herself.

"Looking back I don't know which was worse. Reading her letter or hearing the will read. She said, in the letter ... let me put it this way. She said no word of farewell to any one of us. It was a difficult time. Lily, Rose, Jack. I think if she had died in the normal course of an illness, it would have given us some time, time perhaps to grow up, to take on what seemed anyway to be our preordained roles in life. Then again she could have dropped down dead of a heart attack. We could have found her cold in a field somewhere, as cold as a sheep that fell down dead, perishing of the cold."

James was yet again astonished at the hardness of these people and their language.

Violet looked at him suddenly. "You no doubt know some of this." she said with an edge of bitterness.

Startled, James had to think to what was she referring. At last he fathomed her meaning.

"Violet, I can say to you honestly that not one person—and I have talked to many in this village and its surroundings—has mentioned one word to me about your mother." A look of surprise flickered across her drawn, pinched face, and she leaned back against the chintz cushion of her chair.

"Another brandy?" he inquired pleasantly.

"Yes, Mr. Fleming, please help yourself."

He did so, and poured Violet a generous measure.

"Surprisingly, at least to me, her will divided the property equally among the four of us. But I, being the eldest, was to come into my share very shortly, as she knew. And therefore I was to have control over the property as a whole until each of the others came to majority. As it transpired, the others didn't care in the early years. Somehow we slipped easily into roles that mimicked our previous life. I stood in Mother's place. And they reacted to me in much the same way as they had to her. Life went on as before. But I gradually began to extend myself. I grew in confidence after the shock had worn off. It was as though … as though I had been waiting all my life, as though everything that had gone before had prepared me for this. I began to study and learn, to modernize my thinking, introducing improvements on the farm and with the herds.

"Time passed, and it was as though not a ripple had interrupted our lives. Lily became twenty-one and then Rose. Rose had never been strong—you know what I mean—and Mother's death, the manner of her death, had nearly unhinged her. She led a quiet life, and Lily managed her well. Rose never looked beyond the farm for any sort of life, and that was how it should be. At least I thought so. It wasn't that I said to myself, 'Now what would Mother want?' I simply did it." She sighed again at the gargantuan task of explaining her life for the first time. James nodded to indicate that he understood, that he was on her side.

"Lily, on the other hand, Lily did look beyond the farm. She had never been physically strong or robust. She was never a huntswoman, for example. She didn't like to ride, she didn't like to garden, I'm not sure what she liked. She seemed always to be preparing for a life that was completely unavailable to her. Almost ignoring the fact that she was reared on a farm and not in some suburb of Dublin. She liked to read, she liked theatre. She'd take herself off to Dublin to see a few plays or concerts. She drew or sketched or some such nonsense. Yet she hadn't much time for these pursuits because she had a role to play here on the farm, and to give her her due, she did it and did it well. Apart from looking after the hens, her real job has been the management of our accounts. And she has a fine head for money! But her heart was elsewhere—in the city, I suppose. And then she had hopes, as we used to say. Hopes of marriage, I mean. Ridiculous, really. There were one or two young men that took an interest for a while. She'd go to the occasional local dance, especially at harvest time. She got on well with some of the men who came and went here at the farm. There was a dreadful commercial traveler who actually began to court her, but I sent him packing. Totally unsuitable. Probably was married for all we could tell. Lily cried for days and then we never spoke of it again.

"Shortly after that time, though, she started to ask about her share of the farm, saying it was equal to my own and that I had no right or rule over her. She even began to hint that she would want to take her share in another form. Money, I suppose she meant. Of course that was out of the question. It would have meant selling off to get her fair market value of one-fourth of the estate. If she had insisted, it would have ruined my long-term plans for the farm.

"Meanwhile Rose stood by me. Although she loved Lily, she'd never go against me when it came to the farm and all its concerns. I'd merely explain to her, Mother wouldn't have liked it, and she'd trot off and tell Lily to be a good girl. I think now if Lily had married, I would have been better off. I doubt in her married bliss she would have bothered to seek her quarter share of the estate in any form but an inheritance. But imagine Lily bearing children. She always struck me as being so frail and fearful, not in the least hardy. It would have killed her, and then there'd be a widower and some offspring and endless battles about the inheritance. But it was always in her mind, at least in those days. She had one more romance." Violet paused and sipped her drink before continuing. "A certain local man who had gone up to Dublin and done extremely well for himself. It seems he had a 'gra,' as they say, for Lily. He was on the point of settling down with a Dublin girl, but this thing he'd had for Lily was getting in the way. Imagine! He wanted it settled once and for all. He wanted Lily to marry him."

The obvious question sprang to James's lips. What did all of this mean now? With no one to inherit. What did all of Violet's hard work, what did generation after generation of slaving and drudgery and suffering to keep the farm, to hold the farm and increase it, preserve it and defend it, mean? Three spinsters, with no offspring. Three wizened trees with no fruit, with no seed. Pointless. Fruitless.

He drank his brandy as she continued. He was not going to interrupt her flow.

"So you see, I had Rose on my side, and I'd pretty much got Lily settled into my ways. When she'd get very restless, she'd take a holiday with some local lady from the church, or with a group. France. She was fond of France. But she always returned home. I used to think if she'd had any gumption she'd have stayed there, or wherever she happened to fall on her feet. But oh no, despite what she'd tell you now, she always came willingly back, back to the farm.

"But Jack ... I hadn't reckoned on Jack. He was a mere boy when Mother died. I should have paid more attention. But you see, I knew nothing of men or boys. I never knew any very well. I was indifferent to them. I wanted to be strong like my mother and her mother and her mother before her. I had no time for men. To me they were weak. Well, our history shows us that and more.

"But Jack was growing up, and I didn't pay sufficient heed. I had not ken enough to see what was coming, on any score, for that matter.

"He was a big lad, robust and broad. Very strong. And he worked like a horse. Big head of hair, big broad grin. Energy that outmatched the three of us sisters. And he was cheerful, all the day long. He seemed to enjoy what he was doing. He loved the land, and it was growing inside him like a passion. And finally it began to show. As he grew older, that passion grew stronger. All unasked, he would mention plans he had for the farm, long-term plans. Out of the blue, at the supper table. The fact that I never responded never disheartened him. At first I thought it was idle, boyish talk, silly male dreaming. You know the way, 'Some day I'll do this and then some day I'll do that.' But it was all to do with the farm. It finally penetrated my brain. He never talked of going off to seek his fortune—don't ask me why I thought he would do so.

"There were now these conversations about what he wanted for his children. His children! And he a child himself! We never really got on. I simply had taken over from Mother, and he looked at me in that way. I probably seemed as old as Mother. He did willingly what he was bid. It was all Mother had expected. She had got good results from Jack, and I continued to get good results. And that was all I expected.

"I never anticipated that he would see his life as taking shape on the farm, that he would think of taking an active role, a leading role! But that's exactly what he started doing—introducing new ideas, different methods, buying machinery without so much as even consulting me.

"Then I heard talk around the farm that Jack was a real lad for the girls. I thought, if I thought at all, that that was just as well. Let him see lots of girls. Later I learned he was seeing that Walsh one. He started to talk about her at table. Rose would get all giggly. It annoyed me! Lily—I don't remember much of what Lily had to say. If I had to, I'd say she encouraged him. God knows why. She knew as well as I did that a match there was entirely out of the question. So much so, that that is perhaps why I didn't pay it any heed."

"Out of the question?" James asked quietly.

"Of course. Firstly, she, well, she 'dug with the other foot.' A Catholic. There hadn't been a mixed marriage in the family since the dawn of time. But it was more than that. Those Walsh brothers would have been over the moon to link up with us. They would have seized it as an opportunity to join the two estates, the two farms, possibly the two herds! It was unthinkable. After all the work my family—me, me, sir—had put into keeping this herd the purest in five counties!

"To make a painful story short, Jack got it into his head that he was in love and wished to marry the Walsh girl. He was very determined about it. And that determination seemed to fire him up—he was starting to argue with me over the management of the farm. And now I saw that Lily was siding with him against me. And Rose. Of course, Rose was mesmerized by Jack. There was an air of excitement about the three of them. I'd catch them whispering and giggling; they'd stop talking when I came into meals and there'd be the nod-and-wink sort of thing. They were excluding me!" A look of astonishment passed across her face briefly.

"Rose was the silliest. Going around humming little nursery rhymes. Telling Jack which room would make a good nursery and which room these 'children' would sleep in, and actually saying that Mother's room could be done up for Jack and his wife. And then she'd remember why we'd locked it and she'd have a fit of crying. It was intolerable.

"And then suddenly it all came to an end." Violet was silent for a long time, as though deciding whether to continue.

"You've told me so much, Miss Moore . . . Please, if you will, finish the story for me." James's tone was gentle but not pleading. He knew pleading was useless with Violet Moore.

"Yes, yes. It feels good to talk to someone after all this time. Jack's death has made it all very present to my mind. I had succeeded, truly succeeded, in forgetting about this ancient past. But now I can't seem to put it from me.

"The night that Jack went drinking at the pub, I had no idea where he was. I didn't see myself as his keeper and I never did keep track of him in his free time. I had been working here in this room. It was very very late, and Rose and Lily were upstairs in bed, asleep, I assume.

They were never involved in what transpired, then or since. I heard a noise from the direction of the kitchen and I went out there. I knew quickly that someone was in the back hall and I threw open the door, never expecting to see Jack, I assure you. He cowered for a moment and then came into the light. He was in a terrible state. He was covered with sweat and mud, and yet he was shivering with cold— with shock, now I realize.

"He blurted out almost immediately that he had killed Mike Walsh. Walsh had been waiting for him, and leapt out at him in the dark as Jack was cutting across the field, drunk, of course. They were both drunk, I'm certain of that. He pushed Walsh and Walsh went down heavily and struck his head. When Jack couldn't rouse him, he panicked and ran home—to me.

"I admit it. I instantly saw my opportunity. I had always been quick, you see, to see a chance and take it. That's how I prospered so well in the business of the farm.

"He was ranting and crying. The drink was still on him, yet he was sober enough to know what he'd done. He knew he'd taken another man's life, and he fell to weeping, alternating between wanting to run to the police to confess and run to hide behind my skirts. I told him they'd never believe him, that he'd be sent to prison or worse. Oh, I painted a picture, bleak and black. It was then he told me that the Walsh girl was expecting his child. Mr. Fleming, it was a worse shock to me to hear that news than to hear he'd killed Mike Walsh. I saw instantly that that unborn child stood to inherit, to take away from me everything I had worked for, everything that I would work for. I couldn't allow it, but I had to be careful. And in the end it was easy because Jack was still merely a boy, and a very frightened boy.

"I sent him off to wash himself, and I went upstairs quietly and packed his bag. I put together all the cash I had in the house, which was considerable, and stuffed it in a valise. While I was packing I thought of my plan. It came into my head full formed, like Venus springing from Zeus' head: a beautiful plan.

"I explained it to him in words of one syllable. His eyes focused on my mouth, like a drowning man, like a dying animal. It was horrible, really. I never saw before or since such an expression on a man's face. He was horribly white and shaking. I told him that he would leave the country that night, that he should go through the north and from there to Scotland. I swore to him that I would cover for him. But he said he didn't give a damn about that. His concern wasn't whether he lived or died. It was all Kathleen and the baby. And then I swore that I would care for her and for the child. But that he had to promise me something in return because this for me was such a serious undertaking. He knew that. He knew I hated the Walshes, and he knew that I would hate that child. I asked him to give up his share in the farm. I dictated a piece of writing to that effect. I still don't know if it would have held up legally. I never had to test it.

"He took it so seriously, you see. He was that kind of boy. I think that was the first and the last time I saw what manner of man he might have become.

"All he wanted was that the girl and the child be cared for. I even assured him that he might be able to return someday, but that he had to go, and to go immediately. I imagine the whole scene only took an hour or less. And then he was gone.

"I was stunned. Stunned. In a matter of moments our lives had changed forever. I could hardly take it in. I didn't sleep that night, because the enormity of what I had promised finally came home to me.

"I didn't know if I could provide an alibi for Jack. But the police, when the time came, took down my statement in good faith. I had told them that Jack had come straight home from the pub and had been helping me with a sick calf. I suppose because it was already clear to them that Mike Walsh had fallen and hit his head, rather than been hit on it, the police had pretty much decided that his death was an accident. Anyway, they accepted my statement.

"I also told them, and whoever else asked, that Jack had decided to leave the farm after he'd heard about Mike's death. That he felt bad that his teasing in the pub had led to such a terrible result. I implied that he'd gone off to London to work, and that I expected him to return in six months or a year. Because he was so young and known to be headstrong, people seemed to accept my explanation."

"And Lily? And Rose?" James questioned her sharply.

"They were puzzled. And saddened, of course, that he hadn't seen fit to bid them good-bye. But at no time did it ever enter either of their minds that Jack could have killed the Walsh boy. It was unthinkable to them. He was their baby brother.

"Initially I kept the hope alive that he'd return soon. That he was young, just wanted to see a bit of life before he settled down to marriage and responsibility. That too rang true, and they believed me, because, as I say, I had come to believe in the whole fabrication myself. I actually came to believe that Jack had merely gone off on a flit. Days passed. The three of us adjusted. We'd look for the mail at first, and we trusted he'd be back within a year or so. The talk in the village didn't reach us. After all, who was going to relate to Rose, for example, or myself, the low gossip about Jack killing Mike Walsh?

"So when Kathleen Walsh came to call on me, I was completely unprepared. It was as though she no longer existed. And yet there she was, in the sitting room, here where we are talking now." She closed her eyes as if to see that young girl more clearly.

"She reminded me immediately of Jack. She was deathly white. I thought she would faint on me, and I actually asked her to sit down. She spoke simply and directly. She asked me where Jack was, and I told her I didn't know, that I hadn't heard from him. At that point it was the truth. Her eyes filled with tears, but I give her credit—she didn't cry. She told me frankly that she was expecting Jack's baby. That she needed to get in touch with him so that they could marry as planned. She didn't have to tell me what her brothers would do, or what the talk would be, if she started to show before she married.

"She was seventeen, with no money, and in this situation virtually friendless. It was so simple. I was kindness itself. I could see the surprise in her eyes, but she accepted my kindness like a child. I told her that I would take responsibility for her and the baby in Jack's absence. That I would take care of everything. That no doubt Jack would be in contact soon, and just to give me a little time to figure things out.

"In that week I laid my plans. It was essential that she be got away from the village. I believed her when she told me that no one else knew about the child. She had far too much to lose to gossip with her girlfriends. I knew, as we all did, that there were convents dotted 'round the country who took care of this kind of thing. I contacted a girl I had been to boarding school with, who had had a sister with a similar problem. She was reluctant at first, but I got the information. I contacted the convent in Tipperary and made the arrangements.

"Then I fed Kathleen her story, that she was fed up looking after her brothers and the farm, and now that Jack had done a bunk, she too was going off to London to seek her fortune. She left home, having packed and prepared as she would have if indeed she had been going off to London. Her brothers were livid, but she told them she was determined and that there was nothing they could do about it. They made no move to stop her. I met her in Dublin and escorted her myself to the convent in Tipperary.

"I brought her down on the train and took a local taxi service out to the convent. I could tell from the driver's discreet reaction it wasn't the first time. Kathleen was very weepy, and perhaps resentful too. We had had a few angry words and there was, needless to say, very little friendliness on either side. I installed her with the nuns. They impressed me as competent, and more worldly than I had expected. I have had few dealings with nuns ..."

Violet paused at last and stood up slowly, as though to stretch her legs. She walked to the window and parted the drapes, looking out blankly. James was relieved to have a few minutes' respite, although in truth he was hanging on every word. He went over to the sideboard and poured two more brandies, bringing ice and ginger ale on a tray back to the low coffee table. He pondered that Violet was perhaps a mere ten years older than Kathleen at the time of these events. He wondered at the coldness, the detachment she had felt toward that young unhappy girl, carrying a baby and alone in the world because of it.

Violet resumed her seat, straightening her back and leaning forward. This time she watered her brandy with ginger ale and sipped slowly.

"And what of Jack?" James prompted, virtually reminding her of his presence in the room.

Violet sighed. "I am about to tell you. Jack did escape the country, and in a matter of weeks the furor here had diminished. He had no way of knowing that, of course. He had gone to London and had landed a job very quickly on one of the big building sites. There was a tremendous amount of construction going on then, after the war. There were thousands of Irishmen in London doing exactly the same thing, and no one paid any attention to yet another one earning good money by the sweat of his back. As I recall, he seemed to make good pay, for shortly after he settled he began writing to Kathleen, in care of me here at the farm, and enclosing money for her. I knew because I opened the letters ..." She paused as James shifted in his chair.

"Yes, I opened them and I scanned them briefly. What he said to her was much the same as what he also wrote to me. He was sending the money for Kathleen and the baby. He thought they were here at the farm. I led him to believe that was the case. I told him not to write too often. I was afraid that the Sweeneys or the postman, and of course Rose or Lily, might intercept one of the letters. But I guess no one had the same audacity as myself." She smiled weakly at the irony.

"To be fair, I used Jack's money to pay for Kathleen's needs, supplementing it with my own, of course. It did make me feel better. But my scruples soon faded. Jack had plans to bring Kathleen and the baby over to London. He believed they could get a bedsit or flat and that they could live there until a time came when perhaps he could return to Ireland. I told him the police were still actively looking for him and that it could be years. But he was so young, even the thought of a ten-year absence didn't discourage him!

"Meanwhile I mentioned to Kathleen in one of my few visits to the convent that Jack had written from London to tell me that he was about to emigrate. I was vague about it. I hadn't needed to embroider the story, because she believed it immediately and was devastated. She felt completely rejected and, for a young girl, became very bitter very quickly. That was just as well. The nuns and I thought we might have had trouble persuading her to put the baby—if it lived—up for adoption. She did weaken a bit in her resolve, I understand, at the time of the birth. The nuns had rung me and I went down the same day.

"I remember seeing her in her room. She looked so young and fit and well. It was hard to believe she had given birth just hours before.

"I told her the baby would have a better life with a secure family. That she herself would have no life at all if she kept the child. She was a practical girl and knew that herself. I told her then that I would help, since Jack had not. That we might have been sisters-in-law but for Jack's immature behavior. That was a hard one to force out of my mouth. She was wary of me, but believed at least enough to allow herself to take my money. I told her to go to Australia. She knew girls from her school that had already gone out there. It didn't seem such a farfetched idea. She knew better than I that her life in Ireland was over. I gave her the passage to Australia and money for clothes and a bit of a start. And she took it. That was the last I saw of her."

"Did you see the baby? Your brother's daughter? Your own niece?" James thought wildly of Sarah's striking face and her graceful hands, the music of her violin and the strength of her nature.

Violet looked up suddenly. "No, of course not." She spat out the words. "She was as nothing to me. A scrap of a thing. I never for a moment thought of her as part of Jack or part of the Moore family. She was an unfortunate accident."

James reddened with instant fury at the words. He was very close to losing his control with this heartless woman. He would have to leave the room if the conversation didn't change quickly.

"I see you think I've a heart of stone. I admit that I do, but please remember this: I freely took on responsibility for Kathleen and the baby. I discharged my duty. I believed, then and now, that what I did was best for all of them, for all of us.

"I made sure through the nuns that the adoptive parents were highly respectable, educated–that they had money went without saying. I specifically didn't want a farming family. The family who took her were all that I asked and more. There was just one problem. They were Catholic. I would have preferred ... But then, so was Kathleen. The child had been baptized a Catholic right there in the convent, so there were no difficulties in the adoption process. When I learned the family was Catholic and that all was taken care of ... yes, I admit it, I lost interest. It was a closed chapter to me."

"And for Jack also?" James tried to conceal his tone of distaste at her atrocious callousness.

"Jack? Oh, that was fairly simple. Or so I thought. He knew when the baby was due, of course, and his letters at that time were beginning to be more frequent. As soon as the confinement was over, I wrote and told him that the baby, a girl, had died at birth. It wasn't a lie!" She glared at James, to stop him from speaking, if he attempted. "That child was dead to him. I told him Kathleen was shattered and, in order to put all this sorrow behind her, she was going out to Australia. And he believed it. He believed it because she hadn't written to him in all those months, and now what they had had between them was all over."

"Because she never did write ... because she believed he had abandoned her as you had told her?" James's voice was bitter.

"I told her I wrote to him. Of course, when she didn't hear from him herself, she grew discouraged, especially in the latter months of her pregnancy. She felt that only I and the nuns cared for her. She felt Jack had run out on her, and I did not discourage that idea."

James stood up. Pacing the floor, he tried to confront the reality of Violet's story. A young couple completely manipulated by the woman who sat in front of him. A baby deprived of its parents because of this woman, a woman totally without remorse. He glanced at her with loathing. She seemed neither to notice nor to care, and resumed talking.

"I didn't hear from Jack for months. I assumed he was getting on with his life. One night ... one night months later ... I went out to the back barn to check on a cow that was in a bad way. Suddenly Jack was in front of me." Violet looked up. "I couldn't believe my eyes. He looked older, much older than when he had gone away. And he was sober. He had put on weight and, well, it's hard to describe ... he was different. Older, bigger, more threatening. He had come on a mail boat into the port of Wexford that very night and had made his way on foot to the farm. He told me straight out he hadn't believed me, that he knew Kathleen had loved him. He said he knew that even though the baby had died, she would have come to London, at least to talk, to settle things between them. He had begun to suspect, when he thought about it, that I had prevented her from writing, from seeing him or finding him in London.

"I was truly frightened of him. He was ranting at me, telling me that he should never have trusted me. That his child would be alive if it hadn't been for me. If he had been there with Kathleen when the child was born, if he had married her and taken her off to London with him ... He was moving toward me, screaming at me. I thought then—foolishly—that if I told him at least that the baby was alive, he'd calm down. He seemed so caught up with this baby's death, you see. His dead child. I thought ... I thought he'd be pleased to know the truth at least about that. So I told him that the baby had lived. He stopped in his tracks. It was like stunning a beast, like knocking it on the forehead with a great blow. He stood swaying, his eyes glazing over. I tried to get his attention. I poured out that the baby was well, a little girl, that a wealthy, established family had adopted her and that she would have a wonderful life. When I said adoption, he turned his wild eyes on me. I thought he would kill me—the look that passed through his eyes. And then he began to rave ..."

Violet's chest heaved at this, the only sign of emotion she had shown. James felt the sweat starting up on his face and neck as he saw the scene through her eyes. And he saw a man going through a hell of his own making.

"He screamed at me. He told me I had killed him more surely than if I had shot him, more certainly than if I had handed him over to the police and told them outright that he had killed Mike Walsh, more cruelly than if I had put the noose around his neck with my own hands!

"I thought he would kill me then and there. He saw, as if in a flash of lightning, that I had taken his share of the farm, that I would take away his alibi from him if he tried to return. He spat out the words in a wild jumble. He shook me till my brains rattled and his spittle and his sweat covered my face. He told me I had taken his baby from him, the child of his love for Kathleen and hers for him. That Kathleen was gone, the baby was gone, the farm—gone, life itself. He was crying and shouting how he had lived alone all those months in London, in fear and self-loathing, how he'd starved himself to send money to Kathleen to buy the baby fine little clothes, fine wee things of linen and lace. How he had sent money to pay for their passage to London, where they would be a family together, where they would choose a name for their baby together. He stopped talking for a moment and stared at me. And then he came for me—he lifted me up like a rag doll, he shook me, screaming in my face that word—*family, family.* Then he threw me to the floor of the barn with all his strength and staggered out of the door, crying and ranting ... I lay I don't know how long. Minutes, hours? I was frozen with fear and horror. Finally, I grew so cold that I dragged myself back to the house. I thought he might be there, somewhere, waiting for me. He seemed somehow so near death himself that killing me could be his only satisfaction. I searched the house, I searched the outbuildings in the morning light ... but he was gone. I never saw him again ... alive."

Chapter Ten

Maggie's voice crackled over James's intercom. "Mr. Daley rang five times yesterday, James, about the Hanlon will. The travel agent called in with the outline itinerary for your Peru trip. And the Big F wants to see you ASAP."

James sighed. Exhausted and uneasy after learning the whole story from Violet, he dreaded recounting it all to Gerald.

"Put him off, will you, Maggie?"

"I don't think that's wise, pet," Maggie sagely advised. "I'll tell him you'll be in in ten minutes, will that do?"

Forced into making a decision of some kind, James reluctantly chose to edit Violet's story. In the men's room he splashed some cold water on his face, and gathering his thoughts, walked briskly to Gerald's office, where his greeting was warm and cordial.

"I got your office memo, James. And I was surprised—sit down, my boy—that you'd been down to Kilmartin yet again. You didn't mention you would be going."

"Sorry, Gerald. It was a spur-of-the-moment thing. I was beginning to feel some urgency in this case. I have the sensation ... I feel as though time is running out on us ..."

"And so it is, James. Sheridan spoke to me this morning, but more of that later. Tell me, how did you get on?"

"Better than I expected," James said brightly. "You see, I have been worried about Lily's story ..."

" 'Story'?" Gerald leaned back in his swivel chair and reached for his pipe.

"The story that she had seen Violet at the barn on the night in question. Violet had denied that part of the story from the beginning. And I believed her."

"Why?"

"I suppose because she was your client and, well, because you've known her for donkeys years. I didn't press her about it, and as you know, she has been less than forthcoming. But it kept eating away at me. I couldn't understand how Violet could continue to live with Lily in such close quarters if Lily had been lying. On the other hand, I couldn't grasp why Lily would lie—she has nothing to gain, obviously."

"And what have you learned?"

"This may seem unbelievable to you, sir, but somehow the whole story rings true. Violet talked rather freely, for her."

James looked up and smiled at Gerald. Gerald was nodding in agreement.

"She spoke of her family's long history, of her love for the farm—which to me sounds quite obsessional—and how she, well, in a nutshell, lived for the farm and brooked no interference. You probably are aware of most of this from dealing with her legal matters over the years?"

Again Gerald nodded.

"Well, to put it succinctly, she wanted to control the farm, and consequently, to control Lily, Rose, and Jack. Regarding Lily, it seems that she interfered with Lily's own personal plans. Lily hoped to marry and leave the farm. Apparently there was at least one serious romance—in other words, a chance for Lily to marry. And Violet prevented it."

"That seems preposterous!"

"Which? That Lily had plans or that Violet interfered?"

"That in this day and age Violet could have stopped Lily."

"This happened years ago, Gerald. And I had the impression that she must have pressured her into staying for Rose's sake, and perhaps used the fact that their mother might not have approved. Now that I know Violet, I can imagine too that she undermined Lily's confidence. God, she is incredibly hard. Don't you find her so?"

"Indeed and I have, James. I've dealt with her property transactions, and she's as hard as nails in business. Fortunately we only met occasionally over the years. To be frank, although I was willing to take on this case, I have been only too happy that you've been handling it. Violet is our client and she deserves a sympathetic handling of her case. You were able to give her your unprejudiced attention and concern. I doubt I could have. She puts me off."

"Yes, she puts me off too." James's face grew somber, almost sad, and Gerald caught the change.

"Is there something else? You seem troubled."

James didn't answer.

"Well, presumably Violet believes Lily lied for revenge. That's a pretty serious accusation against Lily, James."

"That's just it. I don't know Lily at all, really." James threw up his hands. "God, I hardly know Violet. But somehow it doesn't seem possible that gentle, considerate Lily could be capable of holding such a grudge, of orchestrating a vendetta!"

"I agree, but our hands are tied. As you know, we can't question Lily, since she's a witness for the prosecution. How about Rose?"

"Oh, God, it never crossed my mind to trouble Rose. You didn't want me to...?"

"Not a'tall. Even if she had some information, she'd make a terrible witness. A cross-examination would demolish her. No. You did right. Yet, I sense that Violet convinced you ..."

"I think she did. While I was sitting in her living room yesterday it all was completely believable, the human psychology of it rang true. Even Violet's manner and voice rang true. She's so acquiescent, so ... almost defeated. She feels Lily's betrayal to such a degree, she will not even mention it to her. Honest to God, Gerald, this case is getting nowhere. Lily will be the most damaging witness."

"I'll reserve judgment on that, James. Now let me hear what else Violet told you."

James recounted most of the story, leaving out, as he had decided, the key fact of the survival of the child. Although he told himself that it was on account of his foolhardy promise to Kathleen in London, it was in truth because he could not yet bear for anyone to know Sarah Gallagher's true identity. And he did not want Gerald to tell him that he must instantly sever his connection with Sarah for professional and ethical reasons. He recounted Jack's last meeting with Violet, but let her original lie—that the baby had died—stand.

Gerald sighed and stood up, pacing the room for some minutes.

"I'm not sure," he said at last, "what you have achieved here, James. It seems to me that Violet's story only blackens her chances. I think what you've done is uncovered a sort of motive ..."

"I don't see that ..." James was heated. Here was Gerald finding a motive, and he didn't even yet know about Sarah.

"I'm sorry, James. But look. Say Violet had heard from Jack, knew that he was coming back. That's certainly possible. Look how she managed it years before. Perhaps Jack had written, or better still, phoned her. He might have threatened her perhaps physically–that at least would give Violet a possible defense of self-defense. But that would be weak ..." Gerald thought aloud. "Yes, weak because, on the other hand, it might leave her wide open to an accusation of premeditation. She knew he was coming, and when, and so planned to kill him. It won't matter if she feared for her life, because there's no way we can show he threatened her."

James cursed his own stupidity as Gerald continued to pace.

"And then, say he didn't threaten her, say he was phoning just to tell her that he was retiring, for example. Jack was still a youngish man. He could have been coming home for good, and would expect to resume his rightful place in the managing of the farm. Violet as much as told you she was obsessed–your word, remember, James–with that farm. She might have plotted to deal directly with the situation by killing him on his arrival, and then managed somehow this ruse of the hearse. It's messy, but with the information you've got, the prosecution would slide over little details like that and go for the jugular. They could connect her past behavior with Jack–the lying, the robbing him of his share–with her present behavior. If she lied then, why not now? If she wanted the farm for herself then, why not now?"

James groaned. Only too well he saw Gerald's point. And he alone knew that the existence of Jack's child, Sarah, would provide an even more powerful motive for Violet.

"James, James, don't blame yourself. Facts are facts. I'm only speculating. I don't necessarily believe in the story I just presented. I'm just illustrating what use could be made of this information, how it could be fitted and tailored by the prosecution."

"What should we do?"

"Frankly, nothing. By that I mean I don't think you should report any of this new knowledge to Sheridan."

"But–"

"I know, I know that is your job right now. But listen, man, we don't want the barrister on the case losing faith. No. Leave well alone ... at least for now. Sheridan's good, and he's got his own investigators. I've already instructed him to follow up Moore's possible connection with the IRA, or should I say IRA support groups. If he learns anything more, let it come from his investigators. Or from Violet herself. They'll be meeting before the trial begins ... No, take it from me, James. You've done enough damage for a while."

"I see your point, Gerald, but there's one more thing. Don't you think the fact that Violet can state Jack confessed to killing Mike Walsh will go in her favor? By that I mean, we now know for certain that Jack did it; even if it was an accident, we know he did it. Mightn't that strengthen the case the other way, since it gives the Walshes a motive for the revenge killing of Jack?"

"Perhaps, perhaps. But we only have Violet's word on that. And furthermore, I have reservations about letting Sheridan in on any of this. If you reveal what you know, it proves that Jack and Violet acted in collusion in the past—something that has caused bad blood between them for twenty-seven years. No, leave the Walsh angle alone. And let's hope something will come out of the investigation into Jack's involvement with the IRA boys."

James nodded reluctantly. It was his own fault. So far he'd done nothing substantial to help his client's case.

He told himself that he often drank at the Legal Eagle—a pub near the Four Courts—but it wasn't true. Sitting discreetly in the far corner, he would, if asked, have said that he was allowing fate to take its own course. The barrister, Sheridan, a prematurely graying but striking man in his forties, came in. Suave and at ease with the many legal types in the lounge bar, Sheridan spotted James at once as a less than familiar face and joined him without invitation or ceremony. Gerald could not gainsay that coincidence.

"You look glum, man," said Sheridan, smiling warmly. "Not used to this kind of case, are you?"

"I confess I'm not. I'll be glad when it's over," James blurted out.

"As bad as that, hmmm? You'll get used to it. I'm glad I bumped into you, actually. I've had news from the States. My investigator there located a small-time lawyer, as they say there. Not the man Moore usually dealt with. Just a shopfront fellow. How and ever, it's this man who is holding what seems to be Moore's most recent will. I was going to ring Gerald tomorrow to tell him, since I believe it's within your firm's venue to inform the family, and if they so instruct you, to probate the will. It's going to be very interesting to see whom Jack named as executor of his will. Or executrix!" Sheridan paused, watching James closely as he sipped his drink.

"I say, why don't you do me and yourself a favor. The will has to be brought over by hand–I don't trust it to the mails at this juncture. I could send one of my people, but it could as easily be you. You could ask a few questions of your own while you're there. I think the experience would do you good."

James was startled by Sheridan's suggestion, and didn't answer right away. The conversation moved on to the topic that most concerned them.

"How does it look?" James asked anxiously.

"Not bad, not bad." Sheridan spoke with confidence. "I was quite interested in O'Shea's nugget of information which Gerald handed on to me–about Moore's contributions to the 'cause.' Even if Jack Moore didn't have any direct connection with the IRA–and I've got some people working on that now–I still think I can bring it in to the case to show that others might have had some reason for wanting Jack Moore dead. The absence of motive on Violet's part is very important, Fleming." Sheridan's voice grew somber. "That's why I'm rather anxious about the will. In the event there is something in it that reveals a connection with Violet about which we know nothing–"

"All right, Sheridan, I'll go. But I want you to proceed as if this meeting never happened. I think Gerald would take this suggestion better coming from you than from me. He's a stickler for form, you know, a bit–well–crusty, since Mrs. Fitzgerald passed away." The lies came easily to James's lips, and he was surprised himself how glibly they did so. Yet there was a germ of truth in what he said. He didn't want Gerald to know he had been talking to Sheridan behind his back.

"Fine. No problem." Sheridan glanced kindly at James as he moved away. "Chin up, old man, you'll get the hang of these things, in time."

James spent a second anxious day at his desk, fully occupied with a family dispute over a six-year-old will that in ordinary circumstances would have tickled his fancy. Usually he relished mediating, or better still, refereeing, convoluted battles amongst well-heeled West Brits greedy over their mother's little bits of land and gold watch chains that Daddy should have left to them and not to her when he died twenty years previously. Normally it amused him to see otherwise respectable people in their sixties fighting like children over a bag of candy. However, his interest in ancient wills was rapidly fading.

Finally Maggie buzzed him to visit Gerald's office. He approached, making his face a complete and innocent blank.

"James, my boy, I have something to take your mind off Violet's immediate problems."

"Yes," James answered doubtfully.

"Sheridan rang me this morning with real news. His man in the States has located Jack Moore's will! I suggested to him that you fly out to Boston ASAP and pick it up yourself. After all, James, wills used to be your specialty until you tried becoming an amateur sleuth."

James detected a definite tinge of annoyance in Gerald's voice, and wondered who in fact suggested he fly out to Boston.

"Now?" he asked neutrally.

"Now, James." Gerald's voice was firm. "This is exactly right. It's what you know best. See the American lawyer, collect the will, use some of that fatal Irish charm and see what you can dig up. Suss out why Jack didn't use his usual firm of lawyers. It's imperative that the defense be given any new information as soon as possible."

"When do I leave?"

"I'd say catch the Pan Am weekender flight from Shannon. Three days in Boston should be enough. I would guess the American lawyer—Solomon is his name, by the way—would be willing to see a colleague out of office hours. Here's his number. Get on to it. Now."

James crossed to his office, and by the time he reached Maggie's desk, felt the old adrenaline starting to pump—the thrill that travel virtually to any place caused to run through his veins. Within moments Maggie had Mr. Aaron Solomon of Brookline, Massachusetts, on James's line.

Solomon's broad Boston accent boomed into the receiver. He would be delighted to meet Jim on the Saturday afternoon. He would even pick him up at his hotel. Jim was to call him when he'd checked in. Had Jimboy ever been to Boston? James relished the chance of seeing an American colleague's workplace, and said so. Solomon gave Jimboy the office address and his home number—he was working on Saturday, he shouldn't be, but he was—and then hung up. James smiled. No one yet had attempted to call him Jim, even in school. He decided to try it on for size.

*   *   *

As James reclined in his business-class seat, glass of complimentary champagne in hand, he debated whether to use the in-flight telephone. He pondered for a moment, wondering who of his circle would relish such a call. Sarah was out, for obvious reasons. Matt was on a school trip to Wales. And his other friends would appear to react indifferently. His mother! She would react. He hadn't even thought to ring her to tell her he was leaving.

The call was a resounding success. But when he rang off, the thought occurred to him that it was a sad day when a man of his age was reduced to phoning only his mother. And he thought fleetingly of the house on the hilltop in Kilmartin, and the nameless, faceless wife who would have answered his call with pride and delight, and the two bonny babes who would have been clinging to her, shouting "Dada" down the phone.

Unselfconsciously he pressed his nose to the window. He had spotted two icebergs below, and was now following the line of the coast from Newfoundland. He recalled what he knew about the Viking explorations of the north Atlantic, and thought then about brave, mystical St. Brendan, setting out from Ireland in a leather boat centuries before Columbus. About his description of the giant turtles that swam alongside him on his terrible journey, and of the fires in the sky that he had seen as signs from God. He smiled. It just went to prove that old truism: Wherever you went in this world, an Irishman was there before you!

His hotel in the newly redeveloped harbor-front area of downtown Boston was luxurious. Colossal bed, tasteful appointments, basket of fruit, flowers. His own refrigerator, a phone every four feet, including one by the toilet. He showered immediately, and appreciated the endless and powerful stream of hot water—when, if ever, would Ireland provide showers that worked like this! The view—he observed as he dressed—was intriguing: the bustle and hubbub of what seemed a giant arcade. But he hadn't wanted new, or even plush. He had wanted class, the kind for which Boston had been famous. The hotel, lovely as it was, could be in any major city. He had wanted age and dust, leather-covered books in oak-lined reading rooms, hotel stationery on an inlaid writing desk. He wanted obscure oils on the walls, not mere prints chosen by the interior decorator to tone with the wallpaper and bed covers. He had wanted originality and he got homogenized comfort. Yes, once this whole business was sorted out, he'd take Sarah to Riders Inn for a romantic weekend.

Having eaten a light meal, James strolled out into the mild evening and found himself nearing the harbor. Caught up in a line, he moved willy-nilly with the crowd toward a ticket booth. BOOZE CRUISE, the sign announced. Two-hour cruise of Boston Harbor, return at midnight. Lights and music from the live band beckoned, and shortly he found himself leaning on the railing of the upper deck, large paper cup of watery beer in hand.

The breeze as the boat picked up speed was stiff and became increasingly cold. He felt the salt on his lips and face and the faint, damp spray saturating his skin. He felt invigorated and refreshed after eight hours inside the airplane. The loud sounds of the lively crowd–people all in their twenties, and all dancing and drinking, and inexplicably yelling–somehow faded as the skyline of Boston took shape, rose up above them like a fairy land and then retreated, leaving only a distant promise on the horizon and a black expanse of ocean that increased with each throb of the boat's engine.

In a way, he was glad when they docked back in Boston. Music and lights beckoned from the various open-air nightclubs as he walked back toward his hotel. But he was tired, and tired of being on his own, so though half tempted, he headed back to his hotel. It was already four A.M. Dublin time.

In the morning–a glorious warm, dry morning–James phoned Solomon at his office, then took one of the trolleys on the underground platform and rode a bare fifteen minutes to Brookline, where the line surfaced and the stops were like miniature English rural railway stations, all neat and scrubbed, with a cozy little shelter on either side of the tracks. The journey was a treat for a train buff, and he wrote down the make and model number of his vintage trolley. On James's request, the driver held the trolley so he could take a quick photo.

Solomon's office was easily spotted, situated as it was on Brookline Avenue in a row containing an insurance agency, an ice cream parlor, and an undertaker. James knocked on the glass door and was instantly greeted by a tall, overweight, jolly man slightly older than himself. They passed through a small waiting room clothed in linoleum and vinyl and into an equally drab inner office. Law books lined every wall, and a commercial water cooler bubbled softly in the corner. Solomon's desk was metal with a Formica top. Jack Moore's brown manila folder was placed prominently in the center. James felt he was taking part in a grade-B movie, but within seconds found he had misjudged his man.

"I know your time is short, Jim, my boy, so we'll get straight to business. If you had more time to visit, I'd show you some of the sights, but a weekend is not much time for you to get a picture of this man Moore."

James smiled at his new monicker and at the man himself, warm, jovial, and shrewd. He appreciated his directness.

"I'll tell you what little I know. The details stand out in my mind because, A, I dealt with Moore only once, and then briefly, and, B, the circumstances to my mind were extraordinary. But before I even get started on that, let me tell you, firstly, how I even came to know about his death. I think you might make something of this.

"About one month ago—I can check the date for you, as I kept the papers—I began receiving air-mailed copies of your *Irish Times,* daily copies. I read them—actually, I skimmed them—thinking it was a promotion of sorts. And I do handle a lot of Irish-American clients who live in this Irish enclave here in Brookline. But they kept coming. I was curious, and phoned their business office, which kindly informed me that no, it wasn't a promotion. I had been put on a three-month subscription list. When they told me the exorbitant cost, I was knocked for a loop and asked if they could tell me who had paid for it. They said they had it on record, it was a gift subscription to me from Jack Moore. They still had the gift card, but it was penciled in that the card was not to be sent.

"Naturally, being in this business, I was curious, and began reading the paper more closely. But you see I had already thrown out the earlier papers I had received. Thinking I might have missed something, I got all the copies I had missed, and in reading them over, finally came across the small coverage that that paper had given the murder of Moore! I phoned the consulate here because I believed that I was holding Jack Moore's last will and testament!"

James was speechless as the complex ramifications of this information filtered through to him. Solomon watched his face closely.

"I see you are having the same reaction I did. Moore had the papers sent. I believe he must have been in fear of his life from the time he made the will—and that time coincides with my receiving the newspapers ..."

"And presumably it coincides with the date he left Boston and traveled via London to Dublin ..."

"Yes. It does."

"You see what this means?"

"Wait, there's more. I couldn't understand it, that day Jack Moore walked into the office, no appointment, no previous recommendation of me by a friend. I do believe he literally saw the sign in the window and walked in off the street."

"Did he live locally?"

"Yes, about a ten-minute walk from here. A good building some fifteen years old—turns out he built it. That was his line ... well, one of them. He walked in and sat down where you are now. He said he wanted to make a very simple will, and he showed me a bit of paper. And it *was* simple. He merely wanted to leave everything in his possession at the time of his death to his closest blood relative. And that was it. No names. Well, you'll see that for yourself. I have the will here for you to take back to Ireland."

James scanned the simple document, becoming increasingly anxious. Apart from Kathleen and Violet, and only recently himself, who else could know that Jack's nearest blood relative was his daughter, Sarah? Motive, motive, motive. He was holding it now in his hand.

"Is it bad news?" Solomon's curiosity was palpable.

"Well, you could say that," James admitted cautiously. "A lot would depend on what Mr. Moore had to leave his surviving relative."

Solomon nodded. "That I can't tell you. But if you look at the attached letter, you'll see why I think it was considerable."

James looked closely at the notation on the second page.

"Do you recognize what you're reading?" Solomon laughed. "It's a Swiss bank-account number!"

After a few pleasantries, including a check for Solomon's consultation fee, James thanked him and returned to his hotel, this time by taxi. He immediately phoned Sheridan's man in Boston, one Joe Sorvetti, and identified himself as Sheridan had instructed.

"I've been expecting your call, Fleming."

"What can you tell me about Moore's financial situation? We know his holdings were considerable."

"*Were* is the operative word, Mr. Fleming. I can tell you what I just phoned through to Sheridan. As far as we've gotten in our investigations, it seems that Moore systematically and over about three months liquidated every holding we've been able to locate: property, bonds, IRAs, stocks and shares, bank accounts, annuities, life insurance. He even took some small losses to enable him to do the thing quickly. He was a careful businessman, took no risks, as far as we can establish.

We've been working from information from the feds–the IRS to you. I doubt there's anything we've missed. I don't think there were any secret holdings, 'offshore' stuff. I don't think it was his way. It's as though he was just going along as usual and then, one day, abruptly decided to convert everything into cash."

"Do you know where it is, this cash?"

"Indications are that it's now residing in Switzerland."

"I see. And was what he did with the cash hard to maneuver?" James was careful.

"Yes indeed. American law on transporting funds out of the country is strict and complicated. So far we can't find anyone who assisted him in doing it."

"So you're saying to do it himself would have taken time and some planning."

"Most definitely."

"Can you give me a figure, an amount, so I know what we're talking about here?" James asked hesitantly, dreading the answer.

"If you'll take a ball-park figure–about three million."

"And legally, I mean, is it okay now? You know–can there be any consequences?"

"He seems to have done it 'right,' if you take my meaning."

"Thank you, Mr. Sorvetti. I'll tell Sheridan how much help you've been."

"Wait! There's someone I think you should talk to while you're here. Moore's doctor. I couldn't get anywhere with him. Close-mouthed bastard. You might try your luck, though. Dr. Vincent. His office is just off Brookline Avenue–do you know the street?"

"I do now ..."

James barely noticed the passage of time on his return flight to Ireland. The information he was carrying in his head was of far greater moment than the simple document that now lay in the briefcase on his lap.

Certainly Solomon's information about Jack Moore and about the mysterious arrival of the newspapers had been significant. And the contents of the will were a potential bombshell. And for now only he knew how great an explosion it could cause. Sorvetti's verifiable documentation regarding the amount of Jack Moore's financial worth–three million dollars!–would contribute to the nature of that bombshell. No one, not even Gerald, had had an inkling of Jack Moore's wealth. But the real coup had been his astonishing conversation with Dr. Vincent.

James smiled to himself as he leaned back and surveyed the night sky, seeing and yet not seeing the play of light on the darkening cloud banks seemingly gliding beneath the plane.

He didn't need to read over the notes he had taken after his amiable dinner at the Ritz Hotel with the eminent Boston physician. One single fact stood out amongst all the others, one of overriding significance. Jack Moore had had terminal cancer–and he had known it.

Chapter Eleven

James, back at his flat, showered in the all too familiar lukewarm water and changed. The elation he had experienced on the plane had not abated. He felt a burgeoning of confidence–in himself and in his sense that a solution of some kind was near at hand.

The information that he had gained in Boston was more than significant. Now he had real insight into Jack Moore. And, to his thinking, he had learned something else. Namely, the level of secrecy that Jack had maintained. Jack had had a definite purpose in mind in the weeks and months before his arrival in Ireland. And he kept that purpose, that intention, secret! Equally important, he seemed to have kept his illness a secret too, perhaps even denying it to himself.

Before his departure from the States, Jack Moore had systematically tied up every loose end. He had consolidated his large financial resources into one lump sum and had, in a sense "stored" it, so he could have access to it anytime, anywhere. Here was evidence of complex advance planning. Secret planning. Why put everything into a Swiss account if Jack were merely retiring to live out his years in his homeland? Perhaps Dublin had only been a stopping-off point. But on his way to where? Why dissolve everything, why leave nothing in place in the States? It was obvious from this alone that Jack had not planned to return to Boston.

What else was new? James shivered as he threw on his overcoat. What was new was the large amount of Jack's wealth. It was more than anyone involved in the case had guessed at.

And that large amount worried him. He knew that on the face of it money and greed would provide a very powerful motive for murder. And Violet, with Lily and Rose under her thumb, stood to inherit those millions. That's how the world would see it. That's how Gerald and Sheridan and the prosecution would see it. Gerald's earlier conversation echoed in his mind—that James had done nothing but provide the prosecution with a motive. And here he was again, seeming to do just that—only in trumps.

But that was because no one except Kathleen and Violet and himself knew of the existence of Jack Moore's actual nearest blood relative, Sarah Gallagher. That it was she who stood to inherit Jack's money.

Sarah. Sarah! If she were the one who was to inherit, then in the best fictional—and factual—tradition, she was the first who should be suspected of murdering Jack. James pushed the thought aside, but it remained a nagging presence in the back of his mind.

He checked his answering machine and was relieved. Sarah was in London taking care of a scheduled recording session for a forthcoming CD. His office hadn't phoned. And Mother was on a bridge weekend in Cork. James suddenly felt a free man in more ways than one. Throwing a few items in a small bag, he locked up the flat and headed in his car for Kilmartin. He sped through the mist cloaking the coastline.

Yes, it was evident from Jack's management of his estate that he had had a plan. It was evident that he knew he was dying and his time was short. He had returned to Ireland, to Kilmartin, his childhood home, the scene of all the gravest events of his life. That, too, must have been part of his strategy. And it was in Kilmartin that he had been murdered.

Questions formed in his mind of their own volition. Jack presumably knew that Mike Walsh's death had never been resolved. Yet he took the chance of returning. Perhaps that accounted for his putting his money in a cache? Jack would know that a great deal of money would be of help to him—either in eluding the consequences of his past actions in his youth or perhaps in facing them. James wondered if he had returned home to Kilmartin to confess, to cleanse himself in some way of the sin of Mike Walsh's death before he himself died. Had he in mind to confess to the police in Kilmartin? Or perhaps to deal with the Walshes directly, perhaps even compensating them financially? All he had to do was write a very substantial check, and he could still leave millions as an inheritance.

Or had he decided to confront Violet and settle the past with her? Only Violet, himself, and Kathleen would have known of Sarah's existence. He and Violet may have dismissed Kathleen, believing that she had been living all this time in Australia.

Was it then possible that Violet had killed Jack? Had he told Violet that it was to Sarah that he was leaving his fortune? Could Violet have figured that no one but the two of them would ever know about the survival of the baby daughter? Jack could have explained the terms of the will, and Violet might have struck him down, knowing that if she weren't caught, she would inherit Jack's money. Knowing that although Rose and Lily would also inherit, she was powerful enough to control them and, through them, their share of the money.

Somehow that didn't ring true for James, despite, or perhaps because of, the amount of money involved. Violet had not yet impressed him as a woman greedy for cash. She didn't need millions to preserve her farm or increase its agricultural value. And would she have killed to prevent Jack's money from leaving her control to go to some girl in her twenties with a life of her own? And if Jack didn't tell her he was dying, she wouldn't have seen even this as an imminent threat.

James's head was throbbing. He needed a better picture of Violet Moore than he now had. He needed to flesh out the image. Something was missing, and he believed that the whole story was still in Kilmartin. And he had decided on who best to ask.

"Mr. Sweeney. It's Fleming, James Fleming ..." James hesitated, not sure if Sweeney recognized him as he peered up distractedly from his ledger book. James was relieved to see that he looked fit and spry and none the worse for his ordeal with the IRA.

"Fleming? Do you want a paper ... Oh my goodness! James Fleming. Of course! Very nice to see you again."

They shook hands warmly.

"Can I help you with something?"

"I think that you might, Mr. Sweeney. If you could spare me a little time, I'd like to ask you a few questions about the old days?" James was conscious that a customer had entered the shop.

Sweeney grew momentarily flustered. "Oh dear, let me see. Yes, you go through to the back, yes, just go around there between the meat slicer and the phone booth, then through that doorway. I'll be with you shortly."

James took the liberty of putting on the kettle, so when Mr. Sweeney entered the small, cheerful room he was able to sit down to a big mug of tea. Sweeney inquired carefully as to how the case was going, and James let the conversation take its own course, listening as Sweeney spoke of Violet and how, in recent weeks, she seemed to be fading before their eyes, those few of the locals who had even glimpsed her.

"Eileen tells me that she's sure she's lost at least a stone in weight. That's never a good sign, my boy. And Brendan made a delivery up at the house recently–something unheard of since my father's day. And now that the mail doesn't come through here any longer, we can't keep track, er ... have another cup of tea?"

James realized abruptly that he had noticed a change in the shop as he had passed through. The glass-and-steel cage was gone. He understood the sadness that Sweeney felt. He knew the old man could only see such a decision by the postal authorities as a reflection on himself, instead of laying the blame on the bastards who had committed the crime.

"I will," James said quickly, and moved on to the subject of Violet. "I'm interested in knowing more about Violet Moore as a young woman, and about Jack too. I suppose Eileen would be the one I should talk to, do you think?" James said casually, but he was watching closely for a desired effect.

True to James's expectations, Sweeney bristled, then bustled around the little room with more energy. He fairly slammed the mug in front of James.

"You must do what you think best, of course. But if you're asking me, then I would tell you that Eileen O'Grady wouldn't know as much about those days as she might let on–if you take my meaning?"

"Indeed?"

Encouraged, Sweeney expanded. "Not a'tall! You see, Eileen, for one thing, she wasn't in our parish. She attends chapel. And for another, she was younger than our general set. And for another"–Sweeney was becoming animated–"she wasn't even *in* our set. Do you read me now?" He peered intently at James, and James saw a humorous image of Brendan peering in just such a manner.

"I do indeed, and I thank you for steering me rightly. But then ..." James paused. Sweeney smiled into his mug. "Perhaps you could help me?" said James.

"Well, that depends."

"On what?" James said, truly puzzled.

"On what you'd like to know." Sweeney said pleasantly, at ease now that he had the reins back in his own hands.

"I just want a–let's say–a picture of those times, that year before Jack Moore went away from Kilmartin, for example."

"You know, Fleming," said Sweeney, taking yet another Ginger Nut biscuit and a second banana to slice on to his small side plate, "*that* I can do, because it's a funny thing, but I can remember that time better than I could tell you what happened in the shop yesterday. They were good times in many ways. Although I mightn't have said that then.

"I had just returned to the village to take over the shop. I missed Dublin very much at first, but by that year we're speaking of, I had begun to settle down. I had married, and Brendan was a very bonny baby on his mother's knee. The shop was doing a roaring trade, and I had bought the house where you visited me. Mrs. Sweeney and I were very happy and got out and about quite a bit. Not to the pub, you understand, but to all the socials and the barn dances and the bonfires. Traveling dinners were all the rage then too."

He smiled at James's blank face. "They were great fun. It all had to be worked out beforehand amongst the people in a certain crowd. One home would host cocktails, another would host the first course—you know, soup and bread rolls—another would do the main course, and another the pudding and coffee. We'd all go together in cars, on tractors, on horses even, rushing around from one house to another. I see you think it sounds a bit mad, but I assure you it was fun, at least to us. The world wasn't so sophisticated then, if that's what you'd call it.

"Violet used to do her bit, though never the main course. But she'd often have the coffee-and-pudding stage of the event. People tended to linger over that one since it marked the end of the evening. She didn't seem to mind, now that I think of it. Although she was not terribly social then or now. She was polite but always kept her distance. Rose thoroughly enjoyed these things. She used to go with Lily to the barn dances too. Now, that's something Violet would never do. Poor Rose. There were many nights I'd leave Mrs. Sweeney and give Rose a dance out of kindness. A good few of the married chaps used to do that ... oh, pardon me!"

Mr. Sweeney bustled out to the front of the shop to attend to the two customers who had been discreetly coughing and clearing their throats. James smiled at the simplicity and courtesy of life in Kilmartin, and stretched out in the dilapidated armchair. His thoughts drifted. He liked listening to Sweeney, and somehow the urgency of his quest became lessened. He leaned back and assured his conscience that he was acquiring background material.

"Having a bit of a snooze then, Fleming?"

James heard Sweeney's voice from afar and stirred himself.

"Not to worry. I've made you another mug of tea. Dear me, now where was I?"

James realized that Sweeney was enjoying talking about the past as much as he enjoyed listening. "Barn dances, I think ..." said James.

"Indeed. But we were more active than that too, during those years. We used to go beagling. Ever done it? Great fun. All of us clad in our boots, running through fields after those yipping dogs, miles ahead of us, of course. Chasing some poor fox or rabbit. We never let them attack. They'd tree their prey or run it to ground, depending on what it was, you see. But we never liked blood sports in our set. None of us rode to hounds for example. Although of course we all knew how to ride.

"You know who was a great rider? Gerald Fitzgerald. We used to say he was born on a horse. He's younger than I, but I quite clearly remember him as a young lad, riding without a saddle up here to the shop to pick up something for his mother. Of course in those days this wasn't the racetrack of a road that it is now.

"Yes, all through his boyhood he was a great rider. Did well at the gymkhanas too. And every weekend that he was down from Trinity, and even after he'd passed the bar, he'd always go for a ride, first thing in the morning, last thing before the daylight faded. He had great natural strength–ran in the family."

James smiled, trying to picture the present Gerald Fitzgerald on a horse.

"I haven't seen Gerald in years. Of course, I always knew when he'd come down to the manor to handle Violet's legal business. And I often wondered why he never called in here to the shop." He reached for another Ginger Nut. "Tell me, Fleming, why has Gerald been so absent during all this excitement with Violet and her family? I must admit I'm curious."

"Curious?" James glanced up quickly.

"Well, considering how close he and Lily were in those days."

"Close?"

"Mmm ..." Sweeney hesitated. "Now that Mrs. Fitzgerald is gone, I suppose it's all right to speak of it. Yes, Lily and he were very thick at one time. Virtually engaged. She was the only reason he'd visit Kilmartin after he'd become established in Dublin. We all could see that. He came down frequently, and it wasn't only to see his family. He and Lily were great at the barn dances–both fine dancers. A pleasure to watch. As was watching Lily blossom. She was quite pretty in those days, in a delicate way, and she fairly bloomed then. We were all waiting for the banns to be read out at church–we were that sure!"

"Except for Violet?" said James, hardly believing his ears.

"Indeed. We could also see that she wasn't exactly urging on the match. She'd snub Gerald whenever they met. I think I remember that she was violently rude to him at the house and he stopped going there. That made it a bit awkward for Lily. It wasn't the done thing for her to go off in his car—when he got his fine new car. But they'd walk the lanes and the fields. We'd all see them on a summer night. And they'd meet at other people's houses. She didn't go over to his home much ... well, it was his parents' home. They didn't take kindly to Gerald being made unwelcome at the Moores', and probably retaliated in like manner."

James's heart was pounding. "What happened in the end?"

"Hard to say. It just seemed to dwindle. Gerald came down less often. Lily seemed to shrivel up over that year. She got thinner and quieter. I don't think it was a big blowout. Gerald's parents died then—within two years of each other. Gerald sold the house and farm, at a loss. A lot of it was bought up by Violet, I might add. He and Lily saw less and less of each other. We all had our suspicions, of course. Most of us believed that Violet had succeeded in coming between them. We thought it was too bad. It's only since I've grown older that I realized it was more than too bad, it was in fact tragic for poor Lily.

"Mrs. Sweeney, now, rest her soul, she could have told you more. But what I do recall is that in the following spring Gerald came down and Lily had gone off—to France, I think it was—on holiday. She hadn't told him. We heard he was terribly put out, and shortly thereafter he stopped coming. And that was the end. He married up in Dublin. And poor Lily, well, as you see, she never did marry.

"It was sad for all of them. Jack Moore missed him. He was just a lad in those days, but he'd taken a great liking to Gerald. He was like the father or the brother Jack never had. Living up there amongst all those women! He and Gerald used to ride together, I remember. Mmm. Jack was very despondent around that time. I saw a change in him when Gerald stopped coming. Like the rest of us, he probably thought Gerald and Lily would marry and there'd be a bit of life, a bit of *family* life, around the place. Ahh me ... Violet's a hard woman."

James hoped that Mr. Sweeney believed his story when he made his departure so abruptly. It *was* conceivable he had forgotten an important client meeting. If he were a dolt!

He wasn't sure himself why he had felt compelled to leave. But he did know that he needed time to think, to fully grasp the information that Sweeney had sprung on him.

Why indeed hadn't Gerald been personally handling this case, considering the relationship he had with the family—with Lily? Sweeney's question had been a good one.

James calmed down as he drove. It was Violet who was in trouble. Not Lily. Now, if Lily had been on trial, the question would have been truly valid.

He'd been overreacting. Gerald hadn't been holding out on him after all! Hadn't Gerald told him that he wouldn't have worked well with Violet, stating that he'd always found her difficult? Gerald had merely omitted how difficult! He'd married and made his life in Dublin. And perhaps he still did occasional legal work for the Moores over the years—not out of friendship for Violet, but out of remembered fondness for Lily.

James sighed. He had thought the answer to everything lay in Kilmartin. Everything that Jack had seemingly done had been drawn to that fine point, that single focus. And yet?

Jack hadn't gone directly to Kilmartin. He could have. His flight from London had landed at nine-thirty A.M. at Dublin Airport. Allowing for travel time, that would place him in Dublin center at around eleven A.M. Why hadn't he gone directly to Kilmartin that morning? Why hadn't he rented a car at the airport and gone straight there? If Kilmartin was his ultimate goal, and ironically, where he met his ultimate end, what had held him in Dublin? James thought rapidly. He couldn't remember the details he now needed. What time exactly had Jack Moore checked into the Shelbourne? Had he mentioned how long he'd be staying? Why did he break his journey and go to the trouble of checking in? He hadn't phoned anyone, at least from his room. That had already been checked. Perhaps he had stayed in Dublin, unsure of his welcome in Kilmartin. Maybe the transatlantic flight had tired him out? It made sense. Or maybe it was the Shelbourne Hotel and not Kilmartin that held the key?

Back in Dublin that evening, James stood up from a small writing table and walked over to the window. He pulled aside the curtain and looked out on the darkness that shrouded St. Stephen's Green. The park was locked. The black wrought-iron railings glistened, their outline picked up in the amber light of the street lamps. He glanced to the left, seeing with an inner eye his own darkened office in Fitzgerald's firm, in the building that lay diagonally across the Green. He glanced down to see the people scurrying, heads shielded by umbrellas, at this hour perhaps rushing to the Gaiety Theatre two blocks away, or to stand in the long line outside the Green Cinema. He pictured the College Club just a few doors up the street on the same side as the hotel. It would be virtually empty now. He thought fondly of Matt. Ordinary life seemed so distant. His office, the club, so near at hand, yet he seemed cut off from them by more than the thick panes of his window and the tiny white decorative balcony that clad that window on the outside.

He glanced around the hotel room. It had been an absolute fluke that the room Jack Moore had taken at the Shelbourne Hotel on the fateful day was actually vacant. The clerk hadn't even shown surprise when James had requested the room by number. Perhaps lots of visitors had favorite rooms. This room certainly was magnificent; its style was heavy, with dark mahogany furniture and Georgian prints of Dublin in gold frames against the dull green matte walls. Drapes of gold fabric dressed the two high, sash windows that offered an impressive view of the Green and of the city and the mountains beyond.

James dropped the curtain and cut himself off further from the outside world. He walked back to the desk and read what had taken him the last few hours in the quiet of this room to put down on paper. Each page bore the name of a person. He drew in his breath and read over what he'd written.

Under the name of Jack Moore he had listed:

· Knew he was dying.
· Consolidated his fortune.
· Designed a will that left the fortune to his natural daughter.

Therefore, it follows:

· He knew of the present identity and whereabouts of his daughter.

Questions:

· Had he contacted Kathleen Walsh about their daughter?
· Had he contacted investigators to locate her?
· Had he contacted Violet or Lily or Rose?

James sighed. And how could he establish if Jack had done any of this? He sat down and underscored the next few points.

- Jack had come to the Shelbourne Hotel, to this room, to meet someone?
- To contact someone?
- Who?

James wrote on the paper what he believed. The turning point in Jack's plan was connected with the hotel. He wrote the word *Hotel* with a question mark. Was it the location of *this* hotel? Could it have been any Dublin hotel? James set the paper aside and looked at the next name, Lily, and listing.

- Lily hated Violet enough to lie. Motive? Revenge?
- Possible other motive: Lily knew about Jack's will and wanted Violet out of the way. Violet as a convicted murderer would lose all rights of property and inheritance. So Lily would inherit Jack's fortune, with Rose.
- Lily knew about the will.
- Lily did not know about Sarah.

James canceled those lines. How could Lily know about the will or about Sarah? Unless Jack had told her? James wrote this possible idea down on the paper and moved to the next. Violet.

- Knew about Jack's visit.
- Knew about the will.
- Knew about Sarah.
- Had the physical strength to stab Jack.

James paused. Why was it he could accept Violet stabbing her brother and not Lily? Because Lily had loved Jack in a way Violet had not. He groaned inwardly. He didn't *know* that. What was missing here? He felt it nagging him, and the nagging was familiar. He pictured Violet stabbing Jack in the barn ... That was it! The hearse.

He took a new sheet of paper and labeled it "Hearse." Of course. That was still the unanswered question. It was the question that had bothered him most at the start of this whole mess all those—what now felt like years—months ago!

He stared at the paper, and then wrote quickly.

· Where did the hearse come from?
· Sinclair was sure it was a Dublin car.

He jotted down from his own notebook the description of the car.

· Had Violet hired the hearse?
· If not Violet, who hired it?

He wrote "Hearse" at the bottom of Violet's page and moved on to the next. The Walshes.

· The brothers hated Jack, planned to kill him, and had hired the hearse.
· Therefore it followed they were in contact with Jack and knew his movements.
· Therefore it followed that Jack had contacted them. Had he arranged to meet them at the Shelbourne?

James smiled at his mental picture of the four Walshes in the elegant lobby of the hotel. No, they would have operated on their own turf.

· Kathleen was in constant contact with Jack over the years, and also knew of Sarah's existence. She wanted his inheritance for her child and plotted with her brothers to kill him.

James paused in wonder at what he'd written some hours before. He pictured Kathleen Walsh's face as he'd seen it in London. As a young girl she'd hated Violet Moore. And she hated her now as an adult even more. But her fear had been genuine. He saw again that look of pleading, asking James not to betray her, not to destroy her life with her doctor husband and her two sons. No. James shook his head. No way. But the combination of greed and hatred was lethal–it could make anybody do anything.

"God!" James said aloud and stood up. It seemed he was capable of suspecting everyone. He felt corrupted and tainted and in need of fresh air. He glanced at the clock. It was near midnight, and he was no closer to a solution. No, he'd work on–all night if he had to. He knew the solution was in front of him, but he couldn't see it. He rang down for a bottle of Black Bush and a basket of ham sandwiches. While he waited, he took a quick shower and changed back into the clothes he'd been wearing, feeling fresher and revived.

The whiskey was good. The sandwiches were good. He took up the next piece of paper.

It was blank. James yawned. He brought the paper and pen over to the queen-sized bed and lay down. He kicked off his shoes and leaned back, and in the best tradition of tired solicitors, slept on the problem.

The doorman was only too happy to talk to James. He would have done so, he insisted, even without the generous tip. Yes, he'd spoken to the poor dead Yank, before he was dead, you understand. He remembered him because of his American clothes, very good quality they were, and understated too. He'd seen lots of Yanks and every other type of foreigner. Mr. Moore, yes, from the newspaper reports. Mr. Moore had stopped on the step for a chat. Nothing important. The usual palaver about the weather. It had been sunny, and so, worthy of comment. About Dublin and how it had changed and how it hadn't changed. Nothing remarkable. He'd remembered it because he had relations in Wexford, but not anywhere near Kilmartin. Oh, yes, Mr. Moore had left on foot. He'd wanted to hail a cab for him, but Mr. Moore said the day was too fine to waste and he would walk. He hadn't seen him after that, as he'd knocked off work around midday.

James stepped out of the hotel lobby and into the stream of people passing up and down the pavement along Stephen's Green, people rushing to work, as he would have to later that day. Already Gerald would be wondering at his absence. He walked slowly, buffeted by the rush of pedestrians. He began to see this part of Dublin with new eyes, a part of Dublin he thought he knew extremely well.

He continued methodically, glancing at the signs over each and every establishment he passed. Using the hotel as the center of a mental circle, he divided the area into four quadrants. Moving north, away from the Green and nearest the hotel, he scoured what would have been the northwest quadrant. He carried his list of undertakers and car-rental firms culled from the telephone directory. He knew it was not complete. But it was a start. Along the canal, near Herbert Place, he located two of the garages, but neither was open to business yet. Turning back toward the city, away from the canal, he found a large establishment that rented wedding cars and hearses as well as daily car rentals. They were open and looked to be quite busy. Unsure of what to ask them, James reluctantly entered the small front office. But he quickly established that the firm did not have any business dealings in Wexford on the relevant dates. Walking on through the southwest quadrant, James found only one car-rental firm, but it no longer handled hearses.

He took a break and a cup of coffee at Bewley's Oriental Café on Grafton Street, and then could not resist two currant buns. He glanced at the small map he had sketched. This was such a long shot. Jack Moore would not have known Dublin well. Would he have had the patience to walk the streets? James had a second cup of coffee and finally moved on. In the southeast quadrant of his sketch he covered George's Street, and there saw a really fine undertaker's establishment, but it was closed. He was amazed that he'd never noticed these places before now, yet he'd passed all of them hundreds of times in his life as a student and since. Shops and cafés he'd never seen, and pubs he'd never even heard of! He made a second mental list of the ones he wished to return to and investigate–in the company of Matt.

The northeast quadrant yielded very little, so James returned to the first car-rental firm. He stood across the street at a bus stop, but he hadn't long to wait. Within minutes a hearse pulled out of the garage that fronted the street beside the business office. James's heart raced until he saw the car bore no physical resemblance to the hearse Mr. Sinclair had described. It was unlikely they used different styles, he thought, and walked on. He visited three more premises, and having inquired, was able to scratch them off his list. Eventually he was drawn back to the undertaker on George's Street which had been closed earlier. Their office fronted the street, but the garage did not. James hunted around one or two side streets and alleys until at last he located the firm's name on a double door made of wooden slats. He waited, but within seconds realized how conspicuous he was, standing in the narrow alley. He returned to the cross street near Mercer's Hospital and lounged along the railing that surrounded the huge granite-clad building. Mightn't he be waiting for a patient, or better still, for a nurse?

After an interminable wait, during which James read the morning paper and ate a Mars bar, he spotted a hearse moving out of the alley. Very modern, very discreet, sloped hatchback at the rear. He started walking, crossing the narrow street behind the hearse and coming alongside. His eyes grew wide. The silver trim, the filigree–and the opaque windows especially–matched Sinclair's description! The car accelerated as the traffic ahead moved forward. James examined the rear door; its hinges were invisible. No curtains on the windows either. He paused on the pavement as a woman with a huge pram full of damp sheets of wrapping paper bellowed at him: "Two sheets for five pence!" He shook his head, and she shrugged and moved on.

Gathering his wits and putting on what he hoped was the face of a bereaved but distant relative, he hurried back to the undertaker's office and entered the small lobby. A bell rang faintly somewhere in the building, and suddenly a slim pimply-faced young man appeared before him.

"May I help you?" he murmured unctuously, and James was startled.

"Yes," he said brusquely. In his most officious manner, James rapidly described how his uncle by marriage had died the previous night at the Meath Hospital, and that his aunt had her heart set on a very good funeral. The problem was that his uncle had particularly requested a simple coffin—plain pine—nothing fancy. His aunt, not wishing to deny his request, at the same time did not want to be "burying him poor," which would look very bad in front of the neighbors.

The young man bobbed and nodded, alternating sympathetic noises with expressions of interest—this was a delightful challenge indeed. The fact that the conversation revolved on the cost and the style they could offer didn't disturb him in the least.

"The aunt, she's very determined to have the absolute latest type of hearse, the most up-to-date. The very best! To compensate for the coffin, you understand."

The young man nodded earnestly. "I think we may have the very solution to your aunt's predicament."

"Then you know exactly what I want?"

"Indeed and I do. You see, sir, we've gone quite upscale. Now I know the older generation, our 'senior citizens' "—his unctuous voice stressed this American import—"sometimes they want the very latest, and *that* we can give them."

"Well, perhaps I could see what you have to offer," suggested James. "I know what the aunt wants and what she won't abide!"

The gaunt young man moved with alacrity, leading James through small rooms and corridors that connected the ancient buildings to each other. They walked along a covered passageway that led ultimately to a small parking lot whose doors opened onto the alley where James had been standing only an hour before. Two more hearses identical to the one he had just seen stood there gleaming. James was shown their features in detail. The young man looked at him expectantly.

"I, of course, see the advantages," James lied blithely. "If only there were some truly unique feature I could mention to my aunt. You see, she's terribly concerned about the neighbors."

"But of course, sir. And rightly so, this is the time in one's life when one must be most concerned with one's neighbors."

James was startled to hear his own accent mimicked so well, so subtly, and yet without the slightest hint of irony. He looked sharply at the young man, who showed no emotion.

"Our selling point with these has been that they are unique in Dublin. If you'll only mention to your aunt that our hearses have completely opaque windows, to prevent the idle onlookers from ob-serving the class of coffin within! No other firm uses them!" he added triumphantly.

James's delight showed on his face as he took the young man's card and promised faithfully to recommend him to his aunt.

Back on the street, he stopped to phone Maggie at the office, hoping his voice, which sounded tired enough, conveyed the extent of his flu.

"Various people were wondering, James." Maggie stressed the word *people*. "It's been a while since we've seen you."

"Tomorrow, absolutely tomorrow. There's nothing urgent on, is there?"

"Well, I imagine that ten-year-old disputed will you've been working on will keep for yet one more day. No, apart from the Moore case, there's nothing else urgent on your agenda."

Rain was beginning to fall as he left the booth. He took a taxi back to his apartment and changed, grateful to get out of the clothes he had been living in for the past two days. Thrilled with his progress, he still realized there was a nagging problem. The young undertaker had insisted they had not handled any funerals whatsoever in the county of Wexford.

James threw on his raincoat and, taking his black umbrella, drove his very conspicuous car back into the heart of Dublin. There was no way around it. He had to park the car near enough to the alley to see the rear doors of the undertaker's establishment. The wait was a long one. James fed the meter every thirty minutes and shrugged off the looks of the passing policeman. At four-thirty he left the car and stood in the downpour near the mouth of the alley. At a quarter to six he was rewarded by the sight of two young men in their chauffeur's livery locking and padlocking the doors. As they ran down the alley with heads bent, he moved quickly to block their path. They glanced up—fearfully, James thought. He showed them the two ten-pound notes in his hand, and they moved with him across the narrow street and into the Little Brown Jug. The pub was filling with after-work revelers and residents and interns from Mercer's Hospital across the street.

"What's this about, then?" said the elder of the two gruffly.

"Are you the polis?" asked the other in a broad Galway accent.

"No, I'm a solicitor. I've nothing to do with the police. I just need some information, and I will pay well for it. If you can't give it to me, then perhaps you can tell me who could?" He smiled warmly. The two men looked at each other, and the elder one spoke.

"Whadya want to know?"

"Anything you can tell me, maybe about a rich Yank, maybe about a trip to Wexford?" James looked expectantly at each of them. He couldn't give too much away, but at the same time he had to let them think that he already knew quite a lot.

"And you'll pay?" said the older youth.

James showed him a wad of notes.

"And you're not the polis?"

James shook his head and ordered three pints of stout. When the drinks came, he put a fifty-pound note under the glasses. The elder one drank and took up the money.

"The polis were already around. They talked to old man Ellis. He told them the truth. This firm has not had any calls down to Wexford—ever. You know this outfit, they only handle the Dublin swells."

"I understand that part. But what can you tell me? A Yank came to see you, didn't he? Much like I did just now. Am I right?"

"Yeah, only it was in the afternoon, see. The other two cars were out. We was just hangin' about. Nothin' was on, but we stay in case there's a call to a hospital or the morgue, you know, or a house for that matter." The younger man spoke rapidly, nervously.

"Shut your mouth. I'll do the tellin'."

He shriveled into his corner and drank his pint, watching with huge eyes. He was very young indeed. The elder slid the money into his hand.

James ordered again and put a second fifty pounds under his own glass.

The older youth spoke again.

"This Yank, he comes up to us and sez, like, he wants to play a great practical joke on his family. I knew he had lots of the foldin' stuff by the way he was dressed, like. So he sez he's home on 'holiers' from the States and that his crew of spinster sisters were alus after 'im. He sez he wants to give them a right fright an' make them see sense. He's roarin' laffin', talkin' to us." The youth smiled at the memory of it. "Jaysus, we thought it was a great gag to pull off and sez we'll help 'im. He said he wanted it to be all cloak-and-dagger stuff and no one was to know and could we pull it off. We sez surely. You see, like, me and him, we keep the keys to the lock-up when we leave at night. We work such godawful hours that we're back here at the crack of dawn. And old Ellis, he trusts us like." He looked sharply at James.

"No doubt." James smiled and moved the fifty pounds toward the center of the now dripping table. Brown sworls of Guinness stout soaked into the thin green paper.

"We was to take one of them hearses and drive it to the Phoenix Park, near the obelisk. He said we'd see a box there. We were to take it and drive to an address down in Wexford, a place called Kilmartin, and leave it on the doorstep of this big house. He said he'd pay us two hundred quid. He was full of the joys, laffin' and jokin'. A nice man, sir, a nice man. For a Yank." His voice fell.

"We took his two hundred quid, and that night we did as we was bid. When we got to the obelisk, there was the box–"

"You mean a coffin?"

"Yes, a wooden one, one of the old-style ones. It was on the grass, and there wasn't a soul around, not even the prossies. I was glad for that. O' course it was pouring with rain. We put the box in the back. It was heavy enough, and nailed shut. We didn't look into it since it was nailed tight. Nor did we see a livin' soul around the place. We stood for a bit, but no one came out to us from the shrubs like. So ..." He took a swig of his pint and lifted the money. The younger one's hand shot forward and folded it into his own palm. The elder shrugged. And ordered again.

"He was a man of honor, sir. A man of honor," said the younger of the two. "The next day we got the rest of the money. Two hundred more quid. A messenger came here–to the back of the premises, I mean. You know, one of them lads on the motor scooters, a courier they're called. He gave us an envelope, 'Jim and Joe' was all that was written on it–that's us, right? Two hundred quid. A man of his word he was." He sighed.

"Did you deliver the box?"

"O' course. Whadya tink we are? We did as we was bid," said the elder. "We'd had a bit o' trouble down in Kilmartin, finding the house. It was breaking daylight when we dumped the box. We fair sped out of that place. We had to get the car back, y'see. And wash it down so's Ellis wouldn't have hint nor hair of what we'd been doin' in the night." He leaned back. "And he didn't. We pulled that off and made us'selfs four hundred quid ..."

"Less the petrol?" added the second youth.

"Right. Bizarre, that's what I call it. Bizarre." He stressed the first syllable.

"And that was it?" The mood was affable, amiable now. The pints and the pounds were having good effect.

"It was. Until we read of it on the papers. The polis were 'round like a shot. They didn't question us, just old Ellis, but natural like, he mentioned it to us. Bizarre, he sez to us, and we agreed."

"You didn't come forward with what you knew?"

"And lose our jobs!" the younger lad fairly shrieked.

James nodded with understanding.

"He was dead, wasn't he? The poor old sod. Just like a Yank. Come home, splash the money around and get hisself murthered."

James didn't attempt to follow this logic, but it seemed to console both of the hearse drivers.

"And you told no one?"

"Hey," said the bigger man, "didn't we say we gave the Yank our word? We told no one. Just like he said. And he paid us well, he did that." He eyed James over his glass.

James took out another fifty pounds and stood up.

"A man of honor, he was. He'd give the Yanks a good name, he would, a man of honor. Just like us," he added, a bit slurred.

"Indeed," said James. "Well, have a drink to his memory, then." He nodded and moved quickly off into the crowd, but they made no move to follow him.

James walked slowly back to the car. He'd lost his umbrella, but he took no notice of the rain, delighted as he was to be vindicated at last.

"I said from the beginning it was the hearse," he told his car, whose window was now blanketed with tickets. He sped back to his flat.

A few phone calls and the stage would finally be set.

Chapter Twelve

James spotted Sarah Gallagher before she saw him. She was seated on one of the comfortable floral-covered sofas in the front lounge of the Berkeley Court. He wasn't the only one to have seen her. He stood leaning with his back against one of the pillars, watching as she spoke briefly but sweetly to the middle-aged couple who were obviously asking for her autograph. When two young women approached on the same errand, he intervened.

"Sarah?" he said quietly as she scribbled her name on the hotel brochures the girls had handed her. She looked up questioningly, and an expression of delight passed across her face. She stood up then and said good-bye to the girls.

"James," she whispered as she put her hand on his arm, pressing it.

"I am so sorry for being late. Something urgent had to be taken care of—at the office."

"It's all right, darling, you're not very late. I'm just so glad to see you."

"Shall we have a drink in the bar before dinner?"

"Certainly," she said simply.

James was proud to be walking by her side. She was dressed in a linen suit of pale blue, her favorite color, a shade that flattered her ivory skin. Her dark brown hair was pulled back in a simple chignon at the nape of her neck. And the style suited her oval face and striking features. She walked with an easy grace, with the gait of a natural dancer. He was conscious of people noticing them, and not only because they might have recognized her as the famous violinist. He knew they made an exceptionally handsome couple. She linked his arm with hers as they walked, and he shivered, thinking fleetingly of what it would be like to be walking down the aisle of some small church with Sarah as his bride. He glanced at her face. She didn't look at all like Kathleen Walsh. But shaken by that momentary thought, he pushed it away, back to the depths where he had buried it.

They both ordered gin and tonics with lots of ice and lemon. The day had been surprisingly hot for the end of April. Dubliners had been strewn about the grassy lawns of Stephen's Green and along the banks of the canal, lying prone and unselfconscious under the welcome heat of the sun. Like young children, they lounged at their ease, shoes kicked off, jackets thrown aside, trousers and sleeves rolled up, as if they'd just discovered sunshine. The mood of the city was a holiday mood, happy, carefree. In contrast to his own, thought James sadly.

"You're unusually quiet, James," Sarah said, her low tones like a balm to his ears.

"Am I? I apologize."

"Don't apologize. You can be yourself with me, whatever self that happens to be, on whatever day it happens to be." She smiled into his face as he blushed slightly.

They ate a very light supper of smoked salmon, a salmon mousse, some very delicate pâté of liver, and thinly sliced brown bread. James had ordered a bottle of light chilled chablis. They chose a fresh fruit bowl and sorbet for dessert, and a bottle of chilled liebfraumilch.

It was an extremely pleasant meal, and James listened intently to Sarah's description of her recording sessions in London, which had gone on for some days. But he watched her face even more intently, noting every expression, memorizing how she held her spoon, the sophisticated way in which she delicately held her fluted wineglass.

"James, although you look as though you are hanging on my every word, I don't believe you've heard a single one of them," Sarah said, laughing, but with a question in her voice.

"Oh, no, I've heard everything you've said. I just love watching you say it!" It was Sarah's turn to blush. She glanced away at the other guests in the dining room. There was a low, pleasant murmur of happy voices, with faint recorded music mingling in. James lightly touched her hand as it rested on the white tablecloth. She interlocked her fingers with his. It was then that they both sensed that somehow this night was different, the mood was different between them. There was a shared sweetness, a tenderness, a sadness almost.

They drove in comfortable silence to Dun Laoghaire. James parked the car and they walked the length of the south pier, merely chatting, holding hands just like the other hundred or so couples who passed them. The heat of the day had freshened with an offshore breeze, light and cooling. Young families were there with babies in strollers, older couples with their spinster daughters, men of all ages who walked briskly and alone. Yes, there was a Sunday feeling about the place, a holiday feeling on the long curving granite pier that thrust itself out into the Irish Sea.

A few boats bobbed at their moorings. And as inevitable as the tide, the nine o'clock ferry for Wales sounded its whistle at a quarter to the hour. A signal of departure, a symbol of partings and of new beginnings. They watched in silence until the ferry was out of sight, and James felt again the primeval soothing quality of the sound and the sight of the lapping waves. They stood a long time at the very end of the south pier, until almost everyone else but the fishing enthusiasts had turned back. They were alone at last. Sarah was still silent.

"Sarah?" James said, looking at last into her lovely face. "I love you."

"I know, James. I think I love you too," she said in return.

They didn't kiss. The moment seemed too full, too tender. James had tears in his eyes and he almost sighed with relief. Sarah leaned her head on his chest and he folded her in his arms as gently as though she would break if he pressed too tightly. And so they stood until the stars began to brighten in the now darkening sky.

Eventually they returned to the car. Initially James had thought they would go to an old pub he knew in the Dublin Mountains, which on such rare, warm days as this, placed tables outside its doors. The shabby little pub commanded a magnificent view of the city of Dublin and the sea that surrounded it. On summer nights the white and amber lights of the city would flicker and shimmer through the evening mist, rendering the city a magical place always. But somehow now James didn't feel it was right. As he turned the car toward Monkstown, Sarah nodded, wordlessly answering his unspoken question.

When they parked in front of her parents' house, he knew she wouldn't ask him in. They sat holding hands like two lovestruck children. Then she kissed him lightly, lingeringly, sweetly on the lips. He stroked her hair for one brief moment and then cupped her face in his hands, memorizing its every lineament.

"Sarah," he whispered hoarsely, "whatever happens, please remember that I love you as I have never loved anyone before. And never will again."

"James, I'll see you tomorrow night ..." she started to say with a question in her voice. "Won't I?"

He kissed her quickly on the tip of her nose. "Go now. Go quickly."

She got out of the car and ran as lightly as a child toward the house, and like a child, she didn't look back. As James put the car in gear, he whispered his final farewell and watched until the door closed.

He drove for a long time, up into the mountains till he reached Killakee, then turned swiftly into the Featherbed that ran the ridge of the Sally Gap. The road, lit by a half-moon, was deserted, and he cruised through the dark, reviewing in his mind what had just transpired and what this very long day had meant for him.

When he had got to the office early that morning, Gerald had already arrived. Within seconds he had buzzed for James. James had sensed his annoyance, but didn't acknowledge it. Briefly, he outlined what he had learned in Boston, his conversation with Jack Moore's doctor, his conversation with Solomon the lawyer, including the news of Jack's immense fortune and the Swiss bank account. He had watched to see Gerald's reaction to the size of Jack's estate, but Gerald merely grunted.

At that point Gerald had said, "And the will, James? All this is very well, but I sent you out to Boston to get a copy of the will."

James handed the papers to Gerald and watched his face surreptitiously. But nothing remarkable showed there.

"Well, it is an unusual document, to say the least," Gerald said at last.

"I haven't seen anything like it in my experience," commented James, and his experience was considerable.

"Mmm, no, I'm sure."

He had spent close to two hours with Gerald, who had been quite annoyed that he had failed to turn up at the office on Monday or Tuesday. But James had not offered any excuses.

As James stood up to leave, Gerald added, almost as an afterthought, "Violet and Lily and Rose are in for quite a surprise."

"Surprise?" James said casually.

"Well, I don't believe they have any idea of the extent of Jack's holdings. I don't think they have even considered that they would stand to inherit anything."

"Personally, I don't think it's even crossed their minds. But I'm glad you mentioned it. I phoned Violet last night from my flat ..."

Gerald looked up in surprise.

"You see, Gerald, even though I was recovering from the flu or jet lag or whatever it was, I was still working," James said lightly, laughing in his usual way. "I told her," he went on quickly, "that I needed to speak to her, and to Lily and Rose as well. And I indicated that it has to do with Jack's will. I'll need to start probating, you know, or the firm will, since as their solicitors, it's our job. And Gerald, I'd like to start as soon as possible, because this will be new territory to me."

"How so?" Gerald was sharp.

"Well, for a start, I imagine I'll need to seek precedents, I don't know how complicated the American tax situation will be. I need to establish if he can be viewed as an Irish citizen residing abroad. He had American citizenship, you see. And I'll need to read up on the Swiss banking laws. You know, I've never handled anything quite like this. I might have to ask for an extra clerk to do some legwork for me, if that's all right with you, Gerald."

"I suppose so. Take that new girl, Miriam. She's bright and she's expressed an interest in inheritance law already. It will be good experience for her."

"There's another favor I want to ask of you. I'd like you to accompany me when I go to see the Moores tomorrow. I made the appointment for five because I thought later in the working day might suit you better. I took the liberty of checking your appointment book." James held his breath for the answer.

"You seem to be taking matters into your own hands of late. What do you need me down there for?"

"My feeling is that the will and its contents will be a shock to them. And that the amount of money involved might merit the presence of the head of the firm. And, I might add, it would give *me* a bit of confidence too. Violet tends to treat me as though I were still wet behind the ears."

There was a long pause. Finally Gerald assented. "All right. Let me know in the morning what time you intend to leave. I expect we'll make better time in your outrageous car than in mine."

"Right, I'll get back to you."

James recalled how he had literally sagged against the door to his office once he was safely inside. All the wheels were in motion now. There could be no turning back.

His head was clearer as he turned his car for home. A good night's sleep was essential. He dreaded the drive alone tomorrow with Gerald, but trusted that if they kept to the other cases the small law firm was engaged on, the time might pass quickly enough. Yes, he would be very very glad when tomorrow was over.

They had only been waiting a few seconds on the granite front step of the Moores' fine manor house when the heavy door swung open and revealed Kevin smiling warmly.

"Mr. Fleming, it's good to see you again." Kevin shook hands with Gerald as James introduced them, Kevin's face showing the proper awe at meeting the famous Kilmartin solicitor. Gerald nodded noncommittally, and looked surprised as Kevin accompanied the two of them into Violet's sitting room.

The three sisters were having tea. Violet, cup in hand, was standing by the unlit fireplace, its empty grate supporting a huge array of lilac sprays. She nodded at Gerald and James but did not greet them. Rose, seated at the low table, also nodded, and smiled shyly.

"Tea? Mr. Fleming? And you, Gerald, it's been so long since we've seen you." Rose poured two more cups of tea, which Kevin handed to the two men.

Lily, who had been standing at the window and had obviously seen them drive up to the house, finally moved from her place and approached them.

"Do sit down, Gerald," she said softly, barely glancing at him. "And you too, Mr. Fleming." She herself sat in one of the wing chairs that faced slightly away from them and toward Violet.

There was a heavy, uncomfortable pause. James waited.

"Well, Violet, Lily, Rose," Gerald finally said, as he shifted his weight on the small straight-backed chair. He nodded at each in turn. "I think my colleague, James, would ..." He glanced at James, who was busy reaching for another piece of tea cake. "James would like me to conduct our business here today. As you know, we had assumed that Jack, your brother, must have left a will. It only stood to reason that a man of his financial astuteness would have done so. Or have been forced to by a sensible American lawyer." Gerald attempted a laugh at his own slight witticism.

He continued. "It seems our assumptions were right. Jack did indeed leave a will. Investigation revealed that it was in the States, in Boston, and James went out to get a copy of it. We did this since we were acting on your behalf as your solicitors. Now I must inform you about the will. But I'd like to also mention that I, we, at the firm would be happy to continue in our capacity and would, as a result, like to begin the process of probating the will ..." Violet stared at him in astonishment. "That is," Gerald coughed slightly, "just as soon as Violet is acquitted at her trial, which of course I fully believe will be the outcome of this unfortunate business.

"Now, to the matter in hand ..." Gerald paused to reach by his side for his briefcase. While he did so, and unlocked it and took out a sheaf of papers, all but Gerald heard the front door bell ringing. Kevin left the room wordlessly, glancing only at James.

Gerald looked up. "I'm glad that young man chose to leave. I was surprised you allowed him to be present ... this information is very much for your ears and eyes only."

· "Then may I see it, Gerald? For God's sake, you're making a mountain out of a molehill ... as usual!" Violet's voice was icy. She strode across the room with her hand extended. Gerald stood up abruptly, glaring at her.

"Violet, if you don't mind. There are three of you involved. Or have you chosen to forget about Lily and Rose—as always!"

The argument was interrupted as Kevin yet again opened the sitting-room door. Gerald swung around, on the point of speaking, when James put a hand on his arm.

"Mr. Fleming?" said Kevin, looking from one man to the other. "Inspector O'Shea has arrived ..."

And O'Shea followed Kevin into the room, shedding his light coat as he did so. Gerald's mouth opened in astonishment. All eyes looked from O'Shea to James, who took a silent and very deep breath.

"Fleming! What is the meaning of this? Did you know O'Shea was coming? Quite obviously you did—I can tell from your expression." Gerald was livid.

Violet stepped back from her confrontation with Gerald, eyeing O'Shea and visibly trembling.

"Please. Please be seated. I know that we are here certainly to discuss Jack Moore's will. But there were one or two matters that I wished to clear up at this time. Certain knowledge ... No, let me say I have come across certain information very relevant to Violet Moore's case. And I wanted all of you together when I brought it to your attention ..."

"This is outrageous," spluttered Gerald. "Fleming, you got me down here on some bloody ruse—"

"But the will—"

"The will my foot, man! I don't like this subterfuge on your part, no matter what the outcome. Fleming, you're fired!"

James winced, but continued after a moment, "Please, Gerald, it would be better if you were here to discuss the issues. I am not leaving. Whether I'm in your employ or not, I must discharge my duty." He glanced at Violet. "Miss Moore, perhaps we could all have some brandy?"

Violet wordlessly waved to Kevin, hardly removing her eyes from James's face. Kevin quickly served large measures of brandy to all but Rose, who continued knitting as though oblivious to her surroundings. Lily stood up to take her glass and positioned herself behind Violet, who was now seated. Gerald at last sat down and drank his brandy slowly, eyeing James and O'Shea.

The mood of tension had lessened slightly, and James continued with more confidence.

"I think perhaps the best way to deal with all I have to say is to tell you a story, a narrative in which I have attempted to fit all of the events, all of the personalities, all of the information that I have.

"This story, which I believe had its roots in years and generations gone by, has its origin with three sisters and a brother. Violet, Lily, Rose. And their brother, Jack.

"When they inherited this farm on the death of their mother, Violet–being the eldest, and perhaps their most strong willed, at that time at least–took over the running of the farm, and yes, the running of her siblings' lives.

"Violet had one single goal: to hold on to the property and improve it in every way. She had little time for her family, less time for a social life, and no time for men." James paused and sipped his brandy as Violet stared at him in silent fury.

"Obsessed by her goal, she failed to note that her sisters and brother did not entirely share her, let us say ... single-minded enthusiasm.

"Lily and Jack ... and Rose too"–James looked kindly at Rose, who had looked up gratefully when he added her name–"they wanted what the rest of the world might term a more normal life. They too wished for the farm to prosper, but not at the expense of the rest of their lives. Lily? Lily had wanted to marry and have a family. Rose, who, I think, might not have looked for marriage herself, at the same time wanted Lily to marry. And Jack too.

"In fact, Lily had a number of suitors. Violet worked hard to discourage all of them. But there was one, one young man who was more persistent, more tenacious, and, I believe, more in love with her than the others. A young man from the locality who had made up his mind to leave the difficult life of farming and who made a great success of his chosen profession, the practice of law." James glanced at Lily, who was watching Gerald. "I know now that that young man who loved Lily Moore was Gerald Fitzgerald."

"In the name of God," exploded Violet, "what has this palaver have to do with us, with anything?"

"It has a very great deal to do with your case, Violet," James said hoarsely, his tone now indicating he would not be silenced by her or anyone else.

"Lily and Gerald, both very young, in their early twenties, saw a life ahead together. A normal, happy life. And during those happy courtship days, Jack, who was rather younger–a boy, really–became very fond of Gerald. Perhaps he saw in him both a friend and a brother–brother-in-law, as he soon would be ... or so thought Jack.

As did Lily. And Gerald. And Rose. Rose too saw Lily's proposed marriage with Gerald as bringing new life into her own life.

"However, there was one family member who did not view the marriage in this way. Violet, who had broken up every other relationship Lily had attempted to have, tried to destroy this one too. There were to be no interlopers in the Moore family. No outsiders becoming involved in the farm. I'm not sure how she achieved what she clearly set out to do. Perhaps one day Lily might tell us ..." James watched as Lily lowered her head, silent as ever. Then the sudden sound of Gerald's voice, hoarse with rage, broke that silence.

"I'll tell you, Fleming," he burst out, looking not at James, but at Violet. "She worked away at her night and day. She picked away at what little confidence and trust Lily ever had. She filled her head with stories of men, men who drank, men who played around, men who abused their wives physically and mentally. But Lily held out. She knew I was not one of those men. And then she started on Lily herself. How Lily would not make a good wife to me, that she was only a clumsy country girl who would be a misfit in Dublin. She convinced her that she would not only not help my law career, but would hinder it. Deny it as you will, Violet, but it's the truth." Violet sat stone still and Gerald turned toward the others. "That was far more successful," he said, his voice sarcastic now. "Lily had self-doubts, but we discussed them and I assured her I had no need of this fantasy Dublin society wife that Violet was creating. But Violet had succeeded in sowing seeds of doubt. Lily was weakening. She now needed time to think, whereas until then we had been rushing headlong into love. Oh, and then Violet saw her advantage ..."

He turned to face Violet again. "How can anyone so thick have been as shrewd as you? How could you have known the right buttons to push?"

He glaceed at James, half seeing him now, looking back with an inward eye. "She wore Lily down. She said I would expect many children. That as I prospered I would want a large family, sons to follow me into the law practice. She talked to Lily of the horrors of sex, the brutality of sex with a man.

"I know you well! You must have made it sound like two rutting sheep in the field. And then she spoke of pregnancy and childbirth. There too you had your bloody rural examples to throw in her sensitive face. Oh, Lily had seen ewes die after dropping twins, and Lily had seen cows dying in agony with two-headed calves protruding from their swollen bodies. I know, because I saw it too, and more, and I chose to leave this bloody awful cruel life behind me!" Gerald's voice was cracking with emotion and his finger repeatedly jabbed the air.

"Oh, yes, I would leave it and take Lily with me. But Violet painted such a picture of the marriage bed and the confinement bed that she was scaring poor, dear Lily half witless. Lily, I ask you?" He glanced wildly around the room. "Lily, so full of affection, so full of fine, delicate feeling ... Lily, who should have been taken away from this rough life.

"Ah, but Lily had no mother to advise her, to assure her that marriage and love and trust and children on her lap and at her knee would bring her happiness, physical happiness, spiritual happiness. As if that unnatural woman who bore her would ever have advised her thusly." Gerald paused, but only for breath. "No, there was no loving mother. Only that bitch who sits there now before you!" Gerald's voice dropped. "There was no one." His voice fell to a whisper. "No one." He leaned back and looked toward Lily, who had hidden her face in her hands. Rose had stopped knitting.

"The result was ..." James's voice was quiet. "The result was that Lily did not marry the man she loved and who ... loved her." Gerald bent his head. "Lily remained on the farm, looking after the accounts, tending the hens, and keeping away from the physical work for which she held a deep distaste. Jack, who had come to have hopes of a happier life, we can assume, was devastated–"

"Oh, he was," Rose broke in unexpectedly. She looked around her. "Why, you must remember, Lily? And you, Violet? Oh, Mr. Fleming," said Rose in her rapid, breathy way, "Gerald wouldn't have known, he was gone then, but Jack, oh the poor boy was terribly sad. He loved Gerald. I knew it. We used to lie in the hay after the milking was done and chew straws, and we'd speculate on the wedding, and how we'd both be able to go up to Dublin for visits. How it would be so good to have a real brother in Gerald. And I used to say to dear Jack that perhaps he too could be a solicitor like Gerald, and that perhaps Gerald would help him. But Jack had no ideas of that. Jack loved the farm. This is where he'd stay, he'd tell me. This is where he'd make his life and fortune." She crossed the room to Gerald. "Gerald, Gerald, sure he loved you like the big brother he never had. And do you know one of the things he loved to do with you most of all? Riding. Remember, Gerald?" She waited. "Gerald, you do remember that, don't you? Jack would ride with you morning and evening. You do remember...?"

"Rose, for God's sake." Gerald groaned and stood up, flexing himself, shaking her off.

"I beg your pardon," said Rose suddenly to James. And she wiped away the tears from the corners of eyes, with her fist, like a young child.

James felt completely overwhelmed with the emotion that filled the room. He wondered if he could go on. He opened his mouth, but no words came.

"Fleming! Please continue," said O'Shea in a civil voice. "Perhaps another brandy would do ..." Kevin returned to the sideboard as James tried hard to settle his thoughts and concentrate on the order of his approach. He started again, slowly, at first, addressing O'Shea.

"Things went on rather as before. Except that now Jack was getting older. Jack as he matured began not only to take an interest in the running of the farm, he was also beginning to express his own ideas, his own goals about the improvement of the farm, the herd, and so on. And around the same time Jack too fell in love ..."

"Love!" Violet snorted. "Is this a love story you're telling us, Fleming? Is it for this nonsense—about love—that we are forced to sit here, prisoners in our own home?"

"Yes, perhaps it is a love story after all," said James quietly, his tone full of a strange foreboding that silenced Violet once again.

"Jack fell in love with one ... well, with a local girl, a young Catholic girl, whose family Violet despised. But Violet wasn't as quick to spot the dangers as she had been with Lily. Knowing and caring nothing about ... love," he glanced at Violet, "she assumed Jack was 'playing around.'

"And so we come to the night that Mike Walsh died. Jack Moore killed Mike Walsh." James waited for the effect of his words.

"Come again?" O'Shea blurted out with rising interest.

"Jack Moore killed Mike Walsh. He confessed it to Violet." At this news both Lily and Rose reacted, Lily moving around the chair to confront her older sister.

"I don't believe it! You'll do anything, say anything to destroy Jack's memory." The words flew out of Lily's mouth.

"It's a lie," shrieked Rose, also addressing Violet, who merely looked past them, stony-faced and staring. "You have no right," she hissed.

"I have every right," said James.

"Go on," said O'Shea.

"Mike Walsh had left the pub after his quarrel with Jack and had lain in wait for him—to have it out, I believe, but not to kill Jack. But they were both drunk. In their brief struggle Jack pushed Mike Walsh, who went down heavily into the ditch and struck his head—"

"He was defending himself!" cried Rose. "Why didn't you ever tell us?" she screamed at Violet. "Never, all these years, and we didn't know why he'd gone away. I thought ... I thought he didn't love us anymore ..."

"Be that as it may," said James, "he knew that he was responsible for Mike's death, and he was frightened. He ran to Violet, his older sister, and told her. She then—in a stroke of evil genius—saw her chance."

"Her chance?" said O'Shea.

"To get rid of Jack from the farm. She used his fear and fueled it. She told him to flee, and she helped him to do it. And after that gave him an alibi the police trusted. But all this time she led Jack to believe he was still wanted by the police."

"Oh my God," said Lily quietly.

"But there was more than just Jack that Violet wanted to get rid of."

"What do you mean?" asked Gerald.

"Only Violet of all of you knew that Jack's girlfriend, Kathleen Walsh, was carrying his child. She saw her chance to get rid of not only Jack, but also to separate him from Kathleen, and from their unborn child ..."

"So Jack had his own child after all," said Rose, smiling through her tears.

"Yes, Rose, but he never saw her. Violet kept Jack in London by feeding him lies. She kept Kathleen in a convent, which took in unwed mothers, by feeding her more lies ..."

"And the child?" Gerald's eyes were bulging from his head.

"Violet told Jack the child died, but in fact their child lived. Violet also convinced Kathleen that Jack had abandoned her and persuaded her to put the child up for adoption ..."

"You know this for fact?" Gerald shouted.

"I know the young woman the child became," James whispered into the silence of the room.

O'Shea began to speak, but thought better of it.

A sigh suddenly escaped from James involuntarily. He saw O'Shea anxiously staring at him.

"And what does all this mean?" O'Shea asked.

"Violet," James began again, "believed all was well. But eventually

Jack had his suspicions in London and returned secretly to her." Lily and Rose stared incredulously at Violet.

"He was demented. He had lost his home, his share of the farm with which he had bought Violet's unneeded silence. He had lost the girl he loved, who had left Ireland forever. And he had lost the baby Violet had told him had died at birth." Gerald groaned audibly.

"He was demented. And he was also violent. Violet, for once frightened of something or somebody, sought to save her skin by confessing to Jack that the baby girl had survived and had been adopted. She thought this would console him. But far from consoling him, this news enraged him further. And when he left, this time it was for good."

James paused, not knowing how to continue, feeling that he was himself in danger of becoming a force of destruction equal to Violet. He sat down and mopped his face.

At last Gerald spoke. "He never told me."

"No?"

"No, he never told me about the child."

"I didn't think so," James said softly, gently.

"Did he tell you?" For the first time Gerald spoke directly to Lily. She shook her head, but held his eyes briefly with her own.

"Can you make the connections for us now, Fleming?" asked O'Shea.

"Yes, I think so," resumed James, staring without seeing the lilacs as they randomly dropped their petals on the hearth.

"As far as we can determine, Jack left London shortly thereafter. Emigration records show he entered the United States through New York and went almost immediately to Boston. There he began working on construction sites. Through friends he made and connections he forged, he worked his way up the ladder in a manner that is very possible in the States. He began his own construction company, which went from strength to strength. To put it briefly, he made a great deal of money and he invested it wisely. He took an interest in stocks and shares, working through a very astute and successful broker. He never married—that I think you'll agree was very significant?" James looked around the room at his companions.

"Meanwhile Kathleen, who had stopped and then remained in London, eventually made a good marriage and put the past entirely behind her." James stressed this fact. "And I believe that she and Jack never had any contact over these last twenty-seven years.

"Within the last year, something happened. Jack Moore discovered that he had an incurable cancer."

Violet gasped, as did Rose. "How do you know?" Rose murmured.

"I met with his personal physician in Boston," James said simply. But he watched for O'Shea's reaction.

"But why didn't this come out at the inquest? What about the autopsy?" Gerald asked.

"Because the immediate cause of his death was so very obvious. The point is, Jack knew he had the disease and he knew how much time he had left to him.

"On the surface he immediately began to deal with his financial and business interests. We have a list of his assets and holdings from his accountant. We also have the evidence of the sale and making liquid of virtually everything he owned. This he transferred into cash ... as far as we know to date, all of this was done quite legally. When the will is probated, we or whoever is involved will be able to learn more. I do have the will and the rough figure that the accountant had given to Jack attached to it. The money is safe and its location is known."

"Well," said O'Shea impatiently, "what is this magic number?"

"It approaches three million dollars." Violet, Lily, Rose, and O'Shea—all but Gerald, who knew the figure—gaped at James, momentarily speechless.

"Three million dollars." O'Shea whistled. He glanced speculatively at Violet. And then caught her eye.

"If you think that I knew of this, if you think this gives me a motive," snapped Violet, "then you are very much mistaken."

"I must agree there with my client, O'Shea," James said, smiling to ease his defensive tone. "You see, I believe that no one, no one but Jack's accountancy firm and perhaps the tax people, had any knowledge of Jack's real worth. Neither Violet nor Lily, neither Gerald nor Rose, knew this. Am I right?" The four nodded.

But Gerald added in a subdued voice, "I knew he was wealthy."

"And you, Lily? Did you not know, perhaps from Gerald, the sum of Jack's fortune, perhaps the terms of his will?" James's expression suddenly hardened, but Lily merely sat as erect as ever and determinedly shook her head. Neither she nor Gerald looked at each other, but O'Shea watched them like a hawk stalking new prey.

"It's not important," said James, to O'Shea's visible surprise. "You see, Jack had devised an underlying strategy. On the surface he was consolidating his fortune in view of the limited time left to him. But underneath, he had a definite purpose for massing his money. Firstly, he needed to use some of it—it turns out, not a great deal. Secondly, he wanted to make it simple for his intended heir."

"Heir ..." echoed Gerald, sagging in his chair.

"I'm afraid I've got ahead of myself," said James, bitterness now filling his voice. "Jack had devised a very diabolical plan. It is my opinion that he had been hatching this plan—or rather, plans—for years. The single end of each, the common goal each shared with the other, was—the vengeance he planned to wreak on the woman who had destroyed his life: his sister Violet. I can only imagine how Jack Moore filled the empty nights and weekends, when he was not occupied with his work, when he chose to remain friendless, unmarried, childless. His revenge was his entire emotional life, he fed it and nurtured it instead of the children he had had a right to nurture and cherish. Perhaps he fell in love with his revenge, almost reluctant to enact it and end it. Because when that plan of vengeance was fulfilled, he no longer had any reason to live."

"Preposterous!" said Violet, but her voice was low.

"I don't think so. You, better than anyone, know that, because you saw him that night years ago, a man destroyed in front of your eyes. But when he was told that he was dying, that he was about to die, it became a matter of urgency to carry out his revenge. Now he was no longer afraid to execute the plan, he was afraid he would leave it too late. It was, you see, a very daring and cunning plan, but he needed help. Some of that help he could buy with money. But the crucial help he needed he could only demand from others who had suffered at Violet's hands, from others who had shared his hatred and his desire for revenge ..."

Suddenly Gerald stood up. James shook his head kindly at him. "Please, Gerald," he whispered directly to him. "Even if you leave, where will you go?" O'Shea had moved unobtrusively toward the door, catching Kevin's eye, but they did not need to act. Gerald walked with dignity to the sideboard and filled his glass and James's. He nodded.

"Yes, Jack needed help. Jack—unknown to the others in this room— had kept in contact only very occasionally with Gerald. Gerald let him know how the farm had prospered, and told him, more importantly, about Violet, her habits, her health ... am I right?" Gerald looked away.

"When Jack learned of his illness, he chose to act. He contacted Gerald, and after obtaining his promise to help—perhaps by mentioning the amount of his fortune and the terms of his will...?" He looked at

Gerald, who did not respond. Lily filled her glass and went unexpect-edly to sit beside Gerald, still without looking at him.

"Gerald promised to help. Only one more recruit was necessary. Someone who lived in this house, someone who could carry out the crucial spadework on which the plan hinged." Still no one spoke. James continued, his jaw tense and tired now.

"Much of the planning was done by phone. When Jack arrived in Dublin in secret, he finalized his plan with Gerald and took care of certain outside details personally—"

"Get to the point, man!" O'Shea boomed, startling James. He hard-ened his heart then, knowing he had been delaying the evil day.

"Right! First, Lily—according to a rough timetable, I imagine—obtained from the kitchen a sharp carving knife with Violet's fingerprints on it. Somehow she conveyed this knife to Gerald, who at this time had led all of us—I mean at the firm—to believe that he was at home ill. Mean-while, Jack himself had hired the hearse which, as we all know, was seen by a number of people in Kilmartin, and which I have located, along with the drivers. He also arranged for a simple wooden coffin to be transported to the Phoenix Park and left at a prearranged spot. On the night, or rather, the very early hours of the day on which the body was found here in Kilmartin, Gerald and Jack went to the Phoe-nix Park. I can only ... no, I can't imagine that scene ..." James stared hard at Gerald.

"All right! All right!" Gerald leaped to his feet, waving away O'Shea, who had moved toward him. He swung on Violet and glared at her. "No, none of you—least of all you, Violet—can imagine that scene, but I will describe it to you. So you, as I, will see it to your dying day. Yes, I drove Jack to the park. I felt as though I were caught in some nightmare, truly, but I made no effort to shake myself out of it. Jack was calm and level-headed, and that helped me. I had brought the knife with me, carefully wrapped. Jack had remembered the gloves."

"Oh God," Rose moaned. "Oh God."

Gerald continued unheeding, staring only at Violet's transfixed face. "We went to the spot, and there was the coffin as arranged. I couldn't believe it when Jack actually stood in the coffin. He actually said this would help me! My God! Yes, he stood there and shook my hand, reminding me to fulfill the solemn oath he made me take earlier, to carry out the rest of the plan. He drew on his gloves and I handed him the knife. He opened his coat ... I didn't watch the rest. I didn't turn around until I heard his body fall against the wood of the coffin.

Can you believe it, he had even made sure the coffin was a light wood to make it easier for me to move. He had thought of everything.

"I was scared witless. I think now I *was* witless. I took the hammer and nails from the car, I straightened his body and clothes, took his gloves and the knife. He was dead. He *was* dead! I know because I checked," Gerald asserted, although no one had spoken.

"You were able to move the coffin yourself?" James queried.

"Yes, I nailed it shut. And I dragged it. We had placed it on a large sheet of heavy plastic. That helped a bit. It took some time, but it was an efficient method. Jack had thought of that too. I removed the plastic sheeting. That was tough. I took the hammer and the knife and the plastic ... and I left the coffin by the side of the road, in the dark. I waited in the rain until the hearse came. Up until that point I was never sure the plan would work. But once the coffin was in the hearse, I felt it was beyond my control."

"And the knife?" snapped O'Shea.

Gerald looked at Lily, who still did not speak. "I had arranged to meet Lily the day after the body was found. In the confusion, no one noticed or cared that she had to run an errand. I met her on a local back road and returned the knife, carefully wrapped."

"And she planted it!" said O'Shea matter-of-factly. "She planted it as she planted the idea of her seeing Violet in or near the barn. Clever! Clever. She even used Kevin's actual phone call, a call she could never have predicted, to buttress her story ..."

"Yes, I had phoned that night," Kevin reconfirmed. "And I was calling about the cow ..." He shook his head almost in shock, staring at Lily.

"You played us for fools," said O'Shea, bitterly trying to evoke a response. "You planted the knife and we found it. You gave us the weapon and, oh, how well-timed, you gave us the damning evidence that you saw Violet at the barn ..."

"Oh, it was easy," said Lily, her voice unlike her own normal tone. She stared at O'Shea. "Fools, you said. Yes, you and all the rest!" She spat out the words. "None of you knew how I hated Violet and my life, and none of you ever knew how I loved Gerald." She briefly touched his arm, but he didn't move.

"Can you tell us, Lily, because I think I know...?" James's voice was tender. For a moment.

"When Daphne, Mrs. Fitzgerald, died, Gerald and I ... we realized that what we had felt, that what our brief meetings over the years had sustained, was still there." Lily's voice was soft now and gentle. "But still we didn't act. It was taking time, I think, to come to realize that we were finally free of all that had prevented us, from oh, so long ago. It was as though our mutual hatred of Violet held us in thrall. When Jack contacted Gerald with the terrible news that he was dying, it was as though his virulent hatred was a catalyst. I hardly questioned what he asked me, had asked Gerald to do. I was only sorry that he wouldn't let me see him when he came to Dublin. He told Gerald he thought I would ... weaken. Maybe I would have ..." Lily suddenly leaned back. Her face looked wizened and wrinkled, and her pallor made her appear waxen and corpselike herself.

James could hardly bear the silence in the room, punctuated by Rose's crying. He couldn't bear to see the vacant faces of Lily and Violet; the worn and beaten face of Gerald, his mentor and boss; the astonishment still registering on the faces of O'Shea and Kevin. He stood up, walked to the window, and stared blindly out at the gravel and the lilac bushes. He couldn't remember the day or the date, his mind was so fatigued.

"Suicide," said Violet with a hint of triumph. Each in turn looked at her. No one spoke. "Suicide," she repeated.

Lily stood up and walked to the window.

"Lily, I swear to God," said Gerald, "he never told me about his daughter. I thought the money would be ours ..."

"After Violet was convicted?" James asked.

"Yes," said Lily. "Yes. It would have been myself and Rose then. And when Gerald and I married, he would have shared in it. We knew it had to be a fortune ... somehow it seemed right ... it was justice finally being done."

Rose seemed to have drawn herself into some protective shell, but yet she murmured to Lily: "You would have let Violet go to jail, you would have used Jack's money to look after me?" Her voice was bewildered and faint.

James began again. "Gerald, there was just one thing you had to leave to fate. You had to assume that Violet would telephone you to take care of the funeral arrangements and so on. You took her call. My, but you must have been relieved! And then you turned it all over to me. You mustn't have thought much of me ..." James's voice was bitter and sad. "And then you arranged to be in London—to make my handling of the case plausible, to remove yourself from the scene of the crime! You used me," James said flatly.

"For your information, Fleming," Gerald said, directing his voice at James's back, "it was not essential that Violet contact us first, or indeed at all, though I guessed she would. It was convenient, yes, because I could exercise control over her defense and monitor developments more closely, but it wasn't essential. Jack's plan was perfect–it had an inevitability of its own. His plan did not require any additional input from me after his body was discovered by Violet!

"And as regards using you as a pawn?" His voice rose. "What I want to know is–how long have you been working against me? You consciously misled me when you let me believe that Jack and Kathleen Walsh's baby died! You knowingly lied to me!"

James said nothing.

"Then tell me this, have you actually traced her? You know that she is alive, you know where she is?" Gerald's voice was nearly as bewildered as Rose's.

"Believe me," said James, without turning. "Yes, I've seen her. We've talked, but she ... she knows nothing."

"Nothing?" O'Shea was skeptical, alert as always.

"Nothing." James's tone was infinitely convincing. He paused for a few minutes and then said, as he turned and looked sadly at Gerald and Lily, "Jack betrayed you both."

Gerald nodded, the full impact of that reality having already reached him. Lily began to speak, but her voice broke and she cried at last–silent, tearless, racking sobs.

"I'm lost," said O'Shea.

"O'Shea–Gerald knew the terms of Jack's will ... from Jack, I might add. It was very simple. It said that he was leaving everything–which turned out to be three million–to his nearest relative. Since Gerald didn't know about the surviving child, Jack's natural daughter, he rightly assumed under those conditions, that Violet, Lily, and Rose would inherit. As the aim of the revenge was to convict Violet of Jack's murder, to send her to prison or worse, for something she didn't do, then only Lily and Rose would inherit his fortune. And Gerald, by marrying Lily as he always wanted–would also share in the wealth. In one fell swoop they would have wreaked both their revenge and Jack's. Violet would rot in prison, slowly going mad from the knowledge that she was convicted of a crime she didn't commit and losing the one thing for which she had lived, her property. Jack would have succeeded in doing to *her* what she had done all those years before to him. He would have taken everything that made life worth living away from her. And Lily and Gerald would in that single stroke have also acquired immense wealth. Wealth that would have freed them. Or so they thought. It was to be the most poetic of poetic justice."

"And now?" O'Shea looked at James.

"And now, Jack's daughter will stand to inherit—if, as I think, Jack did everything legally in the States regarding the disposal of his fortune." James sighed. "Yes, Jack's daughter will inherit his millions ... and inevitably, with his money, the knowledge of who her parents were ..."

O'Shea watched James closely. "You obviously know her. Does she—"

"Absolutely not. I already told you. She knows nothing. Jack never contacted her. I suspect he had her traced by professionals, private investigators. It would have been simple, with his money. If I did, then they could have done it."

Studying James for a long minute, O'Shea said finally, "There's more to you than meets the eye, Fleming."

But James merely shrugged, turning back to his window, his only image of escape from the horrors of this stifling room. He continued to stare unswervingly at the sodden lilac bushes now bent to earth with the weight of the rain and with the heavy wind that had risen and was now rattling the bones of this very old house.

He continued to stare as O'Shea led Lily and Gerald to the waiting car. He stared, and behind him Kevin cleared away the glasses and silently left the room to see to the cows. Natural life went on, thought James wildly. Life outside this room went on. And so he chose to stare out, ignoring Violet and Rose as they finally looked at each other, looked into each other's eyes, and saw nothing there that would enable them to go on together. And yet they would. He stared until they in turn left the room. Only then did he let the tears roll down his face as the raindrops rolled down the glass in front of him.

"So the charges were dropped against Violet Moore?" Matt asked as he poured another cup of tea for James. They were alone in his office, surrounded by towering stacks of homework books and endless team photos on the walls. The school was eerily quiet, the pupils having left for the day. James shut the door.

"Yes, as soon as Gerald and Lily made their statements, their confessions, really. I'm representing them both, but that is merely routine." James sighed. "Gerald's been a real soldier about it all. It bothers me ..."

"What?"

"To see him so ... so beaten."

"For God's sake, James–"

"I know, I know but ... he's asked me to take over the firm. To buy it out. He'll never be able to practice again, being disbarred. I said yes. The name will be changed too ..." He smiled at that, and looked up at Matt. Matt nodded, reassuring as ever.

"My mother's helping out. He's giving me a good price, but I don't have the capital. She says I might as well have what I'd be getting when she died. You know how funny she can be. We discussed it with my brother, and he doesn't mind. He'll be setting up his own practice shortly. I believe he might open his surgery in her house. Now there's an image to conjure with!" James laughed, but halfheartedly. He was tired.

"But tell me this, what do you think will happen to Gerald and Lily?" Matt was anxious for all the details, he wanted every loose end tied up. James sat back and crossed his legs, inadvertently clipping the edge of a towering stack of books. As he went to grab for it, it came to meet him, and in an instant the entire history assignments of Class 2B were in his lap. All twenty-six of them. Five minutes later James answered the question.

"I do believe they'll get suspended sentences ... at their ages. They didn't kill Jack, although it's hard to separate that out from the whole tangled mess. They concealed knowledge, they obstructed justice, they attempted to divert justice–you know–by planting the knife, by incriminating Violet. God! It might have succeeded ..."

"Mad, absolutely mad!" Matt whistled.

"You mean Jack? Yes, I'm afraid so. I think the cancer tipped the balance. Perhaps if he had lived, he just would have continued to fantasize, to plot and plan. I believe the cancer unhinged him ..."

"And hatred and bitterness and greed 'unhinged' Lily and Gerald too?" Matt sounded skeptical.

"Oh, Matt, how else can I look at it and carry on? It's hard, really hard, to see these people in the clear light of day. I had come to know them ... they're names, just names to you."

"So Gerald will retire. And Lily? Don't you think it's unfair that they will be able to live out their lives together in peace ... as though none of this had happened?"

"That, at least, won't be happening ... Lily stayed with Gerald one night in his Dublin house, the night of the day they were formally charged and released on bail. Can you imagine? Gerald a felon, standing before a judge. Gerald, whose whole life was the law!" James shook his head, and Matt saw in that single gesture the disillusionment James was feeling.

"And Lily, you started to say ..."

"Lily went back to Kilmartin, to the house. The three of them are there together, and I think that's how it will stay. Habit is a powerful thing, Matt. The habit of hatred binds them together in that house." He stared in front of him, picturing Violet, Lily, Rose. Picturing them in that house, in the barns, carrying on, unable to speak of what had happened, hate binding them as love might bind another family. Perhaps blood is thicker ... His thoughts strayed to the brief note he had mailed the day before to Kathleen Banks in London, suggesting she might enjoy following the career of the prominent young violinist, Sarah Gallagher. But Matt was asking him a question.

"O'Shea? He thinks I'm the greatest thing since sliced bread!" James laughed out loud. "But that won't last," he added.

"Well, the reports in the papers have given him much more of the credit than he deserved. They barely mentioned you!" Matt laid a plate of stale biscuits on the desk. "The whole thing is virtually a dead issue. It was really hot in the staff room when the papers thought it was a murder, a juicy scandal. Everyone was talking about it, and I didn't even know you were involved." Matt scowled at James, teasing him. "But now, well, once the news was out that it was a suicide, it died a death ..."

"Oh, very bad pun intended," James replied. "Anyway, you know I couldn't tell you what was going on, don't you?" He was apologetic with his old friend.

"Of course, of course. I know, always knew how discreet you were. How discreet you are. In fact, if you're not too tired from all your high drama, there's a small matter I'd like your particular perspective on."

James's ears pricked up with interest. "Yes?"

Matt paused and then leaned across his desk. He lowered his voice. "It's the head of my English department. He's Irish, you see, but he's been teaching in England–in Oxford, as he led me to believe. He only came this year. I was desperate when old Maughan died, God rest his soul, and I hired this man damn quick, too damn quick. I only got around to checking his references recently. They're phony. He's from Oxford all right, but I've been getting some very funny rumors back from my inquiries. It seems there was this young graduate student ..."

Matt's voice dropped as his friend moved closer. James smiled to himself. His Peru journey was postponed for the foreseeable future, but this most interesting development could well make up for that!

James let himself into his flat. He was tired, but pleased with his day. The visit with Matt had been good in more ways than one. And the bank manager had been more than cordial when he saw Mrs. Fleming's substantial savings account. The small Dublin law firm of Fitzgerald's would be his in a matter of weeks. He sighed. He hadn't been able to force himself to go into the office. "Avoiding the issue, Fleming," he said out loud, his voice booming in the silence of the flat. "Not a great way to start off as head of the firm. A raise for Maggie, that's the first thing!" He smiled to himself. He couldn't afford to lose her; she ran the bloody place!

James loosened his tie and threw himself into the chair beside his phone. The blinking red light of the answering machine distracted him. "Maggie, no doubt," he mused aloud, "with an agenda a mile long." He laughed as he punched the button on the machine, but his laughter froze when he heard the voice.

"James, darling, where on earth have you been? I haven't been able to reach you at the office." She paused. "I've just received a very strange letter, telling me I've inherited a fortune. It's postmarked Boston and it's signed by someone named Jack Moore. I was wondering if you knew anything about it ..."

Ǝast Wind

FREEMAN WILLS CROFTS

Inspector Joseph French of the CID had handled in his time a great diversity of cases. Of these, some were remarkable for their dramatic setting, some for the terrible nature of the crimes revealed, and some for the brilliant logical analysis by which the inspector reached his result. The case which had its beginning on the famous 10.30 A.M. Cornish Riviera Limited Express belonged to none of these categories. In it French was shown, not as the abstract reasoner triumphantly reaching the solution of some baffling problem, but as the practical man of affairs, the organiser using with skill and promptitude the great machine of the British police force.

It was towards the end of May and French had been working for several weeks on an intricate case of forgery in South London. He was tired of Town and longed to get out of it. When therefore it became necessary for him to interview an old lag who was doing a stretch in Princetown, he was delighted. A breath of the air of Dartmoor would come as a pleasant change from the drab and sordid Lambeth streets.

It was with pleasurable anticipation that he drove to Paddington and took his seat in the train. He had a good deal of work to do before he reached the prison, and as soon as the express settled down into its stride, he got out his papers and began. For some hours he read and noted, then with a sigh of relief he bundled the documents back into his bag and turned his attention to the scenery.

They had just passed Exeter and were running down the river opposite Exmouth. The previous night had been wet, but now the sky had cleared and the sun was shining. Everything had been washed by the rain and looked fresh and springlike. The sea, when they reached it, was calm and vividly blue and contrasted strikingly with the red cliffs and pillars of Dawlish and Teignmouth.

They turned up the estuary of the Teign and ran through Newton Abbot. From here to Plymouth French thought the country less interesting and he turned to a novel which he had thrust into his bag. For a few minutes he read, then he heard a whistle and the brakes began to grind on the wheels.

There was no halt scheduled hereabouts, the train running without a stop from London to Plymouth. Repairing the line or blocked by some other train, French thought. Since he had done that job on the Southern near Whitness French rather fancied himself as a railway expert.

The speed decreased and presently they stopped at a small station; Greenbridge, he saw the name was. With a slight feeling of displeasure he was about to apply himself again to his book when he heard a faint report, and another, and another.

Three distant fog signals, he supposed, and as he knew this was an emergency danger signal, he lowered the window and looked out. He was at the platform side and down the platform he saw a sight which brought him to his feet in the twinkling of an eye.

A hold-up was in progress. Some four carriages down the train a door was open and opposite it stood a man, a big stout fellow in grey with a white mask on his face and a pistol in his raised hand. With it he covered the passengers, none of whom was to be seen, but the guard had alighted and was standing opposite his van, his arms raised above his head.

As French reached the platform, two men stepped out of the compartment with the open door. One, medium-sized and dressed in a fawn coat and hat, was also wearing a mask and brandishing a pistol. The other, of about the same height, was without arms or mask, and even at that distance French could sense an eager haste in his movements. The three, the two armed men and the eager one, ran quickly out of the station and immediately the sound of a rapidly accelerating car came from the road.

French dashed to the exit, but the vehicle had disappeared before he reached it. Then he ran back to the compartment from which the men had descended, and which was now surrounded by an excited crowd of passengers. French pushed his way to the front.

In the compartment lay two men in the uniform of prison warders. One was obviously dead, shot through the forehead; the other was hunched up in a corner, apparently unconscious, but with no visible injury.

'I'm a police officer from Scotland Yard,' French shouted. 'I'll take charge here.' He pointed to a couple of the passengers who were crowding round. 'Will you gentlemen search the train quickly for a doctor. You others, close the compartment and let no one in except to attend to the man in the corner. Where is there a telephone, guard?'

The moment French had seen the warders' uniforms, he knew what had taken place. Though it was not his business, he happened to be aware that a prisoner was being conveyed to Dartmoor by the train. He was a man named Jeremy Sandes, and French was interested in him because he was one of his own captures.

The crime for which Sandes had been taken was the theft of Lady Ormsby-Keats's jewels from her country house of Dutton Manor, situated about a mile from Epsom. With forged testimonials he had got a job as footman. This gave him his opportunity. It was suspected that Sandes was only one of a gang and that before capture he had managed to pass on his takings to his accomplices, though neither of these assumptions could be proved. At all events not a single pennyworth of the £17,000 odd of jewellery he had stolen had been recovered.

French's inspiring example galvanised the passengers into activity. A doctor was speedily found, and while he was attending to the warder, French and the guard and some of the passengers ran towards the station buildings. The station was little more than a halt, but there was a general waiting-room and a tiny ticket office. Of these, the office was locked. French rattled at the door. 'Anybody there?' he shouted.

For answer a dismal groan came from within. French and the guard threw themselves on the door, but it was strongly made and resisted their efforts.

'The seat,' French pointed.

On the platform was a heavy wooden seat. Willing hands quickly raised it, and using it as a battering ram, swung it back and brought its end crashing against the door. With the tearing sound of splintering wood the keeper gave way and the door swung open.

In the little office was a single chair and on the chair sat a man in porter's uniform. He was securely gagged with a cloth and bound to the chair with a rope. A few seconds only sufficed to release him. Beyond the possibility of apoplexy from suppressed fury, he seemed none the worse for his experience.

'The big man came in with a mask on his face,' he spluttered indignantly, 'and before I could move I found myself looking into the wrong end of a gun. Then the second man came in and I was tied up before you could say knife.'

'Anyone else about the station?' French asked sharply.

'Yes, there's the signalman. They must have tied him up too, else they couldn't have stopped the train.'

The signal-box was at the end of the platform to the rear and the little party hurried down. It was as the porter suggested. The signalman was seated on a stool, bound and gagged, but uninjured.

He had, he said, been sitting in his box, when he noticed two men pacing the other end of the platform, as if measuring. They disappeared, then a few minutes later they suddenly rushed up the box steps and covered him with their guns. He could do nothing and was at once gagged and bound. He had already accepted the express and pulled off the signals, and the men at once threw the latter to danger. They waited till the departure came through for the express, acknowledged the signal correctly, and then cut the block and telephone wires. When the train appeared and was slowing down they pulled off the home signal, leaving the distant and starter at danger. This was correct railway practice and showed that they knew what they were doing. Then they hurried down to the platform, and were ostensibly reading a time bill with their backs to the line when the train came in. Thanks to their skilful operation of the signals, it pulled up as if it had been timed to stop. They evidently knew where the prisoner was, for they had been waiting opposite his compartment and opened its door without hesitation.

French heard the story in the briefest outline and then asked for a description of the men. But he could get nothing of value. Between the speed with which everything had happened and the masks which had been worn, only a blurred picture of their assailants had been left in the railwaymen's minds.

He ran back to the train, and holding up his hand for silence, asked if anyone had noticed any peculiarity about the men by which they might be recognised. For a moment there was no reply, then a lady in the compartment adjoining that of the tragedy came forward.

She had been in the window and had had plenty of time to observe the big man who had kept guard on the platform. She could not of course see his face, but she was able to describe his clothes. These were quite ordinary except for one point. On the toe of his rather elegant black shoe were three small spots of mud forming the angles of a tiny equilateral triangle.

This was the only clue French could get, but it was of an entirely satisfactory nature. If the big man did not notice the marks and rub them off, they might well lead to his undoing.

French turned again to the railwaymen, asking urgently where was the nearest telephone. The wires in the signal-box being cut, the porter advised application to Farmer Goodbody, who lived three hundred yards up the road. It would be quicker, he said, than traveling on by the train to the next station.

In three minutes French was knocking at the farmer's door and in another two he was speaking to the superintendent in Exeter. He had been extremely quick in his enquiries and not more than ten minutes had elapsed since the crime. The fugitives could not have gone more than seven or eight miles at the most, and prompt action should enable a police ring to be thrown round the area before they could get clear. French however asked that they should not be arrested, but only shadowed.

He was able to supply very fair descriptions of the trio. About the prisoner, Jeremy Sandes, he could give complete information. He had worked at his description so often that he remembered it in detail. As to the others, he knew their height and build, and there was that priceless point about the three spots of mud.

The information was passed to Exeter, Plymouth, Okehampton and other centres, as well as to the Yard. Arrangements were made about the bodies of the dead warders and then French rang up the nearest village for a car and was driven into Newton Abbot. There he was fortunate enough to find a train just about to start for Exeter. Forty minutes later he reached police headquarters in the city. Superindendent Hambrook was an old friend and received him with effusion.

'We've done what you said, inspector,' he went on. 'As far as we have men to do it, all roads have been blocked in a circle from here through Crediton, Okehampton, Tavistock and Plymouth, and we are having the Exmouth ferry and all ports in the area watched. That circle is about twenty to twenty-five miles radius as the crow flies and it would take the parties thirty or forty minutes to reach it. With luck we'll get them. But, French, are you sure you're right in not arresting them? If you lose them now they mayn't be easy to get again.'

'I know, super, but I think it's worth the risk. What do you supposed this escape was organised for?'

Hambrook closed his right eye. 'The swag?' he suggested.

French nodded. 'That's it. They'd never have committed a murder just to help their pal. This Sandes had hidden the stuff and the others were left. Now they're going to make him fork up.'

'And you want to let him find it?'

'He's the only one who can.'

'It's an idea,' the super admitted doubtfully. 'But I don't know. If it were my case I think I'd go for the bird in the hand.'

French's reply was interrupted by a strident ring on the super's telephone bell. Hambrook picked up the receiver, handing a second to French.

'Constable Cunningham speaking from the London bypass, Exeter. I think we've identified the big man and the prisoner, Sandes. They're driving towards London in a Daimler limousine Number AZQ 9999. If we're right, they've changed their clothes. The big man is wearing a dark coat and hat, but when we had him out we saw the three spots of mud on his left toe. The driver answers the description of Sandes, though his face has been darkened and he's wearing chauffeur's uniform. The big man gave the name Mr Oliver Hawke, diamond merchant, of 767B Hatton Garden and St Austell's, Grabfield Road, Hampstead. They stopped at once and were quite civil. They said they were coming from the Burlington Hotel in Plymouth and going home. We let them go and Constable Emerson is following them on the motorbike. The tyres are newish Dunlops.'

French was highly delighted. 'If they're being civil and answering questions it means they've fixed up an alibi and feel safe about it.' He rubbed his hands. 'A diamond merchant! The best fence in the world!'

Hambrook agreed and French went on. 'I bet you anything you like Hawke's going home as he says. If so, we'll get him there, and Sandes too. Ring up ahead, will you, super? If he's making for Town we'll call off the pursuit.'

While Hambrook was telephoning French had been studying a timetable. 'There's an express at 5.42,' he said. 'If they go towards London I'll take it. I confess I'd like to be in Hampstead to see them arrive. Just get the Plymouth men to look up that hotel, will you, super?'

The Burlington reported that Mr Hawke and his chauffeur had

stayed there for the past two nights and had left for London that day about noon. They had taken lunch with them and said they would eat it in the car *en route*.

'There's the alibi emerging already,' French declared. 'Why did they take so long between Plymouth and Exeter? Because they stopped for lunch. Why were they not seen at any hotel? Because they took it in the car. Quite. Now the Yard, like a good fellow.'

To headquarters French reported what had happened, asking if a Mr Hawke lived and moved and had his being at the addresses given, and if so, what was this gentleman like in appearance? In a short time there was a reply which showed that the man in the car had given his real name.

French rose. 'I'll just get that train if I look slippy,' he said. 'Well, super, glad to have seen you again. If your people come on that other ruffian, I'd shadow him also. We think there's still another of them in the gang and we may as well have a shot for the lot.'

As French sat thinking over the affair in the up express, he saw that there definitely must have been another confederate. The two men at Greenbridge had known in which compartment the prisoner was travelling. Now it was impossible that they could have evolved this information out of their inner consciousness. It must therefore have been sent to them, and there was only one way in which it could have been obtained. Someone had watched the man and his escort entraining at Paddington. French wondered could he trace a trunk call or a telegram from Paddington shortly after 10.30 that morning.

At Taunton, their first stop, French sent wires in veiled language to the Yard and the Exeter super, asking the former to find out if such a message had been sent, and the latter if Hawke had called anywhere to receive it. Then feeling he had done his duty by the case for the moment, he went to the dining-car for a long-delayed meal.

At nine o'clock French stepped down on to the platform at Paddington and fifteen minutes later was at the Yard. There he found his colleague Inspector Tanner waiting for him.

'I've been handling this stuff of yours,' said Tanner. 'Your friends are coming up nicely. They were seen passing through Chard, Shaftesbury, Salisbury, Andover and Basingstoke. They dined at Basingstoke and left there half an hour ago. They should be in Hampstead between ten and eleven. We'll go out and see them arrive.'

'Get anything about Hawke's business?'

'Small one-man show. Doesn't seem to be much going on. Yet Hawke must be well-to-do, judging by the house he lives in. I went to the office to ask for him. The clerk made no bones about it. Mr Hawke was down at Plymouth on business, but was coming up today and would be available tomorrow.'

'I thought that part of it would be all right.'

'What about arresting him now, French?' Tanner went on earnestly. 'If we find him in the company of Sandes we have him; he can't put up any kind of defence. Once we let them separate we'll find the case a darned sight harder to prove.'

'And what about the swag?' French returned. 'No, we'll take the risk. And there's another point you've missed. As you know, we believe there are four men in the gang. Now we want them all. If we arrest Hawke and Sandes tonight, we may lose the other two. No, let's watch them: we may get the lot. By the way, did you find out anything about that message from Paddington?'

'Yes, we've got something there.' Tanner drew a scrap of paper from his pocket. With eagerness French read it. 'Quotation required Exodus chapter six verse four.' 'It was sent at 10.40 from the telegraph office at Paddington,' Tanner went on, 'to "Anderton, Post Restante, Plymouth". It was called for at 11.45 by a man resembling Hawke. Does that give you any light?'

French nodded delightedly. 'I should just think it does!' he declared with enthusiasm. 'You see it of course? The sixth carriage from the engine and the fourth compartment. That's what the men were measuring on the platform at Greenbridge. If those post-office people in Plymouth can swear to Hawke, that'll come in handy.'

'Pretty sure to, I should think.' Tanner glanced anxiously at the clock. 'Your friends should have been past Blackwater before now. It's only fifteen miles from Basingstoke and they've left nearly forty minutes.' He picked up his telephone and asked for Blackwater. 'No sign,' he said presently. 'I don't like this, French. Have they turned aside?'

French was already examining a large-scale road map.

'Reading or Farnham are the obvious places north and south,' he answered, 'but there are endless roads in between. Give a general call over that area, Tanner.'

Tanner did so as quickly as he could and they settled down to wait. As the minutes passed French became more anxious than he cared to show. Had he overreached himself? If so, and if these two got away, it would be a pretty serious thing for him. Yet, he told himself, they *couldn't* get away.

Once again the telephone bell rang. 'Blackwater at last,' said Tanner with relief. Then his expression changed. 'Oh, you have? Good man, sergeant! Splendid! I'll wait for his report.' He rang off.

'Blackwater reports that when they didn't turn up he sent a man out on a motorbike to look for them and he's found them parked up a side road near Basingstoke. He's watching them and will keep us advised what happens.'

'What's that for on earth?' French queried.

Tanner shook his head and once more they settled down to wait. And wait they did, endlessly and with growing mystification. Twice at intervals of an hour the constable rang up on an accommodating householder's telephone to say that the men were still sitting in the stationary car, but the third message, when it came at half-past twelve, showed that the halt was over.

'Speaking from Farnham,' the constable reported. 'About twelve they started and ran here and have gone on towards Guildford. I've asked the Guildford men to have a look out and ring you.'

'Guildford!' French exclaimed anxiously. 'What in Hades are they going there for?' He glanced at Tanner. On his face was imprinted the same anxiety.

Once again the bell rang. 'They've been seen,' Tanner reported. 'They passed through Guildford four minutes ago in the Leatherhead direction. The Guildford men have already rung up Leatherhead.'

Suddenly French started. Leatherhead! Leatherhead was near Epsom. Not more than three or four miles between them. With a rising excitement he wondered if he could guess their destination.

In a moment his mind was made up. He would stake everything on this idea of his. He spoke quickly to Tanner.

Tanner swore. 'You can go at once,' he answered with equal speed. 'The cars are waiting to go to Hampstead. I'll be here if you want anything.'

A moment later French was racing down the corridor to the courtyard. There, with Sergeant Carter and a number of plain-clothes men, were two police cars.

'Come on, men,' French shouted. 'Tumble in. Hard as you can lick to Epsom.' Ten seconds later the cars glided out on to the Embankment and turned south over Westminster Bridge.

French had done many a race by car, but seldom had he made such going as on the present occasion. Traffic in the streets was at a low ebb and they took full advantage of it. They gave way to nothing, slinging across the fronts of trams and causing other motorists to jam on their brakes and complain to the nearest policemen. Twice disaster was avoided by a hair's breadth, and again and again only profound skill saved a spill. So, leaving behind them a trail of indignant and exasperated drivers, they rushed on through the streets.

Presently they left Town behind them and still further increased their speed. The edge of the road became a quivering line in the light of their headlamps and their tyres roared on the asphalt surface. The needles of their speedometers rose and rose till for one brief moment on down-grade straight they touched 65. Their horns were seldom silent, and more than once as they took curves French thanked his stars the road was not greasy.

At Epsom they swung quickly in to the police station. A sergeant was waiting on the footpath.

'Your car went through seven minutes ago,' he said quickly: 'towards Burgh Heath.'

This news practically confirmed French's idea. Dutton Manor lay about a mile out along the Burgh Heath road.

'Good,' he cried with a feeling of relief. 'After it, drivers.'

Once again their tyres roared over the smooth road. A mile slipped away in a few seconds.

'Steady,' said French presently. 'Stop before you get to that corner.'

Round the corner was a straight upon which the Manor front and back drives debouched. As the cars came to a stand French leaped out and ran forward with his torch, followed by his men. They passed round the corner and reached the straight. No car lights were visible ahead.

This however was scarcely to be expected and they raced on, keeping for the sake of silence along the grass verge. Presently they came to the front entrance.

With his torch held vertically so as not to betray their presence, French made a hurried examination of the drive. It was surfaced with gravel and the recent rain had softened it. He could have sworn that no car had passed over it recently. Calling softly to his followers, he hurried on along the road.

From his investigation at the time of the robbery French knew every inch of the little domain. The back drive was a hundred yards farther along the road and this was his new objective.

When he shone his torch on to the ground at its entrance, he gave a grunt of satisfaction. There entering the drive were fresh tyre marks, fairly new Dunlops. Good for the Exeter constable's observation!

More cautiously they hurried up the drive, the men moving with speed and silence. There was no moon, but the stars gave a certain light. A wind had been blowing earlier, but it died down and now everything was still. Suddenly French thought he heard a voice. A touch passed down the line and all instantly became rigid.

Yes, people were moving a short distance ahead and speaking in low tones. French crept stealthily forward.

'... stopped us at Exeter,' he heard a man say in low tones, 'but they didn't suspect anything and we passed through all right. How did you manage, Taylor?'

'I garaged the car at Newton Abbot and came by train,' returned another voice. 'I reached Paddington at 6.55, got your 'phone from Basingstoke, picked up Gould and came on here. What's it all about, Hawke?'

'The swag. Sandes had hidden it here. I thought we ought all to be here in case—'

The speaker must have turned away, for French lost the remainder of the sentence. Crouching back into the hedge, he could now see four figures moving like shadows in front of him. They were entering the drive from a field, obviously after hiding their car. As they turned towards the house, French and his men dropped in behind.

To say that French was delighted would convey no impression of his state of mind. From the first he had felt that only hope of the recovery of the swag could account for the rescue of Sandes. Now his ideas and his actions had been abundantly justified. A little more patience and a little more care and both men and jewels would be his! Something more than a triumph, this! Out of what had seemed defeat he would snatch an overwhelming victory!

The two parties were now silently creeping up the drive with a hundred feet or more between them. Surely, French thought, the quarry would not go near the yard, where there were dogs and where the chauffeur slept? No, they were turning aside. They left the drive through the small gate which led to the side of the house, and began to work forward over a grass sward containing flowerbeds and a fountain. Here in the open, French's little band had to drop back to avoid being seen, but on reaching some clumps of shrubs they closed up again.

French was growing more and more surprised. It was beginning to look as if the others were meditating an attack on the house itself. They were certainly moving on to the very walls. Then suddenly French saw where they were going. Just in front of them was a loggia. He knew it well. It was a biggish area, some fifty feet by twenty, and was roofed and bounded by the house on two sides, but, save for pillars, was open on the third and fourth. On it gave a passage from the main hall, as well as french windows from the principal reception-room, while a short flight of stone steps led down to the terrace. These steps were in the centre of the longer open side, which faced southwest. The short open side faced southeast. These sides were edged with a stone balustrade and every few feet were pedestals bearing large stone vases, each containing a laurestinus.

French's heart beat more rapidly. The end, whatever it might be, was upon them. He wondered if he were about to witness house-breaking. The french windows would be just the place to try, but as he knew them to be fitted with burglar alarms, he did not think the attempt would succeed. Well, if Hawke & Co. gave back, believing they had aroused the household, he and his men would be ready for them.

Slowly and silently the four men crept up the stone steps to the loggia, and as they disappeared within, French and his followers slipped up against the wall at each side of the steps. The floor was some four feet high, and standing on the grass, the watchers could see in between the stone balusters. Contrary to French's expectation the quarry did not approach the french windows. Instead they moved like shadows over to the northeast corner, where the shorter open side joined the wall of the house. French, slipping round the corner, crept along the outside of that short side till he came opposite where they had congregated. They had turned a torch on the floor, which gave a faint light in all directions.

'All quiet.' The whisper came from the man who had been referred to as Hawke. "Now, Sandes.'

A shadow detached itself from the group and came forward towards French, who shrank down beneath the floor-level. ' 'Ere in this 'ere vase,' he heard in a Cockney whisper. 'It were the nearest place outside the 'ouse I could find and because of the east wind no one sits in this 'ere corner.'

Slowly French raised his head. With a thrill of excitement which he would have died rather than admit, he watched the man put his hand over the edge of the vase and feel about. Then the man gave a sudden grunt, snatched the torch from Hawke, and shone it into the basin. Finally, throwing all caution to the winds, he began to grope wildly. The others had closed in round him.

'Well,' said Hawke, and there was a sharp tenseness in his voice. 'Where is it?'

From Sandes there came a sort of dreadful strangled cry. Then as if reckless from fury and disappointment he swore a lurid oath. 'It's not there!' he cried aloud. 'It's gone! Someone 'as taken it!'

'Silence, you fool,' Hawke hissed. He snatched the torch from Sandes and gazed into the vase. 'You—liar!' he went on, and his voice, low as it was, cut like a knife. 'This soil where you haven't disturbed it hasn't been moved for months! It's grown green scum. See, you others.'

The other two men looked and cursed in low tones.

'Now see, you,' Hawke went on, still hissing venomously like an angry snake. 'You tell us where that stuff is inside ten seconds or this knife goes into your heart. You thought you'd do us out of our shares so that you could have it all when you got out of quod, and now you think you can put us off with fairy tales! I suspected this and that's why I brought these others.' He raised his hand, which held a long pointed knife. 'You won't escape, Sandes, and we'll all be responsible for your death. Now where is it? I'll give you till I count ten. Hold him, you others.'

French wondered if he should take a hand. He believed Hawke was in earnest and he couldn't stand there and see murder done. Then he realised that Hawke would delay in the hope of learning the truth. And as he himself was quite as anxious as the others to hear what Sandes had to say, he also waited, his heart thumping from the suspense.

'One!' Hawke paused, then went on slowly: 'Two! Three! Hold his mouth, will you!' French saw the little knot bunch together. Hawke raised the knife and began to press the point against the little man's breast. Suddenly the prisoner began to struggle violently. Hawke withdrew the knife.

'We're not bluffing,' he whispered in that voice of steel. "If we don't get our shares this knife goes into your heart. I've counted to three.' Again he paused. 'Four!' And again. 'Five!' And again. 'Six!' Then came another voice. 'Try him with the knife again, guv'nor,' said the man who had not previously spoken.

'No, no, no!' came in a muffled scream. 'I've told you the truth, I swear I 'ave. I 'id it there.' He swore by all his gods. 'If you kill me I can't tell you no more!'

'Hold him again,' said Hawke inexorably, once more raising the knife.

French felt he couldn't stand this anymore. He believed Sandes. He recognised the ring of truth as well as of desperate despairing fear in his voice. The man had, French felt sure, hidden the stuff there in that vase and—someone else had got it and was sitting tight. Perhaps a gardener or one of the servants ... He began edging round the wall to the steps.

He had formed his men for the assault and they were about to rush up the steps to take the others by surprise, when there came a terrible scream from above followed by Hawke's savage voice: 'That's torn it, you — fools! Why couldn't you hold his mouth as I said? We may run for it now! Bring him along!'

Dispensing with any further attempt to preserve silence, the three men dashed across the loggia, dragging the fourth with them. So headlong was their flight that they did not see the waiting constables till they were at the steps. Then arose a terrible outcry. 'The cops!' yelled Hawke with a furious oath. 'Leave Sandes and get away over the balustrade!' As he shouted he doubled back, fumbling desperately in his pocket. French, flashing out his torch, rushed forward, followed by his men. As Hawke drew a pistol, French closed with him.

Now the loggia became a nightmare of whirling bodies, of groans and curses, of thuds and—a couple of times—of pistol-shots. The torches had been knocked down and had gone out, and no one could see what he was doing. Everyone clung to whoever he could feel, but he had no idea who he was holding. Three of the policemen found themselves struggling together, and it was a couple of minutes before they discovered it and went to their companions' help. Then French touched a torch with his foot and managed to pick it up. With the light the end came quickly. There were eight police to three criminals, for Sandes was too much overcome to take any part in the mêlée.

'Take them along to the cars, Carter,' French panted.

Presently, handcuffed, the four men were led off, while French remained behind to assuage the fears of those in the Manor.

Next morning French walked up to have a look at the scene of the combat. With Sergeant Carter he stood in the centre of the loggia and looked around.

'Do you see anything interesting?' he said presently, and when the sergeant had failed to give the required reaction, he went on: 'That corner where Sandes said he hid the stuff gets the east wind. You remember he said he chose it because for that reason no one sat there. And yet I notice that the plants there are finer and more healthy than those on the sheltered south side. Does that suggest anything to you? Ah, it does, does it? Then let us see.'

He walked over to the poorest of the plants, which looked indeed as if it had been scorched by wind. In the vase he began to dig with his penknife.

'Ah,' he said in accents of deepest satisfaction. 'What have we here? I think this is Sandes's little lot!'

It was a lucky deduction. In a parcel were the whole of the jewels, and an enquiry from the head gardener showed that only the week before he had changed the vases round, so as to get the poorer shrubs out of the east wind.

At the trial only Hawke and Taylor could be proved guilty of murder, the sending of the telegram not being held to cover compliance with all that had been done at Greenbridge. The first two were executed and the others spent many years in retreat from their normal haunts. In gratitude for French's work Lady Ormsby-Keats contributed £500 to police charities, so for a twofold reason French felt his efforts had not been wasted.

The Tinker's Revenge

D. M. O'REILLY

The sergeant stood at the end of the pier with his hands on his hips, looking at the other policeman who had parked the car. A group of fishermen formed a small circle around the body, and behind, some women and girls looked on.

"Come on now, come on, move back," the sergeant said, moving through the small silent crowd.

The men parted like hands separating after prayer. "Sergeant, Sergeant." A voice came from behind as Father Riordan, cassock flapping in the sea breeze, joined the group. The sergeant slowed, allowing the priest through, and the men mumbled, "Mornin', Father," as the priest walked between them, ignoring their salute.

"Sergeant, I just heard.... What happened?"

"... He's dead, drowned by all accounts," the policeman said, kneeling beside the corpse of the big man.

"It's Mikey, Father," one of the fishermen said.

Mikey Lawlor lay on the cobblestones of the pier, his appearance that of a beached whale. The villagers all knew him and his antics. They studied him now, perplexed to see him so still. The priest moved ahead of the policeman and began to mumble a prayer into the wax-coloured ears of the dead man. The sergeant stood back and removed his hat, wiping the band on the inside with his handkerchief, nodding to his junior to follow suit. Some of the assembled men muttered prayers under their breath and stepped back from the spreading pool

of water that seemed to seep from the dead man. When the priest
had finished, the sergeant looked at the weathered faces still gaping at
the corpse and said:

"Well, does anyone know what happened?" There were mumbles
and Sean Joyce, one of the fishermen, moved forward.

"Sergeant, it was a holy fright. We were mendin' them nets there,
and he comes barrellin' down the pier screamin' and roarin', sayin'
he'd been poisoned. He was demented ... Ye know Mikey, he wasn't
all there; but Lord have mercy, he was in a terrible state. We didn't
know what to do." Some of the other men moved forward, and
nodded in solidarity. The sergeant turned and looked at the big
man, water still seeping from his sodden clothes. "... Well, we was
frightened, and weren't sure if he had taken drink. He was a fright
when he had drink. He was in a lot o' pain and clutchin' at his
stomach, and then he said that the tinker had poisoned him. He
kept callin' that the tinker had poisoned him." Sean Joyce rubbed
his stubbled jaw and, shaking his head, pointed to the end of the
pier and in a hushed tone continued. "The next thing, before we
could do anything, he doubled up and went to sit on the stanchion
over there, and before ye know it he's toppled off the end of the
pier into the water. He was flailin' and screamin'. God, he made an
awful noise."

"Didn't anyone help him?"

"Sure, Sergeant. By the time we realised what was happenin', the
current had pulled him away, tossed him, big and all as he was, like a
cork ... sure he couldn't swim, and with all his screamin' and flailin'
about, it didn't take long. That current pulled him right out. We've
high tides at this time o' year."

"When did this happen?" the sergeant asked.

"Yesterday...."

"Yesterday...? Yesterday, and you waited until this mornin' to call
the Garda in Tralee?"

Sean Joyce rubbed his jaw again and looked at the sergeant, his eyes
glinting in the bright sunshine. "Ye asked me what happened, that's
what happened." He spat past the policeman, his spit making a little
clap as it hit the water. The fisherman pushed past the two policemen,
and the others followed.

"Well, Sergeant," the priest said, "looks like an easy case for you,
worth that five-mile trip from Tralee. I'll take you up to the tinker's
place."

"Wait, wait, Father, who said anything about goin' to the tinker's place?"

"Well, you heard Joyce. Surely you're going to arrest the tinker; it's obvious he's responsible. Those two have been at each other for years. That tinker's no good ... unbeliever," the priest said. "That tinker, we'll be better off to be rid of him, he's a ..."

"You were saying, Father? He's a ..."

The priest looked at the policeman and rubbed his hand across his heavy jowl, his pale blue eyes blazing. "I'll leave you to carry out your duties then, Sergeant. If you need any help, and you will, you can contact me at the presbytery." The priest took one look back at the open-mouthed corpse of Mikey Lawlor and shrugged.

"Why do you think I'll need any help, Father?"

The priest turned and smiled, revealing tobacco-stained teeth. "Oh, you'll need help. You don't know these people, Sergeant; I do. They'll want results. They won't want the likes of that tinker getting away with this. Getting away with murder." Before the policeman could reply, the priest stormed up the pier self-importantly, his cassock billowing around him as he went.

"Well, Sergeant," the younger policeman said, "we seem to have ruffled a few feathers."

The sergeant nodded and walked up to the white, bloated body. The eyes were open and dry, like those of an old fish. Even in death Mikey looked a bit simple, he thought. Mouth gaping open, he seemed to grin up at them. The sergeant shook his head and watched the knot of men now walking across the beach, the priest following. They stood in a group by some upturned boats and tipped their caps as the priest marched past, then continued along the path that skirted the small harbour and disappeared behind the old forge. The sergeant looked across the gently rippling waters and saw the men move away and disappear into Maguire's public house. The group of women, wrapped in shawls and still standing a safe distance away, watched every move. "Did he have any kin?" the sergeant asked.

They didn't answer, but an older woman at the front shook her head, and the sergeant looked back at the corpse, the bright sun now drying out the fabric of the big man's striped, collarless shirt, his old faded braces stretching across his enormous gut like straps securing a heavy cargo. He looked back to the huddled women.

"'Twould be an act of kindness if ye'd wash and shave him for burial." He watched them, and finally the older woman nodded and beckoned to two other women, who moved forward.

"You go up to the village," he said to his colleague. "See what you can find out; see if anyone else heard this poisoning story." The young man nodded eagerly, and walked away. He was new to the job, and from Dublin, with hopes of quick promotion from this backward place, back to his grey city where there was a chance of some serious crime and rapid promotion. The sergeant, on the other hand, was of these parts, from Tralee five miles away. He knew these people and already realised that this was to be a difficult case. He knew the people's weaknesses, and knew when to blink the eye, but he also knew the law. The law to him was the most sacred thing, transcending all other considerations. He took a great pride in his impartiality and fairness. He watched his young colleague stop by some men working on a boat, who with great gesticulation explained what they knew, his colleague furiously scribbling it all down in his notebook. The sergeant looked at the sky as light clouds drifted lazily from the Atlantic, and he turned to see a man in a brown shop coat running frantically towards him along the pier. The sergeant watched the women move around the dead man, their pale nunlike skin appearing and disappearing from beneath their shawls. He saw the blacksmith, his leather apron flapping around his calves, guide a piebald horse and worn-looking cart on to the pier.

"Sergeant," the man in the brown coat said, panting. Stopping, he took off his cap and wiped the beads of sweat from his forehead. "I only just heard. Dear oh dear, what a situation."

"And you are ..."

"O'Mahony. I own the shop in the village. You know, groceries, hardware ... that sort of thing."

The lazy clip-clop of the horse echoed against the wall of the pier, and the blacksmith took his pipe from his mouth and shot a jet of tobacco-stained juice expertly into the gently swelling waters of the harbour.

"I thought ye might be needin' a bit o' help with that," the blacksmith said, jerking his head in the direction of the corpse. "But I tell ye," he said, looking up at the blue sky, "we three'll never lift him, and that's the truth. Sure Mikey must have weighed three hundredweight...."

"Well," O'Mahony said, "I'm afraid I can't help you with that." He rubbed the base of his back. "Doctor's orders say I'm not to lift weights. Sure it's a lifetime of liftin' bags of flour and the like has me poor back destroyed. But, Sergeant, I have some information about ..." He nodded in the direction of the body.

"I saw him yesterday," the blacksmith said, expertly guiding the horse backwards, the animal's eyes wide with fear, but he coaxed each nervous step nearer the water's edge with practised ease. "Yeah, saw him pass right by the forge over there. Looked as pleased as punch, he did. Aye, as happy as a lark, comin' from the direction of the tinker's, he was. I was shoein' a horse for old Joe Finnegan and asked him what he was so happy about, but he just laughed and continued up the road, mumblin' to himself."

O'Mahony, with the enthusiasm of a schoolchild bursting with the right answer, hopped from one foot to the other. "Isn't that exactly why I'm here? Sure wasn't that the reason I wanted to speak to the sergeant? He came in to me only yesterday, it was, and wanted to buy candles...."

"Candles...," the sergeant said, scratching his forehead.

"Aye, candles. Bought them all up ... last dozen ... mad, I thought he was, but he would hear none of it and insisted. But sure you know the old fool wasn't right in the head. He was a bit of an *amadán*, and now look," he said, jerking his head to where the women stood in a circle around the dead man. "But pray," he said, looking at the policeman, "what happened? I hear he took a fit or somethin'."

"I heard the tinker poisoned him," the blacksmith interjected. "That's what the lads are sayin' over in Maguire's ... aye, they said the tinker poisoned him. Can ye believe that? But that auld tinker is a clever creature, begod he is. Used to drive auld Mikey mad, but then I suppose with the bullyin' auld Mikey used to give him, I suppose ... whoa whoa!" he said to the horse who was only too glad to stop. The blacksmith wiped his sweaty hands on his stained leather apron and looked up at the blue sky again. "I better go and get some help from the lads. We'll be shiftin' him presently," he said, walking away.

The sergeant turned to the shopkeeper. "You have no idea why he wanted all the candles."

"No, none at all. Sure the old fella is probably better off now, you know. He's been demented recently, what with the shortages because of the war. Sure he was half starvin' a lot o' the time. There was a time when he worked around these parts and the farmers would pay him in food, but sure some of them wondered if they were gettin' a good return, he'd eat that much. But those two, him and the tinker, always at it, they were. Begod I never thought I'd see the day the tinker ... hard to believe that old divil." The shopkeeper looked around furtively and then faced the sergeant. "But he had it comin'...."

"What?" the sergeant said.

"Ah, Mikey used to make the old tinker's life a misery ... sure he tormented the little fella, never let him alone. The only peace the tinker ever got was when he was on the road, you know, mendin' pots and pans, but sure old Mikey'd ransack his little place when he was away, searchin' for anything worthwhile, but especially food."

The sergeant walked along the pier as the blacksmith returned with some of the fishermen, and as they approached, the sergeant stopped them. "I will need any of you who witnessed this event to give us a statement."

"What need of statements ..." Joyce, courageous with port, said. And there were aye's of agreement from the crowd. "Sure we know the tinker did it. He'd have wanted to do away with Mikey fer years, and now he's done it."

"I'll need statements, now it's for the law to decide. Remember, he's innocent until proven guilty."

"Sergeant," another of the fishermen spoke. "Why waste time? Sure it's only a matter of time before he's brought to court, and sure he's only a bloody tinker, the jury will convict. You'll find it hard to get a jury around here not to convict the likes of the tinker, and for murder ... he hasn't a hope."

"It's for us," the sergeant said, "to decide if there has been a murder. Where's the local doctor? I'll want him to carry out an investigation. He'll be able to tell us what he ate last." He looked into their cold eyes and saw the hate: hate at the fact that Mikey was dead, hate towards the tinker whom they blamed, and hate at the policeman because he was interfering in their ways. He studied their weather-beaten brown faces and decided that if they'd had their way they'd look after matters themselves. But then he wondered, was he being as judgemental? The sergeant walked along the remainder of the pier and saw the priest coming towards him. He stopped, feeling the sweat prickle beneath his black tunic.

"I've just heard, the circuit court is sitting in Tralee next week; the judge is coming down from Dublin." The priest rubbed his heavy jowl, cool blue confident eyes studying the policeman. His jowl indicated the good things in life had come easily. He had that air of smug satisfaction that came from the unearned affection the people bestowed upon him. He demanded respect because of his position, not because he'd earned it, and now he wanted retribution. The sergeant remembered the story in the Bible: "Revenge shall be mine, sayeth the Lord," but perhaps the priest thought differently.

The arrival of the sergeant's young colleague prevented the conversation going further, and the priest hurried away.

"Well, I suppose we better go and give this tinker a visit."

"Right."

"'D you find out where he lives?" the sergeant said.

"Aye ... not far."

They got into the car and drove on in silence for a while, the tyres crackling on the stones as they turned and drove up through the village, aware of the looks of locals as they went.

"The law's the law," the young man said. "It looks like this is a bit open and shut. Sure according to what I've heard, everyone thinks the tinker did it. Sure he hasn't a hope."

"Ah, maybe," the sergeant said. "But I have a funny feelin', there's somethin' nigglin' about this one."

It was hot for September. The tops of the trees, some of which were turning gold against the clear ultramarine sky, swayed gently in the offshore breeze. Chestnuts, almost ready for dropping, hung in pale clusters in the cool lower reaches of the trees. The two stopped outside the gate, and the sergeant took a handkerchief from his pocket and wiped his forehead, then removed his cap and ran the handkerchief around the band inside before he put the hat back on his head.

There was a row of small cottages, and the tinker lived in a sort of caravan on a small neat site. "The end one there is Mikey Lawlor's cottage. I suppose we better have a look there first," the sergeant said. They moved up through the unkempt front garden and, opening the half door, peered into the dirty interior. The dead man's cottage was very shabby, neglected.

Entering the gloom, the sergeant looked about and said to his junior, "Look around for anything he might have eaten, and see if you can find the candles."

They rummaged about in the dirt and disorder.

"Found the candles...," the young policeman said, opening the drawer of an old pine dresser.

"How many there?"

"Eh, let me see ... ten."

"O'Mahony said he bought a dozen. See if you can find the others. I'm going on over to the tinker's place."

The sergeant walked through the long unkempt grass to the rear of Lawlor's cottage and crossed the fence that separated the two dwellings. The tinker's caravan and site were in marked contrast with the condition of its neighbour's property.

"Well well, a sergeant o' the Guards." A thin voice came from behind the sergeant, and he turned to see a small crooked little man standing beside an apple tree.

"I hear there was a lot o' commotion down at the harbour. A man on his way to Dingle told me as he passed the way."

"Yeah, Mikey Lawlor ..."

"Whist the old fool fallen down drunk again? Sure he's always on the drink ... mad, he is, you know that, mad. I live in mortal fear o' the man."

"Well, you have no need to fear him now...."

"Get away, what do you mean?"

The sergeant looked at the worldly-wise face, tanned from an outdoor life, a line at the base of his neck indicating how far the sun penetrated.

"Everyone in the village seems to be fairly sure what happened ... they say you poisoned him."

The sergeant walked around the neat little garden towards a shed at the back, a small chimney stack protruding from the roof.

"Eh, Sergeant, why don't you come inside? I could give ye some tea ... I was just brewin' some up."

"Tea? And where do the likes of ye come by tea in these difficult times...?"

The small man just tapped his nose. "I have me ways ... nothin' illegal, you understand."

"Oh no, of course not," the sergeant said, following him down the neat path to the caravan covered with hollyhock and clematis.

"Come in, come in and sit yerself down, Sergeant," the little man said. "And you a man of the law believe the vicious rumours of that lot. Sure they'd say anything ... how is he anyway?"

"So there's no truth in the rumour then?"

"No, none. I never poisoned the auld fool ... where is he?"

"He's dead. They fished him out of the harbour this mornin'. I have a witness says he saw Mikey comin' out of your place yesterday. Is that true?"

"Aye, true enough. He was here, and I feared fer me life and no one to protect me. But ye say he's dead, really dead?"

"Is there any other way to be dead?" the sergeant said, looking around the neat room.

"Would ye like sugar in yer tea, Sergeant?"

"Sugar? Where the hell . . . look, I won't ask . . . I'm sure it's legal."

"Oh, completely legal."

"Well, in that case I'll have a spoon."

The young policeman knocked on the door, and the tinker turned suspiciously and seemed to stiffen, his eyes shining as he moved cautiously to the door.

"It's all right, he's with me," the sergeant said, taking the cup of brown liquid from the tinker's weathered hand.

"So he's dead? Dead . . . I'm not sorry. No. I'm not sorry. I can have some peace now. All the years that blackguard tormented me. Every opportunity he got, he's tormented me fer years. Stupid oaf, he deserved it. No one to blame but himself."

"He made serious allegations before witnesses that you poisoned him."

"Ha! That'd be him all right. Sure he's been makin' allegations against me all his life. Made my life a misery, and ne'er one o' them Christians down there ever did a thing to help. No, they were all in on it, goading him on. He delighted in it. Could brag down in Maguire's of a Friday night, but I lived in daily fear o' the man. Oh, and fer the years I sat and thought of how I could get revenge, but how could I? There was no way, a little fella like me, and he the big ox, his sole reason in life to torment and make me miserable. When I'd be away doin' an honest bit o' work, he'd be over here ransackin' the place. I went to the priest and he would do nothin'. See, bad and all as Mikey was, he was one o' them, you know, mass every Sunday, takin' the bread an' all. I'm different, that's the thing. I don't go on their ways. There'd be few tears shed in this parish if it was me that'd died and not Lawlor. No, I shed no tears fer him."

The sergeant sipped his tea, listening intently to the information the tinker imparted.

"Well, I tell ye, Sergeant, lately I was really in fear o' him. He was driven mad with the hunger, you know. Mad, he was. You'd hear him growlin' over there, pacin' up and down. He'd shout over the hedge that he was comin' over, and I was petrified."

"Listen," the sergeant said. "He was here yesterday?"

"He was, aye, he was here."

"And what did you give him?"

"I gave him nothin', gave him nothin' at all."

"Well, the doctor will be able to tell us what he had for his last meal, so you might as well tell us now. It will go better for you."

"Sure I'll tell ye that meself."

"Well...?"

"I'd done some fine work fer a farmer over the mountain—fixed some milk churns fer him, saved him a fortune—so he gave me a lovely bit o' bacon and some bacon fat. So the other day I was fryin' up some potatoes in the bacon fat. I wanted to save the bit o' bacon for Sunday, when I knew he'd be down in the pub and I could enjoy the bit o' meat meself with no hindrance from him. Anyhow, he burst in through that door.... Go on there, young fella," he said to the young policeman. "You have a good look at that door, and tell me if it wasn't pulled away from the lock. He did that. He's ... was," the tinker said with a smile, "such a brute. There's the proof. Pulled the door off its hinges, he near did." The tinker reached over to the stove, took the teapot, and filled the sergeant's cup and then his own. He didn't offer any to the young policeman, who was busy making notes regarding the damage to the door.

"'Where's the bacon?' he'd said, after burstin' through the door. 'I've no bacon,' I said, terrified, for he was in a fearful rage. 'You're a bloody liar, tinker. Where's the bacon?' He began ransackin' the place, and so I told him it was candles. He stopped and looked at me and said, 'Candles?' 'Yeah, candles. That's how I'm fryin' up the potatoes.' It was the first thing I could think of," he said, the sergeant noticing the twinkle in his eye. "Sure I had to tell him something or he'd have ransacked the place, might even have done me in. He was in a fearful state. I remember the look on his face.

"'Candles,' he'd said. 'In that case I'll be eatin' fried potatoes meself.' Then he ran out of the house, shoutin', 'Yo ho, auld tinker. I'll be eatin' as good as ye today.'"

The sergeant sat back and shook his head. "You think he ate the candles?"

"I'm sure of it," the tinker said. "Sure he'd eat anything," the tinker said, offering the sergeant more tea.

"May God forgive you, but you're a clever man," the sergeant said. "There is nothin' the law can do to touch you. Aye, you're a clever man all right."

"But, Sergeant," his young colleague said, "aren't you going to arrest him? He was ..."

"On what charge? I can't arrest him on any charge relatin' to the death o' Mikey Lawlor. No crime has been committed. Aye, ye're a clever man, but you'll have to answer to the Almighty for this, you know." The sergeant said, standing stiffly. "Aye, ye'll be judged then all right."

"Ho ho, listen to you, Sergeant," the tinker said. "Isn't it grand that the high and mighty look to God to punish the weak and the poor? But I don't care. A lifetime of abuse I've had to endure at their hands, and now I can laugh, and I will laugh, and I'll fear neither God nor man. If there is a just God he'll know the sufferin' and fear I've endured at their hands. I'll take me chances with him."

"But I am goin' to arrest you," the sergeant said, looking at the tinker, who was still laughing uproariously. "I'm arrestin' you for that poteen still you have in the shed out back, so come on with you."

"Ah, Sergeant, Sergeant, you're a clever man yerself." He continued to laugh, completely unperturbed by the change of events. "Sure I haven't been to Tralee for ages, Sergeant. 'Twill do me good to get away for a while." He stood up and took his coat from the back of the door, still laughing. The sergeant followed him and nodded to his young colleague. "Go out there and bring out the still, and pour away any poteen he's already made."

The young policeman walked up the garden path, shaking his head. "How did you know?" he said, turning on the path. The sergeant tapped the tip of his nose and smiled.

"Experience, and a good sense of smell. I could smell the peat."

The sergeant then turned to the tinker, who was still giggling, "What are you so happy about?"

"Oh begod, that's the best part of all. That batch yer young buck is goin' to destroy, that was fer them in the village. Big Feis comin' up and I'd been workin' night and day to get the stuff ready. Now they'll be singin' a different tune." He jigged around in the middle of the road. "Aye, they hated me all right, couldn't stand the sight o' me, the old cripple, but I made the best poteen in these ten counties, and they were glad to come to me fer that. And you know, Sergeant, the best laugh of all, they paid me fer it in advance. Oh, to see their faces," he said, climbing into the back of the car, still laughing.

Jerry Brogan and the Kilkenny Cats

JON L. BREEN

Jerry Brogan took on the job of entertaining Hiram O'Leary for one September afternoon at the request of the visiting novelist's brother-in-law, Keene Axtell, who also happened to be general manager of Surfside Meadows, where Jerry spent the racing season as track announcer and the rest of the year as a member of the PR staff.

"I can't stand this professional Irishman for another second," Axtell moaned. "His own sister can't stand him, but she won't tell him to go home. Take him off my hands for a day, will you? Go up to Santa Anita and take in the races. Or go down to San Diego and throw him in a tank at Sea World. I don't care."

Jerry agreed without much reluctance. Before the California-born O'Leary had emigrated to Ireland, Jerry had known him slightly and found him agreeable enough in small doses. But when Jerry had asked his girlfriend Donna Melendez to accompany them, she had refused. "Sorry, but I can't take a day in the company of anybody who hates women as much as he does."

"What makes you think he hates women?" Jerry inquired.

"Have you read his novels, Brogan?"

"No, but—"

"Just try one. You don't even have to read between the lines. Read the lines."

So it was that Jerry Brogan and Hiram O'Leary went to the races on the day of the California Cup without feminine companionship. They ended their day at Birraporetti's, an Irish pub cum Italian restaurant in Orange County's South Coast Plaza about halfway home from Arcadia to Surfside. Over the crab cakes, O'Leary gave Jerry all the credit due a master handicapper. Jerry knew O'Leary would have bet on Blaze O'Brien in the California Cup Mile regardless of what he'd said, but why argue with the guy who was paying for dinner?

"What was I to do? What was I to do?" Hiram O'Leary fretted, sounding after a third drink like a bad imitation of Barry Fitzgerald. "As an ink-stained wretch, I could follow the chalk and bet on Journalist, but the green of my adopted homeland offered better odds. If there had been a filly in the race, you may be sure I'd have bet on her—though I never won on a filly yet."

The brogue the California-born O'Leary had always affected sounded thicker but no more genuine since his move to Ireland. A couple of successful novels had permitted him to quit his newspaper job, and the income tax break afforded all artists in the Emerald Isle added strength to the pull he already felt from the land of his ancestors. O'Leary now wrote his novels between greeting guests at the bed-and-breakfast inn he operated in Kilkenny.

"I knew you didn't want to bet on Journalist," Jerry said. "For one thing, you're no longer a newspaperman, so it's not that great a hunch bet. And you told me you never bet favorites anyway. Finally, Blaze O'Brien is a figure you can identify with: a wearer of the green who was bred in California. And his jockey was Chris McCarron—I'm not sure that's Irish, but it's closer to Irish than the rider of Journalist."

"Hah! You think you know so much. McCarron's a Scot, and I have it on good authority Corey Nakatani is half Irish!"

"Still, you knew it had to be Blaze O'Brien. All I did was verify the old boy had a good shot at it and you wouldn't waste your bet."

The big seven-year-old gelding had got the job done, holding off a longshot named Fax News and paying $9.60 for a $2 bet. O'Leary had put considerably more than two dollars on Blaze O'Brien's nose, and the dollar signs gleamed in his eyes across Birraporetti's table.

"You must come to visit me, Jerry," O'Leary said. "A lad with the surname of Brogan, after all ..."

"I guess Ireland doesn't have the same pull for me, Hiram."

"Your mother's side, those filthy-rich Barchesters, pumped too much English blood into you then. But the land has charms for everyone, most particularly for horsemen. You can visit the St. Leger Church and see the very steeple, a race to which gave us the word *steeplechase.*"

"Do I look like an etymologist to you?"

"You're a horseman and don't deny it! I'm only a short drive from the Curragh and the National Stud. And my adopted hometown of Kilkenny is such a lovely, friendly place, with whole blocks full of nothing but pubs."

"Pubs don't have the same attraction—"

"For you as for me, aye, aye, twit me for my imbibing as you must. But remember this, Jerry: for a drunk, one pub is enough. To appreciate several in one block requires sobriety." Before Jerry could question the logic of that statement, O'Leary whisked on. "And the history of Kilkenny, the legends, the stories, the Kilkenny witch, the Kilkenny cats."

"I'm not really a cat person," Jerry said. "My Aunt Olivia might enjoy the story, though."

"It so happens, if you're not a cat person, you might enjoy the Kilkenny cats account even more. There's a famous rhyme about them, goes like this: 'There once were two cats in Kilkenny,/Each thought there was one cat too many,/So they fought and they hit,/They scratched and they bit,/Till excepting their nails,/And the tips of their tails,/Instead of two cats,/There weren't any.'"

"Charming, but what's the point?"

"Not so difficult. A warning of the cost of belligerence, wouldn't you say? Our neighbors to the north should take heed of that."

"San Francisco?"

"Northern Ireland, you young twit. Ah, why do I bother with you?"

"Actually I did like that rhyme more than my aunt would. How did the Kilkenny cats story originate?"

"Come to Kilkenny and I'll tell you. It doesn't play as well over pasta as potatoes."

Jerry didn't expect to take O'Leary up on his invitation, but the following summer, through a combination of circumstances, he made his first visit to Ireland. There were other vacation options. Donna was taking some of her drama students on a performing tour of the Southwest, and he'd been invited along. But the company of that many teenagers for that long a time was more than he could deal with. So, while she was gone, he would take a trip of his own.

Landing at Dublin Airport, he crammed his bulk into an undersized rental car and set out on a nerve-wracking jet-lagged drive on the wrong side of roads that seemed precariously narrow and inadequate to a Southern California freeway driver. Once away from the city, though, the charm and beauty of the countryside took hold. By the time he reached the National Stud, his one scheduled stop before Kilkenny, he was in a surprisingly mellow mood.

Only one of the horses standing at the National Stud was well-known to Jerry—it was Yashgan, once a major winner on the Southern California circuit—but he enjoyed looking around. The Irish Horse Museum was especially interesting, with its somewhat ghoulish display of the skeleton of the great steeplechaser Arkle. More pleasurable was a continuously repeated newsreel of the rivalry between Arkle and his English contemporary Mill House, culminating in the running of the 1964 Cheltenham Gold Cup. Jerry listened to Peter O'Sullivan's BBC call with a fellow pro's admiration.

"It's Arkle on the stands side for Ireland and Mill House for England on the far side. And this is it, with Arkle taking the lead as they come to the last fence. It's gonna be Arkle if he jumps it!" He did, and it was.

Jerry spent a little longer than he'd intended at the National Stud, even having a look at the Japanese gardens that were on the same grounds—it was then he missed Donna, knowing she would enjoy the gardens more than the horse barns—so he was latish getting into Kilkenny. There was still light enough to see some of the ancient buildings of Ireland's self-proclaimed mediaeval capital and the advertised row of neighboring pubs. Jerry noted that the venerable Smithwick's Brewery stood on the grounds of the even more venerable (twelfth-century) St. Francis Abbey, symbolizing the traditional Irish association of church and alcohol.

Hiram O'Leary B & B was called the 'Chase, and it sported a carved wooden sign of a leaping horse in front of the door. The place was easy enough to find in the twilight, but the Garda vehicle parked in front of its eighteenth-century façade was not the welcome Jerry expected. Leaving his bags in the trunk of the rental car, he walked through the entryway to see a red-haired woman sitting at the reception desk. She had the kind of beauty that peaks with middle age, but her eyes were red and her face held a mixture of grief and anger.

"I'm sorry, sir," she said, "but we've no vacancy."

"I—I'm expected," Jerry said. "Has something happened?"

"Would you be Mr. Brogan?" she asked. "Hiram's mate from America?"

"That's right."

She came around from behind the counter and surprised him with a warm embrace.

"I have the most dreadful news," she said. "My Hiram has been murdered, murdered in his bed."

"Would you be, ah, Mrs. O'Leary?" He hadn't known there was one.

A flash of anger crossed her face. "Aye, in all but name. I've shared his bed. I've done his cooking. I've done his accounts. I've run this place, I have, and if there's a Mrs. O'Leary in this world, I am she, whatever you may hear from any other. Linda is my name. Linda Malone."

"I'm very sorry for your loss, Linda. This is a real shock. Is there anything I can do?"

"I'm not sure. But Hiram thought a great deal of you, Mr. Brogan. Even in his dying breath, you were in his thoughts. He asked me to tell you—"

She broke off. A man entered the room a moment later, a thin, balding man who wore civilian clothes but whose bearing said cop in any country or language. Apparently a creak on the stair had alerted Linda Malone to his coming.

"Finish what you have to say, Miss Malone," the man said. "Don't let me impede you."

She whirled on him, her long red hair flying defiantly. "'Twas no message for you," she spat.

"When a man has been murdered," he said, his voice gentle and mocking and menacing all at once, "anything he may have said for any ear but the priest's is a message for me. You, sir, are Mr. Jerry Brogan, the much expected visitor from America?"

Jerry nodded.

"Did your people flee in the time of the famine?"

"I'm honestly not sure." Jerry knew volumes of history on his mother's side but very little on his father's. What did it matter anyway?

"Probably they did, and a pity it is, but they'll get no blame from me. Those were terrible times. Miss Malone has told you what happened?"

"I just got here. She said Hiram O'Leary was—"

"Murdered earlier today. Stabbed in the abdomen by a tool usually employed, I am told, in the gelding of horses. A painful way to die, but may God forgive me, I wish the poor man could have lasted just that wee bit longer, long enough to tell *me* something. Still, if he left a message for his American visitor, that is the message I must settle for."

"Is he...?" Jerry gestured toward the stairs.

"Still on the premises? No. His mortal remains were removed only an hour ago. My name is O'Rourke, and I have been dispatched from our Garda station in Dominic Street to complete a simple task: to identify and arrest the murderer of Hiram O'Leary."

"Is that so simple a task?" Linda Malone asked.

"Indeed. I have but four suspects who might possibly have done it. The visiting jockey. The visiting trainer–"

"And who else might have an implement for gelding on his person?" Linda asked.

O'Rourke shrugged. "I doubt he would bring it on a weekend holiday. You don't often geld a horse in a bed-and-breakfast, do you, Mr. Brogan?"

Jerry shivered. "I don't geld a horse anywhere. If it were up to me, they'd all remain stallions."

"To continue: four suspects. The two guests. Yourself, Miss Malone. Herself, Mrs. O'Leary–"

"She's not his wife! She tried out for a two-week period as cook and manager, same as me. It was a fair competition, a competition that I won. I got the job. She didn't. And now here she is suddenly back here–"

"She says she's his wife. And she has his name."

"She's no right to it, the cow," Linda Malone muttered.

"Tell me, Mr. Brogan," the detective said, a glint of humor in his eye, "am I wrong that it was Mrs. O'Leary's cow that burned Chicago and not Mrs. O'Leary herself."

"That's the story," Jerry said, a bit weary of the badinage.

"So there we are," said O'Rourke. "Only four people could have killed Hiram O'Leary, because only four people were with him in the house at the time he died, and there is no sign of forced entry. We have two rival ladies and two guests. I should think, Miss Malone, the guests would be more unlikely suspects...."

"If we're so unlikely, why won't you let me leave?"

This time Jerry had heard the creak on the stair. The man who came through the doorway was small and wiry. His size coupled with the strongly muscled forearms suggested his occupation just as the Oklahoma accent suggested his nationality, but Jerry didn't need the clues.

"Tommy Nixon," he said. "How are you?"

Nixon looked at Jerry uncomprehendingly. "What are you doing here, Jerry?"

"Vacation. What about–?"

"Business. I was hoping to sign a contract to ride over here. Hiram introduced me to Gary Kelley, a trainer friend of his who'd come down from Dublin, races a big string at the Curragh and other places."

"The other guest?"

"Aye." Another man entered the room, a fair-skinned and ruddy-faced fireplug. "And no, I didn't expect to geld any horses while I was here. I'm ashamed to say I faint at the sight of blood."

Following introductions and handshakes, O'Rourke said, "I have a splendid idea. Rather than stand about here, why don't the five of us have a comfortable seat in the dining room. You put the kettle on if you will, Miss Malone, and I'll ask Mrs. O'Leary to join us as well."

"She's *not* Mrs. O'Leary."

"Certainly, certainly, as you please. You brew up, dear lady, and I'll call her whatever you wish."

Fifteen minutes later, Jerry was enjoying a strong cup of tea and the comfort of a chair, but the dizzying events were whirling no more slowly and his jet-lagged brain was having trouble taking it all in. The walls of the dining room were decorated with caricatures, among them some racing personalities. Trainer Gary Kelley and jockey Tommy Nixon were both included, and the artist had captured their features brilliantly.

"He was good, wasn't he?" Gary Kelley remarked.

"He got you to a T," Tommy Nixon agreed. "But I don't really look like that, do I?"

Looking at the signature common to all the drawings, Jerry learned for the first time that Hiram O'Leary's talents had gone beyond the literary. Also among the caricatures was one of Linda Malone.

"You don't see the so-called Mrs. O'Leary here, do you?" Linda said, following Jerry's eye.

"I don't know what she looks like," Jerry replied.

"Then take my word for it, she's not here. If he really loved her as she claims, would she not be among the gallery?"

"As it happens, the late Mr. O'Leary *did* immortalize the putative Mrs. O'Leary in charcoal," O'Rourke said casually.

"Well, I never saw it if he did."

The woman who claimed to be Mrs. O'Leary had not appeared to join them yet, but the Garda seemed to be enjoying himself immensely, so he was in no hurry. Small talk with the jocular cop had its pitfalls:

the moment Jerry mentioned he had sometimes helped American police with turf-related investigations, he realized it was a mistake.

"Ah," O'Rourke said, "what do I need so much as an amateur sleuth to assist my inquiries? I'll look forward to hearing your theory of the case, M. Poirot." Glancing from Jerry to the jockey and back again, he said, "Did you say you'd been to our National Stud today, Mr. Brogan?"

"That's right."

"Then you undoubtedly saw the film of our great 'chaser Arkle winning a hard-fought victory over the game, but outclassed, English challenger Mill House?"

"Sure."

"And Mill House, I think, is quite similar to the middle name of your late former President. Who in fact shares a surname with the American jockey who had the opportunity, if not any motive we know of so far, to kill Hiram O'Leary. Can that be a coincidence?"

"This isn't funny," Jerry said wearily.

"Funny? Am I trying to be funny? That's not all, you know. Do you happen to know the name of Kilkenny's principal legitimate theatre?"

"No."

"The Watergate, Mr. Brogan!"

Tommy Nixon, who must have been hearing the jokes all his life, wasn't laughing either.

Despite the comic interruptions, Jerry managed to piece together some of the facts of the case. O'Leary had been stabbed in the early hours of the morning. Both women who claimed his undying love had been on the premises, but neither, that night at least, had shared his bedroom. Linda Malone had been managing the 'Chase for several months, while letting O'Leary get on with his novel writing. She had also been sleeping with him and had come to think of herself as his wife for all practical and moral purposes.

Then one day, less than a week before O'Leary's death, a woman calling herself Constance O'Leary had appeared. Linda remembered her as the woman who had preceded her two-week tryout at the 'Chase. According to Hiram, she had merely been another job applicant. But now Constance claimed they had been married during her period of working at the 'Chase and that she had come to claim her share of his writing royalties and innkeeping income. Hiram had seemed more amused by the situation than anything and somehow managed to keep both women at bay for the week. But finally, the day of Jerry Brogan's arrival in Ireland, something had seemingly snapped.

Constance O'Leary was a heavy sleeper and told O'Rourke she had heard nothing, but Linda Malone claimed to have heard O'Leary cry out and, rushing to his side, shared a few words with him before he expired. Tommy Nixon and Gary Kelley had arrived in O'Leary's bedroom shortly after Linda. All three of them swore they would have heard any noise from the street below. Even if opened with a key, the front door creaked loudly, and there were several steps on the staircase that would also have betrayed an intruder. Thus, the possible suspects in the murder were narrowed to the four.

When he had finished his third cup of tea, O'Rourke finally expressed some impatience about the nonappearance of Constance O'Leary, who had told him she would only be a moment.

"The rude cow," Linda said. "Mr. Brogan needs his rest. I'll go get her for you."

Jerry wasn't sure which was more surprising, that Linda would be the one to go after Constance O'Leary or that O'Rourke would allow it. Moments later, his reservations about the idea seemed to be confirmed. Sounds of screaming and scuffling came from upstairs. O'Rourke reluctantly lay down his cup and scurried up the stairway, the other three men following in his wake.

On the upstairs landing, two women were rolling on the floor, locked in a wrestlers' embrace and shrilly screaming at each other. Constance O'Leary was smaller, dark-haired, and surprisingly younger than Linda. Though she was not being seen to best advantage at the moment, Jerry noted she was at least equally attractive.

"Come, come, ladies," O'Rourke said, as he attempted to pry them apart. Jerry, whose bulk transversed a good part of the landing, assisted. The two women shrieked and glared at each other but finally subsided. If they were going to break down in sobs, they'd do it in private.

"Perhaps we are not after all destined to sit down together and smoke the pipe of peace," O'Rourke said. "So why not tell us all, Miss Malone, here and now, just what O'Leary's message for Mr. Brogan was?"

Linda looked at Jerry, as if to ask whether a message intended for him alone should be openly revealed.

"I believe in cooperating with the police," Jerry said, not adding, even with a madman like this, "I'd tell him as soon as you told me anyway."

"Very well. Hiram said, 'Tell Jerry, racing in boats is for rats.' I have no idea what it meant."

"That's not what he said," Tommy Nixon interrupted.

"Oh, but he did," said Linda Malone, turning to the jockey.

"No, you must have misunderstood him. I heard what he said. I was there in the room when he said it. You heard it, too, didn't you, Gary?"

The trainer shook his head. "Can't prove anything by me. I got there a mere second after you, but I didn't hear O'Leary say anything."

"Well, she misheard him."

"I didn't, Mr. Nixon. I heard it plain as day."

"So did I," Nixon said.

"And what did you hear, Mr. Nixon?" O'Rourke asked.

"He said, 'Tell Jerry to remember the Kilkenny cats.'"

Linda shook her head positively. "That's not what he said. I heard him distinctly."

"So we have two possibilities," O'Rourke said. "Any idea what 'racing in boats is for rats' might mean?"

Tommy Nixon looked at Jerry nervously. "If he'd actually said that, he could have been referring to me. But that's not what he said."

"'Rats' was a nickname some of the other riders on the California circuit gave Tommy Nixon," Jerry said. "And a boat race is, well, a fixed horse race, a race where the jockeys agree ahead of time who's going to win."

"I was never involved in a boat race in my life," Nixon said heatedly.

"What about it, Mr. Brogan?" O'Rourke inquired. "Was he?"

"Not that I'm aware of, no. I've never heard any rumors to that effect. As far as I know, Tommy Nixon has always been an honest rider."

"Mr. O'Rourke," said Constance O'Leary in a soft voice. She had not spoken since the breakup of the fight.

"Yes, Mrs. O'Leary?"

"I've just recalled something Hiram told me a couple of days before he died. He was very troubled. He said he had evidence one of his guests had been involved in dishonest racing, that he'd brought two friends together for what should be a mutually beneficial association, then learned that one of them was not the honest person he had believed. I didn't know then whether he meant Mr. Nixon or Mr. Kelley, but now–"

"Do you accuse Mr. Nixon of this crime?" Linda Malone shrieked.

"I accuse no one. But–"

"You killed him yourself, you cow! Then pretended to be fast asleep and thought up this ridiculous story to put suspicion on an innocent visitor."

"I thought up no story," Constance said. "I only tell what I know to help Mr. O'Rourke. And if I had to name a murderer, it would not be Mr. Nixon, it would be *you*, you conniving bitch!"

That led Linda to throw herself in the direction of Constance, but she never got there. Jerry intercepted her before their fight could resume.

"Ladies, ladies, let us discuss this like civilized people," O'Rourke said, not really soothingly. "It seems your evidence gives us a possible opening for some further inquiries, and for that I am truly grateful. But witnesses do not always hear dying statements with perfect accuracy. The ears can deceive. No one need be lying. Let us consider the other alternative offered by Mr. Nixon: 'remember the Kilkenny cats.' Does that have any significance for you, Mr. Brogan?"

"He might very well have said that," Jerry said, vaguely remembering the rhyme O'Leary had recited at Birraporetti's. "He was going to tell me the origin of the Kilkenny cats story when I got to Ireland."

"Or illustrate it," said O'Rourke. The policeman roared with laughter. "The Kilkenny cats! An appropriate dying message. Do you know the story, ladies?"

"I'm not from Kilkenny," said Constance O'Leary, clearly proud of the fact.

"Nor am I," said Linda Malone.

"I'll tell it to you then. In the days of that scoundrel Cromwell's occupation of our fair isle, a troop of English soldiers stationed in Kilkenny practiced a particularly detestable blood sport. With a length of rope, they would tie two cats together by the tails, toss them over a line, one hanging down on each side. It was natural for the cats to blame each other for their painful predicament, so they went at it with a fury only an angry feline can. One day, the story goes, they fought until there were only two tails left hanging there, hence the charming rhyme that finishes, 'Instead of two cats,/There weren't any.'"

As O'Rourke had told the story, Jerry's mind had been working furiously. When the policeman had finished, he said, "Hiram really did hate women, didn't he?"

"He did not!" said Linda. "He loved me."

"He had a good loving heart for a good loving woman," said Constance, "but not for a home wrecker like you."

Jerry laughed. "You two were the Kilkenny cats. He set you up against each other, just to see you go at it, possibly for the entertainment of his guests. It doesn't make me proud of my sex, and I might be just as happy to let you two get away with killing Hiram. But you went a step further and tried to pin your crime on an innocent bystander. You act so hostile to each other that your independent evidence against Tommy Nixon seems to carry more weight. But I noticed something suspicious about that fight I just broke up.

"Where's the damage? Where are the bleeding scratches? Where's the torn clothing? Your fight looked and sounded convincing, but separating you just seemed too easy, and your performance since then has looked a lot like playacting. I think you figured out that Hiram was playing you against each other and it brought you together in a plot to have your revenge on him and cast suspicion on somebody else."

"And how did you figure it out?" O'Rourke chimed in, addressing the two women rather than Jerry. "Did one of you find Hiram O'Leary's latest cartoon?"

The cartoon, which Jerry saw later, could well have been enough to bind the women together against a common enemy and inspire them to murder: It showed Linda and Constance as bewhiskered, bare-clawed cats, tied over a clothesline by their tails, hissing and spitting at one another. It reflected all the misogyny Donna had perceived in O'Leary's novels. Had it not been for their effort to pin the crime on a scapegoat, Jerry would have been content to see Linda and Constance get away with it.

Jerry continued his Irish travels, but before he took his flight back from Dublin, he returned to Kilkenny, where O'Rourke, over a drink in one of the town's numerous pubs, filled him in on some of the details.

"The two women killed him together in relative silence. Then Constance retreated to her room and Linda stood over him watching him suffer until a particularly loud cry of pain awakened both Nixon and Kelley. The two ladies had already planned to frame Tommy Nixon, a handy member of the hated male race. When O'Leary made his comment about the Kilkenny cats in Nixon's hearing, Linda decided to turn it around against the jockey. I don't know which of the women actually had the greater claim to O'Leary's royalties, but neither of them will profit by his passing now.

"Now, Jerry, you must discover one more of the fine products brewed locally by Smithwick's before you return to your California home."

"Sounds good."

O'Rourke whispered something to the bartender, and what the latter produced proved to be the Garda's ultimate joke: a Budweiser.

The Goodly Race

A "Henry Po" Story

ROBERT J. RANDISI

1

They call them the "goodly race."

I was told the term came from an old Irish poem, but nobody has been able to tell me the name of the poem or the poet. In any case they say the phrase was used to describe horses in Ireland, and I say it's as good as any and better than most. I've been around people and horses a lot the past few years, and I have to tell you I like horses better.

Even as I struggled to find my way through Dublin Airport I still couldn't believe I was there. It actually looked the same as any American airport, but the *sounds*–now, they were different. Have you spent much time in airports? There are always announcements being made over the PA system–"So-and-so meet your party at ..." and "So-and-so please dial ..." At Dublin Airport, though, even the announcements had a musical sound to them. The conversations going on around me, whether in Irish or "English," were more like songs.

All of the airport facilities were there as well. A baggage claims area, a bank, a post office, a tourist information booth, shops, restaurants, bars, a hairdresser, "car-hire" counters–there was even a church and a nursery. The difference between these facilities and their American counterparts is that most of these were manned–or "womanned"–

by people with *manners*. Some of them were downright pleasant. A guy from New York could find this hard to get used to.

Yesterday morning I was called into J. Howard Biel's office. Biel is the Racing Secretary for the New York State Racing Club, which operates Aqueduct, Belmont, Staten Island Downs, and Saratoga. I'm a special investigator working for him, along with three others. Recently, however, he had bestowed on me the title of Head of Security. It doesn't mean much. I don't run security for the track. There's a company with uniformed men that does that. I still basically do what I did before: investigate "special" problems for the NYSRC. The only difference is I now make a little more money than the other investigators, and they have to report to me.

Of course, the fact that there were only two of us now, because the other two got better offices, sort of watered down the honor. The other investigator is a woman named Shukey Long, who claimed that my newfound title had also earned me this trip to Ireland—a trip I neither knew about nor wanted yesterday afternoon.

"Ah, Henry," Biel said when I entered his office at Staten Island Downs. "Thanks for being so prompt. Come on in."

"I'm always prompt, Howard," I said. "It's one of my many sterling qualities."

"Most of which I am well aware of," Howard replied, "only I wasn't aware that promptness was one of them."

"Okay," I said, sitting down in front of his desk, "so sometimes I'm late."

"Sometimes," he said, nodding and rubbing his hands together.

"Since I'm on time today, what's on your mind?"

"Ireland."

"I didn't know you were Irish."

"I'm not."

"Then why is it on your mind?"

"Because I'd like you to go there."

"Business or pleasure?" Maybe he was offering me an all-expenses paid vacation.

"A little of both," he said.

"You'll have to explain that to me, Howard," I said. "It's too convoluted a prospect for me to handle alone."

"I'd like you to go there and do a favor for me," Biel said, "and then take a few days to enjoy the Irish countryside. You know, they say there's magic in the ground there."

"Why do I get the feeling there's bullshit in the air here?"

"You wound me."

"Uh-huh. What's the favor?"

"Dublin has two central racecourses, Leopardstown and Phoenix Park."

"What about the Curragh?" That was the only Irish racetrack—or "course," as they call it there—that I knew, because one of our American horses—Fourstars Allstar—went there a few years ago to win a big race. I think it was the 5,000 Guineas.

"There are several other courses within easy drive of Dublin, and the Curragh is one of them. We, however, are concerned with Leopardstown."

"Why are we concerned with Leopardstown?"

"Because I have a friend—my opposite number there—who is having some problems and he needs the services of an outside investigator."

"Outside," I said. "Yeah, I guess bringing me in from the U.S. to Ireland would qualify me as an outside investigator."

"This would be a favor to me, Henry," Howard went on, undaunted, "but my friend, Seamus Kilkenny, insists on paying you. I told him that would have to be between you and him."

I frowned.

"Howard, why would I want to be paid for doing you a favor?"

So I didn't particularly want to go to Ireland. So what? Howard Biel only asks me for a favor once or twice ... a month! It doesn't hurt to have him constantly in my debt.

So I ended up in Dublin. During the cab ride from the airport, the thing that struck me about Dublin was its doors. It seemed that every building had a different door—different style, different shape and, most striking of all, different color. I had never been so fascinated by doors.

There were several ways I could have traveled from the airport—car rental, bicycle rental, bus—but I chose a cab. It was the most expensive, but my expenses were being covered by Seamus Kilkenny.

My accommodations had already been arranged by Kilkenny: a hotel called the Clarence. I found out later that the area was called Temple Bar, south of the Liffey—the Liffey being a river. Temple Bar was one of Dublin's hot restaurant and bar areas.

The hotel itself was pretty big, located on Wellington Quay and actually overlooking the River Liffey. The Clarence was a middle-range accommodation, so my guess was that Seamus Kilkenny had some bucks.

I got a room halfway up, facing front so that I overlooked Wellington Quay and the river. Off to the left—west of me—was a bridge I later found out was called Grattan Bridge. Several blocks to the east was Ha'penny Bridge.

As I was checking in, the desk clerk—as pleasant and polite as everyone at the airport had been—handed me a message slip. I waited until I was in my room to read it. I was craning my neck to see the Ha'penny Bridge as I unfolded it.

"MEET ME AT THE HA'PENNY BRIDGE INN AT 7 P.M." It was signed simply "KILKENNY."

I looked at my watch. It was four, which gave me three hours to wander around and get the feel of the area, maybe even have something to eat. I didn't know whether I'd be eating with Kilkenny or just drinking, so I thought a snack would be in order.

I also could have rested, but I really wasn't that tired. Coming to Ireland hadn't been my idea, and I might never have gone there without Howard Biel asking me to do him a favor. I had somehow gotten into my late thirties without ever having left the United States. Now that I had, though, I was kind of excited about it, and I wanted to see as much as I could.

There was a map of the area in the room for the guests. I took that with me when I left, because I didn't want to get lost and be late meeting Kilkenny at seven.

2

Okay, so I was a little late, maybe ten minutes. I had stopped in several pubs and was surprised to find the people friendly and curious. When they found out I was from America, they had all kinds of questions to ask, and they'd go out of their way to make me feel welcome. I don't think I bought myself one drink, and in one pub they took the time to teach me how to throw darts properly.

And the pubs themselves were an education. The frontages on all of the buildings were different and, again, so were the doors. Each had such an individual look, they were a pleasure to look at.

I had never before found myself so concerned with architecture. I walked and walked, enjoying the ever-changing scenery from building to building. When I finally looked at my watch, it was six-fifty-five. When I reached the Ha'penny it was seven-ten.

I was about to enter when I saw there was some commotion across the street, by the Ha'penny Bridge. I considered crossing to see what it was, but I was late so I went inside.

I looked around for a man of Kilkenny's description, which had been given me by Biel. He said Kilkenny was built like a six-foot fire hydrant. I didn't see anyone who fit that description.

I ordered a pint of Guinness. Actually, I didn't say a pint, but just ordering Guinness or Harp in Ireland will get you a pint.

I sat down to sip my drink and realized I hadn't eaten anything. In all my pub-hopping I hadn't had any food. I also realized, as I sipped my Guinness, that it was either my fourth or fifth of the day.

By seven-twenty Kilkenny hadn't shown up, and now there were police cars and an ambulance across the way. I was feeling uncomfortable, and then a man came walking in who was apparently fairly well-known in the pub. He was wearing a white shirt, a vest, a tweed jacket, a black cap, corduroy pants, and Wellingtons. There were other men in the place dressed similarly. It seemed to be the uniform of the pub or the area.

"Sean, what the hell is goin' on by the Ha'penny, do ya know?" someone yelled.

"Sure, I know," Sean replied. He was a wizened little man who, if I had seen him on the streets of New York, would have brought to mind the word *snitch*.

"Well, will ya be tellin' the likes of us?" someone else asked.

"Fished a feller out of the river, they did," Sean said.

"Anybody we'd know?"

"Nobody I know," Sean said, "but it's a big feller, he is, or so I hear. 'Ave ya got a pint for me, now?"

I didn't wait to see whether they had a pint for him. I was out the door and crossing the street to the bridge. The uncomfortable feeling I had in my stomach had grown into something downright painful.

3

In Ireland the police are called the Garda. To me, though, they were still the police. The detective inspector whose desk I sat in front of was roughly the equivalent of Detective Hocus at home in New York, a hard-working cop with more cases than he could handle.

I'd met him at the foot of the Ha'penny Bridge, where in a sprinkling rain they had dragged Seamus Kilkenny's body from the water. He had a bump on his head, so he had fallen and hit his head, or been hit from behind and dumped in.

It had taken me several minutes to get the local police to let me speak to someone in authority, and that turned out to be Detective Inspector Jack Donnelly.

We spoke briefly by the bridge, and I told him I was waiting to meet someone who was late.

"And you're afraid this poor feller might turn out to be him?"

"It's a possibility, I guess." I didn't bother telling him about the feeling in the pit of my stomach.

"Come have a look, then."

"It might not help," I said, as we walked to where the body lay with a blanket draped over it. "We were meeting for the first time."

"Did ya have a description?"

"Just that he was a big man."

"And his name?"

"Seamus Kilkenny."

When we reached the body, he had the blanket removed and we both looked down at a man who was broad in the shoulders and must have stood six-two when he was upright. From the angle of the body I couldn't see the wound on the back of his head, for which I was grateful.

"Inspector?" a uniformed man said.

"Yes."

He handed the detective a wallet.

"Where was it?"

"In the dead man's pocket."

"Thank you."

I waited while he looked inside the wallet and came up with several pieces of ID identifying the dead man as Seamus Kilkenny.

"Would you be comin' back to the station with me, sir?" the detective asked politely.

And there we were.

I was waiting for the inspector to finish his telephone conversation, during which he must have said, "Don'tcha know?" six or seven times. I'd also heard the phrase countless times during the day in the pubs.

He was dressed simply in a white shirt, black pants, and a dark gray sports coat. The shirt had slightly frayed cuffs and collar, and the jacket was also slightly frayed around the cuffs.

Jack Donnelly hung up the phone and stared across the desk at me. He was a round-faced man carrying about twenty extra pounds here and there on his body, which made him look sort of lumpy. His hair was mousy gray and thinning, and he occasionally ran a hand through it, to no avail. It would never look anything but windblown.

"Now I was askin' ya ... what?"

I reached across the desk and handed him my ID and passport.

"Ah, yes," he said, accepting it. "Thank you."

He studied my papers and then looked at me again.

"A private inquiry agent from America, eh?"

"We usually say private investigator."

"And you had business with this feller Kilkenny?"

"I was meeting with him as a favor to a friend of his in America."

"And what were you meetin' him for?" When he said "for" it sounded like "far."

"I don't know."

"Your friend who you're doin' the favor for, he didn't tell ya?"

"No," I answered. "He said Kilkenny would fill me in when we met."

"And now ya can't be filled in, can ya?" Donnelly asked, handing me back my papers.

"I guess not."

"Will you be leavin' us, then?"

"Hmm? Oh, you mean going back home? Well, I didn't know how long I'd be here, so my ticket is open-ended. I guess I could leave, but ..."

"But what?"

"Your city is very beautiful," I said, "and the people are friendly ... and I'm from New York."

Donnelly grinned.

"I know what you mean, sir, but you know, if you stay even a few days you might not want to go back to New York City, don'tcha know?"

"I think that's a chance I'll take."

"Before you leave, can you tell what business Mr. Kilkenny was in?"

"Thoroughbred horse racing."

"Ah, a trainer, was he?"

"No, he worked at the track. In fact, I think he runs–uh, ran– the track."

"And which track would this be?"

"Leopardstown."

"Ah, yes," Donnelly said. "I haven't been there meself. Been to the Curragh once or twice, though. Beautiful track. You might want to go and see it."

"You're right, I might." I hadn't bothered to fill him in on my real job in New York. It didn't seem necessary.

Until he asked me his next question.

"And your friend, the one you'd be doin' the favor for, who is he and what does he do?"

I explained who J. Howard Biel was and what I did for him.

"Well, then, you'll be wantin' to see our racecourses for sure."

"If I have time, I might."

"So Mr. Kilkenny's problem had to do with racin'?"

I decided to be vague.

"I don't know."

"Well, if your Mr. Biel runs a ... track, is it?"

"Yes."

"–track in New York, and Mr. Kilkenny runs our Leopardstown course here, it would seem logical that the problem had to do with racin', don'tcha know?"

"It would seem logical, I agree, but I'm afraid I can't confirm it for you."

"I suppose I'll finally make a visit to Leopardstown, then, huh?"

"I guess you'll have to," I said. "Is that all?"

"I think so," Donnelly said with a frown ... then he nodded and added, "yes, for now. Where are you stayin'?"

"The Clarence."

"I'll have someone run ya back."

"I'd appreciate it. I'd also appreciate knowing if you find out any- thing while I'm still here, Inspector."

Donnelly smiled and said, "I will try to keep you informed, Mr. Po."

I said, "Thank you," even though I had the feeling that keeping me informed would not be on his list of priorities.

4

By the time I returned to my hotel, I still wasn't quite sure what I was going to do. I went up to my room, put the key in the lock, opened it, and stopped when I saw the man sitting in the chair by the window.

"You don't look surprised to see me," he said.

"I'm not." I entered and closed the door. "Seamus Kilkenny, I presume."

"That's right. How did you know the body by the bridge wasn't mine?"

"The way Howard Biel described you," I said. "The dead man was tall and broad in the shoulders. Not exactly what you'd call built like a six-foot fire hydrant."

Kilkenny was a tall man, but he was thick, like a hydrant. Not at all like the dead man.

"Bein' built like this is hell on gettin' suits," the man said, "but it helped me today. Just before the other feller hit me from behind, I sensed something and started to turn. The blow struck me on the back of the shoulder, where I'm well padded."

"And you killed him."

He nodded.

"We struggled and he fell into the river. I saw him hit his head on the way down."

I stared at Kilkenny for a few minutes, wondering what the hell I was doing there.

"Why didn't you wait for the police?" I asked.

"Somebody is tryin' to kill me, Mr. Po," Kilkenny said. "I was not about to stand around and give them another chance at me, don'tcha know?"

"Them?"

"Whoever it is."

"You don't know who's trying to kill you?"

"No, I don't."

I studied Kilkenny for a few moments. This was Howard Biel's friend, the man I had come over here to help. As far as the police were concerned, he was dead, but how long would that last? Once they checked the cadaver's fingerprints, that would be the end of that.

Or would it?

According to what Biel told me, Kilkenny had money, and had been the racing secretary—or whatever its equivalent was—for the past seven years. The man sitting in my room, looking around nervously, did not fit that description. But then, I was used to seeing Howard Biel in his office, or at some thoroughbred racing function. How would he look sitting nervously in a hotel room?

"So is this what we were going to talk about at the Ha'penny Inn earlier today, Mr. Kilkenny? That someone is trying to kill you?"

"Not exactly," he said. "This is the first attempt on my life, but it just shows how the situation is escalatin'."

I waited, but when he did not continue I asked, "Uh, from what to what?"

"There has been some horse dopin' goin' on at Irish tracks, Mr. Po."

"How long has it been going on?"

"It came to my attention a few weeks ago when a horse died in its stall at Leopardstown, after a race."

"And the autopsy revealed drugs in its system?"

"Yes."

"That must have been a big headline in the papers here."

"Uh, no, it wasn't."

"Why not?"

"It was not revealed to the public that the horse's death was drug in-duced."

"What was the reason for that?"

Kilkenny fidgeted in his chair.

"I was told to keep it quiet."

"Somebody told you to keep the lid on it?"

He nodded.

"Who?"

"I ... can't say."

"Can you tell me why?"

"The trainer is a ... a very big name here, as is the owner."

"And between them they had enough clout to keep it quiet."

"That's right."

"But you know about it."

"Yes."

I sat down on the bed.

"You're telling me they'd kill you to keep you quiet?"

"No," Kilkenny said, "I'm telling you that's the problem I was havin' here."

"That's the reason you needed an outside investigator?"

He nodded again.

"I was thinkin' I wanted to find out if they've done it before," he said.

"Why?"

Kilkenny frowned and clasped his hands, placing them between his knees so that his shoulders were hunched.

"I love horses, Mr. Po," he said, and then he quoted, " 'The Goodly Race.' There's no better name for them. I love the animals, and the game. When someone starts contaminatin' it, no matter how big they are ..."

"Let me get this straight, Mr. Kilkenny," I said. "There's no doubt that this high-profile trainer and owner doped that horse?"

"No doubt."

"And if you spoke up, they'd be ruined."

"Their reputations would be damaged," Kilkenny said. "I don't know that they'd be ruined, but they'd get some dirt on them, to be sure."

I thought about that for a while. Racing was a big business all over the world, a rich man's business. Jenny Craig owned horses, Burt Bacharach, princes, sheikhs, and kings. Would someone kill to keep their reputation intact? To keep some dirt off their name?

Oh yeah.

But there was still something wrong, something that smelled.

"What is it?" Kilkenny asked. He must have sensed something, or seen a look on my face.

"I think we should go to the police."

"No."

"Why not? You're in the right here, Mr. Kilkenny."

"I think you should go home, Mr. Po, and let me handle this."

Something dawned on me then.

"You didn't want me here at all, did you, Mr. Kilkenny?"

"No."

"Biel forced me on you."

"He didn't even tell me you were comin' until you were in the air."

"And you already had your plan in play, didn't you?"

"My plan?"

"Who was the dead man, Mr. Kilkenny?" I asked. "The owner or the trainer?"

He didn't answer.

"They'll find out the body is not you soon enough. They won't be fooled for very long by the wallet."

He unclasped his hands, put his hand inside his jacket, and came out with the gun. I could be excused for not noticing it. It was a small automatic, and not at all visible while he was seated.

"This isn't the way, Kilkenny."

"What have you figured out?" he asked.

"The dead man did not fall into the water during a struggle," I said. "He had your wallet in his pocket. You could only have put it there if you overpowered him, and then tossed him in the river. You arranged to meet him there, didn't you? You planned to kill him."

"He's scum, Mr. Po," Kilkenny said, not bothering to deny it. "Pure scum."

I'd been thinking wrong all along. It wasn't the trainer and owner who would kill to keep their names from being dirtied, it was Kilkenny who would kill to keep the "game" and "the goodly race" from receiving a black eye.

In other words, a fanatic.

"He killed that horse sure as if he'd shot it," Kilkenny explained. "The animal's heart just exploded. It's a wonder it didn't happen on the track, durin' the race. It's happened before, you know. At the Breeder's Cup in America?"

I remembered a race during which a horse's heart literally "exploded," killing it along with the animal who fell over it and had to be put down.

"I never heard anything about drugs in that case."

"It doesn't matter," he said. "It's goin' on all over the world."

"And they dared to do it at your track, huh?"

"They think they can get away with anything."

"And what about you? How do you expect to get away with this? Why'd you put your wallet in his pocket?"

"They'll notify my wife, and she will go to the morgue and identify my body."

"You've convinced her to go along with you, huh?"

He laughed.

"She loves horses more than I do, Mr. Po. In fact, it was her idea, and I readily agreed."

"Kilkenny," I said, "this is murder. You can't—"

"They murdered that animal!"

"And what about me?" I asked. "Are you going to murder me as well? I never harmed an animal."

"You're a danger to me, lad," he said. "I'm sorry for ya, but you are."

He raised the gun as if to fire, and I tensed, getting ready to leap at him in the hopes that I'd get to him before the bullet got to me. There was no need, though. At that moment the door to my room flew open as if kicked, and then the man who kicked it rushed in with two other policemen, one of whom was Detective Inspector Jack Donnelly.

5

ow did you know he was here?" I asked Jack Donnelly, after the other two policemen had led Seamus Kilkenny from the room.

"I didn't, for sure," Donnelly said. "I was just playin' a hunch. I didn't think you'd come all this way from America for nothin', so I made sure I'd be able to hear what was goin' on in your room."

"You bugged my room?" I asked. "You don't need a court order for that kind of thing in your country?"

"Ah, well, I didn't really bug your room." He walked over to the telephone, which I noticed now was off the hook, just slightly ajar enough to keep the line open.

"We were in the room next door," he said, hanging up the phone. "I had one of my men make the connection."

I shook my head.

"What if he wasn't here?"

"Then maybe he would have gotten away with it long enough to make good his escape." Donnelly shrugged. "As I said, it was just a hunch. I thought you knew somethin'."

"Did you hear enough to know that I didn't?"

"Oh, yes," Donnelly said. "I won't be detainin' you, Mr. Po. You can leave anytime you want."

I had wanted to see some of Ireland, but now I couldn't wait to leave.

"Well, thanks for saving my life, Inspector."

Donnelly smiled and said, "It's my job, sir," and headed for the door.

"Donnelly."

He turned.

"What would have happened if I went to make a call and assumed a maid had knocked the phone ajar?"

He shrugged.

"Any number of things might have happened, Mr. Po ... but they didn't. I guess you were lucky you didn't want to make a call."

As he left the room, I went to the phone. I wanted to make a call now, that was for sure. I wanted Howard Biel to know what he had sent me into by trying to force a friend to take his help. If this had taught me anything, it was that being helpful was not always a good thing.

Or a goodly thing.

Jeremiah's Lily

MARY RYAN

Con had never forgotten her. It had been twenty-two years since he last saw her, but her memory was as fresh as though it had been yesterday. She had left in 1929 and after that the time had run around, one year chasing the next as though the years were a figment of the brain. Even the war had come and gone, taking its complement of young men, but except for that, and for the wireless, nothing much had changed in the parish or the whole county. What did the years mean anyway? They came and went, chasing across the meadows and the stretch of woodland, screaming, winter after winter, behind the church and the graveyard at the foot of Mount Tirnagh. They meant nothing; he had always known she would come back.

He looked at the face of the prosecutor under the grey wig and listened as he opened the case. He heard his own name. He sat in the dock examining the courtroom with a kind of wonder. He saw the judge on the bench; he saw the barristers, their black gowns, and their curling wigs with stiff pigtails and white neckbands. He felt, rather than saw, the strangeness, the closed world of the law. It was like a scent or a sound, an ambience which had the power to transport one into a harsh dimension where every word, every sentence, was weighed. He felt its peril in the pit of his stomach. He sensed the curious onlookers crowding the public gallery. He saw his own defence counsel shuffle his papers and turn to glance at him.

*   *   *

He remembered the day twenty-two years earlier, when she had told him, "I'll be leaving soon, you know Con; I'm going to Chicago." She had been cycling home and had met him on the road to the village. When his face did not register any understanding as to where this Chicago might be, she had added, "It's a great big place in America!"

When he still did not respond she added, "They call it the Windy City." She gestured to the blue-green mass of the hills. "Do you think it will have the gales like the ones that come down to us from the mountain in March? Do you think the air will smell of the heather?"

"I don't think it will, Marina."

Marina, he knew, had never been to a city, not even to Dublin. The farthest extent of her travels was Tralee. She was Jeremiah Tracey's daughter, one of five: tall beauties, the lot of them. But the TB had come, and its little cough had hacked the bloom from Jeremiah's lilies, unnaturally rouging their cheeks, corroding the life within until, one by one, they had bowed their heads and sent their souls out into the universe to find God. But not Marina. "Sure there's no one will have me now, you know! With TB in the family!"

"I'll have you, Marina!"

She put her hand to his face. "I know, Con. I know."

Then she looked away, into the clouds massing in the west, gathering up the rain from the ocean. From where they were standing on the high ground above Kilnacranagh, they were able to see the grey-blue inlets where the Atlantic ate its way into the Kerry coast. He saw the curved sweep of her lashes and the gentle swanlike grace to her neck as she lifted her face to study the squall approaching from the west. He took off his old peaked cap, greasy from years of toil, wrung it in his hands, and said, "Will you have me, Marina?"

She looked into his eyes. It was a steady gaze, a gaze that did not condemn him, that did not whisper silently that he was a bit strange in himself, that he was weak-minded, that he was Con O'Driscoll, brother of Dan who had forty acres and a terrible will, that he was of limited intelligence. "The only one of that family to be a bit touched, God help us!" He knew what the country people said about him; he listened to everything. He did not speak much, which in turn was because he knew people spoke *raiméis*, rubbish. He preferred to wander away into the mountains and dream of long ago, when the mythological

Fionn MacCumhaill and his son Oisín had stalked the land (mighty men those, tall as trees). So the people thought him mad.

Marina knew he was not mad.

"If I had you, Con, where would we live? Is it to live in your brother's house and make way for another woman when he brings home a wife? Is it to live, we and our children, on his indulgence?"

"The farm will be mine someday," Con said. "I saw it in a dream!"

Marina sighed, raised her hand to gently touch his face. "Ah, Con ... we can't live on dreams. I will come back someday; I'll come back with money and then, who knows ... are you going to be waiting for me?" she added with a touch of levity, trying to give a lift to the sadness of the farewell.

Con's face, stern and grave, stared into the distance, as though he would force Time to yield up its secrets.

"I'll be waiting for you, Marina. Always!" Then, without another word, he turned and walked away.

After this exchange, Marina cycled the three miles to her home. She lived in the village of Drumcarney, in a small house adjoining her father's shop, where he sold groceries and hardware, new tin buckets, spades, sweets in big glass jars, chocolates, newspapers, candles, sealing wax, twine, rope, ink, pencils, and copybooks. The house was connected to the shop by an internal door, and the three rooms above had been used as bedrooms when Marina's sisters were alive. It was on the street outside this house that the villagers had laid down quantities of straw to deaden the noise of the carts; they had laid it out of respect for the dying, as, one by one, Jeremiah's lovely daughters had sickened and died. The house was white-washed and gave directly onto the street, the only street of Drumcarney. Now, when Marina came home that summer evening, the blue turf smoke hung above it in the evening air.

Her father was in the kitchen, behind the shop, reaching up to the mantelshelf for his tobacco. His old pipe, the briar Marina knew so well, was in his hand. He filled the bowl with plug tobacco from a tin and lit it with a taper, sucking vigorously with small noises. He was a man of medium height, a little stooped, a little too pale from a life spent behind a counter. He had married in middle life and his pretty wife had borne him one daughter after another, until Ellen, the youngest, had arrived, at which point the poor mother had developed complications and died. His girls had all taken after their mother, and for years he had asked for nothing except to work and care for them and see them grow up around him. They were his pride and joy; he knew they were admired and that someone had referred to them as "Jeremiah's lilies," and it pleased him that the name had stuck.

And then, after years of patient love, work, thrift, care, anxiety, and expense, disaster had struck. There had never been TB in his own family and he could not understand why Fate should have so grievously smitten him. His eldest daughter, Kate, had been the first to go, and then the disease had swept through his household, sparing only him and Marina. But now even Marina was to be taken from him, but only by the vagaries of sudden chance. She had the offer of a job in Chicago, a parlourmaid's job with a rich American family. This job had been procured for her by a maternal aunt who lived in the Windy City. She could start a fresh life there. He well knew that no one in the county would marry her with TB in the family. There was no point in trying to keep her. It would be cruel to condemn her to a life of spinsterhood, to force her to invest the joyful sap of her youth in supporting his old age.

Now he turned to the last of his children and said, "You're late, girl. What kept you?" Although he spoke gruffly, he felt his heart lift at the sight of her. Marina was full of life, and her cheery face, despite his heaviness of heart, always made him smile.

"I met Con O'Driscoll."

Jeremiah's face clouded and he looked at her over his spectacles. "Keep out from him. It's stranger in himself, that fellow's getting. He's a wild man, is Con. He's been seen out pacing the fields half the night."

"He asked me to marry him, a Dhaidí. He asked me would I have him."

Her father's face expressed exasperation and something like anger. "Oh, he has great notions, I'll say that for him!"

"I told him I was going to Chicago!" she said slowly. "I don't think he even knew where it was! So I explained that I would be going to America. He'd heard of America!"

Her father sighed and turned away. "Troth if he hadn't heard of that, there'd be little hope for him."

"I told him I'd come back a rich woman and would he wait for me. I thought it would make the parting easier."

Her father turned to stare at her. "Is it mad you are, child? That man will remember it; he might spend years waiting for you! There's no knowing what a man like that would do."

Marina smiled. "Ah no, he won't. He has more sense. Sure he knew I was only joking ... sure we're old friends." Her face became grave. "You see, *a Dhaidí*, for all his strange ways, he is really the gentlest and the best!"

Marina Tracey had been at school with Con O'Driscoll. In those carefree days, they had often walked home together as far as the village, where Marina would say good-by and Con would continue on his way to the boreen that led eventually to the isolated, thatched farmhouse that was his home. At school Con excelled at only one thing—poetry—both Irish and English. He absorbed it effortlessly and regurgitated it with passion; but he was so bad at everything else that he would have been the class laughingstock were it not for the fact that he was feared. There was something about Con that was not to be trifled with. No one could say precisely what this was, because he was never seen to hurt anyone, and was, despite his size, the epitome of gentleness. But there was in him some kind of iron, some vision of reality that was outside of the general ken. He had a way of looking at you that made you feel your soul was under inspection, and people, for some reason, found this disquieting. So, in spite of all his scholastic backwardness, he inspired respect.

He and Marina became friends by virtue of a small accident. Everyone went barefoot, even adults, except, of course, important people—like teachers, bank clerks, shopkeepers—and Marina. Poverty was universal and bare feet, winter and summer, in sleet and sunshine, were the norm. However, it was a point of pride with Jeremiah Tracey that his daughters were well-clothed and -shod, although he himself had but the one good suit in twenty years. One day when Marina was being teased by her classmates, though without malice, for wearing boots, she took them off and said she didn't like them anyway. The children were in the school yard at the time and Marina joined them, barefoot, at their game of tag, running around in her white feet in a brave effort to be as good as the next. But the small sharp stones were agony, and then a large thorn found its way into the soft sole of her right foot and she retired, grimacing, to the wall that bounded the school yard. Con saw her limp from the game, and he followed her, putting a hand on her shoulder and silently turning up the sole of her wounded foot to inspect it.

"Look over there, Marina ... you see the thrush ... the lovely, speckled fellow pushing out his chest on the blackthorn," Con commanded, and when her attention was distracted, he whipped out the aggressive intruder from her foot, squeezing the flesh so that a small crimson drop followed it. Then he fetched her boots, told her to put them on, and then knelt down and tied the laces. Con was without the usual pride of his sex and age; he would kneel to tie a young girl's laces with the same unconscious care that he gave to stacking a load of turf or driving the old chestnut mare to the creamery on a winter morning or doing a man's work in the hay field.

Marina looked into his eyes and smiled at what she found there.

"Thanks, Con. You're great...."

Con was a year older—in sixth class at the time—and Marina invested him thenceforth with the mantle of the elder brother. But she had not seen what he had done with the small smear of her blood that was left on his finger. Properly shod once more, she had returned to her game, and he had turned aside and rubbed the salty red droplet into his lips, looking after her with a strange faraway expression.

After that, Con knew that he had found the woman in his life. His love was but eleven years old and he twelve, but he loved her with the unconditional passion of his whole being. He wove her into the fabric of his epic fantasies, into his dreams, sometimes muttering her name aloud. He saw her red-gold hair and brown eyes before him in all the nooks and crannies of the wild countryside where he lived, as well as in all the nooks and crannies of his own upright and unorthodox soul.

His elder brother, Dan, who eventually inherited the farm, asked him about her. "Did you see Marina today, Con? You're astray in the head about that girl!"

Con knew perfectly well that Dan felt he had no future with Marina. He was sure of this himself, but it did nothing to deter the passion that burned in him, and that continued to burn well after his school days had closed behind him (he left school at fourteen), and right through his adolescence and into his young manhood. He accepted this fire in his soul as his lot, not as something he expected to fulfill; he knew he was no match for Marina. A beauty like her would have her pick. She would marry someone with land of his own, someone clever, who understood the ways of the world. But he was glad he had the pain of longing; he put its fierceness at the core of his life and let it scorch him. Because of it, he knew he was alive.

But then tragedy had visited the Tracey family. Four of the five girls were mowed down by the dreaded tuberculosis, and people, however kind they might be as each individual catastrophe presented itself, began to mutter that there was no luck in that family, that there must be a drop of bad blood. Jeremiah's business began to slacken, particularly the grocery end of it. It might be all right to buy the new bucket and spade from him, but food was another matter.

Marina's potential suitors—and there had been a few—lost interest and disappeared off the mat. No one would choose a wife from a family decimated by TB; that was tantamount to bringing home the plague itself. So, from being the most admired of Jeremiah's lilies, Marina became the pariah, the pitied outcast. It was not her fault, everyone knew that; but death was no respecter of persons, and you did not pause to covet the beauty or the merits of someone who had the Grim Reaper grinning over her shoulder.

"I'd like to marry Marina, Dan," Con said the evening after his meeting with her, when she had told him of her impending departure.

Dan was sitting by the fire, drinking the naggin of whiskey he permitted himself on Sundays. He was a taciturn man by nature, not particularly gifted, a careful farmer, a caustic brother who expected his younger sibling to work seven days a week, three hundred and sixty-five days a year, on the place in which he had been reared, but without any ostensible title to a square inch of it. Con did get an odd bit of pocket money, which he spent on books and his board and keep. He was entitled to live on the property under the terms of his father's will, but Dan had conveniently forgotten this and reminded his brother, in numerous small ways, that he owed him lifelong slave labour because he had a roof and food in return. He also took out on his younger brother the frustrated passion of his own existence. He had been jilted by the girl he was keen on, and Con was the available scapegoat for the ensuing grief and anger. Con accepted it, and when he felt the lash of the old horsewhip across his shoulders, he knew that he deserved it for his contrary ways. He knew how to distance himself from pain, and that made it possible for him to endure the agony when the thongs of the whip bit into his flesh. Even his brother, sometimes privately smitten with guilt for his temper tantrums, was secretly in awe of Con's patience, but it only reinforced his certainty that he deserved what he got. After all if he didn't deserve it, why would he put up with it?

Now Dan, having listened with astonishment to his brother's marriage hopes, said with a dismissive laugh, "What put a notion like that into your thick skull?"

"She's for leaving ... going to America ... she might stay if I had something to offer her!"

Dan stared at him for a moment while his mouth curved into a smile, and then he laughed into the fire.

"Well, you can't bring her here," he said after a moment, in which he considered with private mirth the prospect of his brother marrying. And then with sudden, searing jealousy, he said, "I won't have her here. She's blighted, my lad. The whole family came down with the consumption, like it was the wrath of God ... anyway, she'd never have you. She knows *how* things are with you...."

"*How* are things with me?" Con asked quietly.

His brother turned sharp eyes on him. "*How* you're soft in the head, Con ... *how* you can't count money, Con. *How* you know nothing at all about what's goin' on in the country. *How* you clear off to the mountains when the humour takes you and wander like a lost soul ... *how* you talk to yourself ... all that poetry ... it's all right for a bit, Con, but day after day, year after year! What woman would put up with the like of that?"

"I'm not 'soft in the head,'" Con said equably. "I don't know much about things not worth knowing, that's true enough. But she'll have me yet. She said she would come back ... It may be years, but I don't mind the wait!"

Dan groaned and threw another slug of whiskey down his throat. "Merciful God, will you have sense...?"

Marina went away to Chicago. The years passed. Her father, Jeremiah, sold his shop and went to live with his old sister in Dublin. Con heard nothing more of his love. But she remained for him still bright ... still the young girl with the thorn in her foot, who had put her hand to his face and said, "You're great!" ... still the maiden with the laughing eyes who had touched his face and said, "Ah, Con, we can't live on dreams...." He wandered the slopes of Mount Tirnagh and whispered her name. He stole lines of poetry:

> Last night, ah, yesternight ...
> There fell thy shadow, Marina! ...
> And I was desolate and sick of an old passion,
> Yea, I was desolate and bowed my head.

He tried his own immortal lines, but they never quite progressed beyond:

> Marina of the beauteous eyes,
> Forget me not, forget not I.

He was dubious of his efforts, suspecting that they lacked something critical, that they failed to touch the quick of any experience, poetic or otherwise. So he eventually abandoned his own attempts and opted instead for classic lines from great works, or his own heartfelt and heartbroken sighs; her name torn from his lips and lost in the whistle of the wind: "Marina ... Marina ..."

"Marina, Marina," Dan echoed, having watched his brother down the years. "In the name of Jaysus, will you have an ounce of sense? The woman has been gone these twenty years. She has forgotten your existence. If I hear any more Marinas I'll take to the drink!"

"You wouldn't have too far to go," Con returned in a rare moment of acerbity. "So spare yourself the trouble."

"None of your lip, you bloody fool," Dan retorted. "Living with the like of you would drive a body to worse! Trying to get sense out of you is like trying to crack walnuts with a body's left foot!"

Con hated his brother on these occasions. In some corner of his being, in some central place, he craved, he really longed for, a small morsel of love. He had a memory of his mother, who had died when he was seven, a memory of sitting on her knee. It was like a dream, a kind of paradise. He had mattered to someone then. On his rare forays into the county town, he watched men with children hanging on to them, men with wives smiling into their eyes, and he felt a great void, like the pit of damnation, open in his chest. *Ah, Marina,* he thought. *Where are you, my love? When are you coming back to me?* But he became cagey with Dan and tried to make sure that he never again heard her on his lips. Her name was too good for Dan's ears. And he did not want to antagonise his brother any more than he could help. He knew he needed Dan. It was true he knew nothing of money; it was true he couldn't fend for himself—not because he was stupid, he told himself, but because he had never learnt how. It had never seemed important compared to the ecstasy of poetry in his brain; words, the mystery and power of them, trembling and tumbling like a torrent; words, the music of them sending shivers up his spine, as though language itself were the place of ultimate knowing. That was what interested him, that and the wind talking to him in the gullies of Mount Tirnagh.

And then, when she had almost become as much a myth as old Fionn MacCumhaill himself, she came back.

It was Dan who told him.

"It seems that she's coming back," he announced suddenly one summer evening as he chewed his bit of bacon fat. He had been at the fair that day in the county town and had come home feeling communicative, his pockets full of money. He had got the news at the fair from a local farmer, who had been standing beside him all morning in the marketplace, waiting for buyers for his three bullocks and two heifers.

For a moment Con did not understand his brother. He was eating meditatively and trying to read some of Blake's poetry by the fading light from the window, occasionally rubbing his eyes. His sight had begun to fail a bit in recent years and he needed glasses, but Dan would not bear the expense of them.

Dan realised at once that his hint had not been taken up.

"Do you hear me?" he demanded.

"I hear you. Do you think I'm deaf?"

"Oh no," Dan said. "You're not deaf. Daft you may be, but not deaf...."

Con looked at him mildly. "Who were you talkin' about?"

"About herself...."

"Herself?"

"Yes ... herself ... aul' Jeremiah's daughter ... the girl you had a great notion of once...."

There was silence for a moment, in which Con heard the shiver of the leaves outside the half door and the small sounds of the turf ash settling in the hearth.

"Marina?"

"God help me, yes, Marina ... I had forgotten her name."

"She's back?"

"She's comin' back—on a visit. Maybe she wants to buy back the auld place, the shop? She was in touch with the Kellys beyond in Ballyfagan. She was at school with one of the girls...."

"When?" Con asked.

"I dunno ... but that's what I heard."

Con did not finish his supper. He went into the twilight and walked to his old haunts on the slopes of the mountain.

Looking at the courtroom now—the fuss, the stacks of paper tied in dark pink ribbon, the balding solicitors like vultures, the barristers like exotic birds of rare plumage—Con found it wonderful that so much trouble should have been taken over him.

"My lord," the prosecuting counsel said, addressing the bench, "the State will show that the accused deliberately and maliciously murdered the deceased by inflicting wounds of a nature likely to lead to death...."

Con's mind wandered. What had he done that night on the mountain? He had not come home until dawn. He had walked and sat in the cool night of summer, high up where the clouds were almost within reach and had stretched out his soul to Marina. *You are too good ... I knew you would come back ... you have all of me, all the love, all the longing, all the service of my life ... my Marina.*

In his mind he saw her pale face, rust red hair, and brown eyes twinkling at him; heard her voice, "Is it to live on your brother's indulgence?"

He had told her he would have the farm someday. This seemed likely enough, as Dan was not a marrying man; since the day his own sweetheart had jilted him, he had scorned women. Con, ten years younger, was his heir. Who else could he leave the farm to? But still Con knew that he was not as yet the owner, and he knew too that Dan had often threatened to sell out and turn his brother onto the side of the road. He still had nothing to offer Marina. She had returned, as she had promised; he was the one lacking. He was still the same Con, still without a penny to his name, although he had worked for nearly half a lifetime on the stubborn, stony acres that belonged to his brother. He had never even had a wage.

The following day he walked over to the Kellys at Ballyfagan. His bicycle had a buckled wheel, and Dan had long since refused him the money to replace it.

"Is Miss Tracey here? Marina Tracey."

Eithne Kelly knew him. *Ah, poor auld Con*, she thought, and decided to humour him.

"Con O'Driscoll ... do you not know me ... and I sat behind you at school for six years! Glory be to God, but I feel I haven't laid eyes on you for a century!"

Con shook hands. He had forgotten her and was only half aware of her curious eyes. He was bearded now, and the beard and his hair, which was receding from his temples, was well slashed with grey. He did not know that his eyes were red and staring and that he was breathing quickly like a beast in distress.

"Marina won't be here until Saturday. She's coming down from Dublin," Eithne said slowly, studying him. "Her father died, you know, and she came over for the funeral." Then she added, aware that he was shivering like someone sickening for the flu, "Will you come in for a cup of tea? I was just going to make myself a cup...."

Con refused, said he must be about his business, that he must be off. Eithne frowned, said it was a long way and that her brother Paddy would give him a lift in his car; he would put the bicycle into the boot.

"Where's your bike?"

"I walked."

"Eight miles?"

"Aye, eight miles. I'll come back on Saturday to see Marina. I'm sorry for troubling you."

As he stumbled away, Eithne saw the brown-red stains on his clothes.

Con went home, but Dan was nowhere to be seen.

"Dan," he called, going out to the barn and the cowsheds. "Dan!" But all he heard was the lowing of the cows waiting to be milked. They were in the shed but were standing interrogatively, as though asking why they were being neglected, lifting up their wet, black muzzles and mooing forlornly.

He checked everywhere. The cottage was empty, the door unlocked, as though his brother had walked out for a moment and intended to return. But the fire was dead and the kettle silent on the black crane above the hearth. The picture of the Sacred Heart over the mantelpiece looked at him with gentle interrogation. Jesus pointed to his wounded, bleeding heart, which was festooned in thorns.

Con began to feel that something terrible had happened. He did not know what. But he felt the dread of it, hanging in the air like a judgment, the certainty that he had forgotten a matter of the first importance and could not, no matter how much he cudgled his brains, remember what.

It was only when he had searched the outhouse yard for the second time that he saw something that galvanized him. Sticking out of the manure heap beside the cowshed was a human hand.

Con ran all the way to Garda Sergeant Jim Sheehan's house in the village. This was the police station, if such it could be called. The sergeant's duties were light. There had been no crime in Drumcarney or the parish itself for many years; occasionally there were newfangled old bothers to look out for, like driving licenses or car taxes or broken headlights. But these were rare, as few of the locals had cars, and those who had them ran them into the ground. He had often waved down a car to check the tax disc, only to see the driver's door open and a desperate foot stick itself out onto the road to bring the vehicle to a halt. "You should get those brakes checked, Mike," he might say, before asking after the family and waving him off, chalking an E on the windscreen to indicate to any other assiduous Garda that the car had undergone legal inspection.

Now Con arrived, distraught, trembling, and out of breath. The sergeant was at table with his wife and three children, but he left them to talk to the visitor at the door, recognising him only when he had introduced himself. He knew of Con more by repute than by sight. People spoke of him as a recluse or as someone who was not the full shilling. "A bit strange in himself." People had seen him in some of his wanderings, and the word went out that he was harmless but one of God's elect, one of those chosen for a special cross.

"My brother's been murdered," Con said to the sergeant.

Jim Sheehan sighed. "Sure what would make you think the like of that, Con...? he said placatingly, with the air of a man who didn't want any trouble, not now at any rate with his supper on the table and the black pudding going cold on his plate.

"He's buried at home in the manure heap," Con said. The sergeant considered this, sighed, and said he would come with him. He asked him to wait and went to the kitchen.

"Can't you finish your tea?" his wife asked, and he said he had better go out to the O'Driscoll place, that there was some kind of a problem. He reached into the oven, where his supper was being kept warm, grabbed two pieces of the black pudding that he had been mourning in the course of his interview with Con, and popped them into his mouth. "All eyewash probably; I don't think the man is compos mentis." He liked the words *compos mentis*. They had a nice legal ring to them, a nice educated sound.

He brought Con outside with him and backed his battered Austin out of the gate and onto the deserted road, and drove in virtual silence until he was at the O'Driscoll cottage. Con conducted him in fraught silence to the yard, and there, sure enough, was the human hand Con had complained of, sticking out of the manure heap. The Garda took a spade and lifted some manure away until he found the corpse.

" 'Tis Dan, sure enough," he muttered. "When did you find him here?"

"He was here when I came back this evening. I was over at the Kellys, and when I came back I couldn't find him...."

"Is that a fact?" Sergeant Sheehan said. "How did you know it was him? You didn't take the manure off him!"

"Isn't it his hand?" Con said in exasperation. He looked at the strong familiar fingers, curved forever in death, and the full force of his loss exploded in his head. He began to cry, shaking and trembling, and the sergeant examined him with human sympathy liberally laced with suspicion. He regarded the dark stains on Con's clothes and began to draw the obvious conclusions.

"Well, we'll have to remove the body," the sergeant said. "I'll telephone to Tralee. But you had better come with me, Con, because there'll be questions you'll have to answer."

"I'll stay here," Con said. "Isn't it my home place, and isn't it mine now?"

"Is that a fact?" said the sergeant again. "I suppose you wouldn't have laid a hand on him yourself?"

Con seemed so thunderstruck by this suggestion that Sheehan was almost mollified. *But who else could it have been?* Sheehan's mind demanded. *Is there some monster loose in the townland? It's either that or Con O'Driscoll has murdered his brother.*

Con had not seen Marina. The guards, men he had never seen before, had charged him and taken him away. They had taken his clothes for a forensic examination and the body of his dead brother for a postmortem examination. The machinery of the law had been set in motion and, like a steamroller, it pursued an inexorable course, outside the power of any individual agency to deflect or alter it.

Con denied the charge. He would not murder his brother. He seemed bewildered, but he did not seem surprised by the charge that there was blood on his clothes. He said there often was. People who had known him, like the curate who loaned him books, and others whom he hardly remembered, came forward and said they would give witness to his character; that he was the gentlest of souls, living with a difficult, sharp-tongued, and often violent brother, who got more than his pound of flesh from him. Con was astonished how people he could not remember felt they knew so much about him. They said he was a bit simple. Con knew what this meant, and it hurt and angered him. But they said that he was a good man, a poet of sorts, always with a book in his pocket. Con was touched by this description. A "good man" sounded like someone who had, if only for an instant, inspired some fellow being with recognition and respect.

"What did you do when you came down from the mountains?" the detective inspector assigned to the case asked him.

"I dunno," Con said candidly "I went over to the Kellys."

"Why did you go there?"

"I heard that a lady I once knew was coming to stay with them."

"Who might this lady be?"

Con drew himself up. "Her name is sacred. It is not fitting that it should be bandied about in a place the like of this!" This was the only question that had made Con bridle and raise his voice. The inspector took a deep breath and looked at the sergeant.

"What time did you come down the mountain? Was it early?"

" 'Twould have been early enough."

"Did you see your brother?"

"No."

"So you went straight over to the Kellys."

"I did."

"Can you explain the bloodstains on your clothes?"

Con hesitated. He didn't want them to know that the horsewhip often bit so deeply into his flesh, even through his clothes, that it made him bleed. So he lied.

"No. I didn't know they were there."

The sergeant wrote out a statement, gave it to Con to read, and then asked that he sign it, which he did. He was not permitted bail, although someone had been willing to go surety for him. Then there were doctors from fancy hospitals, psychiatrists, who came to see him. They spoke to him gently and asked him about his life, about his brother. He told them, because they asked, that his brother was a decent man, that he beat him occasionally with a horsewhip because he wandered away at times when he should have been working or annoyed him with too much poetry. He said this as though he understood his brother's dilemma and bore him no grudge. He dealt with intelligence tests they gave him; he answered questions lucidly. They said he was fit to stand trial, that he knew the difference between right and wrong, and that they would testify accordingly.

Con had a young barrister assigned to him to deal with his defence. He told his counsel that he had not killed his brother. The murder weapon was believed to have been the spade stuck into the manure heap, which Sergeant Sheehan had used to clear away enough of the compost to reveal the corpse. In doing this he had helped to obliterate possible evidence. The deceased had died from a blow to the back of the head, delivered with a sharp instrument and under considerable force, shattering the skull. The deceased had died instantly. Con mourned his brother. He did not know who could have done so terrible a deed.

When the case came to trial, Con was glad the delay was over. He knew he was innocent until proven guilty, and how could they prove him guilty of something he hadn't done? He looked around to check the public gallery. He saw people he knew. Eithne Kelly was there, and someone with her, a plump woman with red hair. He saw the woman's mouth quiver for a moment as she whispered to the man beside her, and he, a middle-aged man who had the look of an American, put a hand on her shoulder. Con remembered the school yard and the girl wincing with pain, the girl whose shoulder he had touched, whose white foot he had taken in his hand to free it from the thorn. The years had taken the sapling grace from her, touched her with a kind of settled rotundity, but he knew her. Her eyes were sad, and he saw the man in the beige macintosh pass her a handkerchief. She blew her nose, and as she did, he saw the wedding ring on her hand. Then she looked up and met his eyes.

Con turned and stared into the distance—beyond the well of the court, beyond the bench, beyond the wigs and gowns, beyond the myriad pairs of curious eyes. He saw the slopes of Mount Tirnagh and heard the wind whistle and moan down its rough and sleek aspects; felt its summer benediction; saw the great sky above, wild with clouds. He saw the years ahead, should there be any—not that they mattered now. He saw the years behind. He knew perfectly well the penalty for what he had done. The judge would put on his small black cap before passing the ultimate sentence. He had often read about that piece of theatricality.

It had come back to him in a sudden spasmodic twist of memory when the red-haired woman—his Marina who was lost to him, who had married someone else—met his eyes from the public gallery. He suddenly remembered the early morning, the wet grass, his brother milking in the pungent cowshed, shouting at him as he came back from his overnight sojourn on the mountain that he was a half-eejit, that he'd have him locked away.

" 'Twas years ago I should have had you put away!" he had roared at him. "When I think of how I could have been married grand, only for you ... she'd have had me, yes, she'd surely have had me, if I hadn't had a poor *amadán* livin' in the place...." And then Dan had got up from the stool and reached for the whip with which he took out the frustration of his life. Con remembered it now as though it had happened to someone else, remembered the moment when something had snapped in him, the moment when his own hands had snatched up the spade, striking the fatal blow, covering Dan carefully with the warm manure, and then throwing the old horsewhip behind the big wooden bins of meal in the barn.

He got to his feet in the dock.

"I have something to say," he announced in a loud stern voice, enunciating each word. He saw the judge raise his eyebrows, saw the prosecutor straighten with surprise, saw his own counsel's shocked face turn to him in remonstrance.

"I am guilty," he said, preempting them all. "I did it. 'Tis true that I had forgotten it, but I remember it now this minute. I murdered my brother."

He slapped the varnished dock in front of him to emphasise his words. "So bring the rope and let there be justice!"

In the shocked silence that followed, a woman was heard weeping noisily in the public gallery.

A Stone of the Heart

JOHN BRADY

For Hanna, Julia, Elizabeth and my mother, Mary Brady
—and in memory of my father, Christopher Brady

Chapter One

Too long a sacrifice can make a stone of the heart.
—W. B. Yeats, "Easter 1916"

Mary Brosnahan alighted from the train at Pearse Street station. Although she was going to be late for Miss Black—she could see Miss Black's tight little mouth saying 'nine sharp'—Mary was not one for running. Her only sister, Francie, had had a stroke three years ago and Francie was only fifty-three, three years younger than Mary.

Mary pressed into the Friday morning crowd which was flowing toward the top of the stairs. Behind her, the station began to vibrate and thunder with the starting train's efforts to push itself on to the south suburbs of Dublin. Mary had known these same trains for thirty years. Like most other Dubliners starting into the 1980s in their greying city, Mary had insulated herself with a benign cynicism. No matter what they said, the new electric trains were a pipe dream concocted to catch votes. Never happen, not in a million years.

While Mary was on the train she had caught sight of the headline on the *Independent*. Now it appeared to her again in the stacks of papers by the foot of the stairs: 'Kidnapped RUC man found dead.' Another one, she thought.

Mary's attention was then taken up with negotiating the murderous traffic in Pearse Street. She pressed the button for the pedestrian light and waited. Momentarily, she recalled the headline again and the photograph of something (clothes? a sack?) lying in a ditch, with police-men and soldiers standing around. As the light changed, she scurried through the crowd and made her way toward the back gate of Trin-ity College.

Mary worked as a skip in the college. Her job was to houseclean the students' rooms and other residences. She had been doing this for fifteen years. She entered the grounds and immediately headed for the passageway between the gymnasium and the science blocks. A bicycle hummed by slowly with its chain rattling. Again Mary recalled the photograph in the *Independent*. This time, she summoned up the memory of the daily glimpses of the Dublin mountains she caught as her train crossed the Liffey by the Custom House. Mary seized on this recollec-tion to quell the feather touch of anxiety she felt coming over her.

She emerged from the passageway to face the broad playing fields lined with trees. Mary did not miss the propriety of the flowers and shrubs held in by the tended beds which followed alongside the path. There was care taken here and things were kept in order–at least that could be said for the place, no matter the likes of Miss Black who ran it. Outside the walls, Dublin had gone to pot in Mary's estimation. Where was the polite and decent city she had grown up in? You'd be run over by cars and you on the footpath even, she had concluded. The clerks in the shops didn't so much as look at you these days. People eating in restaurants and houses being knocked down for shops and offices.

"It's them Johnny-Jump-Ups from outside of Dublin has the place gone to hell. What do you call them, the entrepreneurs and the like. Hucksters and bogmen. They take the money and run," Mick said.

The thing was, it was happening all over the world. Like Father O'Brien said in the pulpit, things were changing too quickly. We didn't have our priorities right, he said. That's it, Mary thought, we don't have our house in order, we don't have our priorities right.

Mary quickened her pace. She consoled herself that at least it was Friday. Miss Black and her 'nine sharp.' Little dry old Protestant face on her, Mary thought scornfully. What was it one of the other skips said she'd like to ask her...? "O Miss Black, how's your arse for cracking walnuts?"

Mary imagined the house they'd buy after they retired. It'd be out in Portmarnock with a bit of sea air, near the amenities. A bungalow with a garden for Mick, someplace a person wouldn't be beat up or burgled or run over by traffic. At least it wasn't like up the North, with men shot dead at their doors in front of their families, she thought.

Mary's eye was caught by the sight of a piece of white plastic bag lying in the clump of bushes. Late as she was, Mary was affronted by this. She looked around at the groups of students who passed. None of these youngsters would bother to pick it up of course. Exasperated, Mary stopped and sought a way into the clump which would allow her to get at the bag without getting up to her ankles in muck. She became even more irritated.

Mary walked around the back of the bushes and bent to get into the bag. Bent over, she poked at it with her umbrella, pinning it to the earth. Then she tried to flick it back toward her. She couldn't. The bag was full of something. Mary became angry. She inched in further and looked down at it. It was full of bits of paper. It had to have been some student blind drunk last night who had thrown his notes away. Probably one of them engineers, she surmised, dealing out justice to the anonymous culprit.

Mary picked up the bag. She noticed the sleeve of a coat some six feet away. She hadn't seen it from where she had stood before. She looked at the shrubs nearby. Some of the stalks and branches were showing spots of white where they had been broken. There must have been drink taken last night, she decided. Mary made her way over, her anger now tempered by anxiety and the embarrassment of being in the middle of a bed of shrubs, late for work.

A group of Modern Language students had stepped out of the library to have a smoke and a sit-down in the chairs facing College Park. One of them was ridiculing a psychoanalytic reading of the character of Hamlet when a scream came across the air from behind them. Then another scream.

As they turned, Mary came thrashing out of the bushes with her mouth open and her hat snagged on a bush behind her. She tripped and fell over a waist-high red-leafed bush. Her forearms beat into the ground to save her fall. She scrambled to get up, sliding in the clay again. Mary Brosnahan was quite unconcerned about being late for

Miss Black, moving to Portmarnock or fretting about Dublin's lost civic pride. Her chief concern was to get away from that clump of bushes and shrubs, where her pattern of day-to-day life had been wrecked completely for some time to come by finding the corpse with its head bashed in.

That Friday afternoon saw Inspector James Kilmartin, offices in Dublin Castle, in the company of Garda Tom Connors, of Kevin Street Garda Station but seconded for training to the Murder Squad, sitting in a navy blue unmarked Garda car.

Kilmartin and Connors had just stepped out of the side gate of Trinity College. Kilmartin had listened to Mulholland and then Lacey from Garda Forensic while Connors stood with his hands pocketed, his hair tossing almost in rhythm with the flapping ends of the plastic cordon pegged around the site. The two detectives from Forensic took turns pointing to spots in the bushes. Three other men crouched in the bushes as they talked. Kilmartin watched the three as they inched their ways from spot to spot on their hunkers. He considered that they would make reasonable gardeners but that they'd need something better than tweezers and plastic bags.

"No, sir. No sign of whatever gave him the clout," Lacey had said.

"Nothing like a little hatchet or that class of thing?" Kilmartin murmured.

"Divil a bit, sir. He was brought over here all the same. We might do better now when we find out where he was done in."

"Dragged, is it?" Kilmartin asked.

"Carried would probably be it, sir. He's a hefty lad so ..."

"Did ye take any casts, then?"

"We took two, sir. They were women's shoes."

Kilmartin looked over at Connors and then beyond him to the pallid sky above the Georgian parapets of the college buildings. Connors was staring at the three policemen in the bushes. They reminded him of fowl on the lookout for grains in a farmyard.

Back in the car, Kilmartin sighed.

"Rain, is it, Connors?"

"You'd never know now, sir. It has the look of it."

Kilmartin lapsed into silence. Connors had learned to wait. Two youngsters with skinhead cuts appeared on Connors' side of the car. The two laughed and tapped on the glass. Connors glanced at Kilmartin before rolling down the window.

"How fast does it go?" asked one of them. "A hundred? Do you have a gun? Aren't you a detective? Show us how the radio works. Any bulletproof glass? Give us a bit of the siren."

Kilmartin, a giant to the two and a man who was out of short trousers in Ballina, County Mayo, some forty years earlier, shifted his weight in the passenger seat.

"Who's your man?" said one of the youngsters, eying Kilmartin.

"I'm Kojak. The wheelman here is Danno. Book 'em, Danno. Murder one." Kilmartin said.

The youngsters began laughing again. Connors pulled away from the kerb. Kilmartin wasn't as sour as he looked.

"The telly is a divil, isn't it, Connors?"

"The kids are nice though. You'd never imagine them turning turk on you in a few years," said Connors.

"God, haven't you the black heart in you today. Arra, you'll be all right. Sure isn't it Friday?"

Connors grinned again. "My Ma told me that people in parts of Dublin eat their young, so she did," Connors said.

"God knows now she might be right," agreed Kilmartin. He thought about putting on his seat-belt but decided he'd have too much trouble reaching for his cigarettes.

"Any messages?"

"None, sir."

"Off to Pearse Street. We'll talk to the lads on the spot."

"What was the name of the student?" Connors asked.

"A fella by the name of Jarlath Walsh. Jarlath Walsh."

Kilmartin spent no more than twenty minutes listening to the reports from the two Gardai in Pearse Street station. Kilmartin had worked out of Pearse Street and he hated the building. It gave him the willies. It was old and grimy and cramped. Plenty of action there though, too much. A rough start for a Guard just out of the training college in Templemore. He'd be on the beat right in the middle of Dublin. Kilmartin hated it the day he stepped in the door those many years ago. He had hoped to be posted to a fair-sized town in the West, to be near his folks. He had lived and raised a family in Dublin, however.

He told Connors not to make any notes. It might discourage candour and memory. It would look impertinent too. These two Gardai were well senior to Connors though not in rank. They sat on the wooden chairs poking into their notebooks, their sky-blue shirts making Kilmartin think of Spain.

"About fourteen minutes after nine, sir," one of them was saying. No, no rocks nearby. The body was lying on its back. The forensic team was there at half past ten. Yes, there were some marks in the clay around the body, like shoeprints, dug in at the heel, sort of. *That'd be that woman, Brosnahan, leaping around like a madwoman*, Kilmartin thought. *Shouldn't be so hard on her*. Twigs broken and bent back, yes. Nothing in his hands. Sure it was a he straight away? Yes, the lower part of the face was intact. A bit of a moustache. A white plastic supermarket bag, they'd be for the notes and books. *Why did a student have to use that as a school-bag? Trinity College students not able to afford school-bags? Four hundred years of Anglo-Irish privilege walled up in the place and a student couldn't afford a bag for his books?*

Kilmartin noticed a growing sense of pessimism leaking into his chest. It wasn't a run of the mill one, one of those unglamorous family squabbles that ended in a death with the whole thing more or less wrapped up in twenty-four hours. The public wouldn't be much thrilled to find out how petty the causes were for most murders. No, they wanted the headlines, a bit of sex involved, a name they knew, maybe an international link. This was shaping up to be none of these, it seemed. More like a lunatic on the loose or some panicky young fella on drugs. Twenty years of age, a student.

The two men had stopped talking and, along with Connors, were looking at Kilmartin.

"Thank you, gentlemen. Will you please give your notebooks to the desk sergeant for safe keeping. I'll be requiring them at a later date perhaps."

The two Gardai stood up and left the room without a word.

"How's the old enemy, Connors?"

"Half past four, sir."

Jesus, Mary and Joseph, Kilmartin thought, the traffic would be like the chariot race in *Ben Hur*.

"*Tempus fugit*. Off to the Castle. You can leave me there."

A photocopy of a handwritten Forensic Bureau report lay in a wire 'In' basket on Kilmartin's desk. Under these pages he found a crisp envelope containing fourteen black-and-white photographs and nine smaller Polaroid colour snapshots. Kilmartin had given up trying to get used to the luridly colourful violence he found on the snapshots. Somehow he still expected holiday scenes, people with pink eyeballs at parties.

As he looked through the photographs his pessimism drifted into a stoic pragmatism which was to attend his reading of the draft report. Nothing doing in the boy's bag, save the peculiarity of the bag itself for carrying lecture notes. A train ticket from Dun Laoghaire, bits of things that made up a life. A proper hanky (fresh cotton), six pounds and change, glasses, keys, a watch. Snaps of the site looked like wild Borneo. The body was neater than it could have been; a little care in arranging things?

Walsh, Jarlath Walsh. Student. Kilmartin ruminated for several minutes. It would be late this evening before he'd have copies of statements and a who's-who around the life, now gone but reborn in print in a fattening Garda file, of Mr Jarlath Walsh.

Kilmartin phoned the desk. As the detective answered, Kilmartin languidly wrote down the names of the one detective and four uniformed Gardai who were interviewing Walsh's tutor and his pals in the college. It had fallen to the detective to go to Walsh's parents.

"And have Delaney telephone me at home by eleven tonight, like a good man."

Kilmartin looked through the photographs again. There wasn't much blood on or around the head. Dragged? Carried? The flash had been a little close and the skin seemed to glow with a luminescence which made the gaping mouth all the more odd. Kilmartin noted the tips of the upper teeth showing. His gaze roved to the slight opening between the eyelids, the deceptive sign of life. The forehead was darkened and misshapen, flattened.

An acidy space in his stomach widened. That would be his conscience. Kilmartin became exasperated, but he couldn't settle on a reason for it. "Out with it," he said aloud. Well, sure who else would be able for this one? Shag it. He wrote Minogue's name in his notebook, ripped out the page and stapled it to the reports. Shite, no staples. Rather than sit in Dublin's Friday evening traffic, Kilmartin extricated a poor quality cigar from the back of his desk. He eased his buttocks onto one side and allowed himself a fart, a breezer they called them as children. The fart was in some respects less offensive than the cigar. The world at bay, Kilmartin's stoicism eased a little. Trusting his own mistrust, Kilmartin decided he would give his squad until Monday, but he would call Minogue before then. Kilmartin drew on the cigar. Not for the first time, he tried to understand why he wanted Minogue in on this and why that prospect made him nervous. Because he felt that Minogue was owed something? Maybe he, Kilmartin, was superstitious and wouldn't admit it to himself.

Kilmartin blew a ring across the desk. It was over a year now since the British Ambassador had been blown to smithereens outside the residence in Stepaside. Somehow Minogue had avoided the same fate, by feet, by seconds. Freakish but hardly magical, no.

Even before that, Kilmartin had been conscious of currents in Minogue which marked him apart. Kilmartin believed that his unease with Minogue was the key to Minogue's rank, rather the lack of it. Minogue doubtlessly made his superiors a bit nervous, the same way he made Kilmartin weigh his words or put on the façade of casual conversation. A circumspect man, Minogue, some powerful imminence in him. He was rumored to have a terrific sense of humour.

Some months after Minogue came back on duty, Kilmartin wondered if Minogue had snapped maybe, or had become depressed. Minogue had not been publicly outraged, he hadn't sought vengeance. He hadn't relentlessly questioned his hospital room visitors about the investigation. Minogue seemed to have liked the lying in bed, the long afternoons reading in the hospital. His tall frame humping the sheets up, his head resting on a farmer's hand, his other hand holding a book. Minogue didn't shave for weeks. His wife, Kathleen, didn't fuss him.

When Kilmartin went to see him one Sunday, Minogue was asleep. Kathleen had fallen asleep in the chair next to the bed. The broadcast of the hurling match could be heard from the transistor radio. Clare and Offaly at it. Why did Kilmartin remember that detail? Something had impressed itself on him, this scene of a sleeping couple, one supposed to be watching over the other.

Kilmartin had begun a note to leave with them, rather than wake them. Just as he finished, the daughter came in, Iseult. A name out of the past, a darkly Celtic presence: jet-black hair, the same as Minogue had had, tall. A long peasanty black dress and a shapeless coat. Fashion, is it? The fine arts stuff sent them all a bit off. Minogue stirred awake. His eyes opened and he was fully awake, just like that. A book slipped off the bed and woke Kathleen. She replaced it. A book by that fellow Victor Hugo, *Les Misérables.* What kind of a shagging book was that to be reading and him barely back from the dead after that bombing? A year ago nearly.

Kilmartin stood and looked out the window. The street might as well be a carpark with the traffic. *Les Misérables,* he thought, stubbing out the cigar. Must have been set in Dublin. "Fucking city," Kilmartin whispered, almost disinterestedly.

Chapter Two

On Sunday morning, Minogue and his wife left after Mass in Kilmacud at about a quarter to ten. Mrs Minogue, more devout than any of her family, much favoured the condensed richness of a quick sermon. She infinitely preferred the apt word to the hyperbole which the younger priests seemed to be fond of. Father O'Rourke still gave them the goods though. His sermons lasted about five minutes and they were deceptively simple. Then, on with the Mass and the next thing you knew, you were out the door three quarters of an hour later. That was just about time for Minogue to be more or less awake.

Their children confused Minogue's silence in the mornings with bad humour although he rarely had a cross word to say. He usually said nothing at all if something irritated him. Through twenty-four years, Kathleen Minogue knew almost all the signs: his head would go down, his eyebrows would raise a frown on his forehead. He'd look around for more tea or maybe fiddle with the cup. It was Minogue's idea to make the walk down the pier in Dun Laoghaire after Mass on Sunday. The idea was to let their two children get up late and make all the fuss and hullabaloo they wanted. Iseult could be depended on to come in at about one and Daithi before three every Sunday morning. These hours started when both of them started university. Minogue wondered if that was cause and effect.

Kathleen was for putting the hammer down, 'as long as you're in this house, you'll ...' kind of thing. Minogue's own anxiety about their children brought him to a delicate equilibrium. He persuaded Kathleen to hold off on her plan, but every now and then he had to renegotiate with her. The idea was not to talk about Mass or coming in late but to come back home by about mid-day Sunday after a walk and read of the papers. Iseult would have dinner on and Daithi would be presentable, no questions asked. It worked.

Kathleen had been making the mistake of going to wake up Daithi on Sunday mornings. When she had opened the bedroom door, not only was the room like the wreck of the *Hesperus,* but there was also an appalling smell of stale boozy breath and a night's release of beer farts. Minogue had then been pointed toward the stairs and encouraged in no uncertain terms to rouse their son, express the joint parental disapproval and air the room. Minogue, who had been on a tear manys a time at Daithi's age but now knew better and feared for his insides, worried about Daithi's crowd. A crowd of engineering students put next to a rake of drink brought on a lot of high jinks.

Minogue climbed into the car and handed the *Sunday Press* to Kathleen. The car rocked as it took Minogue's weight. While Kathleen began scanning the headlines, Minogue fumbled the keys into the ignition.

"Dun Laoghaire, for a walk, will we?" he asked.

"Down the pier is it? Tell him Inspector Kilmartin, that is to say, Jim Kilmartin, called. I'll telephone him at dinner-time. Good day to you, now."

In Minogue's Kilmacud home, Daithi put down the phone and cursed his awakening by a policeman, no less. Daithi's neck was stiff and his bowels were groaning. A part of his mind registered that seeing as he had swallowed about seven pints of stout the night before, some issue would have to come of it and rapidly. Iseult eyed him and murmured over her handmade teacup.

"Well, brother. In the arms of Bacchus last night?"

"What?"

"Did you fill up well last night?"

"And if I did? I'm not the kind of yo-yo to sit around like the artsy-fartsy crowd talking about the state of the world."

"Like me?" Iseult said.

"Like your pals, anyhow."

"Did you hear about the Irish homosexual, brother dear? Preferred women to drink."

"Nothing personal, I suppose. You want me married off like the Ma, is that it?"

"Arra no, stay home and look after your mother," she replied.

"You're cracked, so you are. When'll the parents be home?"

"Half past twelve."

"An Inspector Kilmartin will be calling for the Da on the blower."

"Matt, did you read that someone told Gay Byrne to eff off on the 'Late Late' last night?" Served him right, thought Minogue. Byrne and the rest of them were a crowd of yobboes.

"No, I didn't. What prize will the fella be getting? For his candour I mean," Minogue said.

"Now would you lookit," Kathleen said quickly. "I suppose he got a rise out of this fella. Liam Cullen. You know, that painter who makes a religion out of being from Dublin."

"Well, they're your crowd, Kathleen. Good Auld Dublin," quipped Minogue. He inched the car into the line-up leaving the church carpark.

"Well, Dublin or not, there was no call for making a show of us with the language," Kathleen added.

"They give the name of the young lad killed the other night. Inside in Trinity College. Jarlath Walsh. He's not a Walsh we know, is he now, Matt?"

"I can't place him, no."

"Not Jackie Walsh in Bray, his lad?"

"No, that's Brendan."

"God, isn't it terrible, a young lad to be murdered like that?" Kathleen said.

Minogue allowed that it was. As Kathleen read on, Minogue's thoughts ran adrift.

Minogue would have liked to buy one of the British newspapers, like the *Observer* or the *Times*. Minogue used to buy the *Sunday Telegraph* years ago, but since the North, the newspaper had come out in the open as a Tory rag. Minogue tried the *Times* and the *Observer*, but they shoved in enough slurs to turn him away from them. The Irish Sunday papers were rags too.

Approaching Monkstown, Minogue awoke to the understanding that he had not remembered driving away from the church. How had they made it to here and him daydreaming? He glanced over at Kathleen. High cheekbones on her, her eyes disappeared when she laughed. Was she fifty this year?

"Do you know something? I'd love to pick up on the French again. I'll get myself a Paris *Match*," Minogue said to his wife.

The car breasted the hill looking down into Dublin Bay. Howth rested across the postcard-blue water, beyond the East Pier.

Kathleen looked over at him. Senile dementia, it had been called in her mother's day. At fifty-two? Clare people are a bit off anyway.

"Would you now, lovey? Maybe you can teach me a bit and we can go on a holiday to France someday."

She's learning, thought Minogue. Far more effective than coming out with 'Matt Minogue, are you going a bit quare?'

Minogue smiled. He parked the car close to Dun Laoghaire train station. Kathleen and he began strolling toward the pier.

"We're practising for Paris now, Mrs Minogue. We're *boulevardiers*," said Minogue.

*   *   *

Kilmartin turned aside from the hurling match on the telly that Sunday afternoon. It was a slow game. The playing field was sodden. The players were all splatted in mud from the opening minutes and the greasy leather ball slipped from players' fingers and off the ends of their sticks. Maybe the Canadians had the right idea, Kilmartin mused, put it on ice and call it hockey.

He fingered through his notebook and practised phrases silently. He felt awkward talking with Minogue, especially since Minogue's injury. Kilmartin dialled. Minogue answered. As he waited for Minogue to finish the greeting, those two seconds brought the image of the Commissioner confiding over his glass in The Bailey those months ago: *jobs which will take his interest, challenges. He refused the disability pension and he still has another eight years before the pension. No, he's not handicapped at all outwardly. What we need to do, because he's one of our own, is to give him a new hurley stick, a new reason to go back into the game, if you follow my analogy.* That was fine and well, thought Kilmartin in the hissy quiet after Minogue's greeting, but Minogue might translate it as pity. He'd bridle at that to be sure.

"Good day to you, Matt. Tell me, are you following the match on the telly?" asked Kilmartin.

"I'm not, Jimmy, but I might take a look at what the opposition might be like come the final this year."

"Gob now, aren't you Claremen very cocky now? And how do ye know ye'll get by Cork?"

"Well now. I'm surprised at you, Jimmy, and you a Mayoman rooting for the Cork crowd, but the game is the thing I suppose ..." said Minogue.

"And will the Clare team be wearing shoes on the field this year, Matt?" Kilmartin jibed.

"Well now. The thing is, Jimmy, the lumps of raw meat were left in the usual spots in under the rocks. God in his providence will decide what class of person will come down and how they'll be attired. The ones who carry sticks, we call them hurlers and we don't look to the footwear. Fate and natural selection have decided the rest by now."

None of which was true, of course, thought Kilmartin. Minogue's mannerly dissembling was his way of keeping an order. Here was Minogue doing and saying exactly what one might expect, as if he were subtly mimicking the images people had of him, but with no rancour that Kilmartin, at least, could detect. Where was the twist, Kilmartin wondered. How did Minogue get him to think like this?

Kilmartin asked him if he had read the papers. Minogue replied he had. Had he read about the murder of the student in Trinity? He had. On Saturday's paper, it had been: 'Body of student found in suspicious circumstances with foul play suspected.'

"It was in today's paper, Jim."

"Well. I have a feeling about this one. Nothing has turned up from the lads looking to it right now. I have the feeling it requires the likes of yourself to come at it."

Silence. Kilmartin wondered if Minogue saw charity in this, if Minogue felt he was being deeded a case to keep him interested. Maybe to test the waters and see if his brain was on the ball after last year.

"Well now. It has the makings of a good little detective thriller, Jimmy."

Equivocal silence again. Kilmartin, who had large feet and plenty of nerve, went direct.

"Would it be something you could drop your current duties for?"

Minogue realised it was not a roundabout question. He knew that Kilmartin could requisition him. In case Kilmartin had forgotten the hierarchy, Minogue placed the formal step out for him.

"As soon as Jack Higgins gives the imprimatur, I expect."

"I took the liberty, Matt. Although he says his office will suffer while you'd be away."

Indeed, thought Minogue. The conversation had really quite run away with them both. He smiled at the almost mechanical way the pleasantries and face-saving entered, registered and left the talk. Miss me, he thought and smiled again. There'd be plenty more bits of housebreaking today and tomorrow and the day after, and Detective Superintendent Jack Higgins would still manage.

"All right so, Jimmy," said Minogue.

"I have all the stuff that's coming for the moment up in the Castle. Will you come up about ten tomorrow?"

"I will that, Jimmy."

"To be sure. To be sure. Connors, my aide-de-camp, will go over to Donavan, the State Pathologist, with you. Needs the experience. How about one o'clock and ye can meet here and go off to Donavan?"

"Grand, so."

"And how's the family?" Kilmartin asked.

"The usual. They have me driven mad. Business as usual."

"Remember me to Kathleen, Matt."

So, Minogue thought as he began strolling toward the kitchen. *They want to see if I'm the full round of the clock still.* He stopped and looked at the copy of Magritte's *Memory* which Iseult had bought him for his birthday. Now why had she done that? She had said that when she saw it, she knew it was for him. That was the way young people talked, that throwaway, confident exaggeration. Still, he liked the picture's coolness and its stillness. It reminded him, for no reason that made sense, of his father playing "The Moon behind the Hill" on the melodeon nearly a half century ago. Minogue had learned that daughters more or less broke their fathers' hearts effortlessly.

By half past two, Connors and Minogue were sitting outside the State Pathologist's office. Donavan was already late.

Connors was thinking about the new side to Kilmartin he had seen but an hour before. When Connors was called in, Minogue was sitting while Kilmartin was propelling himself around the room with small talk. Signs on, Connors concluded, the two men had known each other for a long time. Minogue managed to say little, maintaining a thoughtful if distant expression.

"And Connors will drive over with you, Matt, and sit in with ye, if you don't mind. Connors is new to the department and will benefit from the experience to no end entirely. Am I right?"

"To be sure, Inspector," Connors had said.

On the way over to Donavan's office, Minogue asked him if he was related to the Horsey Connors or the Hurling Connors. Connors replied that he knew of neither.

"Well there's Connors in Kilrush now and they were born with hurley sticks in their teeth. The Horsey Connors are from East Clare and they break the bookies in England regularly. As easy as kiss hands."

"Maybe I should have claimed relations with them, Sergeant, because I have no luck on the ponies at all. There's nags I put money on in Leopardstown and bejases I'd say they're still running."

"Oh, a bad sport to an honest man, the same horses," Minogue murmured. "There was another family of girls in Ennis but I would never ask if you have any kin with those Connors, not at all."

"Well, the ones in Ennis, are they Connors or O'Connors?"

"Oh they're Connors too, but they'd be nothing to you at all, I'm sure. A family of girls that never married."

"The Horsey Connors, the Hurley Connors," Connors mused.

"And the ones in Ennis," Minogue sighed.

"Who were they?"

"Well they were called the Whore Connors, so they were," Minogue said resignedly. "Silly of me to bring them into the conversation."

Minogue didn't smile but began to stare out over the bonnet of the car as if he were deep in thought.

Footsteps on the stairs and Donavan appeared from around the corner.

"Good morrow, men," said the doctor.

The two policemen eyed Donavan. He was a well-known eccentric. He wore a greying beard under owlish eyebrows with a red face bursting out from behind the hair. Donavan was crammed into a three-piece tweed suit tailored in the manner of suits of Minogue's father's day.

The office was a morass of paper and knicknacks. Connors observed bottles containing yellowy lumps of something, immersed in clear liquids. It dawned on him that these polypy lumps might well be pieces of flesh, preserved to be viewed and pondered over. A faint odour like a chemist's shop came to Connors as his eyes slipped out of focus and he swallowed, trying to rid himself of an unpleasant sweetness near his tonsils.

Minogue studied Donavan as the pathologist took off his jacket. A rugby player of old, exactly the kind of man who could fall down the stairs sober and not hurt himself, Minogue thought.

"Matt Minogue, Doctor. And my colleague, Detective Connors."

"And how is the bold Inspector Kilmartin back at the ranch, men?"

"Oh, pulling the divil by the tail, Doctor."

Donavan sat heavily into his seat. He pulled a file from under a brimming ashtray.

"Do ye want the pictures, lads?"

"No thanks, Doctor. We'll defer to your description."

"The mob in Pearse Street handed this over to you as a matter of course? The deceased was a young man in good health. I suspect that he had been killed on Thursday night at about 9 P.M. Well he was dead between eight and twelve hours. There. Isn't pathology wonderful?"

"To be sure, Doctor," said Minogue.

"Well. To cut a long story short. There's no doubt this young man was killed by whoever set about it. There was no trick acting and playing kiss-my-arse-and-kiss-my-elbow with this. This wasn't a brawl that got out of hand. I found a moderately severe contusion on the left side of the head. My feeling is that this was a blow rendered by some object such as an iron bar, perhaps a good quality bicycle pump or the like of that. It would have been enough to put him out. It certainly wouldn't have killed him at all, at all. What did in this unfortunate lad was the stone or whatever was used on his head. It appears to have been applied several times. The person wielding it would of necessity have to have given good swings at it … maybe from the height of a man's shoulders. Now, I'm speculating here. However, he was given a *coup de grâce,* if you like, with a lot of force applied toward the end of the episode."

"With the same object?" Minogue interrupted.

"To be exact and evasive at the same time, with an object of the same material, surface area and weight. Perhaps another stone."

Connors looked up from his notes, his mouth a little open.

"Scrapings under the nails, nothing."

'*No struggle?*' wrote Connors.

"This young man had had a glass or two of wine and some class of Italian food."

Donavan looked directly at Connors.

"Perhaps the Garda would require to see details…?"

Connors looked up abruptly from the notes and swallowed. Minogue glanced at him.

"Leave it in the file for the moment if you please, Doctor," said Minogue.

"Could have used a bit of exercise. But couldn't we all? Nonsmoker. A bit fond of his rashers and eggs. No signs of sexual activity, if you follow me. Teeth all his own. Isn't the National Health great?"

"One blow, then others?" queried Minogue.

"Exactly. The thing is that the head would have to have been lying on a surface with no give in it when these stones or the stone were dropped. That alone would account for the particular shattering effect at the back too, you see. A simple principle really, no great shakes. Think of nutcrackers. One side couldn't be made of rubber or the like."

Donavan arched back in his chair and filled a pipe. The file lay open on the desk. They listened to Connors' diligent pencil scratching. The window was full of green, like a big sponge, waving slowly. Nothing like a willow tree to show the time passing, thought Minogue.

"Bad cess to the fecking thing," Donavan said mildly. He threw the lighter across the desk. "I don't doubt that Nora paid twenty pound for this bloody gas lighter with the flame thrower thing for the pipe. And you think it works because it cost an arm and a leg? Not a bit of it," he muttered.

Minogue carried a box of matches to remind himself that he was a free man. If he chose to smoke, he would. Minogue offered his box of matches.

As he did so, he caught sight of Connors' glassy stare. That's what it was, the 'arm and the leg' bit. Minogue tried hard not to laugh.

"Detective, would you check with headquarters on the radio to see if there are further matters requiring our consideration, if you please? I'll be down presently."

Connors made no delay in leaving.

Donavan, wreathed in Amphora smoke, laughed gently.

"Is your man just after his dinner?"

"He's new to the department, Doctor. He is a very quick and able officer-in-the-making, I believe."

"Gob, he's quick at getting through doors. Ah, Nora says I have a warped sense of humour. God knows, maybe she's right. Do you know, there's nothing to this really. I mean, I put the radio on. There'd be the news, a bit of music, an interview or the like. I'd be pinning back skin or using the saw or dissecting one thing or another. I work on my own you know, me and the tape recorder with Radio Eireann in the background. I don't like working with an assistant. It seems rude, somehow. I'm trying to help the poor divil there in the room with me, but sure he's dead. Still trying to explain things even after the person is dead. But it helps. It's preventive medicine in a sense. Your pal will get used to it. It's not personal. You're in the presence of some final truth."

Minogue thought for an instant of the stories about Donavan. Maybe it was by default that he seemed to enjoy the living so much. Donavan was no fool. He was a philosopher who knew enough to be able to laugh. Good man at a wake. Maybe invite him to mine.

"Anything worth hanging on to, Doctor?"

"Well, this is the preliminary, you understand. It'll be all typed up and a few more tests will be in but that won't make much difference. You have the gist of it."

Both men were silent for a minute. Donavan turned his gaze from the window to Minogue.

"As an aside, er–"

"–Matt–"

"Yes, er, Matt ... I have the feeling of some kind of intention behind this thing. Some kind of deliberation. Maybe it's the shows on the telly. Still, I think there's something to this one. Don't quote me now. That stuff is not my job at all. I'd expect anything."

Minogue was to remember this remark; not the words themselves, but the speculation on Donavan's face. Have to do some Sherlocking on this one.

Connors was leaning on the boot of the car outside trying to make his attempt at nonchalance outdo his sheepishness.

"Come on now and we'll go back to the Castle. Jimmy Kilmartin says he has a desk for me and odds and ends from the other lads in the Squad who were at it over the weekend."

"To be sure," Connors said spiritedly. He was grateful that Minogue had passed up on that very Irish liking to send a jibe his way.

Chapter Three

On Tuesday morning, Minogue found himself at his new desk in Dublin Castle, HQ of the Garda Murder Squad. 'Found myself' were the words that came to him as he settled into the chair, and those were the words he'd report his day to Kathleen with: 'Well, I found myself at this desk, you see.'

He tried the phone. Glory be to God, it worked. Would he have to start taking seriously the Minister for Post and Telegraph's threat to make the phone system work? He took another sip of tea. Jarlath Brendan Walsh, k/a Jarlath Walsh. He must have had a lot on his plate with a name like that. Saint Jarlath was a Galway saint. Minogue had known but one person before in his life by that name and the fellow had wisely called himself Jer.

A black-and-white photograph of a group of young men and women at a party looked up at Minogue from his desk. This was a picture of a crowd of young ones at Trinity Ball, taken the previous year. Jarlath Walsh looked out from behind glasses. One of his arms disappeared behind the waist of the girl standing next to him. Others in the picture were up to antics and posing, so they must have been into the gargle. Our man Jarlath looked composed, in place, as an older man might.

Next to this photograph was an assorted set of colour snaps, also taken from his parents' box, doubtlessly kept in the same kind of old shoebox on top of the wardrobe as Kathleen kept hers in. A younger fellow with different glasses, standing beside a grandparent; milking a cow somewhere; holding a certificate; seated, posing, at the piano. "Hardly started living really," Minogue murmured, but not the time or place to be maudlin. Stick to the necessities. Well, one of the necessities was to be realistic: this young fellow looked fairly stuffy, bookish and mannered.

Jarlath Brendan Walsh was the eldest of two children, the other one a girl, Maria, away at boarding school in County Kilkenny or to be up to date, currently in the family residence in Foxrock, grieving. Jarlath Brendan Walsh was a twenty-year-old observing Catholic with modest academic achievements behind him as he worked through his second year in the Faculty of Economic and Social Studies in Trinity College, Dublin, Ireland. Jarlath Brendan Walsh had no known reason to get himself bumped off. "He had everything to live for," Minogue muttered.

Soap operas aside, Master Walsh could look forward to some entitlement. His father was a well-do-to fruit importer. The family lived in a big new McInerny house in Foxrock, a fine summit of achievement for a man from the country. *Mustn't get snotty,* thought Minogue. *I'm a benighted peasant myself but, God help me, I have a Dublinwoman and a family of Dubliners in tow.*

Minogue's view from his office consisted of a grey stone wall, patched decades ago with brick and mortar, slashed into a lunatic jumble by the thoughtless installation of distorting glass. He tried to stare through the glass but he became a little dizzy. Jarlath Brendan Walsh studied political science (is there such a thing?) and economics. If Jarlath Walsh wasn't dead and if his passing had not led to Minogue sitting at a desk with several fair-sized reports to read, Jarlath Walsh would be rather nondescript. Shouldn't think that: his parents must be in agony.

The door opened. The arrival was surprised to find someone in the room.

She introduced herself as Brid and announced that she would be adding to the file on Walsh. Minogue turned to the four carbon copy leaves when she left. Detectives from Pearse Street station had found a bloodied rock in the alley which ran next to the Pearse Street side of Trinity's walls. Looks like someone lobbed it over the wall after he'd made use of it. The blood matched. More crucially, there were four strands of hair stuck to it. The stone had apparently come from a stockpile of similarly sized and shaped stones which lay in a heap in Front Square. Trinity College had undertaken the Sisyphean task of repairing all of its historic Front Square. Workmen were ripping up the cobbled square and saving the stones so they could be reset. No wonder stone masons had a reputation for being stone-mad.

No prints that meant anything on said stone. Minogue sat back sipping at the sweet tea. The idea of it, a Catholic lad, parents up from the bog, finally emancipated into some status by attending Trinity College, the bastion of the Anglo Irish, and there he was done in by a stone in these ecumenical times, a stone taken from the squares where scholars walked. Would they find the spot where the boy's head had been smashed though? It had to have been a hard surface, likely cobblestones if it had been done inside the front end of the college. It might rain at any time and wash away clues like blood. At least the rock was something.

Minogue finished the tea. He then surprised himself with the enthusiasm he felt as he pushed off out of his chair. He selected from his files as his intentions required and left the office.

In between sessions with students, which Minogue had purposely set for the morning, his mind worked calmly, fitting details. Killed by a rock is not planned killing. Killed inside a university is hasty killing. Something had happened that very evening, something to precipitate things. It wouldn't have been an unconnected event. It may have been done by more than one person. If it was done by one, then he must have been hefty enough to drag a limp body into the bushes. Presence of mind to brush over the tracks. Professional? Not necessarily, just determined, desperate maybe. But still, if it was the latter, whoever it was, kept cool and saw to little things. Analytical, practical. Does that mean educated? Dragging bodies is not easy. Minogue stopped listening to the student friend of Walsh and remembered the *whump*, the glass flying like sand, the car turning slowly. Then he had felt a terrible silence and stillness as he crawled out of the car, knowing all the time what had happened. He had tried to drag the bloodslick body of the detective, the cheery lad, over to the bush. To what end? He was dead, of course. Minogue had passed out then ...

Minogue had asked to see the president of the Students' Union. Walsh had been a class representative and, as such, should have been known to the president. Minogue looked over his notes in the intervals between students. He had made a point to thank them before starting.

Only one of the young men had wept. Minogue rather liked that young man and he wasn't surprised at such a show of feeling. In a sense that boy had graduated much further than the acerbic self-assurance Minogue detected in the rest of them.

None of these students had been with Walsh in the hours before he died. Minogue found out that Walsh's girlfriend, the one in the picture, if they called one another boyfriend or girlfriend anymore, would not be back until tomorrow. Her friends had packed her off, inconsolable, on the Belfast train. Nothing to it, Minogue thought, even if it was a nuisance that they'd got only brief statements out of the girl last Friday. Plenty of kids from the North attended Trinity. Although it could be done, no one was about to phone the Royal Ulster Constabulary up there to interview her on their behalf or keep an eye on her movements. She'd be rested and ready tomorrow.

The door, formerly ajar, swung open. In walked a tall, bearded president of the Students' Union.

"You wanted a word?" said the newly arrived.

'Intense' is the word, thought Minogue, rising to show some equality.

"If you please, Mr, Mr ..."

"Roche. I'm Mick Roche. My Da's name is Mr Roche. I haven't inherited the title yet. No hurry either."

"Would you sit down please, er, Mick. I won't keep you long."

Roche sat down. His shirt-sleeves were rolled up to his elbows. He smelled of cigarette smoke. His eyes were lightly ringed. No comb had afflicted his hair since rising from his or whoever's bed today. He affected a look of distance and disinterest. He didn't succeed in concealing a keenness and an alertness from Minogue.

"Spelled R-O-C-H-E, is it?" asked Minogue.

"Yes. An agreeable enough name excepting for a prohibition against narcotics of the same name," said Roche without a trace of humour. *Practised that one,* Minogue thought.

"Well now. I'm Detective Sergeant Minogue. I'd prefer you call me Matt. To tell you the truth, Mick, I have no interest in that side of things at all."

"In the consumption or in the law enforcement end of things, Detective Sergeant?" asked Roche.

"Well neither, actually. It's about one of your representatives, your colleagues. Jarlath Walsh, the lad who was murdered."

"Like they say on the telly, I can fill you in on some background, but I knew him superficially really."

Minogue suppressed a smile by diligently writing a word in his notes. He wrote 'superficially,' thinking that this would be a word to bounce back at this president fellow. He'd be smart enough to catch the drift.

"You were in the same class as Jarlath, I understand."

"If you know that, you'll know that there were about two hundred students in that year. It's a general course we all take, then we branch off."

"Am I right in thinking that it is very unusual for a second-year student to hold your office? You must know your onions, Mick."

Roche said nothing, but Minogue detected with a father's acuity the pride which Roche tried to conceal. Minogue was so relieved that he almost burst out laughing. This Roche boy is ordinary, he blooms with praise, Minogue thought.

"Incidentally, what would you be studying if you were an ordinary student?"

"For the files, Sergeant?"

"Well no actually. I have a son and a daughter in college. I'm just interested." That sounded corny, Minogue thought.

"Political science."

"Isn't that one of the things Jarlath was taking?"

Roche's eyes suggested the beginnings of a sarcastic answer.

"It is. There are different types of oddities which call themselves political science. Let's say that Jarlath Walsh's studies would be different from mine."

"I don't understand."

"Well he followed up notions they call consensus theory. Stuff like the rise of the party system or the role of the Senate in decision-making. Jarlath didn't understand the notion of class or the influence of economics. He looked at surface things."

"So Jarlath wasn't afraid to speak up, then? I mean you knew his opinions readily in a class of two hundred."

"We were in the same tutorial group. He stuck to his guns even when it didn't make sense. His position was eventually tautological. He ended up with these unopened boxes like 'culture' or 'nationalism' or 'parliamentary democracy'—American stuff, like Coke. Hymns to the status quo."

Minogue began to appreciate the deadly gifts that brought Roche to where he was. A liking for the phrase matched with a passion and knowledge he tried to conceal. 'Tautological,' if you please.

"I think I know what you mean. 'The best of all possible worlds,' don't they say?" essayed Minogue.

Roche looked at him and grinned, then nodded his head lightly.

"Exactly, Sergeant. He was the property of his class. Why wouldn't he follow that line."

Meaning you don't, because you've seen through it all, Minogue thought.

"Northern Ireland is a rather mysterious set of events for the likes of Jarlath and the parvenus who'd just as soon forget they came from the bog. In one sense they're right when they say that nothing worth learning can be taught ..."

"Oscar Wilde said a lot of things like that. What do you call them?" Minogue murmured.

"Aphorisms. Conceits. Sophistry."

Must be a holy terror for the lecturers here if he has things like that at the tips of his fingers. Minogue wondered if he had made any ground with the dig about Wilde. A fellow who could remember stuff like that would be a favourite with the girls, no doubt, especially with his grim, illusionless sight of reality. Outside the window, Minogue saw the ordered history of the college, all grey and angled with mani-cured lawns, worn steps to the chapel, professors waltzing around in gowns.

"You'll know that Jarlath was in the Fine Gael association here, Sergeant. He bought into them calling themselves social democrats, not fascists. I'm more or less an anarchist, on Saturday nights anyway."

Ah, a joke, Minogue recognised.

"Actually I'm a grumbler in the Labour Party. I spend most of my time trying to get grants for students. I have time for rhetoric usually after office hours. If it's friend or foe with this thing of Jarlath, chalk me up as friend. He didn't deserve what happened. He would have changed, I know it, he would have come round. You know what would have brought him around? His girlfriend. Agnes McGuire. She lived in the real world."

"Isn't she the young lady that accompanied him to the Trinity Ball?" inquired Minogue.

"How did you know that?"

"I might well ask you the same thing," Minogue replied.

For the first time, Roche looked ill at ease. His eyes widened, then he regained his composure.

"Wasn't she my girlfriend in first year?" Roche said with a decidedly emphatic irony. A fraction would have conveyed it to Minogue. So they still called them boyfriend and girlfriend, Minogue thought. Isn't that rich. *Touché,* the atmosphere changed. Minogue asked Roche if he remembered any particularly acrimonious debate involving Walsh. They were all acrimonious, Roche replied. Demonstrations? Out of fashion, said Roche. Other issues? Roche replied after a pause:

"Well, I know that he irritated some people who run the Students' Union magazine with his yarns. We, or rather the editorial board, wouldn't run them because they weren't researched. That's putting it mildly really. They were figments of his imagination. Wild swipes at things."

"Such as?"

"Oh I don't remember a lot of it. Misappropriation of money; you know, the executive filling up on free beer at student expense. Or politics."

"Anything on drugs maybe?"

Roche looked directly at Minogue. Minogue thought he was flicking through his list of possible answers.

"No, I wish he had. Might have brought home some news about the real world."

"I don't get it. Drugs bring you reality?" Minogue asked.

"Do you know what heavy drugs are doing to a lot of kids in Dublin? Well, I do. You wouldn't believe it. No one wants to know about it. Stuff like pot is a joke. It's stupid to chase people for that. I know that heavy stuff surfaces here in college a lot more than people think, but Walsh wasn't going to help anyone with his approach. If you ask me, he was setting himself up for a go at journalism after college. Building a rep for himself here."

"I see. That was Jarlath at his, let's say, most tendentious then?"

"Yeah. He'd jump on the bandwagon with rumours about IRA here in Trinity. No one takes those comments seriously. I mean, look around. What would they be doing here with all the boys and girls from the stockbroker belt going to school here? Ask around. He was just trying to start up some stuff so he would be known."

"Something to think about. Thanks, Mick. If I need to see you again, is it OK to phone the Students' Union office?"

Roche stood up to leave.

"Well, yeah. But just give your name. Forget the Sergeant stuff."

As he listened to the feet clattering down the stairs, Minogue privately remarked upon titles. Hadn't Master Roche been the one who insisted on it in the conversation?

Minogue gathered his papers but left his impressions scattered. He followed Roche down the bare stairs. He was looking forward to dinner. The Junior Dean had arranged everything. They would eat in the Staff Lunchroom, if you don't mind.

Minogue stepped out onto the cobbles and took in some of the sulphurous air of Dublin. He felt sprightly. He eyed a few girls, students, dressed up to look ugly but in a certain good taste which Minogue couldn't put his finger on. This was the new wave, then. He felt the sharpness of the square in the sounds it held and echoed. A blind man was tapping over the cobblestones. A bicycle tinkled by him. Laughs and footfalls came abruptly over the air. Something ascetic about it, like a Protestant chapel, Minogue mused. Then it struck him that he knew nothing about Protestant chapels.

Professor Griffiths was like a man out of the thirties. A gown over a tweedy suit, stiff collar and red brogues. A face like a horse, hair a bit long. He greeted Minogue by lifting his eyebrows and extending an arm in the direction of a door at the front of the dining hall.

"Upstairs, Mr Minoooog."

He wondered if he was putting on the Bertie Wooster stuff. Minogue ate an indifferent dinner at a well-laid table in company with the college Security Officer and Griffiths. Huge painted figures of dead bishops and scholars looked down at them. Cutlery clanked, food was prompt. Captain Loftus, the Security Officer so-called, kept his army rank in conversation as well as in other forms of intercourse, Minogue realised. Well, in verbal intercourse anyway.

Loftus was a Corkman. He liked to dress well. He was one of the few men Minogue had met in the last few weeks of whom it could be said he looked very upright. Minogue had heard that he had done tours of duty with the UN or peacekeepers before springing into this cushy job in Trinity. A modest beeper poked from his pocket.

By way of taking his attention from the metallic taste of the cabbage, Minogue spoke:

"Well now, Captain Loftus. Has there been stuff like this before?"

Loftus affected puzzlement.

"This boy Walsh, done in," Minogue added. Loftus leaned forward and confided that there hadn't. Griffiths, no doubt daydreaming about Homer or "The Rape of Lucrece," looked to Loftus and then began stuffing a pipe.

"Is there anything about politics here amongst the student body that'd go to this extent?"

Loftus looked at him without answering. Griffiths, with a peculiar crack in his face which Minogue suddenly realised was a smile, murmured,

"None other than the boy was a member of the Fine Gael association, Sergeant Minogue. Hardly just cause."

"There was talk of drugs," Minogue said.

"Mr Walsh was a conscientious student, Mr Minogue. His lecturers thought very highly of him," said Griffiths.

The *politesse* and containment began to grate on Minogue. The fun was gone out of this place very quickly. The boy was dead. These two stuffed shirts were sitting on the fence.

"An interest in journalism?" Minogue tried.

"As much as any other student, Sergeant Minogue," replied Griffiths.

"Captain Loftus. How often do patrols of security guards go by that area where the body was found? On average, at night...?"

Loftus looked up to one of the paintings.

"Em, say roughly once every three quarters of an hour after midnight."

"Reliably?"

"Yes. They log in to check-points, a keying system tied to a timer. The college gates were locked. Pretty well impossible to get in over the walls."

"Say, the lowest would be fifteen foot?"

Loftus looked to Griffiths before answering.

"Well, we don't want it known but there are certain parts of the perimeter that can be scaled without assistance. They're in laneways."

Minogue felt resistance. He had been prodding only. This wasn't the place for swipes. He knew well that someone could get over the wall. He had walked the perimeter the previous afternoon. Griffiths and Loftus were reluctant because they couldn't believe someone in Trinity would do this. Loftus didn't want his security and gadgetry to look bad. Griffiths obviously felt the Gardai were barking up the wrong tree. They presumed that some scofflaw from outside the hallowed walls had done it. Minogue looked away to find the eyes of an eighteenth-century judge staring haughtily at him from a painting overhead. The canvas shone dully. *And up yours, too,* Minogue thought. At least he had managed to resist an atavistic urge to prod these two. Master Walsh was done in in a hurry as he headed for the Nassau Street gate of the college to catch the 63 bus home. It didn't matter too much right now whether the killer attended Trinity or not: he or they knew enough to drag the body away to a safe place and make an escape.

*   *   *

In the afternoon, Minogue used a college telephone to make appointments with four of the five lecturers Walsh had had. By half past four, Minogue had chatted with all but one, Professor Allen. No, they weren't being asked for statements, he explained. Perhaps recall the last time you saw him. Any unusual things, conversations, remarks.

The late afternoon was quietly drawing Minogue's energy and interest away. He asked questions mechanically as the feeling grew that even with but one day gone by, he was getting nowhere. He had not realised quite how distant lecturers were from their students. He thought of Iseult and Daithi, how they lived in this kind of world. But, he consoled himself, they had friends. Minogue thanked the lecturer and asked him to direct him to where he might find a Professor Allen.

"He's Psychology," replied the lecturer.

"Yes," Minogue said. He eyed the lecturer's frown.

"Is there something unusual in that?"

"In psychology?" Both laughed lightly.

"No, Sergeant. It's not often that a lad enrolled in things like political science and economics would be doing a psychology course. Nothing wrong with it of course. But would his time allow that?"

Minogue dithered.

"You could phone Professor Allen," the lecturer murmured with a faint smile, waking Minogue from his lassitude.

Minogue found Allen's name in the college telephone book. He counted five degrees after Allen's name. Maybe Allen suffered from an excess of modesty in keeping his other dozen degrees to himself?

A secretary said that Allen was not in his office. Could he make an appointment?

"Are you a student?"

"I'm a Sergeant in the Gardai."

Not impressed. Professor Allen made his own appointments personally, she intoned. Minogue should phone tomorrow. She would leave a message with him to say that Sergeant Malone called.

"And tell him that Sergeant Minogue called too, like a good woman," Minogue said. She did not ask for an explanation. *Sorry for asking,* Minogue thought, *are they all Caesars here?*

Chapter Four

The next morning, Minogue awoke before the clock radio. Amongst other things, he had dreamed of Agnes McGuire. She was the spitting image of Lady Lavery on the old paper money, sitting there looking out in such a melancholy way at the bearer of legal tender. Maybe she realised that the money was going to be exchanged for pints in a pub. Minogue lay still in the cream-lit morning bedroom. He had his fortnightly appointment with Herlighy, the psychiatrist, this morning. There were birds galore outside. The radio popped on and Kathleen elbowed up to look at him. Then she lay down and held her arm over her eyes.

The news came on after the electronic fanfare. Two RUC men had been killed last night in Belfast. They were plain clothes officers in an unmarked car, apparently following a van. The van doors had been kicked open from inside and too late the two realised that they had been drawn into the figures, history, headlines. Nowhere to hide from an M60 machine gun. The van didn't even stop. It didn't need to. Death on the run, a couple of hundred shells fired off in a matter of seconds. Hardly need to aim it.

Kathleen stirred. Belfast was just up the road really, thought Minogue, a million miles away. In Derry, a rocket-propelled grenade had blown in the wall of a garage which housed some city buses. "If it's not American, it's Russian," Minogue murmured. That was psychology, a message, an experiment to show they had got them and it could have been you. Kathleen blessed herself.

"God look down on them and all belonging to them."

And she means it, Minogue knew. At one time she had discounted the death of a British soldier in a gun battle. She had felt there was some fairness in that. He was part of an occupying army. That was back in the early seventies. Minogue agreed with her then, but with a lifetime's practice, had not said so aloud. What could be said now? Gardai had been shot and killed. Whoever had set the mine that day, whoever had tripped the switch had not been indifferent to Detective Sergeant Minogue's fate at all: there was intention there, but *nothing personal. It was the Ambassador we were after.*

Minogue remembered coming home from the hospital. There were neighbours in, tea and cake and whisky. Everything had been taken care of. It was as if he had just been married. Daithi and Iseult were serious and solicitous. Things had changed. There was new china out on the table. There were new bedspreads and sheets and a bottle of Redbreast in the cabinet below. It was only then that Minogue had realised, quite neutrally as he sat in the deck-chair beside the rhubarb, that he had nearly died. He had prepared a list that day which ran to one hundred and eighty-three items:

4. I will not hate my brother Mick for supporting the IRA.
5. I will not cause Kathleen to worry, so I'll accept the transfer out.
12. I will kiss Daithi and Iseult daily, at least once, even in public.
25. I will accompany Kathleen down the pier as often as she requests.
57. I will continue to be a republican in spite of this.
59. I will visit the National Gallery at least once a week and I will see each painting afresh.
114. I will not lean upon the church.
136. I will live in Dublin as long as Kathleen wants to.
147. I will not treat young people as upstarts.
160. I will learn to play Ravel's Pavane on the piano.

Minogue lived again.

"They put me on a case. It's a murder investigation."

Herlighy, the psychiatrist, didn't say anything. Minogue resisted saying more. He let the silence last for a minute.

"To see if I'm serviceable, I suppose. To see if I'm the full round of the clock again. I'm to start this afternoon," Minogue added.

"Can you do it, do you feel?" Herlighy asked.

"Yes. I'm not that leery about it really. They've given me a free hand so far as I can make out," Minogue replied.

It was toward the end of the session. Time had passed quickly for Minogue. He was aware of the hidden expectation that he should talk. That went against his habits and it irritated him frequently. Nonetheless he saw the use of being here.

"And the sleep?" Herlighy asked.

"Oh great. The odd time I wake up early but sure that's normal. If I can use that word. I understand it's not in vogue."

Herlighy smiled briefly.

"You deserve a lot of credit for that, Matt, that you're doing so much," Herlighy said slowly.

Minogue laughed to hide his embarrassment and pleasure.

"Ah sure, time and tide, you know."

"Well, I'm sure you know how much resistance there is to getting proper advice as you have done."

"The wife's idea," Minogue rejoined quickly. "She knows what the score is. She had it herself years ago. I used to think that I should have gone to the sessions with her, you know. I think I was too mad though, and I didn't know it. I shouldn't say mad, I suppose. More like I was raging. Wouldn't listen to anyone. Not much help to Kathleen, I expect, no. But ... that's done with."

"The first child?" Herlighy said.

"Yes," Minogue said softly.

Minogue and Herlighy were walking slowly around Merrion Square. They had stepped out from the psychiatrist's office at Minogue's request. They kept to the outer route where the paths were closest to the railings. The railings were quite buried by the shrubs and trees. Merrion Square held its Georgian grace to all four sides. As the two men walked slowly along the path, views of the eighteenth-century houses emerged between the trees. Here a row of windows, ivy cosseting railings which formed balconies on some, there a door at once simple and refined.

As usual, Minogue did the leading. He was walking slower today, Herlighy noticed. Minogue had not hesitated to ask for an 'out' day today. On his first visit to Herlighy's office, Minogue had gazed out the long windows onto the square. He had been surprised when Herlighy had simply asked him at the next session:

"Do you want to go out there? There's no need for us to be in here at all."

Minogue had been amused too, but not suspicious.

"You mean it's all right to be out there? I thought you had to be in a room, like going to confession."

"Interesting idea. No. I find it helps," Herlighy had replied.

Herlighy was still puzzled. On the one hand, Minogue seemed bound up, complete and self-assured all these months. Then he was speculative and yearning, even playful sometimes. Must play hell with him, having to work as a cop: 'unsuited' written all over him.

Minogue seemed to be thriving, despite the trauma after the explosion. Had he been faking it? Why did he seek out these sessions then?

What did he want to tell? Herlighy still believed in Minogue's need to confess. Guilt was the motor for this, survivor guilt. There was some other story coming through, like a descant, but still faint however. Some old story in Minogue was starting to talk again.

Herlighy often felt nervous with Minogue. He felt that Minogue was ready to confront something soon. Oddly, he also found himself looking forward to their sessions. He had begun hypnosis with Minogue five sessions back. For a cop, Minogue was neither suspicious nor hostile.

"How's your list coming along?" Herlighy asked.

"Great, so it is. Once you get over the first ten or so, you can't stop. I think I could go on to a thousand," Minogue replied.

"Good," Herlighy said.

"I'm working on a few of them actually, bit by bit. Funny, I have the craving for a smoke again," Minogue added.

They walked on in silence.

"Some of them are hard, but I'm doing all right," Minogue murmured.

Herlighy's eyebrows went up, and he slowed the pace so Minogue would notice.

"With the children, like. I'm more ... more: I shouldn't say 'physical.' More direct, like. I always wanted to be. You were definitely right about that, I can tell you," Minogue said.

Herlighy noted Minogue's embarrassment. They resumed their walk, under the trees.

Just after eleven o'clock, Agnes McGuire arrived unannounced at the door of Minogue's office. She stood in the threshold.

"I'm Agnes McGuire. You were looking for me."

Minogue was taken aback. He stood quickly, his mind alive with details. Her accent carried up the ends of words and phrases and it added what southerners mistook for earnestness. A soft hiss on the *s,* a changing of vowels.

Agnes McGuire had dark red hair and a pale face. Her eyes had red edges to them. The centres were gentian. Thin hands joined in front of a handknit cardigan. In a sense which shocked him, Minogue abruptly decided that Agnes McGuire was somehow used to grieving.

"Will you sit down please, Miss McGuire?"

"Agnes will do," she said.

"And you can call me Matt if you wish. Agnes, I'll be asking you questions which you may find very trying. I don't need to tell you that we want to get to the bottom of this thing as quickly as possible and although part will be painful to you, I trust you believe that it'll be worth something in the end. Every little thing counts."

"Well, do you think it was a madman who did this, Mr Minogue?" said Agnes.

"Because, to be quite frank, I don't think it was at all. That is what bothers me the most, you know," she continued.

Minogue decided to level with her.

"I can tell you that we don't have much to go on right now. It's not one of those things that results in an arrest within a matter of hours. Do you know how much of this kind of thing is done by another member of the family, a relative, a falling out among friends? This young man's background suggests none of that at all. Unfortunately Jarlath's parents are too distraught to recall a thing with any clarity, but, to be honest, I expect they will have little to offer to help find a resolution. If you follow my reasoning, or should I say, my speculation, I'm thinking of what happened as an event in this area, not just geographically, but in this part of Jarlath's life. College, his life here. Does that sound a bit cracked to you, Agnes?"

Agnes didn't reply immediately. She toyed with her long fingers and then looked to the window.

"I follow you. I didn't want to think like that. Jarlath was not what you might call an extremist." Was she smiling faintly?

"You're saying that Jarlath would not have been involved with radical student politics, whatever they might be?"

"Far from it. Jarlath was always talking about the Enlightenment. That sounds daft, doesn't it? Well, he thought that Irish people had to become more rational, more enterprising about politics."

Minogue said nothing. He waited.

"I suppose it was like a debating club with him really. But it's no sin to be naive. Or is it? Sure, he was laughed at by some of the students here. You know, the 'bourgeois apologist,' the 'light weight' tags here. I think they were jealous of him, do you know that? He had an optimism that they hadn't. I remember one of the sociology crowd telling him that he needed to visit the North once in a while to get to reality, that he needed to get out of his cosy middle class ghetto in Foxrock. It's like the Malone Road, I suppose. You know what was so silly about that? These radicals came from the same backgrounds. They felt they had to be full of thunder and opinions because they felt guilty about being well-to-do."

Minogue believed in wisdom at twenty for he had felt it stirring in himself at that age.

"Jarlath comes across as a gentle type of lad the way you talk," he said quietly.

Had to do it, damn and blast it, thought Minogue. Of course she began to cry and wasn't that the idea, you cruel bastard? When Agnes stopped crying, Minogue asked her:

"Agnes, can you tell me if Jarlath had any notion of drugs?"

"No. He had nothing to do with them. You can be sure of that."

Although Minogue had read the preliminary statements taken from Agnes that Friday, he needed to go back and flesh out the details. Agnes made no protest. She spoke as if reciting. They had both studied in the library–the 1937 Reading Room–until a bit after eight. They skipped tea-time. Then they went to her rooms where she prepared a meal. *Linguini?* Strips of pasta. A bit of meat made into a sauce. They had a couple of glasses of wine. They talked a bit, then he left. About half past ten. *Did they arrange to meet? Anything out of the ordinary they talked about?* No, a plan for a cycling holiday in France. *Oh, Jarlath wanted to visit Belfast. Curious?* No, she smiled. He had never been there, said he wanted to. *Were they thinking of going steady, getting engaged?* Pause. No. *Did he leave any belongings in her rooms?* No, he took everything in his bag. The bag was falling apart, she said. *Hmm.*

"His school-bag?" asked Minogue, with a slight stir in his stomach.

"No, that was gone. He had it stolen from him. He had to sneak in home with his shopping bag so no one'd see him. The one that was taken was a present from his mother so there'd be wigs on the green if they found out."

"Stolen in college?"

"Right out of his locker, locked and all."

"And did he have valuables in it?"

"Not really. He caught up on the lecture notes by borrowing. Notebooks and bits of things went. A fountain pen he won in debating competition in secondary school. A snap of me." She blushed lightly.

A minute's silence filled the room. It seemed to rest on the grey light which morning had brought to this part of the college. Minogue remembered that it was sunny on the other side of the square when he came in. He felt Agnes willing herself not to cry. He pretended to note things on his sheets. He was thinking of Iseult. Agnes' composure had returned.

"Agnes, if you don't think it's forward of me, may I invite you to come for coffee with me above in Bewley's? I'm allowed some freedom on this case and I intend to sustain myself well. A sticky bun. Maybe we'll risk a large white coffee too, upstairs. If I'm not presuming too much ..."

Upstairs in Bewley's the sun roared in the windows, shocking the wood into showing different hues. The newspapers were luminous sheets in the rage of light. From halfway across the room, he could see where an old man hadn't shaved. Minogue didn't ask any more about Jarlath Walsh. Nor did he mention anything about the North. Emboldened by the coffee, Minogue found himself talking with a young woman his daughter's age about the National Gallery and the recitals he planned to go to.

He talked on and on. Agnes looked from him to the sunlit windows and then back. Sometimes she laughed aloud. Minogue, for his part, kept on talking while the sunlight–in its slow and grudging move through Dublin–graced the next table.

Minogue's profligacy with time still allowed him to see Captain Loftus before dinner-time. He climbed the circular staircase slowly, trying to sort out the impressions. History, an alien history, came to him with the lavender smell of floor polish and the echoes of his own footsteps. As he mounted the staircase, his hand rested at times on a varnished banister. Below and to the left of him always, the flagged floor turned lazily with Minogue's ascent.

He knocked and pushed at a heavy door. Loftus turned from a cabinet.

"Ah, Sergeant ..."

"Minogue."

"Indeed. Is it me you came to see?"

"To be sure. I was hoping to find out more about that boy's locker. It was broken open some time ago. Do ye keep any reports on such goings-on in the college?" Minogue asked.

"Let me see ..."

Loftus opened a drawer and glanced at a document. Minogue worked hard to conceal his humour, or rather his ill humour. He smelled a cloying scent of aftershave off Loftus. Let me see, indeed. Let me see your Aunt Fanny's fat agricultural arse.

"Some three weeks ago, Sergeant. Four lockers were broken open. As a matter of policy we don't trouble the Gardai with these things.

Little enough was lost. Notes, someone's rugby shirt, another lad's lunch." Loftus smiled.

"Jarlath Walsh's bag."

Loftus looked back at the sheet.

"Yes, that too. Yes"

"Do you by chance have a list of the items reported stolen, Captain Loftus? Might I see it?"

"No problem," said Loftus.

Must have learned the 'no problem' stuff off the Yanks. Jarlath Walsh, 24 South Park, Foxrock, County Dublin: one leather briefcase, black, containing two notebooks and various lecture notes, mementoes/ personal, no cash, pens, pencils, a tape recorder.

"A tape recorder?"

"Apparently so. Mr Walsh likely used it for lectures, I expect."

"What's the usual routine on this stuff, Captain?"

"Eventually compensation. We stress that the college is not liable for damage or theft, but we don't like to leave people hanging. Especially in this case. I had authorised payment to Mr Walsh the day I heard the news."

"Yes. I suspect that the thief used a crowbar or the end of a heavy screwdriver. Determined. You'll understand, Sergeant, that manpower needs preclude constant patrols."

"Dublin isn't what it used to be, is it, Captain?"

"Indeed, Sergeant. The needs must. We do what we can. A person desperate for anything to steal really. A drinking problem. Maybe just vandalism."

Yes, thought Minogue, *plenty of that. Drive out by Tallaght in your BMW on the way home to your enclave. You'd probably spend your next few weekends adding glass to the top of your walls.*

"Thank you, Captain."

Minogue phoned in a want card on a tape recorder and a black leather briefcase if any citizen should turn it in. Fat chance. He phoned Kilmartin's office.

"Matt, the hard man."

"Jimmy, how are you? Any give on the spot where this Walsh boy was killed?"

"Divil a bit, Matt. The two lads from Pearse Street scoured the college looking all day yesterday. Did you bump into them at all?"

"No."

"Well, the gist of it is that they found nothing. Tell you the truth,

I think they're praying for rain so that they have the excuse to give it up. They are wall-eyed after a day of that. The fellas in Pearse Street found nothing on the weekend anyway."

"Hmm ..."

"Do you want manpower?"

"No thanks, Jimmy. Slowly but surely. I'll put a few notes together and rocket them over to you."

"Incidentally. Connors is gone to the Walshes to go over things with them. Save you the trouble. He needs the practice in this kind of thing. A bit weak in the shell. Have a look at what he says tomorrow."

Minogue put down the phone. He was glad he didn't have to interview the parents. He thought about Loftus, about how he wanted to show he was running a tight ship. What was he hiding, though? Crossing Front Square toward the room he had been assigned at the college, Minogue passed Mick Roche.

"How'ya, Mick?"

"And yourself, Sergeant?"

"Will you direct me to Dr Allen's place?"

"The headbanger? The psychology fella. Oh yeah, you'll have no trouble finding him. Follow the crowds."

"How do you mean?"

"Just joking. He's a bit of a guru. He has a loyal following, especially in Agnes McGuire."

Minogue followed directions to Allen's office in New Square. Allen greeted him with a tight handshake. He seemed to have expected him.

"Professor Allen. Thank you for your time. I tried to make an appointment but your line was engaged."

Minogue examined Allen's face. He was drawn to the eyes. Unbotherable, confident. The eyes rested on an outdoor face which looked open. A full head of hair, though quite grey. An attractive man to women, Minogue concurred without thinking about it. Allen was dressed casually. He had stepped out of his shoes. His fortyish face smiled in an unsmile, a formal ease.

"I sometimes leave the phone off the hook. Things find me eventually and the more necessary ones will reach me first, I find."

"Sergeant Matt Minogue," and Minogue proffered a hand.

"Not Malone, then. That clears that up," Allen smiled.

They sat. Minogue glanced at the rubbings of figures taken, he guessed, from old stones lying around the ditches of Ireland or from monuments as they were called. These poster-size rubbings were all of whorl patterns.

"They're very nice, Professor Allen. The rubbings. They're hard to do though. I did them as a child."

"Minogue. That's a Clare name, is it not?"

"It is to be sure. And yourself?"

"I'm an Englishman actually. What you hear is an overlay of ten years of being in Ireland, with a heavy foundation of Lancashire."

"You'd never know it."

"More Irish than the Irish themselves you might say, Sergeant."

He had the charm and the small talk too, Minogue reflected.

"Actually, my mother was Irish. An emigrant. Regrettably, she died before she could return for her old age."

"A hard thing to leave go of, the mother country. How well you knew I was from Clare now."

"I do a lot of ethnography, more as a hobby. See this?" Allen pointed to one of the rubbings.

"I got it in West Clare. I went on a dig some years ago in Sardinia and I found a pattern almost identical to this one. A type of mandala. Some people get a bit upset about finding these kinds of similarities, isn't that odd?"

"It is, I suppose," Minogue allowed.

"People don't like to realise that others had the same inspirations or troubles or joys as countless others. Sort of offends against one's sense of uniqueness. Our treasured assumptions about how we control the world."

"You have me there," Minogue murmured.

"It's nothing really. Some of us think that causes and effects are out of our hands. Other people like to think they have more control over things. Illusion really, but it's the belief that counts."

"Superstition, like?"

"In a sense, yes. Look at Americans for instance. They seem to think they can do just about anything. They have a nice, cosy, irrational belief in Progress. Now, Irish people are a bit passive perhaps, but there's history too ... Shouldn't generalise really."

"Well you've given me a lot to be thinking about now, Dr Allen," Minogue said thoughtfully.

"I wonder," Allen replied, "I wonder why I'm telling you this. It's not what you're here for, is it? Maybe you have some facility as a seer, drawing out things."

Minogue affected to be surprised. He laughed lightly.

"Ah, I'm a bit pedestrian at the best of times. But continuing on from what you were saying about people believing they can effect things, can I ask you where you'd place Jarlath Walsh there?"

Allen sat back and crossed his legs at the ankles. His forehead moved slightly and his hair moved with it.

"Hmm. Interesting you should ask. Yes. You know of course that what I say is not in the nature of a report. Mr Walsh attended one lecture a week with me. I hardly knew him. I'm not sure why he chose to do this course."

He paused as if to think deeply. 'Switched into his official style,' Minogue memoed himself.

"I can't say that Mr Walsh was the brightest student in the class. He definitely had an interest in the subject as a whole, but from an essay he wrote me at Christmas I feel that he didn't have the background for attempting what he appeared to be attempting."

"What was that?"

"Well, he was trying to develop a psychology of a typical Irish person, I suppose you would say."

Allen's forehead went up again and he studied his toes. "Let me see if I can explain, Sergeant. Stuff like this might have worked in the last century. No, I should be more charitable about it ... Psychology has come a long way from metaphysics in the last century. Mr Walsh wanted to plug in an easy theory into his understanding of Irish politics. He had taken an interest in the violence in the North, of all things. Let's say more than others in the Republic anyway. I suppose he thought there was a simple psychological solution. He was quite emphatic about this. One can understand naive enthusiasm, but Mr Walsh had not moved from this position. There's quite an attraction for people in this stuff about national character. You hear a lot of it. The Russians are supposed to be dour and bearish people who favour despots, or the Irish are charming dodgers. Any good psychology has to account for individual differences as well as commonalities across cultures. Mr Walsh was tempted to reach for what we call Grand Theory." Allen paused. A trace of amusement passed over his face.

"Am I lecturing?" he asked softly, as if taken aback at a great new understanding of himself.

"Not a bit of it," replied Minogue with conviction.

"It may be that Irish people don't feel they can effect any solutions in the North. Pessimism and acceptance. However, one can't be too careful with those wild, huge hypotheses. With Jarlath Walsh, it was becoming a Pollyanna-ish thing really. Still, he had done a lot of work and he got better than a passing mark."

Minogue was thinking about Agnes McGuire. Maybe she was lying down in her room, thinking of the boy. Perhaps Walsh had been learning something but not something a university could teach. He had found Agnes anyway. Why wouldn't a callow young man believe that some psychology could fix the mess up North? It would have that attractive simplicity, a parallel to feelings which were newly arrived to him with Agnes perhaps, and he could have swept away with inexperience and optimism.

"I think I see what you mean. Tell me, did you know that Jarlath had a relationship, can I say, with a student in your class? Agnes McGuire, she's in your class too, am I right?"

"Yes. You may have touched on the chief reason he was in the class in the first place."

Minogue could detect no trace of sarcasm in Allen's voice. As if in answer, Allen said:

"I'm not being flippant or dismissive. Have you spoken with her yet?"

"This very day," Minogue replied.

"Perhaps lecturers are not supposed to notice, but I think Mr Walsh was very taken with her."

"I had the same impression. Like we say though, she's young."

"Ah but, Sergeant, years aren't everything. I imagine there was a wealth of difference between her and Mr Walsh. Sometimes the facts, big as they are, escape us."

"In. . .?"

"Agnes McGuire has lived through a lot, Sergeant."

"Oh yes. Belfast."

"And more," Allen replied, leaning forward in his chair to ruin Minogue's day.

"Her father was a magistrate in Belfast. He was assassinated three years ago."

Minogue felt as if the afternoon had run in a window and fallen on top of him. It wasn't the faint touch of smugness in the delivery that suggested he hadn't done his homework. It was more the thought of Agnes' composure, the control she had. She had had the cruellest practice.

The silence in the room lasted a full minute.

"Three years."

"I'm Agnes' tutor. We take on groups of students to help and advise them. She was assigned to me alphabetically. My specialty is in the psychology of aggression, of all things. I do public lectures all around Ireland, North and South. Everything's coloured by what happens in the North, of course. Here I was, sitting across the table from her. I'm trained in various therapy techniques, you see. I expected that she'd be a candidate for help. Given the right suggestions, learning is improved, relationships bloom. I cannot disclose anything of our chats, you'll understand, but let me tell you that Agnes McGuire gives credence to some unfashionable notions. Health, freedom ..."

"Strange to think ..." Minogue began.

"That she and Walsh could get along? She's Catholic. Her father was killed by Protestant extremists. Isn't that something in itself?"

"I don't follow," Minogue said.

"You'd think they'd leave him alone, wouldn't you? I mean they talk about law and order and enforcing the rule of law when it suits them. The thing was that McGuire was the one who started the process of getting Loyalist paramilitaries behind bars, not just the IRA. I imagine the other side couldn't countenance a Catholic putting away one of theirs, no matter that he was part of the institutions they said they were fighting for."

Minogue said nothing. A whorl of pity eddied down his stomach. No, not pity: regret.

"So much for rationality and politics," Allen said.

"So much indeed," Minogue muttered.

It was beginning to dawn on Minogue that Jarlath Walsh had been naive all right. Still, there was a pedestrian heroism to his ideas. In the end though, what did this all have to do with his getting killed? Ireland entertained a lot of people with the most lunatic ideas. Some were even elected to promote those ideas.

Minogue made to go. Allen's eyes had gone out of focus. They returned to focussing on his feet. Then he looked up at Minogue.

"Sergeant, I last saw Mr Walsh after last Thursday's lecture. That I've told you. I'm not sure if what I'll tell you now has any bearing on your investigations. For some weeks now, Walsh has been asking me privately at the end of the lectures for books on the psychological effects of things like cigarettes, alcohol, narcotics and so on."

Minogue tried to look unconcerned, but apparently it didn't work.

"That shocks you a little, Sergeant?"

"I'm a bit taken aback to be sure. I'm sure that you can understand how one forms an image as one investigates someone's life." Minogue liked the sound of the way he had said that, very neutral and analytical.

"Narcotics. You mean hash and grass basically?"

"I suppose I do," Allen replied with the faintest of smiles.

Touché, thought Minogue.

Minogue recalled the bland assurances he had had from college officials about this kind of thing not being on their turf, oh no.

Minogue's mind was tired. He was beginning to feel irritable. He felt uninformed. He hadn't really one promising lead, not a sausage. Intuitions meant nothing, less than nothing, because they deflected his attention. Look: he had spent ten minutes talking about Agnes McGuire. Romancing, he was. Go home to your wife.

Chapter Five

Instead of going home to his wife, a contrary Minogue knocked on Captain Loftus' door. He caught Loftus leaving. Loftus stood in the doorway, half-coated, reaching for the sleeve. The office had a strong smell of aftershave.

"A minute of your time, Captain. I'd like to see Walsh's locker."

"Ah, that'll be a job. I'm afraid those lockers were too badly damaged now. They've been replaced."

Minogue felt the beginnings of indignation.

"I had the understanding that the lock was jemmied. They'd be those little locks you get in Woolworth's. There'd hardly be damage to the locker itself though, would there?"

Loftus dodged, pretending to search for keys in his pocket.

"There was a lot of damage done, Sergeant. The hinges were torn out. You can't just weld on a door. They make you buy the whole unit. There was nothing for it but to be rid of them."

"Where are they now?"

"They'd be gone to the dump, I expect. Good for nothing."

"Actually, Captain, they'd be good for my investigation. When did you have them taken down?"

"Last week, sometime," Loftus replied.

"Friday, then?"

"It might have been that late, yes."

"Who gave the order?"

"The requisition...? I did."

"So there'd be a record of the date."

Loftus stopped fiddling. He stood to his full height.

"Sergeant Minogue. I'm beginning to wonder if you're not overworking yourself here."

"Let me enlighten you then, Captain, because I think you're not enlightening me much. Now I didn't get out of bed on the wrong side this morning, but that doesn't mean that I'm interested in getting the run-around. I'm paid to look into all the bits and pieces."

"An empty, damaged locker, Sergeant?" Loftus said slowly to heighten the effect.

Minogue didn't reply. He didn't want to tell Loftus that he'd wanted to look for signs of what might have been in the locker. He wondered if Allen had misread the questions that Jarlath Walsh had put to him. Minogue was beginning to believe that this was the case. Minogue guessed that the boy wanted the information for something more prosaic, like a debate. He caught a little of this Jarlath Walsh and it wasn't encouraging. A boy, not a man, tipsy on book-learning, his trust in the power of reason, boyscout's honour. Knowledge is power for good: Walsh was a dupe for the university. No. He was a trier. Minogue was dried up with cynicism. Maybe. Walsh didn't have the edges smoothed out by experience yet. He noticed that Loftus was eying him. Why not give him a swipe?

"It may look odd to you, Captain. Let me be candid. This student wasn't killed by some random act. All the signs are against it. He had something, he did something or he knew something. He probably didn't know that he did any of these things. At least not powerful enough to warrant his murder. I'm no Agatha Christie, and I don't have a computer to calculate odds. The thoughts I'm having are what they call hunches in the thrillers. The word 'drugs' keeps popping into my head. I hear it a lot. Dublin isn't what it used to be. Nor, might I add, is Trinity College or its students. What do you think?"

Loftus' nostrils had been sucked in. Minogue recognised signs of breath held in. Loftus was staring intently at him, struggling with a decision. Then, abruptly, he turned away. He took off his coat with an air of resignation and he walked around to the other side of his desk. He fumbled with his keys and unlocked the desk. Without a search, Loftus drew out a large envelope. He handed it to Minogue. Minogue saw defiance in the place of the smugness he had read on the face before.

Minogue removed the note and read it. It had been typed, poorly.

JARLATH WALSH MAKES A MOCKERY OF THIS COLLEGE. WHO WILL ACT?
WALSH TRAFFICS IN DRUGS. DRUGS POISON PEOPLE. DON'T BE DECEIVED.
ACT. WALSH'S FRUIT IMPORTS LOOKS AS INNOCENT AS WALSH.

Minogue read over the note again. Loftus sat down.

"Get many hoaxes, Captain? Your students here have a reputation for high jinks."

"My thoughts exactly, Sergeant." Was there a hint of vengeance in his voice?

"I made a decision quite awhile ago. Forbidden fruit is a lot less tasty when there's no talk about it."

"I don't follow your analogy, Captain."

"My chief concern here is not whether this note was written in a serious vein or not. I'm sure there are people capable of trying to ruin someone's good name for spite. I'm sure there are self-appointed people whose paranoia leads them to make serious accusations without any reasonable evidence too."

"So...?" Minogue probed.

"On balance, I think this is just a malicious slur," Loftus said slowly.

"Hmm," from Minogue.

"The way we see it here, Sergeant, the more talk of drugs the students hear, the more glamourous the stuff appears. You know how it is at that age. It's the same thing with the bank robberies and the shooting: glamour. We deal with so-called drug problems in the college in a very low-key way. We're not entirely naive in here about the ways of the world out there. We go through the Drug Squad when we need to. Check that out and you'll find how good our liaison is with the Gardai."

Minogue wasn't listening. He was thinking of the way Loftus was saying "we."

"A person of lesser sophistication might call this sweeping things under the table, Captain," Minogue offered.

"The college doesn't employ such persons, Sergeant," replied Loftus.

Minogue realised all of a sudden that a few years ago he might have gotten on his own high horse with this sparrowfart.

"Uh," Minogue said, trying to appear thoughtful.

"So whether I believe this rubbish or not has little to do with the matter at hand for me. Of course I cannot stop you believing what you will. We're all responsible for the good name of the college in here. It's not so much security as reputation. That is a commodity, once traded, impossible to buy back. This is the college of Edmund Burke and Oliver Goldsmith. Samuel Beckett too, if that's your fancy. Our graduates and our students as well as our staff are our stock of good will."

Minogue was tiring of this speech. He wondered if Loftus had practised this one or had used it before. Minogue also wondered if he should be standing here barefoot and illiterate as his ancestors had been, while this haven of scholarship buttered up the gentry whose daddies had sent the bailiff to batter down peasant houses. Careful, Minogue, your inferiority complexes are showing.

"We see this current fetish with drugs as part of history, you might say," Loftus was saying. "It's a small part of our first four hundred years and we'll ride it out."

A picture of Mary Brosnahan, the cleaning-woman who had tripped across the body, came into Minogue's mind. Her statement read like an apology for nearly having dirtied the college with her discovery. Why this loyalty, and she paid little enough, and her knees probably gone these years? And Walsh, trusting in reasonable propositions, boyscout's honour. Loyalty to those notions on this island?

"I take your point, Captain. I'll be dispensing with pleasantries as such while I effect economical answers to present concerns. Doubtless you'll see to the reputation of the place in your own good time. Now: why did you remove the locker in its entirety only on Friday? When did you get this note? Before answering, be assured that this is a very serious matter and I'm well able to step on toes."

Loftus' answer immediately gave Minogue the impression that Loftus had prepared for this eventuality.

"I take it you've not been in the army, Sergeant. I'd know it if you had been. You don't need to look beyond a man's bearing and general attitude to know one of our own. Finbar Walsh, the boy's father, and I had the privilege of serving together. It was for a short time only and it was quite a number of years ago. Mr Walsh was a senior officer to me and the army lost a valuable man when Mr Walsh left. I was happy for him that he managed to be so successful in business. I don't give a god's curse basically if there's one iota of truth in this note or not. If indeed there is some substance to it, you can be certain that my loyalties are to the college and this man's reputation. Particularly so because the boy is now deceased. Don't mistake me. I want to see the culprit caught too."

Great speech, thought Minogue. He nodded resignedly.

"And something else too. I hope you don't mistake my concerns for obstruction. I suspect that you haven't been adequately briefed by your superiors on this matter. As for myself, I'm not a desk jockey with no backing," Loftus said with a tight smile.

"There are things that matter more than incidents," he added with a tone of finality.

Minogue was sure now that he loathed this twit. Loftus had stopped little short of a criminal offence. The thing was that there was no point in throwing the book at the likes of Loftus. He'd probably been given the lead from someone else anyway.

Loftus wouldn't have said what he did without some umbrella, some nod from a handler. Probably your man with the tweed brain, Griffiths. All sweet eminent reason, of course. What was more, the note might well be rubbish, a bad joke, and nothing would come of tests on the bloody locker anyway. Notebooks and a bag. Far too like James Bond.

Minogue looked at the sliver of sunlight which the late afternoon had carried into the office. It held playing motes of dust and it showed up the grain on the edges of the desk. History rolls on like the afternoon. Time and tide. Jarlath Walsh would be buried tomorrow. The parents would be in no condition to talk tomorrow. Connors would draw a big duck egg there too. Well, Minogue decided, with a finality quite alien to the dreamy light around him, might as well leave this twit hanging.

"Be so kind as to give me that note and an envelope to hold it. It will be returned to you when we have gone over it. Good day to you, Captain Loftus. We'll be meeting again perhaps. You have a way to get in touch with me?"

Loftus nodded once.

Minogue smelled wax and confidence in this building as he walked down the stairs. Immovable, assured.

Minogue awoke to the sounds of rain. It had been raining for some time because the heavy, slow *pat-pat* of the drops oozing from under the gutter was a steady pattern of sound. Minogue swore silently. He could see the rain washing away the traces of a murder. He saw the water swirling toward a drain, a face grinning. It was Loftus' face.

The dawn light came into the bedroom like smoke. Minogue crept out of the bed and went downstairs. He made tea and turned on the radio low. Then he switched on a bar of the electric heater and leaned closer to the radio. He craved a smoke. Not even the stay in hospital had given him the urge as strongly as this.

It was too early for Radio Eireann. Minogue turned to the BBC just in time to catch the tail end of a sentence.

". . . at his front door in Limavady about seven o'clock last night. A spokesman for the RUC confirmed that Mr Elgie had received death threats in the past. Mr Elgie was active in the Peace Now movement in Northern Ireland. He is the forty-seventh civilian to die of violence in Northern Ireland this year. Security forces are reportedly stepping up searches and surveillance in the area in the wake of several shootings in this area within the last fortnight. A spokesman for the Army did not deny that all the shootings appear to be part of a pattern as similar weapons have been used in recent incidents. Concern was voiced during question period in the House of Commons that more weapons appear to be entering Northern Ireland. Rocket-propelled grenades and heavy calibre machine-guns have been used in ambushes in South Armagh. Police believe that Mr Elgie was killed with a Russian-made semi-automatic rifle. So far, no organisation has claimed responsibility for the murder. Conservative MP Mr Stanley Robinson accused the government of the Irish Republic of being lax in border security. Mr Robinson said that the IRA is indiscriminate in its use of weapons and sources of supply and this indicates how bankrupt their politics are. The Prime Minister today visited . . ."

Minogue felt awake enough to want to go back to bed. Words like 'terrorist' and 'security forces' rolled off the announcer's tongue just like that. Indiscriminate, lax. It was all loaded of course, we can expect no less, Minogue thought. His wakening mind rambled on to an image of Allen and the work he was doing. Seemed so calm, so rational, even confident. Did he really believe that his lectures could change people?

In many ways, Allen was a man to be admired. He didn't hide in the academic cloister. Instead, he went out and gave ideas their acid test, to see if they could make change happen. A composed man, a bit cautious, but with assurance. He didn't miss much. Imagine an Englishman knowing so much about Ireland. Well it just went to prove that the Irish and the English were not inevitable enemies due to some chemistry or geography.

Agnes McGuire had composure and pride too. She seemed to be able to take it all in and to transcend it, but a sadness lingered. It actually shone out of her. Maybe Allen, as her tutor, had been able to help her make sense of things. But hadn't Allen said that she didn't need him to sort things out for herself? She had begun to soften and shape poor Walsh even, the son of parents and a country who didn't want to know about the North but wanted to be left alone with their lawns and their holidays.

Minogue abruptly realised that he hadn't touched on the relationship between her and Jarlath. Reserve, politeness? A cloud of doubt passed over the prospect of the day's work ahead. He could spin it out in the college for another day or two and that would be that, unless Connors had something from the parents or prints showed on the note.

Kathleen shouldered the door open gently.

"Matt. You're up."

"Good morning, madam," Minogue replied, the advantage of tea resting him on the high ground of talk. "I awoke early. I may be entering my dotage."

"Is it the job?" Kathleen asked.

"No, lovey. The rain woke me, so it did."

Later, when Daithi and Iseult appeared at the table, Minogue couldn't keep his eyes off them. It occurred to him that he might indeed be going dotty to be scrutinising them like this. Daithi looked up from his cornflakes several times. Finally he raised his hands.

"Honest to God, I didn't do it," he said.

"What?" Minogue said.

"Whatever it is, I didn't do it. If you're looking at me bloodshot eyes, it's the library to blame."

As they left Minogue's car outside the university, Minogue managed to kiss both of his children. Iseult blushed and drew away a little, her eyelashes down. Daithi was more than bashful and he tried to ease his father's caprice as well as his own irritation.

"We can't go on meeting like this, darling."

There might be something in that remark, Minogue thought as he drove off.

Kilmartin was sitting behind a copy of the *Irish Independent*. It crumpled down as he began his effusive greeting. Greeks bearing gifts, Minogue figured.

"Matt, me old ball and socket," Kilmartin said. "How is she cutting?"

"Fair to middling. Nothing to write home about."

Both sat. This is not like him, Minogue registered. For his part,

Kilmartin felt a companion gas pain. Its occurrence marked awkward moments in his life, a constant sentinel these days. He hoped he wouldn't have to fart here in this office. Better hurry it up, Minogue knows there's something in the wind.

"I took the liberty of bringing along Connors' notes of the interview with the Walsh boy's parents. A very sad business to be sure, to be sure. The missus is under sedation. She might have to go into hospital. Do you know, her memory is gone almost completely. She remembers the boy as a youngster and little else."

"An interview? Yesterday?" Minogue said.

"Well, a few words to be exact. Connors just kept his ears open."

"The Da?" Minogue led.

"Oh he's a very busy man, you might say. Very busy, yes," Kilmartin said with reluctance.

"Not saying he wasn't a good father at all, don't get me wrong. Let's say he let the wife look after domestic things. And the family sort of fell under that heading. At the moment, Connors said he doesn't know whether he's coming or going really. That's the gist of it," Kilmartin concluded.

"Thanks. I'll go through it myself later."

"And the bloody rain has put the kybosh on searching for the murder-site. Isn't that the divil?" Kilmartin said.

"It is," Minogue allowed.

"And I have to sit in on these meetings to do with the latest stuff in the North. Would you credit it but we're all involved? There's to be some of that crowd from A division up in the North—you know, the joint RUC and Special Branch thing they have up there. They'll be sitting in too. They have the wind up, so they do. I don't mind telling you, Matt, that that particular crowd has hooligans in it, what with the way they treat people in Castlerea ..."

And what about our own Heavy Gang here in the South, Minogue mused inwardly. Banana republic. Kilmartin lit a cigarette and inhaled. Minogue glanced over the transcriptions of Connors' notes.

"Not so hot, is it?" Kilmartin offered.

"Best he could do, I suppose," Minogue replied.

"You're managing OK though," Kilmartin said tentatively. "Overall, like?"

Minogue studied the desktop. So that was it. Kilmartin wanted to be reassured.

"Fine, thanks. I'm always quiet like this when I'm Sherlocking cases."

"Right you be, Matt, right you be. Sure didn't I know that when I had you put on the case?"

Kilmartin smiled, affecting contentment. His belly rumbled and the pain burned him again.

"The Commissioner was inquiring after you. Asked to be remembered to you. 'Glad to hear Matt is on this one,' says he. 'The man is out on his own, so he is,' he says. 'And don't I know that myself?' says I. Isn't that the trick, Matt, picking the right people and then getting a pat on the back for the results, hah?"

It was Minogue's turn to smile. Out on his own is right. Did he mean outstanding or remote?

"Oh and he says to tell you that Wexford will wallop Clare when their turn comes," Kilmartin said with some satisfaction.

Minogue had to hand it to Jimmy Kilmartin. He was making the best of it, trusting Minogue to fill in the lines. Letting Minogue know in a low-key way. A bit of chat about what the patricians were hatching, keep in touch. He liked Kilmartin. He didn't envy Kilmartin's go-betweens, his rank, his obligations. They had known each other for twenty years. Still, Minogue was growing frustrated at waiting for the rest of it.

"So Loftus put a flea in someone's ear?" Minogue asked.

Kilmartin didn't balk.

"Yep. He was on the blower. Nothing direct, you see. Polite enquiry and exchanging pleasantries."

"And ..." Minogue waited.

"Wondering if maybe you were concentrating too much on something. You gave him a bit of heat about a locker the other day?"

"Lucky I didn't run him in for destroying evidence. There might be a drug angle to this so—"

"—and you're the man on the spot, Matt. Tell you the truth, I haven't the time of day for the likes of your man, Loftus. Just to let you know. Now if you need staff to work on this part with you, say the word. We're stretched but, you know."

"Thanks."

"Loftus was peeved. The Commissioner got the impression that you might have felt under pressure to produce results and that you were pushing a matter of little consequence."

"Sounds like Loftus talking," Minogue said. "Tell me, was the Commissioner ever in the army himself?"

Kilmartin hesitated.

"Matter of fact, now that you mention it, he was. In the early fifties. Did an unusual thing, changed career. Paid off."

"The contacts are always there," Minogue observed delicately.

"Look, Matt. That note–I know about it–is from a crank or some yo-yo who didn't like Walsh. As for his Da's importing fruit and the like, well you can't get much for bananas on the drug market here. Walsh wouldn't know one end of a reefer from the other. Neither would the young lad, God be good to him. It's just a student thing. You know how the papers would lap up any stuff like that though. That's Loftus' peeve, I'm sure."

"One of the boy's professors told me he had an interest in the effects of various drugs," Minogue said.

"Ah," Kilmartin sighed. "Well, that's how I tend to think about it meself. He probably wanted to have something ready to say to his pals if they were poking fun at him for not smoking up. A debate maybe. He was well able to talk, by all accounts."

Neither man spoke for several seconds.

"Be that as it may, though," Minogue said quietly, "Loftus won't be the one to determine whether police work should or shouldn't pursue something, no matter how far up the bog it might look."

"Absolutely," Kilmartin said. "But listen. Maybe you did rub Loftus the wrong way, maybe a personality thing. The Commissioner is wondering if maybe your own views on things aren't squeezing in on things a bit."

"You mean Loftus and where he works? The old school tie stuff and the gentry beyond in Trinity? No."

"It's been a rough year for you, Matt, more than a lot of people could take. Wouldn't you prefer to work on another angle? Look, I can get Connors to do the legwork for you. He's a smart lad. He has his wits about him."

"No thanks," Minogue said, in the quietness which seemed to fill the room after Kilmartin's remarks.

Kilmartin turned back to the pleasantries. He did not want to leave any friction in his wake. He suffered for his understanding, however, with the knifing pain in his bowel as well as with the knowledge that Minogue read his strategies.

Chapter Six

With no plan in his head, Minogue went to Trinity College. Driving into the centre of the city, the buildings passed him in a grimy, purgatorial progression. The rain greyed everything. Women's stockings had splash marks on them. Motorists were drowning people at the streetcorners. The buses seemed to go even faster than usual. Tramps stood sodden in the streets downtown, their hair matted on their foreheads. The parking practices of Dubliners were bad enough on days you could philosophise about them, but today they were three deep in Leeson Street. Grafton Street was blocked.

Walking from his car finally, Minogue felt the gloom approach closer. No doubt it would meet him and swallow him whole in the room. Burying Walsh today. What a send-off in this downpour. Minogue shivered.

Closer to the door of the room he had been assigned, Minogue had a little change of heart. He headed off toward Agnes' rooms. Breathless after three flights of stairs, he tapped at her door. He heard footsteps inside. She opened the door and smiled faintly.

"Well, Sergeant. Come in."

She was dressed in black and grey. The outfit was a size or two too big for her, probably borrowed. The dark colours made her face even paler.

Minogue stepped in. Sitting at the table was Allen, uncharacteristically dressed in a jacket and tie.

"I was just about to leave," Allen said, rising. He turned to Agnes. "I'll be back at a quarter to. The car is parked up near Pearse Street Gate."

"Sit down, will you, Sergeant. Will it be tea?" she asked. Minogue was taken with the accent again: sot dine.

"I had hoped to carry on our conversation from yesterday, Agnes. But if I'm intruding ..." he trailed off.

"Not a bit of it."

"Well," Minogue began, "yes, tea would be grand."

He felt his heart pushing still after the climb. Agnes lit the gas, walked back into the room and sat across the table from Minogue. A picture of two people dressed up as clowns on their way out to a party hung on the wall behind her. It was at dusk and the two figures were dwarfed by the black branches of a winter coppice. Between the branches was a sky of light blue which fell imperceptibly to cream behind the trees. Miraculously, a moon held the stillness and peace without a trace of a message for the astonished Minogue. A Rousseau?

The place was very neat without being fussy. Minogue noticed that all the books were shelved alphabetically. Rain beaded the window. Drops broke away with the help of gusts and they gullied down the glass. A faint smell of gas came from the kitchenette. It was mixed with a light staleness of age, maybe a trace of bedwarmth. Nobody smoked here.

"You'll be off soon then, Agnes?"

"Dr Allen's giving me a lift out to the funeral. So ..."

"I'm still trying to figure out details, so I am. Every little thing can have a bearing. I don't know if this is the day to be pursuing it though."

"I can try in the next twenty minutes or so. I'm in one piece now. I can't say about this afternoon though," Agnes said. Her voice had the questioning quality which Minogue was familiar with from listening to Northerners. Hers had none of the suspicion or dare-me he associated with the talk he heard in that accent. He was quite mesmerised by her voice. The silence finally jolted him back from staring at the poster.

"Em. Agnes, did Jarlath ever discuss things to do with drugs with you?"

"Drugs?" she asked. Drugs. She shook her head, not taking her eyes from Minogue's.

"He wasn't the type of person. I would have known," she added. "Jarlath talked about a lot of things. I'm not sure I was listening to him all the time. It wasn't what he said or anything, it was more that he liked ideas, liked a listener."

"He had notebooks that were stolen. Would you know anything about what he used the notebooks for?" Minogue asked.

"Well, he wrote down ideas. He was full of them. Anything really, I suppose. Quotations, references maybe ... He said it made him look organised, like Woodward and Bernstein, documenting everything," Agnes said.

"Who?"

"The men who blew the whistle on Nixon. The Watergate thing. Jarlath was very interested in that stuff. He wanted to get a scoop, he said. He used to joke about it. He'd keep me in suspense, you know, pretending he had found out something big and I'd be dying to know. It'd turn out to be a yarn, having me on. He had a sense of humour.

People didn't see it very often though. They didn't give him much of a chance. He'd have me on the edge of the chair with it, and it'd turn out to be something like the Provost's cat peed on his shoes. Silly, but he did it for laughs. He wasn't the way others here thought of him, you know."

"Yes, your president beyond in the Students' Union mentioned Jarlath's interest in the journalism," Minogue said.

"Mick Roche? Not too complimentary, I'd suspect," Agnes said wryly.

"Not really. Said Jarlath had potential," Minogue said.

In between talking, he could hear the kettle gathering strength. Soon it would whistle. It dawned on Minogue that he liked this room. He would like to try this other life out for a while. Going to lectures, chatting, making friends, reading. To be this age, to be going to libraries, to be in touch. Minogue wanted to do silly things, to make mistakes.

Agnes went to the kitchenette to make the tea. Minogue listened to the numerous domestic sounds. His mind reeled effortlessly back to his own youth. Had he had a youth? Maybe that's what it is, he speculated: he didn't have a youth and he spent his adult life trying to make up for it. He didn't mind being thought of as a bit eccentric. It served as well as any other dressing. Over the years he had watched some grey creep in, even into his beard. Kathleen had bought him an electric razor. With some fascination he observed the dust of hairs which he blew out the bathroom window. His hands had lost their strength. His shoulders weren't back. Stairs reminded him of his age. His new friends looked old sometimes, straitened, very usual.

Minogue had gone all the way through school to the Leaving Certificate. He and his brother, Mick, had run the farm. Their father could do little enough after the bouts of TB. The boys were a new generation in the Irish Free State. The war on the continent had brushed them in their early teens. Big things happening abroad, the names of battles and towns and generals coming across the wireless. The Local Defence Force hanging around in ditches trying to look fierce at the occasional roadblocks. Cars were scarce on the roads.

The Christian Brothers had done their anointed task and Minogue had endured. He could almost carry on a conversation in Latin. At least he could entertain a few Romans with recitations from Livy. He remembered the stupidest things even yet: which forms took the subjunctive, expressions like *iter fecerunt,* Hannibal with the vinegar, breaking boulders in the Alps.

The odd teacher along the way indulged him. He read out parts of the *Aeneid* by gaslight at home in the kitchen. His parents listened with a reverence for the holiness that Latin brought to the house. His father would cough and say that Virgil borrowed his stuff from the Irish stories.

They heard about camps for Jews on the continent. A lay teacher risked George Orwell, God forbid, and even loaned Minogue books by Steinbeck and Sinclair Lewis. The wet fields waited for them in the spring. One of the fields might flood. A pig might get stuck in a dike. They bought a tractor, the talk of the townland.

In school, the civics classes taught you codes of conduct. May brought the altar to the Blessed Virgin into the classroom, lilacs inevitably. The Catechism showed him how to answer hypothetical questions which a Protestant might ask you if you were in a bus, say. No opportunity for converting was to be lost. Minogue's mother thought that one of her sons might have a vocation for the priesthood. She fastened her hopes on Mick and he turned toward her hope. Minogue watched his sisters grow up, do Civil Service exams, go to dances, get a job in the bank and more. Minogue stayed on the farm while Mick deliberated.

More cars appeared on the roads. There was a change in the music at the dances. Minogue began to favour pints of stout and he found that he was well able to drink them all evening in the pub. Coming home on the lane, the drink tidal in his belly, he'd stop for a piss in the ditch. He'd hear the rustlings in the hedges when the stream stopped. Swaying in the dark, he'd be pissing on his shoes as he looked up for stars. He was twenty and tired of waiting.

At night he'd hear the cattle lowing or the hens being disturbed. Up at six, the clang of the milking buckets, a cigarette in the mouth early, the rhythmical swish of the teats squirting into the bucket.

What decided it finally was not his father's deteriorating condition or his own frustration. Rather, it was the questioning of his brother by the Garda one evening. It was a casual thing, to look as if they were doing something about the IRA. Mick came home late. He was triumphant, Minogue realised. He had been questioned in the barracks in town about his connections with the IRA, a proscribed organisation. It didn't matter that it was moribund, maintained by diehards and barstool heroes. Mick had found his vocation, Minogue understood. Ireland was to be his religion.

Maybe, as Mick accused him, it was the books he read. Books full of pessimism and anti-religious feeling. Maybe it wasn't fashionable to be devoted to your country anymore, Mick would sneer. Youth? Mick didn't have it either. Curious though, Kathleen had remarked after they had all met at a neighbour's funeral years later, Mick didn't seem to age.

Minogue tried his hand at bartending in Dublin. His mother wanted him to do the Civil Service exams. He spent a lot of time in the libraries. He saved money for a trip to America. He met Kathleen O'Hare who was new to the Civil Service. She poked fun at his accent, knowing his irritation to be waxing love. He in turn complained about Dublin people. She teased out his plans. She said she had to be fair with him, not to lead him on, because if he was serious about America, she couldn't go. Her family needed her and America frightened her, she admitted.

"You're nobody there, Matt," she'd say.

Minogue was reading the Frenchman, Sartre, and he felt that he wouldn't mind being a nobody for a while. Maybe a holiday in America, Kathleen said.

She had been very fair to me, Minogue thought. He was determined to repay her honesty with a loyalty the intensity of which surprised him. Minogue didn't fancy himself as a man who went in for the lovey-dovey stuff, but not because he wanted people to think he was a hard man. He would be happy with loyalty and company. Within a year, he was through the Garda training in Templemore, surprising himself even more by doing well at it. They married. With the America money and Kathleen's economy, they saw themselves into a new house in Kilmacud. Minogue didn't mind it at all, not even the cliff-heights of a mortgage.

In that same year, Minogue's father had died, leaving Mick the man of the house. Their mother grieved for a long time. The doctor called it reactive depression. Minogue's sisters and their husbands called on weekends. One sister, Maura, gently asked him what he thought about her moving to Canada and how would their mother take it. Families grew. Something was stirring in the country, money.

Kathleen delivered a baby boy, Eamonn, a big hairy child. Eamonn died unaccountably some seven months later, forgetting to breathe, it seems. The death precipitated the worst years of Minogue's life. For all their cleverness, the poems and the books meant nothing after that. Kathleen overcame her dread and went to see a psychiatrist. Minogue was helpless, encumbered. They promoted him to detective.

It wasn't until six years later that Kathleen conceived again. Minogue felt frightened being an expectant father again. None of their acquaintances joked with them. Minogue had been marked as different already.

Iseult was a different baby from the start. Kathleen took heart. The coldness leaked out of Minogue. As if to remind them that it wasn't chance, Daithi was born the following year. Minogue was always watching. He was careful not to live for his children but his determination was manic. They would have university, the loan of the car, good teeth, pocket money, clothes, French, parties, books. Fearing his own intensity, Minogue immersed himself in it all the more.

As they grew, Minogue wondered—but didn't much care about—his promotion. He became a detective sergeant. Others passed him on the ladder.

Optimism seeped into Ireland in the sixties. One evening he watched civil rights marchers being beaten up near Derry. Was that still going on? He knew vaguely that the civil rights people were Catholics and that the Unionists controlled the North. The police beat up the marchers. That Paisley lunatic and his huge lips and mouth sneering on the television, a hysteric from another century. A new IRA appeared in the streets. Minogue was relieved. The people he worked with and the people he met were glad too. There were rumours of sending in troops to Derry to protect the Catholics. Hooded bodies turned up in ditches. Bombs demolished shops and factories. Men were shot to death at their doors. Troops went berserk. Petrol bombs arced lazily and burst in the night on the evening news. British Ministers recoiled at the hatred. Minogue's brother called in and had a glass of whisky.

"Majority my foot. How is it that a country that's held up to be the birthplace of parliamentary government can give in to a crowd of seventeenth-century bigots who represent about two percent of the population of Great Britain. How is that, can you tell me?"

New laws and courts, armed guards and the army at trials. The word 'terrorist' showed up in the news a lot. The old guard of the IRA, well clear of Belfast and Newry and Derry, lauded their northern heroes. Mick exhilarated in talk. He was well-to-do now. The country was to join the European Economic Community although Mick didn't agree with the move in principle. Still, Mick was not an activist, Minogue knew. Mick was for Ireland going it alone and his zeal couldn't countenance socialism. He couldn't approve of guns from Libya or Russia or from the madmen in Germany.

The brothers met intermittently at hurling matches. In Hayes' Hotel in Thurles, they'd be pressed together by the swell of men trying to get to the bar, eager for pints after the game. Both locked into the throng of countrymen in the streets and pubs of provincial towns. Minogue would catch sight of his brother through the struggling mass; the strong smells of his own youth–the porter, the cowshite, the hair oil–rising up around him. They never quarrelled.

Minogue knew that his brother knew more than he'd tell. The mannered ambiguity and the lifetime's practice with evasion meshed the two men. Ah, Minogue thought sometimes as the stout hit his stomach, we have the same sisters and mother and father, isn't that the strangest thing? How's things, Matt? Grand and how's yourself and yours? Can't complain, Matt, back to the wind. And how's Kathleen and the two children? Good, thanks be to God. *Not thanks be to God at all, to Kathleen probably.*

Minogue had felt a God in the singed grass at the side of the road, in the slowness of things winding down. The young fellow with the scattered blots and freckles of blood thick all over his face and everything silent and slow and slower as the smoke moved off. Minogue had spent a long time thinking about it in hospital. It was never fear really, more a surprise, especially so because there was something so familiar there at the time. It was like a face maybe. Maybe like those Zen fellas, a face he had before he was born. Not smiling or puzzled or anything at all really, more a feeling that something was there. A watchful presence, interested and disinterested at the same time. Great calm, silence. Maybe a trace of regret as it receded. Life marches on, each wave of people full of themselves, but less so as they get closer to the edge with the years. Then it's our turn.

Lying in the hospital bed, Minogue had imagined all the life, plants and animals, all the plankton in the sea, all the organisms in his body. This small hating island off the coast of Europe ... There were people dying of hunger elsewhere, without the time or the energy to be on their mad summer marches, without any dirty little pubs to plot in. Ah, but that wasn't the half of it even. People are nice here a lot of the time. More inane phrases drifted by Minogue and he'd turn aside to sleep.

Then, driving back up to Dublin after the games, Minogue would sometimes dream what life would have been like had he left for the States those years ago. He might be a cop on the beat in New York City. He might be a farmer in Montana with a Ford pick-up truck and steers. His wife would be a blond with big white teeth and a skin that'd tan. Maybe two cars. The kids would have American accents.

No end in sight to this business, is there, Matt? That is if the English insist on being blackmailed by those Orangemen. No, Mick, it doesn't look like it.

Mick didn't shoot the guns, but Minogue was sure he cheered the count of soldiers or loyalists killed.

Maybe it'll spread, Matt. It may well, but we'll do what we can, Mick.

Minogue listened to the things his brother left unsaid. Minogue had by then given up any ambition of rescuing his brother or indeed any of his countrymen from whatever threw them effortlessly between savagery and kindness.

Agnes laid the vapouring cups on the table. Slowly the two of them sipped their tea. Occasionally, a gust sprayed rain on the window and rattled the frame. Finally, Agnes spoke:

"A great day for going to the library ... or a funeral."

Minogue couldn't deny her. He had been sitting there as a visitor drinking tea. He was afraid to intrude upon her by asking her questions about her own family. That was none of his business. She had told him as much as she could about Jarlath Walsh. Agnes prepared to go. He couldn't stay here. He was supposed to be detectiving, not sitting here with a girl, daydreaming.

He walked down the flights of stairs ahead of her and side by side to the carpark. Allen leaned over and pushed the passenger door open for her. When Allen fussed with attaching her seat-belt, Minogue believed that this was a different Allen, a solicitous man taking custody of a precious cargo. A fatherly concern? Easy in a man with no brood at home to be keeping him in the real world, a part of Minogue's mind jeered.

Minogue closed Agnes's door. It closed with a solid clap. Beads of rainwater quivered on the waxed paintwork. A nice, big, new Toyota without an excess of chrome, Minogue mused. He would have had to put his boot to his own door on the Fiat to get it to close first time. As if reading the thoughts of a poor but secretly favoured suitor, Agnes looked up briefly and smiled through the glass. Unreachable, going. As he walked aimlessly back into the college, Minogue worked at persuading himself that he was not somehow envious of Allen. A moment of juvenile insecurity, he chided within.

What Minogue could not put aside, however, was the belief that the case had left him beached with the ebbing tide no longer touching him. Funerals. The last funeral Minogue had attended was that of an old IRA man from 1916, one who had survived the Civil War and a spell interned in the Curragh, to write memoirs and die renowned as one of the last of the hard men. There couldn't be many left. Three old men, propped up by their relatives, had stood over the grave. Mick had been among the hundreds of mourners there. Minogue had caught his brother looking over at him several times. He thought it was a look of some satisfaction on Mick's face, as if to claim the damp countryside and its people as his inheritance, not Minogue's.

Chapter Seven

Back in his room, Minogue doodled. He wrote down names and events. Then he tried to join them with lines so he could work out cause and effect later. Nothing.

They'd be burying the boy now. There'd be beads of rain on the coffin. The wet would give the bouquets more colour. Minogue reached a disagreeable decision. He phoned the Drug Squad.

While Minogue doodled, thought and telephoned, a well-dressed man in his late thirties took up a padded barstool in the Bailey public house. He held a copy of the *Irish Times* under his arm. He had stepped from a taxi but feet from the door.

The barman prided himself on recognising customers' occupations by the way they dressed. He took the order for a small Paddy, and he registered some surprise at an American accent, soft but there all the same. The customer unfolding the paper had the ruddy tan of a robust Yank with any amount of rhino for holidays and grub. Took care of himself.

The barman put him as a legal eagle, but that was a long shot, he realised, as he poured the water into the jug. Irish-looking, all the same, probably in the early thirties. The barman recognized a forty quid shirt when he saw one. The plain grey suit had the looks of having cost three hundred quid. Although he hadn't seen the customer hang up his coat, the barman guessed an Aquascutum.

The customer opened the paper to the editorial, which concerned itself with a condemnation of the murders of policemen, culminating in another one yesterday. He sipped at the whisky. The barman returned to his preparations for the lunch-time crowd.

When the customer's pal showed, the barman pegged him for a journalist or a theatrical type. Maybe not though. He served him a pint and returned to setting up glasses. He felt the light grab at the

small of his back, the twinge that would grow to an ache by lunch-
time. The barman's name was Gerry, and he wasn't any more interested
in politics than he was in soccer, but he talked about both endlessly
every working day. He heard enough guff. The tanned and fit-looking
barrister who was not a barrister was likewise disinterested in what
passed for politics. He was so antipathetic toward the way politics ran
on this island that he carried a large-calibre automatic pistol holstered
under his armpit. The magazine was fully loaded and there was a bullet
in the spout. The man wanted nothing to do with talking politics or
any other conversation which policemen might wish to engage him in.

Before starting out on this project, he had weighed the things he
felt were necessary and those which he could get around. Daily, and
with no sense of excitement, he cleaned the gun in his hotel room.
Carrying it was a non-negotiable item in his list and he felt quite at
home with yet another hard and fast rule in his life.

Gerry the barman's guess about the other fellow, who was dressed
half as a farmer and half as a priest, was partially correct in that the
man was a playwright. The playwright had spent the best part of a
half hour making sure he was not being tailed.

The tanned man disliked the playwright, not least for the maudlin
viciousness of his nationalism. He regarded him as a fool whose brains
were stewed by decades in fifth-rate theatricals. He did not trust the
playwright, but he knew that having to work with him was a test
which others were watching.

"You can see that results come quickly," he began.

"There's no gainsaying that," agreed the playwright. "So it went
smoothly this time and the volunteers got away. Maximum effect, oh
yes, I can see that."

"But...? You have reservations?"

The playwright observed the bubbles rising to the ice in his glass
before replying.

"I'll say this much. All this firepower and technology are fine and
well. You are well able to do the fancy footwork. But I've been in
this thing for most of my life. I know how the lads on the ground
feel. I can tell you that they're not too excited about the Russians
getting in on this like they've started to."

The tanned man saw the beginning of a faint irony in the smile on
the other's face. Patronising.

"What don't they like?"

"Don't get me wrong. The movement is all for arms supplies, even from the man in the moon. As long as there's no strings attached. What do I say when they ask what we're supposed to hand over in return? Some of the lads'll think maybe it's too much of an assembly line thing. They wonder what we had to give to get this kind of support."

The tanned man looked directly at the playwright.

"Does it really matter to the active service units where the stuff comes from? It's a command council decision. I haven't traded away the place to get this stuff. And that consideration has really nothing to do with either of us, has it? I'm here to monitor things. I have to report to them at some point, otherwise they won't hand over any more," he added.

"Risk," the playwright said.

"Everything has risk. It was even a risk trying to persuade the council to go along with this scheme. The drop to the trawler went off without a hitch, didn't it? The Soviet boat didn't pick up on anyone. And they're stuffed with monitoring gear. It went off perfectly. The guns were in use and even safely back across the border within a week."

"Could be the Yanks are stringing them along and waiting for a big haul so they can tip off the Brits. I read where those satellites can read the paper you have in your hand from up there," the playwright said.

Testing my patience, the tanned man thought, *to see how far he can go with me, how much he can find out.*

"Could be," he began. "But we're not talking of sheer numbers of weapons. The risk of detection is not as high as you might think. It's a matter of having the right weapon at the right time. Look at all the publicity about the grenade launcher. Let them think we have these things coming out our ears. They think we have any amount of nightsights. That's what works. Effectiveness, economy. There's more yet."

"Another toy?" the playwright asked.

"You don't need to know details. Just get your guys to set up a car to take something the size of a suitcase. The guidance and the sights fit into the suitcase too. It looks like a typewriter case. Light, portable; about twenty-five pounds."

"A suitcase?" The playwright had become very attentive.

"Have you heard of a Sagger?"

"I've heard of a shagger. I've met a lot of them ..."

"They were big in the Egypt and Israel war in seventy-three."

"What is it?"

"It's a guided missile, an anti-tank missile. It'll go a mile and a half. If it hits dead-on, it'll go through 400 mil plate."

The tanned man watched the playwright lose his battle to keep his composure.

"Jesus, Mary and Holy Saint Joseph. Is it here?"

"It was in, as of eleven o'clock last night."

"Same stunt?" the playwright whispered.

"Same route, different boat. I told you they're serious about this. It's a whole new approach. You've missed out on the global picture here. They're peeved with the Americans sending in stuff to Afghanistan. There's Central America. We're all part of the big picture. It's not just a local squabble."

"So it could be released a mile and a half from target?" the playwright asked.

"It's proven accurate to that. It needs two men, one to sight and control as it's in flight, the other to set up behind. It's wire-guided. Not for space cadets. It's reliable. It works."

The playwright frowned. He wondered yet again what this Yank, or whatever he was, had as a stake in this. The rumour was that the Yank was actually Irish, even born here. Another part of the mythology which had gathered around his arrival was that he was a tycoon businessman. That was too much to hope for, that image of Ireland's emigrant sons renewing the struggle. In any event, the council had put their suspicions aside and allowed this newcomer some rope. So far, to their astonishment, he had delivered. Although they had no way of checking, few could doubt that indeed he had enough links to set up the deliveries right from the Soviet Union. Still, no one could fathom his motives enough to allay their suspicions. He hadn't approached any of the movement in the States. A search on him had turned up things that the leadership had kept to themselves, causing the rumours to fly around even more. Some suspected a plant, but again they were discredited when the guns went into use in the North.

As the playwright tried to digest this news, the tanned man observed with some scorn. Resentful, befuddled. This remnant of a green peasant Ireland was out of his depth.

The playwright and his like didn't want a rational solution to the mess, because they wouldn't be the kings of the pygmies anymore afterwards. He had no commitment to unloading the mess, the national inferiority complex, the energy deflected into 'politics,' the bitterness.

Like any neurotic, the playwright didn't see how he was clinging to the neurosis itself.

"And will you be wanting those couriers still...?" the playwright asked.

"You sound like you want to tell me there's some hitch," the tanned man said.

"It's not a hitch."

"Well, what's the big deal then?"

"There's no big deal. I hope you've got a car lined up yourself for this. I don't have anything in the garage right now. Seeing as you don't like Mercedes and all that."

"Get your guys to boost something a lot less conspicuous next time, that's all I said. You ditched it like I said, right?"

"Almost."

"What does that mean?"

"Some of the boys are down from Belfast and I had to give them a car. The only one in the garage was the Merc, so I gave it to them for today and tomorrow. What's the point of torching a perfectly good car?" the playwright answered.

"Look. You know the cars are for this operation." The tanned man's voice began to rise.

"I know, I know. Don't be getting yourself–"

"Shut up for a minute. I say what goes here. Just because I say dump that car, that doesn't mean it's yours and you can loan the goddamn thing out. Get it back off those hoods straight away. Tell them to boost their own transport if they have to. I want this operation watertight. Get it back and burn it, OK?"

The playwright held his palms up in mock surrender.

"Anyway. I have the guy I need for this one. Good cover and a car thrown in as well, all legal. I want you to use the gas–the petrol tank for the package."

The playwright finished his drink and got up to leave.

"Better get the car to me soon. Can't do much at the garage until they have the exact dimensions. It's a very precise thing. The cars are not as big over here," the playwright said.

The tanned man turned aside the veiled jibe and merely nodded his head. You must be kidding, he thought. Whip off the gas tank and secure the thing inside another one. No doubt this loser favoured putting it on his shoulder and running across the fields. Or taking chances on the roads even when they didn't know which roads the

Brits were likely to crater from one day to the next. The British Army had infrared and thermal surveillance as well as roving patrols out in the fields at night.

When the playwright left, the tanned man took up the newspaper again. Much to the chagrin of the barman, he ordered a coffee. Gerry was twenty years in the trade and still couldn't get used to serving up tea and cake in a public house.

As the lunch-time crowd began coming in, Gerry noticed the well-dressed fella get his coat and leave. The man crossed Duke Street and entered the shopping arcade. He went to a phone booth, deposited the money and dialled.

"I'm calling about the matter we discussed on the weekend. It's ready to go."

"Have you got a day on it yet?"

"No. But I'll know by tomorrow evening probably. It'll be your fellow doing it again."

The other person paused.

"Is there a problem with that?"

"Not really. We might need to let some things blow over."

"Like?"

"That business about the student. My fellow balked a bit. It scared him a lot."

"Is that it?"

"We have an irritation which prevents things from, shall we say, healing over. The dick who's looking into it. Not what you'd call a sleuth, but I had a bad feeling about him. Deceptive kind. Behind the scenes."

"Did you spin out the drug thing?"

"Yes. I think it's working."

"Well, we can't wait forever."

"No. I'm thinking that we should maybe nudge more things on him, set him going on the trail."

"That's your affair. Just make it work. We have to work this thing to show we can deliver. Then we can relax."

While the tanned man left the arcade, the person he had called sat wondering what to do about Minogue.

For his part, the playwright was not a happy man. He sat in a taxi which had been caught in a traffic jam in College Green. A bloody bomb scare, wasn't that funny? The playwright did not like the man he had met in the Bailey. He didn't like him one bit. He was a snotty, smart, pushy, well-to-do Yank. Telling him who he could give out one of the cars to. What was this well-connected Yank going to get out of this anyway? What would the Russians get out of it? Surely they knew that Irish people wouldn't accept their way even if they did help to win in the Six Counties. Although it was tougher and tougher to get in the stuff from the States, at least it didn't alienate the rank and file. What if the Yank was an undercover, a set-up?

It had come hard to the playwright to be told by the leadership to give this man all assistance. It might even be that this new thing could change everything. The taxi inched around College Green, under the portals of the Bank of Ireland and the haughty Trinity College. He smiled grimly at the sight: god-damn it to hell, he decided, if that institution can claim to have any say in the business of Irish liberation. He knew then what he would do. The preparations would go ahead, but the weapon would find a different route to the North. *We'll test out this fancy scheme,* he thought. *Well and good if they make it through, then he'll have been wrong and he'll admit it.* No one would blame him in the end for being so vigilant. He'd find a way to get the weapon in by his own route.

More and more as he thought about it, the playwright began to believe that this was the acid test. The Brits would have stepped up searches with the latest incidents. Any number of things could banjax this whiz kid's operation and all its glamour. A tip-off was the worst danger, of course. Tip-offs. At least such betrayals sent the command council scurrying around trying to find the traitors and made them rely again on the proven loyalty of men like himself. Tip-offs, yes. A constant worry, something that high-flying boyos with their shady deals overlooked.

The taxi-man swore long and loud.

"Everything'd be just dandy if people just knew the ropes in this city," he muttered. "The trouble is you have drivers who think they know bloody short-cuts and fancy moves. They're the ones that jam up the shagging place when a street is closed with a bomb-scare. Fuckin' iijits, pardon me language."

The driver switched off the engine. Exactly, the playwright thought. The war is being fought by Irishmen and women here in Ireland. For their own homes and families, their own country. Ordinary people like this taxi-driver, born and bred here. Living here, enduring, persevering. And the Yank, or whatever he was...? The playwright didn't need to deliberate any longer. He caught sight of the tired face of the driver as he turned in the seat to share his exasperation. Right, he thought, certain now about the Yank: our Ireland, not his.

Minogue had that stupid feeling again. Anytime he was on the phone for more than a minute or so, he felt stupid. He became bored talking into it, no matter how important it was supposed to be or how well known to him the person on the other end. Minogue's attention wandered all the more because he knew he was getting a long and polite no with many hints and reasons.

He liked the man on the other end, Denny Byrne from the Drug Squad. For a Wicklowman he was a good old stick.

"The chances are very much against it, Matt. The crates and things do be open, you see, to air the goods. There does be a lot of loose stuff in them, compared to other things, you see. It used to be popular enough a number of years ago, I don't mind telling you, but we copped on. I shouldn't say it was us who copped on. It was others, like fellas unloading and finding burst bags of things. I remember even a fellow out in Fairview who ran a shop phoning up and telling me he had 'drugs' in a box of bananas. 'Go way outa that,' I says to him, thinking like bananas is the word for him. God, do you know he was right. So I says to him, 'How did you cop onto the fact that these were bags of heroin, then?' You know what he says? 'Why wouldn't I know they were drugs? Sure don't I see it on shows on the telly?' "

Minogue smiled.

"So, a slim chance."

"Yep. That's about it. I'm not saying we're sniffing around the port of Dublin every day. But I don't mind people thinking we are. We go through people, people we know about or hear about. We can't afford to go the random route alone, do you see."

That was that, Minogue thought. Walsh was an unwitting accomplice in a deal, then he stumbled on something? Wild guessology. Still, Minogue had had the direction from two people independently, and they were not the sort to be romancing. Loftus for all his prissy speechifying about law and order was not a fool, nor was Allen. Allen. What was it about Allen? Was it that he was so organised, so controlled?

Minogue decided that it was time to dose himself with a large white coffee in Bewley's. He stepped out onto the greasy cobblestones and felt the drops of rain pat against his coat. The air freshened him. He

wondered if he was being played elaborately by somebody or somebod-
ies. Even Mick Roche, the Students' Union president, had turned in a
fine performance, one might think. As Minogue shouldered into Bewley's on Grafton Street he wondered: and Agnes?

After his second cup of coffee, Minogue had decided to return to
Agnes McGuire. She wasn't popping up again and again in his mind
for no good reason. There was something she hadn't said, he was sure
of that. Maybe it'd turn out that what she'd say would not help him.
Maybe she'd cry out her loss and break down, shed the stoicism and
sadness and show her anger. It must be there, he thought, she's only
human.

Minogue's timing worked. Agnes had returned from the funeral some
minutes before he climbed the stairs and knocked. She didn't seem
surprised to see him. She let him in.

"Agnes, I've held off asking you certain questions. God knows, I've
never had much sense of timing so I'd like to try them now. It'll speed
things up a lot. Or it will close off some distracting angles anyway."

"I think you want to ask me if there was a Someone Else. Isn't that
the way it goes?"

"That's about the size of it, Agnes. Can you help me? You see, this
thing has hallmarks of what might be called a crime of passion. It's an
avenue I have to explore sometimes."

Minogue saw reluctance in her. She examined her fingers before
she spoke.

"It's a funny thing, I suppose," she began, "but when you least
expect it you have something you never expected to have. Would it
surprise you to know that I didn't have a boyfriend until I started
college here? You'd think the opposite, wouldn't you, that the local
thing would win out and that you'd go out with someone from your
own background...? Well, my father was assassinated when I was
sixteen. You can imagine what that made of our lives."

Minogue watched her eyelashes as signs and when they stopped
flickering, she continued.

"Well, I came here and, you know, I liked it. I didn't think I would. I
felt that people in the South were not very sincere, if you know what I
mean. This thing about violence. They didn't have to go through the
results of their thinking. They just don't understand. It's not like 1916. I
suppose you could say I was cynical." 'Son-e-col,' Minogue heard.

"At first when Jarlath started following me around, I was annoyed.
He was such a puppy. Embarrassing."

She smiled. Minogue was attentive at the same time as he was lost in thought. His mind raced on from her words, from her accent.

"Odd how things work out. Feeling sorry for him, I mean. The politicos used to tease him a lot here. You know how it is, the students who have a lot of ideas about society, have read a lot. Can you imagine how surprised I was when I heard myself defending and explaining Jarlath to Mick Roche? You know him?"

"The president of the Students' Union."

"Yes. Well, I was sort of going out with Mick. Or at least that's what he thought. I think he felt sorry for me, did Mick. Maybe even more than Jarlath. He knew my background. I felt I had to thank him somehow for feeling sorry for me. God. You know, I found out that people with any brains here in the South seem to be just hypnotized by the North. All Mick's talk is organised around it. There's a lot of fellas here in the South feel like that too, but all the most of them want is a bit of excitement or something like that. Mick is different. I think he felt guilty or something. Ashamed ... How did I get to talking about this? Sounds like a soap opera."

Minogue smiled in return this time.

"... Anyway. I felt I was some kind of specimen. A ghost to haunt them here. But Jarlath didn't try to mine me for info like the others. Not head-over-heels or anything like that. He was very naive. Very. And, you know, I didn't mind that. He wasn't putting on like he knew or understood everything. Oh sure, he probably was opinionated, but he could feel things. That was the difference; he had a stomach. I felt bad for him when they laughed at him. His ideas used to get him into trouble."

"Dr Allen mentioned that Jarlath had a stake in something which wasn't in favour, academically at least," Minogue said.

Agnes' eyebrows arched.

"Something about a psychological model of Irish character that we could use to solve some of our, em, problems," Minogue offered.

Agnes turned to look at the window. Her hands were clasped together. Her head dipped as if to concentrate on her twining hands. Her hair fell to conceal her cheeks. Minogue waited. He saw a tear drop onto her arm. For no reason his sluggish mind could settle on in that room, he felt appalled. He shouldn't be doing this. This could be Iseult by chance of birth or geography. Without raising her head, Agnes picked a paper hanky from her sleeve and dabbed her eyes. Then she tossed her hair back. Minogue saw the film still on her eyes.

"It's all right," she said. "Just some things. Some people would say he was just thick or that he was a part of a class who helped cause the stuff up North so he'd never admit to the 'reality' of the situation. He hadn't been to the North once in his life. So there he was trying to build a big theory up for ... for I don't know what. His family took care of him all his life. I mean what did he know about poverty or civil rights? Really?"

Agnes looked inquiringly at Minogue and then continued:

"The thing was—and I don't care what anyone else says—he was trying. I suppose it'd look sort of clumsy to an older person. When I think of it. Cooking Italian food and trying out wines. The Student Prince." Agnes' teeth showed in her smile this time. Then she frowned and looked straight at Minogue.

"Maybe I was the only one who noticed he was changing. I'll bet his parents didn't notice. I met them today for the first time. And the last time probably. I shouldn't say it maybe ... but I felt I had seen them before. They didn't seem like strangers."

Minogue was thinking about Mick Roche. Could hardly call him jilted though. He had been circumspect, not the opinionated termagant Minogue had expected in a student leader. Perhaps give him credit for being able to conceal his feelings. Still, Roche had recognised the changes in Jarlath.

"Agnes, did Jarlath experiment with drugs at all?"

Minogue looked closely at her to try and gauge the risk. He had said it out of context, watching. Would she switch to anger? Minogue waited, seeing the frown on her face, not knowing if he had asked at the right time.

"Are you joking?"

Minogue didn't reply.

"Like I said this morning: *No*."

After a pause of returning his gaze, Agnes spoke slowly.

"Maybe I had better save you some embarrassment, Sergeant. You talk about drugs. Well, Jarlath didn't so much as experiment with sex. He was all for cuddles and going to the pictures and walking me home. As for trying to stay the night ... and it isn't even that I wanted things that way at all. But you know fellas, trying to prove things to themselves. Jarlath got pissed out of his brain after three pints. I mean, nothing doing. Can you believe that?"

"Yes," Minogue said simply. He turned away from the intensity of her gaze. She had decided in his favour by the slightest of margins.

She still retained the challenging candour in her voice as if daring him to push his luck into rudeness. "Yes." Minogue needed to believe as much about Iseult and Daithi, that they weren't part of the touted libertine rubbish which the magazines fed to the middle-aged on their stale weekends.

Minogue heard a little *ping* in the back of his head. It came from remembering Allen's reluctance in telling him about Jarlath's interests. Had Jarlath kept it to himself, this business about the effects of drugs? Wouldn't Agnes know? It just wasn't likely that he'd keep it to himself. Minogue found that Agnes was still looking directly at him, awaiting the signs of another challenge. No, he decided, he couldn't ask her now.

Chapter Eight

The south side of Dublin being snotty, plenty of the cars which passed Gardai Kehoe and Cummins cost more than twice their annual salaries, before tax. The two were sitting in a Garda squad car near the Bray Road, the main thoroughfare south from Dublin. There was an agreement between them that their priorities would be given to Jags, BMWs, Mercedes and anything made in Italy that wasn't a Fiat. Speed traps were rare on Irish roads, but such a potential source of revenue as the billiard table expanse of the new Bray Road couldn't be ignored.

Kehoe and Cummins had been sitting in the car before morning rush hour some weeks previously, and they had observed a reddish projectile rocketing under the bridge in Belfield. Kehoe burned his fingers as he tried to get the cigarette out of his mouth, looking for the ignition. The UFO had obliged them by mounting a curb near Stillorgan, ripping off the front of the car and grinding to a stop after it had rubbed itself like a drugged, frantic cat along a wall for over two hundred feet. All this at ten to seven in the morning. Later, the authorities were to report that the showband star inside, one Malachi O'Brien of O'Brien's Country Treasures, a band enjoying a large following in all parts of the Republic except Dublin, was too drunk to get out of the car. O'Brien expressed his gratitude at being rescued by the officers and added that it was only because the new Bray Road was so well constructed that his life had been extended. The car had been travelling at speeds close to a hundred miles an hour.

"It's the bloody telly. *Smokey and the Outlaw,* or whatever you call it. Did you hear him? 'Arra boys, the blessin's of God and his Holy Mother on you. Amn't I only delighted to see ye. Sure the bloody car took off by itself and I couldn't stop it,'" Kehoe mimicked to his colleague.

"Blind drunk, I suppose, was he?"

"Man dear, he was nearly speechless with the drink. He didn't know what century he was in. I wouldn't mind but he's a favourite of the wife's. She was surprised, I can tell you."

"Pop stars? A pack of iijits. That's a nice how do you do."

Both Gardai guessed that the motorists had been flashing lights up ahead. In ten minutes, they hadn't heard the alert from the speed gun.

"We'll head off so," Kehoe muttered.

Kehoe clipped on his belt and started off on the slip road which joined the dual carriageway a hundred yards ahead. Cummins radioed in and sat back. Kehoe noticed a large car which had been coming up fast behind them. It had braked when the driver had realised he was passing a police car, itself doing the legal limit. Kehoe saw the bonnet of the car, a Mercedes, dip in his mirror. That'll learn you, he thought. For divilment, he slowed the police car. The car, a yellow Mercedes, was obliged to pass. Kehoe nudged his partner. Both looked over to the right at the slowly passing car. The car was no more than a year old.

The Gardai knew that the occupants would pretend not to notice them. There were three men in the car. It was a kind of play: the driver knew he had been speeding, the Gardai knew it, they all knew that each knew it, but the radar wasn't on. The driver and passengers stared ahead. As the rear passenger drifted by the police car, he darted a glance at the two policemen. Both Cummins and Kehoe noticed this. Kehoe, closest to the passing car, was the first to say it.

"Well, Lar. Will we give it a look?"

Cummins didn't answer immediately. Cummins was a Dublin-man, an exception on the Garda police force. He came from Crumlin, a working class district. He had had to take a lot of stick for joining the police. Crumlin didn't harbour many Mercedes. Cummins didn't mind that many of the policemen he worked with were bogmen, even though he knew they acted the heavy sometimes because they wanted to get a dig at Dublin hooligans.

Cummins had a new house in Templeogue and his wife, Breda, had a job in the bank. He had bought a new car. Cummins and the wife had been to Greece on their honeymoon. He didn't think he had any reason to resent rich people. Cummins could not ignore the internal radar, that intuition which he and Kehoe, who was a Kilkenny bogman, along with other police had. Three men in a car starts you thinking.

"Keep an eye on him anyway, I suppose."

Cummins reached for the microphone and called in the registration, a Dublin one. A 280 SEL. He wondered if that was a six-cylinder model. Waiting for the reply, the Gardai could hear the chatter of the other units. Kehoe had sat in, two cars behind the Merc. They'd have to decide soon because the turnoff to Booterstown was coming up soon.

"Blackrock, Unit Fourteen ... a yellow Mercedes, number is ... Meath. Hold on a second until I get the number ... reported stolen yesterday in Dunboyne. Model 280 SEL, year ..."

"Blackrock, Unit Fourteen. Meath, is it?"

"Yes, Fourteen. Hold on a sec now ..."

Cummins looked over at Kehoe. Kehoe nodded. Cummins wrote down the number anyway. Cummins radioed in their location and that they wanted to look over the car.

Kehoe pulled out and drew alongside the Mercedes. Faces turned to the two Gardai. Cummins had put on his hat and he had opened the window. He signalled the driver to pull over. One of the passengers leaned forward and spoke to the driver. The driver looked over to the policemen and nodded briefly. The Merc slowed. Kehoe pulled in ahead of the car.

He unbuckled his seat-belt as he watched Cummins walk back toward the Mercedes. There were about two car lengths between them. In the mirror, Kehoe noticed that the three men were sitting quite still, watching Cummins approach. Just before it happened, Kehoe had a sudden understanding of something, like when he had fallen on the ground during a game of football as a child.

Cummins heard the engine race and he chose the right direction to run. He leaped over the kerb as the Mercedes shot forward into the traffic lane. It surged into second gear and Cummins heard the deep burr of the six cylinders pick up the load again, rocketing the car into the light traffic. By the time Cummins had run to the car, Kehoe had it moving.

The Vauxhall squealed out from the kerb. Kehoe switched on the siren and threw his hat into the back seat. Cummins worked the radio. He felt calm even when Kehoe threw the car around in traffic. He glimpsed the tail of the Mercedes already racing by Booterstown Avenue. The traffic light there was turning orange.

"Ah shag it," Kehoe said. He skidded to a stop and leaned on the horn. Then he started off again.

"Be better off on me bike," he added, disgusted.

Cummins knew enough about cars to put his faith in the two-way radio. Blackrock and Donnybrook stations were the closest, unless there were cars out on the road ahead. Maybe a Garda on a motorbike. Cummins began figuring the chances as he listened to the radio, waiting. A Merc could easily do the ton and it could peel the door handles off this car on its way too. The Vauxhall could wind up to a hundred or maybe a hundred and ten if it was going down the side of the wall with a strong tail wind. Main thing was to keep it in sight and get the job done by radio.

Cummins saw the Merc veer sideways across a lane ahead. The chances might be even better, he thought. Suddenly the Mercedes darted across three traffic lanes and took off over the kerb down Merrion Avenue. Over the siren, Cummins could hear tires squealing still. Someone blew on a horn. Kehoe, with his tongue caressing his lower lip, dodged the cars, their brake lights popping on, their drivers up over the steering wheels. With a sense of timing and dexterity which surprised and pleased him, Kehoe crossed over the three traffic lanes in the wake of the Mercedes, now but a couple of hundred yards ahead.

Kehoe shot a glance at Cummins. Might actually be able to stay with it, Cummins thought.

Merrion Avenue is a broad, straight avenue which runs toward Blackrock and the sea. Off Merrion Avenue run various avenues and roads which draw out the most florid prose in auctioneers' sale ads. A tidy amount of money is to be made installing and updating burglar alarms along the Avenue.

In theory, one can drive down the Avenue at a wicked speed. The risks involved in doing this include an uneven road surface, the entry of other roads onto the Avenue and the presence of several schools at the bottom of the Avenue, just before it joins onto the coast road.

Cummins and Kehoe knew the Avenue. Each separately wondered if the driver of the Merc did. There was a good chance that there were some kids knocking about at the bottom of the Avenue.

Kehoe was travelling at eighty and the Merc was still pulling away. The Vauxhall bottomed out on a dip in the road surface. Kehoe had put the odds at about even: the Mercedes had the power and the handling, but it had to open a path in the traffic too. Dispatch, a girl

with a Cork accent, told them there was a unit turning up Merrion
Avenue to meet them. She cut off and the other car radioed that it
was passing Sion Hill School. The driver of the Merc didn't use the
brakes at all now. He swung it across the road or even passed on the
inside. The distance between the cars was widening. Then Kehoe spotted the flicker of blue light atop the other police car in the distance.
At the same time, the brake lights on the Merc glowed. In an instant,
the Mercedes had turned off to the right. The driver had almost lost
it. The yellow car had skidded to face almost completely up the Avenue. The tires left greying smoke in the wake of the car. Time yet,
Kehoe thought.

The Vauxhall roared into the street behind the Mercedes. Cummins
shouted that there was a cul-de-sac up on the left. Kehoe looked in
the mirror to see the other police car come swaying into the street at
speed. Ahead of the Merc, a County Council dustbin lorry was backing
out onto the road. The Mercedes swung wildly to the left and careened
into the cul-de-sac. Kehoe laughed aloud. Cummins groaned inwardly
because it looked like another episode of leaping over walls and
through bushes. They might be lucky. Maybe the Merc would crash
and give them the chance to put the heavy hand on these fellas. The
other police car was closing in behind them. Four against three. Shag
it, Cummins thought, and he hoped to God that there was some fit
lad in the car behind to do the leaping and jumping. Lucky there was
no one on the street. The Merc sped up.

"How far ahead?" Kehoe shouted.

"Around the bend there's a crescent and that's it," Cummins replied.

The Vauxhall rocked and squealed over the concrete roadway. As
it swayed around the bend, Kehoe saw a housewife look up from the
plants near her front door, her hand full of weeds and a trowel in the
other hand. Then a yellow shape appeared across the roadway ahead
of them. Two men were jumping out the doors on the far side of the
car. The driver was shouldering his door on this side. Kehoe stood
on the brakes and with screaming tires, the Vauxhall dredged into
the road.

Cummins was thinking: watch out, the lads are coming up fast behind. Kehoe was looking at the heads which appeared over the roof
of the Mercedes. They're not running, Kehoe thought. They're not
running; isn't that a queer turn of events?

The Vauxhall was slowing, skidding sideways. Cummins felt and
heard a pat somewhere in the body of the car. Pebbles? More. Then

something like one of those sticker things against the window, those joke bulletholes. One of the men ran out from behind the Mercedes. He was carrying some kind of torch, flashing it at them. The windscreen whitened and a chunk of it fell out onto the bonnet. The Vauxhall was almost stopped now, grinding down on the suspension on Kehoe's side. Kehoe grunted and sighed. Something went through the car, then another and another, in and out the windows.

Isn't that odd? Cummins thought. *It's me who should be leaning up against Kehoe the way the bloody car is going, not the other way around. Anyone would think he was trying to give me a feel. His hands are all over the place.* Something hit Cummins in the side of the face. *A warm snowball, like a sod you'd clip from the field when you missed with your kick at the ball. Sore thing, that ...*

The siren had stopped. Someone was breaking glass. Before the car had stopped–at the very instant that Cummins looked at his partner–their car was hit by the patrol car which had come into the cul-de-sac behind them. Cummins' belt bit into his neck and his head shot out in reaction to the shock. The door was coming in at him. Everything became suddenly glarybright and the world turned sideways, then over. Cummins' car rolled but once before it hit the Mercedes. It came to rest on its side. Without turning his head, Cummins could see Kehoe half hung in his belt above him. His head and shoulders had slipped out and lay partly on Cummins. Bright red splashes covered the roof of the car and Cummins could feel the absurd drip soaking further into his navy blue uniform. Cummins felt uncomfortably hot as the darkness which welled in through the windows from the sideways world outside gathered him.

Minogue stood in the doorway of the building which housed Allen's office. He stroked his upper lip between thumb and finger. A group of passing students looked at Minogue and awoke him. Loftus he discounted. He was engaged in the administration of his fiefdom and his loyalties to the university and an old army buddy of his. Chivalry my royal Irish arse. Allen? Minogue gave it a chance.

He walked up the staircase slowly. On the way he stepped around a woman on her knees, washing the steps. That could be that Brosnahan woman doing that, Minogue thought. Maybe her knees'd give out soon or she'd have arthritis for her pains. He knocked, expecting and hoping that Allen wouldn't be there. Bugger: Allen's face appeared in the doorway.

"Sergeant," he said.

"Good day to yourself, Doctor. I hope you can spare me some of your time."

"Just a few loose ends, Sergeant?" Allen asked.

"I beg your pardon," Minogue said.

A smiled crossed Allen's face briefly. Minogue thought he saw irritation replace it. Maybe something else.

"Nothing really. It's just that I expected you to say something like that. Like the films or the television. Yes, I can spare you about ten minutes. Will that be enough?"

Minogue marvelled at the mixture of sentiments which Allen's remark could conceal. There were touches of sarcasm undoubtedly, and even a little arrogance too. There were also traces of relief and apprehension. In a strange sense he seemed relieved to see Minogue, almost resigned in some way, but he was guarded.

Minogue stepped into the room. The place was cluttered with books. Some order informed it all though, Minogue's glance affirmed. Allen sat next to his desk. Minogue noticed Allen's eyes. They seemed bigger than normal, whiter. Perhaps they were more opened. He looked as though he had just run up the stairs or he had been walking for some time.

Behind Allen, a view of the greenery and trees of New Square was framed in the tall window.

"Oh, I think I get it all right. I really should polish up my lines. You're quite right about the loose ends, I don't mind telling you. I'll be calling them straws soon enough. Where there's life ..."

Allen, his arms folded, was displaying a patience which was not easy for him, Minogue realised. He was privately pleased that Allen should be uncomfortable.

"To follow up on every little thing," Minogue continued. "I need to convince my superiors and myself that this is not some lunatic random thing."

Allen frowned.

"Yes. I suppose that I've hidden my light under a bushel, Doctor. Do you know that I hadn't even admitted to myself out loud in the middle of the day that this simply couldn't be a random thing? Well, there you have the gist of it. We can't escape it. I feel badly that I don't have some class of solid stuff for my superiors to digest, you know. It's like I can trace out elements, but I can't put things together in a way that appears rational. I'm waiting for a part of my brain to catch up with me," Minogue allowed himself a grin before continuing.

"Yes. What do you call it, free association. Like we allow ourselves to believe certain things without even stopping to think. We don't know the half of it, do we? A hint here, a suggestion there. It's my experience that people are easily led, if you know what I mean."

Allen eased himself in his chair a little.

"I think I follow you. Your technique for thinking out loud is a very good exercise. What I'm asking myself though is why you do it here."

"Ah, there's a good one indeed, Doctor. I confess I was drawn to your office by the need of your insight. I mean that I think I'm up the garden path at the moment. For instance, the drug thing you mentioned to me. I'm stymied by it. Agnes McGuire knew nothing of his interests in that line. He wasn't the kind of lad to hold back, was he? I mean, that was almost a failing in him, the way he had so much to say, to offer. He was naive, like."

"Well, he'd hardly advertise it to someone he wanted to impress, Sergeant," Allen observed.

"So you put some store in the whole thing then?" Minogue asked quickly.

"Actually I'm almost sorry I mentioned it at all. You seem to be saying that it is a red herring."

"Were you aware that an anonymous note had come to the college security officer, Captain Loftus, suggesting that Jarlath Walsh might be involved in drugs?"

"Matter of fact I was. I'll grant it may have coloured my interpretation of the questions he was asking me. Like I said, I'm almost regretting having told you about this in the first place ..."

Allen sat back in the chair and folded his arms again. Then, like a cloud passing over his face, Minogue watched the idea come to Allen. Allen leaned forward slowly.

"I have the distinct feeling that you're not asking what you really want to ask me, Sergeant, but you're trying to provoke me in a way."

Full marks, Minogue thought. *Go to the top of the class.* Did it really look that obvious?

Minogue said nothing. He watched what looked like indignation loosen Allen's manner. Finally he said:

"Doctor, I'm sorry if I left you with that impression. I wonder if I might ask you to sleep on the matter. Any small details or memories that come to you. A remark in class, a fellow student, anything."

"You think I'm concealing something, don't you?" Allen said.

"Not at all. I haven't been able to firm up anything on this effort about the drugs, you see, and it's distracting me. I must be a very suggestible person."

Not fooled for a minute, Minogue thought. Allen's gaze suggested a knowingness but an amused ambivalence too. Maybe he was working hard at not being rude, Minogue considered. Hard to blame him, with a detective who is flying by the seat of his drawers.

Minogue returned to the room he had been lent in Front Square. He determined to make an early day of it. At least it had stopped raining. Walking to the carpark, he found himself searching the faces of passing students for any signs of a son or a daughter. Were they all the same, students?

Climbing into the car, he assigned the day a four out of ten. Little remained of the rain except a saturated city and oily roads. Could it be that they might get a bit of sun?

Minogue wanted to sneeze but the sensation passed. A police car with sirens and lights going full blast went by him as he rounded into College Green. Damn and blast it, he thought. It would be better if he at least phoned Kilmartin's office and checked in. Go by the book. Minogue stopped at two phone-boxes in succession. Both had been vandalized. Reluctantly, he drove up Dame Street toward the Castle. Another police car passed him at the lights at George's Street, screaming away. Maybe it was a bank robbery, another one.

Outside Kilmartin's office there was no work being done. Several uniformed Gardai sat on the edges of the tables, smoking. Minogue could hear the monitored voices of men out in the streets, patrolling. The voices and clicks drifted down from the dispatch room. Nobody in Kilmartin's office. Minogue strolled toward the dispatch room, nodding at several Gardai as he passed them.

"Inspector Kilmartin, lads?"

"He's above in dispatch, sir," a Garda replied.

Kilmartin was sitting in a chair next to one of the girls. She was studiously concentrating on her earphones, nervous at his presence. He was smoking a cigarette. He stood up when he noticed Minogue and he walked over to the doorway.

"Did you hear about it?"

"What now?" Minogue asked.

"They shot our lads out in Blackrock. It's still going on. They got the driver, but the two fellas with the shooters are on the loose still."

Minogue felt an approaching swell. He waited. Kilmartin was mooching about for someplace to kill the butt of his cigarette. His arm was wavering. Minogue felt light, cold. The day was transformed. Somehow the room looked lurid. It pressed in on him.

"The IRA or the INLA or whatever crowd, I'll wager. One of our lads was killed outright. The other one's alive," Kilmartin murmured, still wandering around the room. Minogue was taken up with watching the girl's nervousness as Kilmartin paced.

"Only a pack of animals would react to a uniform like that. They have automatic rifles. The place is upside down so it is. They have a cordon up. The army and the whole shebang is there."

"Where?" Minogue heard himself asking.

Kilmartin stopped walking.

"Out near the bottom of Merrion Avenue, near enough to Blackrock."

As hard as he tried, Minogue couldn't get the taste out of his mouth. The fear was like cheese on his breath. *It sticks in your throat, it actually chokes you,* he thought. *Smell it on your breath.*

Chapter Nine

The tanned man replaced the phone and walked over to the window. His room at the Shelbourne overlooked St. Stephen's Green. He watched couples and children and old people enter the Green. They haven't a clue, he thought, about what goes on less than a hundred miles from here.

Parked cars glutted the streets around the hotel. No one feared that one might contain a bomb. No searches, no midnight raids by troops. The shops were full, the pubs were open. A soft city in a soft country. It even made visitors soft. People became so flaccid that they feared slight changes to their self-satisfied equilibrium. A decision had to be made within the hour. The danger was in over-reacting, of pouncing too soon.

The Green was swollen with trees and shrubs, all dense with the day's rain. The tanned man was thinking of Minogue. The photo showed a tall man in a cheap suit walking in the Front Square of Trinity College. Totally out of place. A redneck. There was something cautious and reluctant about the face. Soft, maybe. He didn't put his hands in his pockets walking. Certainly not stupid. Was it possible that this Minogue had a hidden sense of an adversary out there, that this boy's death was linked to another world of events? It didn't matter now, be pragmatic. Kill Minogue or not?

Why kill? To be sure. Take such a risk, just get this one crucial delivery across the border to prove he was right. The place would be crawling with cops if that happened. That moron playwright would leak eventually. Get him too. No, needed him for this.

The tanned man decided that Minogue would live. He would stick with the story about drugs and build one more block onto it. It had to be something fairly dramatic, a bit of Mafia or something to it. Like being done in with a stone. The papers would say, 'Assault the work of drug-related criminal element' or 'Suspected drug link in assault of Garda.' It would have to do, even though the tanned man didn't like it. As he waited for the playwright to answer the phone, he wondered if Minogue knew that his probing was forcing somebody's hand.

"Are you getting the car ready for that trip?" he asked.

"Yep. He'll bolt on the goods tomorrow," the playwright replied airily.

"Another thing. Minogue, remember? Like we discussed. Get a car, that way. Leave something behind."

"Yep."

"You know how important this is. We're buying time until we can deal with the other thing that's come up. I'll be dealing with the other asshole before his knees give out completely."

The playwright laughed. He hadn't heard the Yank using bad language until now. It didn't fit with the suit. Could it be that Mr Whiz Kid might be human after all?

"Yes. I'll do the other thing myself. Kilmacud, is it?"

"Yes. No Roy Rogers stuff now. Think of it as a part. Imagine yourself as a gangster."

The tanned man hung up. He suppressed the little ice of anxiety which was rising in his stomach.

He returned to gazing out the window. The waiting was the worst of it. He acknowledged the burrowing truth that ultimately, no one was completely reliable. No one should be trusted in extremity. As the stakes rose with the latest dangers, he had felt his own control slipping, his sense of agency diminish. Like a bank of clouds, chance and circumstance were drifting in to conceal the elements. He had no choice but to wait and see what came in from the fog. He thought about Minogue again. Would his nerve go after a bit of pushing or would he dig in his heels?

He was drawn out of his speculations by the rising *wawa* and the car horns which came in over the trees in the Green. Two police cars, an unmarked van and an army Land Rover sped by the hotel. Reflex- ively, he pushed his elbow into his side to feel the belt at his shoulder better and to feel the butt of the gun meet the inside of the his jacket. *Not for me,* he thought. *Only in the movies.* He felt slightly claustrophobic with the noise filling the air.

He took his gabardine and went to the hotel foyer. He stepped out into the street. On the footpath outside the Shelbourne, a newspaper seller squatted on an orange box. The radio beside her chattered on and then broke into a monotonous disco beat. He walked over to the woman. The doorman from the hotel was watching the Mercedes and the Jags strewn along the double yellow line. The doorman rubbed his hands. The woman looked up at him.

"Looks like a nice how-do-ye-do, now. Shoot first and ask questions later, I say. Thugs down from the North is what they are. Disturbing the peace."

"Right enough. Thugs isn't the word for them. And them driving around in a Mercedes like they owned the bloody country. Unarmed pleecemen, I ask you. Where's the fairness in that. Shoot the buggers I say," said the doorman.

"I have a nephew out in Monkstown. I wonder if he's caught in the cross-fire," the newspaper woman said.

The doorman tried to ease the full weight of his sarcasm.

"Jases sure Monkstown is miles away. Cross-fire is it? What fillum was that in. Your cousin is under the bed if he's not inside in the shaggin' bed itself."

The tanned man stood quite still. He felt the ripple pass right to the top of his head. He turned to the doorman.

"What's going on with all these police cars?"

"Ah sir. There's some class of gunfight going on in Blackrock. There's a Garda after being killed and there's two of them on the loose—"

"—with tommy-guns," the woman interrupted.

"—and they think that they have the two of them boxed in. Turn over to Radio Eireann on that box of yours and you'll get it on the news ... Hanging is too good for them. You see we're doing fine down here as you can see for yourself, sir. It's that crowd giving us a bad name abroad ..."

"Indeed," the tanned man replied.

"Well, they have one of them captured so they have. I'd like to get a dig at him myself. In cold blood. What's the world coming to?"

The tanned man turned to walk toward Kildare Street. He was almost dizzy with the anger. The doorman had said there was a Mercedes involved ... It couldn't be a coincidence. Some incompetents in a useless shoot-out. No discipline, probably free-lancing on a bank job. That proved exactly what he had been busting a gut trying to convince them, that personnel like the damned playwright couldn't run things. After getting them to set up a proper garage and a mechanic to do the cars for the couriers, the playwright had blithely turned over one of the cars to some amateur thugs down from Belfast. All the work and preparations and the moron had given them a car, a toy to amuse them. A car gone to waste, weapons probably captured or abandoned. Cops on edge all over the city. He'd have to close the place down right away. If one of the losers knew about the garage and he talked, the cops could be kicking the door in fast.

The tanned man tried to rescue some benefit from this episode. At least it might divert some attention away from his operation for a few days anyway. When he finished with this part, he'd have the playwright's head on a plate for this.

Minogue felt light-headed and pukey after the cigarette. It was like learning to smoke all over again. It left him feeling bloated and nervous after even the first few pulls. Kilmartin sat with his elbows on his knees listening to the odd parts of the drama that were interspersed with the other messages.

The two gunmen hadn't been sighted since the shooting. They had taken off across the gardens. The danger was in cornering them where they might use hostages. Two units from the army had set up in the area. The Special Branch and the Gardai were running down streets and behind houses. There still wasn't enough manpower to get to all the houses and evacuate people. Just over thirty-five minutes, Kilmartin reflected, and the damage was done. There was a maze of streets just south of the cul-de-sac, just a few gardens over. It was likely that they had split up and ditched the guns. Aside from a thick lip and a bang on the head, the driver was in one piece and in custody.

Minogue decided to phone Kathleen. She'd have heard something on the radio anyway, he guessed. Fair play to her, Minogue pondered as he heard her talking, she's determined not to show anything now.

" 'Tis a bad state of affairs to be sure. Lookit, I'm not much help here so I'll be off home soon. Do you want me to stop off at the shopping centre for anything?" Minogue asked her. The phone was greasy in his hand. He smelled his own fetid breath curling out of the mouthpiece.

"A bit of black pudding and some sausages," she said.

Kilmartin looked to him as he re-entered the dispatch room.

"Do you want a few smokes for the way home, Matt?"

"No thanks. Sure it'll be another while before I take them up again, I'm thinking. They're a great comfort though ... I'd forgotten that. I'm off home now. You should go home yourself. The Special Branch lads will have the matter well in hand," Minogue murmured.

Kathleen Minogue answered the phone for the second time in five minutes. This time she didn't predict right because it was neither Matt nor the children.

"Em, no. He's due home though. A school reunion? Well, isn't that rich," she laughed. "But sure that's years ago."

Kathleen thought the caller must have moved well away from County Clare himself. His voice had a polish to it, deliberate like Richard Burton, with a trace of country accent. "Indeed and you should, Mr...? Mr Murphy. Oh I'm sure he'd be tickled. We have the tea about six. In actual fact I'm waiting for Matt to stop off at the shopping centre to bring home sausages and the like. I wasn't out on account of the rain. Yes, do. About half six and you'll be sure to get him."

The playwright left the booth and got into the Granada. The car was no more than a year old and it had been in his possession for approximately twenty-seven minutes. It would remain in his care for about another three quarters of an hour, then to be ditched. With luck, he wouldn't leave a mark on it.

He drove off out the Bray Road, in the direction of Stillorgan Shopping Centre. He was pleased with his performance. It would look like he was giving every assistance to Mr Whiz Kid. The car insulated him from the road and the sights which slowly swept by him as he stop-started in the traffic. He observed the frustration on the faces of people standing at bus-stops. Cars inched by him, then fell back again to pass him again. He made studies of the faces in the cars. Bank managers and accountants on their way home to the vacuum of suburbia. This was the Ireland which we had fought the British for?

A woman laughed behind glass in a Jaguar. She looked like a carnival mask with that sinister leer. Made up to the hilt and wearing those stupid glasses, copying anything and everything American.

No one would have the nerve to even think that he'd tip off the Brits. After they'd taken the car apart, the council would know that he'd been wise not to entrust such a valuable weapon to the Yank's scheme. Him and his cars and his couriers. We haven't come through the lean years just to hand over the reins to some jumped-up Houdini opportunist who was trickacting with the Soviets.

In a room on the second floor of Blackrock Garda Station sat two hefty middle-aged men. One, Galvin, remained on his feet, pacing the room in a measured pattern. Formerly dark-haired, he was now balding. He had found suits disagreeable these thirty years and more and it showed. A shelf of shirt stuck out from his belt and gathered the end of his tie, itself at half mast. Galvin had the face you'd see squinting on the steps of a Sunday church in Tipperary as he'd edge out into the daylight before the end of Mass. When he moved, however, no fat jellied around him. Removed from the company of farm animals these thirty years, nature had compensated him with the attributes of a suspicious bull.

His companion, Moroney, remained seated. He contented himself with picking imaginary pieces of lint from the knee of his pants. Moroney lacked the physical presence of his colleague Galvin; his body was beginning to sugarloaf at the belt. His face, mounted on thin lips, was completely out of place. Where one could reasonably expect swarthiness and a ruddy, heart attack complexion, a marbled model of cerebration rested atop the collar. To the side of Moroney was a pitted wooden table salvaged from a civil service department. The sole window in the room had been painted over with a heavy cream on the inside. A grid of wire mesh had been screwed to the window frame some years ago. The room smelled of damp and waiting. Under the window, a radiator which looked like a failed bellows tried to heat the air. The floor was made up of cracked and worn lino tiles which were flecked with cigarette burns.

On the table lay a portable tape recorder with a microphone attached. The seated man sat with his arms folded now. Occasionally he'd uncross his legs and then cross them again. He didn't speak to Galvin who was circling the room like a wrestler before the bout. They had been waiting for ten minutes. Every now and then they could hear the sounds of the building, the ticking of the radiator, steps outside. Five minutes ago, a young Garda had stuck his head in the doorway.

"Momentarily now, sir. He's on the way."

Galvin and Moroney had travelled from Dublin Castle. They had made their arrangements for the proceedings in the car. Galvin stopped pacing as he heard footsteps outside. The door opened. Two uniformed Gardai walked in, followed by a young man in handcuffs. Another two Gardai followed in his wake and after an interval a plain-clothes Garda, whom neither Galvin nor Moroney recognised, followed.

Moroney stood up slowly, watching the young man's face intently.

"Right, thanks," he said to no one. The uniformed Gardai left. The plain clothes stood leaning against the wall and ensured that the door closed fully.

Moroney looked at the elastoplast over the man's left eye.

"Sit there," he pointed to the chair he had vacated.

Galvin stood behind the chair. The young man turned slightly to look at him. Then he sat on the edge of the chair. His hair looked wet. His skin reminded Moroney of a jail-bird. Which is probably what he was. Moroney put him at about twenty-four.

The prisoner held his handcuffed wrists up from his knees. Moroney ignored the gesture. Instead, he switched on the tape recorder.

"Your name in full."

"Volunteer James Duffy," the man replied with assurance. Moroney glanced over the prisoner's shoulder at Galvin.

"And where are you from, Duffy?"

"The Six Counties," he answered.

Without warning, Galvin grabbed him by the hair and lifted him out of the chair. As Duffy reached to his head with his arms, Galvin punched him under the ribs. Duffy wheezed and tottered sideways as Galvin released his grip on his hair. He squirmed on the floor, his face knotted. His sharp intakes of breath stopped abruptly as he was lifted into the chair. He sat crazily leaning with his eyes watering through the slits of his eyelids.

"I insist on medical treatment, to be examined by a doctor, that's my right," he wheezed. He was beginning to open his eyes more to let the tears escape. He didn't open them in time to avoid a knee in the side of the face. The blow filled the room with a *thock* sound just before the screech of the upturned chair. He fell uncontrolled to the floor.

Galvin raised his eyebrows slightly. He nodded to Moroney who was now standing over the prisoner. Duffy was breathing through his nose in bursts.

"Up," Galvin said.

Again he was lifted up by the hair. He was determined to keep his eyes open. Duffy sat shakily, fearfully checking the man standing to his side in the edge of his vision. His body was like a spring, arching away from the threat.

"We'll try again now. Your rights as you call them don't mean anything here. The policeman who was killed had rights too. Common sense should tell you to say all you know. There's no one else, just the three of us," Galvin said quietly.

Duffy edged onto one buttock and darted his eyes from Galvin to Moroney standing beside him. He could feel his cheek thickening already, pressing up to his eye. He probed with his tongue and found two loose teeth. A glaucous liquid was leaking into his mouth from somewhere.

"Don't delude yourself. Your outfit talks about a state of war, so stop playing public house solicitor and bellyaching about your rights. You answer the questions put to you and I'll see what I can do about you leaving here in one piece," Galvin added.

"Now. Where are you from?" Moroney asked.

"Newry," Duffy said thickly.

"What were you at this afternoon?" Galvin asked.

"Well–"

The chair was kicked from under him and he fell heavily to the floor. Before he had time to cover it, Galvin kicked him in the side of the head. A flare of light exploded in his brain and he heard a sound like a waterfall. Dimly he tried to roll onto his knees and get away. Halfway up he felt steadying hands on his back. Then a tremendous kick in the stomach almost lifted him off the floor. As though from a long way off, he heard someone telling him to get up. He decided that he wouldn't. A blinding pain in the small of his back made his legs tingle. He heard a yelp. He found himself back on the edge of the seat. Something was in his way as he looked to the side where he expected the cop to be.

"What were you at?"

"As true as God, nothing," a voice said. His own voice, like out of a pipe.

"Continue." No kick.

"We're down for a while to get a rest. Fun, a bit of a holiday," he whispered. He looked up into the impassive face of the policeman.

"Are you part of an active service unit in your area?"

The prisoner hesitated. Then he recoiled at the slight movement of that shadow to his side which could only be that other cop.

"I'm a driver," he blurted out. He swallowed more of the liquid in his mouth. "I don't do the other stuff at all."

The policeman by the door lit up a cigarette.

"Just a driver," murmured Moroney. He looked at the prisoner's feet as if he were studying them. Then he returned his gaze to Duffy's bruised face.

"There's no just-a-driver here. Killing a policeman is a capital offence. You did just as much as your friends. That's the way the law looks at it too. Your two pals are singing like canaries. According to them you do a lot more than driving."

Duffy tried hard not to show some relief. He knew this cop was lying. He kept his head down. Maybe he'd get out of this one.

"Where'd you get the car?"

"In Dublin."

"Where'd you get the car?"

"Like I–"

The chair leg shrieked as Duffy rolled toward the wall. The plain clothes at the door kicked him in the shin. As he tried to roll away, Galvin kicked him in the small of the back. His legs went numb. The light in the room began to pulse and run up to him. He remembered the name they gave these cops in the South, The Heavy Gang. He felt himself pulled up and he was left trying to stay standing. He couldn't. He fainted.

When he came to he was in the chair again. A smell of baby came to him, strong. He had puked down his shirt, he realised. He looked up. Nothing had changed. He tried to turn slightly and check where the other cop was. How much time had passed?

"Where'd you get the car?"

"I swear to God," Duffy began. The voice, his voice, resonated through his skull. He was sure it was someone else's voice. He knew what he wanted to say, but his hearing wasn't picking up what he thought the voice was saying.

"... I came down on the train is all. That's all. I was told to meet the others at a hotel."

"What hotel?"

"The Bur ... the Burg. The Burlington."

"When?"

"The day before yesterday, yes."

"Who told you?"

"I just got a phone call. A fella phoned."

"Where did you meet these two before?"

"As true as God, I never did. They're from Belfast."

Vaguely, Duffy wondered if he could control what he was saying. It was like being stoned—you didn't know if you said it or just thought it. He understood he had to keep the shared illusion about the other two being caught. He doubted they'd be taken. They were hard men and they were wanted, so they had little enough to lose. They had made him nervous the way they hardly said a word all day.

"All I know," the voice continued, "is that they told me to lose that patrol car. I remember we ran into a dead end and they jumped out of the car. I remember them shooting. And me trying to get out the door on my side. I was halfway out. I was lucky not to get me leg sliced off so I was."

"What were you at this afternoon?"

Duffy hesitated. Like a magnetic force, he could feel the closeness of the cop behind him. His skin tickled alarms.

"I think it was a bank job. The boys was bored."

"Where?"

"Cruising is all. They never told me anything, as true as ..."

"Where have you been staying?"

"At that hotel. Same as them," Duffy added.

A light knock at the door. Plain clothes opened it. Galvin left the room. He closed the door gently behind him.

In the hallway, the Special Branch man whispered, "No sign of them or the guns. We think they got out of the area right away."

"This yo-yo says they're Belfast and that's all he knows. They'll be headed back into the city now. They were staying at the Burlington so set the place up overnight anyway, though I doubt it. Get in first and have a look around. Remember who you're dealing with. They might have handguns."

"What about your man inside?"

Galvin stroked his chin.

"Ah, he's only a dummy. He's not trained at all. He has the willies with Moroney in there."

"We have the check-points up on the Bray Road and Merrion Road. Nothing yet. We're starting the house-to-house about now," the Special Branch man said.

And there'll be nothing from the check-points either if that little shitebird is telling the truth, Galvin added silently. Hard men.

"Set up something for this fella in the Bridewell, would you. They can't keep him here. We'll be done with him in a few minutes. For the moment anyway. Make sure the door-to-door thing is kept up. And I want every house on our lists visited by a policeman tonight, especially on the south side of the city. Sympathisers, politicos, hangers-on, I don't give a shite. Show the flag. They'll know that they can't hide out there."

"Yes, sir."

"And get a bit of first aid for this fecker in here. Maybe a concussion or eardrums. Don't take any guff out of him. He fell down a few times and hurt himself."

"Yes, sir."

When Galvin re-entered the room, Duffy looked over to him. Duffy was hunched over in the chair. The room smelled bad. It was hot now.

"Duffy. In between now and the time we see you again, you have some thinking to do. You should opt for self-preservation if you have any savvy at all. Your mates are in the same boat. And here's something else to dwell on while you still have fond memories of my colleagues here. Your outfit will be told that you're singing away here, so you'll have to square it with them in the clink when you get there. Who knows, we mightn't have you alive enough after that to hang you anyway. Doesn't matter what you say. We have the finger on plenty of your lads here and all we have to do is lift a few of them and drop your name, Volunteer Duffy. You don't know the half of it. Start remembering quick. You're up to your oxters now so all you can do is buy your way into some kind of protective custody. And even that won't mean much unless we see our way to some allowances later on. Remember: you killed a Garda officer. We can have you looking like a Hallowe'en mask at the end of a rope."

Moroney saw the wariness in the prisoner's eyes. The side of his head was swollen already and there was a drying film of blood at the corners of his mouth. Galvin felt a final rush of contempt for this pathetic fool. *He thinks he has one up on us because we're codding him about his cronies being in custody,* Moroney reflected. *No training. Maybe it'd never dawn on him how suggestion worked. We know that he thinks he knows, that's the control.* Moroney believed Duffy would get his story in soon enough. He also believed that it wouldn't amount to much.

"Get this worm out of here," Moroney said.

Chapter Ten

Minogue felt it was taking him forever to reach the shopping centre. His mind was cluttered with dark forms whose details escaped him as he tried to concentrate. He felt cold and he felt old. Maybe this is how it is when you lose your nerve, or when you let yourself admit you've lost your nerve, he thought.

Minogue parked his Fiat two rows away from the supermarket. He checked his pocket for money. He stopped walking and stood between parked cars, fingering coins to the side of his palm. The air was thick and moist around him. He pocketed his find and resumed walking. An expanse of glass confronted him beyond the rows of parked cars. He could see himself, head and shoulders above the car roofs as he stepped out onto the roadway. He felt damp and creaky out of the car. The sky was low, greyed and browned. He smelled a faint diesel scent hanging in the air. In the gutter ahead of him lay a discarded umbrella, like a broken bird. He stepped across rainbowed splashes of petrol now quite prominent after the rain.

Ahead of him, his figure became larger. This is how I must look to other people, he realised. People were moving behind the reflections in the glass. He heard the baskety metal clash of the shopping carts shoved away. Minogue thought of Debussy. Music under water, shimmering. Everything slow. Iseult had taken Kathleen and himself to a recital in the Art Gallery some weeks after he had come out of the hospital. Minogue had been astounded at what he had heard. He was sure the doctor had been wrong about the hearing loss. There in the hall, with the musicians warming up, the sounds had been like a dream. They walked toward the great hall, Minogue hardly feeling his feet move under him, quite lost to the gathering sounds which washed over and enveloped him. Was that what it was like when you kicked up your heels and your soul took off? Like a big underwater cave and everything changed and shining.

Silly to be thinking of Agnes McGuire and that at the same time. And then that young Guard in the car, dead now, just like that, like he never lived, another gravestone being made, an editorial on the outrage. What was the use of it all?

To Minogue's left, a movement between cars caught his eye. Ahead of him, the glass was now a darkening mirror. Rows of cars to his left and right in the mirror. Minogue wondered if he should go to a record shop later. A flicker of movement registered in Minogue's unconcern. He stepped over a worn yellow line. *Debussy was like breathing under water, so it was.* Minogue was vaguely aware of a soft hiss of tires on the tarmac. *As if you could swim next to the dolphins and go into coral caves.* Minogue realised that he was not surrounded by cars anymore. In a ridiculous second, he was standing on the strand in Lahinch, again a child, with the ebbing tide pulling the grains away from under him. He'd feel the tug and he'd turn and realise how far away the others were. All the way to Boston, Mam said as she pointed out over the waves.

Minogue heard the squeal as the tires bit in. He stopped. He looked to his left to see the car bearing down on him. A silhouette and beads of old rain on the glass. The engine roared and gulped as the automatic grabbed onto second gear. A pulse ran up to Minogue's scalp. Where? Minogue's body was all wrong for heading for the kerb ahead.

Still he moved a foot awkwardly in that direction. He dropped onto his flexed knees with his arms spread in a move from a deadly Chubby Checker dance. *This can't work,* he was thinking, as his body ran ahead of him, shifting from foot to foot awaiting a decision. *I can't stay here, I'll be run over and killed.* Where? Don't think. Minogue's take-off foot wrenched him back toward the parked cars. His brain followed. He could feel rather than see the speeding car change direction. His legs seemed so long and so slow. They weren't really propelling him, he was tottering. The car was a breath away, bigger, final. The space between the Fiesta and the Mini parked ahead of him seemed huge but unattainable. The colours of the cars were now almost luminescent. The rush of the approaching car filled up all the space under the clouds.

Then Minogue was on his knees, pitching forward. His palms grazed along the wet tarmac. His shoulder bounced off a panel. His legs took him over on his side and he catapulted over the downed shoulder, heels drumming a door on a car and the tar grinding and pulling his hair as his head came over. The cars trembled and wavered as the white car shot by the gap. Tiny drops of water sprayed up from its wake fell lightly over Minogue's face as he lay there. A dull burning came from his forehead. He tried to get up, his hands splayed on the tar. *They might come back, I don't know.*

His leather soles slipped and he fell down again. It felt dangerous to be so near the underside of cars, so close to the wheels. As he elbowed up again, he felt wetness at his knees and in his socks. He crouched between the cars. Then he darted to the back of the car and looked up through the back window. A white car was speeding out onto the Kilmacud Road. It bounced on a kerb and moved abruptly around cars. As it passed out of his sight, Minogue heard horns blowing. He was trembling, ready for doing something but there was nothing now. His body was twitching. He began to breathe deeply as he leaned on the Fiesta. He looked up to find a middle-aged woman, head and shoulders, two car roofs over from him.

"Are you a'right now?" she called out.

Minogue's body was beginning to tighten and ache.

"Did you see that, missus? Did you see that car?"

"What car, now?" she said, softer.

"A white car. This minute."

"No, I didn't."

Minogue swore.

"And your head. Is your head all right?" she asked.

Minogue reached up to the burning. His fingers showed orangey blood.

"Here, I have an elastoplast in the car. Come here. What happened to you at all?"

Minogue leaned on the bonnet of the car. His neck was beginning to hurt.

"Well, missus, unless I'm mad entirely, someone tried to run me over."

The woman stood away from Minogue and raised a hand to her mouth. Her eyes widened.

"On purpose? Go away, you're codding me," she whispered.

"Indeed and I'm not, ma'am," Minogue said resignedly.

"But that sort of thing only goes on in ..." she hesitated.

"In America? In the movies is it? I wish you were right," Minogue replied.

"Shouldn't we call the Garda then?" she whispered.

Minogue had found enough control over his trembling to flick at the particles of wet dirt which had been ground into his coat. He looked quizzically at the woman who was suspended, tongue over lip, in that ageless motion of trying to get the sticky parts of the elastoplast away from the wrap without dropping the whole thing or sticking her thumb into it. He bowed to let her apply it to his forehead.

"Thanks very much now. Sure I am the police, there's the rub," Minogue murmured.

* * *

The tanned man hissed as he spoke into the phone.

"I don't give a shit. Take anything that'll lead them further out of there and get to hell out of the place as fast as you can."

The tone of the man on the other end turned more petulant.

"After all the trouble we went to? There's a lot of me own tools in there as well. That'll take time. I mean to say, I can't just walk out the door. Look–"

"Shut up for a minute and listen. There's been a royal screw-up with that Mercedes you had in the place. Sooner or later the cops will trace that car to your place, and you won't be whining about your tools then. Just get them and get out. Go take a holiday or something."

"Here, it wasn't me who handed over the car. And those tools cost me a fortune, mister. Lookit, whoever you are, I don't care. I just did the plates and built hidey holes for a few cars. I don't ask any questions."

"Exactly. You don't ask any questions. No one will know you worked out of that place. We looked after everything else. If you did what you're supposed to do, there'll be nothing to tie you to that place. It's all a dead-end, the cheques and the rental thing. Christ, you couldn't have been in the place more than half a dozen times."

"But who'll pay for me tools?"

"Look. You've never been fingerprinted so no one can trace you unless you damn well hang around! Don't you know they have one of those guys in custody?"

"Here now, hold on a minute," the mechanic said. "I don't want to know who I'm doing this for. A job is a job. I do the work and I gets me pay. Ask me no questions and I'll tell you no lies. I'm like the three monkeys, you know what I mean? And I don't like being let in on this stuff either. It's none of my shagging business."

The tanned man spoke quietly into the telephone now.

"Listen here now. It'll become your business if you don't get out of there inside of five minutes. If by any little remote chance, I get the slightest irritation because you screwed up somewhere ... you'll be getting a new face knitted for yourself. You'll be playing with fucking Lego for the rest of your life, do you hear me?"

"I'm not deaf."

"Where did you leave that Merc off for those guys anyway?"

"Ah sure I didn't have to leave it off anywhere. Just outside in the back lane here. I left the key under the wheel like that other fella told me. Your pal, whatever his name is."

The tanned man almost threw the phone across the room. His hand tightened around it. Outside the bloody garage, of all the places on this island. Outside the garage. That was the bitter end.

The mechanic listened but heard only breathing on the line.

"Are you still there...?"

"When did that other car go out, the one with the new tank?"

"Yesterday. Picked up, no bother."

At least the main part of the operation was intact, the tanned man thought. He eased his grip on the phone.

"No hitches?"

"No. Your pal must have come over some evening and packed in whatever it is. All I know is I came in and there was a note saying bolt the thing back on, the thing is packed in and sealed. That's what I did. Dirtied it up good like I was told and left it parked on what-you-me-call-it Street, er ... Nassau Street."

The tanned man felt his body ease into the chair more. So that part had gone fine.

"Look. We'll pay you for your tools or whatever you can't get out of there in five minutes."

"Five minutes?"

"The cops will look around the lane first probably, damn it! Just make sure there's nothing with your initials or that sort of thing. Go to the post office in Rathmines tomorrow. There'll be an envelope in your name."

The mechanic's voice lightened.

"Right you be, chief."

"And remember what I said. If I get so much as a ripple because of anything you do, the organisation will take care of that too. There's nowhere to hide."

The tanned man hung up. He surveyed the hotel room. The problems amounted to little more than a few stones falling away. There would be no avalanche. Maybe in the future he might have the leisure to rethink this. By then he might even see that this series of mishaps was very functional. It plucked out the gangsters in the movement, the inept. If anything, the old guard in the movement would be discredited even more for not being able to control the mobsters they brought south for R & R.

He didn't feel any sympathy for any of those men. In fact, it would have been better if the two were shot out of hand. As for the third one, he'd probably spill but he was just a gofer. He might even distract the Branch with a few yarns.

He rose and walked to the bathroom. He felt sweaty. While the bath was filling, he hung his jacket. He took out the gun and laid it next to the telephone. He unhooked the harness, cursing inwardly at the sweat dribbling through the Velcro. The phone was still warm as he spoke into it again:

"A beer. Any kind. Has to be cold."

Such habits, he mused, as he put down the phone. Bathing at the first signs of sweat; a cold beer. He returned to the bathroom and laid the gun next to the handbasin. In the mirror he saw a strong and youthful man. His mother had said it well, 'If you don't look after yourself, no one else will.'

The bellboy wore an outfit that made him look like a New York leprechaun. He tipped him a pound at the door out of spite.

"Thanks very much, sir. Anything you want now, just give a little tinkle." A little bow, the door closed.

He swallowed a cold draught from the neck of the bottle. Roll on the future, he thought, that we may never have servile Irishmen like him born here again.

Minogue stood aching in the telephone booth.

"Uh-huh, yes. A white Granada, newish. Yep. The new model. No, I didn't get it. Call me at home, so. Anytime."

Agnes McGuire had heard police sirens at intervals while she studied in her room. It took little to distract her. By times, she awoke from a trance, exasperated that she had not turned a page in the book for ten minutes. She was thinking of her family and Italy. The two scenes alternated. She imagined herself walking with a packsack through dusty roads in Tuscany. It'd be dusk, an infinite orange world, glowing and washing into pinks. She'd stop at a farmhouse and be welcomed. She'd chat with the family for hours, listening to their stories. Agnes would be a pilgrim of sorts and people there would understand that.

Then Agnes was walking through streets in Belfast. It was raining. She had messages to get. Her arms ached from carrying groceries. Her fingers were numbed by the handles of the plastic bags which bit into them. Her mother was waiting at home. She was afraid to go out herself.

In the mornings, Agnes would bid goodbye and shoulder her bag now laden with homemade wine, bread and cheese. It would be no weight at all. She might even sit at the side of the road for a half hour and watch the mist dissipate, revealing an ancient land.

Agnes looked out over the sodden garden three floors below. Enclosed by enormous railings, Trinity resisted the bustle outside. Traffic was clogging Nassau Street. Agnes could see forms behind the steamed windows of the double-decked buses as they crawled by. A hand would work to clear part of a window, a face look out.

In Tuscany there'd likely be animals drawing wagons of some description.

Leaving the Belfast supermarket, an armoured carrier they called 'pigs' drove by like a sightless dinosaur and, gone by, the hard and challenging faces of soldiers appeared, looking to the wake of the vehicle's passage. Itching to play with their guns. Maybe somewhere nearby men were watching from a window too, deciding if they would shoot.

Piazzas at dusk, candlelight on the faces of the working men as they sat at tables, gathering in the cool of the evening.

Agnes was aware that Jarlath had no presence in these journeys. She could see him clearly, besuited, walking the streets of his own city here in a few years. He might wind up doing law or concentrating on economics. He'd work in an office. He'd be kind though. He mightn't get far on the ladder so his Da might pull him into the fruit business quickly to get him set up. Maybe Jarlath would take the year off like he said he would. Still, Agnes could not see him so changed as to be out on those roads and streets in Italy, or leaning on the railing of a ferry leaving Brindisi ...

Lights were now gathering strength out in the streets. Traffic was easing. Behind her, the room was obscured. Agnes switched on the light. It was time to eat. She returned to the table and sorted the photocopied pages. Agnes, who could not now summon up the golden landscapes of Tuscany, began to shiver. Her eyes salted as she worked. She made no attempt to stop the steady roll of the first tear.

What straightened Minogue out was the unforeseen arrival of Iseult for tea. Kathleen's mock chiding, now that she had to include Iseult in the pan, helped him to land.

"What happened to you?" Iseult said breezily. "Ma, did he make improper advances, is it?"

Iseult turned to him and play-punched him in the shoulder. "You're a bit of a devil I'm thinking, Da. At your age. Ma you did the right thing. Feminism is coming of age. Down with patriarchy. What's in the pan?"

"Hafner's sausages. Do you want an egg, lovey?" Kathleen asked.

"I think Da has the duck egg. Give me a look. Did she hit you with the pan or what?"

"Very smart, I'm sure," Minogue said. He reached to touch the elastoplast and the lump which swelled it out from his forehead.

"Have a bit of sympathy now. Your daddy fell down in the carpark. A terrible day all around," Kathleen murmured.

"Did you spill any out of the bottle, Da?"

"Any what?"

"Whatever it was. Powers or Jameson."

Kathleen looked over from the cooker at her daughter.

"How well you know the names of all the whiskies. Is that the sum total of third level education these days?" Kathleen asked.

Minogue poured the tea. He was careful to keep his finger on the lid so it didn't fall off. This heartened him, this familiar precaution bedded into the rituals of the household. All the little idiosyncrasies of the house were shared knowledge. How to get the lawnmower started. How to tighten the shears and keep them sharp. How to get the garage door to close properly. Which ring on the cooker didn't heat up well. How to make sure you didn't bugger up the washing machine because the switch was contrary.

"Did you hear about the Garda being killed out in Blackrock?" Kathleen asked.

"I saw the headlines. Was it a fella you knew, Da?"

"No, actually."

Kathleen scooped sausages, black pudding and a fried egg onto Minogue's plate. Iseult leaned her chin on the heels of her hands, and elbowed into the plate exactly the way her parents had tried to train her out of doing for years. She watched her father attack the sausages. He looked up at her.

"Isn't it awful entirely?" he said quietly.

Kathleen sat down. She watched Minogue pour her tea.

His shirt-cuffs were dirty. He had missed a bit shaving under his ear. Hair was bushing out of his nose. She looked over to Iseult and saw her looking back. Her vision changed with the salty film which came between them. When she blinked, a drop popped on the table-cloth. Kathleen kept her head down then. The odd time, when she looked up, Iseult was looking at her, a big open face like the moon on her, as if she knew.

"Tell us now," Minogue said at last. "Any chance you'd set us up for one of those music recitals again?"

As was his habit when working to a deadline, Allen skipped his tea. He felt that his public lectures needed to be revised now. The danger, he felt, was in routinising the delivery. He had noticed his own inner voice telling him that he was drifting into clichés. His metaphors strained him. He was actually tiring himself out by trying to suppress the inner critic. He tried to persuade himself that every audience was a new one, but that didn't satisfy him.

This time it wasn't just a matter of setting up some new idiom or sprinkling in new anecdotes and metaphors. He had come up with a good one during the week: 'We cannot live in the subjunctive or pluperfect any more than we can live in the future. Mental illness is also a case of people largely living out false histories. Living out life in the wrong tense. Wrongs done us in childhood, wrongs done in history must not put blinkers on the future ...' That'd certainly strike a chord in any audience.

Allen sat back. He wondered if this sounded a bit academic. Where would he deliver this one? Newry? Allen remembered that Newry was largely a Catholic town. He determined to blot this understanding out so that he would not skew the lecture because of the fact. He would not pander to partisan learnings. He had spoken in Newry before and he had been heckled a lot, but he had also been applauded. There was an informal committee there to welcome him and to put him up.

Allen switched on the radio for the half-six news. Two armed men were still at large in the Blackrock area after a shooting incident today. A Garda was dead and one of the group was in custody. Police believed that they had intercepted the group en route to a bank robbery. All roads in the vicinity had road-blocks manned by armed Gardai and members of the armed forces.

He stiffened in his chair. The small of his back began to ache. He began his habitual inner talk to relieve the stress. He tried to loosen his muscles but couldn't. Abruptly he switched off the radio. He noticed that his hand trembled slightly.

Allen tried to return to his notes. He could easily take six months off. Greece, say, or Sardinia; someplace warm, distant. Maybe the break could be complete: he might never come back.

At this notion, Allen's thoughts of the lecture all but fled from his mind. He could not afford to think of this possibility. It threatened to burst completely through the dike he had built to staunch such thoughts. Again he tried to rescue his former life by concentrating on his notes. It wouldn't work. Allen threw his pencil across the room. He let his arms hang loose over the arms of the chair. The silence after the radio seemed to indict him as he looked at the refined clichés in his notes. He saw the hopeful, expectant faces of his audiences, those thoughtful, law abiding citizens–exactly the ones who were not involved in the violence. Those others were out in the night some-where, planning, watching, waiting. They had waited for Allen. Now they had drawn him into their cycle of malignant atavism.

Daily he had checked to see if he was drifting into that helplessness and passivity which his training led him to expect. He had noticed a distance growing between his waking thoughts and his work. Some sleeplessness too, but he had preserved a spark by dint of his own powers. He could not always staunch the fear which came to him when he was reminded of where he now stood.

Allen willed himself up from the chair. He stood for a count of twenty, barely quelling this bout of panic. He knew that it would get worse too. How many more crises could he withstand, keeping up the manic façade of a normal life? How long before he broke ... or before he would make his break? Maybe now, this evening, this miserable evening, the reckoning had come. He hadn't risen to being a professor of psychology in Trinity College from a poor emigrant family in Bir-mingham just to go under meekly, another victim.

Allen felt the fear and hatred ebb and a determination setting in in their place. He looked about his office, at the remnants of what was his old life. He could phone travel agents for a start.

Allen reconnected the phone. It rang almost as soon as he took his hand off it. "Allen?"

"Yes?"

"I've been trying to reach you for some time now. You should stop this childish business of unplugging your phone. We must meet. As soon as possible, actually."

"Your office?"

"No. It's better if we meet outside Trinity."

Loftus paused as if trying to sense the atmosphere for cues.

"OK, then. I'll be dining alone in the Granary. I'm leaving now. I'll expect you there presently."

Allen put down the phone without answering. The image of Agnes

McGuire came to him. He had watched her from a distance in the church at Walsh's funeral. Her face radiated a calm, even when she paused to whisper to Walsh's parents. There was an irreducible truth to her which Allen had recognised in a handful of people he had met over his lifetime. She was an enigma to him but overwhelmingly of this world at the same time. Not the longing for a matriarchal comfort in him, no, more a feeling he remembered as a child, on a visit to Liverpool. He had seen a great tanker anchored offshore, mysterious and inaccessible to him. Promise.

Outside, puddles at the edges of the pathways held sections of Trinity buildings, moving them as Allen walked by. Parts of the cobblestones had dried. The grass seemed to breathe. The air was close. Students were calling to each other across the echoing stone square. A gowned lecturer helloed him in the gathering gloom, pipe smoke smell trailing him. Lights swelled soft yellow out onto the stones. Allen felt that he had let down a load, a load that had clung to him for most of his life. He did have a choice, one choice at least, and he was determined to use it.

Chapter Eleven

Moroney and Galvin, the two Special Branch detectives, stepped from their car in Baggot Street. They had been preceded by plain-clothes officers from a surveillance unit some hours before.

Neither of the detectives was happy with what they had heard. The driver of the Mercedes had picked up the stolen car with its plates doctored in a lane behind Baggot Street. On the way in from Blackrock, they had been radioed that the garage had been located. They had had to decide whether to keep a lookout on the premises or whether to go in right then and there. Curiously, it was Galvin, the detective who had done the heavy with the prisoner, who was in favour of keeping watch.

"You never know. They mightn't have heard ..." he had said.

"It's been on the radio and the telly" Moroney replied.

"But they mightn't reckon on our pal telling us anything. They might be kind of slow on the details. Might come in a hurry to tidy up or something."

Moroney wondered if perhaps they hadn't an embarrassment of riches. Perhaps they had done their job too well, getting the driver to tell them what he had.

"Ah, give them credit now. They'll have been mobile and ready to get the hell out at a moment's notice. I have an idea that there might be something useful in this place for us. My guess is that it's part of a network. I think we have to move fast. We have to get some results, that's the politics of the thing right now. The shootings and bombings are on the up and up. Can't wait."

Galvin said nothing.

"We'll go in, what?"

"All right," Galvin said.

The two men walked by the entrance to the lane. The light was poor. They recognised the old coachhouses, garages and sheds which had formerly been servants' quarters, stables and the like. Now they were used as storage buildings or for parking. Often they were gutted and turned into pricey mews houses. They wondered if they hadn't gone to the wrong lane. There was nobody about, no cars. A man in a light raincoat stepped out from the shadows.

"Sergeant?" he said.

"Hello. Special Branch. Yes. We're just in from Blackrock. What's the story?"

"Very discreet. We met a fellow up the lane who has an electrical shop there. He knew the place."

"Are you sure?"

"I am. He even remembers walking by and the door was half-open. Said he saw the Mercedes in there."

"See anyone?"

"He didn't. We haven't seen anyone either. There's men over beyond and a few in the garden there with night glasses. We're ready to go."

The way he said it irked Moroney. These fellows were more like paramilitaries. They didn't let you know they were in the area half the time. Strolling about the place with submachine guns, like they were out walking the dog.

"Hold on there now. What's the chain of command here?"

"We were called in sir. Told to wait for your instructions."

"Who?"

"Superintendant Reynolds."

Moroney almost smiled. They had been given a surprising amount of leeway. That'd be one in the eye for those yobbos.

"And you're...?"

"McAuliffe, sir."

"Right, McAuliffe, give them the billy."

McAuliffe fingered his earphone more securely into his ear. He turned back a lapel and bent his head toward the mike.

"We are going when I say. Have you got a clear field up there? OK. Back up 1 and 3. Clear? Any lights in there? Right 9 and 10, back door to yard opens inward all right? Ready units 2, 4 and 6. What? Yes, jemmy it."

He paused and looked down the silent lane. Only the centre of the lane was in light.

"Stand to the side, gentlemen," he whispered to the two detectives. Leaning to the mike, he said, "Go, now."

He reached under his coat and drew the sling tight to his shoulder as he poked an Uzi out. He ran on his toes down the lane.

The detectives saw a half dozen men sit upright on the roofs of sheds to the front and sides of the garage. Three more men in what looked like jogging suits ran to the door. One produced a crowbar and levered a crack between doors until a loud splintering sound echoed down the lane. The man swore and quickly inserted the crowbar again. This time the doors gave way and the crowbar fell to the ground. Another figure yanked open the door and leaped in, shouting. The men on the roofs jerked their heads slightly from side to side, listening intently to their earphones, all the while training their weapons on the doors. A can was kicked over inside. The shouting died down. A light went on. Still no one appeared in the lane. No one had noticed, the Special Branch men realised. They recognized McAuliffe's silhouette in the light which spilled from the door. He beckoned to them.

Inside, the men who had stormed the place stood around looking both disappointed and relieved. One of them was speaking into his radio and staring off into space as his head inclined to listen to the reply.

The garage was not really a garage. It was a dusty shed. Some planks lay haphazardly on the floor. They could see right up to the rafters. There was a faint smell of paint. Some rusted garden tools lay piled in a corner. A homemade stool made of rough plank scraps lay on its side. A car pulled up outside. In it were two uniformed Gardai. A small old man sat in the back.

"He's the one up the lane. The electrical shop," McAuliffe said.

The detectives walked over to the car.

"Hello. We're police officers," Moroney said, leaning in the window. "You're the man who spotted that the place was being used as a garage...?"

"I am that."

"Anything unusual at all lately?"

"Not to speak of. No. But didn't I see a fella working on that Mercedes Benz the other day."

"Yesterday, like?"

"The day before."

"And did you know him? Did you know his face, like?"

"You know, I never even seen him. I saw his legs I think. He was doing something at the front of the car, down near the bumper. 'Hello,' I says to him. And he says 'Hello' back. That was it. The only time I seen him and I didn't see him at all."

"Never saw his face at all?"

"Not a bit of it," the old man said with a look of satisfaction.

Moroney looked away to his colleague. The two Gardai remained in the front seats listening to the dispatcher on the radio. Galvin's eyes went toward a heaven he privately doubted.

"Tell you what," the old man said suddenly. "I saw him, or actually didn't see him fiddling with another car."

"And...?"

"And nothing. I don't know what class of car it was at all."

"No idea? When was this?"

"Early in the week. He had it up on one of those jacks. He had the back up, I know that. He had the car backed in that time. I heard him wriggling around under the back. 'Hello' I says–"

"–and he says 'Hello' back," Galvin interrupted.

"How did you know?" the old man asked.

"Was there a colour?"

"Let's see. You know when something is crimson and purple at the same time...?"

"Magenta?"

"Ma what?"

"Was it new?"

The old man's face took on an indignant look.

"And how would I know? Do you think I'm an encyclopaedia of cars or something?"

"How well you know the Mercedes, though."

"Sure that's a quality car, mister. There was a singer in Dublin by that name back in the thirties. Would you credit that? Mercedes McNamara. A bit of an actress too. Before your time, I'm thinking."

Moroney looked down the lane. He was aware of McAuliffe standing next to him.

"Will you be wanting the fingerprint brigade in, sir?"

Moroney wondered if McAuliffe was being bloody-minded. 'And should I try picking my nose, sir? Or maybe will I let a fart, sir?'

"Where are they?"

"The van's out on Baggot Street, sir. I think you passed it on your way in," McAuliffe replied.

Moroney scrutinised McAuliffe's face for any visible trace of insolence. He could find none and this irritated him all the more. These lads had been trained in leaping about like the Chinese, living off the bog, killing people with paper cups and that sort of effort. Very modern men entirely. Toughs who'd probably never have to start on the beat and get promoted into plain clothes.

"I'll be needing you to bring this man here to the station and go through the car book with him," Moroney said.

"I took the liberty of assigning that work to the two Gardai here from Harcourt Street station. It's my understanding that we've done our part," McAuliffe said.

"What?" said the old man in the back of the car.

"Here, leave me off at the bus, the number 10. I have to get home. The missus'll be wondering if I've run off with a young wan. Hee hee. Are we right?" the old man continued.

The Garda behind the wheel looked wearily at McAuliffe, then at Moroney.

"We need you to look through a few pictures of cars for us," McAuliffe said to the old man.

"Are you joking? Sure I've done what I can. I have to get home. Jases."

"You can call the wife from the station. We'll drive you home. You'll get your tea too," said the Garda in the passenger seat.

"Feck it, lads. God forgive me for cursing. *Magnum P.I.* is on the telly. I never miss it."

McAuliffe waved the van into the laneway. His men were putting on jackets and dispersing. A couple who had walked into the laneway stood staring as the van disgorged wires and lights and boxes. McAuliffe made himself scarce in the hubbub. When Moroney went off to look for him, he was gone. Moroney was still angry.

He found Galvin, gawking like an adolescent looking at donkeys at it in a ditch, a far cry from the heavy who had thrown the Duffy fella around that afternoon.

"Here. Leave these fellas alone. Do you know what I'm going to do? I'm going to buy a pint of stout apiece for yourself and myself and a big fuckin' sandwich below in O'Neill's. What do you think of that?"

Galvin frowned. It wasn't like Moroney to be so coarse.

As the two detectives walked out under the arch to Baggot Street, they passed several people looking down the alley at what must have looked like people making a film. There were three squad cars parked beside theirs now. As they passed one Garda, Moroney said:

"The hard man, is it yourself. How's things out in Blackrock?"

"Divil a bit," the middle-aged Garda replied and shook his head.

They walked on. As he opened the door of the car, Moroney's pessimism rolled up relentlessly behind him and broke over him. The birds had flown, he realised. It was dark now.

The following day being Friday, Kilmartin did not feel too aggrieved at having slept poorly. He had had a feeling which persisted into his dreams that something was unravelling nearby, but that it couldn't be detected. Were there a forced choice, Kilmartin would have preferred 'prosaic' to 'man of fantasy' on his gravestone. Nonetheless he felt as a child felt upon awakening, knowing it had snowed in the night, even before opening the curtain. This morning, Kilmartin's snow was quite invisible. He felt gruff. He smoked four cigarettes in the car on his way to work. Eight hours ago, the two gunmen in Blackrock had not been found. He had gone home after midnight, despondent and furious by turns.

Of the two men who waited outside his office, he would have preferred not to see Minogue. Connors he could send on some errand. Minogue's odd face gave Kilmartin a tiny pop in his stomach. He groaned inside at the thought of a morning's gas.

"Good morrow, Matt. Tea, then?"

"Good morning yourself," Minogue replied, fingering the folders under his arm.

"Step in, step in. Connors, would you kindly root out some tea?"

Minogue sat lightly in the chair. Kilmartin sat on the edge of his desk, wondering if the *clackety clack* of the typewriters would now add a headache to his woes.

"Any big moves, Matt?" inquired Kilmartin gently.

"Well now. This thing will be eclipsed by other concerns, I'm sure, so I'll make a long story short. Someone tried to run me over yesterday. They could have tried a bit harder too, I've been thinking."

Kilmartin started. He stared at Minogue.

"Odd, isn't it? In a carpark. Of course I didn't tell Kathleen, but someone phoned the house masquerading as an old school friend, if you please. Some yarn about a reunion. All rubbish of course, but he knew where to find me and what I looked like."

This was it, Kilmartin was thinking. Minogue has gone batty. The signs were there and it's only now they're coming together.

"Yes. All part of an elaborate play. I'm thinking someone is trying to push this drug thing on me."

"I don't get it, Matt ..."

"I'm being led. That's what I'm saying. I believe that boy's girlfriend or whatever you'd call her. I'm not sure why."

"Her account of the boy...?"

"Yes. I'm not happy with the two yobbos in Trinity pushing those hints about drugs."

Kilmartin thought for a minute. Minogue seemed relaxed and somehow resolute about this. Had he changed a bit somehow? "What makes you feel that you're being led down the garden path, Matt?"

"There's the rub now. I haven't an inkling. Well, actually now I shouldn't say that at all. I have the feeling that something is happening and that time is a factor. Like while the show is on, someone is picking pockets in the cloakroom."

Kilmartin stood up and walked to the window. He risked a small burning fart for relief. Minogue's thing was contagious, damn it all. Hints and inklings, suspicions. What Kilmartin really wanted was to be called to help in this business last night, not to be left eavesdropping in the radio room for great events which made careers for other men. Something you could leap into and work at and get credit for.

"Anyway. I'm hoping the car was stolen and that it'll turn up. There's no reason for people trying to bump me off, you know. The old grey matter is nagging at me to believe there's something in this to do with that boy Walsh."

Indeed, thought Kilmartin. *Well now, Matt Minogue, I'm not going to come straight out and tell you what I think, but I'll give you a hint.*

"Tell you what, Matt. Give it until this evening or over the weekend. Then we can get someone else to start from scratch and rehash it."

Kilmartin caught wind of his newborn fart. It had emerged and lain in waiting only to burst when he had congratulated himself for his discretion. Holy God, it was a killer. The window was stuck. So was

Kilmartin. A sulphurous aroma rose around him. Minogue uncrossed his legs and brushed lightly across his nose with his fingers.

"Right so. I'll look over the parents' statements again and rethink it," said Minogue, rising from the chair.

"Good, Matt. Look, do you want me to follow up on this thing yesterday? Where that car came at you?"

Minogue recognised the challenge. *Minogue is gone loony, right?*

"No. I'll go through the thing myself."

"Sergeant Minogue? Doherty here. You asked about a car."

Doherty? Right, the one from the Vehicle Bureau.

"Yes. Are you Pat Doherty's brother?"

"I am."

"Tell him they haven't a ghost on Sunday in Nenagh. The Wexford crowd will take the day. Ye'll have to play the wings and pass the ball more."

"Go on out of that," Doherty said. "If the rain comes again, we'll scalp that crowd. The Wexford crowd hate the rain."

"My eye," said Minogue.

"I'll put money on it," Doherty replied.

"I don't want to be robbing you."

"Well. A white Ford Granada was stolen on Churchtown Road in the afternoon. Are you with me?"

"I am."

"Reported at 10:53 last night. Some old bollocks had been in a pub all that time. And then he wanted to drive home, but he couldn't find his bloody car."

"Comical."

"The country is gone to pot," Doherty said. His Galwegian indignation came softly to Minogue, who thought of the long, open bogroads by Clifden with the clouds rolling in over the horizon, sea on the air.

"Well, it turned up today in Dundrum. Next to a bus-stop. The cheek of it, I ask you. Do you know, it caused a bit of havoc in the traffic this morning."

As if he intended we find it, Minogue realised.

"Where is it now?"

"Store Street Station."

"Good luck."

Minogue's years on the Drug Squad afforded him the chance to track down a pal, Jack Currelly.

"And how's the family, Matt?"

"Oh, pulling the divil by the tail, Jack."

"Where, now?"

"Store Street. Don't bother with the kit. Let's keep it informal for the moment. You'd know what I'm looking for straight away."

Minogue stood in the yard leaning on a freshly crushed Capri. Currelly rested on one knee on the driver's seat as he checked the interior. To Minogue, the white Granada looked threatening.

A uniformed Garda stood by, clasping a clipboard.

"Rain do you think?" a garrulous Minogue said.

"God knows now, sir. It's as like as not."

A fresh-faced lad up from the farm, big sky-blue eyes on him and a razor cut next to his chin. Trying too hard to be perfect.

Currelly kneed his way out of the car. He showed Minogue the remains of a joint nestling in the palm of his hand.

"One roach. In the ashtray, if you don't mind. Well, Sherlock. What do you think? Will we call in Dr Watson or what? Joy-ride, I'd say. Still though you'd expect the car would be done in a bit. Want me to give it the once-over in earnest?"

"No thanks." Minogue turned to the Garda.

"Do ye dust these yokes for prints or that class of thing?" Minogue asked.

"If requested, sir. If the items are part of a body of evidence. Commission of a crime, like."

"How about this one?"

"No, sir." The Garda pointed to the Comments on the sheet as he held out the clipboard for Minogue. Minogue read 'Joy-ride?' and, below, 'No apparent damage.'

"So?"

"Well, it's a question of volume really, Sergeant. Your man should be glad he got it back in one piece. There's a lot go missing in Dublin."

"And if we find a narcotic substance in it?" Minogue pressed.

"Oh in that case I'm sure that'd warrant full treatment, sir."

Whatever the hell 'full treatment' meant these days.

"To tell you the truth, sir, the car was just given the once-over very quick, like, when it came in. The real examination would be done later in the day, I'm thinking."

Good lad, Minogue thought, at least you're covering for your pals and that's no bad thing. Not the end of the world.

"Could you arrange to have it done, if you please? And have that Garda Doherty call me as soon as he has anything?"

"Yes, sir."

Currelly and Minogue strolled over to their own car.

"Is this a big deal, Matt?" Currelly asked.

"Ah you know, I'm just pulling on bits of things really."

"Terrible bloody mess that thing yesterday. Out in Blackrock."

Both men got into Minogue's car.

"And tell me, Matt, how have you been since that other business?"

"Could be worse, Jack, could be worse," Minogue heard himself reply.

The traffic on Friday in Dublin had staggered an already shaky system. Soon they became enmeshed. The sun came out and Currelly rolled down his window. On the path beside him, a well-dressed couple walked by speaking French loudly over the noise of the cars. Minogue knew there wouldn't be any prints worth a damn in the car and he was still being bobbed around on a string. He'd call Trinity to see if anything had shown up in lost and found.

The *Irish Times* headlines lay across Allen's desk, barely held in by the width of the newspaper itself. The picture of a Garda in uniform stood next to a picture of a car on its side, leaning against a Mercedes. He was sure of his decision now. Surprisingly, Allen had slept well. He had not dreamed. He felt light now. The sun threw light in the window, over his notes and against the bookcases. It was as good a time as any.

Allen was certain that he could persuade her. He returned to his notes and began trying to memorise the outline. Allen gathered his notes. He couldn't concentrate. He removed mementoes from a drawer—a pen won in grammar school, a medal of his father's. He looked around the room. There was little or nothing personal in it. A few plants—they could stay—a radio alarm clock, a poster of an old phrenology diagram. The books had been expensive but they could be allowed no weight now.

Allen fingered through the files in his desk. Anyone could take his place, marking tests, going to conferences, meeting with colleagues. Committees, proposals, luncheons. Student counselling, research, administration. Evaluation, theses, recommendations. Evisceration. Yes, that too. His friends? Allen's reserve and self-sufficiency had allowed him distance. He sat at his desk and began writing a list of what he had

to do: *'Bank, letter, solicitor.'* He'd go whether she agreed or not. He
went through his office again, selecting and discarding.

The committee met in a carpeted room in Dublin Castle. Army intelligence arrived in civvies. The only uniforms present were those of two
district superintendents from Dublin. Almost half of the eleven men
present were from Special Branch. A civil servant who looked more
like a priest, and knew it and cultivated it, sat at the table also.

"The basics are these," a Special Branch detective was explaining.

"We have a man in custody, one James Duffy, native of Newry. He
has no record of criminal activities with the RUC. The most he has
done in his life is thrown stones during riots, live on the dole and,
the RUC suspect, drive other people's cars without their permission.
He is on a list of theirs as under suspicion for involvement in IRA
activities. Admits to driving the car yesterday. Claims not to have
known the other two. Not even their names. You know the routine.
Admits to being a 'volunteer.' He says he was here on a kind of
holiday. We think he's small fry and that he will be no loss to them.
That's probably why he was sent down here. Expendable."

"What does he know, Sergeant?" army intelligence asked bluntly.

"Yes, he picked up the car–incidentally the plates were fakes–in the
vicinity of a lane behind Lower Baggot Street. We found the garage
that probably hid the car and fixed the plates. So, to answer your
question, he knows bugger-all. He's more or less a stooge. He says the
two were bored so they wanted to crack a bank in south county
Dublin."

"How did he get his instructions?" the army man persisted.

"Over the phone. As for the garage. We got in yesterday evening.
It was decided by the boys on the spot. As it turns out, nothing
would have been gained by setting up a surveillance. They had flown
the coop."

"They?" said the civil servant.

"Whoever. The owner rented it out, paid in advance. He says the
man who rented it was, what was his word, 'civilised.' Well-to-do.
Youngish and fit-looking." The detective flicked to a page: "... *'well
groomed' ... 'obviously a businessman'* ... The man told him it was for
preparing antique cars for restorations. The name doesn't mean anything and the address is rubbish. The man was 'refined.'"

"In other words, nobody."

"Has the owner been through the books?" one of the superintendents asked, more to get a word in than to advance the understanding of the meeting.

"Yes, sir. Nothing." The detective sat down. The man next to him stood and put his hands in his pockets. He had no notes to brief him.

"A man who used one of the sheds up the lane identified the Mercedes straight away. He couldn't be sure about another car he saw there earlier in the week though. He settled on a Japanese car and that's as good as we'll get. The thing which may be of concern is that one of them was getting some substantial attention. Some alteration or repair job."

"What's the significance, Inspector?" queried the superintendent.

"Well, we believe the car or cars are being prepared for some operation. If this old man is right, a car has been modified most likely. We're working on the worst interpretation here."

"With respect, Inspector, I have to explain to the Minister why you are considering this. Seems tenuous to me," the civil servant said. The inspector, who had twenty years on the bureaucrat he was silently eying all the while, continued.

"Fair enough. We discount legitimate purposes. We don't think that this outfit went to the trouble of getting a place just to switch plates on a stolen car. A babe in arms could do that blind drunk on a wet night. We think there's some kind of a shift on but to be quite honest," he paused and looked directly over to the man from army intelligence, "we don't really know more than the next man."

He didn't have to spell it out. Sources in the British Special Branch and anti-terrorist squads had been unusually communicative lately. This was the case with the Brits only when they were grumbling. They grumbled because there was little they could do about it from their side, and they grumbled because the RUC's grumbles weren't listened to as keenly in the South. Ergo there was something going on in the South they wanted to stop but couldn't do it themselves. The increase in shootings and the sophistication of the weapons and techniques involved had them stymied. Their usual sources knew nothing about how the weapons were getting in. They had stepped up the border patrols and they had undertaken aerial surveillance with helicopters. The inspector let the silence sink in with its eloquence. Then he reminded them:

"There are signs that there's a new twist to the arms supply. You all know that our department feels the political pressure very quickly. We're pulling out all the stops. This business yesterday has turned up the heat even more."

"Will you outline the courses we can follow, gentlemen?" the civil servant asked.

"We're at a disadvantage. Our sources have either dried up or they don't know anything. There seem to be new men in the game. Whoever this 'refined businessman' is, we don't know. We should acknowledge that. We think that there's a connection between yesterday and our current problems. A slip. The human factor, if you like. No organisation is completely watertight. I'm suggesting that every available man be on a surveillance roster for each and every so-called republican on our books. The two murderers have to go to ground somewhere. I want taps on phones ... I have a list here and it's as short as I can make it."

He pre-empted the civil servant whose face was already taking on a set of disapproval.

"And I don't like it either. There's no point in picking them up and interrogating the whole lot of them."

He slid the list across the table toward the civil servant And he sat down. Nobody spoke for a half minute. The civil servant looked up from the list and said:

"Inspector, can I see you after the meeting?"

A rustle of papers moved the committee on. The army intelligence had reports of sightings of Russian trawlers just outside the boundary last week, the week before and again this week. They had left the area before fishery protection vessels could get there and confirm the sightings. Nothing special, he said, time of year perhaps. A report from British Intelligence that it was almost certain one of their men had been killed by a sniper who used a Startron nightsight. Nothing else could explain him being shot in the head at nearly three hundred feet in the dead of night. Queried to the States because it was restricted on the Munitions List from their State Department.

Toward the end of the meeting, the inspector looked up from his fingerplay to find the civil servant's limpid gaze fixed on him. The civil servant was absent-mindedly drawing a thumb to and fro over the edge of the sheet which listed the names for the telephone taps. He looked away as the inspector met his stare, affecting attention to the speaker.

Scared, the inspector reflected. *He feels things are slipping, but he doesn't want to tell his Minister that, because the Minister would rather believe otherwise.* The inspector gave him a lingering look, knowing the civil servant would be aware of his mild scrutiny. *Not as scared as some of my men, he's not*, the inspector guessed. *Probably not as scared as me.*

Chapter Twelve

The playwright listened to what he knew were Americanisms. He looked around the pub for some relief from the tight-lipped anger of the Yank.

"I had to close the god-damn place down right away after I heard about your goons," the tanned man hissed. "So much for you loaning out a hot car to those assholes."

"Who gave you the job of deciding what I do?" the playwright retorted. "I gave them the car because I didn't want them trying to lift one for themselves and getting caught. We need those men up there—"

"Right. We don't need them screwing up the works down here, I tell you—"

"—They're coming from a battle zone, mister. Maybe you don't realise that. Your crowd can have your Vietnams and your Chiles a thousand miles away. Our men on the ground are under pressure all the time. They need a break. We do what we can for them—"

"—Like tell them to take on a bank? Shoot cops?"

"That's out of bounds and they know that. They'll answer for it. To the appropriate authorities."

The tanned man heard the changed inflexion in the playwright's words now. So that was it, his trump card, the appropriate authorities. At least it was more out in the open now. He felt a grim satisfaction take the place of his anger. He'd have the playwright's head on a plate after he got through with this.

"Look, let's drop it for now," said the tanned man. "We'll be bringing the present for Aunt Maggie tomorrow. Everything is settled isn't it?"

"That car? Yes," the playwright replied.

"No screw-ups, OK?"

The playwright returned the Yank's glare but said nothing. *The only other detail really is that you are out of the running, my fine flowery mid-Atlantic fancy man. You're washed up as of tomorrow.* He smiled up at the Yank.

"By the way, your home phone is being tapped again, so go through your list consecutively if it's on business," the tanned man said. *Show-off,* thought the playwright, as he smiled more broadly at the departing pest.

*   *   *

Minogue had sought refuge in Bewley's. Needed something to keep him going. He had been on his way out to Walsh's despite the reception he had gotten on the phone from Mr Walsh. A mixture of tentativeness and arrogance which mystified Minogue had been his reward for phoning. Mrs Walsh was under sedation and the doctor was ready to send her to hospital at the drop of a hat. Did Minogue really need to see her today? She couldn't stand to be around the house with memories. Mr W. hadn't been to work in the last week. What good would it seem to talk now? Hadn't they told the police everything they could?

A large white coffee and a gooey bun brought some solace to Minogue. He ensconced himself near the window in the non-smoker's section on the first floor. Sun streamed in over the rooftops opposite. Between Minogue and the office windows across Grafton Street lay the paralysed traffic below, a snake of exhaust and metal.

Minogue began to observe the waitresses. They were perked up by the arrival of Friday. Some of them appeared exceedingly gorgeous to Minogue. He attributed his rush of feeling to the coffee. Then he began to go further and understand that he had been gladdened and emboldened somehow. The near miss with the car had brought him another taste of the calm perspicacity which had cradled him for those weeks in hospital. Minogue saw the cashier throw her head back and laugh at something a customer had said. A tramp snored lightly at the far end of the room. Each woman seemed stubbornly real to him. They'd be tired after the day, their backs, their feet. But look at the one still laughing. Maybe some of them were married to slobs, ah-good-ould-Dublin characters who came home late from the pub. Dublin. It dawned on Minogue that he was almost free. There was an ungetaroundableness to things now. Sequestered truths awaited him here in Dublin, which was neither Clare nor Montana ...

Truths? Did we always have to believe that things turned out well, that there were answers and happinesses ahead? Maybe they were badly paid here. Maybe someone was being shot in the North. Maybe Daithi might fail his exams. Maybe his brother Mick was unforgivable.

Minogue opted for a second cup of coffee. Confidence welled in him, barely overshadowed by his sense of the puzzle of the murder waiting for him beyond this happy afternoon, the body of one Jarlath Walsh waiting for answers.

Leaving Bewley's, Minogue reinserted himself in the traffic jam. As he finally made some headway beyond Merrion Square, his precarious caffeine optimism dulled and then died. Pulling into the manicured driveway of Walsh's house, he saw a curtain drawn back slightly to show a man's face, more disapproving than curious.

Portly, Minogue thought, like out of a book. He expected to see Walsh dressed in a three-piece with a pocket-watch in his fob. Hair in place, thinning, no suggestions of sideburns. Walsh preceded Minogue into another carpeted area.

"Step into the living room, Detective Sergeant."

Minogue tried to trace the accent but failed to get beyond a vague understanding that it was from some part of Munster.

The curtains were half drawn. Minogue was looking at a face which was used to being resolute but was now wavering. The man looked almost curious. Still, he was keeping together. Minogue noticed no decanters around. The room was large and tidy. The diffused light made pastels of most of the colours, themselves mainly beige or blue anyway. Minogue wondered if they lived in this living room. His eye was caught by a stand-up thing for holding magazines. *Time* and *Newsweek* looked out of it.

"Mr Walsh. Please accept my condolences."

There was a few moment's silence between the men. Minogue felt himself sinking into the upholstered chair.

"I'd offer you a drink, Sergeant ..."

"Thanks, but no. It's semi-official."

"Semi?"

"Well, I'm looking for something or someone to fill the holes in my investigation. I'm less inclined to believe that your son was a random victim of violence."

Walsh seemed to sit up more in his seat.

"Random?" he said.

"I don't believe in a master plan or that class of thing. I'm guessing that Jarlath was in the wrong place at the wrong time, that he may unwittingly have been involved in something."

"Sergeant. I know my own son. He was not involved in gangs or whatever it is you're describing."

Minogue heard himself speaking and he was taken aback by his own tone. This man, whom he had met but minutes before, rankled him somehow.

"Allow me to say, Mr Walsh, that I have built up a fair picture of your son over the last week too. What I need now are some little details which might not have seemed important enough to mention before. A hint."

Walsh's face had changed. He licked a lip. Minogue wondered if he had been a farmer's son, big as he was, a big neck on a body going fat inside a few more years. A face you'd see under a cap herding cattle down a lane. The striped shirt and the marble fireplace belied that.

"Now, Sergeant, I had an inkling you–not you exactly now–but one of ye would come to that. I think that your crowd have run out of steam and now ye're worried about looking bad with no one behind bars for this.

"So what do you do?" Walsh continued, sitting forward in his chair and clasping meaty knuckles together. "Ye try to insinuate that there's something amiss with my son. Almost like he had it coming."

"Now Mr Walsh, that's not the way it is. What I'm saying is that many investigations are successful due to the remembering of details which initially seemed of no consequence."

"Oh that's a nice thing to say and a nice way to say it, Sergeant, but let me tell you. I think the place is out of control. That's what I think. I think you lads don't know whether you're coming or going here in this city. Ye're afraid to deal firmly with the likes of criminals walking the streets. Do you know, I don't care whether it was a lunatic or some gang. I want the fella or fellas caught. Punished. That's the size of it."

Minogue stared idly at the television in the corner while Walsh talked on. He realised that Walsh had to be allowed to vent his frustration on someone. At times Minogue nodded in a show of sympathy to hurry him up. It wasn't working.

"Sergeant Minogue. I came to Dublin over twenty-five years ago and I had nothing at all. Now those were not the best of times. But the first thing I learned was that Dublin people are not the same as us. They don't like us doing well for ourselves. They want to sit around over pints and complain. So you know what I think is the pity of it though?"

Minogue was tempted to say he did.

"That every year the Gardai on the beat are learning the same thing. Young lads up from the farm like myself. A bit too trusting, I'm thinking. Didn't know how to deal with hooligans and vandals. Afraid of the firm hand. Oh don't get me wrong, I don't blame the Gardai entirely. I'm well aware of the way this country is going. I'll tell you that a spell of army service would do the youth of this bloody city a lot of good. What galls me is that these vandals here can hang around the pubs on the dole and never get told to shape up or ship out.

They're getting so brazen they're robbing people on the streets. Drugs and everything. Look, I don't mind telling you that, same as yourself, I had some high jinks when I was a lad. A few glasses of porter, a bit of divilment. But I never in my life thought that the rest of my life could be like that. There was always hard work the next day. 'Work hard, play hard.' That's my motto."

Walsh seemed to have spent himself. He was probably on the edge and confused for the first time in his life, Minogue guessed. How could a woman live with a man like that? He'd scarify her for any signs of weakness.

"Did Jarlath discuss any of his hobbies or interests, Mr Walsh? His girlfriend?"

Walsh's eyes widened, then narrowed and he shook his head gently. Damn, Minogue thought, set him off again.

"Girlfriend, is it? You mean that red-haired young one at the funeral? With the Northern accent?"

"Agnes McGuire," Minogue said pointedly.

"Look, no one minds young people having a fling. These are different times than when we grew up. I always say play the field as long as your conduct is good, no one can fault you."

Minogue was struck by the word 'conduct.' he hadn't heard it in years. He associated it with sentences or warnings, school or court-rooms.

"I said that to him. I said, 'Jarlath, you are a free man. You don't owe anything to anybody so you're beholden to no one. You pick your own studies now and you make friends. Male and female alike. Your mother and I are a bit old-fashioned but you'll know later on what we mean. There's time enough for responsibilities later.'" Walsh paused.

Minogue felt a breeze of despair.

The words turned over in his mind. He thought of Daithi, foolish man-boy half astride a fence in these years. A mistake to call him a man. Kathleen had been at him to take Daithi aside. What did that mean, to 'take Daithi aside'? To prepare him for life with a little chat? Like those stupid American shows on the telly, 'Well, my boy, it's time we had a little ...' A little what? A little man-to-man chat? About what? Passing on the secrets of males, the pathetic bullying ways of half the world who threw children into wars and sat around pubs uttering platitudes.

"Freedom. They used to talk about it a lot more. The hippies and the rest of it. Freedom doesn't mean that some gutty has the choice to kill my son out of turn. That's not freedom. Jarlath picked his courses. He had his own politics and I never said boo to that. I worked in this bloody city so he can have those choices. I can tell you that it took a while for me to learn it, but Jarlath had as much right to go socialist as I did not to–"

"Socialist?" Minogue interrupted.

"Well, left or whatever they call it. You have to understand that Jarlath had no experience of the world. He didn't know what socialism was in practice. 'We're all socialists at heart,' I told him. 'Even Jesus Christ was a socialist,' I told him. I pay the lads well at work. Not that I have much choice with the unions ..."

Experience being the name we give our mistakes, Minogue's inner voice copied Wilde's mordant truth.

"Anything about Irish politics? The North?" Minogue said.

"You're back to that girl again, aren't you? He told me once that we didn't know anything because we hadn't lived through it. I mean that's all fine and well to say. The enthusiasm of youth is a thing that can be easily turned to bad ends."

So that was another gem, Minogue thought. He imagined father and son shouting at the foot of the stairs, Mrs Walsh trying to intercede. Mother Ireland.

"Anyway, I'd not describe her as a girlfriend. To answer your question," Walsh said and sat back defiantly in his chair.

"Why not?"

"Well, we never met her. She was never introduced to us. In a formal way."

Minogue's pessimism deepened. The boy had learned enough to be ashamed of them probably.

"I was just thinking, Sergeant Minogue. Doesn't the Bible say 'an eye for an eye'? Don't you think there's something in it all the same? Where's the justice even if the fellow is caught? Jarlath had a great future ahead of him with the business. Sure the university was just a general training. Did I insist he do accountancy or the like? No, I did not. 'Every lecture has something for everybody,' I told him. A liberal education as they say. Strange as it may seem, I believed in that."

Minogue realised that he was probably the first and perhaps the last visitor to the house since the funeral. The man looked like a bachelor somehow. The place was spic and span, unused. Walsh's face held an intensity which was still disbelief as to how the world had fallen apart.

Soon it would turn to anger. Walsh would want answers and no one would be able to provide them.

Walsh was fingering his lip now. His voice had dropped and he was staring at a print on the wall.

"The North. Well, that's part of it, I'm sure. Not directly of course but it sets the thermostat, you could say."

He looked intently at Minogue and continued.

"They're not the same as us, Sergeant. Not one bit. They're a different race entirely ... My suppliers sometimes ask things but I explain that it's like another world up there. It could be another continent. Still they ask. What about the vast majority though, I ask myself. They're trying to make a living and keep their businesses going, like the rest of us. They're the same as us in that respect. Unsung heroes I might say, the ones who put the food on the table and keep the economy afloat. Where's the justice in that though? Bitter people. Too much politics. We don't need that here."

Minogue's mind echoed with 'vast majority.' He heard it often, usually to do with bad news. He felt weak in the company of this man, surrounded by his achievements. Walsh stood up and pocketed his hands. Minogue, no psychologist, recognised his chance.

"Mr Walsh. I'm wondering about your son's briefcase. It was stolen in the college. Did he mention it at all?"

"Matter of fact he did. I haven't told his mother at all on account of it being a present she gave him. I suppose no place is safe now, not even Trinity College Dublin."

"Any strange phone calls or visitors looking for your son this last while?" Minogue tried.

Walsh looked carefully at Minogue, considering his answer.

"No, Sergeant. And your insinuations can stop at that point. You're trying to suggest that our son was a stranger to us. We made it our business to know what he did. We were interested in how he did and not just with the books. We knew our son. We talked and discussed things with him. If you leave here with nothing else aside from that fact, well that'll be fine with me."

Minogue stood. Too far, he thought. Yes, this Walsh was a country man and no stranger to Minogue. Minogue had been meeting these men less and less over the years. He remembered a line of a poem but couldn't remember the poet.

'Will it be the bourgeois coma or the bully's push?'

Walsh had enough of the bully in him not to be comatose in the suburbs here. Yes, Walsh had the age-old dislike for the peelers and the law. Walsh led him to the door. Brass fittings caught Minogue's soupspoon head in passing. *You're wrong, Walsh. Your son was a stranger to you because he was learning to know you too well. Familiarity ...*

"Thank you, Mr Walsh. I regret the inconvenience."

"We all do our job, Sergeant. Good day now."

Another bloody clumsy hint, Minogue realised as he heard the door clunk behind him. A cement statue in the middle of shrubs reminded him of a cemetery. Who had educated Jarlath Walsh really? Agnes McGuire, that's who.

Within a mile of the Walsh house, Minogue was faced with a choice. The Friday traffic was flowing south. Minogue's home was but three miles in toward the city. Couldn't he justify staying out here rather than returning to the city?

At this same time, the playwright had executed his choice. He replaced the phone. Maybe, on reflection, he should have phoned the Brits instead of the Gardai. A car of a given make and colour would be worth inspecting. It would be going through Dundalk tomorrow. It wouldn't be exactly full of petrol.

Minogue pulled in beside a shop, aching for a cigarette. He sat in the car for a minute, listening to the engine. Then he drove off onto the Bray Road toward his work. On his way to the city centre, there were times when he couldn't remember how he had driven this far, paying no heed to what he was supposed to be doing. By the time he reached Trinity, his mind had caught up with him. He was surprised to find himself parking there. He gathered his notes and checked the drawers. He locked the door behind him. He wrote a thanks, slipped the key into an envelope and sealed it. He walked under cooing pigeons at Front Gate and handed the envelope to a porter.

"And thank Captain Loftus for me. We'll be in touch," Minogue said.

Instead of returning directly to his car, Minogue turned toward Allen's office. The heavy varnished door took his knuckles and offered nothing. Minogue put his ear to the door but he heard no sound. He felt relieved and disappointed at the same time.

In truth, Minogue felt washed up. Almost unknown to himself he was lying in wait on the bank for some moving thing to pass, something he couldn't predict or control. Like waiting for a bus after you've had a few jars, idly detached from things. The implacable closed door and the bird song coming in from the square made him feel silly and lost. Walsh was right, he'd run out of steam.

He gathered his papers better under his arm and turned to leave. Turning, he caught sight of a faint sliver of brightness under the door. He bent to look and noticed that a folded sheet of paper had been slipped under the door. Minogue fished it out with the end tooth of his comb. The note was from a secretary apparently, reminding Allen to phone Captain Loftus when he got back. 'When you get back Sun/ Mon.' Minogue slipped the note back under the door.

Minogue explored his way to the back of the building. Turning a corner, he heard a typewriter. He knocked and entered. No, Dr Allen would not be in for the remainder of the day. Who was looking for him. Mr Who? Minogue. Had he an appointment? No. Well Dr Allen is very fussy about that. No less fussy than yourself, Minogue thought. Where could he reach him? He had rooms in college but he wouldn't be there either. How come...?

His lectures took him away at least twice every month. And where would he be delivering his next one? That's a private initiative on his part. Sorry for asking.

"Well, more power to his elbow. I'll be seeing you," Minogue said to annoy her. A face on her like a plateful of mortal sins, Minogue thought.

Chapter Thirteen

Detective Garda Connors was trying to unbunch the large muscle group which comprised his arse. Connors welcomed the break from Kilmartin's company. Kilmartin had become morose and then angry by turns. Connors could feel Kilmartin's imploding anger and helplessness. The two killers were still at large. It looked like every single Garda in Dublin would be on the job following suspects around. Suspects indeed. Connors had drawn surveillance on an old-timer, a playwright, who had been active nearly thirty years ago. He had faded into the background more and more as the war in the North became a city war. The playwright hadn't been under regular surveillance for over three years. The file read like a story about a film star in decline.

Connors tried to remember some of the plays this fella had written.

All with a nationalist bent or some bloody propaganda. Well, at least it was only playacting. Maybe he'd be flattered to think he was being followed. He could boast about it to his cronies, be a fecking hero.

Connors' backside began to ease. He ordered another glass of Harp and looked around at the Friday afternoon crowd in the Bailey. Oh very poosh. More like a crowd of gobshites. And the women dressed up, laughing like actors on the telly. Mutton dressed up as lamb. Vixens, they'd take a lump out of any honest man in their path. Hardly ideal company for the patriotic playwright. Who was the fella with him though?

Connors took a slug out of the glass and watched the playwright talking. The other one looked like a Yank. The playwright might be softening him for a few jars or maybe a bit in the theatre line. That was one of his plays, *At the Wall*. Connors was pleased with his memory. A play about what might have happened if the leaders in the Rising hadn't been shot in 1916. Maybe it'd go down well in the States. Hardly though. That fella had a good tan, typical Yank. Looked after himself with the hair and the clothes. How did the Yanks make good suits like that?

The way he sat on the chair suggested to Connors that he was fit and stronger than the suit might indicate. There was something about the consistency in his posture. They had been in the pub for fifteen minutes, but the tanned man didn't slouch. He still looked none too happy about something, but the vexed look he had when he came in was gone now. He now looked merely annoyed at a nuisance of some kind. Hard to put an exact age on the Yank.

Connors wished he had heard the few sharp words the two exchanged when the Yank had come in first. All he could make out was the Yank—or whoever he was—saying something about screw-ups. The playwright had snapped back at him once or twice. After that they seemed to settle down a bit, with the playwright giving him a few big salesman smiles. Wouldn't trust him as far as ... Aha, maybe the playwright had fixed him up with a colleen, but she hadn't obliged when push came to shove. No, there was more to it. The Yank looked like he was working at staying polite. Like Paul Newman after missing a honey shot in *The Hustler*. Cool dude. Under control ...

The tanned man made his call from a phone in the hallway leading to the pub. He spoke slowly.

"Your job is on for tomorrow. Confirmed. Follow your normal route.

Your car will withstand even a minute search so don't sweat it. It's right inside part of the vehicle's structure."

"Why are you telling me that?" The voice was less anguished than bitter.

"So you'll have confidence. So you'll look confident. Is that too simple a proposition for you?"

"When I get there...?"

"You leave the key, just the car key, under the right front tire. The car'll be back in the same spot within the hour."

The tanned man heard breathing over the line.

"Why did you tell me this? Why not just get me to do it without knowing about it?"

The tanned man recognised the bitterness clearly now, but he didn't resist the sarcasm in return.

" 'The unexamined life isn't worth living' and all that."

He hung up.

Connors watched as the Yank stood up abruptly. He gave a parting glance to the playwright. Another big crooked smile from your man. Must have one up on the Yank: probably stuck him for the price of the drinks. Connors was out the door before him. He put on his raincoat and a cap to alter his appearance outside. He stood looking into a window full of crafts, waiting for either or both of the men to come out. Almost three minutes passed before the Yank came out. Must have gone to the jacks. No sign of the playwright though, damn and blast him. So what about this Yank, Connors thought. So what? He had hoped that the playwright would be with him, but that'd be too tidy by far. He saw the Yank squint in the daylight as he paused by the door to the pub.

Connors decided to follow the Yank. He could always say that this Yank had acted suspiciously. The playwright might still be in the pub for hours. Connors watched the Yank cross Dawson Street and then step into a lane which was a short-cut to Molesworth Street. He thought that for a Yank, the tanned man stepped out nicely and seemed to know his way better than the rest of them who stood around Dawson Street with their snake-skin wives blocking the path, lost just a few hundred yards from the hotel. Connors bet on the Shelbourne Hotel.

*   *   *

The tanned man had already taken in the skulking presence of the man pretending to be interested in the shop opposite. He had been in the pub too. He became aware of a little congestion in his sinuses. He felt the shoulder strap bite as he shrugged. He was certain this was the first time he had been followed since he arrived. The guy was either a cop or a heavy that the playwright had called in. Not drinking enough to be serious about his stay and not meeting anyone, which is why he'd have been nursing his drink so long. Didn't look like a cop.

More pieces fell into place in parallel lines of thought as the tanned man took up a brisk pace. He began a flush-out. There was no way that the Brits would have a man tailing him here in Dublin. He stepped into the arched passageway with a piece of Molesworth Street framed in light at the end. He felt he should decide by the end of this tunnel. The playwright had been almost ingratiating by the time he left the pub. Was that a prelude to being set up? And he had been all too obliging about putting the fear on that cop with the stolen car and the dope.

He approached the end of the tunnel and, without turning to look behind, headed for Kildare Street. He thought of his time frames for what he must do. By tomorrow, Saturday, at about two o'clock in the afternoon he would know whether he could report success or failure. He'd be on the plane to Amsterdam, armed with this success, to lever agreement out of his liaison. A unit in Armagh had guaranteed to target a patrol for Sunday as conclusive proof. They'd hear of it before the evening was out from Hilversum or the BBC and the liaison would set up the meeting with the cover from the embassy.

Ahead of him was Leinster House, the Parliament. Laughable that the National Museum was next to it. Could they be distinguished really? He knew that there were armed guards and army units in the Parliament and he allowed for that. His mind cleared with the arrival of his chance.

As he walked into the foyer of the museum, the thought struck the tanned man that his follower might well be looking for a chance to kill him. The image of the playwright's face with its barely hidden condescension went through his mind. Was he capable of sending in an assassin? The museum was surprisingly bright. Light fell in from the large expanse of skylight. It made the tanned man think of a church. He could see but four other visitors in this large hall. On the balconies which faced out onto the main exhibition hall, he heard the talk of other unseen visitors. An elderly museum guard nodded at him and

resumed his measured, meditational walk. He stepped into the floor
proper and strolled by the cases with early Christian artefacts in them.
He passed spearheads and pots from the Iron Age. He tried to remember the run of the museum from when he had visited it as a child. It
was probably all changed.

He mounted steps leading to a balcony overlooking the hall. There
he was, this rather tired-looking follower, now in shirt-sleeves gazing
too intently at golden necklaces, of all things. Why would he follow
him around the museum and not wait near the front door? Must be
expecting some cloak-and-dagger meeting. He looked at his watch. The
museum closed in another twenty minutes. He turned the corner to
meet with a museum guard who looked restive, whistling faintly between tongue and teeth. He had come circuitously back to the stairs.
With luck, the guy following him would be a few rooms behind him
now. Across to the entry hall. His shadower would be checking rooms.

Connors' feet were bothering him. The Yank looked as if he had just
got out of bed and could run a few miles. In all honesty, well, to
himself at least, Connors admitted that the Yank hadn't acted in any
suspicious way. There was still time to go back and check on the twit
he was supposed to be following. Likely if he checked out a few of
the pubs like O'Neill's or Davy Byrne's, he'd soon find what's-his-face
again. The Yank hadn't so much as looked around. This struck Connors
as a bit odd, that he should know where he was going. But he ended
up going to the museum, so that was that. Why go to the museum
when it was ready to close? He should have phoned in. He should
have stuck with the other fellow. He should have watched outside the
bloody museum. What class of meeting could a body have in a museum
anyway? He should have spent the extra tenner and bought real shoes.

Connors had seen the Yank go up the stairs and into a room before
he himself crossed the floor of the hall. He stood behind a display
case near to the toilets and watched for the Yank. Follow-around
be damned.

What Connors saw in five minutes sparked a faint lightness in his
chest. The Yank had come back down the stairs and looked around
once before leaving. Either the Yank knew he was being followed or
he was looking for someone he expected to meet. Connors counted
to thirty. Then he crossed the hall and retrieved his coat and jacket.
He wondered if his guess about the Shelbourne Hotel would prove
true. He could check this fella out from there.

Connors left the museum, elbowing into his coat. It was nearly five o'clock. There was no sign of the man. Connors strode to the railings which girdled the museum as it ran along Kildare Street. He looked up and down the street and across at Molesworth Street. The Yank was gone. The dying leper's vomit, the curse of the seven snotty ... Had he stepped into a taxi or a doorway? Connors was about to let go a volley of curses aloud when a movement in a shop window opposite caught his eye. An assistant was taking an antique plate from a display in the window, all the while talking to a customer. Though Connors could not see the face well, he recognised the suit. The Yank: if I can see him, by Jases he can see me.

Connors' brain raced. He could not appear to be faltering. There was no phone nearby to get another detective to switch the surveillance. Connors walked up Kildare Street with a purposive swing to his gait, raging inwardly. His best hope was to get to St. Stephen's Green and wait for however long it took for the Yank to return to the Shelbourne. Connors felt the presence of the Yank behind the glass opposite as he passed up the street and wondered if they both shared some new knowledge now.

Connors reached the top of Kildare Street excited and angry. He dodged traffic and stepped into St. Stephen's Green. He found a seat just inside the railings which afforded him a view of the front of the hotel and, to his left and almost directly ahead of him, the tops of Dawson Street and Kildare Street as they led up to the park.

As the assistant reached into the window, the tanned man saw his follower looking up and down the street. He had looked up and pretended not to notice the antique shop. He had been seen and he knew it.

He listened to the assistant but watched the man recovering and heading up Kildare Street.

"It's from a set. It's Belleek china. Do many people in America know about Belleek?" the assistant inquired.

"Well, I'm from the West Coast, ma'am, so I can't speak for collectors on the Atlantic side," he replied.

"Ah, I detect an Irish influence though," she said conspiratorially.

"How discerning of you, I'm sure. Yes, my mother is Irish."

"Isn't that rich now," the assistant said.

The irony was not lost upon him. He'd as soon throw the goddamned plate through the window.

"I'll take your card if I may, ma'am."

"Oh, I see. Well, all right," she said, visibly taken aback.

He retraced his steps back along Molesworth Street. He was surprised to find that his armpits were sweating. The tail might have an out somewhere. He decided to go up Dawson Street to St. Stephen's Green. As he walked by late shoppers and cars, he tried to control his unease.

Minogue's week was over. He'd not be called in on the weekend even with the sweep for the murderers of the Garda. Kilmartin would have him nixed off the list, because Minogue had some vague status as an invalid. It has its advantages, Minogue reflected. Someone had tried to run him over; he had found out that there were powerful old boy networks in the army and in Trinity. They wanted their reputations left glowing even if it meant sullying others. That Loftus was a bad egg, an organisation man. Minogue realised that Agnes McGuire entered his mind as an image, a face, unclouded by things she had said.

This was quite contrary to how Loftus and Walsh's father came to mind. Where she came across as singular, Minogue's distaste for the others made his recollections of them amorphous, webby.

Kilmartin probably didn't believe him about the attempt. There was nothing he could do about it really. No clues came from the car. Maybe it was some headbanger who was on the lookout for anyone to frighten. Minogue found that his resistance to certain thoughts had weakened. Dublin was a different place. There was a lot of heavy drug addiction that no one wanted to talk about, a lot of lunatics on the loose. It was the times. Maybe some deranged addict had finally unhinged when he had seen this Walsh boy, a well-fed student with his future ahead of him, a boy who didn't know that the likes of Coolock or Finglas existed. On balance, however, people with drug dependencies were usually more passive than violent. General rules didn't explain every incident. Could a boy like Walsh inspire such violence otherwise? Maybe whoever did him in panicked before they got to the boy's wallet. Maybe the realisation of what they had done broke through their frenzy and hatred.

Minogue had felt the violent impulse himself in recent years, the rush of contempt that came over him at times. The most he had done was jump out of his seat and switch off the television when the inanity overwhelmed him. A narcissistic rock star comparing himself to Bach, someone whining about their oppressors, oppressors they needed to nourish their own weakness. On *The Late Late Show,* the accents did it. He had exploded once, unable to even laugh it off, when some ex-airhostess who had been appointed to promote tourism in the States started talking in her *hoi polloi* southside fakery.

"And now joining us on the show is Mrs Blah, wife of the auctioneer Michael Blah, all the way from New York, USA. My, Deirdre, what a gorgeous tan you've got ..."

How could it be that people who were so insipid and grasping could inspire such disgust? His own anger, so vital and huge a hammer, stood looming over these fleas of contemporary Ireland.

The slats of the seat bit into Connors' thigh. He sat forward, his elbows on his knees. He watched scattered groups of pedestrians waiting for the lights at the top of Dawson Street. He looked over to Kildare Street and checked his watch. His gamble should pay off within fifteen minutes or not at all. He had three minutes left in his limit. He stood up and strolled toward one of the entrances to the Green.

Again he scanned the footpath. The traffic was moving fast, swirling around the Green. Connors wondered what would happen if one of the cars stopped suddenly. Everything would be haywire all over the city. The place wasn't built for cars. Connors turned at the sound of a horn. Someone had tried to run through the traffic to get to the Green. Probably a tourist, taking their lives in their hands. Connors saw it almost daily in the summers. Some poor old divil from Minnesota or someplace after a near miss, with that expression you'd see on a donkey chewing barbed wire and just beginning to realise it, trying to laugh it off. 'Oh Elmer nearly got run over in Dublin. Charming city.'

A near miss by the sound of it too, down the far side of Dawson Street. The pedestrian skipped through parked cars to the safety of the Green. Connors could not see the person very clearly. In the instant that the pedestrian ducked into the Green, Connors' brain eclipsed his eyesight and he began running down the path toward where the person had entered. He had made out that it was a man, a man in a hurry too, a man in a suit.

Connors ran across the grass, scattering seagulls. Coming around a hedge he almost collided with a woman pushing a pram. He stopped and looked around him. He could find no trace of the man who had entered the Green. Connors' rational sense began to catch up with him and nag him. The woman had stopped. She looked him up and down disparagingly. If he's in a suit, then it's no bother to speak your mind to him, she thought. Still, he was harmless-looking, not like the gurriers, the thugs who'd do the same and dare you to complain.

"You don't have to jog all over me and the child, mister. Watch where you're going, would you."

"Sorry, missus. I'm looking for a friend of mine. I saw him come in, but I don't know what way he went. I have an important message for him."

The young mother had Connors taped as a bogman who had nearly trampled on her child. Still, a nice look about him.

"Your pal seems to do his jogging here too then," she said and indicated with her head.

Connors ran. He rounded the pond and headed up a hill to where he knew there was a statue of Yeats. Connors stopped near the statue. The statue, in the abstract style, made Connors feel he was on the moon. Various granite blocks had been laid down to provide steps and benches around the statue. He felt his legs twitching. He looked around at the trees which enclosed this area. There was nobody here.

Connors stepped slowly off the granite blocks and began walking under the trees. The grass had been worn away here, what little could grow in the shade. For a moment, Connors lost his bearings and imagined himself far from the city. Only the constant hush of the traffic as it filtered into the Green reminded him. He had been diddled, but what excited Connors now was that this man must have had a reason for running. Connors could now justify his trailing the man. His next step was to report in and have that playwright fella picked up and questioned about the Yank he had met, then to go looking for him in earnest.

This is indeed what was to happen, but Connors' intentions did not effect these steps. Connors was surprised to find a man in a well-cut suit standing with his back to him next to a tree. The man turned and stared at Connors. The face was indeed tanned. A mixture of pity and irritation animated it. Connors though it was odd to see a man so well dressed standing there in the trees. Maybe he'd stopped for a piss, not knowing where there was a proper jacks. The man's hand came up abruptly from his side.

"Hey!" Connors said.

The man's hand jerked and Connors was falling back before he heard the *phutt*. As the back of Connors' head hit the clay, the sky's light became intolerable. He wondered how he could have been pushed from so far away. He remembered the lightness in his chest when he'd leap down into the hay. "Up and awaaay" his brother would shout, "Up and away."

Kilmartin listened to Minogue's voice over the phone.

"Yes, I'm just leaving Trinity. The idea is to throw the bits up in the air again and look at it all from a different angle."

"Yes, Matt. I follow."

"What about that lad you have, what's his name."

"Connors?"

"Yes. He's on the up and up, isn't he?"

"He's very quick, there's no doubt, Matt. Are you saying you want to give him a crack at this?"

"Yes. A fresh approach."

"Sorry now, but you'll have to take your turn. He's out on surveillance now if you don't mind. It's this murder out in Blackrock," Kilmartin said.

Minogue looked around. The foyer to the library was empty. Students kept office hours too, apparently. He felt chastened at having all but forgotten that other events took precedence over his concerns. Was this a sign of old age, retreating into one's own preoccupations?

"Well, do—"

Minogue heard clicks on the line as an operator interrupted.

"Inspector Kilmartin, line two. Hello?"

"Hello?" Kilmartin said.

"A priority call on line two, Inspector."

"Hold, Matt, you hear," Kilmartin said.

For thirty seconds Minogue listened to his own breath bristling through his nose into the mouthpiece. There was a faint smell of peppermint off the phone.

When Kilmartin spoke again, his voice was very different.

"Matt. Be over here directly now. Something has come up. Drop what you're doing immediately. We'll need all the manpower we can get."

Chapter Fourteen

Allen watched her balancing the coffee as she took the change from the cashier. She sat down across the table from him.

"You know best, I mean," she said.

"By half past, it should be OK. It's just that I'm allergic to traffic jams," he said.

Agnes smiled.

"It'd surely spoil the impulse if we ended up in a traffic jam so it would," she agreed.

"Does your family know you're coming?" Allen asked.

"No. It'll be a surprise, I can tell you," Agnes sipped her coffee and sat back. Allen had watched her sling a packsack into the boot and had felt a strange thrill.

"Well," Allen said, "I decided to go tonight and not wait. They're expecting me tomorrow but ... too much routine. How are the books, Agnes?"

"What a question." She smiled. "I shouldn't tell you. I forget you're one of them."

He laughed.

"Well, aren't you?" she teased.

"On come on now. This isn't school. You don't have to pretend," he said.

"Ach, I wonder. I could do with a break from the books."

"Sounds normal to me. You'll pick up again."

Agnes sipped at the brim of the cup speculatively.

"Yes. I know that. It's just that sometimes I think of the future, you know. Jobs and all that. It's better than thinking about the past," she said.

Allen smiled.

"I really like the placement though. That's real social work. When I started out I couldn't understand it, you know. People here–the South I mean–are so different from back home. I used to think they were worse off here sometimes."

"How do you mean?"

"They couldn't blame it on the troubles is what I mean. There's no reason for people to starve in Dublin, but they do."

Allen understood. Life had been whittled cleaner for people in the North. Their uncertainty was kept at bay by this constant involvement.

"You know, like you talk about rationalisation in your lectures? It's the national pastime really, isn't it?"

Allen laughed and nodded his head. She got straight to the point, he thought. Would he though? Later, after they crossed the border. Maybe her reserve was a defence to hide her feelings for him.

By the time Minogue reached Kilmartin's office, he had dropped his files once. He caught Kilmartin just as he was about to step out the door, followed by a uniformed sergeant. Kilmartin's face was tight.

"Put 'em away in my office." Kilmartin nodded at the papers under Minogue's arm. Minogue looked at the sergeant. He appeared to be angry. He was flicking car keys on his fingers. Minogue tripped out in their wake.

"As true as God, Matt, this is the limit. I'll do it myself if I have to."

"What?"

Kilmartin stopped abruptly and shouted.

"They've shot Connors. He's dead. They shot him."

Minogue could smell Kilmartin's breath. Later, Minogue would remember striding behind Kilmartin and his driver and sinking into the seat. The sergeant drove at speed with the siren on. He mounted footpaths and swore. His sweat smell permeated the car. Nobody spoke. The city looked hostile to Minogue as it sped by. Kilmartin sat looking out the opposite window. As they reached St. Stephen's Green, Minogue heard other sirens behind. Ahead of them, Gardai on motorcycles were shouting at motorists. Groups of pedestrians stood staring over at the growing numbers of police cars and vans.

There were fifty or more uniformed Gardai keeping an area free of gawkers. Minogue caught sight of a few faces he knew, plain-clothes police. His tension increased. Those men were surely armed. The whole place was falling apart. The Green should have a few people strolling around, some youngsters necking, not this.

Detectives were unrolling red plastic, twining it around trees and shrubs to mark off the area. The body was gone.

"I'm Kilmartin."

A detective stood aside from a group and helloed Kilmartin. Minogue stood behind Kilmartin.

"Inspector–" the detective began.

"What I need to know is this," Kilmartin cut him off. "I need to know who did this. I don't care who or how many."

The detective looked over Kilmartin's shoulder at Minogue. Minogue began to understand why he had been brought along. He felt a tenderness for Kilmartin. Kilmartin could never say it, but he needed Minogue along because he, Kilmartin, was frightened. This was not Kilmartin's Ireland any more than it was Minogue's.

"I can tell you that there were no witnesses to the shooting, sir. He was shot once, it appears, in the chest. We haven't turned up a shell yet, so we don't know if it's an automatic. It looks like a fairly large calibre, sir."

The detective took a step back, glancing at Kilmartin and then at Minogue.

"Is one of these lads from the Branch?" asked Kilmartin. The detective frowned in puzzlement.

"The Special Branch. They're the ones who'd know who Connors was tailing. They borrowed him from me."

"Oh yes, sir." The detective turned and tapped one of the group on the shoulder. The man turned and looked at Kilmartin. The detective stood back, eying Kilmartin.

"Kelly, sir. You're Inspector Kilmartin?"

"Yes."

"We're looking for the fellow. You know him, McCarthy, that bloody playwright. He's not in his flat."

"Kelly, tell me why a man seconded from my department was on a surveillance assignment on such a dangerous suspect."

Minogue saw Kilmartin's hands fist in his pockets.

"Sir, with respect, it's not like that. That McCarthy is the last fella to do this. It had to be something else, sir. He wouldn't have done that, sir."

"My arse for a yarn, Kelly," Kilmartin snapped.

Minogue heard the chatter from a handset the sergeant was carrying. Kelly looked down at the ground, then back at the rigid Kilmartin.

"Understand this, Kelly: when we finish our job, there'll be ructions. Unarmed Gardai are paying the bill with their lives for what's going on. I won't stand for that. Inspectors in other departments won't. Neither will the public. This is Dublin, the capital of Ireland, for fucks' sakes, not New York."

Minogue watched Kilmartin stalk away. He turned to look around and watch the men securing the plastic rail.

Kelly glanced at Minogue.

"He's right, you know. That fella in Blackrock and now this? Where's it all going to end?"

"Are we talking about an organised series of killings here?" Minogue asked.

Kelly shook his head and looked over at Kilmartin, now holding a handset. What a place to die, Minogue was thinking.

The plastic-covered ID had slipped from the man's fingers. It lay face up on his chest. The tanned man saw the Polaroid with some print to the left side. He felt suddenly seized, unable to move. A cop. *Jesus.*

The tanned man rolled off the silencer and buttoned his jacket. He walked to a path nearby and within two minutes was leaving the

Green by an entrance which faced onto a taxi rank. He decided against taking a taxi. His back prickled in a sweat, vulnerable. Still he heard no shouts or sirens. Mentally he counted the people he had met as he left. An old woman who had fallen asleep in a chair. Two teenagers entwined, trying to walk on a path.

The rush hour had eased to the degree that cars were moving into third gear between traffic lights. He walked across to the College of Surgeons and turned right toward Grafton Street. He had to work hard at not running. He knew that he had to get in the hotel and then out as soon as possible. They'd find McCarthy.

The tanned man stepped into a pub and went to the Gents. In the remaining fraction of a mirror, he saw his own face, strange and wide-eyed. He could not stop his hands from shaking. He did some belly breathing. Then he combed his hair and straightened his tie. He checked for any mud on the sides of his shoes. He went back outside and bought a newspaper. He tucked it under his arm and, taking a deep breath, strolled toward the Shelbourne Hotel. And still there was no sign that anyone but he knew that there was a body lying under the trees not two hundred yards from where he was walking.

"Picked him up then?" Kilmartin said into the microphone. "Pearse Street station?

"Well, tell them I'll be there. I want in on this."

The sergeant jammed the car into the traffic and headed down Kildare Street. Kilmartin turned to Minogue.

"Yes. They found what's-his-face, McCarthy, him in a pub. O'Neill's. So they took him in for questioning in Pearse Street."

Minogue still found it hard to believe where he was and what he was doing. He should be phoning home. What was for tea? Did he have to buy sausages? Connors was dead, dead.

"That was quick," Minogue said, trying to fan away the fear.

"He'd better have something for us quick. Those boyos from the Branch may be full of fancy footwork, counter-terrorist this and counter-terrorist that, but I'll wager they won't know how to make do with this fella."

Minogue knew that the Special Branch could be extra-legal and they could get away with it. They'd be all the more urgent because it looked as if they hadn't looked after a policeman who had been on loan to them: faulty intelligence had occluded the danger, bad work.

Kilmartin's fear and anger were not abating. They had grasped his guts, squeezed and held. A vast indigestion had control of him. He couldn't fathom what had happened, no more than Minogue. His neck and shoulders were knotted. He wanted to shout, to hit someone. For an instant he recalled a mannerism of Connors' and it tightened his chest. In desperation, he turned to the sergeant driving.

"Coincidence be damned, hah?"

The sergeant looked over and said gruffly, "That's too much to swallow, sir. I know that fella Kehoe out in Blackrock. I know his parents too. I'm thinking we have to decide who's running the bloody country, them or us?"

Kilmartin wasn't listening. The sergeant's eyes sought Minogue in the mirror.

Speeding and braking along Pearse Street, Minogue saw a dirty, heartless city. The sergeant swore aloud and bullied the engine, himself a countryman trying to wrestle with this brooding dump.

Minogue recognised the playwright. He looked younger than his years, preserved by a fanatic's purity. He didn't look in the least intimidated. A knot of policemen cluttered the corridor, a mixture of Special Branch, uniformed and hard chaws from the Technical Bureau. Minogue saw the door close on the playwright and two plain clothes.

"This way men," a desk sergeant said. "Come on now, it's set up for sound so ye can listen over beyond."

Minogue saw resentment burning in Kilmartin's face. They sat in the briefing room along with three others who nodded and produced notebooks.

"Tea, lads?" the genial desk sergeant said.

They listened to preliminaries. McCarthy was not going to be man-handled in this session with the mikes on.

"You're obliged to tell me under what Section I'm being held," the playwright said.

"You'll be told sometime during the next forty-eight hours. Where were you this afternoon?"

"Where you found me. In a pub."

"How long?"

"How long does it take to drink two pints of ale?" the playwright asked.

He's enjoying this, Minogue realised. A threshold hiss came across the speakers. The men in the room looked at one another. The sergeant stepped in with a tray of tea.

"Technical problems, lads?" he said and smiled.

No one replied.

The hiss stopped and they heard the playwright's voice again.

"You shouldn't have done that. That'll show. This isn't Guatemala you know. Or Belfast," the playwright said. The men in the room heard him breathing out of turn.

"What time did you get in?"

"About a quarter past four."

"Anybody see you come in?"

"I was with friends. You can ask them."

"Where were you before that?"

"I was in another pub."

"Where?"

"The Bailey."

"With who?"

"With anybody, is who. No one specific. I do the rounds."

"Name any of them."

"Ah, they're regulars, I hardly know their surnames. What am I supposed to have done?"

"How long were you in the Bailey?"

"I don't know. A half hour, three quarters. Since after the Holy Hour. I moved on. There was no one there of any interest."

"You know the barmen there?"

"Yes."

"Who was on?"

"I don't know their names."

"He saw you come in?"

"Well, he said hello."

"Who did you talk to?"

"There was no one there really. The regulars had moved on. I caught up with them in O'Neill's. It's a moveable feast."

"Nobody?"

The playwright didn't answer for a moment. Then he said:

"I know what you want. You want to know about that Garda that was killed the other day in Blackrock. You're going at in a roundabout way, aren't you?"

"Shut up and answer the question."

"I hadn't planned on meeting anyone specifically. Is that the right answer?" Minogue stood up and left the room. He dialed home from a phone on the front desk.

"I'll be kind of late, sorry."

"What's up, Matt?" Kathleen asked.

"Well. You'll find out sooner or later. A Garda was shot. Another one. I'm with Jimmy Kilmartin. We're sort of observing right now. He'll be wanting me for something, I'm sure."

Minogue's ear prickled against the phone. He listened to the sound of his wife breathing. He could hear the radio in the background.

Barely audible, she said, "All right so."

"I'll be all right now. Don't worry. Leave it in the oven for me, whatever it is."

By the time they reached Swords, Allen noticed that Agnes had relaxed into the seat.

"Let the seat back if you want," he said.

She smiled.

Allen thought that this must be what a honeymoon couple felt, the man at least. He wanted to believe that they belonged like this, she sitting beside him in the car, not needing to talk. If his instincts were right, soon they'd be laughing about it. She would laugh and say, 'And I thought it was only me.' Or would she?

Sleepily, Agnes said, "You don't have to drive me to Belfast you know. I can get the bus from Newry. What's the point, you have to drive back to Newry again. Really."

"It's nothing, Agnes," Allen said, relishing the echoed name in his memory. "I'm a day early. I'll probably stay over in Belfast anyway."

"I write plays and articles. Didn't you read my file? I talk to anyone and everyone."

Minogue sat down again. Over the speaker he heard someone walking, opening a door and then closing it. Minogue recognised one of the two plain clothes who had been in the room with the playwright.

Without being asked, one of the men at the table said, "Can't tell. He knows the routine, that's the thing."

The other at the table nodded. Kilmartin folded his arms.

"Check with the barmen and his pals anyway."

Kilmartin cleared his throat and said in a quiet voice:

"Tell him why he's here. He won't be expecting that. Just tell him."

"I don't think he did it either," Kilmartin continued, "but I'll bet that our patriotic bloody playwright will see he's in over his head with this. The man is a complete hypocrite. He's probably never been in on

a shooting or the like in his life. Tell him. Put the fear of God in him
and stop farting around. We don't have too much time if whoever did
it is on the move."

Plain clothes left the room. They heard him returning to the interview room.

"We're holding you on suspicion of murder. A Garda officer was
murdered today in the middle of Dublin. Murder of a Garda who's in
the course of his duty is a capital offence in this state. You'll be tested
for evidence that you discharged a firearm recently—"

"You'll find out then that I didn't," the playwright interrupted.

"You won't be able to worm out of being an accomplice. Same
thing in the end and you'll not find the climate too sympathetic
when it comes to sentencing. Judges don't like policemen being
shot dead."

"You're out of your mind," the playwright said slowly.

There was a minute's silence over the speaker.

"Anything to add, McCarthy?"

Minogue listened keenly. When the playwright spoke, Minogue felt
a mixture of relief and loathing. McCarthy had lived up to Kilmartin's
expectations. He had realised that the rules had changed. Like Kilmartin
and Minogue, this was suddenly not his Ireland either.

"Look. I meet all kinds of people. I didn't know I was being followed. There's plenty of lunatics out there. There's this fellow who
started to tell me his story. He's an American. Said he knew of me
and wanted to get in touch with republicans or something. I tried to
give him the brush. Who knows what kind of a nutcase he might be?"

Minogue's sixth sense told him this was only part of it. McCarthy
was parcelling out bits to sell off.

"I don't know the first thing about him."

"How did you meet him?"

"He came over to me in the pub."

Minogue saw Kilmartin shaking his head slowly. He wondered what
infinitesimal signs had brought Kilmartin to the same conclusion as
himself that McCarthy was lying. There was something else to it.

"Just walked over? Never saw him before?"

"Never."

"Describe him."

"Youngish, I'd say. He'd be in his late thirties. He dresses fancy,
sort of."

"A man with no name?"

"Never told me a name. I didn't ask. I could care less what his name is."

Kilmartin turned to the detectives listening to the speaker.

"What's the story on the business in Blackrock?" he asked.

"We've picked up more suspects off the lists anyway. No sign of the actual killers, but they have to turn up somewhere. They might steal a car or turn up at a house under surveillance," one of the detectives replied cagily.

"See any links with today?" Kilmartin murmured.

No one answered. *This is the belief,* Minogue thought, *that is why nobody can say it.*

"The place is full of Yanks, that's the thing. It'd be like McCarthy to work up an imaginary Yank to explain everything," the Special Branch man said.

"Yes, but what kind of a Yank would pull a stunt like this? Assuming this Yank really exists at all and McCarthy isn't spinning out rope for someone else's neck...?"

Kilmartin's belly ached. It was like someone had stabbed him. He stole a glance at Minogue. No awkwardness rubbed against them now. They listened again to the speaker.

"How do you know he was American?"

"Accent."

"Drawl? New York maybe?"

"I don't know anything about that. He didn't sound like a cowboy."

"Where is he staying?"

"Jases, I don't know. He just came up to me out of the blue," the playwright replied.

"How did he know to go to you?"

"How would I know? Maybe I have fans out there and they put him my way."

"What did he talk to you about? You said he wanted to meet republicans."

"Said he wanted to write a piece on the Troubles here. Wanted to get 'the real story,' he says. I told him to shag off but he kept on yapping and asking me things."

"What things?"

"It's hard to know where to start ..."

The playwright was back in role now, Minogue thought. The confidence was returning to him. He was off acting again. The wall between his inner landscape and the real world had collapsed years ago. Maybe he wanted drama, anything on the blade edge of life whether it was to do with guns or props. But this man sounded normal, even witty. As sane as the next man. Yet he didn't keep budgies or go along with superstitions or worship the sun: he was part of an organisation that killed people. Is that what mad means, when you can't tell the difference anymore?

Minogue's chest leadened when he felt the truth of this. He thought of Dublin in the fifties, moribund and discoloured. No wonder there was so much emigration. This fool had emigrated all right, but inwardly: he had willed his life away to The Cause.

"What exactly did he say, then?"

"I don't remember his exact words."

"Try."

"Like I said, he said he wanted to meet republicans."

"Why?"

"Just to meet them. To do a story on them, I suppose."

"What were his interests?"

"I don't know. Maybe a tourist looking for excitement."

"Married?"

"How would I know?"

"A ring?"

"Didn't look."

This could go on for hours and it would. He was lying, probably buying some time for this fellow. Give away a little so they believe the big lies.

Kilmartin leaned back, balancing on the back legs of the chair and said, "Well, are ye out looking?"

"Hotels, airports and ferries, sir. The whole bit," a Special Branch man answered.

"So. It appears to me that a) there's enough truth in this business about an American to allow us to bugger up by wasting time; b) there's some element of betrayal here. McCarthy would like to spill all the beans, but then he'd be a marked man if he sold someone out. McCarthy understands the business about being implicated in a capital offence so he'll let go stuff a bit at a time."

"Time's the thing," the Special Branch man echoed.

"I'm thinking," Kilmartin said slowly, "that you fellas charged with pursuing this investigation in the murder of one of my men should find some way to eliminate this time factor. This would effect a speedy resolution, I'm thinking."

No one answered. Although the interrogation went on over the speaker, Minogue believed that no one was listening anymore. Pencils were being fingered and shoes observed.

"Go over your description again."

"Medium height. He wore a suit," the playwright answered. He was talking too readily, Minogue understood. A command performance.

"And...?"

"There was nothing special about him. In his thirties."

"Eyes?"

"I dunno. I suppose they were blue."

"Balding?"

"No he had a full head of hair. Trimmed, looked after."

Kilmartin seemed to be examining his fingernails minutely. Minogue wondered how many Americans would be in the country at this time of year. Thousands?

Chapter Fifteen

He slipped the Canadian passport into the inside pocket of his jacket. Again he checked his recall on the dates and events of his new self. He didn't need an inbound airline ticket stub because Professor Levesque had come across as a foot passenger from Holyhead and he had one-wayed it to London from New York on a cheap flight.

He looked at himself in the mirror. Above the glasses, his hair was parted more to the centre now. The light Gore-Tex jacket and the lumberjack shirt added to a stereotype. Behind him, he noticed the suitcase he'd be leaving. Inside, neatly folded, was his suit. Everything else had fitted into the shoulder bag. For a few seconds he wondered if he had omitted anything from the routine. Yes, he had gone over the bathroom fixtures; the television, the suitcase. OK. He turned and allowed his eyes to take in the room. The window? Yes. Door? Yes. Glasses or bottles? Gone.

He couldn't afford to worry about things like a hair in the bathroom. He zipped the bag. As he bent over, he felt the gun detach itself slightly from his chest. That'd have to go too but after he was on the boat. They could bellyache all they wanted about the trouble it was to get one for him and then him just dumping it. Bellyache, he thought, snared for a moment on memory. His father had used that word often.

When he had cried on their first visit to his boarding school, his father had grabbed him by the arm:

"Don't bellyache. You'll look back and thank us."

When he got clear, he'd find a way to do for McCarthy.

Kilmartin stood up.

"Gentlemen, I'll be staying in the station here while you listen on to this drivel. If you have any news for me, kindly relay it to me within the next half hour. Anything after that will be all but useless, I'm thinking."

Minogue saw embarrassment on the men's faces. They nodded. Minogue joined Kilmartin as he turned and walked through the door. As he closed the door behind him, Kilmartin murmured:

"Well, do you think they have the idea?"

Minogue didn't answer. Their driver, the sergeant, was leaning on the back of a chair in the canteen, smoking. The desk sergeant, who had come off duty but was hanging around for news, sat opposite.

"More tea, men?" he said

Minogue and Kilmartin declined.

"The back of the neck is what it is," their driver continued, putting out smoke as he talked.

" 'Yank' my arse. Leading us up the garden path, he is," he muttered. The off-duty sergeant nodded.

The talk dried up. Other policemen came and went in the canteen. When Minogue looked at his watch, twenty minutes had passed. He had thought of asking the driver for one of his cigarettes. Before he did, one of the three men who had sat with them listening to the questioning came in. He walked to their table. Kilmartin looked up sardonically.

"Well? Has the cow calved?"

"Sir. If you could step into the room beyond, we can brief you."

Kilmartin and Minogue returned. No sounds came over the speaker. So that was what they'd done, Minogue thought.

"The suspect has informed us that he believes this American may have more, er, significance than was first thought, sir."

"Go on," said Kilmartin.

"McCarthy stresses his minimal knowledge and involvement."

"And all the rest of it," Kilmartin said grimly.

"But he understands that the American is here to do with some transporting of something or other to the North."

"What exactly does that mean?" Kilmartin's voice rose.

"His guess is that this man is involved in weapons."

Kilmartin snorted and headed for the door.

"Let me talk to Mr Shakespeare and we'll have it out in detail. I know how to deal with the likes of him," he hissed.

The Special Branch officer moved to stop him and Minogue heard the man call out:

"That isn't possible right now, sir."

Kilmartin wheeled around and looked at him, then to Minogue.

"McCarthy is indisposed at the moment, sir. Fainted."

Kilmartin stared at the nervous officer blocking his way.

"But we have a better description of this Yank, sir."

"This hypothetical Yank, you mean. My money's on some gun-happy slug down from the North and Connors came on him."

"And thinks the Yank mentioned something about the Shelbourne Hotel, sir."

Kilmartin stepped back and looked to Minogue. Minogue noted the glimmer in Kilmartin's surly gaze now.

"Maybe there is something to this Yank then ..." Kilmartin said. "They'll know him at the Shelbourne, sir, if he's staying there. Nothing as sharp as a good desk-man in a fancy hotel, is there, sir?" the detective said, mollifying. His efforts did not break the cast of skepticism on Kilmartin's face.

Just before they reached Drogheda, a glaring sun appeared from between the evening clouds. It flooded the car with gold. It ran along beside the car, through the trees and the bushes, full on Agnes when they had fields to the west of them. Allen knew they wouldn't meet the sea again until close to Dundalk. By then it would be dark. Agnes' eyes were closed. He smelled a faint perfume in the car. The light set her hair a-dazzle.

Under the trees and in the ditches the shadows were broadening out. Already the sun couldn't get over a hedge here, the roof of a house there. Where the sun still hit fields, the green was luminous. They passed a tinker camp, the men on hunkers next to a fire. Every second or third vehicle was a lorry. The edges of the road were greyed by their passing. Sometimes Allen would find the mirror filled with the dinosaur front of an eighteen-wheeler, out of nowhere. When they stopped for petrol, the boy stood by the car looking over the inside, curious about Agnes.

"A good evening for travelling now," he said. "There'll be no rain."

"How do you know?" Allen said.

"Oh sure we've had our ration for the week. Sure wasn't it a terrible week? Wasn't I drownded myself here several times in the one day," the boy answered.

Allen heard Michael Jackson coming through the half-open door beyond the pumps.

"I suppose," said Allen, "you might have something there."

When Allen sat back in the car, Agnes said:

"Where are we?"

"Near Drogheda. It'll be dark soon," Allen replied. "God," Agnes said yawning, "Drogheda. This is the longest road in Ireland so it is."

Agnes looked out at the town. Already some streetlights were glowing purple, a prelude to the glare of yellowy light which disfigured towns all over Ireland. The sun was gone now. Over head, puff carpets of grey clouds showed pink edges. The world was straining toward the west. As the car passed pubs, she saw shadows and soft lights in the windows. The shops and supermarkets were busy. Cars parked up on the kerb. Agnes thought of what Jarlath would have done tonight. He'd have suggested a foreign film probably. Reluctantly, Agnes would have agreed to go along. His callowness would make her feel guilty. Then she remembered that she had arranged to avoid a date with him by going to a friend's flat. She didn't want to go there, but she didn't want to encourage Jarlath either. An icy breath ran through her chest. To think that this could have happened. Was it only sinking in now?

She forced herself to think of Tuscany. A moon would be up. The stone walls would be warm. The sky would be full of stars. She could sleep in a barn or in the fields to be awakened at dawn. That was the way to live, sleeping from dusk to dawn. None of those noises at night, the sirens or the floodlights. *La Luna, mi amore.*

"Daydreaming, Agnes?" said Allen.

She glanced at him. What was different about him? She was too used to seeing him deliver lectures.

"A bit, I suppose."

"You think being restless is exclusively the preserve of persons under twenty-five? Or perhaps a sign of early senility?"

"Aye. We all could do with a break," she said.

Agnes thought of the city waiting for her, her bedroom, the telly with the news blaring out one more miserable day for the city. She had trouble remembering her father's face, seeing only the crumbling face of her mother. With no warning, her mother could be stricken helpless with crying. Watching TV, reading a book or eating, her mother's face would suddenly contort. Agnes understood it was the commonplace things that could upset her, the vertiginous understanding that her husband was dead. No shaving soap in the bathroom, no other person in bed, no need to make sure the toast wasn't underdone. Agnes could comfort her mother again and again, but the weight seemed to increase. Sometimes she felt that she was nothing, neither young or old. When would it all end?

The sergeant started up the car. Minogue sat in the front passenger seat. He felt Kilmartin's impatience as a palpable weight in the car. Minogue noticed that the sergeant's uniform was spotted with cigarette ash. His breath came across stale, penetrating.

"Well, the Branch didn't so much say it as let it be known," Kilmartin began. "They got a phone call. Somebody claiming that there's going to be a car going north with weapons aboard. Tomorrow. They think it might have to do with that other car or cars in that garage."

Minogue contented himself with looking out at the dusk over College Green.

"They know the heat's on. I don't doubt they want results fast," Kilmartin murmured.

"Yes," Minogue allowed. He was tired. Drifting through the traffic made him sleepy.

"They've bought into McCarthy's Yank business anyway. I still have me doubts. Yank or not, you can't persuade me there isn't a connection though," Kilmartin said.

"What?" Minogue said reflexively.

"The shooting in Blackrock. The place is gone to hell in a wheelbarrow. I can see the news tonight and the bloody headlines: 'Murderers still at large,' 'Armed men on the rampage in Dublin,' 'Gardai draw a blank in search for killers.' "

"You think the same people are involved," Minogue said.

"Maybe not the actual same people. Did I tell you we got a rocket about being alert for new types of weapons and a new network for getting them in? That's what has the Branch looking for this mysterious Yank and taking crank calls seriously. The fella who called described a car that sounds like the one in the garage. And the way McCarthy was hinting about arms smuggling got them going in a big way," Kilmartin said.

"Well in anyhow: the other thing is a no-go. Those two fellas have gone to ground. Between me and you and the wall–" Kilmartin nodded in the direction of the sergeant's head, "those shaggers are back in the North by now."

"Signs on," Minogue said.

"And as for the thing about the garage, well I'm sure we closed it down before anything became operational. I say it was a mistake to raid it," Kilmartin said.

Minogue elbowed onto the seat and turned to Kilmartin. He was wary of the sergeant driving because he would be all ears, like anyone else, for an inspector's candour. Minogue imagined the sergeant going home to his wife: 'Wait 'til I tell you what I heard today ...'

Minogue was surprised to find himself alert. He noticed that Kilmartin was frowning at him. The front gate of Trinity College fell away behind the car, as the sergeant wheeled the car around into Dame Street.

Minogue's knees began to itch. He strained further to look out the back window at Trinity College receding behind them. It looked magical, a place apart. The lights gave it an air of churchiness. Students emerged from the archway, out onto the centre of a city which Minogue believed had gone mad. They could always go back in to the squares and the classic proportions, to the insulated clarity of that island. Stone buildings and edged lawns answered the bullydom of Ireland. But no: that was false, too facile. Minogue was thinking as a peasant. In the week he had been in and out of the university, he had felt it had a vulnerability, despite the intellectual and physical architecture which held it in place. No amount of pretty young girls with baskets on the handlebars of their old bikes could stop history. No amount of paintings hanging down over the dining tables could exempt this place from the present.

Agnes McGuire carrying her terrible burdens. Mick Roche trying to work through the place, not cynical enough to give up on the well-to-do students there. And Allen, for all his academic manner, he was trying in his own way to change things. Was he jealous of Allen? Minogue recalled Agnes smiling briefly as she went off in Allen's car, under his care. Maybe it was that he, Minogue, had felt stuck on the sidelines again, a spectator to events, with Allen's swanky car hissing away to the funeral in the rain. Allen's car: Jesus, Mary and Joseph ...

"Pull over here, if you please, Sergeant," Minogue said.

Kilmartin was staring at Minogue.

"That other car in that garage. You said whoever called gave a description which might match that one in the garage."

"The Mercedes, the canary yoke," Kilmartin said.

"No. The other one,"

"We don't know. A Japanese car, fancy, was the best we got on the one in the garage."

"And the one in the tip-off?"

"I don't know. A Branch man just told me it was awful like the description of the other one," replied Kilmartin.

"Are there any reports of stolen cars of that type?"

"Now, Matt, you know as well as I do ..."

"But it was checked against the reported stolens, wasn't it?"

"No doubt. But, here, hold on a minute, Matt. The one in the garage might have been legit anyway, a fella fixing a car. Anything. It was only that oul' lad thinking he saw one. Let the Branch worry about it."

The sergeant was assiduously trying to prove he was deaf. Minogue opened the door.

"Sergeant, could I ask you a favour, please."

The driver's head shifted around.

"Anything I can do, Detective Sergeant."

"Would you find out what you can on the radio about this car business. Inspector Kilmartin here will furnish details."

"But Matt," Kilmartin leaned over to look under the roof as Minogue stepped out onto the kerb.

"That can wait. We have this thing on the boil."

"Sure what can we do about this evening, Jimmy, except, kill time waiting for something?" Minogue said.

He had actually been reprimanding in his tone, the driver realised. Now if he himself tried that with an Inspector ...

"I'll be back in a few minutes," Minogue said. He began striding down the footpath toward Trinity.

As if Minogue's newfound vigour had by default led him to lassitude, Kilmartin slouched in the back seat listening to the driver. He was becoming aware that Minogue was more than merely contrary. Because Minogue did what he had just done so rarely, it appeared almost aggressive. Kilmartin decided he needed some time in the near future to sort out how to deal with Minogue. The sergeant was stroking his neck in anticipation of a reply on the radio.

"Takes 'em long enough," the sergeant muttered.

Kilmartin idly watched two drunken men staggering arm-in-arm down Dame Street. They didn't even notice the police car.

Then Minogue was climbing into the front seat, breathing heavily.

" 'A magenta Toyota Cressida,' he said."

"What?" said Kilmartin.

"It's a magenta Toyota Cressida. It's on its way north tonight."

"What are you saying?" asked Kilmartin.

"All this talk of a big Japanese car. I was thinking about that McGuire girl, the Walsh boy's girlfriend. Allen gave her a lift to the funeral in a fancy car, I'm sure it was a Toyota, and I think it was a magenta colour. You know, the one you don't know if it's crimson or purple. I could kick meself, so I could."

"But how in the name of Jas–" Kilmartin began.

"–I asked one of the porters, one of the fellas who works in the college. He checked the parking passes off a list."

A voice yowled on the radio.

"No reported thefts of that type. A magnet ... a magan–a magenta Toyota Cressida or Datsun. Over."

"Tell them," Minogue said. His wide eyes bored into Kilmartin's.

"Hold on a minute," Kilmartin leaned over. "Tell them what?"

"The suspect car is heading for the border."

"But the tip-off was for tomorrow, Matt."

The driver looked to Kilmartin.

"Over," the radio said.

"Allen has a car like that. He's gone up north to deliver a lecture. He left a day early. He's the one."

Kilmartin's frown bit deep into his forehead.

"The professor fella who does the peace lectures?"

"Allen. Dublin registration. A Professor Allen."

He ate in McDonalds in Grafton Street. His throat was still tight, barely letting food down. The restaurant was full. He looked around and realised that almost all the customers were young people. The older folks didn't trust hamburgers. So this was freedom and progress. He looked down at the shoulder bag under the table and he thought back to his exit from the hotel. The shift had changed for the evening and he hadn't been noticed. He had peeled off the moustache in an alley. The glasses irritated the bridge of his nose. He could discard them later.

The food tasted the same as stateside. Near the bottom of his coffee cup, he decided that he should try to get out tonight from Dun Laoghaire. There was nothing else for it. Either he left tonight or he waited for a week or two. His disguise was foolproof up to the point of someone checking when he had entered the country. They'd never go that far.

He stepped back out onto Grafton Street and crossed onto the footpath which led to the Front Gate of Trinity College. Busses and cars swept by him. The lights of shops spilled out over the path opposite. He remembered that the ferry left at nine o'clock.

He felt quite alone for the first time since he had landed. This bothered him all the more when he wondered as he passed people if they knew he was carrying a gun or that he had killed someone. There was no one he could phone or say goodbye to. This is absurd, he thought: get some control. Nothing would be served by an attack of nostalgia on top of the fear. As he passed the front of the college, he noticed a police car turning into Dame Street. The doubts began to creep in again. What could McCarthy tell them if he was picked up? His thoughts turned to wondering how much surveillance there would be at the dock in Dun Laoghaire. Had they installed a metal detector there since he got the OK?

Ahead of him, the bustle of O'Connell Street lit up the bridge. A tinker woman with a baby shawled next to her breast sat by a cardboard box on O'Connell Bridge.

"A few ha'pence, sir, to feed the child," she said.

He walked by her thinking of O'Connell, the Liberator, with beggars in his liberated land. In the distance he heard a siren. It came from behind him, from College Green and it faded quickly.

As the police car sped up Dame Street, Minogue watched the red light spilling and wiping along the buildings. The siren seemed to vibrate inside the car. For a few moments he wondered if this was real at all. In five minutes he'd be aloft in a helicopter from Dublin Castle on the way to the border. Ridiculous, to be sure. Was that him who shouted at Kilmartin to get him a place on it with the Special Branch men? And why had he insisted so? He wanted to see Allen's face, to tell him something, not to ask him questions. Minogue didn't know what it was that he should tell Allen. His mind struggled, looking for a grip on some words.

"Have you ever been up in one of those things before?" Kilmartin asked.

"Never in my life," replied Minogue.

The car shuddered over the kerb and stopped abruptly at the gate to Dublin Castle. Walls loomed over the car. A uniformed Garda walked over to the car. The driver knew him. The Garda nodded his head and returned to the booth. The barrier lifted soundlessly.

"Who owns it?" Minogue asked.

"Who else but the bloody army. They can get what they want these days."

Minogue stepped stiffly from the car. He was excited and nervous at the prospect of being whisked away into the night in this contraption. Kilmartin called out to him and he paused. Kilmartin half lay on the seat looking out under the window at Minogue. Looked like a child, Minogue thought.

"Matt. Don't bite any of your company in that whirlygig thing. Remember you're on the trip on sufferance. I'm a bit out of order insisting on you going along so don't poison the well for me. The Branch men will make the arrest and have him driven back to Dundalk most likely. I'll be arranging from this end that they give you a few minutes with him. You know this fella better than I do."

"So: observe," Minogue said.

"Now you have it."

Minogue recognised one of the men who had sat with him in Pearse Street listening to McCarthy. He walked over to Minogue.

"Are you the one who hit the button on this?" he said.

"Sort of," said Minogue, anticipating trouble.

"Be the living Jases you must be some kind of magician. Would a bit of it rub off on me now?" he said.

Minogue smiled despite the excitement. It felt like he hadn't smiled for days. He fleetingly recalled the moments in Bewley's, the talk around the tea-table at home: worlds away.

He followed the Special Branch men out through the building to a tarmacadam pad. Eerily, a light helicopter sat there. To Minogue it looked like a big insect. Its blades were claws, its Plexiglas screen a giant eye. Two men in jogging suits stood next to it, smoking. In the floodlights the smoke writhed Hallowe'enish toward the machine. Both men looked up when Minogue and his companion neared the helicopter. *Just like that,* Minogue was thinking. *We're going to walk into this thing, like a bus.* One of the two eased into the seat and switched on what sounded like a ventilator fan.

"Are we right?" the other said.

"As right as we'll ever be," the Special Branch said. He looked at Minogue and said:

"It'll be cold, er ..."

"Minogue. Matt Minogue. I'll be all right. How long will this yoke take?"

"We'll be landed and sitting in the customs post within fifty minutes. Less even."

"Be the hokey fly," Minogue marveled. What was that expression? 'I have seen the future and ...'?

As the craft lifted and bowed away over the city, Minogue was again stunned. It was incomprehensible that no wires held this thing up. The city was completely changed from here. It fell away under the belly of the helicopter like glowing embers of a coal fire. To the east the sea was in blue darkness. Ahead of them, then veering away, he saw runway lights at the airport. Minute moving lights of cars pulsed along the veins of this thing below. The lights petered out as they tended to the mountains. Minogue sat between the pilot and the Special Branch man. It felt as if he were in their care. The helmeted pilot was shockingly casual about it all, drawing lightly on the stick, commenting into the stalk microphone which stuck out from the gladiator helmet. Over the rotor noise, the Special Branch man shouted:

"I'm Scully, Pat Scully. I forgot."

Minogue nodded vigorously. This was like a carnival. He tried to identify the constellation of lights ahead of him. Swords? It occurred to him that he wasn't exactly sure what would be happening when they landed. Would they pick up Allen along the road or would they wait until the border? They had time, just about though. The porter at the Pearse Street Gate in Trinity said that Allen had taken his car about an hour ago. He couldn't have made it by then. He'd know better than to try an unapproved road especially after dark. Roving patrols of the British Army and SAS were on the move after dark.

"What's the story up ahead?" Minogue shouted into Scully's ear.

"We're all set up," Scully replied.

What did that mean? Minogue returned to thinking out the possible outcomes. Did Allen know? Allen would not hand over his car like that. It hadn't been stolen so Allen must have voluntarily given it over. Could it all be a coincidence though? What was there in it for Allen?

The pilot reached over and tipped Scully on the knee, then he pointed to a headset. Scully put it on. Minogue lip-read the pilot saying 'go ahead.' Scully searched for a volume control but giving up, cupped hands over his ears. As he listened, he nodded several times. Then he said OK. He looked over at the pilot who nodded once. Minogue noticed the pilot glancing quickly at him and then back to Scully.

"The car has been spotted. This side of Castlebellingham. Plenty of time," Scully shouted.

Minogue looked out over a town, marooned in light. A slash in the sky to the west was flooding a scarlet ribbon in the grey.

"Drogheda," the pilot said, pointing.

"There's someone else in the car."

"What?" said Minogue, leaning.

"There's someone else in the car. A woman," Scully shouted.

"What's the plan?" Minogue asked.

"We'll stick to the original," Scully announced and turned to look at the town passing below. Minogue looked out too. He followed car lights on the outskirts of town. They looked like a video game. A woman. Minogue's heart stopped, then a cold wash fell down through his chest. No, it couldn't be.

Minogue nudged Scully.

"Where will they be picked up?" he shouted. Scully paused before answering.

"At the border."

Minogue felt an alarm, like waking in the night to a strange sound. He stared at the side of Scully's face. Scully turned again.

"The situation on the ground," Scully shouted. "It may change. We have to be ready," he added, and returned to looking out over the Belfast road. Any minute now, they'd be overtaking the car.

The cold was biting into Minogue's shoes and under his chin. He no longer noticed the noise. He began to count but his heart was racing. He thought of Ravel and the tea at home in the oven waiting for him. Allen's face kept interrupting his images. Then he saw Agnes McGuire's face clearly in the darkness below.

Chapter Sixteen

Agnes sat up on the seat as they slowed, entering Dundalk. "They called it El Paso, the locals," she murmured.

"I shouldn't wonder," Allen replied.

"Doesn't look bad at night, does it?" Agnes said.

Allen guessed it was eight miles from the border, give or take.

"Tell me, Agnes, do you get nervous crossing the border? Going North, I mean."

"I'm going home, so I am. What's to be nervous about?" *Touché*, thought Allen. Stop treating her like she's wounded. As they pulled away from a traffic light, Allen noticed a car parked in a sidestreet. It was half up on the kerb. A double yellow line ran under the car. Briefly he noted the outline of two figures in it. He caught a momentary glint of an antenna as he accelerated through the junction.

"I suppose 'irritated' is the word. I don't like men with guns and costumes or uniforms looking at me. It's all so silly. Sometimes you forget it's serious. I find myself laughing, then crying," Agnes said.

Part of Allen's mind discounted what he had seen. Dundalk was a border town so you'd expect police.

"It's like a game, isn't it?" Agnes murmured.

That had to be routine here. He looked in the mirror but no car emerged from the street.

"Yes. I suppose," Allen replied.

That was the way it had been those years ago, a game. At least that was how he looked at it. In an instant he had felt the full weight of an adult world when the girl's parents opened the door to the garage. He had run, but he knew that he could run nowhere but home. Despite admitting it to the policeman who sat in the kitchen chair where his father used to sit, his mother kept saying it was impossible, that she knew her own son. She didn't listen at all.

Allen felt the beginnings of a headache grasping the back of his neck. Of course he was nervous, he couldn't deny that. Which was he more nervous about, asking her, or facing these soldiers and RUC at the border?

"Are you OK?" Agnes was asking.

"Oh. Yes. Just tired, that's all," he replied.

Minogue followed Scully over to an unmarked car. Behind him the blades were slowing and the monster was bathed in light. His legs felt like pieces of wood. The blower was on in the car. The driver reminded Minogue of Connors. A creased coat, the shirt half out of his pants probably.

"I'm Scully. Sergeant Minogue here is along for the ride. He's investigating a link here."

"Geraghty, sir. I'm to take yous to the customs post."

So they were going to wait, Minogue thought. That was odd.

"Away, so, Geraghty. What kind of time do we have?" Scully asked.

"The suspects are in Dundalk, sir. They're probably ten minutes back the road."

"Timing, hah?" Scully said, rubbing his hands.

"Were they waiting for us before they make the pick up?" Minogue tried.

Scully didn't answer. Minogue felt his tension edge into anger.

"Who's the other suspect?" he said.

"A woman, sir," Geraghty answered, suddenly aware of a brittle atmosphere.

"Reddish hair, young?"

"We don't know, sir," Geraghty said cautiously.

Traffic was light as they passed the sign for the border. Minogue remembered Kilmartin's injunction to him about meddling. Scully turned to him and said:

"Not to worry, Sergeant, everything will go well."

The mention of his rank skittered away in Minogue's mind. A warning? The floodlights at the customs post ahead filled up the windscreen. A lorry was parked off to the side, facing south. Minogue could see figures in the shed through the screens. They pulled up on the gravel behind the shed. Minogue noticed two cars and a Land Rover in the shadows. It'd be the same up the road, he guessed, on the northern side. RUC armed and some soldiers off to the side of the road; invisible from within the arena of floodlights. Minogue stepped out of the car. He felt ropey.

Scully walked over to the car and began talking in the window. Minogue heard a man laugh. The car creaked on its suspension. The lorry which had been parked drove off. No other vehicles could be heard. Minogue saw a movement in the shadows behind the customs shed, then another. He recognised the outlines of soldiers carrying automatic rifles.

Headlights appeared, coming from the south. It was a van. It slowed and a hand waved toward the customs shed. Probably a local who made the crossing every day. It accelerated slowly away to the north. Minogue stood at the side of the road. He saw a group of lights on the northern side which filtered dimly through the yellow-white glare of the customs post. He heard a car door open behind him. A big man climbed out awkwardly. In the weak light which shone from the car's interior, Minogue saw the man heft a strap on his shoulder inside his coat. He was carrying a submachine gun, Minogue realised. More cowboys.

Scully walked over to Minogue.

"Any minute now," Scully said.

"I don't see all your lads, is there more of them?" Minogue asked.

"Ah we don't need an army now," Scully said smoothly.

"Are they obliged to stop here? Heading north?"

"Not obliged. But people slow down."

"Do you put down some barrier?" Minogue persisted.

Scully shook his head.

"You're making a lot out of this now. Leave the details to me. Everything's in place. We're here to just see that everything goes smoothly. Don't be worrying," Scully soothed.

Minogue could smell the sea. It was mixed in with the smell of turned soil. He looked to the north again, at the lights of their customs post. A few hundred yards away were British soldiers like on the telly, with real guns and real uniforms.

"Oi," said Scully behind him. Minogue turned. The lights of one vehicle were approaching from Dundalk.

"Over here," Scully said. Minogue followed him to the customs post and stood next to him in the shadows. The big detective joined them. A radio squawked under his anorak and he reached in to turn it down. Minogue caught a few words before the volume went.

"Car's through, maintaining speed. Roadblock in place—"

"What roadblock?" Minogue whispered.

Allen had the road to himself. Only one lorry passed him going south. No lights appeared in his mirror. He felt some relief that he wasn't being followed. He wondered why there were so few vehicles on the road. Ahead of him the lights of the Irish customs post formed an island in the darkness. The place looked deserted. Allen knew that this post here at Killeen had been blown up a half dozen times in the past. Often it was closed down at night.

He could see lights on the far side of the border now. He slowed the car and let it coast up to the light. He knew he didn't have to stop. There was someone on duty in the office. Yellow glare filled the car interior. Agnes was squinting. Allen noticed an army Land Rover and several cars parked some distance behind the customs post. For a moment he felt a bolt of panic, but nobody was out on the road. There was no barrier. He drew abreast of the shed and looked in.

A customs officer looked out at the car through the grid of wire. Should he stop? The customs man made no gesture but continued looking dully out at the car. Allen's eyes were straining to see better.

"God, what a pack of iijits," Agnes said. "They don't know whether they're coming or going."

Allen was almost at a standstill.

"Go ahead," she said, "you don't have to stop, so you don't. It's just that everybody slows down to a crawl. If they want you, they wave."

Allen clutched into second gear.

"What roadblock? I don't see a roadblock," Minogue hissed. The car was pulling away from the customs post. Minogue saw a profile of the driver, yellow light on his shoulder. There was someone else too. Agnes. Minogue felt an aching in his shins and knees. His mouth was dry. The night was suddenly lurid to him with the lights and the evasions. He fixed his eyes on the red lights of the car drawing away.

The detective took out his portable, squelched it and handed it to Scully.

"Gone through now. Over," Scully said.

"What's going on?" Minogue said, louder.

"A success. That's what's going on. What do you want?" Scully said. Minogue looked at Scully's shadowed face. It confirmed what Minogue had felt from the voice: a changed man.

"Who's going to stop them?" Minogue said.

"The other crowd. The Brits," Scully replied. He turned and nodded to the others who began heading for the door of the customs post. Minogue overheard one of them saying 'big deal.'

Minogue grabbed Scully's arm. Scully's head darted around.

"It's a set-up, isn't it?"

Scully looked disparagingly at the hand holding him. He shook himself free.

"Your superiors didn't burden you with too much info. Leave well enough alone, now. Your job's done, so's ours."

"What's going to happen?"

"Look, Minogue. There's reasons."

Minogue stood in front of Scully.

"I want to know, Scully. I'm involved."

Scully stared a hole in Minogue before replying.

"We have to give the Brits something. They're moaning about security this side. They're expecting this. We had that tip-off about the car and we passed the ball to them. It's a token. They get the credit and so do we for delivering. We'd have a job convicting them in the South probably. Trade, tit for tat," Scully said.

"But you would have missed the car if I hadn't come up with Allen," Minogue protested.

"If, if," Scully repeated, looking out into the darkness. "Fair dues to you, we would have missed him all right. I'm not saying we're not beholden to you for it. That's why you get to be here, sitting next to me," Scully murmured.

He turned abruptly to Minogue.

"A day here, a day there, what does it matter in the end? We're all on the same side, Minogue."

Panic ran up from Minogue's knees and prickled his scalp. He looked at the red lights of the car. He heard the engine pick up speed. Scully ignored Minogue and looked at the car too.

When Minogue heard himself speak, the voice seemed to belong to someone else. Scully's frown had eased as he stared at the small bowl of light in the distance.

"What if he tries to run it, Scully?"

"He'd want to be a terrible stupid gobshite to try that class of a stunt, I'm thinking," murmured Scully. "Their border lads are sharp little thugs."

Scully hadn't taken his gaze from the car lights ahead. Doesn't care, Minogue realised dully.

"The girl," Minogue said. "The girl in the car with him, she's—"

"The girl in the car is the girl in the fucking car, Minogue. For all you know, she's in cahoots with him somewhere along the line," Scully snapped. "Maybe you didn't twig to her."

"She's not, I tell you," said Minogue hoarsely. "I know she's not."

"We'll find that out then, won't we? Let them sort it out."

Minogue grasped Scully's arm. He felt the muscle tense. Scully turned to him.

"Get your shagging hand offa me or I'll drop you, Minogue."

"These are cowboys, these border patrols, Scully. You know that. They're trigger-men. They're volunteers, they're just itching to take the law—"

"Get back in the car, Minogue. I've had enough of this rubbish. I'm going to lodge a slip on you for this. Shut up and get—"

Then Minogue ran.

He heard Scully's shout hang in the air behind him as the night air brushed over his face. With the glare ahead, Minogue was running blind. The road thumped the soles of his leather brogues. His coat flapped behind him. The raised voices behind him mixed with the sounds of air rushing into his nostrils. His shins cracked with each slap of his feet on the tar. Beneath him was darkness and all around darkness, just the glow of light ahead, like a magnet drawing him. It occurred to Minogue that he might well be shot at. The night seemed full of his breathing and flapping. Ahead of him the tail-lights glowed stronger as the brakes were applied.

Minogue prayed for the brake lights to stay on. He saw a figure step into the light ahead. It looked like the figure was carrying a stick, a hurley maybe. Minogue's chest was bursting, his legs jellying. Old, old. He was slowing. Spots of light danced all around him, a crazy swirl swarming around the lights ahead too. As though floating, Minogue took note of the low hedge running along beside him. For an instant Minogue thought the dream would end. He was getting no nearer the lights. It was an endless treadmill where he lost ground quicker than he gained it. He hoped he wouldn't trip. He knew he wouldn't be able to talk if he caught up to the car and that could be dangerous. The thing was, he must get her out of the car.

Allen felt as if his chest was being squeezed. From the recesses of his mind, he observed himself there in the car, slowing. He saw the soldier bulked with a flak jacket step into the light. Allen wondered where the RUC were. The soldier was holding the automatic rifle almost level. Off to his left Allen caught a glimpse of a vehicle in the ditch, a Land Rover. Where were the RUC?

Agnes turned around and looked out the back window.

"Do you see it?" she said.

Allen was rolling down the window. She looked at him and he turned to her. He saw her frown and her face go loose. *Now she knows,* he thought. *This is it, all of it.* She tried to say something but couldn't. Her back pressed into the door, looking across at Allen.

There was no traffic. The car was rolling to a halt, endlessly. Allen felt blood rush around his head. He looked out at the soldier who was not moving toward the car. Allen could see the kid's face clearly. He was no more than twenty-five. He wore his beret low on his forehead. Allen grasped the slicked wheel with both hands. His upper arms began to tremble. He thought something passed behind the car, a flicker in the mirror. The car stopped and rocked back slightly as the suspension returned it level after the braking. All Allen could hear was the regular infuriating tick-over of a well-tuned car.

"Switch off the engine. Then step out of the car," the soldier said. Allen couldn't take his eyes off the rifle.

"Surely–" he began.

The soldier looked over the roof of the car. He glanced at Allen again.

"Out."

"Really," Allen said. "Is this necessary? Don't you–"

"There's something out there," Agnes whispered.

The solider backed away from the car and levelled the rifle.

"Out of the car!" he shouted.

Allen saw the soldier look behind the car again, frowning. Time stopped for him. A rush of understanding settled on him. He felt a finality, close. Something was wrong. He could feel Agnes' alarm. It was dark outside this bowl of light. Was there nothing outside this terrifying oasis? He laid his hand slowly on the gearshift and looked to his right.

Minogue wondered why nobody had stopped him. Each of his feet was landing flat and heavy now. His breath was in hoarse gasps. Maybe if he shouted, they'd hear him from there. A stitch like a cold knife was slicing under his ribs, jabbing. He saw the man with the stick move back from the car. Another two men came up behind the car, sticks raised to their shoulders. Minogue stopped. He was within a hundred yards of the car. He saw the back of the car dip. The tires squealed. Minogue shouted with all the wind he could hold. The light was pulsing in front of him. He swayed with the effort.

"Wait! Police!" he shouted. "Wait!"

The soldiers turned and crouched. Minogue shouted again. One of the soldiers turned back and Minogue heard the *pop pop,* a staccato. Minogue dropped to the ground. Seconds ticked by. He heard more shots. The car lights were moving from side to side. Then, lazily, the tail-lights straightened out their course. Minogue heard shouting. The lights leaned to the left and followed, shuddering, the grass highlighted by the beams ahead of the car. Floodlights froze the slowing car in their glare. Minogue leaned on his elbows in the road, dumbfounded. The red lights leaned more as the car mounted the ditch and came to a standstill.

*   *   *

Figures ran to the doors and pulled them open. Minogue saw them pull the two passengers out to the ground. He heard more shouting. Suddenly he was blinded by light.

"Stay where you are." He heard the English accent through the loudspeakers. "Do not move or you will be fired on."

Minogue heard the siren warbling stronger from behind. He felt completely vulnerable, spreadeagled on the road. He waited for the *whack* of a bullet. Minogue thought of all the minute indentations in the tar. It smelled of petrol and rubber and farms. He closed his eyes. A car pulled up behind him.

"Police!" someone shouted, an Irish voice. "One of ours! Police!" Minogue heard footsteps in the ditch next to him.

Again the voice. "Police, don't shoot!"

A faint blue light swept around in the glare. To his left Minogue saw a British soldier. He looked around and saw Scully cupping hands to shout again. The soldier's face was blackened. He was squinting down the sights of the rifle. Under his eyes, the small black hole of the muzzle seemed to rest on his hand. Minogue wondered if this boy was going to shoot him. He couldn't miss. Minogue could hear the boy's breathing.

The soldier said, "OK," and lowered his rifle. "OK."

"He's one of ours. He's OK."

"OK," the soldier said. "Just get the bastard out of here. Just get him out of here."

Minogue elbowed onto his knees. The soldier was shaking his head. Another soldier appeared from outside the glare.

"Get up, Minogue." Scully's voice, thickly.

"John fuckin' Wayne," the soldier said.

The boat train to Dun Laoghaire was only three minutes late. It emerged from between the houses and gardens by Merrion Gates at a rush, rumbled over the level crossing and seemed to relax as the bay opened up to to east. Howth with its necklace of lights shouldered out into the sea across the bay from the swaying train.

Three men sat ahead of him. They looked like navvies on their way back to England. They smoked constantly and spoke little.

He tried to maintain the appearance of a tired tourist. He had held off the bouts of panic, but the effort left him jittery. He tried to block out images which were coming to him constantly now. He saw the playwright, that expression of disdain on his face, talking to a policeman. Then he saw that cop's hands reaching for his chest as he lay on the ground. It looked like he was trying to pull the slug out. The cop's head arching back, digging into the ground and then falling back as the hands went limp.

"That's the end of the holidays now, hah?" a navvy said. "Back to the grind, hah?" he added, and returned to staring out through the grass.

The tanned man tried to smile and he nodded. He was relieved to have escaped wordless from this. Then it occurred to him that he might be passing up something. In his caution he might be losing out on an advantage. If he got in with these men, it might help him. They might adopt him if he bought them some drink. It would take effort, but it would be worth it.

"Excuse me but are we close to Dun–Dunleery?" he said.

"I'm telling you now, Minogue. When we go over you better mind your p's and q's. You're bloody lucky you didn't collect another hole in your arse off those fellas," Scully said.

Minogue's legs were cramping, but his breath was back. He felt like an errant schoolboy sitting in the back of the car with the big detective eying him.

"Seems to me it's your arse is in the sling, Scully," Minogue said quietly. Scully turned to look at Minogue. His eyes flickered to the detective and then back to Minogue.

"You've said enough, Minogue. You're a loose cannon. Bloody iijit, you nearly banjaxed the whole thing."

"You're forgetting something, Scully. I have a mouth on me. You're just the pot-boy with the piss-bucket here along with these cowboys. The arrest should have been made here. You know and I know that the Brits are trigger-happy. They've been given the green light. They're just itching to have a go at anyone. You threw those two to them," Minogue said.

"Watch who you're calling a piss-boy, Minogue. We heard about you." Scully's voice rose.

"This was a planned operation–"

"–And you're just here to execute it. Or them," Minogue said.

"–so get it through your head!" Scully shouted.

"So what are you going to say to them? You don't even know yet if Allen was shot or what happened," Minogue retorted.

"Was that the deal? You throw them to the wolves for public

relations and the Brits let you question him for ten minutes. If he's still alive. And the passenger?" Minogue continued.

"You don't get holy on me, Minogue. I'm doing this stuff every day of my working life and more besides. Don't give me the innocent bystander bit. They're all at it."

"I'm telling you that she's not involved!"

Was that himself shouting, Minogue wondered. How long since he had shouted at someone?

"Look, Minogue. All I know about you is that I'm to assist in you getting an interview with this Allen fella. I don't know or care who your mother is or whether you're the full shilling or even whether you got your arse shot off or not. If I have to revoke this because you've gone off the deep end, I will, and I can live with the bloody consequences."

Before Minogue could reply, headlights flashed twice ahead. The driver flashed back and accelerated toward the light. Minogue looked behind as the car started off. He saw men in battle dress in the ditch. Back at the customs post, blue lights whirled.

Ahead of them, Minogue saw three vehicles blocking the road. One was an ambulance. As they slowed, the ambulance moved off. A soldier waved them down. Scully rolled down the window.

"We're to see a Sergeant Davies," said Scully.

The magenta Cressida stood like an abandoned toy. The doors hung open and the lights were still on. The back window had been shot out. Minogue saw a half-dozen holes in the boot and a ding in the bumper. Scully stepped out of the car and Minogue followed him. Minogue realised there were people standing off in shadows, soldiers. Two cars started up almost simultaneously beyond the floodlights. A Land Rover equipped with a crane drove slowly toward them. It turned away from them and began reversing into the ditch behind Allen's car. More soldiers and men in plain clothes appeared out of the darkness. Minogue thought that there must be a lot more of them out in the fields too. Behind them their car, with the two detectives still in it, backed slowly to the side of the road, followed by the soldier who had waved them down, cradling a rifle.

Two men in plain clothes approached Allen's car and looked inside. One of them walked to the back of it. He bent over, his face inches from the back lights, examining the boot lid. Then he closed the doors slowly. He guided the Land Rover in. The other man walked over to Scully and Minogue. Minogue felt nervous and exposed.

Sergeant Davies was a slight man with pale features which were whitened further by the glare off the lights. His hair was neatly trimmed. He wore a V-necked jumper over a collar and tie. Minogue guessed him to be in his early forties. Looked like he had just put down the paper after tea and come out for a stroll. His face suggested a minimum of surprise at guesting these coppers from the Free State.

"Davies," he said.

Minogue wondered why he had not learned to distinguish regional accents in the North. For an instant he was back watching the news at home, listening to the inquiring and querulous tones of the North. Another shooting, more condemnation, more bile. Why did he feel they were so foreign?

"Detective Sergeants Scully and Minogue," Scully said. Minogue nodded. There were no handshakes. No love lost here.

"In the van here," Davies said.

Minogue's heart was pounding. He had restrained himself from asking about the ambulance. He noticed his hands were in fists.

"What was that little problem ye had there with some fellow running along the road?" Davies asked.

Scully paused a moment before answering:

"Nothing to it. It's settled now."

"Uh," Davies said. He stopped at the back of a Sherpa van. "Ten minutes or so. We have to get out of here. Too much lights, do ye know. It's not the safest of places," Davies said.

Allen's face was white. Minogue crouched for a few seconds, paralysed, at the door. Allen's shirt hung out over his pants. He was shivering. Looking at Allen's strained and damp face, Minogue doubted that he was the same man he had spoken to recently.

Davies leaned in the doorway. Scully sat down opposite Allen. Minogue noticed flecks of blood on Allen's face. There were cuts on the back of his hands. He looked out under his eyebrows and the toss of hair at Minogue, then at Scully.

"I'm Detective Sergeant Scully. Sergeant Minogue here will be asking you questions. If you make things awkward, there'll be trouble. Just tell what you know."

Allen's pupils were tiny. His eyes seemed to bulge wider. He didn't know what to do with his handcuffed hands.

When Allen spoke, Minogue was shocked at the voice. It was a high, child-like register, with none of the assurance Minogue had expected.

"I might have known," Allen said.

"What about the girl?" Minogue whispered. Allen didn't answer but looked at Scully and Davies instead.

"What about the girl? Agnes," Minogue hissed. Again, all they heard were the engines outside. He's in shock, Minogue realised. He's out of it.

"She's gone in the ambulance," Davies said. Minogue reeled inwardly. He turned to Davies.

"Is she badly hurt?"

Before Davies could reply, Allen said:

"Agnes is taken away. They took her away, you see." His voice trailed off. Then he stared at Minogue.

"She was hit," Davies said. Minogue concentrated on the accent: 'hot' for hit.

"Minogue," Scully said.

Minogue heard the reprimand in Scully's voice.

"Loftus. I know I don't have to tell you anything. You know Loftus? Yes. Loftus. You could say he is ... very resourceful. He is quite without any ..." Allen whispered.

He looked up at Minogue.

"No. You needn't ask. It wasn't voluntary on my part ... Not at all, I can assure you."

"Who else?" Minogue asked.

"People on the phone. I don't know."

"Was there an American?" Minogue asked.

Allen's brow knitted over.

"An American," Minogue repeated.

"I'm not sure. I don't know."

"What's in the car?" Minogue said.

Allen grinned but his eyes held the fright, unchanged. Minogue saw that Allen's eyes were blinking rapidly.

"I don't know. I really don't," he whispered.

Minogue looked at Scully. Davies was pushing back the cuticle on a nail.

"But there was something."

"I suppose.. They said–"

"Who?"

"On the phone ... that's all."

Minogue waited before asking. Then he spoke slowly.

"Where does Jarlath Walsh fit in?"

Allen stared at his handcuffs. Minogue asked again.

Allen looked up at Minogue. His eyes were wet, blinking. "That wasn't my decision at all. You should understand that," he whispered hoarsely. "I had no hand, act or part in it."

"In concealing evidence you did."

Allen stared at him for a moment. Minogue saw some defiance in the stare before the eyes slipped out of focus again.

"You don't know half of it, Minogue. Nothing," he said.

"Tell me then," Minogue said. "You've nothing to lose now."

Chapter Seventeen

The train jolted to a halt with the rattle of couplings. The older man stood and stretched.

"Canadian? Are they fond of their beer there, tell me."

"Fairly."

The tanned man followed them out onto the platform. Groups of people were wrestling luggage down toward the rear of the platform.

He looked at some of the others walking down the platform. A couple with a sleeping child and too many bags. A heavy-set man, his suitcase tied with a belt, walking unsteadily.

"Is there a big line-up here?" he asked the red-faced navvy.

"Ah no. Nothing to it. Sure they know the half of us going across."

"What about a ticket?"

"Go round the corner there. There's a sweet shop and a ticket office at that gate in. Here, hold on, I'm going meself."

He saw no police. He couldn't ask the navvies about the police. The red-faced navvy was paying for his ticket ahead of him.

"Cabins?" The red-faced man was saying to the woman behind the counter.

"Do I look like Jack Tar or something, like Moby Dick? What would I want a cabin for? Here look after your man here, he's a Canadian. He's a long way from home."

The tanned man grinned, but he felt an icy touch. He didn't want any attention drawn to himself.

After he bought the ticket, they rejoined the other two. They were now leaning against the wall at the end of the passageway leading to the passenger entrance to the ship. He smelled the pungent air, a mix of fish and engine oil. Through the window he saw Dun Laoghaire pier and the waving masts of moored yachts. Isolated figures walked from light to light along the pier.

"Me belly thinks me throat is cut," the short navvy said.

"Give over bellyaching, Joey. There's plenty of gargle on the bloody boat. We'll be on in a minute," the older navvy said.

A uniformed member of the crew opened the doors leading to the gangplank. Two men in grey overalls stood next to the gangplank, idly looking at the waiting passengers. The line began to move.

The tanned man practised his breathing to ease his tension.

"No big deal, is it," he said. "They don't make a fuss, do they?"

"Why would they? Sure aren't they glad to be sending us back? There's no jobs here," the older navvy remarked wryly.

Another member of the crew walked down the gangplank. Still, the tanned man saw no one that looked like the police. He shuffled along beside the red-faced navvy. They were within a dozen people of the doors. Then he saw a stocky man standing to the side of the doors, outside. He looked to the other side of the door, but he could not yet see far enough around the jamb.

"Aye, aye, Captain!" the red-faced man called out to the two crew members. Both looked over at him. One of them grinned.

"Here, lookit," he said to the other one.

"Well lads, did you fix the hole in the boat?" the older navvy asked loudly.

Both crew members were grinning now.

"Where would a fella get a bit of refreshment here, Admiral?" the small navvy called out.

"Yiz could try a swim. That's very refreshing," one of the crewmen said.

"Very funny. Pass the chicken, the feather's worn out. We'll see yiz later, hah?" the small navvy said.

The tanned man had lost the breathing routine. His neck felt as if it were in a vice grip. As he stepped through the door jamb he saw the other cop, his hands in his pockets, looking over the faces. He cursed the wit of the three navvies for drawing attention to themselves. Better now try to avoid their eyes. Look surprised, a bit puzzled. The cop on the left was looking at him. Without thinking about it, the tanned man had drawn his elbow in so that he could feel the gun under his arm. He couldn't see any metal detector. He stopped breathing.

*   *   *

Minogue did not speak on the way back to Dundalk. Agnes McGuire's face kept pushing his thoughts aside. Occasionally he noticed that the detective beside him was watching him. Scully sat in the front looking ahead. The most that Minogue knew about her came from Davies, who reminded him somehow of a stale room. Davies was making little of it, as an object lesson for what he saw as Free State clodhoppers who needed instruction in the violent ways of the North. Davies probably wouldn't admit that the whole thing was out of his hands anyway, that he was dragged in to front the operation for the British Army.

Minogue had stood beside the customs post back on the Republic side while Scully radioed in a report to be passed on to Dublin. He watched as the vehicles drove out of the aura of light back up the Belfast road. The floodlights turned off all at once. There were more troops and police on the Republic side than when they'd crossed. They had stood around, not sure what to do. Then they began dispersing.

Allen had asked him what he could do. Minogue told him he'd try to get news of Agnes to him but that he, Allen, was going North. As Davies slammed the door he said to Minogue:

"There ye hove it. For a perfesser he's a torrable stypud mon."

Minogue's loathing for the broken man in the back of the van broke through his own numbness and threatened to overwhelm him. For a few moments, Allen's face had communicated the strain he had been under, but then Minogue's mind reddened with anger. He might be a step closer to Walsh's murderer, but who paid in the end?

When the car stopped, Scully got out and walked over to Minogue.

"You got what you wanted, Minogue. So far as I'm concerned that episode is over. There's no need for it to be written into the record. It was quite understandable when you think about it. I mean, you had your priorities. The word from on high was to pass the ball. That's hard to live with these days, I know."

Minogue looked beyond Scully to the helicopter.

"What with policemen being shot in the streets. I put two and two together you know, even if nobody told me all the ins and outs of it. It's connected with the things in Dublin, isn't it, the murders? You don't have to tell me," Scully continued.

Minogue began to walk off. Scully walked alongside.

"Just ask yourself this: if it helped to find the killers of those lads in Dublin and if it helps stop more police being killed, shouldn't you weigh that in the balance?"

Minogue stopped and faced Scully.

"You know, Scully, you sound exactly like a brother of mine. He talks the exact same way. The same kind of logic, but he's on the other side. Does that bother you at all? Allen and the girl were thrown to the wolves just so the various custodians of this bloody island can tell all of us to sleep soundly. You know and I know that car should never have crossed the border. But you're just doing what you're told to do, same as the rest of us. That stuff doesn't work in the long run you know. Our kids can see through that rubbish as easy as kiss hands."

Scully frowned.

"Nice speech, Minogue. Except it doesn't fit in this world."

As the helicopter lifted off, Minogue reflected that Scully was right, but it shouldn't be Scully saying it. It was after nine now. As they came in sight of the northern suburbs of Dublin, the message was relayed from Kilmartin that the Special Branch were outside Loftus' flat, waiting for the word to go in.

He felt claustrophobic as the passengers crowded closer at the door. He met the cop's gaze for a few seconds. The cop's gaze rested briefly on the tanned man and then it moved on. He began walking toward the gangplank railing. The other cop had not looked at him.

The first cop glanced at him again. He felt the skin at the back of his neck prickle. He patted his jacket to make sure it was zipped. As his feet started up the metal tongue of the gangplank, he risked a look at the cop. Unbelievably, the other cop was stepping onto the gang-plank as well, timing it to match his arrival. The tanned man froze as the two cops met on the gangplank directly in front of him. He realised he had left it too late. He looked directly into the face of the cop who was blocking his way. The cop flicked a glance at him but looked over his shoulder. The passengers had come to a standstill. The two cops edged around the tanned man and one grasped the arm of a teenager behind.

"Will you step aside for a moment, please," the cop said.

The tanned man turned to see the teenager dart a look from one cop to the other. Then he shook his head and stepped off the gang-plank. The tanned man resumed his climb. The navvies looked behind.

"What's with your man there. Is he mitching from school or what?" red-face said.

"Maybe he did in the budgie at home," the older navvy replied.

The tanned man realised he was breathing heavily through his nose. His legs were lazy springs that barely carried him onto the ship.

"Here lookit, where's the gargle?" the short navvy yawned.

"Jases, you're a divil," the older one replied. "It's a wonder those fellas didn't take you aside. You're not out on bail for something, are you?"

"Out on bail is right. It's baling out is what I'm doing. Bloody place."

"What was all that about?" the tanned man managed to ask.

"Your man? The young fella?" red-face said. "I don't know. Maybe he was skipping the country or something. Looks like they were waiting for him."

"Here, do you miss the place already?" the red-faced navvy said. "Come on up and I'll stand you a drink. You have to have something to puke up if it gets choppy."

The tanned man forced a smile.

"Do they let Canadians buy drinks on this boat?" he asked. The older navvy laughed.

It had begun to rain in Dublin. Kilmartin's face was streaked with the shadows of rain which clung like eyelashes to the windows of the car. The constant hush of rain washing up under the car made Minogue sleepy. Kilmartin's face brightened and darkened alternately with the passage of the streetlights as he talked.

Minogue turned to him.

"I want to ask you something about that business earlier on," Minogue said.

Kilmartin returned Minogue's steady gaze.

"I want to know if you knew it would turn out like that."

Kilmartin blinked and said:

"You mean the girl being shot? Of course I didn't–"

"Not that," Minogue interrupted. "I mean dumping them with the Brits."

Kilmartin paused. He took in Minogue's darkened face, the tiredness and the wariness gathered around his eyes.

"No I didn't, Matt."

Kilmartin let his eyes go out of focus as he gazed out beyond the driver and the squeaking wipers.

"They don't tell me that stuff. They're a law unto themselves, so that's that," Kilmartin said softly. He wondered if Minogue believed him. Kilmartin's unease impelled him into talking.

"Our mystery man stayed at the Shelbourne. One of the porters put a good face on him, right down to the shoes he was wearing. 'Looks a bit like a bank manager,' says he. Between what McCarthy told us and what the nosey staff up above in the Shelbourne say, we have a rough-and-ready Identikit of this fella. There were clothes left in a room and there's no sign of the man who stayed. No visitors. He was there for a while," Kilmartin was saying.

"What will he do?" Minogue asked.

"I don't know. Something tells me he is a very polished performer entirely. The Branch are quite up in a dander about him. They don't know anything about him. Came out of nowhere. I'd say he'll lie low here. I wouldn't put it past him to have other passports and things."

Minogue imagined a well-groomed, confident American. He'd have good teeth anyway, probably aftershave, one of those diver's watches on an expandable strap. Hairs would poke out under the strap. He might chew gum. What was he doing here though?

"Irish American. A true son of Erin," Minogue murmured.

"Seems likely, doesn't it?"

"If he's so well set up, then why would he shoot someone?" Minogue wondered aloud.

"Strictly speaking, we don't know that he did," Kilmartin answered. "It's a lead."

"Hardly coincidence then about Walsh," Minogue said.

"Well what do you think, Matt?"

Minogue didn't answer immediately. Then he said:

"I'd better fill you in on Allen."

After he had finished, Kilmartin said:

"God, isn't that the back of the neck? Great oaks from little acorns grow. How long ago was this?"

"Well, Allen is getting on fifty. So let's say nearly forty years ago."

"And what happened?"

"Took psychiatric treatment. Made to. And it worked, he says."

"So he changed his name ..."

"... and turned out to be a model. Got interested in the psychology and took it up. He's a very smart fella, Allen."

Kilmartin harrumphed.

"–Not smart enough to deal with Loftus I'll warrant. He had nothing to fear. Jesus God in heaven, people are nearly getting credit for any kind of perversion these days. Sure what age was he?"

"Thirteen," Minogue said.

"And didn't he pull himself up by the bootstraps ever since. I can tell you I couldn't hold it against him. He should have skinned Loftus when Loftus put the pressure on."

"Well," Minogue murmured as a bump interrupted him, "he had to gild the lily, or so he thought. He wanted to measure up, you see. His father was dead these years, probably the only one who could tone down the mother."

"Go on," Kilmartin said. "A real bloody cop-out. 'It started with me mother' and all the psychology stuff. And he told you this in a van in the middle of nowhere?"

Minogue wondered if he could tell Kilmartin how relieved Allen had been to let out with the intolerable stresses he had endured. He had said it all in a matter of minutes. Minogue had felt less disgust than some vague and frightening acceptance of Allen's story. He didn't need to tell Kilmartin the real, the simple and the quite absurd truth which Allen had communicated to him. Allen, elbows on his knees and looking at the handcuffs, had told him in so economical a way as to be devastating, that he could not have Agnes McGuire know about his past. Ordinary, like the rest of us, Minogue had understood, he wanted deliverance and love too. There had been no accounting for that.

On the way back to Dublin, Minogue shivered and spent most of the time wondering how it would come out, how much damage would be done to Allen's work for peace. All come to nothing, probably.

"Pressure," Minogue said. "You never know what people'll do."

Kilmartin did not miss the tone of Minogue's remark. Had Minogue known all along that everyone was watching him to see if he was the full shilling? Maybe he even played on it, controlling it in his own way. Kilmartin gathered himself in the seat.

"Anyway. Allen is small fry. I want Connors' killer and you want whoever killed that lad in Trinity. We may well be talking about the same character, hah? We'll root him out in short order and there'll be no bones about it."

Loftus looked quite different without a tie, Minogue observed. Still, he retained the appearance of confidence mixed in with a knowingness and a contempt. He had not ranted and raved but slipped on a coat and gone to Donnybrook Station with the three Special Branch detectives. He appeared almost relaxed. His hair had been oiled by the rain. He sat in his coat some six feet from the table. When Minogue entered, an amused glance of recognition came from Loftus. Then he returned to observing the desk and walls. Minogue nodded to the Branch man standing outside the door as he closed the door gently. He stood next to the desk looking at Loftus' face. Loftus smiled.

"Unorthodox. And melodramatic too," Loftus said.

"These are dramatic times, Captain Loftus. Less comedy though, I'm thinking."

"You're wrong there. I was at home watching the television and now I'm here. It's fairly comic, wouldn't you agree?"

"Do you want the rigmarole about what you're doing here and what you're being held under?"

Loftus didn't answer.

"I requested to interview you alone."

"I recall you doing that in my office last week, Sergeant. Am I supposed to be disoriented and confess to something now that I've been dragged down here?"

"You'd know about that stuff, Captain. I mean you've been trained. How long were you in the States on your training?"

Loftus raised his eyebrows.

"Really now, you haven't brought me down here to get me to start an autobiography. I've been out of the army for eleven years."

"When did it all turn sour for you?" Minogue asked.

Loftus laughed briefly.

"Get someone in here to get on with whatever I'm supposed to be here for. And make it good. After I get amused, I'll be none too pleased and heads will roll about this."

"Is that so, now? I have convinced the Special Branch crowd and even my superiors, who are all waiting to talk to you, that I can get you to help us. Now I don't mind telling you that they think I'm cracked. I don't even want to tell you that they are in a fierce hurry to talk to you. Pressure, you see. We're all under pressure. So I'm here to pass on some pressure to you."

Loftus' bemused look had changed to one of curiosity.

"Everyone seems to believe that systems can be designed to rule out human weakness. Perversity, maybe I should call it. I mean nothing is ever watertight. People don't behave according to plan. Isn't that really banal, Captain?"

"You're putting it mildly."

"The best-laid plans and all that. You think you can depend on people. Especially if you control their motivations. I mean, young people are called cynical the way they scorn the carrots dangling in front of them—the job, the car, that stuff. What happens when the incentive isn't there though?"

"You're nearly as entertaining as the programme I'm missing at home," Loftus said.

"Weakness, though. Some people can live with it and some can't. Some despise weakness, don't they? They fall in love with efficiency, action. Any action if it comes to that. Looking for to be heroes of some description."

Loftus drew in a breath and expelled it noisily through his nose.

"Or was it Captain Loftus, the great nationalist, who has all the ready solutions at hand...?"

Loftus' eyes glittered with contempt but he said nothing.

"... If I had to place my bet, though, I'd not put money on your brand of patriotism, Loftus. Not even your love affair with the problem-solving know-how that you learned off the Yanks when you were there ... Oh no, I see the dark horse as the one for this course. You're a good, upright lad who probably still goes to Mass and visits his mother, are you? But every day in the college you rub up against what's left of the Anglo Irish. And you find that you're not really their equal, no matter what the job description says ... You're just not a college boy, are you? A Catholic lad, up from Cork, you have your wits about you, but you find it's not quite enough to be acc-"

Minogue saw Loftus' nostrils flare. Loftus leaned forward in the chair.

"Easy does it now, like a good man, Loftus. There are men outside here who have had friends killed by the types of people you favour with your politics. Do you follow the gist of what I'm saying?"

What would have been a sneer had Loftus not controlled it eased into a strained grimace of a smile. He sat back stiffly in the chair.

"I'm getting tired of this ramble, Minogue. I've been patient. I have an idea how things work for security organisations. The more you talk, the bigger a stink I'm going to make about this. I'm not your common or garden-variety citizen who has to put up with this. I maintain enough links through the college with people who can have you on the carpet-"

"So Murphy's Law of Damage is true again," Minogue continued.

"What?"

"You know. If there's a one percent chance of something going wrong, it'll go wrong ninety-nine percent of the time and cause one hundred percent damage."

"That's rich all right. I'll remember that. Now–"

"Now we'll talk about Allen, Captain."

"Who?" asked Loftus.

"Allen, the one who's putting the finger on you. You don't have a lever on him anymore. Something else came up. Didn't you know? I'm sure you did. Agnes McGuire? Well she was in the car with him, but he didn't make it this time. Someone tipped off the Brits. They were waiting for him. Yes. Allen tried to make a run for it, but they shot up the car. Yes. Don't know if she'll live or not."

Minogue stood up and crossed his arms. He began to stroll slowly around the room, watching Loftus out of the corner of his eye. Minogue felt the day would never end. He had an ache like a kick in his belly. The tea would be burned by now and he'd reneged on one of his resolutions. Kathleen would be worried. As he paced the room, he recalled the blades beating the air as he bent to walk to the cockpit of the helicopter. Rust-coloured blood on Allen's face and shirt, but not Allen's blood. He stopped and sat on the desktop.

"He has nothing to lose now, you see," Minogue murmured.

Inspector Colm Quigley arrived at a run from the car which had raced through Dun Laoghaire. Even before he stepped from the car, he had been breathing heavily. The drizzle came as a relief to him. Somehow the smell of the sea calmed him. He reminded himself to be more regular with his exercise as he approached the van.

Other policemen were jealous of what they thought was glamorous stuff that Quigley's Emergency Response Team did: hostages, shootouts, surveillance. Often arriving unannounced, Quigley walked heavily on many toes. His teams were called cowboys. At meetings, Quigley spent a lot of time returning the gazes of senior uniformed Gardai whose looks indicted his forty-three years as well as the paramilitary operations he reported on.

Three other cars stood next to the van, their engines running. He tapped on the window of the van. A face behind the drops widened in recognition.

"They're ninety percent sure," the driver of the van said, rolling down the window.

"Come in outa the rain, sir," Sergeant O'Rourke added.

Quigley declined.

"He was in the crowd getting on," O'Rourke said.

"And how did it get this far?"

"Came out on the train, sir. We don't have anyone actually on the train."

"Are the two detectives down there armed?" O'Rourke asked quickly, nodding toward the ferry lights, half hidden in the trees which lay below the carpark on Marine Road.

"No, sir. A fair crowd on the boat tonight," O'Rourke said.

Quigley recognised the tact and he privately admonished himself.

"Right. How many are we?" Quigley said.

"Gibbons, Maher and meself here, sir. There's eight more in the cars outside. All the stuff is here."

Quigley thought for a minute. This could be buggered up very easily. If it was the fella, then there might be shooting. There were a lot of confined spaces on the boat. Too many places to cover as well. The drizzle was soaking down his hair now, settling, cool.

"Anybody told the Gardai yet?" Quigley asked.

O'Rourke shook his head.

More trouble, thought Quigley. He'd have to tell them sooner or later. Maybe this fella was standing up on a deck looking around for police. Imagine a crowd of yahoos tearing down here with the lights flashing ...

The ferry was due to leave at a quarter to nine. They had twenty minutes before having to ask for a delay and arouse the man's suspicions. Now: if they could coax the fella out on a deck alone. No one would be out in this weather.

Quigley could see the beginnings of the pier's lights below. The rest of it hid behind the trees, curling around to meet the East Pier at the mouth of the harbour. Behind him he could hear music coming from the lounges in the seafront hotels. The idling engines reminded him that time was running out fast.

"O'Rourke, listen. This fella may have the same gun on him. It's a 45 calibre, an automatic, so it'll put out a lot in a hurry. Under no circumstances are you or any of these lads to challenge him if there is another party present. Bystanders and it's out, completely. That doesn't leave us much leverage. No one is to take submachine guns on board."

O'Rourke raised his eyebrows, then he nodded twice, slowly. "Moloney, you get a call through to the bridge for the captain or first officer only. Tell them we're coming on board. Don't tell them why. Tell him

I'll go directly to him so have someone meet me and tell any crew at the entrance."

O'Rourke paused. He was aware of a slight tremor in his voice.

"Then you'll wait for ten minutes and you'll radio in for Garda assistance. If there's any questions asked of you later, you'll refer them to me, and me only. Gibbons, I want a vest. You and O'Rourke and myself are going to go ahead, one by one at a half minute apiece. I'll go first. The two lads at the gangplank say he might be with a crowd of navvies, but I don't get it. He has a red outdoor jacket, like an anorak, like something for climbing mountains. One bag. When you get on, just disperse, move around. We don't have much time. He'll be suspicious if the boat is late. If you spot him and there's none of us near, then use the radio. If he's clearly on his own and you've got the space, well and good. Assume he is armed so follow procedures. I repeat: assume he is armed."

Quigley paused before continuing. He looked from face to face and worried lest the men see his own fear.

"Have you some kind of duffle bags to carry? Something casual...?"

"What about the other lads, sir?" Gibbons said.

"Too much. We can't take that chance. Moloney: tell 'em to scatter around the dock and maintain radio silence. We'll be wired up, but we can't use an earpiece. We'll only use it if we have to. Just be ready to get on board in a hurry if you hear anything on your set."

O'Rourke was looking down at the gauges on the dashboard. He's not happy, thought Quigley, but he won't say anything. This was the worst kind of operation. A not-so-hot description, a boat half full of people, a million cubby-holes to get lost in. They hadn't even got a plan of the decks. The suspect wouldn't hesitate to use a gun. In a small space the jacket wouldn't mean much. He could even go for a head shot. There'd be ricochets.

Quigley hunkered into the back of the van and slipped off his anorak. He undid the strap and elbowed out of the harness. Where the leather had warmed, now felt exposed. He banged his head off the panel as he got into the Kevlar vest. Before he put on his anorak, he unclipped the Browning and checked the magazine. He remembered O'Rourke looking at it one day.

"They let you have one of those things? That's a very all-or-nothing yoke if it's the one I'm thinking of, sir. Bit of a whack to it for a nine millimetre."

Quigley hadn't had to use the standard automatic off the firing range, but the double action had never jammed yet. He took a deep breath. He zippered his anorak right to the neck to cover the vest beneath.

He closed the van door behind him. Men were getting out of the parked cars. Two he recognised, Lacey and Doyle, strolled over to take over the van when Gibbons and O'Rourke left. As O'Rourke stepped lightly onto the tarmacadam, Quigley noticed the sergeant was blowing air around his tightly closed lips, running bulges around his gums. Nervous. Quigley touched O'Rourke on the shoulder.

"All right, Donal, give me a half minute. No radio contact until we need to, all right?"

O'Rourke nodded. He shifted from foot to foot as if winding up for a race. Quigley felt a slippery warmth like pins and needles at his knees as he descended the glistening steps toward Marine Road. As he got under the trees, more of the ferry came into view. Its gaping maw, beak upturned, seemed to draw the cars into its yellowed belly. He looked up at the decks and railings but could see no one there. The floodlights floated above triangles of light, misted by the drizzle.

Chapter Eighteen

Minogue's eyes roved around the room. The worn green and white lino tiles stretched to a wall painted yellow. The wall gleamed dully with the oil paint. The room contained two chairs and a desk. Innumerable hieroglyphics were etched onto the desktop. They had been done with some care though, Minogue realised. Probably the work of a civil servant, one of many who had occupied the desk. Funny the things you do and you don't notice, like dancing around the place when you're talking on the phone. Minogue glanced at Loftus. Loftus was looking straight ahead, but Minogue knew that he was alert.

Minogue thought of Iseult on the phone at home, twirling the wire, poking at a picture on the wall, pulling on strands of her hair. Sometimes she scribbled things on the phone book, strange signs left behind after a conversation. Nerves? Daithi fiddling with something when he was talking to him: irritation, concealment? As if Minogue had something terribly important to say and that he should sit up and listen? But it wasn't that, ever. It was merely a furious desire to see these strangers' faces, grown people. Genes my arse, Minogue thought. He was different from the children. A whisper would have woken him in the night and Kathleen awake beside him too; to tiptoe as best as a

size ten countryman's feet can, to the little room over the stairs. An
ammoniacal smell of piss, but even stronger was the curious baby
breath warm air; a struggle to turn over, a frown; lips licked, maybe
a grunt. He'd wait to hear the rhythm of breathing start up again. 'All
right?' Kathleen would whisper, neither awake or asleep herself. 'Yes,'
and back into the bed: will I sleep now? It's hormones is what it is,
Minogue thought, time of life to be lusting after girls. Five minutes
gone now, he realised. He was wrong about Loftus. Maybe Loftus
didn't have a blind side.

"It's a matter of time really, Loftus. We know you're not going to
open your heart to us. Don't forget Allen. He'll testify and you won't
be able to get at him. Know a fella by the name of McCarthy, one of
our playwrights?"

Loftus seemed to smile faintly at the mention of the name.

"Can't stop that man from yapping, I can tell you. I'll bet you a
fiver he'll stick another needle into you. Ah, if only they were all as
perfect as yourself, Captain Loftus," Minogue said. "But you can't deny
me. They'll trip you yet. You know I was going to begin our interview
here by getting right down to brass tacks, straight from the word go.
I was going to ask you directly, 'Captain Loftus, did you murder Jarlath
Walsh?' And I expected you to give me an honest answer, just like
in one of those melodramas on the telly. You know, a burst of violins
after it, the case solved. But I'm not going to ask you that at all,
because I know you didn't do it. All I will ask you is who you gave
the key to."

"What key?" Loftus asked.

"Whoever did it had to get out of the college at night after the gates
were locked. Only higher-ups have keys to the sidegates. Whoever did
in young Walsh could slip in and out when he wanted," Minogue
replied. Loftus laughed.

"You know, Captain, I have this picture in my head of the fella we
want. We've started calling him the mystery man, but we know what
he looks like. You met him or at least you've talked to him on the
phone. He is a Yank, we think. The fella who killed the guard in St.
Stephen's Green. In a sense I think he's like you. Went to the States,
didn't you, and fell in love with the efficiency thing? They call everything 'problem solving' over there, don't they? Still I bet you came
back a convert. Am I right? But what I don't get is when it all turned
bad for you here, when you decided to get into this from the other
side. What was it?"

Loftus' gaze rested on the wall behind Minogue. Thinking about it later, Minogue believed that Loftus was about to speak when Kilmartin stuck his head in the door and motioned Minogue out.

The four of them sat at a plastic-topped table bolted to the floor facing the bar. Underfoot he could feel the hum of the ship's engine. The three were anxious for the screen to come up from the counter.

"And what do they drink in Canada now?" the older navvy asked.

"Oh, beer and lager. I'm not much on them myself—"

"No more than myself," the smaller navvy added.

"—but I can toss a few back in the summer," the tanned man continued.

"'Toss a few.' Hah, that's a good one. We say 'sink a few' so we do. Same thing only different. All goes the same way, amn't I right? I hear the pubs do be open until all hours in America, I mean Canada."

"Longer than they should, people say," the tanned man parried. He ached for some sign that the ship was preparing to go. A blast of the siren, a rumble below, maybe. He looked around at the passengers who had come straight to the lounge. Altogether about twenty-five people. Sitting opposite one another over a table by a window too big to be called a porthole, a young couple was the only exception to the general air of brooding tiredness which the men in the lounge had brought with them. Some sat on their own, watching the steward, yawning. The train from Holyhead would get the passengers into Euston Station in London by seven the next morning. A sense of loneliness gathered itself at the edges of his thoughts, surprising him. That Irish people have to do this, that the country is so bathed in this habit, he thought.

"Any minute now," the older navvy said, nodding toward the bar.

"Are there delays on this trip fairly often?" the tanned man asked.

"The weather can slow you down, that's a fact. It can speed you up too though. I was on this a few times, and I'm not joking you, I was the only one not spewing me lights up all over the place. Even your man, the barman or the steward or whatever you call him, officers, the whole lot. All puking goodo all over the place. We were three hours late getting into Dun Laoghaire. Wait 'til I tell you, they wanted to close down the bloody bar. 'Hold on there a minute, brother,' I says. 'I'm a paying customer and I can guarantee you that yous won't need to be mopping up after me. I was well reared. So hand me a pint of stout there and keep the oul flag flying.' Not a bother on me." The older navvy fisted gently on the tabletop and wagged his head with pride.

"Jack Tar," the red-faced navvy said.

"Yeah. Mutiny on the what-che-me-call-it," echoed the smaller one.

"Ah go on, yous are only jealous," the older man derided them.

The four men fell silent as if each knew that the talk only served to distract them from waiting. Another few passengers—again all men—trickled into the lounge. The tanned man felt his radar sense ease with each arrival. Then the sound of the screen sliding up returned him to the present.

"Aha. What'll you have, " the old navvy said to him.

"Hold on, it's my twist," said the red-face.

"You buy later. I'm flush. A pint of beer?"

The tanned man wasn't listening. He was trying to supress any outward signs of the alarm that was yammering in his head.

The man had walked in just as the screen was going up. Instantly, the tanned man was aroused. He felt his pulse push at his collar. The man had glanced at his group and then affected to look around. He was a tallish man with a full head of hair. His gait suggested an attempt to look slovenly, but it didn't come off. The face was a little too impassive, his glance a little too neutral. The man's coat was darkened at the shoulders by rain and his hair was stringing. His duffle bag should have bit into his shoulder but it didn't: it was probably half empty. Who would travel with a half-empty duffle bag?

"Beer. You can have Smithwick's, though personally I wouldn't drown a cat in it. How about Harp? That's a lager ..."

"Yes."

"The Harp?"

"Yes. Please."

It was as if there was a stage director in his head pointing out all the moves. *See how he is being too casual? Walking so slow? He's trying to look sloppy but look at the shoulders. Face is too bland by far, because he's not tired. He's trying so hard not to look ... excited.*

The red-faced man leaned over.

"Oi. We haven't got going yet. Don't look so thrilled."

"Pardon?" said the tanned man. He watched the man disappear around the corner, back out toward the stairway.

"You look a bit peeky so you do. Go out and stick your finger down your neck. Honest to God it works."

The tanned man looked directly at the red face. He saw a dissolute, loose face. Written on it were evasions and self-pity. The shallow banter was a poor attempt to mask the weakness. Instantly he loathed these men and the inanity which formed their lives. They were carica-tures and they didn't know it, half-alcoholic, petulant children. Their humour had a manic, follow-on quality. The red-rimmed eyes above the bristles, puzzled and wary, the very pith of the simian Irish peasant in *Punch*. He looked at the smaller navvy, whose face showed a mix of cowed agreement and resentment at the world, tempered with antici-pation for the drinks on the way. He felt a rage against them. All he had risked and hoped and: not for these.

He left the table without a word. He didn't turn to the "Oi" from the older navvy who was carrying pint glasses of beer and stout to the table. He felt himself walking almost on his toes, ready to break into a run. The cop was not there. He unzipped his jacket three quar-ters of the way and he opened the door which led out on deck. Immediately a spume of drizzle came in out of the night at him. Dun Laoghaire pier ran out alongside the boat.

He looked over the railing. The gangplank was still down. It was the only way off the ferry unless he was to jump into the water. He began walking toward the steps which, he supposed, led to the back of the boat. There was no one on deck. He passed portholes and windows where he saw passengers settling listlessly into chairs. A seagull flew through the lights and into the darkness overhead. Above the back of the ferry, he saw the lights of the hotels half hidden by the trees. Stepping closer to the railings, he looked down at the dock. Several porters and men in overalls stood around, sheltered by the roof of the railway terminal. A faint cloud of drizzle hung over the rail tracks in the light which came out under the roof. Two men appeared from a doorway and walked hurriedly to the end of the platform.

He thought about the lifeboats or storage, but they'd search them. The ship's engine droned up through his feet. Maybe the car decks, there might be a car open. Or a truck. They'd want to isolate him in a set-up like this. Dump the gun and brazen it out with the Canadian passport: the playwright ... *Trust in no one. Well, Father, what would you do?*

"Here come on. Is the job done?" he heard behind him. The older navvy stood at the door.

"In a while," he managed to say. Turning around again, he noticed a movement behind the navvy. The navvy made to step aside and let the person pass. The tanned man called out:

"Come on over for a second, would you?"

The navvy stepped over the jamb, scratching the back of his neck. As he began walking, the tanned man realised he might not have the time to put the silencer on.

"I'm a bit groggy," he said.

The navvy came over reluctantly. Whoever had been about to come out the door had not appeared.

With the navvy between him and the door, the tanned man turned back to looking at the town and reached into his jacket. He felt, rather than heard, the navvy's footsteps approaching him reluctantly across the deck.

"What's the story?" the navvy began.

The tanned man turned and brought the gun away from his chest.

"We're getting off the boat. Don't say anything, just listen to me."

Quigley saw the older man freeze, with his arm out a little from his sides. He heard Gibbons breathing close to his ear. Quigley's finger pushed out at the trigger guard, the muzzle touching the side of his knee. His arm felt heavy as if the gun were hanging from it.

"He has a gun on him," whispered Gibbons.

"He'll probably bring him down on the stairs outside as much as he can. There's no one on deck," Quigley murmured. Quigley tried to guess the distance from the door to the railing. Probably the best part of fifty feet. The door opened out and there was a jamb to jump over too. The Yank was right-handed. Quigley watched the Yank's hand come down on the navvy's shoulder, the navvy's arms go up almost horizontal. Must be an instinct, to raise your hands like that, he thought. Anything could happen here. This was what they had feared, a hostage. For a second he remembered the stoicism on O'Rourke's face, well in control of the skepticism. Even in broad daylight you couldn't shoot accurately at fifty feet with only one chance. So: the Yank had copped on when he had walked into the bar. Quigley leaned back against the wall, flattening his back.

"Which deck is the ramp on again?"

"For passengers on and off, sir?" Gibbons asked. Quigley nodded.

"Two decks down. If he's going to try and get off the boat, he'll have to take at least one stairs inside the boat, sir. The deck right below us is the last one with a promenade outside ..."

Would he jump to the dock? Quigley wondered. Fifteen ... eighteen feet; bad light ... hardly.

"Fuck it, fuck it!" Quigley hissed. "Go down one deck you, Gibbons. Wait by the door there. That's where he'll make his move to come inside if he's really headed off the boat."

"Right."

"Now listen, man. I'm going to get behind him from here, so's I can take him at that door if I have any safe angle at all. I'll call out to him. You see him turn around, grab the oul lad he has with him. Through the door, if you can. By the hair if you have to. Just get him to the deck as fast as you can, I don't care. We'll have a clear take-down on the gunman if it works."

"Lookit, you have the wrong man. Where's the cameras? Is this *Kojak?*" the older navvy said.

"Shut up. Walk slowly. You'll know it's for real if I have to use it."

The navvy turned and began walking slowly to the pier side of the boat. The tanned man stared at the door and then to the stairs ahead. Had he been mistaken?

When the navvy reached the stairs, he grasped the rail and stopped.

"Look, mister, it's none of my ..."

The tanned man nudged him with the gun and stepped down after him.

"Slow down." The navvy stopped at the bottom of the stairs.

"We have to go inside now," the navvy said quietly. "It's the only way off without breaking your neck. If me mates see me, what'm I going to say to them?"

"Tell them you're looking after me."

The two men stood four steps from the door. The tanned man looked around and listened. He looked toward the stairs they had come down.

"The door opens out, so no funny stuff," he said to the navvy. As the navvy grasped the handle, the tanned man hid his gunhand under the left side of his jacket. The navvy yanked the door open with ease and lifted his leg over the jamb. The smell of cigarettes and the *opep-opep* of a video game came through the door. And something else: the tanned man turned and looked back up the stairs. He knew instinct-ively that he had to hold out his hand to stay the closing door, but it would have to be his left hand. The sound from inside drowned out the voice from the top of the stairs.

Someone had knocked the navvy over inside. The heavy door had snapped almost shut. It was hissing slightly in the closing gap. The tanned man stepped back from the door and fired up the stairs. More shouting inside, the door clicking shut and the huge *daanng* as the bullet hit off a rail, whining off into the dark. The figure at the top of the stairs stayed flattened against the wall. The tanned man began backing away on his toes. A face appeared in a window next to him and reflexively he squeezed off a shot. The glass webbed instantly. Someone screamed. He watched the door where the navvy had been swallowed up. Overhead he heard footsteps running along the upper deck. Things were happening too fast, at least three men. Turning, he ran.

Quigley waved O'Rourke on toward the stairway forward of the ship. He heard O'Rourke's crêpe soles squeak softly as he began running down the wet promenade. Quigley started down the stairway slowly. Three steps down he saw the two men at the doorway below. Quigley shouted as the navvy opened the door. The Yank turned toward the stairway as the door closed abruptly ahead of him. Quigley heard muffled shouting from indoors. He saw the flash as his back pressed into the plate which formed a wall section to the upper stairway. The second shot was from further away, Quigley guessed.

He eased himself down one step, then another and took aim at the doorway. Outside the door at the bottom of the stairway, the prome-nade deck was empty. Drizzle had gathered into droplets at the rims of the overhang, and they fell off slowly onto the railing beside him. Quigley strained to listen: the hush of sea, a breeze, drizzle. His arms were hurting. Images of passengers walking into a line of fire flashed on and off in his mind. He crouched near the railings, still pointing the gun at the doorway.

"Gibbons?" he called out, still pointing.

"Sir!"

"You got your man in?" he shouted.

"I have him here!" Gibbons shouted back.

"Where's the target?" Quigley didn't care that the edge of panic in his voice was quite plain now. He looked down the promenade. He thought he saw a flicker of movement, a shadow in the dimness beyond the lifeboats. Running? Gibbons' head appeared in the doorway. Quig-ley looked in at the navvy still sprawled on the floor, pale.

"Looks like he's headed for the stairs up ahead. Go inside, now and quick. O'Rourke's up there, maybe ahead of him, up above. Don't let the Yank inside!"

Quigley went forward in a crouch, his left hand on top of his right to keep the barrel down when he fired. He felt the beginnings of a cramp grasp the palm of his right hand. As he passed a window, a glance showed him some passengers on their knees, others running for doors from the lounge. The ship swayed very slightly from side to side. Faintly, a siren, two. Quigley swore aloud.

The tanned man stopped abruptly. Ahead of him was the other stairway descending from the deck above. It ran against him. A perfect spot to command entry to the doorway at the foot of the stairs. He strained to hear footsteps above him. Nothing. He looked behind. There was someone or something moving quickly around the lifeboat stanchions. He felt the ship's engine at idle, resonating underfoot. And something else, he sensed: the slightest tick, a vibration nearby. A footstep on the stairway? Through a window he glimpsed a figure running inside. Another one. Had to move now.

He stepped abruptly to the foot of the stairway and aimed up. The figure had one foot tentatively on the step down and he was already turning sideways. The first shot staggered O'Rourke. The tanned man saw something fly up from the head with his second shot, as the head jerked. The arms flopped and O'Rourke fell, as a puppet dropped. He tumbled down the stairway flopping loosely, without any attempt to slow. O'Rourke's pistol clanged, fell down a step, then another, and lodged. His leg caught in a support and the rest of him fanned bumpily against metal, pivoting around head first.

The tanned man had three steps to the doorway. He was through the second and reaching for the handle when a blow to his left side danced him sideways. *Shot,* he thought remotely. *Must be the one coming up behind me. This is what it is like to be shot? No pain yet, why?* He almost lost his balance.

The shout from behind seemed to be coming from the far end of a playing field. Must have been the guy behind. The other one inside would have reached the door by now too ... yes. He felt himself swaying. Dizzy a little, but things were clear, not like being drunk even.

He turned and fired, wondering. He heard the shot ricocheting angrily off metal. The ejected shell *pinged* and rolled lazily along the deck toward the door. He felt hot, things were loud. *Can't even try to go up the stairs,* he thought. He wondered if he had spoken aloud. He tried to grasp a railing again, but he couldn't feel it. Another shot, but this didn't hit. He strained to see where the one who had shot him was.

The after-image of the flash wavered as his eyes scanned dully along the deck. *Someone crouched by that big box near the stanchion... ? Not sure, keep looking, a movement* ... For a moment the tanned man was back in the water again, a child, listening to the voices of people on the beach, so far away, a plane droning overhead in the blue Florida sky. *Ah, shot. Mistakes but tried, tried hard.* Yes, there was someone crouched down there ... The tanned man levelled his pistol. *A chance,* he thought. *Done tougher shots on the range a couple of times anyway* ... He thought of his father's face turning back to the newspaper, tight lips: his mother kneading her hands at the door, always defending, *'He couldn't help it, Seamus, he's only a boy.'*

Out of the corner of his eye, the tanned man saw the door fly open. He started to draw his gun arm around toward the doorway, knowing he was too late.

Already braced in the doorway, Gibbons fired. The shot caught the man behind the ear and his chin rocked onto his chest as he fell forward. His knees hit first and Gibbons heard the *thunk* of his fore-head hitting the deck. A spray of blood flicked onto the deck around the head. The body rolled slightly but then seemed to right itself, face down. Gibbons stared at the gun next to the right hand, and he walked slowly over the jamb of the door. He looked up the stairway at O'Rourke. The side of his head showed purple in the light. A steady stream of blood had run across two steps and was draining onto the last step. Gibbons could see it moving like there was no end to it, edging and pouring over onto the deck now, mixing with the wet gleam left by the rain. Quigley was running toward him, shouting. How could people have so much blood?

"Jesus, Mary and Joseph," Gibbons whispered. He remembered something out of his youth, long gone now, and not knowing what else to do for O'Rourke, he started on the Act of Contrition.

Chapter Nineteen

On Wednesday, Kilmartin had met him for dinner in the Civil Service Club in St. Stephen's Green. After the soup, Kilmartin winked at Minogue.

"Will you take a glass of whisky with me beyond in Dwyers' pub afterwards?"

"No thanks, Jimmy," Minogue murmured.

Kilmartin nodded slightly and toyed with his fork.

"It'd put me to sleep for the afternoon, so it would. Thanks anyway," Minogue offered.

"I see, I see," said Kilmartin, still observing the fork studiously. "To be sure, I understand."

The waitress clumped a plate in front of Kilmartin.

"Cod?" she said to Minogue. Kilmartin forked a piece of stringy beef.

"He flared up only the once yesterday, Loftus. But then he shut up very quickly," said Kilmartin. Minogue worked on the batter around the cod.

"Something about 'duty.' I asked him if he thought it was the duty of an officer in the Irish Army to resign his commission and work against the laws of a democratic state just because he didn't agree with the way the country was being run. I thought he was going to spit at me, so I did. But he clammed up then after a dirty big sneer at me. That's as far as we've got with that boyo."

Minogue nodded but stayed silent. By unspoken agreement, they had given up on Loftus. They had tried to lever him with news that the Yank had been caught and that he was telling all. Loftus, it seems, knew better. He said nothing. He had withdrawn, leaving a composed expression. It struck Minogue that Loftus seemed relieved now that he had done his duty.

"Some duty," Kilmartin said. "Ah, but something will turn up on this Yank, you'll see. Then Loftus'll say his piece."

Kilmartin had been wrong to date. The most that Loftus said in the days after his arrest was couched in a mixture of disdain and a half-hearted effort to explain by allusion. He soon stopped that, even, apparently sure in his mind that the audience of interrogators would never understand. That left Kilmartin to wonder if the Irish Army really would have gone into Derry in '69 like Loftus said. They had field hospitals and vehicles gathered up near the border, everyone had known that. Should they have gone in? Against the British Army, could they? Loftus had resigned within the year.

"I think maybe his trip to the States is what turned the corner for him," Minogue said finally.

"You mean all the hardware and blather they have over there? And where did it get them in Vietnam I ask you, Matt?" Kilmartin replied.

"America is a country full of savages. They don't know what they're at half the time. Look at the telly, I mean. Or should I say, don't look at the telly," Kilmartin said indignantly.

" *'Dulce et decorum est pro patria mori,'* " Minogue murmured.

"What?"

"It's about dying for your country."

"I have a brother out in the States. The wife is always at me to go over and have a look at the place. What about yourself, Matt?"

"I don't think so. I don't think I could manage over there at all. It's a different life entirely," Minogue replied.

Kilmartin affected to be considering some other matter and attacked the limp broccoli. Minogue waited. After several minutes' silence, Kilmartin looked up from the wreckage of his dinner. Minogue met his gravely gentle look reluctantly. Kilmartin's voice was barely above a whisper.

"Matt. What did you tell the Walshes out beyond?"

Minogue remembered Mrs Walsh dropping cup and saucer on the fireplace. A stain started in the carpet, her shaking hands reaching under cuffs for a hanky. Walsh had changed. No speech from him. He sat across from his broken wife, not wishing to be involved in weakness before a visitor. He told his wife she mustn't upset herself and she stopped. Minogue told them the truth. No, he couldn't be sure, but it was the most likely turn of events.

"How did they react, I mean," Kilmartin probed.

Minogue's anger turned the potato quite tasteless, an obstruction in his mouth. He waited, disguised in eating.

"I don't know how they reacted, Jimmy."

And he didn't. His thoughts went back to the Walshes' sterile living room, his attempt to explain the run of events to them ... How Jarlath Walsh's knock on the door had probably not been heard by Allen because he was on the phone. The door was ajar, visualise. Jarlath puts two and two together and sees several things. Your son Jarlath sees credibility, a scoop if he can bring Allen to admit things out in the open. He doesn't know Allen is being blackmailed. Jarlath seems to have wanted to keep this all to himself. An exclusive. He tells nobody. He drops hints at Agnes. It's his secret, he's working on it. It's something he'll be proud of. Jarlath brings a tape recorder with him to talk with Allen, but Allen says nothing directly. Jarlath may have tried to wear him down probably, hints, winks. Allen is under terrible pressure and tells Loftus. Loftus tells him it'll be looked after. Loftus is the one who has checked into Allen. Allen's original name is O'Donohue and Loftus trips him up on what happened a long, long time ago. So, Mr and Mrs Walsh, these people severally and individually have helped to have your son murdered. Outburst of tears from Mrs, glares from Mr: did you have to be like this, Minogue?

"And did Loftus murder Jarlath?" Mr had asked then.

Minogue can't pick careful enough words.

"We know he didn't actually kill him. He has an alibi for that night. But in law, he did, because he helped arrange it. Allen will be on the stand to testify to that."

"Who killed him...?"

"We don't know. Loftus is saying nothing at all. We doubt he'll even be induced to tell, if indeed he knows, at his own trial for capital murder. We think your son was killed by the same person who killed two Gardai within the last week."

Mrs Walsh, perking up: "And who's he?"

"We're trying to find out. We think he's American."

Minogue, leaving, had felt the cold stare on his back all the way down the driveway.

"Well, you let them know we're continuing on the case. Doing our best," Kilmartin said. Minogue shook his head. The case was technically open, but Minogue's papers had been removed, the office was being painted. Minogue wondered if Garda inspectors spent more than half their time worrying about the management of impressions for the public.

"Yes," Minogue offered. Kilmartin was suspicious again.

"Doesn't that beat Banagher though," Kilmartin went on. "His prints are not on file with the Yanks. We're going through the airline lists now. My bet is he'll turn up to be a dud as regards the passport he came in on too. We have the pictures sent out, that's all we can do. Some of the lads thought he looked familiar, but they couldn't put a finger on it. Looked kind of Irish they all said."

Minogue tried the stewed apple but turned it away after one spoon.

"Think he did it, do you?" Kilmartin said.

"Yesterday, yes. Today, I don't know. There's the temptation to shove all the pieces together, to tidy up, I suppose," Minogue said in a conciliatory tone.

Minogue wanted to allow the unspoken intimacy to drift back to them. He made an effort to leave clear answers and comments for Kilmartin. The waitress banged their plates onto the trolley. She returned and plonked two cups of tea down. Minogue looked up at her, but she had turned and gone. Kilmartin offered his packet.

"Do you want a smoke?"

"No thanks, Jimmy. I'll try and steer clear of them."

"And Allen, how long ago was it...?"

"He was thirteen at the time," Minogue answered. "He was babysitting and the parents walked in on him. I don't fully understand the wording from then, but I think it amounted to an aggravated rape on the child."

"Jesus, Mary and Joseph," Kilmartin whispered with a grimace.

"So he went to juvenile court, but they didn't send him to reformatory. Took counselling afterward and never looked back since. That's where he got the interest in psychology."

"That's not one bit funny at all," said Kilmartin.

"It caught up with him," Minogue speculated. "The whole thing."

"Like...?"

"His mother. Nothing he did was ever good enough for her. He couldn't be Irish enough for her. No wonder his Da died young. Allen, or O'Donohue, was left to her mercy more or less. It's no wonder he did what he did."

"You don't believe that stuff about Irish mothers or parents in general, Matt, do you?"

Minogue didn't answer.

"What possessed that fella to be like that? I ask you. Couldn't he leave things well enough alone. I mean to say this hop-off-me-thumb helped to get people killed, do you follow me?" asked Kathleen.

Minogue was following a lorry on the road into Tulla. The hedges and trees almost met over the road. The ditch was full of grass and brambles. Small fields, stonewalled, secretive patching over hillocks. Clare: fields like a quilt.

They had passed the holy tree on the Limerick road, coins jammed into the bark, pieces of cloth tied to its branches. Minogue was daydreaming, waking, daydreaming. Words and verses had stayed circling in his head since he had woken up, thinking of his own parents.

> Will you come out tonight, love
> The moon is shining bright, love

His mother hanging clothes across the bushes from the haggard, air sweet and close on a May morning, the birds filling the air with sound.

"I mean. All this lu-la would never have happened. He must be a twisted man entirely. In Trinity College Dublin with them nobs. There one in the eye for that crowd. I'm glad Daithi and Iseult go to UCD, I don't care what they say. Where's your man from? Loftus is it?"

"He's Cork. Well-to-do, I suppose. A career soldier who should have stayed in," Minogue murmured.

"They all want power, isn't that the be-all and end-all," Kathleen asseverated.

"I suppose. Some notion of duty mixed in with an inferiority thing, I'd wager. A powerful mixture, that ..."

"And he didn't budge," Kathleen added.

"Even after your man being shot out in Dun Laoghaire," Minogue said.

"Go on. Tell us a bit," Kathleen said.

"Well. There was a watch on for this fella. Very brash he was, brazening it out by trying to get on the boat to Holyhead. It's not that he was stupid or anything. He calculated things, that's my feeling. But he got annoyed at some point."

"How do you mean?" Kathleen asked

"Well, frustrated maybe. He shot that Garda Connors. Maybe they were hounding him."

"Who's 'they'?" Kathleen asked.

"The likes of that gangster, McCarthy. The old crowd. Maybe he just imagined it though."

"Isn't it the strangest thing?" Kathleen said.

Minogue was half driving, half looking around, half thinking. There were cars behind now. One had a Clare flag stuck out the window. No sign of the Kilkenny mob; the Kilkenny Cats, a sharper crowd of hurlers hadn't been let on the face of the earth. The Clare goalie would have to do Trojan work today.

Minogue had smelled deep from a cattle lorry on the way into Portlaoise. They had been unable to pass for ten minutes. The smell was still with him. It had left a lingering unease which surprised him. He wondered if he had detected a fear in the animals, perhaps knowing they were on the way to be slaughtered. Minogue tried to laugh off the persistent memory still locked in his nostrils. Middle age, dotage— he tried all the sneers to keep himself in line.

By the time they turned off the Limerick road to Killaloe and the Shannon, he had let his efforts slide. Though rested and jockeying a desk for a week, he felt the strangeness flood through him again. He had the baffling notion that things had changed again, that old things had faded and been eclipsed by something new. It was like waking up to know something was gone but that something else was imminent, a rejoinder. Without looking at her, Minogue sensed that Kathleen's thoughts had gone elsewhere too. She stared out the side window at the drumlins, the hedges, the tight and secret fields. Worrying still, Minogue knew.

Within ten minutes, Minogue and Kathleen were in sight of the village of Tulla, home of the resurgent Clare hurling team. The overcast sky hung still over streets glutted with cars. Men with caps down over their eyes, dogs, children with ice cream. The pubs had just closed. Sunday hours. They'd have to go out the Ennis road to get parking.

"You should do this more often, so you should," Kathleen said. "The rest is a tonic, isn't it? Does for the both of us."

Minogue's thoughts edged onto irritation. He didn't want reassurance this way, people circumspect as if he were an invalid again. He couldn't even think of the questions he wanted to ask. The words fled away on him like pigeons disturbed off a roof. He fought off the resentment.

"Well now, if I'd known you were a fan, I'd have brought you here a long time ago, wouldn't I?" he said.

"I'm getting pointers for the Dublin team so we can leather ye when we get the chance," Kathleen replied with a laugh.

The traffic had been stopped for nearly five minutes. Minogue switched off the engine in the middle of Tulla. People walked around between the stranded cars on their way to the pitch. Then the cars ahead began to move. Stop again, wait.

"Look," Kathleen said. "It's Mick. Maura—and Eoin."

Minogue looked out and saw his brother about to walk beyond the car.

"Mick. Maura!" Kathleen called out.

Mick turned, recognition dawning on him. He looked beyond Kathleen to Minogue. Maura came over too. Eoin, their oldest, looked on.

"Off to the match, so we are," Kathleen said.

"God bless ye," from hearty, pious Maura. Minogue imagined Maura tying bits of cloth onto the twigs over the holy well, polishing statues of the Blessed Virgin around the house. He watched his brother's face.

"Aye, aye," Mick said.

The wives began talking. Mick strolled around the driver's side. Minogue listened to Maura and Kathleen laughing. Eoin stood away. Like his Da, Minogue thought.

"How'ya Matt?" and his arm resting on the door of the car.

"Struggling," Minogue said, protected in ritual.

"Great goings on above in Dublin I hear," Mick said.

Minogue nodded and looked ahead. Maura and Kathleen were touching each other, laughing. Eoin stood like a sentry, frowning off into the distance, his arms folded.

"Hard to know these days, isn't it? Who's who, I mean?" Mick said. Minogue nodded.

"I saw your name in the paper, Matt, in connection with it."

"Marginal, Mick. Very marginal."

"We all do what we can, I suppose. Or do what we must?"

Minogue saw cars moving ahead.

"A bit of both, I'm thinking," Minogue said.

Mick nodded his head slowly and studied the chrome rim on the gutter.

Minogue started up the engine.

"That's the way of it, isn't it now? There's always another day, so there is," Mick said.

"God bless ye!" Maura waved.

That day, Clare beat the socks off Kilkenny, thereby overcoming a superstition about losing vital games on their home ground of Tulla.

To Minogue the land, the hills, the hedges, the clouds were as parts of a stage. Kathleen had done more cheering than he had. Minogue began reciting "The Ballad of Tommy Daly":

> On the windswept hill of Tulla
> Where the Claremen lay their dead,
> Three solemn yews stand sentinel
> Above a hurler's head ...

The crowds began to disperse. The pubs were opening, cars starting up. Only once during the game did he feel himself falling away, but he recovered quickly. His chest felt like a damp house for a while afterward.

He bought Kathleen and himself a steak in Portlaoise and he was picky about the wine. Kathleen was excited.

During the meal she told him she wanted to find a job and would he mind, bearing in mind that Iseult and Daithi would be gone soon. And speaking of which, Daithi was too embarrassed to broach the subject, but could we see our way to paying his fare to the States in the summer. If he gets the visa that is. He could visit his cousins up in Canada. It'd do him good, so it would. And why not, because everyone else was going there these days and he'd learn to look after himself and couldn't be worrying about every little thing that might happen to him. Good experience for him.

Kathleen drew him out. He said let's go to France and why the hell not. She laughed and blamed it on the wine when she couldn't stop laughing. Oh didn't I marry the right one, she laughed, romantic nights in gay Paree, go on you're joking me. He said he wasn't. She laughed against her breath. Spluttering, laughing again. He said look at the Dublin crowd making a show of themselves down the country with drink. You can do what you like in Paris, she croaked in reply, even see the Follies but don't tell anyone.

In the valley after the wine, they were crossing the Curragh in darkness. Like the plains or the prairies, Minogue thought. His throat was dry. He did not resist when the memory changed tense for him again that day. He knew this might be the last time it erupted over him before he could finally house it and think about it without the anger or the desperate urge to be forgiven, to try again. He wondered if he could bear to look at Allen again as he would probably have to during Loftus' trial.

Chapter Twenty

Herlighy showed no surprise at Minogue's request. He followed Minogue out of the office.

"I'll be back within the hour, Mrs Sullivan," Herlighy said as he passed the receptionist. There was no one in the waiting-room.

"You're sure I'm not inconveniencing you, now," Minogue said as he grasped the hall door handle.

"Not a bit of it," Herlighy replied lightly. "I've been cooped up inside all day. Pardon the expression. Glad of a bit of fresh air, such as it is here."

Minogue pulled the heavy door open. The brass plaque on the door caught his eye as the wan afternoon light moved across it. Dr Sean Herlighy in black, the brass clear and polished. No mention of Herlighy's stock-in-trade, psychiatry, Minogue mused again.

Minogue paused before descending the half-dozen steps to the footpath. He looked out on Merrion Square ahead. Two days of wind and rain had left the trees bare of leaves.

"Hold on a minute," he heard Herlighy from behind. "I forgot my cigarettes."

Minogue leaned against the railing and looked down the terrace. Merrion Square was still a showpiece of Georgian architecture. Railings everywhere, granite edges to the steps, the wide doors with fanlights above. The rain had left the tree-trunks blackened. Cars hissed by on the roadway. The grass inside the square would be completely sodden, Minogue calculated vacantly. Stick to the paths.

Herlighy had a lighted cigarette in his hand when he opened the door. The two men crossed the street and headed for the pedestrian gate. Minogue felt his nervousness as something unnecessary, a leftover from the anticipation which still clung to his thoughts even now beside Herlighy. They entered the Square. They had the place to themselves.

"I half thought of slipping into the National Gallery beyond and having a cup of coffee or the like," said Minogue.

"That'd be grand too," Herlighy said neutrally.

"Ah but I'd spend the day there looking at the pictures, I don't doubt."

Herlighy smiled tightly and blew out a thin stream of smoke. They walked slowly on the gravel path. Herlighy seemed to be studying the path ahead of him. Minogue knew it was up to him to start.

"So I was thinking I'd like to postpone things awhile," he began. "Wait and see what way the cat jumps, do you see."

"The sessions we have?" said Herlighy.

"Yes. What I mean is that ... I think I'd like to try out things for myself now," Minogue added quietly.

"I understand," Herlighy said after a pause. "If you say you are ready, that's fine by me."

"You're not going to be idle now that I'm taking a break from the sessions, I hope," said Minogue.

"There's always plenty of work in my line," replied Herlighy.

"It's not that I didn't get a great deal of value out of our ... you know," Minogue looked to Herlighy.

"Our chats."

"Our chats. I got a great deal of good out of them, yes indeed ..."

"Are you staying on in the job, so?"

"If you had asked me that two weeks ago, I would have said no. I don't think I would have even gone back to Vehicles."

Herlighy stopped and glanced at Minogue.

"You had offers of doing something away from the front-line, I

remember. Crime prevention, a bit of training for in-service or new re-
cruits...?"

"Ah, I'd be bored stiff with that stuff, I have to admit," Minogue
shrugged.

"Tell me why you're staying on, then."

Minogue blinked. He looked beyond Herlighy to the dripping trees.
Were psychiatrists supposed to be this direct? A test?

"I haven't quite worked it out completely but ... I didn't want to
throw in the towel because of what happened. What you explained
about trauma was very good, you see. I got so as I knew what was
happening better. It's more like I don't want to be sitting at home
watching the news, being able to switch off the telly or change the
station if I don't like what I see ... It's hard to express, you see ..."

Herlighy nodded once and began walking again.

"I don't want something like this happening again, I suppose you
could say," Minogue added. "I wish I could ..."

"About Agnes McGuire, you mean?" asked Herlighy without slowing
his stride.

Minogue felt the tightness close on his chest again. He drew a deep
breath. The air was full of the dank smell of rotting leaves.

"Yes," said Minogue hoarsely.

He stopped walking. Herlighy sensed he was walking on alone now
and he turned. Minogue was standing with his hands deep in his coat
pockets, staring out over the wet lawns. Herlighy took a long drag on
his cigarette. He thought of some of the comments he had written in
Minogue's file after the first sessions. An overly sensitive cop, care-
taker personality quite dominant. Herlighy had been pessimistic at the
start. A bogman, this cop, plainly out of place in this fraying city.

He walked over to Minogue.

"You'll be trying again then, Matt. Is that how I should write it in
me file?"

Minogue searched Herlighy's face for any humour.

"You know that I can sign you for the full disability. There'd be no
problem in the world in you getting the full salary until you qualify
for the pension at retirement age," Herlighy added. "Have you considered that aspect?"

Minogue didn't reply immediately.

"I'd still like to keep on at the job," Minogue murmured. "If they'll
let me."

It was Minogue who started down the path first this time. Herlighy flicked the cigarette butt into the grass and followed him. Minogue seemed to be more relaxed now as he walked next to the psychiatrist.

"I don't need to tell you that you're welcome to stop by anytime," said Herlighy.

"Thanks very much."

Herlighy reached for the packet of cigarettes again. Minogue stopped when he heard the scratch of Herlighy's lighter. Herlighy eyed his patient over his cupped hands as he flicked at the lighter again. Minogue's gaze was straying out over the acres of grass again. Gone already, thought Herlighy. The gas ignited this time and Herlighy tasted the first papery burn of the smoke. He caught up with Minogue.

"Did I tell you that Kathleen and myself are going to steal away to Paris for a little holiday?"

"Paris?" asked Herlighy. "Why Paris?"

Minogue smiled and scratched behind one ear.

"Oh there's a sort of a story to it ... do you want to...?"

Herlighy said he did. They walked on under the trees, Herlighy silent, listening to Minogue.

When tired, Herlighy often had an image of himself sitting in his office here in a country on the periphery of Europe, trying to sort out the Byzantine web of sophistry and evasion. Sometimes he had to remind himself that he, Herlighy, was searching, himself. He wondered if Minogue would visit again. Herlighy put the packet of cigarettes back in his pocket. So Minogue was ready for more. More what? Another drag on the cigarette reminded him of his envy.

EpiLogue

Minogue had walked around Dublin on Friday, from church to church, museum to gallery. He had sat in the chill caves of cathedrals for a rest, unable to pray.

There had been nothing in Allen's car. It had been taken apart: nothing at all. They didn't want to charge him with anything, just dump him. All a mess, dump it back on Dublin.

Agnes McGuire had died early on Friday morning, *letting go and casting off for where she'd not be let down again,* Minogue thought. Did Allen know yet? And Loftus, now silent and remote, the little Napoleon, the one-eyed king, did he care? Minogue had not run fast enough or far enough. Again and again he saw the soldiers pulling two out of the car that night, then Allen's grey face in the back of the van.

Instead of a Mass Card, Minogue bought a card with a copy of Walter Osborne's 'Scene in the Phoenix Park' on it. He got them to use it as a Mass Card in Clarendon Street. He thought about going to visit Mick Roche, but he felt he should wait.

Walking through Trinity College, nothing had changed except the film of suspicion and resentment which had come across his vision. Gowned lecturers billowed past him in Front Square. Minogue turned away from his path and wondered if he should tear up the card.

The Rose of Tralee

BILL CRIDER

The pale moon was rising above the green mountain and shedding her pale rays through the trees in the Tralee Town Park. It was a beautiful sight, but Sonya Morning suddenly wished that she had never come to Ireland.

It wasn't that the park wasn't lovely; it certainly was, with the green grasses and red roses silvered by the moonlight.

The company was wonderful, too. Michael O'Brian had black, curly hair, eyes as blue as the Irish Sea, and a smile that could melt the polar ice caps. His wonderful liquid voice sent chills down Sonya's spine every time he spoke. For most of the week since she had arrived, she had been thoroughly grateful that her parents had insisted on her accepting the chance to become the Rose of Tralee at this year's festival.

But the dead body lying not more than ten feet in front of her added a deeper chill to the cool shades of the evening and took away any pleasure that she might previously have felt. Sonya knew the man was dead. She had never seen anyone lie that still before.

"I ... I think I know that man," Michael said, after clearing his throat several times.

His voice sounded not nearly so wonderful as it had earlier, and his mild remark reminded Sonya of another of the minor disappointments that Tralee had provided for her: Not one single person spoke the way she had hoped. Not one *bejabbers* or *begorrah* had she heard.

"Who is it?" Sonya asked, staring at the corpse that was dappled by the dark shadows of the leaves that rustled above. She could see well enough to tell that the back of the man's head had been bashed in. "And what's that in his hand?"

Not far from where the dead man lay flowed the pure crystal waters of a fountain dedicated to the memory of William Mulchinock, who had written the song that had brought Sonya to Ireland. The man's hand was stretched toward the fountain.

"It's Liam Kelley," Michael said. "And I believe that's a rose he's holding."

"Liam Kelley," Sonya said. "Oh dear."

She walked a little closer and peered down. Michael was correct about the rose, and she looked around to see where the flower had come from. There was a rose bed nearby, bordered by stones, and the man had obviously fallen very close to it. He hadn't died at once but had managed to pull the rose and crawl a few feet toward the fountain. She could see the marks he had made in the grass.

"I should notify the police," Michael said, apparently not as interested as Sonya in looking at the body. "There's a telephone in the tourist office."

"All right," Sonya said. The tourist office was at the entrance to the park, and not too far from where they were. "I don't mind staying here."

"Why should you do that?"

"Because someone else might come by and disturb things. The police wouldn't like that."

"But what if the killer comes back?"

"Why? To revisit the scene of the crime? That never happens except in movies."

Michael shook his head. "I don't think it's a good idea."

"I do. Now go make your call."

Michael looked at her, and she returned his gaze steadily.

"Very well," he said. "But it will be quite dark soon."

"I don't mind," Sonya told him, and he turned back the way they had come.

Sonya looked down at the body again. Who would ever have guessed she would come to Ireland and come upon a dead man? That certainly hadn't been in her family's plans for her. All her father wanted was for her to be a part of the Rose of Tralee International Festival. He didn't even care whether she won. Just to have her chosen to participate was honor enough, he said.

It wasn't that her father was a professional Irishman or anything. He was a pharmacist in Chicago, but he did enjoy the fact of his Irish ancestry, and every St. Patrick's Day he rented a video of *The Quiet Man* and insisted that the whole family watch it. As Sonya was now very well aware, the movie didn't give a very realistic picture of Ireland, but she thought it was wonderful anyway. The scene with John Wayne and Maureen O'Hara in the wind and the rain always got to her.

At any rate, Sonya's father was proud of his heritage and of the fact that his family had in the distant past lived in County Kerry. He liked to sing "The Rose of Tralee" in a quavery tenor and tell his daughter that she was just like the woman in the song—"lovely and fair as the rose of the summer."

For some reason, however, Sonya had never developed much of an interest in Ireland. She wasn't sure she could tell the difference between a shillelagh and a nightstick or between a leprechaun and a Smurf.

So it had come as a surprise to her when her father had asked her about trying to become the Rose of Tralee. He had kept up with the festival since its beginnings in 1959, and when his own daughter had been invited to enter, he had been ecstatic.

"It's a great honor," he'd said. "And it's not just a beauty contest. It's like the song says, ' 'Twas not her beauty alone that won me.' There's a lot more to it than beauty."

Sonya, who was majoring in math at Marquette and had a 3.75 average, certainly hoped so, and she finally allowed herself to be persuaded. Up until now she had been glad she had.

Now she wondered if the festival would even continue. After all, Liam Kelley was—or had been until quite recently—the extremely popular "King of Chat" and the host of the two televised nights of the festival. Who would they get to replace him?

Sonya looked at the rose in his clenched fist.

I wonder why he picked it? she thought.

Lieutenant Donovan wondered the same thing. He asked William O'Grady about it.

"I have no idea." O'Grady was a thick man with a shock of gray hair and eyes that Donovan thought were set entirely too close together. "Stopping one last time to smell the flowers, do you think?"

Donovan didn't like O'Grady's attitude, but he had to tread carefully.

O'Grady was one of the largest local contributors to the festival and a powerful man in Tralee.

"Can you think of anyone who might have disliked Liam Kelley enough to kill him?" Donovan asked.

"I can't think of anyone who *didn't* dislike the man," O'Grady said.

They were in O'Grady's office at festival headquarters, which was where O'Grady spent most of his time in the two weeks prior to the beginning of activities. He liked to be close to the action so that he could see to it that his money was being spent appropriately.

Donovan brushed at the wrinkles in the right leg of his suit. There were no wrinkles in O'Grady's suit at all.

"There's Carlton, for one," O'Grady said, meaning Peter Carlton, Kelley's manager. "Kelley treats him like a bloody Englishman. Of course, he *is* a bloody Englishman. I've heard rumors that Carlton was dipping into the till."

Donovan had heard the same story from several sources.

"What about Fitzgerald?" he asked. "Didn't he like Kelley?"

"Fitzgerald's a sod," O'Grady said. "And a drunk. And the worst tenor in all of Ireland. Why Kelley demanded that he sing on this year's program is a mystery to me." He stroked his chin thoughtfully. "Unless, of course, Fitzgerald had a bit of information that Mr. Kelley wouldn't want the world to know, which wouldn't be too surprising when you consider the kind of man that Kelley was. He's had his hand up half the skirts in Tralee town by now."

"Do you think a woman killed him?"

O'Grady shook his head. "I believe you said that Kelley was seen entering the park with a man."

Donovan regretted having imparted that little bit of information. He shouldn't have done. But it was so. One of the workers in the tourist office had seen Kelley and another man going into the park late in the afternoon.

"But the other man's face was in shadow," O'Grady continued, "which means the information was not as much help as it might have been."

"True," Donovan said. "Perhaps Kelley was killed by a jealous boyfriend."

"God knows, there should be enough of them to go around. Have you found the murder weapon?"

Donovan shrugged. He wasn't going to give anything else away, but the fact was that the murder weapon was indeed in the possession of the police. It was a rock from the border of the rose bed, which had been replaced after the killer was done with it.

O'Grady smiled thinly. "Keeping things to yourself, I see. Very well. Is there anything else I can do to help you?"

You haven't helped at all, Donovan thought, but he said, "Not today, thank you. But I might be back."

"Please come any time," O'Grady said.

Donovan didn't think O'Grady really meant it, but he didn't comment on that fact. He merely took his leave.

Charlie Fitzgerald was tall and bulky, and he looked to Donovan a lot more like a baritone than a tenor. Liam Kelley had been his best friend. Or so he claimed.

"Like brothers, we were," he said, dabbing at his eyes with a handkerchief that was none too clean. Donovan suspected that Fitzgerald might have had a drop or two to drink.

"I'll be singing at his funeral, you know," Fitzgerald said, putting the handkerchief away.

"I didn't know," Donovan told him, looking around Fitzgerald's kitchen. There were dirty dishes in the sink, and the tabletop was none too clean.

"Best of friends, since childhood." Fitzgerald suppressed a sob. "Not like that bleeding O'Grady. Hated Liam's guts, he did."

Donovan, who was sitting in an uncomfortable wooden chair, crossed his legs.

"Why?" he asked.

"Kelley stole his woman, that's why. Nora Malone. It wasn't general knowledge, so you mightn't have heard."

Donovan hadn't heard. O'Grady obviously hadn't thought to mention it.

"You seem to know a lot about Mr. Kelley," Donovan said.

"Best of friends," Fitzgerald repeated. He pushed away from the square table and said, "I could use a wee drop to cut the dust. And you?"

"No," Donovan said. He didn't drink on the job. "Since you know so much, tell me who might have wanted Mr. Kelley dead."

Fitzgerald took a half-full bottle of single malt from a cabinet and poured a generous dollop into a dirty glass. Donovan thought that was a hell of a way to treat good whiskey.

Fitzgerald took a sip and licked his lips. "Ah, mother's milk. And what was that you were asking just now?"

"Who might have wanted Mr. Kelley dead?"

"Poor Liam. He had a talent for friendship with the ladies, but the men never cared for him. I'd say Peter Carlton was the one. If Liam hadn't paid him so well, he'd have left long ago. It could be that Liam pushed him too far at last. Called him every vile name under the sun, you know. Slapped him and accused him of stealing, I believe. A sad mess, when friends fall out."

Fitzgerald took another drink, more than a sip this time.

"Or it might have been O'Grady," he said. "Nora is a fine figure of a woman. Very fine."

Donovan watched Fitzgerald drink. There wasn't much left in the glass now.

"What about roses? Did he like flowers?"

"Not in the least," Fitzgerald said. "I know he had a rose in his hand, but he was a sentimental man. His last thought was of the festival, I'd wager."

He took another drink. His interests didn't seem to lie in women or roses so much as in whiskey. When Donovan left, he was crying softly, with his head down on the smeared tabletop, the nearly empty whiskey glass held tightly in his hand.

Peter Carlton was offended that Donovan was in his apartment.

"I had absolutely no reason to kill Liam," he said, standing stiffly in his living room. "He was my employer, and I was diligent and exacting in the performance of my duties. Liam bloody well knew that, and he knew that he couldn't find anyone to replace me. I was invaluable to him. And as for my part, I might never find another job that pays quite so well."

"Does the money mean that much, then?" Donovan asked. He too was standing, not having been invited to sit.

"Of course it does. What else is there?"

"Humane treatment, for one thing. I've heard that Mr. Kelley didn't treat you very well."

"Who said that? The man was a saint. He hardly ever raised his voice."

Donovan didn't even blink. "Not even when he found out you'd stolen several thousand pounds from him."

"That's a bloody lie!" Carlton's neck swelled, and his face reddened alarmingly. "I never took a penny, and Liam knew it. Who told you that? I'll have his guts for garters, by God!"

"You seem to have quite a temper, Mr. Carlton. Why don't you take a deep breath and think about what you're saying?"

"Don't tell me what to do, you bleeding peeler. If you think I killed Liam, you're starkers."

"I'm not saying you killed him, just that you had a motive. Several people heard him accuse you of stealing from him."

"He might have accused me, but I never stole a sou. Not from him or any man."

"Who took the money, then?"

"How should I know? I've been making inquiries, but so far I haven't been able to find out. That bloody Fitzgerald was much too thick with Liam, however, if you ask me. He could easily have dipped his drunken fingers into the loose currency."

"Did Mr. Kelley like flowers, do you know?"

"Flowers? He never thought about flowers unless some fan sent him a bouquet. As often as not, he'd dump it in the trash rather than look for a vase and water."

"Why might he pick a rose before he died, then?" Donovan asked.

Carlton's color was slowly returning to normal. "I have no idea. Did you ask his friend Fitzgerald?"

"He didn't know either," Donovan said.

Sonya Morning thought that she knew, however. Michael, on the other hand, didn't want to talk about it.

"It's a matter for the police," he said, trying to take Sonya's hand. "They know about these things, and we should leave it up to them."

Sonya pulled her hand away. "But it was a dying message," she said. "Just like the Ellery Queen stories. It must have been. Otherwise, why would he have tried to crawl to the fountain with a rose in his hand? It all means something. I'm sure it does."

"Perhaps." Michael looked hurt that she had removed her hand from his. "But if it does, the police will discover it."

Sonya wasn't so sure. The man who had questioned her, the somewhat rumpled Lieutenant Donovan, had not seemed interested in hearing her theories. All he wanted to know was how she and Michael had come upon the body, whether there had been anyone else about, and whether they had seen anyone else since entering the park—boring things like that. She hadn't even had a chance to tell him her idea about the dying message.

"I think we should call him," she said. "I'm sure that if I explain things in the right way, he'll listen to me. Please."

Michael hesitated. He wasn't so sure that Donovan would want any help from a prospective Rose of Tralee, but Sonya looked at him with hurt green eyes, and he picked up the telephone.

"Don't you see?" Sonya said. It was the morning after the murder, and she had been thinking about it all night. "He was trying to tell us something. We just have to figure out what it was that he wanted us to know."

Donovan, unlike Michael, was sure that Sonya was right. The crime scene analysis showed that Kelley had fallen near the rose bed, crawled to the nearest bush, plucked the rose, and started his crawl toward the fountain, dying before he could reach it.

"What do you think he meant?" Donovan asked.

Sonya shook her head, and her dark hair danced. "I don't know who the suspects are, but I was wondering if one of them could be a woman."

"No," Donovan said. "All the suspects are men."

The field had been narrowed to Carlton, who may or may not have been stealing from his boss; Fitzgerald, who seemed to know quite a bit, and maybe too much, about Kelley's private life; and O'Grady, who had lost Nora Malone to Kelley's charms.

"That's too bad," Sonya said. "I thought that the killer might have been a woman, maybe someone who was a former Rose of Tralee."

"Kelley was seen entering the park with another man," Donovan said. "It's logical to assume that the man was the killer."

"He had the rose in his hand," Michael said. "The idea that it was a woman is certainly logical."

Sonya didn't feel that she needed Michael to defend her.

"There's another possibility," she said, the truth dawning in her eyes.

"And what might that be?" Donovan asked.

When she told him, he thought that she might very well be right, and as it turned out, she was.

"He confessed?" Sonya asked when Donovan returned later that afternoon. "Just like that?"

"It wasn't 'just like that,'" Donovan said. "We had to press him quite hard. But in the end he admitted it. It was your clue that led me in the right direction, I must say."

Sonya smiled. "Thank you. It was a logical conclusion to reach. If he wasn't trying to tell us that the killer was a woman, a Rose of

Tralee, he was surely trying to tell us *something*. Maybe that the killer's name was Mulchinock."

"Or William," Donovan said, matching her smile. "Mr. O'Grady was certainly surprised when we confronted him with that idea. Of course, the fact of the fingerprints on the rock didn't hurt. He really didn't have much respect for the police. He never thought we'd find the rock, and he certainly didn't think we'd find the prints on it after he had wiped it."

"He should have wiped harder," Sonya said.

"He should never have picked it up, but he was already upset that Kelley had taken Nora Malone away from him. When Kelley taunted him with it in the park, O'Grady let his temper get the better of him."

"He should never have gone to the park with O'Grady in the first place," Sonya said.

Donovan agreed. "But they were scouting locations for the outdoor part of the television program. Kelley saw no harm in it, and there might not have been, had Kelley not mentioned Miss Malone."

"I hope you don't think any the less of Tralee town for what has happened," Donovan said.

"Of course not. It's not the town's fault. There are men like William O'Grady everywhere."

"Unfortunately true," Donovan said. "And let me say that I hope you become this year's Rose."

"Thank you," Sonya said. "But the competition is quite fierce."

"I'm sure that it is," Donovan said, bringing his hand from behind his back. He handed her a perfect rose. "But you'll always be the fairest flower in the vale to me."

Sonya took the rose and held it carefully. Lieutenant Donovan did not look nearly so rumpled as he had a day earlier. She realized that he was as young as Michael, and she was suddenly glad again that she had come to Ireland.

The Hanging of Myles Joyce

JAMES JOYCE

There is less crime in Ireland than in any other country in Europe. In Ireland there is no organised underworld, and when one of those events which the journalists, with atrocious irony, call 'red idylls' occurs, the whole country is shaken by it.

Five years ago an innocent man, now at liberty, was condemned to forced labour to appease public indignation. But even while he was in prison the crimes continued.

Some years before this a sensational trial was held in Ireland concerning a family bearing the same name as my own. The case had its origins in a lonely place in a western province called Maamtrasna where a terrible murder was committed.

The facts were these. A man named Joyce, his wife and three of his four children, had been murdered in County Galway by a party of men who believed they were informers. Four or five townsmen, all belonging to the ancient tribe of the Joyces, were arrested and charged with the crime and brought before the court.

The oldest of these men, a seventy-year-old named Myles Joyce, was the prime suspect of the outrage. Public opinion at the time, though, thought him innocent and today considers him a martyr.

Neither the old man nor the others accused knew any English. The court had to resort to the services of an interpreter to hear their evidence. The questioning, conducted through the interpreter, was at times comic and at times tragic.

On one side of the courtroom was the excessively ceremonious interpreter, while on the other stood the patriarch of a miserable tribe unused to civilised customs, who seemed stupefied by all the judicial ceremony.

At one point, the magistrate said to the interpreter. 'Ask the accused if he saw the lady that night?'

The question was referred to him in Irish, and the old man broke out into an involved explanation, gesticulating, appealing to the others accused, and to heaven. Then he quietened down, worn out by his effort.

At this the interpreter turned to the magistrate and said, 'He says, "No, your worship".'

'Ask him if he was in that neighbourhood at that hour?' the magistrate went on.

The old man again began to talk, to protest, to shout, almost beside himself with the anguish of being unable to understand or to make himself understood, weeping in anger and terror. At last he fell silent once more.

And again the interpreter said, 'He says, "No, your worship".'

When the questioning was over, the guilt of the poor old man was declared proved by that court. He was remanded to a superior court, where, with two others, he was condemned to the noose.

On the day the sentence was executed, the square in front of the prison in Galway was jammed full of kneeling people shouting prayers in Irish for the repose of Myles Joyce's soul.

The story was told that the executioner, also unable to make the victim understand him, kicked at the miserable man's head in anger to shove it into the noose.

Murder at Cobbler's Hulk

SEAN O'FAOLAIN

It takes about an hour of driving southward out of Dublin to arrive at the small seaside village of Greystones. (For two months in the summer, it calls itself a resort.) Every day, four commuter trains from the city stop here and turn back, as if dismayed by the sight of the desolate beach of shingle that stretches beyond it for twelve unbroken miles. A single line, rarely used, continues the railway beside this beach, so close to the sea that in bad winters the waves pound in across the track, sometimes blocking it for days on end with heaps of gravel, uprooted sleepers, warped rails. When this happens, the repair gangs have a dreary time of it. No shelter from the wind and spray. Nothing to be seen inland but reedy fields, an occasional farmhouse or abandoned manor, a few leafless trees decaying in the arid soil or fallen sideways. And, always, endless fleets of clouds sailing away towards the zinc-blue horizon.

Once there were three more tiny railway stations along these twelve miles of beach, each approached by a long lane leading from the inland carriage road to the sea. The best preserved of what remains of them is called Cobbler's Hulk. From a distance, one might still mistake it for a real station. Close up, one finds only a boarded waiting-room whose tin roof lifts and squeaks in the wind, a lofty signal-cabin with every window broken and a still loftier telephone pole whose ten crossbars must once have carried at least twenty lines and now bear only one humming wire. There is a rotting, backless bench. You could scythe

516

the grass on the platform. The liveliest thing here is an advertisement on enamelled sheet metal, high up on the brick wall of the signal-cabin. It shows the single white word STEPHEN'S splashed across a crazy blob of black ink. Look where one will, there is not farmhouse nor cottage within sight.

It was down here that I first met Mr Bodkin one Sunday afternoon last July. He was sitting straight up on the bench, bowler-hatted, clad, in spite of the warmth of the day, in a well-brushed blue chesterfield with concealed buttons and a neatly tailored velvet half collar that was the height of fashion in the Twenties. His grey spats were as tight as gloves across his insteps. He was a smallish man. His stiff shirt-collar was as high as the Duke of Wellington's, his bow tie was polka-dotted, his white moustaches were brushed up like a Junker's. He could have been seventy-three. His cheeks were as pink as a baby's bottom. His palms lay crossed on the handle of a rolled umbrella, he had a neatly folded newspaper under his arm, his patent-leather shoe tips gleamed like his pince-nez. Normally, I would have given him a polite 'Good day to you,' and passed on, wondering. Coming on him suddenly around the corner of the waiting-room, his head lowered toward his left shoulder as if he was listening for an approaching train, I was so taken by surprise that I said, 'Are you waiting for a train?'

'Good gracious!' he said, in equal surprise. 'A train has not stopped here since the Bronze Age. Didn't you know?'

I gazed at his shining shoes, remembering that when I had halted my Morris Minor beside the level-crossing gates at the end of the lane, there had been no other car parked there. Had he walked here? That brambled lane was a mile long. He peeped at the billycan in my hand, guessed that I was proposing to brew myself a cup of tea after my solitary swim, chirruped in imitation of a parrot, 'Any water?', rose and, in the comic-basso voice of a weary museum guide, said, 'This way, please.' I let him lead me along the platform, past the old brass tap that I had used on my few previous visits to Cobbler's Hulk, toward a black-tarred railway carriage hidden below the marshy side of the track. He pointed the ferrule of his umbrella.

'My chalet,' he said smugly. 'My *wagon-lit*.'

We descended from the platform by three wooden steps, rounded a microscopic gravel path, and he unlocked the door of his carriage. It was still faintly marked FIRST CLASS, but it also bore a crusted brass plate whose shining *rilievo* announced THE VILLA ROSE. He bowed me inward, invited me to take a pew (his word for an upholstered carriage seat), filled my billycan from a white enamelled bucket ('Pure spring water!') and, to expedite matters further, insisted on boiling it for me on his Primus stove. As we waited, he sat opposite me. We both looked out the window at the marshes. I heard a Guard's whistle and felt our carriage jolt away to nowhere. We introduced ourselves.

'I trust you find my beach a pleasant spot for a picnic?' he said, as if he owned the entire Irish Sea.

I told him that I had come here about six times over the past thirty years.

'I came here three years ago. When I retired.'

I asked about his three winters. His fingers dismissed them. 'Our glorious summers amply recompense.' At which exact moment I heard sea-birds dancing on the roof and Mr Bodkin became distressed. His summer and his beach were misbehaving. He declared that the shower would soon pass. I must have my cup of afternoon tea with him, right there. 'In first-class comfort.' I demurred; he insisted. I protested gratefully; he persisted tetchily. I let him have his way, and that was how I formed Mr Bodkin's acquaintance.

It never became any more. I saw him only once again, for five minutes, six weeks later. But, helped by a hint or two from elsewhere– the man who kept the roadside shop at the end of the lane, a gossipy barmaid in the nearest hamlet–it was enough to let me infer, guess at, induce his life. Its fascination was that he had never had any. By comparison, his beach and its slight sand dunes beside the railway track were crowded with incident, as he presently demonstrated by producing the big album of pressed flowers that he had been collecting over the past three years. His little ear finger stirred them gently on their white pages: milfoil, yarrow, thrift, sea daisies, clover, shepherd's-needle, shepherd's-purse, yellow bedstraw, great bedstraw, Our Lady's bedstraw, minute sand roses, different types of lousewort. In the pauses between their naming, the leaves were turned as quietly as the wavelets on the beach.

One December day in 1912, when he was fifteen, Mr Bodkin told me, he had entered his lifelong profession by becoming the messenger boy in Tyrrell's Travel Agency, located at 15 Grafton Street, Dublin. He went into Dublin every morning on the Howth tram, halting it outside the small pink house called The Villa Rose, where he lived with his mother, his father, his two young sisters and his two aunts ...

The Villa Rose! He made a deprecatory gesture–it had been his mother's idea. The plays and novels of Mr A. E. Mason were popular around 1910. He wrinkled his rosy nose. It was not even what you call a real house. Just two fishermen's cottages, joined front to back, with a dip, or valley, between their adjoining roofs. But what a situation! On fine days, he could see, across the high tide of the bay, gulls blowing about like paper, clouds reflected in the still water, an occasional funnel moving slowly in or out of the city behind the long line of the North Wall; and away beyond it, all the silent drums of the Wicklow Mountains. Except on damp days, of course. The windows of The Villa Rose were always sea-dimmed on damp days. His mother suffered from chronic arthritis. His father's chest was always wheezing. His sisters' noses were always running. His aunts spent half their days in bed.

'I have never in my life had a day's illness! Apart from chilblains. I expect to live to be ninety.'

The great thing, it appeared, about Tyrrell's Travel Agency was that you always knew where you were. The Tyrrell system was of the simplest: everybody was addressed according to his rank. (Mr Bodkin did not seem to realise that this system was, in his boyhood as in mine, universal in every corner of the British Empire.) Whenever old Mr Bob wanted him, he shouted, 'Tommy!' at the top of his voice. After shouting at him like that for about five years, Mr Bob suddenly put him behind the counter, addressed him politely as 'Bodkin' and shouted at him no longer. Five years passed and, again without any preliminaries, Mr Bob presented him with a desk of his own in a corner of the office and addressed him as 'Mr Bodkin'. At which everybody in the place smiled, nodded or winked his congratulations. He had arrived at the top of his genealogical tree. He might fall from it. He would never float beyond it. Very satisfactory. One has to have one's station in life. Yes?

The summer shower stopped but not Mr Bodkin. (In the past three years, I wondered if he had had a single visitor to talk to.) There were, I must understand, certain seeming contradictions in the system. An eager ear and a bit of experience soon solved them all. For example, there was the case of old Clancy, the ex-Enniskillener Dragoon, who opened the office in the morning and polished the Egyptian floor tiles. Anybody who wanted him always shouted, 'Jimmy!' Clear as daylight. But whenever old Lady Kilfeather came sweeping into the agency from her grey Jaguar, ruffling scent, chiffon, feather boas and Protestant tracts, she clancied the whole bang lot of them.

'Morning Tyrrell! Hello, Bodkin! I hope Murphy has that nice little

jaunt to Cannes all sewn up for myself and Kilfeather? Clancy, kindly
read this leaflet on Mariolatry and do, for heaven's sake, stop saying,
"Mother of God!" every time you see me!'

The aristocratic privilege. The stars to their stations; the planets in
their stately cycles about the sun; until the lower orders bitch it all
up. Meaning old Mrs Clancy, swaying into the office like an inebriated
camel, to beg a few bob from Clancy for what she genteelly called her
shopping. Never once had that woman, as she might reasonably have
done, asked for 'Jim'. Never for 'Mr Clancy'. Never even for 'my
husband'. Always for 'Clancy'. Mr Bodkin confessed that he sometimes
felt so infuriated with her that he would have to slip around the corner
to The Three Feathers, to calm his gut with a Guinness and be reassured by the barman's 'The usual, Mr B?' Not that he had ever been
entirely happy about that same B. He always countered it with a stiff
'Thank you, Mr Buckley.'

It was the only pub he ever visited. And never for more than one
glass of plain. Occasionally, he used to go to the theatre. But only for
Shakespeare. Or Gilbert and Sullivan. Only for the classics. Opera?
Never! For a time, he had been amused by Shaw. But he soon discarded
him as a typical Dublin jackeen mocking his betters. Every Sunday, he
went to church to pray for the king. He was nineteen when the
Rebellion broke out. He refused to believe in it. Or that the dreadful
shootings and killings of the subsequent Troubles could possibly produce any change. And did they? Not a damned thing! Oh, some client
might give his name in the so-called Irish language. Mr Bodkin simply
wrote down, 'Mr Irish'. Queenstown became Cobh. What nonsense!
Kingstown became Dun Laoghaire. Pfoo! Pillar-boxes were painted
green. The police were called Garda. The army's khaki was dyed green.
All the whole damned thing boiled down to was that a bit of the
House of Commons was moved from London to Dublin.

Until the Second World War broke out. Travel stopped dead. The
young fellows in the office joined the army. He remembered how old
Mr Bob—they ran the office between them—kept wondering for weeks
how the Serbians would behave this time. And what on earth had
happened to those gallant little Montenegrins? When the Germans
invaded Russia, Mr Bob said that the czar would soon put a stop to
that nonsense. Mind you, they had to keep on their toes after 1945.
He would never forget the first time a client said he wanted to visit
Yugoslavia. He took off his glasses, wiped them carefully, and produced
a map. And, by heavens, there it was!

There had been other changes. His mother had died when he was forty-three. His two aunts went when he was in his fifties. To his astonishment, both his sisters married. His father was the last to go, at the age of eighty-one. He went on living, alone, in The Villa Rose, daily mustering thousands of eager travellers around Europe by luxury liners, crowded packet-boats, Blue Trains, Orient Expresses, Settlebellos, Rheingolds, alphabetical-mathematical planes. He had cars waiting for some, arranged hotels for others, confided to a chosen few the best places (according to 'my old friend Lady Kilfeather') to dine, drink and dance, and he never went anywhere himself.

'You mean you *never* wanted to travel?'

'At first, yes. When I could not afford it. Later, I was saving up for my retirement. Besides, in my last ten years there, the whole business began to bore me.'

He paused, frowned and corrected himself. It had not 'begun' to bore. His interest in it had died suddenly. It happened one morning when he was turning back into the office after conducting Lady Kilfeather out to her grey Jaguar. Observing him, young Mr James had beckoned him into his sanctum.

'A word in your ivory ear, Mr Bodkin? I notice that you have been bestowing quite an amount of attention on Lady Kilfeather.'

'Yes, indeed, Mr James! And I may say that she has just told me that she is most pleased with us.'

'As she might well be! Considering that it takes six letters and eight months to get a penny out of the old bitch. That woman, Mr Bodkin, is known all over Dublin as a first-class scrounger, time-waster and bloodsucker. I would be obliged if you would in future bear in mind three rather harsh facts of life that my aged parent seems never to have explained to you. Time is money. Your time is my money. And no client's money is worth more to me than any other client's money. Take it to heart, Mr Bodkin. Thank you. That will be all for now.'

Mr Bodkin took it to heart so well that from that morning on, all those eager travellers came to mean no more to him than a trainload of tourists to a railway porter after he had banged the last door and turned away through the steam of the departing engine for a quick smoke before the next bunch arrived.

Still, my duty was duty. And he had his plans. He hung on until he was sixty-five and then he resigned. Mr James, with, I could imagine, an immense sense of relief, handed him a bonus of £50—a quid for every year of his service, but no pension—shook his hand and told him to go off to Cannes and live there in sin for a week with a cabaret dancer. Mr Bodkin said that for years he had been dreaming of doing exactly that with Mrs Clancy, accepted the fifty quid, said a warm goodbye to everybody in the office, sold The Villa Rose and bought the tarred railway carriage at Cobbler's Hulk. He had had his eye on it for the past five years.

The night he arrived at Cobbler's Hulk, it was dry and cold. He was sweating from lugging two suitcases down the dark lane. The rest of his worldly belongings stood waiting for him in a packing-case on the grass-grown platform. For an hour he sat in his carriage by candle-light, in his blue chesterfield, supping blissfully on the wavelets scraping the shingle every twenty seconds and on certain mysterious noises from the wild-life on the marshes. A snipe? A grebe? A masked badger?

He rose at last, made himself another supper of fried salty bacon and two fried eggs, unwrapped his country bread and butter and boiled himself a brew of tea so strong that his spoon could almost have stood up in it. When he had washed his ware and made his bed, he went out onto his platform to find the sky riveted with stars. Far out to sea, the lights of a fishing smack. Beyond them he thought he detected a faint blink. Not, surely, a lighthouse on the Welsh coast? Then, up the line, he heard the hum of the approaching train. Two such trains, he had foreknown, would roar past Cobbler's Hulk every twenty-four hours. Its head-lamps grew larger and brighter and then, with a roar, its carriage windows went flickering past him. He could see only half a dozen passengers in it. When it died away down the line, he addressed the stars:

'"O Spirits, merciful and good! I know that our inheritance is held in store for us by Time. I know there is a sea of Time to rise one day, before which all who wrong us or oppress us will be swept away like leaves. I see it, on the flow! I know that we must trust and hope, and neither doubt ourselves nor doubt the good in one another ... O Spirits, merciful and good, I am grateful!"'

'That's rather fine. Where did you get that?'

'Dickens. *The Chimes.* I say that prayer every night after supper and a last stroll up the lane.'

'Say it for me again.'

As he repeated those splendid radical words, he looked about as wild as a grasshopper. 'Thinner than Tithonus before he faded into air.'

Had he really felt oppressed? Or wronged? Could it be that, during his three years of solitude, he had been thinking that this world would

be a much nicer place if people did not go around shouting at one
another or declaring to other people that time is money? Or wondering
why Mother should have had to suffer shame and pain for years, while
dreadful old women like Kilfeather went on scrounging, wheedling,
bloodsucking, eating and drinking their way around this travelled world
of which all he had ever seen was that dubious wink across the night
sea? He may have meant that in his youth, he had dreamed of marriage.
He may have meant nothing at all.

He leaned forward.

'Are you sure you won't have another cup of tea? Now that I can
have afternoon tea any day I like, I can make a ridiculous confession
to you. For fifty years, I used to see Mr Bob and Mr James walk across
Grafton Street every day at four-thirty precisely to have afternoon tea
in Mitchell's Café. And I cannot tell you how bitterly I used to envy
them. Wasn't that silly of me?'

'But, surely, one of the girls on the staff could have brewed you all
a cup of tea in the office?'

He stared at me.

'But that's not the same thing as afternoon tea in Mitchell's! White
tablecloths? Carpets? Silverwear? Waitresses in blue and white?'

We looked at each other silently. I looked at my watch and said
that I must get going.

He laughed happily.

'The day I came here, do you know what I did with *my* watch? I
pawned it for the sum of two pounds. I have never retrieved it. And
I never will. I live by the sun and the stars.'

'You are never lonely?'

'I am used to living alone.'

'You sleep well?'

'Like a dog. And dream like one. Mostly of the old Villa Rose. And
my poor, dear mamma. How could I be lonely? I have my beautiful
memories, my happy dreams and my good friends.'

'I envy you profoundly,' I said.

On which pleasant little coda we parted. But is it possible never to
be lonely? Do beautiful memories encourage us to withdraw from the
world? Not even youth can live on dreams.

He had, however, one friend.

One Saturday evening in September, on returning from the wayside
shop on the carriage road, he was arrested by a freshly painted sign

on a gate about two hundred yards from the railway track. It said FRESH EGGS FOR SALE. He knew that there was not a house nor a human being in sight. Who on earth would want to walk a mile down this tunnelled lane to buy eggs? Behind the wooden gate, there was a grassy track, leading, he now presumed, to some distant cottage invisible from the lane. He entered the field and was surprised to see, behind the high hedge, an open shed sheltering a red van bearing, in large white letters:

FLANNERY'S
HEAVENLY BREAD

After a winding quarter of a mile, he came on a small, sunken, freshly whitewashed cottage and knocked. The door was opened by a woman of about thirty-five or forty, midway between plain and good-looking, red-cheeked, buxom, blue-eyed, eagerly welcoming. She spoke with a slight English accent that at once reminded him of his mother's voice. Yes! She had lovely fresh eggs. How many did he want? A dozen? With pleasure! Behind her, a dark, handsome, heavily-built man, of about the same age, rose from his chair beside the open turf fire of the kitchen and silently offered him a seat while 'Mary' was getting the eggs.

Mr Bodkin expected to stay three minutes. He stayed an hour. They were the Condors: Mary, her brother Colm—the dark, silent man—and their bedridden mother lying in the room off the kitchen, her door always open, so that she could not only converse through it but hear all the comforting little noises and movements of her familiar kitchen. Their father, a herdsman, had died three months before. Mary had come back from service in London to look after her mother, and poor Colm (her adjective) had come home with her to support them both. He had just got a job as a roundsman for a bakery in Wicklow, driving all day around the countryside in the red van.

Mr Bodkin felt so much at ease with Mary Condor that he was soon calling on her every evening after supper, to sit by the old woman's bed, to gossip or to read her the day's news from his *Irish Times* or to give her a quiet game of draughts. That Christmas Day, on Mary's insistence, he joined them for supper. He brought a box of chocolates for Mary and her mother, 100 cigarettes for Colm and a bottle of grocer's sherry for them all. He recited one of his favourite party pieces from Dickens. Colm so far unbent as to tell him about the bitter Christmas he had spent in Italy with the Eighth Army near a place

called Castel di Sangro. Mary talked with big eyes of the awful traffic
of London. The old woman, made tipsy by the sherry, shouted from
her room about the wicked sea-crossing her husband had made during
'the other war', in December of 1915, with a herd of cattle for the
port of Liverpool.

'All travelled people!' Mr Bodkin laughed, and was delighted when
Mary said that, thanks be to God, their travelling days were done.

As he walked away from their farewells, the channel of light from
their open door showed that the grass was laced with snow. It clung
to the edges of his carriage windows as he lay in bed. It gagged the
wavelets. He could imagine it falling and melting into the sea. As he
clutched the blue hot-water bottle that Mary had given him for a
Christmas present, he realised that she was the only woman-friend he
had made in his whole life. He felt so choked with gratitude that he
fell asleep without thanking his spirits, the merciful and the good, for
their latest gift.

What follows is four-fifths inference and one-fifth imagination: both,
as the event showed, essentially true.

On the Monday of the last week in July, on returning from the roadside
shop with a net bag containing *The Irish Times,* tea, onions and a bar
of yellow soap, Mr Bodkin was startled to see a white Jaguar parked
beside the level crossing. It was what they would have called in the
travel agency a posh car. It bore three plaques, a GB, a CD and a blue-
and-white silver RAC. Great Britain. *Corps Diplomatique.* Royal Automobile Club. He walked on to his platform to scan the beach for its
owner. He found her seated on his bench, in a miniskirt, knees crossed,
wearing a loose suede jacket, smoking a cigarette from a long ivory
holder, glaring at the grey sea, tiny, blonde (or was she bleached?),
exquisitely made up, still handsome. Her tide on the turn. Say, fifty?
He approached her as guardedly as if she were a rabbit. A woven
gold bangle hung heavily from the corrugated white glove on her wrist.
Or was it her bare wrist? Say, fifty-five. Her cigarette was scented.

'Fog coming up,' he murmured politely when he came abreast of her
and gave her his little bobbing bow. 'I do hope you are not waiting
for a train.'

She slowly raised her tinted eyelids.

'I was waiting for you, Mr Bodkin,' she smiled. (One of the sharp
ones?)

Her teeth were the tiniest and whitest he had ever seen. She could

have worn them around her neck. Last month, he saw a field mouse
with teeth as tiny as hers, bared in death.

'Won't you sit down? I know all about you from Molly Condor.'

'What a splendid woman she is!' he said and warily sat beside her,
placing his net bag on the bench beside her scarlet beach bag. He
touched it. 'You have been swimming?'

'I swim,' she laughed, 'like a stone. While I waited for you, I was
sun-bathing.' She smiled for him. 'In the nude.'

Hastily, he said, 'Your car is *corps diplomatique!*'

'It is my husband's car. Sir Hilary Dobson. I stole it!' She gurgled
what ruder chaps in the agency used to call the Gorgon Gurgle. 'You
mustn't take me seriously, Mr Bodkin. I'm Scottish. Hilary says I am
fey. He is in the FO. He's gone off on some hush-hush business to
Athens for a fortnight, so I borrowed the Jag. Now, if it had been
Turkey! But perhaps you don't like Turkey, either? Or do you? Athens
is such a crummy dump, don't you agree?'

'I have never travelled, Lady Dobson.'

'But Molly says you once owned a travel agency!'

'She exaggerates my abilities. I was a humble clerk.'

'Eoh?' Her tone changed, her voice became brisk. 'Look, Bodkin, I
wanted to ask you something very important. How well do you know
Molly Condor?'

He increased his politeness.

'I have had the great pleasure of knowing Miss Mary Condor since
last September.'

'I have known her since she was twenty-two. I trained her. She
was in my service for twelve years. But I have never looked at Molly
as just a lady's maid. Molly is my best friend in the whole world. She
is a great loss to me. Of course, as we grow older, the fewer, and the
more precious, our friends become.'

He considered the name, Molly. He felt it was patronising. He had
never lost a friend—never, before Mary, having had one to lose. He
said as much.

'Too bad! Well! I want Molly to come back to us. My nerves have
not been the same since she left.'

He looked silently out to sea. He was aware that she was slowly
turning her head to look at him. Like a field mouse? He felt a creeping
sensation of fear. Her nerves seemed all right to him. He watched her
eject her cigarette, produce another from a silver case, insert it, light
it smartly with a gold lighter and blow out a narrow jet of smoke.

'And then there is her brother. Condor was our chauffeur for five years. It would be simply wonderful if they both came back to us! I know poor old Hilary is as lost without his Condor as I am without my Molly. It would be a great act of kindness if you could say a word in our favour in that quarter. Hilary would appreciate it no end. Oh, I know, of course, about the mother. But that old girl can't need the two of them, can she? Besides, when I saw her this morning, I had the feeling she won't last long. Arthritis? *And* bronchitis? *And* this climate? I had an old aunt just like her in Bexhill-on-Sea. One day, she was in splendid health. The next day, her tubes were wheezing like bagpipes. For six months, I watched her, fading like a sunset. In the seventh month ...'

As she wheedled on and on, her voice reminded him of a spoon inside a saucepan. He listened to her coldly, with his eyes, rather than his ears, as for so many years he used to listen to old ladies who did not know where exactly they wanted to go nor what they wanted to do, alert only to their shifting lids, their mousy fingers, their bewildered shoulders, their jerking lips. Crepe on her neck. French cigarettes. Sunbathing nude. Bodkin. Condor. Molly. 'Poor old Hilary.' What did this old girl really want? Coming all this way for a lady's maid? My foot!

'And you know, Bodkin, Molly has a great regard for you. She thinks you are the most marvellous thing she ever met. I can see why.' She laid her hand on his sleeve. 'You have a kind heart. You will help me, if you can, won't you?' She jumped up. 'That is all I wanted to say. Now you must show me your wonderful *wagon-lit*. Molly says it is absolutely fab.'

'I shall be delighted, Lady Dobson,' he said and, unwillingly, led her to it.

When she saw the brass plate of THE VILLA ROSE, she guffawed and hastened to admire everything else. Her eyes trotted all over his possessions like two hunting mice. She gushed over his 'clever little arrangements'. She lifted pot-lids, felt the springiness of the bed, penetrated to his water-closet, which she flushed, greatly to his annoyance because he never used it except when the marshes were very wet or very cold, and then he had to refill the cistern with a bucket every time he flushed it.

'I find it all most amusing, Bodkin,' she assured him as she powdered her face before his shaving mirror. 'If you were a young man, it would make a wonderful weekend love-nest, wouldn't it? I must fly. It's nearly lunchtime. And you want to make whatever it is you propose to make with your soap, tea and onions. Won't you see me to my car? And do say a word for me to Molly! If you ever want to find me, I'm staying in the little old hotel down the road. For a week.' She laughed naughtily. 'Laying siege! Do drop in there any afternoon at six o'clock for an aperitif,' and she showed half her white thigh as she looped into her car, started the engine, meshed the gears, beamed at him with all her teeth, cried, 'À *bientôt*, Bodkin,' and shot recklessly up the lane, defoliating the hedges into a wake of leaves like a speedboat.

Watching her cloud of dust, he remembered something. A chap in the office showing him a postcard of *Mona Lisa*. 'Ever seen her before? Not half! And never one of them under fifty-five!' Indeed! *And* indeed! 'I am afraid, Lady Dobson, we must make up our minds. A cool fort-night in Brittany? Or five lovely hot days in Monte Carlo? Of course, you *might* win a pot of money in Monte Carlo ...' How greedily their alligator eyelids used to blink at that one! He returned slowly to his *wagon-lit*, slammed down the windows to let out the smell of her cigarette, washed the dust of yellow powder from his washbasin, re-filled his cistern and sat for an hour on the edge of his bed, pondering. By nightfall, he was so bewildered that he had to call on Mary.

She was alone. The old lady was asleep in her room. They sat on either side of the kitchen table, whispering about the hens, the up train that had been three minutes late, the down train last night that was right on the dot, the fog that morning, both of them at their usual friendly ease until he spoke about his visitor. When he finished, she glanced at the open door of the bedroom.

'I must say, she was always very generous to me. Sir Hilary was very kind. He went hard on me to stay. He said, "You are good for her." She had her moods and tenses. I felt awfully sorry for him. He spoiled her.'

'Well, of course, Mary, those titled people,' Mr Bodkin fished cun-ningly and was filled with admiration for her when she refused to bite.

All she said was, 'Sir Hilary was a real gentleman.'

'They are married a long time?'

'Fifteen years. She is his second wife. She nursed his first wife. But I *had* to come back, Mr Bodkin!'

'You did quite right. And your brother did the right thing, too. I mean, two women in a remote cottage. Your brother is never lonely?'

She covered her face with her hands and he knew that she was crying into them.

'He is dying of the lonesome.'

From the room, the old woman suddenly hammered the floor with her stick.

'Is he back?' she called out fretfully.

Mary went to the bedroom door and leaned against the jamb. It was like listening to a telephone call.

'It's Mr Bodkin ... He went up to the shop for cigarettes ... I suppose he forgot them ... About an hour ago ... He may be gone for a stroll. It's such a fine night ... Och, he must be sick of that old van ...' She turned her head. 'Was the van in the shed, Mr Bodkin?' He shook his head. 'He took the van ... For God's sake, Mother, stop worrying and go to sleep. He maybe took the notion to drive over to Ashford for a drink and a chat. It's dull for him here ... I'll give you a game of draughts.'

Mr Bodkin left her.

A nurse? It was dark in the lane, but above the tunnel of the hedges, there was still a flavour of salvaged daylight. He started to walk toward the road, hoping to meet Condor on his way back. The air was heavy with heliotrope and meadow-sweet. A rustle in the ditch beside him. Far away, a horse whinnied. He must be turned forty by now. Behind him, Africa, Italy, London. Before him, nothing but the roads and fields of his boyhood. Every night, that solitary cottage. The swell of the night express made him look back until its last lights had flickered past the end of the lane and its humming died down the line.

But I have lived. An old man, now, twice a child.

By the last of the afterlight above the trees of the carriage road, he saw the red nose of the van protruding from the half-moon entrance to the abandoned manor house. He walked to it, peered into its empty cabin, heard a pigeon throating from a clump of trees behind the chained gates. He walked past it to the shop. It was closed and dark. He guessed at a lighted window at the rear of it, shining out over the stumps of decapitated cabbages. Condor was probably in there, gossiping. He was about to turn back when he saw, about a hundred yards farther on, the red tail-lights of a parked car. Any other night, he might have given it no more than an incurious glance. The darkness, the silence, the turmoil of his thoughts finally drew him warily toward it along the grassy verge. Within fifteen yards of it, he recognised the white Jaguar, saw the rear door open, the inner light fall on the two figures clambering out of it. Standing on the road, they embraced in a seething kiss. When he released her, she got into the driver's seat, the two doors banged and everything was silent and dark again. She started her engine, floodlit the road and drove swiftly away around the curve. Crushed back into the hedge, he heard Condor's foot-steps approach, pass and recede. In a few moments, the van's door banged tinnily, its head-lamps flowered, whirled into the maw of the lane, waddled drunkenly behind the hedges, down toward the sea.

Before he fell asleep that night, Mr Bodkin heard a thousand wavelets scrape the shingle, as during his long life, other countless waves had scraped elsewhere unheard—sounds, moments, places, people to whose lives he had never given a thought. The Irish Times rarely recorded such storms of passion and, when it did, they broke and died far away, like the fables that Shakespeare concocted for his entertainment in the theatre. But he knew the Condors. This adulterous woman could shatter their lives as surely as he knew, when he opened his eyes to the sea-sun shimmering on his ceiling, she had already shattered his.

It was his custom, on such summer mornings, to rise, strip off his pyjamas, pull on a bathing slip and walk across the track in his slippers, his towel around his neck, down to the edge of the sea for what he called a dip: which meant that since he, too, swam like a stone, he would advance into the sea up to his knees, sprinkle his shoulders, and then, burring happily at the cold sting of it, race back to the prickly gravel to towel his shivering bones. He did it this morning with the eyes of a saint wakened from dreams of sin.

On Tuesday night, he snooped virtuously up the lane and along the carriage road. The red van was not in its shed. But neither was it on the road. Lascivious imaginings kept him awake for hours. He longed for the thunderbolt of God.

On Wednesday night, it was, at first, the same story; but on arriving back at the foot of the lane, there were the empty van and the empty Jaguar before him, flank to flank at the level crossing. He retired at once to his bench, peering up and down the beach, listening for the sound of their crunching feet, determined to wait for them all night, if necessary. Somewhere, that woman was lying locked in his arms. The bared thigh. The wrinkled arms. The crepey neck.

Daylight had waned around nine o'clock, but it was still bright enough for him to have seen shadows against the glister of the water, if there had been shadows to see. He saw nothing. He heard nothing but the waves. It must have been nearly two hours later when he heard their cars starting. By the time he had flitted down to the end of the platform, her lights were already rolling up the lane and his were turning in through his gateway. Mr Bodkin was at the gate barely in time to see his outline dark against the bars of the western sky. As he looked at the van, empty in its shed, it occurred to him that this was one way in which he could frighten him—a warning message left on the seat of the van. But it was also a way in which they could communicate with each other. Her message for him. His answer left early in the morning at her hotel.

On Thursday night, the van lay in its shed. But where was Condor? He walked up the grass track to the cottage and laid his ear to the door. He heard Mary's voice, his angry voice, the mother's shouting. He breathed happily and returned to his bed.

On Friday morning, the Jaguar stood outside Mary's wooden gate. Laying siege? That night, the scarlet van again lay idle in its pen. Wearied by so much walking and watching, he fell asleep over his supper. He was awakened around eleven o'clock by the sound of a car. Scrambling to his door, he was in time to see her wheeling lights hit the sky. He went up the lane to the van, looked around, heard nothing, shone his torch into the cabin and saw the blue envelope lying on the seat. He ripped it open and read it by torchlight. 'Oh, My Darling, for God's sake, where are you? Last night and tonight, I waited and waited. What has happened? You promised! I have only one more night. You are coming back with me, aren't you? If I do not see you tomorrow night, I will throw myself into the sea. I adore you. Connie.' Mr Bodkin took the letter down to the sea, tore it into tiny pieces and, with his arms wide, scattered them over the receding waves.

That Saturday afternoon, on returning from the shop with his week-end purchases in his net bag, there was the Jaguar beside the level crossing, mud-splattered and dusty, its white flanks scarred by the whipping brambles. Rounding the corner of the waiting-room, he saw her on his bench, smoking, glaring at the sparkling sea. She barely lifted her eyes to him. She looked every year of sixty. He bowed and sat on the bench. She smelled of whisky.

'What an exquisite afternoon we are having, Lady Dobson. May I rest my poor bones for a moment? That lane of mine gets longer and longer every day. Has everything been well with you?'

'Quite well, Bodkin, thank you.'

'And, if I may ask, I should be interested to know, you have, I trust, made some progress in your quest?'

'I could hardly expect to with that old woman around everybody's neck. I have laid the seeds of the idea. Molly now knows that she will always be welcome in my house.'

'Wait and see? My favourite motto. Never say die. Colours nailed to the mast. No surrender. It means, I hope, that you are not going to leave us soon.'

'I leave tonight.'

'I do hope the hotel has not been uncomfortable.'

'It is entirely comfortable. It is full of spinsters. They give me the creeps.'

He beamed at the sea and waited.

'Bodkin! There is one person I have not yet seen. For Hilary's sake, I ought to have a word with Condor. Have you seen him around?'

Her voice had begun to crumble. Eyes like grease under hot water. Cigarette trembling.

'Let me think,' he pondered. 'On Thursday? Yes. And again last night. We both played draughts with his mother. He seemed his usual cheerful self.'

She ejected her cigarette and ground it into the dust under her foot.

'Bodkin! Will you, for Christ's sake, tell me what do young people do with their lives in Godforsaken places like this? That lane must be pitch-dark by four o'clock in the winter!'

He looked at his toes, drew his handkerchief from his breast-pocket, and flicked away their dust.

'I am afraid, Lady Dobson, I no longer meet any young people. And, after all, Condor is not a young man, I suppose you could call him a middle-aged man. Or would you?'

She hooted hoarsely.

'And what does that leave me? An old hag?'

'Or me? As the Good Book says, "The days of our years are three-score years and ten; and if by reason of strength they be fourscore years, yet is their strength labour and sorrow; for it is soon cut off, and we fly away".'

She spat it at him:

'You make me sick.'

From under her blue eyelids, she looked at the clouds crimped along the knife of the horizon. He remembered Mary's twisted face when she said, 'He is dying of the lonesome.' She turned and faced him. Harp strings under her chin. Hands mottled. The creature was as old as sin.

'Do you happen to know, Bodkin, if Condor has a girl in these parts? It concerns me, of course, only insofar as, if he has, I need not ask him to come back to us. Has he?'

Mr Bodkin searched the sea as if looking for a small boat in which to escape his conscience.

'I believe he has,' he said firmly.

'Believe? Do you know? Or do you not know?'

'I saw them twice in the lane. Kissing. I presume that means that they are in love.'

'Thank you, Bodkin,' she said brightly. 'In that case, Hilary must get another chauffeur and I must get another lady's maid.' She jumped up. He rose politely. 'I hope you will have a very pleasant winter.' She stared at him hatefully. 'In love? Have you ever in your life been in love? Do you know what it means to be in love?'

'Life has denied me many things, Lady Dobson.'

'Do you have such a thing as a drink in that black coffin of yours?'

'Alas! Only tea. I am a poor man, Lady Dobson. I read in the paper recently that whisky is now as much as six shillings a glass.'

Her closed eyes riveted her to her age like a worn face on an old coin.

'No love. No drink. No friends. No wife. No children. Happy man! Nothing to betray you.'

She turned and left him.

The events of that Saturday night and Sunday morning became public property at the inquest.

Sergeant Delahunty gave formal evidence of the finding of the body on the rocks at Greystones. Guard Sinnot corroborated. Mr T. J. Bodkin was then called. He stated that he was a retired businessman residing in a chalet beside the disused station of Cobbler's Hulk. He deposed that, as usual, he went to bed on the night in question around ten o'clock and fell asleep. Being subject to arthritis, he slept badly. Around one o'clock, something woke him.

CORONER: What woke you? Did you hear a noise?
WITNESS: I am often awakened by arthritic pains in my legs.
CORONER: Are you quite sure it was not earlier than one o'clock? The reason I ask is because we know that the deceased's watch stopped at a quarter to twelve.
WITNESS: I looked at my watch. It was five minutes past one.

Continuing his evidence, the witness said that the night being warm and dry, he rose, put on his dressing-gown and his slippers and walked up and down on the platform to ease his pains. From where he stood, he observed a white car parked in the lane. He went towards it. He recognised it as the property of Lady Constance Dobson, whom he had met earlier in the week. There was nobody in the car. Asked by a juror if he had seen the car earlier in the night, before he went to bed, the witness said that it was never his practice to emerge from his chalet after his supper. Asked by another juror if he was not surprised to find an empty car there at one o'clock at night, he said he was but thought that it might have run out of petrol and been abandoned by Lady Dobson until the morning. It did not arouse his curiosity. He was not a curious man by nature. The witness deposed that he then returned to his chalet and slept until six o'clock, when he rose, rather earlier than usual, and went for his usual morning swim. On the way to the beach, he again examined the car.

CORONER:　It was daylight by then?

WITNESS:　Yes, sir.

CORONER:　Did you look inside the car?

WITNESS:　Yes, sir. I discovered that the door was unlocked and I opened it. I saw a lady's handbag on the front seat and a leather suitcase on the rear seat. I saw that the ignition key was in position. I turned it, found the starter and the engine responded at once. At that stage, I became seriously worried.

CORONER:　What did you do?

WITNESS:　I went for my swim. It was too early to do anything else.

Mr Bodkin further stated that he then returned to his chalet, dressed, shaved, prepared his breakfast and ate it. At seven o'clock, he walked to the house of his nearest neighbours, the Condors, and aroused them. Mr Colm Condor at once accompanied him back to the car. They examined it and, on Mr Condor's suggestion, they both drove in Mr Condor's van to report the incident to the Guards at Ashford.

CORONER:　We have had the Guards' evidence. And that is all you know about the matter?

WITNESS:　Yes, sir.

CORONER:　You mean, of course, until the body was found fully clothed, on the rocks at Greystones a week

later; that is to say, yesterday morning, when, with
Sir Hilary Dobson and Miss Mary Condor, you
helped identify the remains?'

WITNESS: Yes, sir.

CORONER: Did you have any difficulty in doing so?

WITNESS: I had some difficulty.

CORONER: But you are satisfied that it was the body of Lady
Constance Dobson and no other.

WITNESS: I was satisfied. I also recognised the woven gold
bangle she had worn the day I saw her. The teeth
were unmistakable.

Dr Edward Halpin of the sanatorium at Newcastle having given his
opinion that death was caused by asphyxiation through drowning, the
jury, in accordance with the medical evidence, returned a verdict of
suicide while of unsound mind. The coroner said it was a most distressing case, extended his sympathy to Sir Hilary Dobson and said no
blame attached to anybody.

It was September before I again met Mr Bodkin. A day of infinite
whiteness. The waves falling heavily. Chilly. It would probably be my
last swim of the year. Seeing him on his bench–chesterfield, bowler
hat, grey spats, rolled umbrella (he would need it from now on), his
bulging net bag between his feet, his head bent to one side as if he
was listening for a train–I again wondered at a couple of odd things
he had said at the inquest: such as his reply to a juror that he never
emerged from his railway carriage after supper; his answer to the coroner that he was often wakened at night by his arthritis ('I sleep like
a dog'), he had told me; ('I have never in my life had a day's illness,
apart from chilblains'); and he had observed by his watch that it was
five past one in the morning ('I live by the sun and stars'). Also, he
had said that from the platform, he had noticed the white car parked
at the end of the lane. I had parked my Morris a few moments before
at the end of the lane and, as I looked back toward it now, it was
masked by the signal-box.

He did not invite me to sit down and I did not. We spoke of the
sunless sky. He smiled when I looked at the sky and said, 'Your watch
is clouded over.' I sympathised with him over his recent painful experience.

'Ah, yes!' he agreed. 'It was most distressing. Even if she *was* a foolish poor soul. Flighty, too. Not quite out of the top drawer. That may have had something to do with it. A bit spoiled, I mean. The sort of woman, as my dear mother used to say, who would upset a barracks of soldiers.'

'Why on earth do you suppose she did it? But I shouldn't ask; I am sure you want to forget the whole thing.'

'It is all over now. The wheel turns. All things return to the sea. She was crossed in love.'

I stared at him. 'Some man in London?'

He hesitated, looked at me shiftily, slowly shook his head and turned his eyes along his shoulder towards the fields.

'But nothing was said about this at the inquest! Did other people know about it? Did the Condors know about it?'

His hands moved on his umbrella handle.

'In quiet places like this, they would notice a leaf falling. But where so little happens, every secret becomes a buried treasure that nobody mentions. Even though every daisy on the dunes knows all about it. This very morning, when I called on Mary Condor, a hen passed her door. She said, "That hen is laying out. Its feet are clean. It has been walking through grass." They know everything. I sometimes think,' he said peevishly, 'that they know what I ate for breakfast.'

(Was he becoming disillusioned about his quiet beach?)

'How did you know about it? Or are you just guessing?'

He frowned. He shuffled for the second time. His shoulders straightened. He almost preened himself.

'I have my own powers of observation! I can keep my eyes open, too, you know! Sometimes I see things nobody else sees. I can show you something nobody else has ever seen.'

Watching me watch him, he slowly drew out his pocketbook and let it fall open on a large visiting card. I stooped forward to read the name. LADY CONSTANCE DOBSON. His little finger turned it onto its back. There scrawled, apparently in red lipstick, was the word *Judas*. When I looked at him, he was smiling triumphantly.

'Where on earth did you find it?'

'That morning at six o'clock, it was daylight. I saw it stuck inside the windscreen wipers'—he hesitated for the last time—'of the Jaguar.'

My mind became as tumbled as a jigsaw. He was lying. How many other pieces of the jigsaw were missing? Who was it said the last missing bit of every jigsaw is God?

'You did not mention this at the inquest.'

'Should I have? The thought occurred to me. I decided that it would be more merciful not to. There were other people to think of. Sir Hilary, for one. And others.' He replaced his pocketbook and rose dismissively. 'I perceive that you are going for a swim. Be careful. There are currents. The beach shelves rapidly. Three yards out and the gravel slides from under your feet. And nobody to hear you if you shout for help. I had my usual little dip this morning. Such calm. Such utter silence. The water was very cold.'

He bobbed and walked away. I walked very slowly down to the edge of the beach. I tested the water with my hand. He was right. I looked around me. I might have been marooned on some Baltic reef hung between an infinity of clouds and a lustre of a sea gleaming with their iceberg reflections. Not a fishing smack. Not even a cormorant. Not a soul for miles, north and south. Nobody along the railway track. Or was somebody, as he had suggested, always watching? If he were concealing something, why had he admitted that he had come out from his railway carriage at all? Why did he choose to mention one o'clock in the morning? Did he know that she had died around midnight? Was he afraid that somebody besides himself might have seen her lights turn down the lane? A timid liar, offering a half-truth to conceal the whole truth?

Above the dunes, I could just see the black roof of his railway carriage. I measured the distance from where I stood and let out a loud 'Help!' for ten seconds; nothing happened. Then his small, dark figure rose furtively behind the dunes. When he saw me, he disappeared.

Soft Day

WENDI LEE

The morning came too early for Rachel. She felt as if she might be coming down with Michael's cold and wondered whether they would have to stay at the Ballygesh hostel for another day while she recovered. She staggered out of bed and splashed cold water on her face. As she was getting dressed, she noticed that Hazel, the British woman whom she had met late last night, was still asleep in one of the bunks. She looked at her watch and wondered whether she should wake her.

"Hazel," Rachel called softly, going over to shake the woman's shoulder. "It's nine-thirty–" Hazel flopped over, her face blue, her sightless eyes staring at nothing in particular. Rachel yelped and stepped back, her thoughts still a blur from waking up. Something under Hazel's sheets moved. At first Rachel thought maybe Hazel wasn't dead after all. But when Eddie the cat emerged, Rachel screamed and jumped. The cat purred and rubbed its face on Hazel's cold cheek.

The dorm door opened and Maire, the houseparent, took in the scene. "What in heaven's name–?" Maire turned pale at the sight that greeted her.

"She's dead," Rachel said numbly. "I–I found her that way. The cat–"

Maire collected herself, and brusquely grasped Rachel by the shoulders and guided her out of the dorm. "We must call the constable."

*   *   *

"It'll be fun, Rach," her boyfriend, Michael, had said when they started planning their trip to Ireland. "Just the two of us, walking Ireland's roads from one coast to the other. Jim and Helen did it last year and Jim told me it only took them two days to walk from Dublin to County Galway. What do you say?"

It had taken five days for Rachel and Michael to get to County Galway. Rachel had originally suggested they plan the trip with bed-and-breakfast inns in mind. But it wasn't rustic enough for Michael, a college linebacker and health nut who wanted to camp out the entire way. The only problem with camping out was that it rained practically the entire time and weighed them down with soggy camping gear.

Then Michael caught a bad cold. When they went in search of a warm, dry hotel where he could recover, they discovered that even flashing Jim's American Express card didn't get them a room. At the height of tourist season, even the little B & Bs along the way were filled to capacity.

Finally, the owner of a small B & B took pity on them and called ahead to a nearby An Oíge hostel in Ballygesh–An Oíge being the Irish equivalent of the American Youth Hostel–and reserved beds for them. Fortunately, Rachel had had the foresight to pack her hostel card.

The Ballygesh hostel was a series of small whitewashed cottages. One cottage served as the common room and kitchen area with an attached peat shed. Two served as dorm rooms, one for men and one for women. The fourth cottage served as the residence of the caretakers, a young Irish couple, Maire and Dennis. When they arrived, Maire noticed Michael's cold and sent him packing off to bed with a hot whiskey and water–"It'll take away the chill"–and several blankets. Dennis signed them in.

"It's a soft day today," he said to Rachel, "and on days like this, we leave the common area open for the hostelers."

Rachel had heard the term "soft day" often enough during the last week to know it meant that it was gray and rainy. It was a pleasant surprise to learn that the hostel was open during the day–most hostels were not required to stay open between ten in the morning and five in the evening. But the Irish hostels out in the country tended to bend that rule, considering how many soft days Ireland had and how few places there could be to take shelter.

After claiming one of the bunks in the women's dorm, she went to check on Michael. Calling out to make certain that the men's dorm was empty, Rachel received no reply, so she sneaked in and found

Michael sound asleep, the empty whiskey glass by his bed. An orange and gray cat with green eyes sat nearby, looking up at Rachel with curiosity.

"Don't mind me," Rachel told the cat as she picked up the empty glass to take back to the houseparents. The cat blinked slowly once, then stood up and arched its body in a long stretch before padding over to a red backpack that was propped precariously against the bunk next to Michael's. Emitting a loud purr, the cat rubbed its face hard against the material, causing the backpack to fall onto the rough plank flooring. The cat rolled over on its back, grabbing the backpack with its claws and trying to pull it closer.

"You careless rascal," Rachel said with a chuckle as she crossed the room to right the backpack and swat the cat away.

"What are you doing here?" a sharp, German-accented voice demanded.

Rachel straightened up quickly. She turned around to face a large man with a red face, blond hair, and a beard. He was standing on the other side of the bunk, where the red backpack had been propped. She noticed an open pack of Gauloise cigarettes on the mattress. Without taking his eyes off Rachel, he picked up the pack and slid it in his T-shirt pocket.

"I, uh, the cat–" she looked around, but the cat was smarter than Rachel and had taken off at the first sign of a confrontation. "I was checking on my boyfriend, and the cat knocked over your backpack." Rachel held up the empty whiskey glass as proof that she had legitimate business in the men's dorm. She could feel her face growing hot as the silent German fellow continued to glare at her.

"It's the truth," she said loudly, glancing at Michael, who snorted peacefully in his sleep. He would be of no help if she needed to defend herself. The whiskey concoction must have knocked him out.

The German strode around the bunk toward her. Rachel shrank back as he brushed brusquely by her to check the pack. Rachel slunk out of the dorm and went over to the common room.

Three other people occupied the common room: a young French couple and an older American man who looked like a businessman on vacation. Rachel wondered whether he'd brought his whole family.

The French couple were oohing and aahing over a pot of boiling water. They introduced themselves to Rachel as Françoise and Jean-Marc. She promptly forgot their last names, but she figured she probably wouldn't see them after tomorrow. Jean-Marc took a cigarette from his Gauloise pack and lit it. The pungent tobacco cut through the clean Irish air. Jean-Marc offered one to Rachel, which she politely declined.

"See what we bought from a fisherman down by the Ballygesh wharf," Françoise said, proudly holding up a limp lobster that had only one claw. "He told us that he couldn't sell it to a restaurant."

"Mmmm," Rachel murmured, wondering what she was going to eat for dinner. She hadn't stopped to get supplies. "It looks wonderful."

Françoise grinned and turned away to check the salted boiling water. Rachel wondered who would get the claw.

The American had been watching her. "I'm Bob from Chicago." They shook hands. Without much prompting, Bob began to tell her about his mail-order business back home, and his divorce, and the revelation he had that he had missed so much of life by marrying early.

"So now I'm doing what I never had the chance to do when I was young; hiking around Europe."

"Why aren't you staying in hotels and B & Bs?" Rachel asked. "You can certainly afford it."

Bob scowled. "What makes you think I can afford more than this?"

Rachel averted her eyes. "Well, I just thought, with your business and everything–"

He sneered and stood up. "Well I can't afford even this, but I'm doing it anyway."

Rachel stared blankly at his retreating back, puzzled by how touchy he'd been over an innocent comment.

"Don't pay any attention to him," Jean-Marc said with a laugh. "He's done nothing but complain since he got here this morning. I just wish he'd get back in his little Fiat and go find a hotel."

"What about the German fellow?" Rachel asked.

"Wolfgang?" Françoise had joined them. The lobster was nowhere to be seen. Rachel assumed it had met its fate. "He just got here. What about him?"

Rachel explained about her visit to the men's dorm to check on Michael. Jean-Marc and Françoise frowned.

"Well," Françoise began, "it is not common practice to allow women to visit the men's dormitory. But we are in Ireland, and rules have been broken here many times. He is a German–" Françoise and Jean-Marc exchanged a knowing look, "–so I suppose he was startled to find you breaking the rules."

Rachel shrugged it off and continued to talk to the young French couple until the lobster was ready to eat. Then she left the common room to take the empty glass back to Maire and Dennis.

"I met your cat," she said. "He was in the men's dorm."

Maire tilted her head and raised her eyebrows. "That's rare. Eddie doesn't usually stray too far from our cottage. She's very territorial." Rachel noted that Eddie was a she.

Rachel's stomach growled, reminding her that she hadn't eaten since that morning. Dennis suggested a pub called the Black Swan, which was located half a mile down the road. "They serve a very nice oxtail soup and a good colcannon with bacon."

Rachel thanked them and went down the road to the Black Swan. Inside, it was warm and smoky and smelled of stale Guinness. Seated in a corner of the pub, a young man played the tinwhistle while an older man accompanied him on fiddle. Rachel enjoyed the quick airs and slow laments, even recognizing one contemplative lament as "Brian Boru's March." She felt a little out of place in a pub that seemed to cater mostly to local men. Still, it was nice to sit by a warm peat fire and relax over a half-pint of Guinness.

By the time her meal arrived, she was sleepy with Guinness and the warmth emanating from the fireplace. She had ordered the colcannon, which turned out to be steamed cabbage and potatoes with lots of salt and a little pepper. Rachel found herself picking out the limp bacon, which seemed to be there mostly for flavor.

On her way out, Rachel spied Bob and Wolfgang huddled in a booth by the entrance, both smoking. Realizing that she would have to pass by them, Rachel found no reason to be cordial to them, since they had both acted rudely in her presence.

"We can make the trade tomorrow morning–" Bob was saying before he caught sight of her. He motioned to Wolfgang, who craned his neck to glare at her, then started to get up. Rachel turned away from them and quickly left the pub, her heart beating rapidly. Was it her imagination or had there been a menacing look in both Bob's and Wolfgang's faces? She wondered what they were planning to trade in the morning.

The walk was brisk, erasing the sluggishness that had overcome her during the meal and the Guinness. But when she got back to the dorm, the day's activities caught up with her and she decided to crawl into her bed after checking the common room one more time for Michael. Jean-Marc and Françoise were gone, which meant they were either out walking or had retired to the dorms, but there was a new hosteler, a woman about Rachel's age.

"Hi," she said with a British accent, looking up from a steaming mug. "Want some tea? I just made a pot."

Rachel smiled and shook her head. "I'm afraid I'm ready to retire."

"You wouldn't happen to be Rachel, would you?" the woman continued.

"Yes, I am," Rachel replied, caught by surprise.

"A man recovering from a very bad cold shared some of my dinner and asked about you." The woman poured a cup of tea for Rachel despite her protests. "That nice young French couple told him they thought you had gone out to the pub."

"I suppose he went back to bed." Rachel sipped the strong, bitter tea.

The woman smiled. "Yes, I expect he did. He didn't eat very much, but he seemed as if he were on the other side of a cold. My name is Hazel, by the way."

They sipped tea in silence for a minute, then Hazel spoke again. "God, I'm dying for a fag and I'm all out. You wouldn't happen to have one on you, would you?"

Rachel shook her head, congratulating herself on knowing that the term "fag" meant cigarette in England. "I'm afraid I don't smoke."

Hazel waved away Rachel's apology. "Well, there's nothing for it, is there? You've got your health, and I've got a filthy habit." Then she grinned and Rachel relaxed. They talked pleasantly for a few more minutes before Rachel made her excuses and went back to her dorm room to crawl into her bunk in the dark.

Now it was morning and Hazel was dead. Rachel stood in the doorway, looking around the common room. Jean-Marc and Françoise were doing their chores—Françoise was sweeping the floor and Jean-Marc was wiping down the tables. A bleary-eyed Michael was wrapped in a blanket, seated by the fireplace, warming his hands over a mug of tea. Wolfgang was seated at one of the tables, hunched over a breakfast of eggs and toast. Bob was missing. Remembering what Jean-Marc had said the night before, Rachel glanced out the window. The Fiat was gone.

Maire had gone back to her cottage to call the constable.

Michael was looking up at her. "What's wrong, Rachel?"

"I–I found one of the hostelers this morning, dead."

Jean-Marc and Françoise stopped their chores. Wolfgang stopped eating. "The American, Bob?" Wolfgang asked.

"N-n-no," Rachel replied, realizing that her teeth were chattering—not from the chill of a soft day, but from the chill of death. "It was a British woman. I met her briefly last night." She wondered why Wolfgang would think Bob was dead—did he think she had stolen into the men's dorm again for some illicit activity that involved his backpack? And why was Eddie the cat hanging around the men's dorm? She turned her attention back to Wolfgang. "I don't see Bob's Fiat outside. He must have left already."

Wolfgang jumped up, upsetting the table and his breakfast, and sprinted to the door to peer out. "Why that two-timing, double-dealing—" He switched from English to German, spouting a stream of bitter invectives that made Rachel wince, even though she didn't understand a word of it.

From Rachel's vantage point by the window, she could see Dennis coming up the walk with the village constable, a tall young man in uniform. Wolfgang had calmed down and was cleaning up the mess he had created, when Dennis introduced the constable to the hostelers.

"I'd like you all to remain here while the doctor makes his examination of the young woman," Constable Barnes said. "Is there anyone missing?"

Wolfgang was quick to point out the missing Bob. A second constable was dispatched to search for the American.

Barnes started his questioning with Rachel. "I understand that you found her."

Rachel launched into her story, trying not to leave anything out. The constable listened with great interest, interrupting her only to ask one or two pertinent questions. When she was finished, he leaned forward and asked, "Tell me, do you recall anything unusual happening yesterday?"

She bit her lip. "Well, actually, when I went to the men's dorm to check on Michael, who was asleep, Eddie the cat was in the dorm. As I was leaving, Eddie went over to a red backpack and rubbed her face against it, and it fell over. The housemother told me that Eddie never goes into the dorms. She thought that was unusual." Rachel told the rest of the story, lowering her voice slightly and glancing at Wolfgang occasionally. The truculent German sat across the room, his sullen face red, his arms crossed in a defensive position.

The constable frowned and looked at Wolfgang briefly. "Well, Miss Birney, I've always trusted in cats' behavior. Let's go have a look at that backpack."

As they stood up, the constable casually told the room, "Miss Birney and I are going to take a look at some of the backpacks in the men's dorm to see if she can identify one. Does anyone have any objections?"

The white-faced group shook their heads uncertainly. Michael looked pale and drawn, and Rachel just wanted to get them both back to Dublin, although she would settle for Galway City or Limerick.

She got up and followed the constable to the men's dorm, which he surveyed with a critical eye. "Which backpack was it?"

There were only two backpacks in view—Michael's tan pack and a green one. Rachel poked around, looking for the red backpack. She shook her head. "I don't see it. I wonder if it was that other American's pack."

Barnes frowned, grabbed both packs, and escorted her back to the common area. He approached Wolfgang. "Show me your pack."

Wolfgang smiled and pointed to the green pack. Rachel half-stood. "B-b-but, that *can't* be yours–" she started to say.

Wolfgang's smile was triumphant. "Ah, but it is. I only went over to the red backpack yesterday to make sure you had not tampered with it."

It was Rachel's turn to glare.

An hour later, an official-looking car drove up with Bob in the back. He was taken out of the backseat, as was his backpack. Barnes brought Rachel out to look at the backpack, which was red. She shook her head. "That isn't it. The pack I saw yesterday was smaller. Eddie knocked it over and acted all goofy as if he were smelling catnip. Maybe if Eddie were here, I bet she could find it."

Constable Barnes called Maire and Dennis out of their house. "Is Eddie about?" he asked.

Maire smiled and nodded, ducking back inside, and soon returning with a sleepy orange and gray cat. "She was catching a few winks on our bed."

Rachel cradled the sleepy, warm cat in her arms and followed the constable back to the dorms. They let Eddie into the men's dorm, but after a perfunctory look around, Eddie seemed inclined to leave. Barnes picked the cat up and they went into the women's dorm, where Eddie took another apathetic turn.

"I wonder what made Eddie so crazy the other day," Rachel said as they took Eddie into the common room. Wolfgang had lit a cigarette that, Rachel noted, smelled stronger than the Gauloise he had been smoking the day before. Bob looked morose. Françoise and Jean-Marc looked pale and worried. Michael just looked exhausted.

Constable Barnes turned Eddie loose. The cat sniffed the air, then made a beeline for Wolfgang, who looked down at Eddie with scorn.

Eddie rubbed her face against Wolfgang's pants leg and the German tried to move his leg. Eddie followed, flopping down on Wolfgang's shoe and grabbing it with her paws.

Rachel blinked. The thick smoke stung her eyes and the heavy smell made it hard for her to breathe. Wolfgang was staring at Eddie as if she were an alien creature. "Get it off my leg!" He stood up suddenly and tried to move away. Eddie seemed to be attached to Wolfgang's leg, however. "Keep the damn monster away from me!" Wolfgang's eyes were wide with panic. Rachel thought it was a strange reaction to a cat.

"Open the window," Constable Barnes ordered. Rachel quickly opened a window, wondering what was going on. Barnes strode over to Wolfgang and confiscated the half-smoked cigarette.

"Hey! Why do you take my cigarette?" Wolfgang asked, standing up and blinking furiously. "I–I–" He collapsed back in the chair, his eyelids drooping. Then he shook his head. "I–I think I need to lie down." The constable helped the German to the window and ordered him to breathe the clean air.

"What happened to him?" Rachel asked. Michael was half-standing. Bob had leaned forward. The French couple had moved to a corner of the room, cringing.

Constable Barnes ignored her question, continuing to frown. "There were only two backpacks in the men's dorm. And the American had his with him. Someone's pack is missing."

Rachel turned to the group. "Wolfgang's and Michael's packs have been accounted for. So has Bob's." Everyone looked at Jean-Marc and Françoise. "The red backpack has to be yours, Jean-Marc."

"What's going on, Rachel?" Michael asked. He looked uncertainly at her and then at the French couple, who had suddenly become morose.

She glanced at her boyfriend. "I'm not sure, Michael, but I think we're about to find out."

A loud, plaintive meow came from the open door of the peat shed next to the kitchen. The constable and Rachel rushed there to find Eddie pawing desperately at the pile of dried peat.

"It looks as if it's been rearranged in the middle here," Barnes noted.

They removed bricks of peat to reveal a red backpack. Constable Barnes opened the flap and inspected the contents. Sure enough, he pulled out several bricks of cocaine from among the clothes, books, toiletry items, and cigarette packs.

Rachel thought it was odd that most of the cigarette packs were open. She picked up one and sniffed it. "This smells sort of like mari-juana, only—" she thought for a moment, "—different."

Constable Barnes took the pack from her and inhaled deeply. "Cat-nip," he said. "This is laced with catnip."

"Whatever for?" Rachel asked, amused at the thought of catnip being brought in illegally to sell to cats like Eddie.

A racket in the other room brought the constable and Rachel run-ning into the common room. Michael was sprawled on top of Jean-Marc, who struggled to get from under. A bleary-eyed Wolfgang held a sullen Françoise, who was halfheartedly trying to get away.

Michael looked up and grinned at Rachel. "It's a good thing I know how to tackle. This guy almost got away."

Rachel smiled. "My hero."

It was later in the day, after Jean-Marc and Françoise had been taken away, that Bob got up, ready to leave. Rachel was heating some canned chicken soup for Michael when Wolfgang's heavy hand came down on Bob's shoulder.

"And now we complete our business transaction," Wolfgang said.

Bob turned pale and started to sweat. "Er, the fact is, Wolfgang, um—"

Rachel saw Wolfgang's hand squeeze Bob's shoulder until pain regis-tered on Bob's face. "I don't have them. I lied. I took your money and was planning on getting away."

"What don't you have?" Michael asked. He stood next to Rachel.

Wolfgang regarded them. "Blue jeans. He promised to sell me two dozen blue jeans cheaply. I could take them back to Germany and sell them for a profit. He took my money and left." He suddenly let go of Bob, who sagged into a nearby chair.

"I lost my job back in Chicago and I'm going through a divorce. I couldn't face the fact that I couldn't pay my child support, so I took off for Europe, thinking I could hide out, avoid my responsibilities for a while. Then I discovered that Germans frequent Ireland and they love anything American. So I've been going around the country, to hostels, selling nonexistent blue jeans to Germans."

Wolfgang's hands had turned into fists, but instead of going for Bob, the German turned away and hit the table. Then he turned back and gave Bob a look of contempt. "Get out of here before I break every bone in your body."

Bob threw the pound notes on the table, backed out of the common room, and hurried to his car, then took off.

Rachel and Michael went back to the dorms and packed their things, then stopped by the caretakers' cottage. Maire answered the door, a sad smile on her face, Eddie twining herself around Maire's ankles.

"It looks like Eddie saved the day," Rachel told her.

She brightened and gathered Eddie in her arms. "She has, at that."

Dennis came up behind his wife. "You're leaving now?"

"We have to get back to Dublin," Rachel said.

Just then, Constable Barnes pulled up in his car. "You look like you're both ready to go. Don't you want to find out what happened?" he asked with a twinkle in his eye. "After all, you were instrumental in solving the murder."

Rachel nodded. "Who killed Hazel and why?"

"It was an accident. Jean-Marc and Françoise came into the common room not far behind you and offered Hazel a cigarette. Unfortunately, it was one laced with catnip oil."

"Catnip oil?" Michael asked dubiously.

"It was discovered in an experiment in the 1960s that tobacco laced with catnip oil can cause hallucinations similar to LSD," the constable told them. "It's not common, but some people still like to smoke catnip-laced cigarettes. Apparently Jean-Marc opened the wrong cigarette pack. Hazel began hallucinating, much like Wolfgang did earlier today. Françoise quieted her down and brought her into the dorm, intending to tuck her in. Unfortunately, Hazel panicked and Françoise covered her face with a pillow."

Rachel winced. "And I was asleep the whole time? How could I sleep through that?"

"It was done quietly," Constable Barnes explained. "And the Irish air has been known to make even insomniacs sleep like newborns. I don't think Françoise intended to kill her; she just wanted Hazel to pass out. But it doesn't take long to smother someone who's in an hallucinogenic panic."

Rachel had an inspiration. "So that's why Wolfgang acted so strange earlier. I saw him take a pack of open cigarettes off a bunk yesterday. That's the cigarette you confiscated from him."

"That's right," the constable nodded. "Fortunately, he didn't smoke much of it, and I think it was lightly laced with catnip, so his reaction was mild." Constable Barnes thanked them again for their help and bade them good-bye before taking his leave.

Rachel leaned against Michael. "Let's go home," she suggested. "I don't think I'm in the mood for traveling anymore."

All in the Way You Look at It

EDMUND CRISPIN

Seven o'clock ... the gathering darkness was accentuated by a fog which had appeared dispiritingly at about tea-time. Looking across the river, you could no longer make out the half-demolished Festival buildings on the far side; and although October was still young, the sooty trees on the Embankment had already surrendered their stoic green to the first spears of the cold, and there were few homekeeping folk hardy enough to resist the temptation of a fire. Presently, to a servile nation-wide juggling with clocks, Summer Time would officially end. In the meanwhile, it seemed that Nature's edict had anticipated Parliament's by a matter of several days; so that more than one belated officer-worker, scurrying to catch his bus in Whitehall or the Strand, shivered a little, and hunched his shoulders, as he met the cold vapour creeping into London from the Thames....

In a room high up in a corner of New Scotland Yard, a room where the lights had had to be turned on more than two hours ago, Detective-Inspector Humbleby produced a sherry decanter and two glasses from a filing cabinet implausibly marked JEWEL THEFTS, and displayed them to his visitor, who said: 'I didn't know you were allowed to keep drink on the premises.'

'We're not.' Humbleby poured the sherry without any special sign of perturbation. 'And I,' he added, 'am the only officer in the entire

building who does. There's discipline for you.... But look here,
Gervase, are you sure you wouldn't like to go on to the club, or
wherever we're dining, and let me join you as soon as this call has
come through?'

'No, no.' And Gervase Fen, Professor of English Language and Liter-
ature in the University of Oxford, shook his head emphatically. 'It's
perfectly comfortable here. What's more, your sherry'—he sipped exper-
imentally and his face brightened—'your sherry is too good to leave.
But what is the call? Anything important?'

'A routine report. From a pleasant enough though rather ponderous
colleague called Bolsover, of the Mid-Wessex CID. They dragged me
in to work with him on a case,' said Humbleby, without relish, 'arising
out of primitive rustic passions. Tuesday and Wednesday I was on
the spot where the thing happened, but then yesterday I had to travel
back here so as to give evidence this morning at the Elderton trial,
and Bolsover promised to telephone me here this evening and let me
know if there was anything new.'

'What sort of case?'

'Murder. It makes my twentieth this year. There are times when I
wish I'd specialised in art forgeries, or something peaceful and infre-
quent like that. Lloyd Jones, who's our best man for that kind of thing,
has done practically nil for the last six months.... However, it's no
use moaning, I suppose.'

'Will you have to go back to Wessex?'

'Yes, tomorrow—unless in the meantime Bolsover's solved the thing
on his own. I'm rather hoping he has, and that that's why he's late
with his call.' Humbleby raised his glass to the light and contemplated
its contents with solemn gloom. 'It's been an exasperating business,
and the sooner it's done with, the better I shall be pleased. I don't
like Wessex, either. I don't like any bucolic place.'

'Well, but what is the problem?'

'An alibi. We know who *did* the killing—we're morally certain, that
is—but the wretched fellow has an alibi and I can't for the life of me
see the flaw in it.'

A little superciliously, Fen sniffed. His long, lean form was sprawled
gracelessly in the office's only tolerable chair, his ruddy clean-shaven
face wore an expression of credulity, and his brown hair, ineffectually
plastered down with water, stood up, as usual, in mutinous spikes at
the crown of his head.

'Perhaps there isn't a flaw in it,' he suggested. 'It wouldn't be the first time a moral certainty had been turned out to be a total delusion. What sort of a moral certainty is it, anyway?'

'It's a question,' said Humbleby, 'of fingerprints. A certain man's fingerprints were found on the weapon with which the murder was committed. The prints were slightly blurred, I'll grant you; someone wearing gloves *could* have used the gun subsequently, and left the prints intact. But then, this man's explanation of how they came to be there is a demonstrable lie—and what's more he has a strong motive for the crime. So you see how it is.'

'I'm not sure that I do,' said Fen. 'Not so far. But since we've got to wait for our dinner, we may as well pass the time usefully: tell me about it.'

Humbleby sighed, glancing first at his wrist-watch and then at the telephone which stood mute by his elbow. Then, abruptly reaching a decision, he got up, pulled the curtains to across the windows, dispensed more sherry, and finally settled himself back into the desk chair with the air of one who is now prepared to stand a long siege. 'Cassibury Bardwell,' he began suddenly, 'is the scene. I don't know if you've ever been there?' Fen shook his head.

'Well, it's a hybrid sort of place, too big to be a village and too small to be a town. The houses are almost all built of a damp-looking grey stone, and the rainwater pours down the surrounding hillslopes into the main streets from all points of the compass, all year round. The nearest railway station is miles away, and the people are in every sense inbred. They're chiefly occupied with—well, *farming*, I suppose,' said Humbleby dubiously. 'But it's not, in any event, a very prosperous locality. In the countryside, round about, there are, apart from the farms, a few remote, inaccessible, horrid little cottages, and in one of these, tended only by a sister of advancing years, lived the protagonist of my tale.'

'More matter,' said Fen, somewhat restively, 'with less art.'

'Unconscious of his doom'—Humbleby had at last found a cheroot, and was applying fire to it from a desk lighter—'unconscious of his doom, the little victim, aged about 30 and by name of Joshua Ledlow, which goes to show the potency of the tradition of biblical nomenclature in these less accessible rural places—the little victim ... What was I saying?'

'Really, Humbleby ...

'Here is this Joshua, then.' All at once Humbleby abandoned frivolity and became businesslike. 'Thirty years old, unmarried, of a rather sombre and savage temperament, socially a cut above the farm labourer, and living modestly on money left him by a farmer father. He is looked after by his sister Cicely, a good ten years older than he is, who shows no particular fondness for him and who would in any case prefer to be looking after a husband, but who remains unwooed and, having no fortune of her own, housekeeps for Joshua as a respectable substitute for earning a living. Joshua, meanwhile, is courting, the object of his fancy being a heavily built girl called Vashti Winterbourne, who appears to have cast herself for the role of Cassibury Bardwell's *femme fatale*. She didn't seem to me, when I met her, to be physically very well suited for this task, but the local standard of female beauty is extraordinarily low, so I suppose ... Well, anyway, you see what I mean.

'Now, as you'd expect, Joshua isn't alone in his admiration for this rustic charmer. He has a rival, by name Arthur Penge, by vocation the local ironmonger; and it is clear that Vashti will soon have to make up her mind which of these two suitors she is going to marry. In the meantime, relations between the two men degenerate into something like open hostility, the situation being complicated by the fact that Joshua's sister Cicely has fallen in love with Penge, thereby converting the original triangle into a sort of–um–quadrangle. So there you have all the ingredients for a thoroughly explosive mixture–and in due course it does, in fact, explode.

'With that much preliminary,' continued Humbleby rather grandly, 'I can go on to describe what happened last Saturday and Sunday. What happened on *Saturday* was a public quarrel, of epic proportions, between Joshua, Cicely, and Penge. This enormous row took place in the entrance-hall of The Jolly Ploughboy, which is by just a fraction the less repellent of Cassibury's two pubs, and consisted of (a) Penge telling Joshua to lay off Vashti, (b) Cicely telling Penge to lay off Vashti and take her, Cicely, to wife instead, (c) Penge telling Cicely that no man not demonstrably insane would ever dream of marrying *her,* and (d) Joshua telling Penge that if he didn't keep away from Vashti in the future, he, Joshua, would have much pleasure in slitting his, Penge's, throat for him. Various other issues were raised, apparently, of a supplementary kind, but these were the chief items; and when the quarrellers at last separated and went home, they were all, not unnaturally, in a far from forgiving frame of mind.

'Note, please, that this quarrel was quite certainly genuine. I mention the point because Bolsover and I wasted a good deal of energy investigating the possibility that Penge and Cicely were somehow in cahoots together—that the quarrel so far as they were concerned was a fake. However, the witnesses we questioned weren't having any of that; they told us roundly that if Cicely was acting, they were Hottentots, and we were forced to believe them, the more so as one of them was the local doctor, who had to be called in to deal with Cicely's subsequent fit of hysterics. No chance of collusion in that department, then. Mind you, I'm not saying that if Penge had visited Cicely afterwards, and abased himself and asked her to marry him, she mightn't have forgiven him; she's not, poor soul, of an age at which you can afford to take too much umbrage at the past behaviour of a repentant suitor. But the established fact is that between the quarrel and the murder next day, he definitely didn't visit her or communicate with her in any way. With the exception of a single interlude of one hour (and of the half hour during which he must have been committing the crime), his movements are completely accounted for from the moment of the quarrel up to midnight on the Sunday; and *during* that one hour, when he *might* (for all we know) have gone to make his apologies to the woman, she was occupied with entertaining two visitors who can swear that he never came near her.'

'I take it,' Fen interposed, 'that this hypothesis of Cicely and Penge working together would have solved your alibi problem for you.'

'It would have, certainly, if there'd been evidence for it. But in actual fact, the evidence completely excludes it—and you must just accept that, I'm afraid.... But now let me get on with the story. The next event of any consequence was on Sunday morning, when Cicely broke her ankle by falling out of a tree.'

'A *tree?*'

'An apple tree. She'd been picking the fruit, it seems. Anyway, the effect of this accident was of course to immobilise her and hence, in the event, to free her from any possible suspicion of having herself murdered her brother Joshua, since his body was found some considerable distance from their cottage.'

'You think the killing was done at the place where the body was found, do you?'

'We're certain of it. The bullet went clean through the wretched man's head and buried itself in a tree trunk behind him—and that's a set-up which you can't fake convincingly, however hard you try; it's no use just firing a second bullet into the tree, because it's got to have traces of human blood and brains on it.... Cicely, then, is in the clear, unless you feel inclined to postulate her hobbling a couple of miles on crutches with a view to doing her brother in.

'The crime was discovered at about 10 o'clock that evening by several people in a party, one of whom fell over Joshua's corpse in the dark: none of these people features in any other way in the affair, so I needn't specify them at all. The *place* was a little-frequented footpath on the direct route between Joshua's cottage and the centre of Cassibury, approximately two miles from the former and one mile from the latter. And I may as well say at once, to avoid describing the scene in detail, that all the obvious lines of investigation—footprints, position of the body, threads of clothing on brambles, and so forth—led absolutely nowhere. However, there was just one substantial clue: I mean the revolver—a great cannon of a thing, an old .45—which Bolsover found shoved into the hedge a little distance away, with a set of prints on it.

'Now, we haven't, I'm afraid, so far discovered anything about this gun—its ownership and history and all the rest of it. It may belong to the Prime Minister or to the Archbishop of Canterbury, for all we know. But in view of the fingerprints we could afford to defer the problem of the gun's origin for a few days anyway; our immediate plan of action was, of course, to uncover possible motives for Joshua's death, get by guile the fingerprints of anyone suspicious, and compare them with the prints on the gun—and that led us straightaway to Penge, because it was impossible to be in Cassibury five minutes without hearing about the Penge-Vashti-Joshua triangle in all its sumptuous detail. Penge, then, had the motive of jealousy—Vashti isn't the sort of girl I personally would do murder for, but then, I've known a *crime passionel* be committed for possession of a penniless old lady of 68, and statistics show sex to be the motive for quite half the murders committed in this country, so that in that particular department I try not to be surprised at anything—Penge had this motive, then. And a comparison of his fingerprints with those on the revolver showed the two sets to be same.

'When eventually he was asked to explain this circumstance he told, as I've mentioned, a demonstrable lie: saying that he'd handled the gun three days previously when Joshua (of all people!) had brought it into his ironmonger's shop to ask if a crack in the butt could be repaired. On its being pointed out to him that Joshua had quite certainly been in Dorchester during the whole of the day mentioned, and so couldn't have visited the Cassibury ironmonger's, he wavered and started contradicting himself and eventually shut up altogether; in which oyster-like condition he's been ever since—and very wise of him, too.

'However, I'm anticipating: we didn't ask him about the gun until after we'd gone into the problem of the time of Joshua's death. There was delay in getting a doctor to look at the body, so that the medical verdict was too vague to be helpful—between 6 and 10 was the best reckoning we could get. But then two women came forward to tell us they'd seen Joshua alive at 7. They said that on hearing of Cicely's accident they'd visited the cottage to console with her, and had glimpsed Joshua on arrival; though he'd disappeared almost at once (having met the two ladies, I can see why) and they hadn't set eyes on him again. So clearly the next thing to do was to talk to Cicely herself. By early Monday morning—the morning after the murder—Bolsover had taken over, and the local Sergeant, an intelligent lad, had the sense to warn him before he set off for Cicely's cottage that she was a hysterical type who'd have to be handled carefully if her evidence was to be of any use—a diagnosis which the event confirmed. However, it turned out that by a great stroke of luck she hadn't heard of the murder yet; the reasons for this being (a) the fact that Joshua had planned to be away from home that night in any case, so that his absence had not alarmed her, and (b) the fact that the local Sergeant, a temperamentally secretive person, had sworn everyone who knew of the murder to silence until a higher authority should release them from the vow. Consequently, Bolsover was able to put his most important questions to Cicely *before* telling her his reason for asking them—and a good thing, too, because she had a fit of the horrors as soon as she heard her brother was dead, and the doctor refused to allow her to talk to anyone since. Anyway, her testimony was that Joshua, having seen her settled for the night, had left the cottage at about 8.15 on the Sunday evening (a quarter of an hour or so after her own visitors had gone), with a view to walking into Cassibury and catching a bus to Dorchester, where he was to stay with friends. And that, of course, meant that he could hardly have reached the spot where he was killed much earlier than a quarter to 9.

'So the next thing, naturally enough, was to find out where Penge had been all evening. And what it amounted to was that there were two periods of his time not vouched for by independent witnesses—the period from 7 to 8 (which didn't concern us) and the period from 8.30 to 9. Well, the latter, of course, fitted beautifully; and when we heard that he'd actually been *seen,* at about a quarter to 9, close to the place where the murder was committed, we started getting the warrant.

'And that, my dear Gervase, was the point at which the entire case fell to pieces.

'Penge had lied about his whereabouts between 8.30 and 9: we knew that. What we didn't know was that from 20 past 8 to 10 past 9, two couples were making love no more than a few feet away from the place of the murder; and that not one of those four people, during the time they were there, heard a shot.

'It's no use talking about silencers, either; even a silenced report would have been heard, on a quiet night. And so that, as they say, was that. Penge certainly shot Joshua. But he didn't do it between 8.30 and 9. And unless Cicely was lying in order to help him—which is inconceivable; and in any case, Bolsover's ready to swear on the Book that her brother's death was an unspeakable shock to her—unless that, then he didn't do it between 7 and 8, either.'

Humbleby stubbed out his cheroot and leaned forward earnestly. 'But he worked it out somehow, Gervase. His lies alone would make me certain that he's guilty. And the thought that he's invented some ingenious trick or other, which I can't for the life of me see, makes me writhe.'

There was a long silence when he had finished speaking. Presently Fen cleared his throat and said diffidently:

'There are lots of things one wants to ask, of course. But on the evidence you've given me so far, the trick looks fairly simple.

'If Penge's alibi is watertight,' Fen went on, 'then it's watertight. But just the same, it's easy to see how he killed Joshua.'

'Indeed,' Humbleby spoke with considerable restraint.

'Yes. It's all in the way you look at it. You've been looking at it upside down, you see. The situation, as I understand it, *must* be that it isn't Penge who has the alibi. It's the corpse.'

'The *corpse?*' Humbleby echoed.

'Why not? If Cicely was lying about the time Joshua left the cottage—if, in fact, he left much earlier—then Penge could have killed him between 7 and 8.'

'But I've already explained—'

'That it's inconceivable she'd lie on Penge's behalf. I quite agree. But mightn't she lie on her brother's? Suppose that Joshua, with a revolver in his pocket, is setting out to commit a crime. And suppose he tells

Cicely, if any questions are asked, to swear he left her much earlier than he did. And suppose that a policeman questions Cicely on this point *before* she learns that it's her brother, and not the man he set out to kill, who is dead. Wouldn't that account for it?'

'You mean—'

'I mean that Joshua intended to murder Penge, his rival for the young woman's affections; that he arranged for his sister (whom Penge had just humiliated publicly) to give him, if necessary, a simple alibi.'

'Well, one can't be sure, of course. But it looks as if Joshua's plan misfired—as if Penge struggled with Joshua, got hold of the gun, and killed his assailant in self-defence. Behold Penge, then, with a water-tight alibi created—charming irony—by his enemy! If the lovers hadn't been hanging about, he would have spoiled that alibi by going back afterwards—and one wonders why he *did* go—'

'Morbid attraction,' Humbleby interposed. 'I've seen it happen time and again.... But good God, Gervase, what a fool! It *is* the only explanation! The one trouble about it is that there's no *proof.*'

'I should think there will be,' said Fen, 'as soon as Cicely ceases to be incommunicado and learns what's happened. If what you say about her dislike of Penge is true, she won't persist in the lie which exonerates him from killing her brother.' All at once Fen was pensive. 'Though come to think of it, if I were *Penge*—'

Shatteringly, the telephone rang, and Humbleby snatched it from its cradle. 'Yes,' he said. 'Yes, put him on ... Bolsover?' A long pause. 'Oh, you've seen that, have you? So have I—though only just ... Allowed to talk to people again, yes, so you—WHAT?' And with this squeak of mingled rage and astonishment Humbleby fell abruptly silent, listening while the telephone crackled despairingly at his ear. When at last he rang off, his face was gloomy.

'Bolsover thought of it, too,' he said sombrely. 'But not soon enough. By the time he got to Cicely's bedside, Penge had been there for hours.... They're going to get married: Cicely and Penge, I mean. She's forgiven him about the quarrel—I told you she doted on him, didn't I? Bolsover says he's never seen a more obsequious, considerate, dutiful, loving bridegroom-to-be. And, of course, she's sticking to her story about the time Joshua left the house. Very definite about it, Bolsover says.'

Fen got to his feet. 'Well, well,' he said, 'you'll never put him in the dock now. And yet I suppose that if he had the courage to tell the truth he'd probably get away with it.'

'All I can say is'–Humbleby, too, had risen–'that I hope it really was self-defence. In the interests of justice–'

'Justice?' Fen reached for his hat. 'I shouldn't worry too much about that, if I were you. Here's a wife who knows her husband killed her brother. And here's a husband who knows his wife can by saying a word deprive him of his liberty and just possibly–if things didn't go well–of his life. And each knows that the other knows. And the wife is in love with the husband, but one day she won't be any longer, and then he'll begin to be afraid. And the wife thinks her husband is in love with her, but one day she'll find out he isn't, and then she'll begin to hate him and to wonder what she can do to harm him, and he will know this, and she will know that he knows it and will be afraid of what he may do....

'Justice? My dear Humbleby, come and have some dinner. Justice has already been done.'

A Couple of Acres and a Few Wee Beasts

MICHAEL JAHN

Captain Bill Donovan of the New York Police Department sat in the village pub and stared at the bottle of Kaliber nonalcoholic beer with bitter irony but slight regret. "My first visit ever to the land of my forebears would come at a time when I've been on the wagon seven years," he complained to Jimmy the proprietor, a jovial man of seventy whom he had just befriended. "All my adult life I've dreamed of sitting an afternoon in an Irish pub downing Guinness and smelling the scent of new-mown hay coming in the window." As he neared the end of his first full day in Ireland, Donovan found his voice lilting and the sentences turning up toward the ends, Irish style. "Not only can't I have a real drink, I'm developing this fraudulent brogue," he said.

"In my opinion you have a fine American accent," the proprietor said.

Donovan nodded. "Last month, for the first time in years, I spoke on the phone to my cousin from these parts. I asked him if he had a big farm. He said ..." Donovan switched voices to an impression of his Irish cousin's nearly impenetrable brogue. "He said, 'Jissa coopla ackers enna few wee basts.'"

The Irish bartender laughed, less at Donovan's attempted brogue than at his cousin's fake modesty. "'Just a couple of acres and a few wee beasts.' Is that how your cousin described his farm?"

"What are 'wee beasts'?"

"Small cows. But your cousin has one of the largest properties in the county."

"It impressed me," Donovan said, gazing out the window not at new-mown hay—it was the wrong time of year—but at an old tractor rusting atop a rolling hill, alongside a stone fence. "My cousin's kingdom for a pint of real Guinness," he said wistfully.

"As for drinking a nonalcoholic brew, let me tell you a story of that tractor you've been admiring and the time ten years ago when Timmy Carey, one of your cousin's hands then, was in his cups from an afternoon spent raking hay and drinking whiskey. He got off that very same vehicle to relieve himself in the bushes and the machine ran over him and mangled his foot, making it drag behind him very much like the hay rake that did the damage. He's been on the dole since ... and warring with your cousin, whom he blames for the accident. That machine has never been fixed—either before the accident or since. The moral is that no one in his right mind drinks to excess anymore."

"My God, the health craze has reached even these shores. Well, so much for Ireland as revealed in The Quiet Man."

"That motion picture is, shall we say, an anachronism."

"So am I," said Donovan. "Now tell me that I can sit here all day and no one will come in and sing 'A Wild Colonial Boy,' accompanying himself on the accordion."

"No one shall," Jimmy said. "But I put several new CDs in the jukebox this morning if you're inclined to hear the new Michael Jackson."

"I'm not," Donovan said with a friendly, resigned sort of scowl. Out in the street, a modern two-lane road in reasonably good repair, two black Mercedes sedans and a maroon Honda Accord cruised by. They were followed a moment later by a BMW and two Lexus LXIs. "And there's no vicar on a bicycle either, is there?" Donovan said.

"He drives a Celica," said the proprietor, adding, "I see that the politicians have begun to arrive for the funeral Mass."

"I had better go," Donovan said, finishing his bottle and laying some money on the bar.

"Your great-aunt lived a good, long, and happy life and is in God's arms now," said Jimmy. It was the most Irish-sounding thing Donovan had heard all day, and he mellowed. Jimmy then said, "When you get to the church, give my regards to Himself."

That would be Donovan's cousin, John Finney, the politician. A member of the Dial, which is the Irish parliament, and a deputy minister, Finney was the ruling Fine Gael party's expert on international finance. As such, he had come to represent Ireland in the European Community. No doubt he had gotten a bit of a swelled head about it, Donovan thought. The appellation "Himself" was an Irish put-down used on someone with too big an ego.

Finney's mother was Donovan's great aunt, the Irish generation that came to America typically marrying much younger than their siblings who stayed at home. When the grand old lady died, her passing was mourned by every member of the cabinet—including the prime minister, who warranted the Mercedes and a security detail. Donovan didn't come to Ireland just for the funeral, though it was the deciding factor. As chief of Special Investigations for the City of New York, he had handled enough major cases in the previous year to have earned a few weeks off. He came because he had been meaning to for years, and also because Cousin John promised to help him get joint citizenship—Americans with grandparents born in Ireland are so entitled—and the EC passport that came with it. Donovan thought that, someday, he might like to work in Europe.

He had done a minor bit of detective work the day before. Waking early at the Mead & Flynn Bed & Breakfast (rooms at his cousin's house had gone to politicians), he followed the morning repast with a stroll across a meadow and into the old village burial ground, seeking the plot where, later the following day, his great-aunt would be laid to rest. He found that newly turned soil quickly enough, but then his eyes were drawn to the ruins of an abbey that sat in the middle of the cemetery. When first he stepped into the burial ground, Donovan had noted an old sign warning of "uneven ground." The land about his great-aunt's grave was firm enough, so perhaps the sign referred to the abbey.

Donovan walked to it and read an ancient sign. It read: THIRD ABBEY OF KYRIE ELEISON. BUILT IN THE YEAR OF OUR LORD 1047, BEFORE THE NORMAN CONQUEST. DESTROYED IN THE YEAR 1152. BELIEVED BUILT UPON A CELTIC SITE DATING TO THE NEW STONE AGE. PART OF THE PROPERTY OF THE FINNEY FAMILY SINCE THE 17TH CENTURY.

The walls were of roughly hewn stone mixed with found bits of slate and held together with ancient mortar. They rose thirty feet in places, all blue and brown (depending upon the angle of the sun) with algae and moss. A Roman arch still stood above the entrance. But the ceiling of the abbey had long since fallen down and the dirt floor inside had been turned to good use as an extension of the burial ground. Half a dozen plots filled it, all of them holding remains of Finneys, the earliest being a Hannah Finney buried in 1816. Donovan didn't recognize any of the surnames, but felt a twinge of closeness nonetheless. They were all ancestors, no matter if he couldn't identify them.

Against the north wall, a tree grew from what appeared to be a pile of rubble. Donovan walked to it, passing along a path that was overgrown with wild grass mixed with large patches of undisturbed thyme that led through the gravestones and crunched beneath his feet, emitting a fine perfume that clung to his shoes and pants cuffs. Cobwebs tickled his face. He recognized them as having been strung up overnight between convenient vertical objects, headstones in this case. He had the feeling he was the first in years to disturb their delicate grace. Upon reaching the wall, he realized that what he thought was a pile of rubble was actually an ancient mausoleum that had collapsed in on itself. The three-foot-high roof was largely caved in, and the walls had also fallen in on two ends. As a result, Donovan was able to bend low and peer inside. A skull had rolled out of a coffin the wooden walls of which had long ago disintegrated. It lay in the mold-covered dirt alongside the spreading roots of a medium-sized tree. A black trash can liner and a blue-and-yellow sandwich bag lay near both, blown into the burial chamber by the winds that swept across the meadow from the river.

"The poor bastard must have been buried with an acorn in his pocket," Donovan recalled thinking at the time.

After he recounted the previous day's experience to the bartender, the man shook his head. "When I was a lad, my grandfather told me that we ought to do something about the condition of that poor man's grave. Every few years we agree to make things right, but it never gets done. Perhaps next year."

Donovan's cousin looked nothing like him. The captain was tall and well-built, in good health and reasonably fit due to seven years of sobriety as well as to healthy habits and daily workouts. Now into his early fifties, Donovan retained most of his hair, though it was turning white at the temples. He had about him the air of a man who had examined his life and pronounced it successful. He was comfortable with himself. In contrast, John Finney was short and a bit heavy, with a round red face made all the more pronounced by the loss of most of his hair. While a few years younger than his American cousin, he looked quite a bit older. This difference was, in a way, offset by his habit of driving about the countryside in a red Alfa Romeo roadster while wearing outlandish hats collected during trips made abroad on behalf of the EC. One week he sported a black French beret; another a red Moroccan fez from which swung a golden tassel. The effect was that of a man a bit uncomfortable with himself but perfectly able to compensate through the forces of his outgoing, if somewhat nervous, personality.

Still, he had become an important man in Irish politics, as evidenced by the official presence at his mother's funeral Mass and wake. Donovan approached the former with a certain apprehension, having run away from the Catholic religion years before and now calling himself an atheist. Yet the old-fashioned Latin Mass was lulling, and he left it with vaguely nostalgic feelings for a lost childhood during which it had been possible to believe in heavenly spirits and the redemptive power of ritual.

If the Mass left him with mixed feelings, the wake included moments that thrilled Donovan. It embodied everything he enjoyed: good food, the company of family, the reminiscence about a well-lived life, and the chance to learn something new—in this case, how to hold up his end of numerous conversations on the subject of European Community politics. His official position in New York City life—which his cousin had, of course, inflated tremendously—put Donovan in the position of defending American policy. That was fun for an iconoclast, and by day's end, when the cabinet members and their entourages had left leaving only a few local Garda officials eager to chat with their American counterpart, Donovan was tired but completely happy with his first two days in his ancestral homeland.

"If only Mr. Murphy hadn't chosen to disappear," Cousin John said, with a roll of the eyes that told Donovan that trouble accompanied the person named. Thomas Xavier Murphy was nominally Finney's boss, the holder of an important cabinet seat that Cousin John was said to covet. Murphy was a political risk-taker, perpetually on the outs with the prime minister but too well connected to fire. It was common knowledge that, should Murphy retire or drop dead of a heart attack, Finney would succeed him. And from that position Donovan's cousin would be a short step away from the prime ministership itself.

Murphy was among the cabinet ministers who came to the village for the funeral. Like the others, he stayed overnight at Finney's home. But unlike the others, he seemed uncomfortable, shunned most conversations, and retired early and alone. By sunrise he had disappeared—clambered back into his BMW and driven off, apparently unseen. Too bad, Donovan thought; it was Murphy he was counting on for help with his dual citizenship.

"He didn't say where he was going?" Donovan asked.

"Mr. Murphy was not in the habit of telling me his travel plans," Finney said, opening a bottle of Guinness and bringing it close enough to Donovan's nose to set off sensations of nostalgia, longing, and irony. "Perhaps he has again taken up with Flanagan's daughter—despite my best efforts."

At that suggestion, Peter Malone, the local equivalent of a homicide investigator, opened his eyes wide.

"I sense a scandal," Donovan said.

"A very old one," replied Malone. "The esteemed Minister Murphy once had an affair with Mary Kate Flanagan, then the twenty-year-old daughter of our local pub owner."

"By the name of Jimmy? I met the man."

"The same."

"He said to give you his regards," Donovan said to his cousin, who shrugged. "I don't think he likes you much, though."

"Nobody here likes John," said the Irish policeman, with a mischievous smile. "He's too rich, and the Irish are a very envious and suspicious race when it comes to persons of wealth. Such is the continued legacy of the British occupation."

"I am not wealthy," Finney said.

"I've seen your beasts," Donovan said. "They're not as wee as you made them out to be. And I like that old abbey you own in the burial ground."

"I own the burial ground too, but the rents I am allowed to charge are relatively modest." He sat back down in an old but expensive armchair and sipped his stout.

"To finish the thought, I like your cousin but only because his speeding tickets pay my salary."

"You're quite welcome, Peter," Finney said. He took off the fairly ridiculous kepi that had adorned his pate for the better part of the evening and put it on an end table alongside his collection of meerschaums. He sputtered, "What the devil happened to my beret?" He addressed the question to no one in particular, or to such spirits as may have inhabited the old, comfortably furnished room. "I left it on the table two days ago and it disappeared."

"Better you should lose that stew pot you were wearing all evening," Malone said.

"At the risk of sounding American, so what if Murphy once slept with Mary Kate Flanagan?" Donovan asked.

Finney offered an uneasy laugh. "He was married to someone else at the time, a fact he kept from her. And she became pregnant, forcing her to go to Britain for an abortion. She was a delicate girl who never recovered after Murphy went back to his missus's bedside."

Malone added, "Her father threatened to kill him. That put the fear of God into the man...."

"No, what did that was the possibility of his wife and the press finding out. Mr. Murphy paid off Jimmy Flanagan."

"Bought him that pub. Before that he worked your cousin's land, as did many local people."

"Milked the wee beasts, did he?" Donovan said.

"I have tried, throughout my life, to help the less fortunate when I can," Finney said grandly, picking up a meerschaum and toying with it. "The fact that a few of the locals resent my ability to do so is beyond my control. Anyway, Mr. Murphy was a guest at this very house when the unfortunate assignation took place."

"Plots just get thicker and thicker around here, don't they?" Donovan said.

"As a result of which, I offered to employ the poor girl—despite the sad fact her mother makes Lady Macbeth seem like Mother Teresa. Mary Kate has been my housekeeper ever since. Maybe she knows what happened to my hat—although I sent her home to her parents temporarily so as not to cross paths with her old paramour. I hired a commercial service to take messages and run errands and the like for my guests. But she's back now, and thank God too. Mary!"

"New York City politics pale in comparison," Donovan added.

Finney pushed his well-fed frame out of the chair with a grunt, walked to the door, and again called the name. Mary Kate Flanagan presently appeared, bringing a hint of perfume to the otherwise manly and smoky study. She looked pale but hardly as delicate as she had been described. Donovan supposed that his cousin meant emotionally delicate. She didn't look that either, but you could never tell.

"Have you seen my beret, Mary?"

"I haven't," she said quickly, then hurried off to answer the telephone, which was ringing off the hook down the hall.

"I had it all worked out so that Mr. Murphy would have gone home after the wake and she would not have come to work until sundown. So the minister leaves before dawn, even, missing the Mass and the wake and his beloved Mary Kate."

Donovan liked the sound of that. It had the lilt and bounce of an Irish song. He hummed to himself, "Missing the Mass/and the wake/and his beloved Mary Kate." However, before he could imagine Tommy Makem singing those words, the woman mentioned in them returned to call Peter Malone to the telephone.

"And my beret is gone too," Finney said, finally stuffing some Sir Walter Raleigh tobacco in the meerschaum and lighting it.

Malone had a few terse words, out in the hall, that Donovan couldn't make out. Then he returned to announce, solemnly, "Mr. Murphy's car was just pulled out of the Langdon Pond." Finney burned his fingers and Mary Kate fainted dead away.

It was the old tractor that Donovan had admired that served to pull Murphy's BMW from the murky, peat-brown water of Langdon Pond. That modest body of water—little more than a good watering spot for the cows—lay at the far end of Finney's property, adjacent to the burial ground. Dawn broke anew over the rolling green fields, dotted here and there with groves of trees and laced with stone fences, just beyond one of which stood the old abbey.

Donovan watched as water gushed from the open door on the passenger's side. Malone supervised two uniformed policemen who, in turn, watched over three local men as they hauled out the car, then loosened the chain that hooked it to the tractor. Finney sat on a folding chair, looking as a man does when he sees disaster spread its wings over his life. The others assembled were Jimmy Flanagan and his daughter (who wore black). Nearby hovered nearly everyone else in the village.

"There's no one in the car," a policeman announced, and Malone leaned forward to see for himself.

"Start dragging the pond," he said.

Donovan asked Malone, "Do you mind?"

"I'd welcome your help, Captain." Malone stepped aside and let Donovan inspect the muddy sedan. After a brief look, he scanned the pond, walking carefully around the edge of it, then returned to the car. A policeman had begun throwing a grappling hook into the water and drawing it back in. The Flanagans had sat down on the grass.

"Any thoughts?" Malone asked.

Donovan shrugged. "I'll be back in a few minutes," he said, and headed across the field in the direction of the burial ground and the old abbey. He found the ancient ruins almost exactly the same as when he left them. The cobwebs had been restrung, but the path he trod two days before now showed evidence of something having been dragged through it. Carefully skirting the path so as not to disturb any new footprints that might be revealed by the forensics technology that would inevitably arrive from Dublin, Donovan made his way to the tumbledown mausoleum.

He bent over and peered inside, the better to see the interior of the open-air tomb. As he half expected, Donovan saw staring at him the ashen and very dead face of Thomas Xavier Murphy. He lay atop the old body of an ancestor of the Finneys and Donovans, his fingers giving the illusion they were grasping at the roots of the interloping tree as if to clutch back life. Beneath the other hand lay what looked, at first, like a bit of the black plastic garbage bag Donovan noticed the day before. But on closer examination Donovan found that Murphy's other hand was resting upon Cousin John's black beret. Using the tip of a pen, Donovan plucked it out.

Below legs twisted from having been shoved last into the tomb, Murphy's hand-stitched, meticulously polished black wingtips had acquired a patina of dirt. From the look of the corpse, the man had been strangled. The exact details of the body and the scene about it were nice to know and would clinch the conviction. What mattered now was the identity of the murderer. Finding the beret beneath the body appeared to make things look bad for his cousin. Or did it? Donovan examined the beret for a long time and sniffed it intensely. He stared at the corpse and the ground around the tomb for an even longer time before taking the news of his find back to those assembled by Langdon Pond.

An hour later, when things had settled down and those villagers not directly involved in the investigation had been sent home—most of them reassembled at the burial ground, however—Malone seated the suspects on folding chairs that Finney had brought from his house. Arrayed in a semicircle with the pond as backdrop, they struck Donovan as resembling altar boys dreadedly awaiting the moment to approach their Maker.

Cousin John was a wreck, his face redder than a tomato in August. His head was conspicuously bare. The subject of fancy foreign hats had recently lost all its luster. He puffed furiously at an especially old meerschaum, sending bursts of white smoke into the warming air. He pretended not to notice the two policemen who had been stationed behind his chair ever since Donovan returned with the beret.

Jimmy Flanagan sat with arms crossed. His face was a mask of stoic defiance. Donovan saw a man ready to go to the firing squad to protect his daughter, who sobbed quietly into a handkerchief that her mother had hurriedly brought forth before retreating to the sidelines to glower.

Malone cleared his throat and announced, "Mr. Murphy's watch stopped just past six yesterday morning, as did the dashboard clock in his automobile. I'll need to know where you were then. Mr. Finney?"

"In bed, of course."

"Witnesses?"

"I'm not married and you know it. I have a housekeeper–Mary Kate here–but I let her off that night, so she can't tell you where I was. I had guests in the house, but all were asleep in their beds. And rightly so. I fed them well the night before."

"And of course I'll take an explanation of how your beret got beneath the dead man."

"I have none. I say only that I didn't kill the man. Find whoever took my beret and you find your killer."

With that, Mary Kate let out a wail that prompted her mother to rush up once again and speak quietly to her.

Malone sidled closer to Donovan and said quietly, "He has no alibi, his hat was found with the corpse, and he stands to gain politically from Murphy's death."

"If Ireland is anything like America, he can't get too much political capital out of being suspected of murder," Donovan said.

"You're his cousin and hardly an unbiased witness."

"I found the beret, didn't I?" Donovan said, displaying it, still at the end of his pen.

Turning to the woman, Malone said, "And you, Mary Kate. Where were you at six yesterday morning?"

"At my father's house," she said between sobs, dabbing at her eyes with a corner of the handkerchief.

"In bed as well?"

"Not at so late an hour. I was helping my mother make breakfast."

"And she'll swear to that?"

"She will and I will too," said Jimmy Flanagan, unfolding his arms and folding them again.

"No doubt," Malone stage-whispered to Donovan. "The members of this family alibi one another. But they all have a motive—revenge for what Murphy did to the daughter."

"Can a grudge of this kind really turn homicidal fifteen years later?"

"I assure you it can. If you take your Catholicism seriously, as many do around here, Murphy endangered her immortal soul. Condemned her to hell, he did."

It was Donovan's turn to fidget. The moment soon passed.

Malone returned his attention to Finney, saying, "On the matter of your fancy foreign hat: How do you suppose it got under Murphy's corpse?"

"I have no idea. I left it on the table by my pipes."

"You have no one who can say you were home at the time of the murder. Your hat was found beneath the victim. Furthermore, you stand to gain high office by his demise. John Finney, I have no choice but to order you held."

The two uniformed policemen moved forward, toward their man, but before they could approach Donovan's cousin, Mary Kate Flanagan's demeanor changed like the spring weather. "John didn't kill anyone!" she shouted, quite as far from being delicate—emotionally or otherwise—as one could imagine.

Finney twisted toward her. "Be still, Mary Kate," he snapped.

"I will not! You're a good and decent man and I won't have you unfairly charged!"

Her father also warned her to silence, to little avail. She said, "I won't let John be convicted of a murder he didn't commit."

She caught her breath, as if summoning up the courage to go further and say what she wanted. But Donovan beat her to it. He said, "You took John's beret before he sent you home the night before last."

Everyone looked at the American detective.

"You may have begun as my cousin's housekeeper, but that's changed, hasn't it?"

Astonished, she nodded. She had stopped crying.

"You're in love with him. You couldn't bear to be away from him even one night, so you took his beret home with you. To remind you of him, you know? I would guess you slept with it on your pillow."

"I did just that," she said in amazement.

"How on earth could you know that?" Malone asked.

Donovan dangled the much-traveled chapeau beneath the Irish detective's nose. "It has her perfume on it," Donovan said. "White Shoulders, isn't it?"

"Yes."

"How do you know so much about perfume?" Malone asked.

"I have a well-documented fondness for women."

Malone turned back to Finney, asking, "Did you know anything about this?"

Sighing profoundly, Finney pushed himself out of his chair and walked to the woman. He picked up her hand and held it in both of his.

"We've been in love for several years. I've been waiting for the right moment to ask her father for permission to marry her."

"What's been keeping you?" Donovan asked.

"I'm only forty-five. A man can't rush into these things."

Malone said, "Mary Kate, you've gotten your man off the hook, but I'm afraid you've gotten yourself and your father onto it. The two of you have a motive—vengeance—for killing Murphy. The hat was last in your possession. Explain to me how it got under the corpse."

Donovan said, "My guess is that Jimmy here found out about the romance between his daughter and Himself"—Donovan nodded in the direction of his cousin—"when he found the beret in her room. Wanting to be rid of it before yet another scandal hit his family, he took the hat to the pub. His intention was to throw it out or else to keep it hidden until Mary Kate could slip it back onto John's pipe table."

Malone asked, "Is that correct?"

Flanagan nodded. "I put it on the rack with the other customers' hats. I figured, where better to hide a tree than in a forest?"

"Very wise, generally speaking," Malone said.

"And from there it disappeared. Just before closing time the night before last."

"The night of the murder."

"I assumed one of the other customers walked off with it," Flanagan concluded.

"And that is precisely what happened," said Donovan. Turning to Malone, he asked, "Would you do me a favor?"

"If I can."

"Would you send some men to round up one Timmy Carey?"

"Carey? The village drunk?"

"The same. I don't know what the man looks like. Was he among that crowd of onlookers before?"

"No, actually. I was surprised by his absence. He's a busybody. I'll have some men bring him around."

"Make sure they also bring every piece of footwear he owns," Donovan said.

Timmy Carey stared down at fingers that he clenched together, in a gesture resembling prayer, in order to keep them from shaking. A thin man the right side of whose torso bulged as the result of a diseased liver, he was, to Donovan, clearly incapable of getting through the day shake-free without a drink. Malone had, of course, made things harder on the man by seating him alone, on a folding chair, near the still-dripping BMW. The Flanagans and Finney stood in a knot behind the detectives. Finney and Mary Kate had begun holding hands.

Malone asked, "Where were you at six yesterday morning?"

"Sleeping one off." The man spoke the words nervously, then calmed himself by lighting an unfiltered cigarette.

"Was anyone with you?"

"Not in years."

To Donovan, Malone said softly, "This man is a loudmouth. Over the years he's spoken ill of everyone, from Yuri Gagarin through Bill Clinton. Jimmy Flanagan bars him from the pub at least once a week, but always relents and allows him back. I know that Carey blamed your cousin for his downslide, but do you really think it adds up to a motive for murder? A motive for killing Murphy to frame Finney?"

"A man who's drinking himself to death and taking decades to do it needs someone to blame it on. By killing Murphy and framing my cousin—and dragging the Flanagans into it as well—Carey could get revenge on all his enemies."

Donovan turned to Carey, asking, "Were you in the pub at closing time that day?"

"Who's this?" Carey asked Malone.

"A famous detective from New York, and you'd best answer him quickly."

"I was."

"And afterwards?"

"I went straight home."

Donovan said, "It was common knowledge that Murphy would be among the politicians staying at John Finney's house. You saw your opportunity when you spotted Finney's famous beret at the pub. When you got home carrying it, you concocted something to get Murphy to

where you could get at him, I would guess a phone call either threatening further blackmail or arranging a meeting with Mary Kate. I'm sure
the phone records will show a call from your house to Finney's. After
you killed the man, you did two things to make sure the police went
straight to Finney. You stuffed the corpse in the grave of one of his
ancestors, a grave well-known to be open to the air. And you stuck
the beret in there as well. You might as well have painted a sign."

"There's no proof for anything this American says," Carey said.

"I have a feeling that when you inspect Carey's shoes you will find
that the space between the sole and the toe of one of them—a right
shoe, certainly, for the man drags his right foot—contains bits of thyme."

"Thyme? The garden herb?" Malone asked.

"It grows wild in the old abbey. I got some on my own shoes the
day before the murder while walking around there. The scent is very
strong. Twenty-four hours later I could still smell it."

Carey sprang from his chair with surprising agility and tried to make
it across the meadow. But one of Malone's policemen tackled him and
took him, in handcuffs, to a police car.

When things had calmed down, Cousin John came up, with his
bride-to-be tucked firmly under his arm. She was beaming, with a bright
smile and a blush on her cheeks that Donovan would remember always.

"The next prime minister should have a wife," Donovan said.

"I'll expect you at the wedding. In the meantime, I'll work on your
papers for your dual citizenship. But tell me one thing: how come
Carey didn't just say, 'Well, there must be thyme growing all over
the place'?"

"He knows that isn't the case," Donovan said. "If you spent more
time on your farm and less in Dublin, you would know that you can't
have such strong herbs growing wild when there are milk cows
around."

Finney sighed, and said, "Of course. I had to have some ivy pulled
up for the same reason."

"It spoils the milk," Donovan said. "And you don't want that happening to the poor wee beasts."

The Dublin Eye

CLARK HOWARD

Kilkenny heard the phone ring as he was unlocking his office door. He hurried in to answer it.

"Kilkenny," he said.

"Is this Mr. Royal Kilkenny?" a hesitant female voice asked. The caller sounded very young. "Mr. Royal Kilkenny, the query man?"

"Yes. How can I help you?"

"Mr. Kilkenny, my name is Darlynn Devalain. I'm the daughter of Joe Devalain, of Belfast."

An image mushroomed in Kilkenny's mind. Not of Joe Devalain, but of the woman Joe had married. Of Sharmon. This girl on the phone was probably Sharmon's daughter.

"How is your dad, then?" Kilkenny asked. "And your mother?"

"My dad's not so good, Mr. Kilkenny," the girl replied, and Kilkenny, though he had never laid eyes on her, could almost see her lip quivering as her voice broke. "He's been in a bad accident. An explosion in his shop. They've got him over at St. Bartholomew's Hospital, but it's not known if he'll live or—"

"Did your mother tell you to call me?" Kilkenny asked, frowning. It had been eighteen years since Sharmon Cavan had picked Joe Devalain over him and he had gone off to America to try and forget her.

"No, she doesn't even know I'm after calling you," Darlynn Devalain said. "Me dad told me once that he knew you before you went to America. When he heard you'd come back and set up as a query man

573

down in Dublin, he told me you were a man he could always count on. He said if I should ever find myself in serious trouble of any kind to get hold of you and tell you I'm the daughter of Joe Devalain. You'd help me just as if I were your own. So that's why I'm calling, sor. Not for me, but for me dad. He needs somebody to look after his interests. The police, they don't seem to care much about who blew up his shop."

"How badly was he hurt in the explosion?" Kilkenny asked.

"As badly as one can be and still be called alive," the girl said. "Oh, Mr. Kilkenny, he's in terrible shape. Can you come, sor? Please."

The girl's voice reminded Kilkenny of Sharmon. Sharmon, with her deep-rust-colored hair and dancing emerald eyes, the smile that showed crooked teeth that somehow made her even prettier, the wide, wide shoulders, and the strong peasant thighs that even at sixteen could lock a man where she wanted him, for as long as she wanted him there.

"Yes, I'll come," Kilkenny said. "I'll take the train up and meet you at the hospital this evening."

Kilkenny bought a first-class seat on the *Enterprise Express,* which made the Dublin-Belfast run in two hours and twenty minutes. Dundalk, an hour north of Dublin, was the last stop in the Irish Free State. After Dundalk, the train crossed into Country Armagh, which was part of Northern Ireland.

At Portadown, the first stop in Armagh, British soldiers boarded the coaches and checked all passengers. From Portadown on into Belfast an armed British soldier rode at each end of every coach. Most passengers didn't leave their seats even to go to the lavatory during that leg of the journey.

At Belfast Central the passengers stood for a pat-down baggage search and questioning at a British Army checkpoint in the middle of the station.

"Identification, please," a pink-cheeked young lieutenant requested. Kilkenny handed over his billfold. "What's your business in Belfast, sir?"

"To see a friend who's in hospital."

"What's the duration of your stay, sir?"

"I don't know. No more than forty-eight hours, I shouldn't expect."

"Your occupation is listed as a 'personal enquiries representative.' What is that, exactly?"

"I'm a private investigator. A detective."

The young officer's expression brightened. "You mean like one of those American private eyes? Like that Magnum bloke?"

"Yes, sort of. Less hectic, though."

The lieutenant frowned. "Not armed, I hope."

"No." Kilkenny wondered why he asked. A sergeant had already patted Kilkenny down and two privates had rummaged through his overnighter.

"Pass through," the officer said, returning Kilkenny's billfold.

Outside the terminal Kilkenny got into a square black taxi. "St. Bartholomew's Hospital," he said.

The driver glanced at him in the rearview mirror, then looked out the side window at the darkening late-afternoon sky. "That's in the Flats," he said.

"The Flats?"

"Aye. Unity Flats. The Catholic section. I'll take you in, but I can't wait for you or come back to get you. I'm not Catholic, so I can't risk being in the Flats after dark."

"Just drop me at the hospital," Kilkenny said. "That'll be fine."

On the way through the city, it started to rain—one of those sudden, blustery rains that seemed to be forever blowing in off the North Channel and turning the already dreary gray streets a drearier black. Kilkenny hadn't thought to bring a raincoat—it had been so long since he'd been to Belfast he had forgotten how unpredictable the weather could be.

"Bit of a heavy dew out there," he said.

"Aye," the driver replied, turning on the wipers. He made no attempt at further conversation.

Kilkenny wasn't familiar with the section called Unity Flats. He, Joe Devalain, and Sharmon Cavan had grown up in a slum known as Ballymurphy. It was a savagely poor place, worse than anything Kilkenny had seen during his ten years as a New York City policeman. In New York he had worked both Spanish Harlem and the South Bronx, and neither of them was nearly as poor, ugly, or deprived as Ballymurphy. Ballymurphy wasn't the gutter, it was the sewer. Both Kilkenny and Joe Devalain had sworn to Sharmon that they would take her away from the life of poverty in which they had all grown to adolescence.

It had not been Kilkenny Sharmon picked to do it. "I've decided in favor of Joe," she told Kilkenny one night after they had made love under the back stairs of Sharmon's tenement building.

"I thought you loved *me*," Kilkenny had said.

"I love you both," Sharmon had answered. "Do y'think I'd do this with the two of you if I didn't love you both? It's just that I can't *have* you both, so I must choose, mustn't I? And I've chosen Joe."

"But why? Why him and not me?"

"Lots of reasons," she said lightly. "I like the name Sharmon Devalain better than I like Sharmon Kilkenny. And I think Joe will do better in life than you. He's got a good job at the linen plant–someday he'll probably be a foreman. While you've done nothing at all to better yourself."

"I go to school," Kilkenny protested. "I want to be a policeman, someday–"

"I don't like policemen," she said loftily. "They're a smug lot. Anyway, Joe'll earn lots more when he works his way up to plant foreman than you'll ever earn being a policeman."

Kilkenny had been sick with disappointment. "If it's just the money, maybe I could be something else–"

"It's not just that," she said.

"What else, then?"

"Well, y'see," she replied with a little reluctance, "Joe is–well, *better* at–well, you know–" She sighed impatiently. "He's a bit more of a man, if y'know what I mean."

Kilkenny had thought he would never get over that remark. It left him impotent for six months. Only after leaving Ireland, going to Southampton and boarding a ship for America, and meeting on board a fleshy Czech girl just beginning to feel her new freedom after escaping from behind the Iron Curtain, was he able to function physically as a man again. He had never had a problem since–but he had never forgotten Sharmon's words.

"Here you are," the driver said. "St. Bartholomew's."

Kilkenny collected his bag and got out. The driver made change for him, glanced up at the waning daylight again, and sped off.

From the front steps of the hospital Kilkenny looked around at what he could see of Unity Flats. It was a slum, as Ballymurphy had been, though not quite as stark and dirty. But definitely a ghetto. Sharmon hadn't made it very far with Joe, he thought.

In the hospital lobby, a young nun, wearing the habit of the Ulster Sisters of Charity, consulted a name file and directed Kilkenny to a ward on the third floor. He waited for the lift with several women visitors. The women in the north were not as attractive as the women down south, he noticed. Most of them wore white T-necks that clearly outlined their brassieres, wide-legged, baggy slacks or skirts that were too short, no stockings, and shoes with straps that made their ankles look thick. Their hair seemed to be combed and in control only down to their cheeks, then appeared to grow wild on its own, as if it was too much to take care of. They were poor women, clearly. As they grew older, Kilkenny knew, they would all become noble mother figures who would strive to keep their husbands sober, their children God-fearing and Catholic, and their homes decent. They were the silent strength of the poor Northern Irish Catholic household. Kilkenny wondered if Sharmon had become like them.

At the third-floor ward, Kilkenny stepped through double swinging doors and looked around. The instant he saw Darlynn Devalain, he knew who she was. She looked nothing at all like Joe, but though he saw only a trace of Sharmon there was enough so there was no mistaking who she was. Burnt-blonde hair, eyes a little too close together, lips a little crooked, almost mismatched, there was something distinctly urchin about her. That touch of the gutter, Kilkenny thought. It never entirely leaves us.

She was standing just outside a portable screen that kept the last bed on the ward partitioned from the others. She was staring out at nothing as if in a trance. Kilkenny put his bag by the wall and walked down the ward toward her. When he came into her field of vision, it seemed to break her concentration and she watched him as he walked up to her. Their eyes met and held.

"You're Darlynn," he said. "I'm Royal Kilkenny."

She put out her hand. "Thanks for coming." She bobbed her chin at the bed behind the screen. "Me dad's there. What's left of him."

There were a doctor and two nurses on one side of the bed, the nurses just turning away with covered aluminum trays in their hands, walking past Kilkenny on their way out. When they left, Kilkenny had an unobstructed view of the bed. What he saw did not look like a man at all; it looked like a large pillow under a sheet with a head placed above it and several rubber tubes running down to it from jars of liquid hung on racks next to the bed. There was an oxygen mask over part of the face. Kilkenny saw no arms or legs under the sheet and felt his mouth go dry.

"Who are you, please?" the doctor asked, noticing Kilkenny.

"A friend. Up from Dublin. His daughter called me." Kilkenny tried to swallow but could not. "Is he still alive?" he asked. The form did not appear to be breathing.

"Yes. Why or how, I don't know. The explosion totally devastated him. Apparently he was right on top of whatever detonated. The flash of the explosion blinded him; the noise destroyed his eardrums so that he's now completely deaf; and the hot gases got into his open mouth and burned up his tongue and vocal cords, making him mute. The force of the blast damaged his lungs and shattered his limbs so badly we had to amputate both arms above the elbow and both legs above the knee. So here he lies, unable to see, hear, or speak, unable to breathe without an oxygen mask, and with no arms or legs. But he's alive." He led Kilkenny out to where Darlynn stood. "I've sedated him for the night," he told the girl. "You go home and rest, young lady. That's an order."

Kilkenny took Darlynn by the arm and gently led her out of the ward, picking up his bag on the way. There was a snack shop still open on the ground floor and Kilkenny took her there, found a remote table, and ordered tea.

"How's your mother taking it?" he asked.

Darlynn shrugged. "It's not the end of the world for her. She and Dad haven't got on that great the past few years."

Kilkenny decided not to pursue that topic. "What kind of explosion was it? How'd it happen?"

"We don't know. It's supposedly being investigated by the RUC. But you know how that is."

The RUC was the Royal Ulster Constabulary, Northern Ireland's civilian police force. Like all other civil service in Ireland's British-aligned six northern counties, it was controlled by London and more than ninety percent Protestant.

"They're trying to put the blame on the IRA," Darlynn added.

"Of course." It would be the natural thing for them to do, Kilkenny thought. But he knew, as most Irishmen did, that for the IRA to be responsible for every crime attributed to it, the outlaw organization would have to be fifty thousand strong instead of the less than a thousand it actually was. "Was your dad still active in the IRA?" he asked.

Darlynn glanced at him and hesitated a beat before answering. Kilkenny expected as much. He was, despite her father's recommendation, still a stranger to her, and to speak of the IRA to strangers could be dangerous. But something about him apparently prompted her trust.

"No, he hadn't been active for about five years. He still supported the organization financially, as much as he could afford, but he no longer took part in raids or anything like that."

"Had he any trouble with the Orangemen?" Kilkenny asked, referring to the pseudo-Masonic order of Protestants that opposed a united Ireland. Their activities were often as violent as the IRA, though never as well publicized.

"Dad had no trouble with them that I know about," Darlynn said. "Except for his IRA donations, he stayed pretty much out of politics. All he cared about these past few years was that shop of his. He was very proud of that shop."

"What sort of shop?" Kilkenny asked. The last he'd heard, Joe Devalain was still trying to work his way up the ladder at the linen factory.

"It was a linen shop. Tablecloths, napkins, handkerchiefs, a few bedcovers, a small line of curtains. If there was one thing Dad knew, it was cloth. He worked in the linen factory for eighteen years and never got a single promotion, but he learned all there was to know about cloth. Finally he decided to pack it in. He drew out all his pension benefits and opened the shop. Mum was furious about it, said those benefits were half hers, for *her* old age as well as his. But Da did it anyway."

"Was that when things started going bad between them?"

"Not really. They'd been at each other off and on for a long time." Darlynn looked down at the tabletop. "Mum's had a boy friend or two."

"Did you tell your mother you were calling me?" Kilkenny asked.

"I told her after."

"What was her reaction?"

"She got a funny kind of look on her face, like I haven't seen in a long time. When I was a little girl, she used to get a look like that whenever Da would bring her a bouquet of posies. When I mentioned your name, it was like I had done something special for her. Were you and my mother close?"

Kilkenny nodded. "Your mum and dad and me were all three close. Your dad and me were best friends, but we were rivals for your mum, too. Your dad won her. He was too much a match for me."

"He wouldn't be much competition now, would he?" she asked. Suddenly tears streaked her cheeks.

Kilkenny calmed her down and got her to finish her tea, then walked the two miles home with her because she didn't feel like riding a bus. It had stopped raining and the bleak, poorly lighted streets smelled wet and the air was heavy. Kilkenny's palm sweated from carrying the suitcase. There was something about the way Darlynn's hair bounced in back that reminded him of Sharmon.

Somewhere along the way, he promised the girl he would look into the matter of the explosion that had destroyed everything about her father except his life.

The Devalains lived as tenants in a little timeworn house that looked like wet newspaper. As Kilkenny and Darlynn got to the door, Sharmon Devalain opened it for them.

"Hello, Roy," she said.

"Hello, Sharmon."

The sight of her reduced him to astonishment. She seemed not to have aged as he had. There were no plump cheeks, no wide hips, nothing even remotely in common with the women he had seen at the lift in the hospital. She didn't look a day over thirty, if that.

"Come in, Roy. I'll make tea."

"We've just had tea, actually. And I've got to go get a room."

"You can stay here. I can sleep with Darlynn. The place isn't much, but it's clean."

"Thanks anyway, but I'd better stay downtown. I told Darlynn I'd try and find out about the explosion."

Sharmon threw her daughter a quick, irritated glance. "She's quick to ask for anything she wants. Even with strangers "

"I don't really feel like a stranger to her. After all, she is yours. And Joe's."

"Yes. Well, I'm sure the RUC will appreciate any help you can give them." Her eyes flicked up and down his tall frame. "You're looking well, Roy. Prosperous."

"Hardly that. I make a comfortable living is all. But it's what I want to do."

"Well, you're one of the lucky ones, then. Most people never get what they want out of life. Are you sure about tea? Or staying the night?"

"Yes, thanks. I'll be off. Is there a bus at the corner?"

Sharmon nodded. "Number Five. It'll take you to Great Victoria Street. Will I see you again?"

"Sure," Kilkenny said. "I'll be around."

Only when he was walking down the street did Kilkenny realize that he had not said he was sorry about Joe.

*　　*　　*

He got a room at the Europa Hotel downtown and spent the night alternating between restless, fitful sleep and sitting on the windowsill, staring out at the night city, remembering.

When the night finally ended and daylight broke over Belfast Lough, when from his hotel window Kilkenny saw smoke rising from the great stacks of Harland and Wolff, the mammoth shipbuilding complex, and when civil servants began hurrying along Howard Street to their jobs in nearby Donegall Square, he showered and shaved and went down for breakfast.

After he ate, he walked over to Oxford Street where the Royal Courts of Justice were located and found that the Royal Ulster Constabulary headquarters were still situated nearby. After telling his business to a receptionist in the lobby, he was sent up to the first floor and shown to the desk of Sergeant Bill O'Marn of the Bomb Investigation section.

"Well, well," O'Marn said, looking at Kilkenny's identification. "A real flesh-and-blood private eye, just like on the telly." He was a handsome man of forty, with great bushy black eyebrows. One of the "black Irish" that women seemed to find so attractive. He wore a sprig of light green heather on the lapel of his Harris tweed jacket. Dapper, Kilkenny thought. "You realize your detective license is no good up here, don't you?" O'Marn asked.

"Certainly," said Kilkenny. "I'm only making inquiry at the request of Mr. Devalain's daughter."

"Who, I believe, is a minor."

"Yes, I believe she is. As I started to say, though, I haven't been retained or anything like that. The girl just wants to know who detonated her father. As I'm sure you do also."

"We already know," O'Marn said. "It was the IRA."

"I see. May I ask *how* you know?"

"The explosion was caused by gelignite. Nobody but the IRA uses gelignite. Every time we raid an IRA headquarters, we confiscate a footlocker full of the stuff."

Kilkenny nodded. "What reason, I wonder, would the IRA have for blowing up Joe Devalain."

"They don't need reasons for what they do," O'Marn scoffed. "They're madmen, the lot of them."

"Are you saying they simply decided to blow up a shop—any shop—and picked Joe Devalain's place randomly?"

"Looks that way to us."

This time Kilkenny shook his head. "I'm sorry, Sergeant O'Marn, but I can't accept that premise. It's always been my understanding that the IRA was much more precise in its operations than that. I thought it only set off bombs in strategic locations where the British Army mustered or patrolled, or where the explosion would produce some subsequent economic impact. I don't see how blowing up a small linen shop is going to do them any good at all."

"Neither do I," O'Marn agreed with an artificial smile. "But then, you and I aren't IRA terrorists, are we?"

"Is the matter still under investigation?" Kilkenny asked, ignoring the sergeant's question.

"Technically, yes."

"But it isn't being worked?"

"I didn't say that, Mr. Kilkenny."

Kilkenny rose. "You didn't have to. I wonder what you'll do about your crime statistics if the IRA ever disbands. Anyway, thanks for your time, Sergeant. Good day."

From RUC headquarters, Kilkenny rode a bus back out to Unity Flats. On the way he became aware of some of the graffiti that scarred the city. NO POPE HERE! read one. NO QUEEN HERE! countered another. PROVISIONALS FOR FREEDOM, GOD SAVE OUR POPE! was offset by NO SURRENDER, GOD SAVE THE QUEEN! Some city blocks warned: ARMY KEEP OUT! SOLDIERS ARE BASTARDS! Others proclaimed: ULSTER WILL FIGHT! The most ominous said simply: INFORMERS BEWARE.

Twice along the way, the bus passed moving Saracens, big six-wheeled armored vehicles that carried three soldiers and patrolled the Catholic sections. The great tanks lumbered past children playing on the sidewalk. They didn't even glance at it, never having known streets without such patrols.

At St. Bart's hospital, Kilkenny found Darlynn sitting by her father's bed, gently stroking the stump of one arm above the bandage. She looked scrubbed and fresh, like a schoolgirl. Kilkenny drew a chair around and sat by her.

"When your dad was active in the IRA, did you ever know any of his contacts?" he asked very quietly.

Darlynn shook her head. "The only time the organization was ever mentioned was when he and Mum would fight about it. She claimed it was because he was suspected of being IRA that he never got promoted at the linen factory. According to her, it's been the IRA that's kept us in Unity Flats all these years."

"Did you ever know of any meeting places he went to?"

"I'm not sure. There was a pub out on Falls Road–Bushmills', it was called. I used to find match boxes from the place when I emptied the pockets of Da's trousers for the wash. I know after he left the IRA I never found them again."

While she was talking, Darlynn had unintentionally stopped stroking her father's mutilated arm. To Kilkenny's surprise, the reduced figure on the bed began emitting from under the oxygen mask a pitiful, begging noise. Darlynn resumed stroking at once, and what was left of Joe Devalain calmed down.

"I don't even know if he's aware of me," Darlynn said.

"I'm sure he is," Kilkenny told her, though he wasn't sure at all.

"I wish there was some way to communicate with him," the girl said. "Maybe he'd know who did this to him."

Yes, Kilkenny thought, he might. But how did one communicate with a living soul who could not see, hear, or speak, and had no hands with which to write or feel or make signals?

"Would you like to come for supper tonight?" Darlynn asked. "Mum's going out, but I'm a better cook, anyway–at least, Dad's always said I was. It wouldn't be anything fancy, you understand."

"I'm sorry, I'll be busy tonight, Darlynn. I want to make contact with the IRA if I can."

She put her free hand on his knee. "Stop by later, then. Just so I'll know you're all right?"

He promised he would.

As he left the hospital, Kilkenny imagined that his leg felt warm where she had touched him.

Bushmills' was not unlike a hundred other neighborhood pubs in Belfast. It had a stained-glass window or two, a few secluded nooks, one private booth with frosted glass, and a bar as shiny as a little girl's cheeks on First Holy Communion Day. There was always an accordion player about, and always a stale beer odor in the air. Anyone ordering anything except a pint of stout drawn from the tap got a sidelong glance. All conversation ceased when a stranger entered.

Kilkenny stood in the silence at the end of the bar and ordered his pint. When it came, he paid for it and drank it down in a single, long, continuous swallow. Wiping off the foam with the back of his hand, he then spoke to the bartender in a tone that every man on the premises could hear.

"My name is Royal Kilkenny. I'm a detective down in the Free State, but I grew up here in Belfast, over in Ballymurphy. My father was Doyle Kilkenny. My mother was Faye Quinn Kilkenny. My grandfather on my mother's side was Darcy Quinn, who was Padraic Pearse's man in County Longford and served four years in His Majesty's prison at Wormwood Scrubs for the privilege. I'm up here because a friend of mine named Joe Devalain was blown up in his linen shop three days ago. He's still alive, what there is left of him, but that doesn't include eyes, ears, voice, hands, or feet. The RUC tells me the IRA did it. I don't believe that. But I want to hear it from the mouth of a man who knows for sure. I'm at the Europa Hotel, room seven nineteen. I'll be back there within the hour."

As Kilkenny suspected, it worked. Two men came for him just after dark, escorted him to a panel truck parked near the hotel, put him in the back, and blindfolded him. The truck was driven for about thirty minutes, on rough streets, making many turns. When finally it stopped, Kilkenny was taken out, led into a building and down some stairs, and finally had his blindfold removed in a small, cluttered room in which a white-haired man sat behind a scarred desk.

"My father was in prison with your grandfather," the white-haired man said. "I'm Michael McGuire."

"It's an honor to meet you, sir," Kilkenny said. Iron Mike McGuire was a legend in Northern Ireland. A third-generation Irish freedom fighter, he was the most wanted man in the country. There wasn't a child over six in Belfast who didn't know his name, yet fewer than a dozen people had seen his face in nearly a decade.

"I know about Joe Devalain's misfortune," Iron Mike said. "I was saddened to hear of it. Joe was once a loyal soldier fighting for a united Ireland. He left the cause some years back, for reasons of his own, but I understand he continued to contribute money to us, for which we are grateful. There was no ill will when he left us. There never is. A man does what he can, for as long as he can, and that's all we ask. If Joe still had been one of us, actively, we'd right now be after finding out who bombed him. Since he was not, we choose to stay out of it. I can assure you, however, that the IRA had nothing to do with the incident."

Kilkenny nodded. "I see. Well, I thank you for telling me, sir, and for the trouble of bringing me here."

"It's not been that much trouble. I'd be particular, though, if I were you, where I made that little speech you gave in Bushmills'. There's some pubs you'd not've walked out of. Pubs that are patronized by the other side."

"I understand," Kilkenny said. "I appreciate the advice. May I ask for a bit more?"

"A man can always ask."

"How would I go about contacting the Orangemen?"

McGuire exchanged a fleeting glance with the two men who had brought Kilkenny. "For what purpose?" he asked.

"The same purpose as my coming here. To see if they were responsible. If it was political, what happened to Joe, then I'll let the matter go. But if the Orangemen also disclaim the act, then I've still got work to do."

Pursing his lips, McGuire silently drummed the thick, stubby fingers of one hand on the scarred desktop. "All right," he said after a moment. "I don't believe the Orangemen were involved, but I could be wrong. At any rate, the only Order of Orange faction that is authorized to take lives is the Black Preceptories. It's an internal terrorist group that specializes in kidnaping, torture, and houseburning. It was them that torched the two hundred Catholic homes in Bogside back in '78. The leader of the bunch is Black Jack Longmuir. He works in the shipyards. You can usually find him through the union office." McGuire smiled as cold a smile as Kilkenny had ever seen. "When y'see him, tell him I'm thinking about him. Day and night. Always thinking about him."

With those words, McGuire nodded and Kilkenny was once again blindfolded and led away.

The union office was open around the clock, because Harland and Wolff Shipbuilding was running three shifts. The office was situated in a little corrugated metal building just outside the shipyard entrance. There was no doubt where the union's sympathy and support lay. Immediately inside the door was an Order of Orange flag and a framed rhyme:

> Catholics beware! For your time has come!
> Listen to the dread sound of our Protestant drum!
> In memory of William, we'll hoist up our flag!
> We'll raise the bright orange and burn your green rag!

William was William of Orange, who married the daughter of the last Catholic king of England, James II, then betrayed him, drove him from the throne, and turned Britain into a Protestant country. Five years later the Orange Society was formed in Ireland by the new gentry to whom William had distributed the land. Its purpose, by its own charter, was to maintain the Protestant constitution of the country. Nearly two hundred years later, it was still trying to do that, although it had since met failure in twenty-six of Ireland's thirty-two counties. The organization was strongest in Belfast, where it controlled the trade unions. Nowhere was there a better example of that strength than at Harland and Wolff, Ulster's greatest single industrial complex. Of ten thousand employees, only one hundred were Catholic.

"Might I be of some service, sor?" a bulldog of a man asked Kilkenny when he entered.

"I was told I might find Jack Longmuir here," Kilkenny said. Several men in the little office glanced at him, then looked away quickly.

"May I ask what your business is, sor?"

"I'm a detective from Dublin. An old mate of mine was seriously injured by a bomb in his shop three days ago. I'd like to ask Mr. Longmuir's advice about how best to go about finding out who did it."

The little bulldog cocked his head. "What makes y'think he'd give you advice on a matter like that?"

"What makes *you* think he wouldn't?" Kilkenny countered. "Or are you authorized to speak for him?"

The little man turned red. "I'll see if he's here."

Several minutes later, a young man in coveralls, with metal shavings and dust on his sleeves, came to fetch Kilkenny. Giving him a visitor's pass, he led Kilkenny past a security gate and into the shipyard. They walked in silence for two hundred yards, then the escort guided him into a welding hangar where at least thirty men were working on sections of steel hull. Pointing, he directed Kilkenny up a metal ladder to a catwalk where a tall man stood with a clipboard in his hand.

Kilkenny climbed the ladder and moved around the metal catwalk until he was near enough to speak. But the tall man spoke first.

"I'm Longmuir. What d'you want?"

"Do you know of Joe Devalain?" Kilkenny asked.

Longmuir nodded. He was a cadaverous man with a jaw that was steel blue from a lifetime of using a straight razor. His eyes looked like two perfect bullet holes.

"I'd like to find out who did it to him," Kilkenny said. "But only if it was nonpolitical. If it was a political act, I'll leave it be."

"Why come to me?" Longmuir asked. "I'm a law-abiding British subject. I work, take care of my family, and support the Presbyterian Church and my trade union. I know nothing of bombings and such. Who sent you to me?"

"Michael McGuire."

For just an instant Longmuir's face registered surprise, but he quickly contained it. "Iron Mike, eh?" he said, as if the words were a foul taste in his mouth. "You saw him, did you?"

"Yes. He assured me the IRA wasn't involved in what happened to Joe. He said only you could tell me whether the Black Preceptories did it."

"How does Iron Mike look?" Longmuir asked curiously. "I've not seen even a photograph of him in ten years"

Kilkenny thought for a moment, then said: "He looks old. And tired."

Longmuir grunted softly. "Aye. Like me." He squinted at Kilkenny. "Did he say anything about me?"

"Yes. That he thinks about you a lot."

Longmuir smiled a smile as hateful as McGuire's had been. "I hope he's thinking of me when he draws his last breath." The tall man stared out at nothing for a moment, deep in thought. Then he emitted a quiet sigh. "No one associated with the Order of Orange had anything to do with blowing up your friend," he told Kilkenny. "You'll have to look elsewhere for them that's guilty."

Kilkenny thanked him, and Black Jack Longmuir had him escorted out of the shipyard complex.

It wasn't too late, so Kilkenny rode a bus out to the Devalain house to ask how Joe had fared that day and to question Sharmon and Darlynn, now that a political motive had been eliminated, about who else might have reason to harm Joe. When he got to the house and knocked, no one answered right away. Kilkenny thought they might already have gone to bed. The past few days had to have been very trying for them. Darlynn, especially, looked on the verge of exhaustion. Kilkenny had just turned to leave when Sharmon opened the door, wearing a housecoat.

"Hello, Roy. Darlynn's not here—she's staying at the hospital all night.

Joe's mind seems to be going. He's bucking up and down on the bed, making that pathetic sound he makes, raising havoc. The only thing that seems to calm him is to have Darlynn there, patting him. The doctor says her touch is all he relates to now; he's been reduced to the primitive level, whatever that means. I'd offer you tea, but I'm just out."

She had not stepped away from the doorway or invited him inside.

"Tea's not necessary," Kilkenny said, "But I would like to ask you a few questions."

"I was just ready for bed, Roy. Can we do it tomorrow?" She must have noticed the curious expression that came over his face, because she amended her reply at once. "I suppose we can do it now. It won't take long, will it?"

"Shouldn't."

She led him to the modest parlor with its threadbare sofa, worn rug, and scratched coffee table. She conducted herself very much like a lady, keeping the housecoat well around her, even holding it closed at the throat. Her reserved demeanor brought back Darlynn's words to him: "Mum's had a boy friend or two." Kilkenny had expected Sharmon to make advances on him first chance she got. Now it appeared she was doing just the opposite.

"I'm sorry Darlynn isn't here," she said. "She'll be sorry she missed you. She fancies you, y'know."

"Nonsense," Kilkenny scoffed. "She's only a girl."

"Look again, Roy. She's older than I was when we first went under the stairs together."

"That was different. I'm sure she only looks on me as an uncle or something." He sat down. "Now then, to business. I've made contact with the IRA and the Black Preceptories. From both quarters I've been assured that there was no involvement in blowing up Joe's shop."

"And you believe them?" Sharmon asked.

Kilkenny nodded. "No reason not to. If either group had done it, there would have been a purpose—the IRA because Joe had betrayed it in some way, the Black Preceps because he was still providing financial support to the IRA or some other unknown reason. Whatever, the bombing would have been to make an example of him. Not to take credit for it would be defeating the purpose of the act. If either group had done it, they'd have claimed it and said why."

"So who d'you think did it, then?"

"That's where I go from here. Who do you think might have done it?"

"I haven't a notion."

"Did he have any enemies?"

"Joe? Not likely. You have to *do* something to make enemies. Joe never *did* anything. Sure, he joined the IRA, but only because a lot of his mates was doing the same. And he ended up quitting that. The only thing he ever done on his own was leaving the linen factory and opening up that silly shop. That was the only independent decision he ever made in his life, and you see how that turned out."

"Was he gambling, d'you know? Could he have been in debt and you not know it?"

Sharmon grunted scornfully. "He didn't have the guts to gamble."

"Do you think there could have been another woman? A jealous husband or a boy friend?"

She shook her head. "Never."

"Well, *somebody* didn't like him," Kilkenny said. "Can't you think of anybody?"

"Just me," Sharmon answered evenly.

"You?" Kilkenny had known it, but had never expected her to be so candid about it.

"Yes, me." With just a hint of defiance. "And why not? Look around you," she challenged, waving an arm. "This here is what my whole *life* is like. Worn, tattered, musty, colorless. This here is what I gave up my *youth* for, Roy. This here is all I *have*. It's all he's ever given me. Oh yes, I disliked him. And if he'd been poisoned or cut up with a kitchen knife, I'd be your number one suspect. But I wouldn't know how to make a bomb even if I had the proper stuff."

"No, you wouldn't," Kilkenny said. He thought he heard a noise from the rear of the house—a creaking, as if someone had stepped on an unsteady floorboard. "Could that be Darlynn home?"

"No. She always uses the front. It's probably a loose shutter. Listen, can we finish this another time, Roy? I've a raging headache and really would like to get to bed."

"Sure."

On his way to the front door, Kilkenny noticed an ashtray on one of the tables with something purplish in it. He saw it only for a second, for just as his eyes came to rest on it Sharmon picked it up and emptied it in a wastebasket under the table. "Goodnight then, Roy," she said. "God bless."

"Goodnight, Sharmon."

He did not return her "God Bless" because it had just registered in his mind what the purplish thing in the ashtray was.

Irish heather. Green Irish heather. It turned purple when it died.

Kilkenny went to the hospital and found Darlynn asleep on a couch in the waiting room. "She was all wore out," the nun in charge of the ward told him. "When her father finally got calmed, we made her come in here and lie down. She was asleep that quick."

"Is he asleep, too?" Kilkenny asked of Joe.

"We never know, do we?" the nun replied quietly. "He doesn't have to close his eyelids to sleep."

Kilkenny went into the ward and stood by Joe's bed. Devalain's form was still, his eyes wide and fixed. "I might know who did this to you, Joe," Kilkenny whispered. "But I must be sure before I do anything."

Stepping to the window at the end of the long room, Kilkenny stared out at the blackness, seeing only his own dim reflection from the night-light next to Joe's bed. If only I could ask him simple questions he could answer with a nod or a shake of his head, he thought. But how in bloody hell can you communicate with somebody who can't hear or see? If he had fingers, he could use children's wooden alphabet blocks. Joe could feel the letters.

If, sure, Kilkenny thought with frustration. *If* he had fingers, *if* he had eyes. If I could work goddamned miracles, I could read his bleeding mind! He turned from the window and looked at Joe again. Sighing, he walked into the hall, wondering if he should wake Darlynn and take her home. Across the hall, above the door to one of the other rooms, a red light was blinking on and off. One of the patients had pressed the call-button to summon a nurse. Kilkenny walked away from it. Then he stopped, turned, and stared at it.

Blink-blink. Blink-blink.

Dot-dash.

Hurrying back into the ward, Kilkenny drew a chair up to Joe's bed and sat down. It had been a long time, thirty years, perhaps too long. Yet if there was a chance—

Gently, Kilkenny placed the palm of his hand on Joe's sternum, just below the clavicle. Joe stirred. Kilkenny thought back thirty years. Thought back to the blue neckerchiefs and khaki caps, the gold patches they pinned to their shirts with the letters BSI on them. Boy Scouts International. It was the only youth organization that had ever come into the Ballymurphy slum to help the kids there. The first thing they had learned in the Morse Code class, Kilkenny remembered, was how to do their names.

With his index finger, he began to tap lightly on Joe Devalain's sternum. Dot-dash-dash-dash. That was J. Dash-dash-dash. That was O. Dot. That was E. J-O-E. Joe.

Joe Devalain frowned. Kilkenny began tapping again. He repeated the same letters. J-O-E.

Under the oxygen mask, Joe's lips parted. He began breathing a little faster. He's got it, Kilkenny thought. *He understands it!*

Kilkenny rubbed his hand in a brief circle to indicate he was erasing and starting a new message. He tapped dot-dash-dot for R. Dash-dash-dash for O. Dash-dot-dash-dash for Y. His name. Roy.

Joe's lips parted even more and he forced a guttural sound from his throat. All it sounded like was a long "Aaaggghhh," but it was beautiful to Kilkenny. It meant he had reached Joe Devalain's mind.

Kilkenny began tapping again, slowly, carefully. Making his message as brief and simple as possible. He tapped: Use eyelids. Dot short blink. Dash long blink. Then he waited.

For a brief, terrible instant, he was afraid Joe wasn't going to be able to do it, his lips remained parted, his sightless eyes unblinking. But then the eyelids closed, remained closed, opened, blinked once, closed again and remained closed for a second, and opened. Dash-dot-dash. That was the letter K. He was doing it!

Kilkenny watched the eyelids as they closed, opened, blinked. The letters they were making etched in his mind. K-I-R-R-G. Then the blinking stopped.

K-I-R-R-G? What the hell did that mean?

Kilkenny took out his pen and tore a sheet of paper from the medical chart hanging on the end of the bed. Turning the paper to its blank side, he wrote down the entire International Code that he and Joe had learned as Boy Scouts. Then he went to work breaking down the blinks Joe had used. The K and the I were all right, he decided. But the two R signals had to be wrong. Unable to quickly decide *how* they were wrong, he moved on to the G. That, in all likelihood, was M-E. One of the most common mistakes in Morse was to misread M (dash-dash) and E (dot) as G(dash-dash-dot). Simply a case of too short a pause between letters, causing the receiver to think it was a single signal.

Kilkenny now had K-I-R-R-M-E. Frowning, he scanned the code symbols he had just written. What was similar to R (dot-dash-dot)?

Then it hit him. Dot-dash-dot-dot. Two dots at the end instead of one. The letter was L. Joe had signaled K-I-L-L-M-E.

Kill me.

Kilkenny tapped a new message: No.

Devalain blinked back: Please. Pain. Going crazy.

Kilkenny: No.

Why?

Kilkenny tapped: Darlynn.

Joe shook his head furiously and blinked: Burden.

Kilkenny tapped: Sharmon.

The answer came: Finish me. Please.

Who bomb? Kilkenny wanted to know.

Why?

Pay back.

Again the emphatic shake of the head: Hurt Darlynn.

How?

Sharmon.

She bomb?

No.

How hurt Darlynn?

Sharmon.

Involved?

This time Joe nodded as he blinked: Maybe. No matter. Finish me.

No. Who bomb?

Then finish me? Joe asked, blinking a question mark at the end of his signal.

Kilkenny thought about it for several long moments. Then he tapped: Okay.

Joe's next message read: O-M-A-R-N.

Kilkenny nodded to himself. O'Marn. The Bomb Investigation sergeant. Neat. He had access to explosives that had been confiscated from the IRA. He knew how to use them. And he was in a position to bury the case without resolving it.

O'Marn. Yes, Kilkenny had suspected as much when he saw the sprig of dying heather in Sharmon's ashtray. The same kind of sprig O'Marn wore on his lapel. He wondered how O'Marn and Sharmon had met. How long they had been lovers. Sharmon, who didn't like policemen, who had picked Joe over him when he told her *he* was going to become a policeman.

He wondered exactly how much Sharmon knew about the bombing.

Not that it mattered. If she was still seeing O'Marn after what had happened to Joe, that was enough. And Kilkenny was sure she was still seeing him. That noise he had heard earlier from the back of the Devalain house. Along with Sharmon's eagerness to send him on his way. O'Marn had been there, listening.

Another guttural sound from the bed drew Kilkenny's attention back to Joe. He was blinking rapidly, repeating a message over and over. Do it. You promised. Do it. You prom—

Kilkenny put his hand back on Joe's sternum. He tapped: Later.

Darlynn was still deeply asleep on the couch in the waiting room. One of the nuns had covered her with a blanket. Kilkenny quietly opened her purse and took her door key.

It was very late now, dark and quiet in Unity Flats. He walked the two miles to the Devalain house, passing no one, seeing no one. When he arrived, he let himself in and stood just inside the door. The house was silent. A night-light burned dimly in the hall. Kilkenny moved slowly toward the rear of the house, taking care to stay close to the wall where the floorboards were less likely to creak.

At the door to a bedroom, he saw in the faint glow two naked bodies asleep on the bed. On the doorknob hung a Harris tweed sportcoat. Kilkenny moved into the room and over to the single window. It was shut tight and locked.

Slipping back out of the bedroom, he edged along the hall until he found the kitchen. Its window was also shut. Pulling a handkerchief from his pocket, he turned on all the gas jets on the stove.

Before he left, Kilkenny shut the door to Darlynn's small bedroom and the parlor, closing off all the house except the kitchen and the bedroom in which the two lovers slept. Then he let himself back out.

He waited down at the corner, concealed in the dark doorway of a small store, watching the house. No light came on and there was no sign of movement anywhere. Kilkenny gave it an hour. Then he returned to the hospital.

Darlynn was still asleep when he put her door key back in her purse. But Joe was wide awake and responded instantly when Kilkenny tapped his first message: Paid back.

Who? Joe blinked.

Kilkenny signaled: O'Marn. Sharmon.

A great, weary sigh escaped Joe's chest, the first sound Kilkenny had heard from him that sounded human. Then he blinked: Now me.

And Kilkenny answered: Yes.

Kilkenny reached over and pinched the tube that was feeding oxygen to Joe Devalain's lungs. As his breathing started to become labored, Joe blinked: Darlynn.

With his free hand, Kilkenny responded: Yes.

Joe's throat began to constrict, his face contorting as what was left of his body struggled for oxygen. He had time for only one more message.

God bless, he blinked ...

Kilkenny sat in the waiting room watching the sleeping Darlynn Devalain until daylight came and the buses began running. Then he woke her and they left the hospital together. On the bus downtown, he told her how her parents had died, but not who killed them. Her mother and O'Marn would be considered suicides. Her father simply had not survived his trauma.

When the bus reached Great Victoria Street, they got off.

"Where are we going?" Darlynn asked.

"First to the hotel to get my things."

"And then?"

"The part of Ireland that's free. Dublin."

Darlynn accompanied him with no further questions.

Acknowledgments

Grateful acknowledgment is made to the following for permission to reprint their copyrighted material.

"Hemlock at Vespers," by Peter Tremayne. Copyright © by the author. Reprinted by permission of A.M. Heath & Company, Ltd.

"A Gift for Friendship," by Morris Hershman. Copyright © 1995 by the author.

"A Study in White," by Nicholas Blake. Copyright © 1949 by the author. Reprinted by permission of the Peters Fraser & Dunlop Group.

"Blood Is Thicker" by Ann C. Fallon. Copyright © 1990 by the author. Reprinted by permission of Pocket Books, a division of Simon & Schuster.

"East Wind," by Freeman Willis Crofts. Copyright © 1938 by the author. Reprinted by permission of A.P. Watt Ltd. and the Authors' Contingency Fund.

"The Tinker's Revenge," by D.M. O'Reilly. Copyright © 1995 by the author and his agent, International Scripts.

"Jerry Brogan and the Kilkenny Cats," by Jon L. Breen. Copyright © 1995 by the author.

"The Goodly Race," by Robert Randisi. Copyright © 1995 by the author.

"Jeremiah's Lily," by Mary Ryan. Copyright © 1995 by the author and her agent, International Scripts.

"A Stone of the Heart," by John Brady. Copyright © 1988 by the author. Reprinted by permission of the author and his agent, Curtis Brown Ltd.

"The Rose of Tralee," by Bill Crider. Copyright © 1995 by the author.

"The Hanging of Myles Joyce," by James Joyce. First published in *Piccolo della Sera*, 16 September 1907. Originally appeared under the title "L'Irlanda alla sbarra" ("Ireland at the Bar").

"Murder at Cobbler's Hulk," by Sean O'Faolain. Copyright © 1971 by the author. First published in *Playboy* magazine, July 1971. Reprinted by permission of the author and his agent, Curtis Brown Ltd.

"Soft Day," by Wendi Lee. Copyright © 1995 by the author.

"All in the Way You Look at It," by Edmund Crispin. Copyright © by the author. Reprinted by permission of A.P. Watt Ltd. on behalf of Jean Bell.

"A Couple of Acres and a Few Wee Beasts," by Michael Jahn. Copyright © 1995 by the author.

"The Dublin Eye," by Clark Howard. Copyright © 1984 by the author. Reprinted by permission of the author.